DRAGON MAGE

DRAGON MAGE

Map by M.L. Spencer

STONEGUARD PUBLICATIONS

Cover Illustration by Sutthiwat Dechkmphu

Cover Design by STK Kreations

Edited by Sarah Chorn

Character Illustrations © 2020 by Wojtek Depczynski

Maps © 2020 by ML Spencer

ISBN: 978-1-951452-04-9

Printed in the United States of America

DRAGON MAGE

ML Spencer

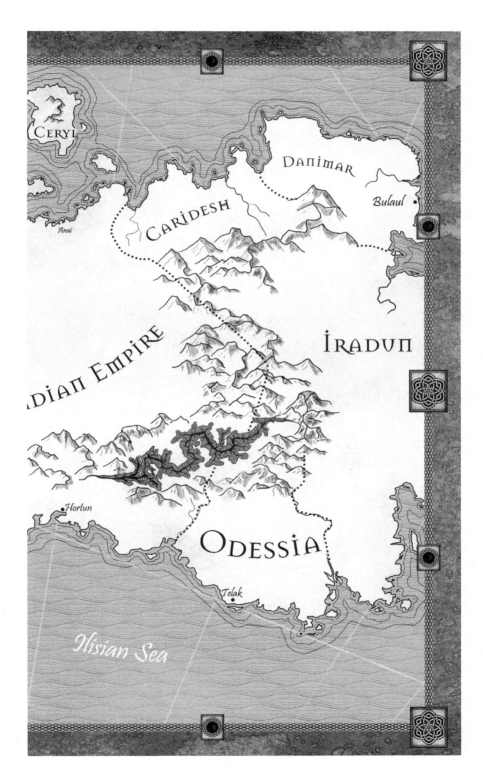

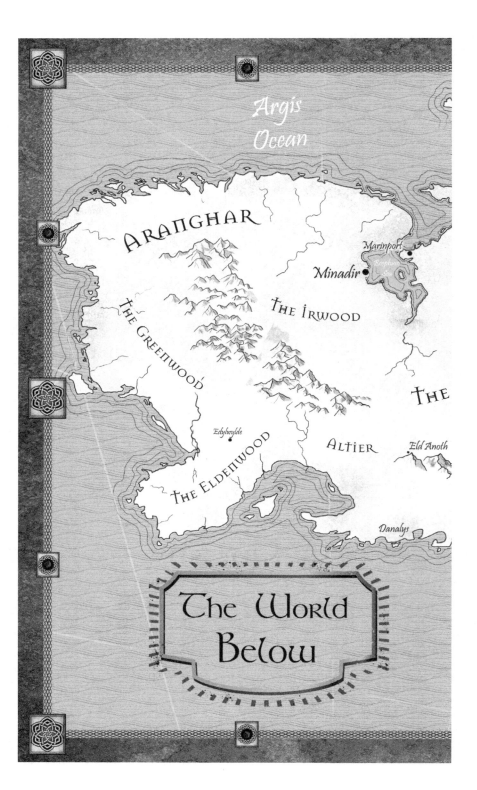

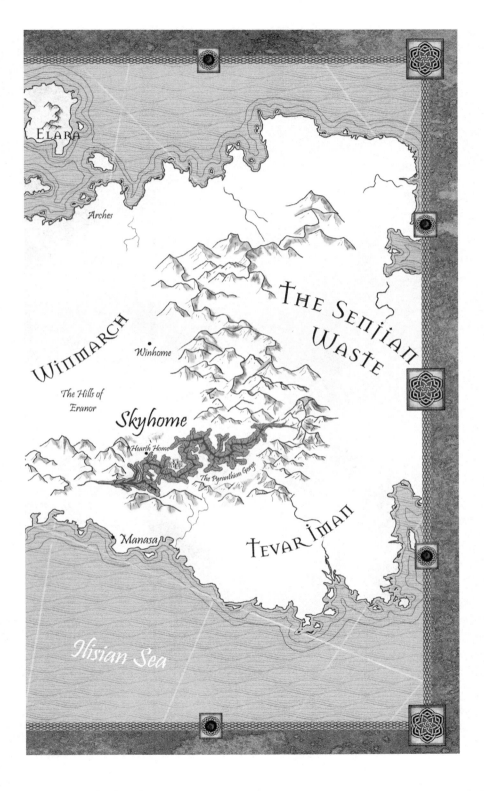

It was said the gods weep every time a dragon falls from the sky.

But it wasn't true.

Maranth the Black fell on a cloudless, rainless day, the event of his death unmourned by the divine. Only his rider remarked his fall, for he felt it like a knife-thrust through his soul.

Tears welled in his eyes, fed by a kind of grief most mortals who have never known the love of a dragon will never experience. He cast himself back from the cliff's edge with a wail of torment, sinking to his knees as his strength fled. It was not only for his soul-bound companion that he mourned, but for all the creatures of the Greenwood, whom his failure had doomed.

His mighty star-steel blade hung limp at his side, and his shoulders stooped beneath the crippling weight of his despair. His spirit had died along with his dragon, for no human could survive such a mortal loss. He was certainly no exception.

An Archon stood across the rift from him, haloed in purple flames, swathed in silken robes, a therling's snakelike body tangled about him. Against such a foe, he had never stood a chance. Only an Auld Champion able to bend the colors of the world could prevail against such a demon, and the last one had fallen four hundred years before.

He may not be a Champion, but he was all they had, even if he wouldn't be enough. He couldn't defeat such a monster, but he had to die trying.

Wiping his tears, he rose to face his adversary.

1

PART I

THE OLD BLOOD

The seaside village of Anai awoke this morning the same as it did every other morning; only, this day was unlike any other. It was rumored that a bard was coming, and the entire village was abuzz with anticipation.

On the docks, the fishing boats remained tied to their moorings, their rowdy escorts of gulls squawking riotously at the change of routine. Spice-scented smoke poured from the curing houses, though the great treadwheel crane on the wharf stood idle. The marketplace was feverish with folks readying for the occasion, scrambling to purchase fresh milk and butter, barrels of beer and hearty ale. The pig sellers were having one of their best days of the season, as were the chandlers, though the peat merchants were bemoaning their losses.

There were many reasons why the people of Anai were anxious for the bard's arrival. As always, the old women would be ready to swoop in first, pecking like seabirds at the bard, eager for crumbs of information about eligible young men and women to add to their matchmaking lists. The young children were excited for stories and the occasional magic trick, while the adults awaited tales of a much more serious, and secretive, nature. However, it was the older boys who awaited the bard's arrival with breathless anxiety, for word had it that this particular man was looking for an apprentice.

Morning was getting on by the time the shout finally came that their eagerly anticipated visitor had been spotted on the seafront road. Flocks of children flew like starlings from their huts, racing to the edge of the village to be the first to cheer his arrival. They collected atop the wall behind the smithy and lined the sand-drift dike along the roadway. There was a general sense of bubbling exuberance in the air as young folk bobbed their heads and stood on tiptoes to vie for a better view.

One of the older boys was not among the other children, but instead sat upon an overturned boat at the edge of the marketplace, showing no interest whatsoever in bards or festivities or anything that involved a crowd. His attention was riveted on a bit of hemp twine in his hands, over which his fingers danced eagerly with the dexterity of one long acquainted with knotwork. He was small for his age, with reddish brown hair that constantly fell into his eyes—eyes that were the color of mother-of-pearl, which held a stare most found intense and unnerving.

Aramon Raythe, or Aram, as everyone liked to call him, had no interest in becoming a bard's apprentice, for that would involve interacting with strangers, an exercise he found particularly terrifying. No, he was meant for the comforting seclusion of the sea. When he reached the age of choice, he would become a sailor, and he would spend the rest of his life in the forecastle of a ship, where he would tend to the running rigging, for ropes and cordage were what he loved best. He had studied knotwork his entire childhood and spent most of his spare time at the wharfside communing with sailors, whose lives depended on knots far more than any other craft.

The sound of cheers made it known that their long-awaited visitor had arrived at the outskirts of the village. Aram was indifferent. The twine in his hands was starting to take shape, and the refinement of that shape was far more deserving of his attention. Working a knot was both artform and adventure, and this particular piece, more than any other, he had to get right. Nothing short of perfection would suffice.

The piece he was working on would be a clothes bag lanyard when it was finished, which he intended for Mora Haseleu, the kindest girl in the world. Mora's father owned one of the local salt shops, where they mixed burned peat dug from local bogs with heated seawater to make salt for curing herring. Whenever Aram looked at Mora, he saw around her a yellow aura the color of primroses, the most beautiful color of all. The aura was a reflection of her personality, for she was generous and gentle and always free with kind words. She was one of the few girls in the village who didn't look away whenever he came near, and Aram would always be grateful to her for that.

The sound of cheering was growing louder and harder to ignore. Biting his lip, Aram applied all his concentration to his knotting, and the twine flew through his fingers. Soon, even the sound of the commotion blurred in his ears, his focus narrowing until the bit of string in his hand was the only thing that existed in all the world.

"What is it you've got there, son?"

Aram glanced up from his last knot, his attention broken. His hand opened spontaneously, and his careful work fell from his fingers onto the hull he sat upon, sliding to the ground. His jaw relaxed and his eyes widened in terror, his thoughts staggering to a halt.

The bard stood in front of him, surrounded by a mob of eager children who, one and all, stood staring at Aram.

Bending, the bard picked up the lanyard and spread it between his hands. He turned it over, holding it before his face, squinting to examine its intricacies better. All the while, Aram sat gaping straight ahead, paralyzed by fright. Not because of the attention he was receiving from his peers, which would normally horrify him, but because of the bard himself, who stood surrounded by an aura of deepest, screaming red, a color he had never in his life seen around a man.

"This is fine work," said the bard. "Fine work, indeed."

Sound returned to Aram's ears, and the motion of the world started forward again. Along with it came the knowledge that every stare in the entire village was trained exclusively on him. Worst of all, on the far side of the road stood pretty Mora Haseleu, her kind gaze riveted on him. The bard knelt until his face was at a level with Aram's, peering intently into his eyes. Aram squirmed, his gaze locked on Mora's like a buck confronted by a hunter. He couldn't dare look at the man.

"You have the most interesting eyes," the bard whispered, low enough so only Aram could hear. "Tell me, what color am I?"

Aram blinked in surprise, for no one had ever asked him that before. Breathless, he muttered, "Red."

The bard's lips drew into a smile. Aram hardly felt the lanyard return to his hand, and his fingers squeezed closed around it. Patting him on the shoulder, the bard rose.

Only then did Aram dare to really look at him. He was a man in his late thirties or so, his complexion the color of cinnamon, his hair slightly darker and tousled by the sea breeze. Like everyone else of Vardic stock, his eyes were gentle and glinting with intelligence. As the bard moved on, children and adults alike fell in behind him like goslings, leaving Aram sitting on the hull of the bark, staring across the road at Mora Haseleu, who, for some reason he couldn't fathom, had remained behind.

He remembered what he was holding in his hand: the clothes bag lanyard he had made especially for her. He had intended it as a gift, but just the thought of approaching her with it made his hand tremble and his stomach twist. After all the days he had spent dreaming up the perfect gift for her, he had never decided upon the way he should present it. He had entertained the idea of leaving it on the brick doorstep of the hut where Mora lived with her parents and brothers, but then she'd never know the lanyard came from him. He had imagined finding her alone somewhere away from the other children and handing it to her (he had actually rehearsed this strategy over and over in his mind). In the end, he always discarded the idea as a fancy he'd never be able to work up the nerve for.

But now he was confronted with exactly that situation, and it was terrifying. For there she was, standing alone in the dirt of the marketplace, the rest of the children swept away in the bard's wake. Worse, her attention was focused solely on him.

Aram swallowed, feeling like a drawcord was tightening around his throat. Mora was the loveliest creature in the world, and he was odd and ugly—at least, that's what everyone kept telling him. He didn't know how she might react to the gift of the lanyard, and he was petrified to find out. In his daydreams, she would smile and thank him and perhaps

even kiss his cheek. In his nightmares, she would shove him and call him a lackwit.

But she was here now, and she was waiting. For *him*. The sky had gone to rainbows and the world was floating. She was staring at him, the softest smile on her face.

Oh, help.

Gritting his teeth and girding his courage, Aram lifted his feet and slid off the curving hull of the boat—and stood frozen, unable to take even one step toward her.

No. He wouldn't let this happen. He couldn't let his own cowardice spoil this the way it spoiled everything else. He was going to give her the lanyard, and that was that. Biting his lip, he forced his legs to carry him forward, step by step, on the longest and most arduous journey of his life. It took all of his nerve and most of his childhood to arrive before her but, eventually, he was there, and she hadn't run away yet or called him an idiot.

Instead, she gushed, "You're the luckiest boy in the whole village!"

He knew he was, for Mora Haseleu was speaking to him. Aram's knees almost buckled, for the road was suddenly yawing like a bark rocked by ocean swells. He gripped the lanyard as though it were a lifeline.

She went on, "The bard spoke to you! I bet every boy in this village wishes he was in your shoes right at this moment!"

That was unlikely. No one would touch him, let alone his shoes, and certainly no one would want their feet *in* his shoes. Besides, he doubted his shoes would fit most of them; all the boys his age were taller than him. But he didn't want to tell Mora this because she might laugh, so he held it in, along with all the other things he wanted to tell her.

Trembling, Aram offered her the lanyard. Mora took it from his hand and held it up, appearing to inspect it. The braided cord was a tapered sinnet decorated with a variety of diamond knots of increasing complexity, finished with his proudest accomplishment, a turban knot of eleven leads, molded into a square shape. He couldn't look at her as she examined it, instead wanting to crawl under the boat and never come back out.

"It's beautiful," she pronounced at last, offering it back. "I understand why the bard admired it."

Tingling euphoria drained the feeling from his face, and for a moment, Aram teetered dizzily on his feet. Emboldened by her praise, he offered the knotted cord back to her.

"I made it for you," he whispered in a voice just as shaky as his courage.

"You did not!" she exclaimed, her words dashing his hopes like a keel grounded on a reef.

Instantly, he was transported back to his bleak reality, from where he should have never tried to emerge in the first place. It had always been a thin chance that she would accept such a gift, coming from someone like him. Tears burned his eyes, and his hand dropped to his side. He started backing away.

"Wait!" Mora cried out, taking a step toward him, her pretty hair tossed by the ocean breeze. "I didn't mean it like that! Did you really make it for me?"

"I...I..." *did,* he wanted to say, but his tongue was stuck to the roof of his mouth, and his jaw was trembling.

"May I...?" she asked, reaching out.

He raised the lanyard again, which looked suddenly crude and ill-made to his eyes. But before she could take it, his handiwork was jerked right out of his grasp.

A hoot of laughter behind him made him whirl. To Aram's horror, he found Jory Kannet standing behind him along with three other miscreants, the same group of boys who patrolled the village on a daily basis looking for problems to cause. They seemed to despise everything most people valued, returning kindness with cruelty. If they found a lizard, they were prone to smashing it, and if they found an injured dog, they were likely to beat it. Three of the four boys had auras the deep green of a lagoon—except Jory, whose aura was streaked with indigo.

"What's this?" Jory held up the lanyard, which dangled, swaying, from his hand.

Aram reached out to grab it but, quick as a cat, Jory tossed it to Galrad, who in turn tossed it to Lorin, who tossed it to Kasry. Wadding it into a ball, Kasry held it over his head just out of reach.

Aram was unable to speak, so violent was the anger boiling within him. He jumped as high as he could, but Kasry was taller, and he kept jerking his hand away. Aram jumped higher, but Kasry just threw the lanyard to Galrad, who tossed it to Jory, to the boisterous amusement of them all.

"Got to be faster than that, moron!" Jory shouted while the others laughed.

Aram glanced at Mora, and the look of disgust on her face squeezed tears from his eyes. *Why?* Why did they have to pick this moment to torment him, right when Mora was watching? Now all she would see in him was a coward and a wretch, for that's all he was. Tears slipped down his cheeks, dribbling from his chin.

"Look at him! He's crying like a baby!" shouted Kasry. "Is that why your father abandoned you, because you're a sniveling halfwit?"

"Stop it!" Mora screeched.

It was too much. Aram couldn't stand it. His legs gave right out from under him, and he crumbled to the dirt in a ball, covering his ears and squeezing his eyes shut as tightly as he could, desperate to block them out—to block the entire *world* out.

They started kicking him. He cried out as a foot took him in the ribs, another striking the back of his head. Then the blows were raining down from all directions at once.

"Stop it! Stop it!" Mora howled. "You're hurting him!"

The blows landed harder and smarter. His head thundered with pain. Someone rolled him over, while another boy stomped directly on his privates. Aram cried out in anguish, clutching himself and rolling back and forth in the dirt.

"What the hell's going on here?" bellowed a new voice.

The beating ceased, the mongrels scattering. Aram lay crying and moaning in the street, dazed and shaking. The odor of urine hit his nose, and he thought he had wet himself. It took him a moment to realize that one of the boys had piddled on him. Strong hands rolled him over, grappling his arms away from his face.

"Easy. You're all right."

It was a kind, gentle voice, and one he recognized. It belonged to one of the older boys, Markus Galliar, whose father owned several fishing boats. Looking around blearily, Aram saw that Mora wasn't there anymore. She must have fled, disgusted by his cowardice. In the dirt lay the lanyard he had woven for her, dirty and trampled. The sight of it was revolting enough to turn his stomach.

Leaning over, Aram vomited into the dirt.

Choking, he spat the rest of his breakfast out of his mouth. His vision still swam with tears that showed no sign of letting up. It wasn't like he was a stranger to a beating—he'd gotten more than his share over the years. But he'd never felt so humiliated. The shame hurt worse than the beating, and he feared it would leave even deeper scars.

"Thank you," he said in a trembling voice.

He raised his eyes to look at his rescuer's face. The image of a tall youth with shaggy dark hair and a lopsided smile came into focus. Looking at Markus, he felt an overwhelming surge of gratitude accompanied by an almost painful feeling of devotion. Never before had anyone near his own age ever championed him. Within him grew a budding hope that he had somehow found a friend.

"They're cowards, one and all." Markus spat over his shoulder then turned to look back at Aram. When he did, his jaw dropped, his face slackening, his eyes going wide and round. "Your blood…"

Mortified, Aram quickly wiped the blood and snot from his face with his shirtsleeve.

"No. Look." Markus took Aram's arm and, holding it up, showed him the bloodstain. "Your blood's not red. It's *brown.*"

Markus blinked several times. The blood coming out of Aram was all wrong. It was a dark, muddy brown that looked like syrup spilling down his face. It came from a wound just above his left temple where Kasry Hamlen had kicked him in the head.

"We need to get you to Mistress Dayslin!" Markus gasped, still not quite believing what he was seeing, or how a person could even be *alive* with blood that color.

Taking Aram by the arm, he helped him to his feet. The boy was a little wobbly at first, as he had every right to be. Jory and his thuggish friends had given him a sound thrashing. His nose was bloody, and he had a cut on his cheek beneath his right eye, which already showed signs of swelling.

"Come on, now!" insisted Markus, taking Aram by the shoulder and pressing him gently forward.

He guided him out of the marketplace, leading him in the direction of the village gate, the boy following along willingly enough. They made their way past rows of workshops that produced barrels of salted fish and hurried past the bakehouse, where Mister Pedieu stood with his arms bared, working dough in a large trough, the smell of baking bread perfuming the street. As they passed by the village green, Markus glanced at Aram's brown-smeared face and picked up his pace.

Mistress Dayslin was the closest thing Anai had to an infirmarer, but she lived out beyond the mudflats to the north of the village. She'd been

widowed several years before; her husband had been the mate of a herring bark that had capsized, and all aboard had drowned. Now she lived
alone in a hut by the tide pools, where she tended her vegetable patch as
well as any sick or injured that came her way.

Markus helped Aram down a short flight of stone steps onto the wet,
sandy mud that lined the beach. The salty smell of the ocean thickened
the air, and the sound of waves breaking against an offshore reef was a
consistent, droning refrain. They picked their way across the wet runnels that drained the low-tide flats, at last gaining the footpath that led
up the rocks to the widow's home.

Fortunately, they found Mistress Dayslin kneeling in her vegetable garden. She was a stout woman in a wool dress and a traditional
headscarf, her perpetual scowl an indicator of her sour personality. She
looked up from her weeding, eyes squinted by the sun. One look at
Aram brought her to her feet.

"Inside." She motioned them toward the door of her hut.

Dusting off her skirt, she followed them within, closing the door firmly behind her, which made dust rain from the ceiling. The interior of the
hut was dim, the only light coming from a small, slatted window and
holes in the wattle and daub walls. It smelled of mildew and old straw,
and as they entered, a wood mouse skittered into a gap in the wattle.

"Sit him down there." Mistress Dayslin nodded toward a cane chair
in the corner, wiping her hands on a rag.

Markus guided Aram to the chair, where the boy sat with his eyes
locked on the wall in front of him, his fingers drumming his thighs.
Mistress Dayslin bent over him and started dabbing at his scalp with
the rag. As she tended the wound, Aram rocked slightly in the chair, the
motion making the legs creak.

"Sit still," she commanded. "How long's your blood been brown?"

"All my life." Aram sucked in a hiss of pain, his back stiffening, but
his fingers maintained their tempo.

The widow gave a grunt then dipped her rag in a bowl of water.
She proceeded to wipe the blood from Aram's face none too tenderly
while the boy just rocked, staring straight ahead as though transfixed by

something on the wall. Markus looked on, burning with curiosity even though he was anxious to be on his way. If he lingered too long, his father would start missing him. He was supposed to be down at the docks inspecting their small fleet of fishing vessels for needed repairs, but he felt somehow responsible for the boy, so he felt compelled to stay.

Even though he'd lived in the same village as Aram all his life, he didn't know much about him, for the boy had always kept to himself. People said he'd been born addled, but Markus wasn't sure he agreed with that assessment. Aram looked just like any other boy from the North Coast. A trifle smaller than most twelve-year-olds, with warm brown skin and ruddy brown hair. If it hadn't been for his eyes, he might have been a good-enough looking lad. But Aram's eyes were...*disturbing* was the best word Markus could think of to describe them. They always stared fiercely straight ahead, and if you looked at them hard—really *looked* at them—you could tell they were made of little flecks of every color, almost like opal stones.

"There," the widow said with one last dab of the cloth. "Now, try not to bleed when people are looking."

"What does it mean?" asked Markus.

Mistress Dayslin scowled, the expression cleaving deep lines into her jowls. "It means his blood's brown."

Markus rolled his eyes. That hadn't been the answer he'd walked a mile and risked a switching to hear. "But *why's* it brown?"

The widow wrang her cloth out into the bowl, which, by now, contained water the color of dark sludge. With two fingers, she scooped something that looked like orange jelly out of a jar, smearing it over the abrasions on Aram's face.

"Sometimes it happens. Not often. But it does happen. Just don't let the Imperials see you bleed," she admonished Aram with a raised finger. "They take people with the Old Blood."

Aram sat with his back stiff and straight, unmoving as she applied the balm to his scrapes. His eyes hadn't stopped staring at the same patch on the wall the entire time.

"Where would they take me?" asked Aram.

The widow glanced at him with an irritated expression then tossed the brown-stained rag into a corner. "Never you mind that. Now, run along, both of you."

Aram rose from his chair with a muttered "thank you" and dodged out of the hut before Markus could react.

"Thanks," Markus gulped and headed after him. It took him a few long strides to catch up, for Aram was already headed for the trail back to the village, seemingly without a care for the widow's dire warning.

"Wait!" Markus called, catching up with him. "Does anyone in your family have brown blood?"

Without looking at him, Aram shrugged.

Markus tried to remember what he knew of Aram's father. Darand Raythe had left the village years before, never to return. No one knew why. He'd just sneaked off one night and never came back. There was lots of speculation, of course, but most people agreed that he'd likely fled to escape the responsibility of raising a slow-witted child. Though, after what the widow had just said, Markus wondered about that. Perhaps the Imperials had gotten hold of him.

He asked, "What did the bard say to you?"

Aram shrugged. "He said he liked my eyes."

"Oh." He'd been hoping the bard's interest in Aram would provide a clue about the boy's peculiarity. Aram's eye color was certainly unusual, though not nearly as alarming as syrup-brown blood.

"Well, still, that's fantastic. Maybe he'll pick you for an apprentice."

Markus couldn't keep his disappointment from his voice, for he felt that his own chances of becoming the bard's apprentice had just been diminished considerably. He was desperate for the bard to pick him. He'd lived his entire life in Anai and couldn't stand it any longer. He despised everything about the village—the constant bad weather, the everlasting smell of fish, the goodwives forever in your business, full of judgement for everyone but themselves. Above everything else, he hated his father. He wanted away from him, and he couldn't leave soon enough.

"I don't want to be picked," Aram said, a statement that shocked Markus.

"Why not?"

"I don't want to be a bard."

Markus flashed him a look of disbelief. "You need to stop and think about that. I mean, can you imagine a better life? Traveling from village to village and talking to different people, eating loads of…"

He let his voice trail off when he realized no one was listening to him. Halting, Markus turned to see that Aram had stopped a good fifteen paces behind him. Brow crinkled in confusion, Markus walked back to him across the wet sand of the mudflat.

"Why'd you just stop?" he asked.

"Because you told me to."

"I did not—"

But he had.

Markus brought a hand up, scratching the back of his head roughly. He'd told Aram to stop and think, but he hadn't meant *right now*. What kind of person would take such an expression so literally?

Aram's kind of person, he decided. Markus stared for a moment at the peculiar boy he'd gotten himself entangled with, starting to get an idea why everyone considered him slow. But he wasn't slow. Just different, in some significant way.

"Come along, then." He started forward, hoping Aram would follow him. Turning around, he walked backward a few steps. "So, if you don't want to be a bard, what *do* you want to be?"

With a smile that brought his face to life, Aram jogged forward to catch up with him. "I want to be a sailor!"

Markus scrunched his nose. Practically everyone he knew was a fisherman or a sailor, and he knew for a fact that it was a miserable life. Very few sailors had families, and those who did never saw them more than a few times a year. Life at sea was wet, cold, and solitary. And all it took was one look at Aram to see that he didn't have the personality for it. Sailing was a hard life, and it took a hard man to lead it.

He asked, "Why would you want to be a sailor, of all things?"

"Because sailors spend all day tying knots."

"Knots…?" Markus's feet slowed as his brain struggled to process the remark. Knots were certainly useful but not something to build one's life around. Then he remembered the knotted piece of twine Aram had shown the bard. It had looked well-made.

"Well, you seem to be good with knots," he allowed.

Aram's exuberance roiled like a boiling pot on the verge of bubbling over. "I know more about knots than almost anyone in the world!"

The statement caught Markus by surprise, for not only was it outlandish, but it was also awfully boastful. If any other boy Aram's age had made such a claim, Markus would have called him out for being a braggard, but one glance at Aram's face made him think that the boy wasn't bragging. He stopped in his tracks, but Aram kept walking, either not noticing or not caring.

"Why knots?" Markus called after him.

Aram paused and turned back. There was something burning in his eyes that hadn't been there before. Was it yearning? Hope? Markus couldn't be sure. But whatever it was, it looked as timid and delicate as a caterpillar, and just as easily squashed.

"Do you want to see?" Aram whispered.

Something told Markus that he really *did* want to see. But then he thought about his father and the work he was supposed to be doing back home, a thought that made him squirm. If he didn't return home soon, he'd get more than just a switching. But curiosity got the better of him, and he couldn't resist.

"All right, then," he decided. "Show me."

The smile that bloomed on Aram's face was a beautiful thing. Without a word, he hastened back toward Markus, but strode past him back in the direction of the widow's hut and the woods beyond. Markus hurried after him, having a hard time catching up with the boy's eager strides. They walked along the wet sand of the shoreline, the waves breaking nearby, rushing toward them with white froth and a sizzling sound, only to retreat again to be absorbed by the sea. A number of gulls circled overhead, some two-dozen or more. They hung like kites in the air, using the steady ocean breeze to hold them in place until the waves retreated, then dove with piercing cries to scoop up sand crabs before the next wave could reclaim them.

It wasn't to the grove beyond the widow's hut that Aram led him, but to the dark cliffs beneath it, and the tide pools that extended out away from the cliffs into the sea. When Aram started climbing across a wide tumble of volcanic rocks, Markus hesitated. The rocks were sharp, and the waves crashing against them were large enough to knock a boy right off and carry him out to sea. They were breaking further out, though a large enough wave could come along at any time and sweep them both away, a thought that made his heart beat faster.

"Where are we going?" Markus climbed onto the rocks after Aram, picking his way carefully and trying hard not to get gouged.

"You'll see!"

Markus wasn't sure he liked that answer, for it contained no information about time or distance, both of which concerned him greatly. Nevertheless, he scrambled along the rocks, following his enthusiastic guide, picking his way around sea urchins and anemones, sharp outcrops and fiddler crabs. The strong odor of kelp filled his nostrils, and the cold sea breeze bit his face, misting him with spray.

At length, they reached a place along the tidepools where the adjacent cliffs bowed inward. Aram climbed down off the rocks, jumping to the sandy beach. Following him, Markus glimpsed the thin opening of a cave ahead, just large enough to crawl into, almost hidden by a massive boulder that had broken off and fallen from the cliffs surrounding it.

"That doesn't look safe." Markus paused, realizing by Aram's trajectory that the cave must be their destination. "If the tide comes up, it could fill that cave and drown us."

"It doesn't ever get that high." Aram dropped to his hands and knees and crawled inside without hesitation.

Markus stood still for a moment, considering the dark opening, then glanced back over his shoulder in the direction of the village. He really should be getting back. His father was surely expecting him by now, and to say he didn't like to be kept waiting was an understatement.

"Come on!" came Aram's voice, small and echoing.

Markus drew a deep breath and mumbled, "This is a bad idea," before dropping to the dirt and following him in.

The passage was low and narrow, just tall enough to crawl through on all fours, with a sandy bottom that swallowed his palms. And it was dark. The light faded completely after a short distance, until he couldn't see anything in front of him. A cold shiver inched across his skin, a sudden and intense feeling of foreboding. He felt the weight of the ceiling pressing down, the hungry ocean rising behind him, the monster surely lurking ahead in the darkness... But he bit his lip and pressed on, hearing Aram's sharp breathing echoing ahead of him. Knowing the boy was safe made him feel a little better.

He wasn't sure how far they'd gone when a light appeared ahead and Aram announced, "You can stand up now."

Markus stood carefully, holding one hand over his head lest he bump the ceiling. The cave had widened substantially, and the light coming from a turn ahead was heartening. Aram stood and motioned him forward, excitement glowing on his face.

Markus hesitated, glancing at the bleak walls. "Why are we here, Aram?"

"Because this is where the cave leads."

Markus felt like knuckling his brow. "I meant, what's here that you want to show me?"

"Come see!"

Aram disappeared around the bend in the cave. Despite the nagging urge to leave, Markus followed. He turned the corner and halted, sucking in a sharp breath.

They stood within a wide cavern with tall, curving walls. The roof had partially collapsed in the middle, admitting a bright shaft of light that shone down onto a small pile of rubble. All around the walls were drawings of animals and sea creatures that looked to be the effort of a small child.

But it wasn't the cavern that stunned him.

It was what lay on the ground.

Aram stood on the pile of dirt in the center of the large space, surrounded by a ring of stones he must have placed himself. All around him, twisted jute rope had been laid across the floor in both directions, marking out small squares of perfectly even sizes. Within each square was displayed a short length of knotted cord. Some squares were broken up into smaller squares, containing knots tied with thinner string. Markus let his gaze slide down the first row of squares, then the next row, then the next—hundreds of squares, hundreds of knots, filling the entire cavern floor.

His eyes snapped back to Aram, widened by shock. "Did you…make all this?"

Standing with his arms crossed within his ring of stones, Aram nodded avidly. "I told you I'm good with knots."

Markus gazed around the cavern in dismay, grappling to comprehend the implications of what he was seeing. The time it would take to tie so many knots…the time it would take to *learn* so many knots…

"How many knots are there?"

Without pause, Aram answered, "One thousand two hundred and forty-three."

Markus blinked, astonished by both the preciseness of the number and the stupefying effort that had gone into amassing such a collection.

"That's a lot of knots…" he whispered.

An understatement.

Aram pointed to the far side of the cave. "On this side are knots made with a single cord." He moved down to the next group of squares. "Over here are knots made with multiple cords." He stooped, moving his finger along one of the rows. "These here are splices, for tying two ropes together. Over here are hitches, for anchoring a rope to something else. These are knob knots, those over there are multiple-loop knots, the ones next to them are binding knots—"

"Wait!" Markus threw his hands up, his mind reeling. "How do you know all this? How did you make all these knots?"

Aram gave him a confused look. With a shrug, he said, "I learned them. From sailors, mostly. Sailors know their knots—they're experts! Knots are what they do every day. Some even know *secret* knots! Sometimes, if I show a sailor a new knot they haven't learned, they'll show me one of their secret knots. Here, look! Over here I've got—"

It was too much. Markus's brain already felt like it was drowning under the tide of information coming at him, and all the types of knots were blurring together. "This is...this is incredible," he stammered. Bending, he picked one up, a large, beautifully symmetrical knot that had an elaborate basket-weave pattern.

"Don't touch that!"

Markus flinched, dropping the knotted cord, startled by the outright panic in Aram's voice. He looked up at him, his heart thrumming against his ribs.

"Don't touch that!" Aram repeated, but this time, it sounded more like a whimpering plea. "Every knot has its place, and if you touch them, they might get out of order!"

Markus fought to get his breathing back under control, his alarm turning to anger. The boy had given him a fright, and for no good reason. Huffing, he rose and started back toward the mouth of the cave.

"Wait!" Aram called after him. "Where are you going?"

"Back," Markus responded sharply.

"You're angry."

Markus stopped and looked at him. "Yes. I'm angry."

"I'm sorry..."

There were tears on Aram's face. He was actually crying. Markus flung out his arms, exasperated, not knowing what to do. The sight of the boy's tears drove home the fact that, no matter how exceptional Aram was, there was something that was just not right about him.

"Please. Don't go," Aram whimpered.

"Fine." Markus sighed, walking back to the center of the cavern. "I'll stay a little bit longer. But I do have to go soon."

"Thank you," Aram whispered, looking at the ground between Markus's feet.

A long silence followed, during which Markus's gaze roamed the hundreds of knots in the cavern while Aram just stood staring at the ground.

"This is so much work," Markus said, prompted by a need to fill the empty space. "I can't imagine. What inspired you to do all this?"

Aram looked up, though not at him. His gaze narrowly missed Markus's face, instead looking off to the side. "I needed a place to organize them. To keep them all straight."

"But…why knots? Why not something else? Like…something practical? Or interesting?"

Aram looked crushed. "Knots are the most practical and interesting things in the world!"

"How's that?" Markus truly didn't understand. Knots were just knots, just everyday things. No one ever gave a second thought to them.

Aram looked at him with an incredulous expression. "Knots are everything! I mean, everyone's life depends on them! Look at your clothes. The fabric's made out of little knots. Your trousers are tied with a knot. If you think about it, all of civilization is held together by knots!"

Markus didn't think Aram had taken a breath the whole while all those words had been tumbling out of his mouth. "So…how did you… discover knots?"

Aram's cheeks flushed, and he glanced down. "Ma says my hands are busy. I used to tap on things, but she couldn't abide it. So she started giving me pieces of string to fiddle with. That's when I started tying knots."

Markus indicated the expanse of the cavern with a broad motion of his hand. "What are you going to do when you outgrow this cave?"

"Someday I'm going to be a sailor, and I'm going to sail around the world and search for every knot there is."

Somehow, Markus had no doubt that Aram could accomplish exactly that. "And what are you going to do when you learn all the knots that exist?"

Aram looked crestfallen. His gaze dropped back to the ground and, for a moment, he seemed on the verge of tears. "I don't have enough years in my life to learn every knot that exists."

Markus had no idea what to say to that, and another long gap of silence followed, during which his thoughts turned back to the inspections he was supposed to be making, fearing his father's anger if he didn't get them done in time. He shifted awkwardly, made uncomfortable by the heaviness between them.

"I'm sorry, Aram. I have to get back."

The boy nodded, wiping his nose. Softly, he whispered, "Will you be my friend?"

Markus managed a smile. "I thought we already were friends."

For a moment Aram just stood there staring at him, his eyes filling with moisture. Then he rushed forward and slammed into him, catching Markus up in a crushing bearhug that made him stagger. Taken off guard, Markus didn't know how to respond, so he stood with his arms out, feeling wretchedly uncomfortable. But pity finally got the better of him, and he let his arms drop, returning the embrace.

By the time he got back to the village gates, Markus was so anxious that his stomach felt like it had rocks tumbling around in it. A stifling fear had hold of his chest, and a sweat had broken out on his forehead. He'd been gone a long time, far longer than he ever should have been.

He turned up the dusty road between huts, at last arriving at his own home, which stood in the corner of the village. It was built entirely of wood, two stories tall, with six different rooms and even a stable out back. His father owned the biggest fishing fleet on the North Coast, and he was the wealthiest man in Anai. He was also a merciless taskmaster and an unbridled drunkard.

Quivering, Markus pushed the front door open slowly, carefully, taking pains not to let it squeal on its hinges. In the end, it didn't matter. His father was standing across the room, a cup of grog in one hand, a thick length of tarred rope in the other.

"Where you been, boy?" His voice was heavy with drink.

"I'm sorry…" Markus whispered, his eyes fixed on the rope.

Aram rushed through the streets of Anai, his spirits lifted higher than the treetops, face flushed with excitement, for he had a friend! An actual friend—a *true* friend!—who hadn't called him simple or odd and had taken the time to admire his collection. It had been so long since someone had paid him any mind. Back when he was six, Paite the miller's son had been his friend. But then, one day, Paite had stopped wanting to play. Aram had never understood why. He'd asked Paite many times if he'd done something wrong, but Paite refused to answer, no matter how hard Aram begged and apologized.

No one else had ever taken an interest in him. When the boys of the village collected in circles for games, they would just ignore him, even when he sat down right behind them or tried to press his way into the ring. Some boys would simply avoid him, while others would make sport of him. Others, like Jory, went much further, though Aram never understood why. He knew he was different; he just wished he understood how. There was something about him that put other people off, and he had no idea what it could be.

Over the years, he'd tried to change everything about himself. He grew his hair out. He cut it short. He tried smiling all the time. He tried not smiling ever. Either way, nobody noticed. He'd asked his ma what she thought was the problem, but all she would ever say on the matter was that he was just like his da and left it at that.

Aram didn't like hearing that. Thinking about his father hurt, and often made him cry. Because, just like everyone else, his da hadn't wanted him—so much so that Darand Raythe had fled the village and left everything behind, including his beloved wife.

Aram didn't know what was wrong with him. He only knew it must be terrible to drive even a father away. Every time he thought about it, he ended up with a big knot in his throat. No, not a knot—he'd be able to untie that. The emotions that always strangled him were a horrific tangle.

But now he finally had a friend, and that made all the difference in the world.

When Aram reached his cottage, his mother wasn't there. The goat was on the turf roof again, which was supposed to be his problem, but he hated getting it down. The goat always jumped onto the roof from the hill behind their house to nibble the new shoots of grass. It could get back down but, sure as fate, the spindly-legged thing usually forgot how. This time, it stood up there on the edge of the roof, legs splayed, bleating at him emphatically.

So he climbed. Aram pulled himself up onto the stone wall that rimmed the village, which buttressed the hill behind his house. From there, he jumped down onto the soggy muck on the other side that stuck to his sandals and made oozing noises when he walked. He climbed the hill to its apex, his muddy feet slipping on the new grass, and from there jumped down to the roof. The small goat was black and white and bearded, and when it saw him it lowered its head, looking to ram him. It took him a few attempts to corner it, as the goat had a way of dashing past. When he scooped it up in his arms, the goat struggled and tried to bite.

"Hey, now!" he gulped. He'd already taken enough beatings for one day.

With the goat in his arms, he slid from the roof to the wall and from the wall to the ground. With one last, human-sounding bleat, the goat jumped down, butted him in the thigh, then trotted off. Aram stood picking straw off his sweater with a smile, thinking of his new friend.

Aram spent the rest of the afternoon telling his ma about Markus, to which she replied, "Hmm" before scrubbing at his face with her kerchief.

The night passed slowly, for he couldn't sleep, he was so excited. He was up until the wee hours, rolling around in the straw, and then he slept too late the next morning and woke to find the hut empty. There was a bucket of clean water by the hearth, and his ma had left him a plate of bread and cheese. He settled down on the rush-strewn floor and stuck his bare feet near the fireplace to warm them. The fire in the hearth was never allowed to die; his ma kept the embers alive by covering them with ashes overnight then rekindled them in the morning.

Aram arranged his bread and cheese on his plate the way he liked to eat it: the cheese on one side and the bread on the other, all perfectly aligned. One slice of bread had the crust torn off, so he tore the crust off the other piece, so that they matched. Only after he was sure everything was neat and symmetrical did he start eating: first, all the bread. Then, the cheese. After breakfast, he pulled on a soft linen shirt and then set off to find his ma, hurrying through the dirt streets past villagers feeding chickens, drawing water, or hauling sacks of flour and armloads of straw.

He found his ma in the space behind Nedam Brahm's house, carding wool with the usual crowd of goodwives, who sat on low stools around a large fire built to heat pots of boiling water. With her was Mistress Brahm, an older woman who was terminally exhausted from bringing a dozen children into this world. There was also Mother Groon, who was prone to fainting whenever Aram showed her a pet salamander or toad. And then there was Miss Bomeu, who had a long, narrow face only a horse could love. She'd been betrothed to Darden Walen, at least until Darden loudly proclaimed his love for another—any other—and departed forthwith for the city. Aram felt bad for Miss Bomeu.

"Where you been, lad?" his ma exclaimed. She was sitting on a stool in the corner of the hay-strewn lot, brushing wool between two fine-toothed paddles. "Get over here!"

Aram scampered forward and stopped before her, hands locked behind his back, hips twisting slightly back and forth. Mistress Braham inclined her head in greeting, a tart look on her face. She sat dry-picking lumps of wool, pulling the fibers apart handful by handful and separating out bits of hay and debris.

"Where you been, I asked!" Ma demanded.

"I overslept," Aram admitted.

"Overslept. Hmm." Her eyebrows shot up. "Well, you're here. Now, start washing fleece!"

With a groan, Aram went to the pile of sacks where the raw wool was kept. Mister Braham purchased fleece from the low country, where sheep wool grew longer and thicker. Most of the fleece produced were bundled and carted to the port cities, where they were sold at wool markets. It was said that the Abadian Empire was built on wool, slavery, and opium. Aram had always wondered about that, because wool seemed too soft to build anything on, and he didn't know what opium was.

Pulling out a raw fleece bigger than he was, Aram tore it apart and placed half onto a rug that had been laid out for the purpose. He then searched the fleece until he found the part that had once covered the sheep's backside and began plucking out pieces of caked-on dung with his fingers. He settled in and got comfortable, knowing he'd be at it for a while.

"There's a new governor in Telibak," said Mistress Brahm, who would know because Mister Brahm made frequent visits to the city. "It's said that he's ambitious, and that he's a whore of the Exilari. His men have been sacking villages up and down the North Coast."

Aram's ma nodded absently, intent on the carders in her hands, using long strokes to comb one over the other. Her gaze flicked up and met Aram's for just a moment before jerking back again to her work.

"My father thinks the bard's come spreading seeds of insurrection," said Miss Bomeu, looking up from her wet picking.

"Your father wouldn't know an ass from a bull's foot," proclaimed Mother Groon.

Miss Bomeu shrugged. "Still, you have to admit, it's odd timing."

"Rubbish!" snapped Mistress Brahm, looking scandalized. "Ebra of Starn does nothing more than remind us of who we are and where we come from. The Imperials have always seen us as a threat—that's nothing new. They're scared shitless and witless of the Old Blood. And the Exilari have hardly helped. All they do is brood in their cellars and stir the pot."

Aram's ears perked at mention of the Old Blood.

"Obviously, you haven't met an Exilari sorcerer," rasped Mother Groon. "Believe me, they can do far more than just stir a pot."

"That's enough," Aram's ma snapped, lowering her carders and looking sharply from face to face. "This is not a conversation for young ears."

Aram was sure she meant *his* ears, even though they weren't any younger than the rest of him.

His ma waved him away with a broad sweep of her carder. "Off with you, boy. Just make sure you're home by supper. And stay away from ruffians!"

Aram was torn. He hated not finishing something he started, but he was filled with a thrill of excitement, for he would be able to visit his new friend. In the end, he obeyed his mother, though leaving all that wool made him feel agitated. As he scrambled out of the circle of women, he heard Mother Groon mumble, "You shouldn't trust him alone, Marna. Just look at his face!"

He didn't hear his ma's reply, for he was off, rushing through the streets past rows of huts and cottages. He jogged past the farrier's and the leatherworks, where Mister Ranner toiled all day tooling leather. He ran all the way to the other side of the village, where Markus lived alone with his father.

His new friend wasn't in the stable yard, so he walked up to the window of the house and leaned inside, peering into the dim interior. But he didn't see Markus there either. Instantly disappointed, Aram decided to go looking for him. He tried the stable first, which was empty, save for two carthorses and Mister Galliar's prized courser. Then he went down to the wharf, where the fishing fleet was moored, but the boats were out, and Markus wasn't there either.

He was about to give up and retreat to his cave when he saw his new friend walking up the lane, back hunched under the weight of a small fishing net, which was still an enormous weight for one boy to carry. He looked to be struggling, so Aram ran to him and took half the net onto his own shoulders. Sweat streaming from his brow, Markus nodded his thanks. Aram helped him lug the net back to the yard beside the stable, where they put it down and laid it out to repair. It was only when Aram put the net down that he noticed that Markus's face was pinched in a peculiar way, and he was moving stiffly.

"You're in pain," he said.

It wasn't a question, for Aram knew the look of someone in pain. He'd once had a hard time telling one emotion from another, but then his ma had started pointing out the expressions on people's faces in different situations, which had helped a lot.

"I'm fine," Markus muttered, but that just confused Aram more.

"You're in pain," he repeated, wondering why his new friend would lie to him.

Markus closed his eyes and let out a deep sigh, puffing out his lips. "Yes, I'm in pain. But I don't want to talk about it."

"All right," said Aram, glad he'd been right, but saddened Markus wasn't feeling well. He had a suspicion that Markus's father had given him a beating. Baldur Galliar was a cruel man. Aram knew this, for his aura was indigo.

"Do you want a dram of whiskey?" Aram asked, for that's what his ma always wanted whenever her hands ached.

"No." Markus gave him a funny look. "I've got to mend this net and get it back before supper."

Aram perked up immediately, for mending nets was what he did best. The nets the fishermen used were made of nettle-hemp and used only two types of knots: the clove hitch and the sheet bend. Not his favorite knots, as there wasn't much to them, but they were serviceable knots and therefore worthy of respect. So he sat with Markus in the dirt of the yard, each with a part of the net spread across his lap, and got right to work.

By the time Markus was finished with his first section and started moving on to the next, Aram was already finishing his third section. He was starting to feel anxious, because the whole time they sat there, Markus hadn't said one word, and his motions were stiff and mechanical. From the way Markus kept shifting his weight from one hip to the other, Aram thought maybe there was something wrong with his back, but Markus had said he didn't want to talk about it, so he kept quiet.

"Did you know the bard is performing this afternoon?" Markus asked at last.

"Uh-uh," Aram muttered, close to finishing his portion of net.

"He'll be in the market. If we can get done on time, maybe we can go see him?"

"Uh-huh." Aram redoubled his effort, knowing that seeing the bard was important to Markus. His fingers flew through the knots, weaving as furiously as they could, never tiring. It took him only another couple of minutes to finish his half of the net and most of Markus's.

Markus laid the heavy net across his lap, staring wide-eyed at Aram. "How did you do that so fast?"

Aram didn't know what to make of the look on Markus's face. He thought the expression was either fear or surprise, though he couldn't tell which. He hoped Markus wasn't afraid of him. He became panicked, worried that he'd done something wrong, just like he always did.

"What's wrong?" he gulped. "What did I do?"

"Nothing." Markus's eyes were still wide. He shook his head slowly. "Nothing. You did everything right, Aram."

A euphoric relief swept over Aram, so strong it made him dizzy. He let out a great, long sigh, sagging visibly.

"Let me just get this net back." Markus folded the net and heaved it over his shoulder with a grimace of pain. "I'll meet you at the market."

"Let me help you," Aram offered.

"No. I'd better do it myself. I'll meet you there."

Disappointed, Aram left Markus to his net and wandered back toward the center of the village. He found the marketplace swarming with a crowd of people, all waiting for the bard to make his appearance. He drew up at the back of the crowd, straining to look over the heads of the people in front of him, toward the wood platform the men of the village had erected for the bard to perform on.

He waited for long minutes, but finally a great cheer went up—a din that made Aram moan, for he hated loud noises. The crowd parted to admit the bard—Ebra of Starn, Mother Groon had called him—who came forward, smiling and waving, holding a thick-necked instrument that he raised over his head, displaying it for the crowd. With a healthy leap, he arrived atop the makeshift stage already strumming, and, throwing his head back, started to sing.

The lyrics of the song were in a different language, one Aram had never heard before, its refrain both beautiful and haunting. Spellbound, Aram hung on every note, straining to understand. The occasional word would hit his ear just right, and he thought he might understand it. It was almost as though the language was one he had once known a long time ago but had forgotten.

"Hey, there!"

Aram turned, smiling happily at the sound of Markus's voice. His new friend looked as though his spirits were up, perhaps lifted by the bard's song. Around them, the crowd started clapping along with the tune and both boys joined in. The bard's fingers flew agilely over the short neck of his instrument, and he tapped out the rhythm of the song on the soundboard with his hand. When the song was over, the crowd cheered and whistled, prompting the bard to launch immediately into the next.

"What language is he singing in?" asked Aram.

"I don't know," Markus answered, clapping along with an eager smile on his face. "Maybe Cerylite."

"It's ancient Aulden," said an old woman standing next to them, her hair covered by a blue headscarf. "The High Speech."

"Aulden," Aram whispered, a faint shiver coming over him. He didn't know much about the Auld, only that they were an ancient race of people who were no more. One and all, they had been slaughtered by the Empire or harvested by the Exilari. He didn't know what that meant, to be harvested, but it sounded awful.

"How does the bard know the High Speech?" asked Aram.

"Because that's what he's trained to know. That's what bards are for: to remind us of what was lost."

With that, she moved away through the crowd, clapping and singing along to the strange-sounding music. Aram scooted closer to Markus. He had stopped clapping and now stood considering the bard with acute interest. The ever-present flurry of knots that occupied his mind had gone still, and for once, he found himself intrigued by something different.

As the bard sang, his gaze fell upon Aram, and he gave a knowing smile, as though the two of them shared a secret.

"Let's go," said Markus unexpectedly, catching Aram's shoulder.

Aram glanced at his friend, wondering what had caused Markus to want to leave—he'd so been looking forward to the performance. Nevertheless, he followed him as Markus wound back through the crowd to the edge of the marketplace, then jogged to keep up with him as he retreated down the street.

"What is it?" Aram asked, once again afraid he'd done something wrong.

Markus shook his head. At first, he didn't look like he was going to answer, but at last he stopped, hanging his head.

"He's going to pick you." His voice was coarse and ragged.

Aram stared into Markus's face, gauging his expression. "You're angry."

"Not angry," Markus corrected with a heavy sigh. "Just disappointed."

That made Aram sad. He didn't want his new friend to be disappointed, and he certainly didn't want him to miss out on something he wanted more than anything in life. Why had the bard smiled at *him*? Why hadn't he smiled at Markus, who wanted—no, *needed*—that smile so much more?

"What if I can help you?" Aram asked.

Markus frowned. "What can you do to help me?"

Aram glanced around to make sure no one was close enough to overhear what he was about to say. He was scared of telling his secrets to

Markus, secrets he'd never told anyone, not even his ma, because people already thought he was strange, and he didn't want to give them more reasons to think so. But Markus had seen his cave and hadn't ridiculed him...so maybe, just *maybe*, he was a good enough friend to accept this part of him, too.

Softly, Aram asked, "What if you could do a magic trick that no one else can do? Do you think the bard might pick you then?"

Markus's brow furrowed in an expression that could have been either puzzlement or disgust. Seeing his face, Aram felt his stomach tense and his skin grow cold. He had taken a chance. Perhaps it was too big a chance...

"What kind of magic trick?" Markus asked.

Aram whispered, "The kind that's real."

Aram trembled, fearing he'd gone too far. Markus was staring at him with the kind of look people gave him when he'd done something *really* wrong. Only, unlike most times, he knew exactly what he'd done, and he was terrified that Markus would think him addled and wouldn't want to be his friend anymore.

"What do you mean, *real* magic?" Markus asked. "Do you mean, like Exilari magic?"

Aram shook his head emphatically, not wanting Markus to think *that* of him. The Exilari were sorcerers who worked for the Empire. He didn't know much about them, other than that they lived in cellars and practiced a kind of magic that caused a lot of people a lot of pain.

"No! Not like them," Aram said quickly. "I do things with knots. Knots of air."

Markus's brow pinched. "What kinds of things?"

Aram shrugged. "Just little things. But if the bard thinks it's you doing it, maybe he'll pick you."

Markus reached up and scratched the back of his head. Then he glanced over his shoulder at the market, where the bard was still performing. "How does it work?"

"I see in color," Aram replied.

"Everyone sees in color."

Aram's face scrunched as he tried to find the right words to describe what he did. "This is a different kind of seeing. It's like…the world's made up of millions of tiny threads. I see those threads in color. Sometimes I see people in color, too. Like your color is..."

He blinked, startled, then peered harder at Markus. For the first time, he realized that his new friend had no color at all. He stood speechless for a moment, not knowing what to say. *Everyone* had an aura...unless they were dead. Dead people lost their color quickly, within seconds. A slow, creeping fear came over him. What if Markus was dead? Could that be possible?

"What?" Markus demanded.

Aram gulped. "You don't have a color."

Just then, Mother Anilla strolled by with a pail of milk and nodded at them cordially. Markus smiled back at her and mumbled a greeting. After she was out of earshot, he leaned close to Aram.

"What does that mean, if I don't have a color?"

"I don't know," Aram admitted, careful to keep his voice low. "Everyone has a color, like a glow about them. Some people are brown, some are orange. My favorite color's yellow. People like Jory are usually blue or purple. If someone's purple, it means something's wrong with them. They're bad."

Markus frowned hugely. "So, you're telling me that everyone in the world has some type of aura—everyone except me. Are you making this up?"

"No!"

"Prove it."

"I can't." Aram sighed, deflated. "The only time I can do magic is when someone's in danger."

Normally, he couldn't touch the colored strands of air that he could see. But if someone was in danger, then the threads became more solid. Like when the large post had almost fallen on Mister Cray's head. He'd been able to deflect it just a little. Not much, but enough. He just couldn't do anything if *he* was in danger.

Markus's eyes narrowed. "Then, how could you help me impress the bard, if I'm not in danger?"

Aram looked at him sadly. "I know what your father does to you.

You *are* in danger."

Markus had a hard time sleeping that night. His back ached even worse than it had earlier, and his mind was too agitated to rest. Aram's confession had bothered him on many levels. Foremost was the revelation that the boy thought he could work magic. Aram had been blessed with a bountiful imagination, but it was going to get him into trouble. If he went around telling people that the air was made out of colored strings, people would think he was mad, and the village elders might even order him restrained.

But that wasn't the only reason he couldn't sleep. He was also scared because the bard was making his choice in the morning, and he was *terrified* that Aram was going to ruin his chance by doing something stupid in a misguided attempt to be helpful. That, or by being selected himself. Markus knew he had no talent to display at the audition; he couldn't sing or dance, and he didn't play an instrument or juggle. His muscles had always served him best, and he'd been hoping the bard would want a travelling companion who could use a sword, with all the raids that had been happening lately. It was a small chance, but it was still a chance, unless Aram blew it.

There was one last fear that was keeping Markus awake, the fear that disturbed him most of all. What if Aram *wasn't* imagining—what if he really *could* work magic? It was a frightening possibility, and one Markus couldn't idly dismiss, for he had been to Aram's cave and had seen firsthand that the boy was capable of astonishing things. If Aram really could work magic, then Markus feared for his life.

Markus rolled over in bed, hoping with all his heart that Aram was wrong.

By the time morning came along, Markus was exhausted. Sometime in the night, he'd admitted to himself that he wasn't going to be picked, and he'd made his peace with it. He would have to wait until he was eighteen to escape the village and his father. Or maybe he could run off and become a mercenary or a sailor. Either one would be a hard life, but better than the one he was currently living.

Aram really did deserve to become the bard's apprentice. And whether or not he could really do magic, Markus could think of no safer place for him.

When the knock came at the door, he wasn't ready for it. Exhausted, Markus rolled out of bed and donned his trousers, tying the drawstring with a new appreciation for the overhand knot. Opening the door, he saw Carince Hanary standing in the predawn gloom, holding a glass-paned lantern.

"Get ye to Flanters'!" Mister Hanary ordered upon seeing his face. "The bard's making his selection!"

Markus's heart skipped. He closed the door and tugged his roughspun shirt on over his head. Then he paused, collecting himself. His father was still asleep—even Mister Hanary's hollering hadn't been enough to wake him. He'd spent most of the previous day at the tavern and had returned deep in his cups.

Markus's pulse thrummed in his veins. His hands were suddenly quivering.

"All right. I can do this," he mumbled, even though his voice was full of defeat.

Opening the door, he emerged into the pre-dawn darkness. The lane was empty, though the air was already filling with the scent of bread from Mister Dareau baking the morning loaves. Up ahead, Markus saw a shadow skitter around a corner. Probably one of the other boys who'd been roused from sleep. He thought about going to collect Aram, then thought better of it. Mister Hanary was moving in the direction of the docks, so he would have already knocked on Aram's door.

Best get moving.

He walked in the long shadows of moonset, the stars fading above him. The sounds of the waves were a gentle and lulling refrain, bringing him some measure of comfort. He could hear the occasional morning birdsong, but even the roosters weren't awake yet. The silence around him seemed somewhat prophetic and he tried not to let it unnerve him. But his courage started failing as he drew near the large two-story house that belonged to Mister and Mistress Flanter, the closest thing the village had to an inn.

In the green area behind Flanters' stood a row of children who'd arrived there ahead of him. Behind the children, a crowd of parents and onlookers waited, an anxious-looking lot. He didn't see Aram, for which Markus didn't know if he should be sad or grateful. Taking his place at the end of the line, he turned and faced the plank wall of the inn.

To his right stood Jan Larule, a tall and scraggly lad who could play the flute. Next to Jan was Mavry Torne, a capable youth who had an uncanny knack for locating shoals of herring. Galrad Fost, one of the miscreants who'd given Aram the thrashing, came to stand next to him, taking his place at the end of the line. Galrad fell in beside him with a derisive smirk and a taunting nod.

"Here to make a fool of yourself?" Galrad whispered, too low for anyone else to hear.

Markus whispered back, "Actually, I'm here to make a fool of you. Again."

Galrad's lips peeled back, baring his teeth. But he didn't say anything further, just stood staring straight ahead with reddened cheeks, for there were too many eyes on them.

The sky warmed and the roosters took up their morning cries while the songbirds made a racket from the trees and rooftops. The sea breeze blew, making Markus shiver. In the shadow of the inn, the warmth of the sun didn't touch the grass, which was heavy and wet with dew.

When the inn's door finally opened, Markus glanced up and down the line of boys. There were fourteen of them in all, every boy in the village between the ages of twelve and sixteen. Every boy but Aram, who was unaccounted for. Markus wondered if Mister Hanary had purposefully skipped his door.

Hands behind his back, long cloak fluttering in his wake, the bard walked forward and stood in front of them, his gaze sweeping over the line of young men. He wore a felt hat with a long feather, and the wool tunic he wore was embroidered with fine thread. He looked far more somber than he had the previous day, and much more intimidating. Every thought Markus had of impressing him swiftly melted away.

Ebra of Starn walked toward Markus's end of the line and stopped beside the last two boys who had arrived late and stood to Galrad's left.

Peering unblinking into the first boy's eyes, the bard asked, "What is your name, and what can you do?"

"Percil Canry, Master Bard. And I can sing," the boy answered, his voice cracking. A glistening sheen of sweat had broken out across his brow.

Ebra of Starn crossed his stout arms and nodded curtly. "All right, then. Let's hear you sing."

Percil swallowed heavily, his Adam's apple bobbing up and down in a convulsive movement. Then he opened his mouth and started to sing. His voice was rich and clear, and even though the song he sang was Caradeshi, it was evident that it was a melody full of sadness and grief. He let the last note linger then drop into a silence that remained pure and unbroken for seconds after the song had faded.

Ebra of Starn nodded, his lips pursing. "You sing well," he pronounced, then moved to the next boy in line. "What can you do?"

"I can juggle," said Tamen Parish with an eager smile.

"Let's see."

The boy stepped forward and, from a pouch tied to his belt, produced three perfectly round stones, the kind one might find on a river bottom. Without hesitation, he launched them into the air and sent them dancing, first in circles then in figure-eights. He kept them going for a full minute before the bard interrupted him:

"Can you do four?"

The rocks tumbled to the ground, and Tamen lowered his head in defeat.

"No," he muttered and returned to the line without retrieving his stones.

The bard moved to stand in front of Galrad, whom he had to look up to address. "What can you do?"

Galrad's cheeks were already flushed, but now they took on a blotchy shade of red. "I can whistle."

The bard motioned for him to begin.

Closing his eyes, Galrad squeezed his hands into fists and puffed his lips out like a fish. A breathy whistle wheezed from his face in an uncooperative tune that petered off quickly. An apologetic half-smile squirmed across his lips.

The bard said nothing and moved on to Markus. "What's your name, and what can you do, son?"

Markus drew in a deep breath, his mind freezing like jammed gears. His mouth opened, and he tried to force meaningful words out, but none came to him. He shook his head, his chin drooping to his chest. "Markus Galliar, sir, and I can't do anything."

"That's not true," came Aram's voice from behind him. Markus turned to see the boy emerge from the crowd of adults. He approached and stopped next to Markus with a wide smile on his face.

"Markus can do magic tricks," Aram proclaimed. "Watch him throw a stone!"

"Oh?" The bard's eyebrows lifted, and he turned back to Markus. "Let's see."

Markus gritted his teeth, feeling his cheeks redden like swollen apples. Casting Aram a look of spite, he stepped forward and, bending, selected one of the round stones the juggler had dropped. He stood there staring at it in his hand, half-hoping the rock would do something, all the while doubting it would. A trickle of sweat dribbled down his brow, and he flicked a glance at Aram.

The bard motioned impatiently for him to begin.

Markus stared harder at the rock. Of course, nothing happened. It was just a rock. Breathing a sigh of disgust, he tossed the rock away and turned to get back in line.

A gasp from the crowd halted him between strides. Looking up, he saw that everyone was staring wide-eyed at something behind him. Scared to look, Markus turned around slowly.

And found the rock he had tossed hanging suspended in the air.

Markus sucked in a gasp.

As he watched, the rock started moving. It glided back toward him and dropped into his outstretched palm.

The crowd burst into rowdy cheers. For seconds, Markus just stared at the rock in his hand, blinking, too frozen to react. Then, mouth hanging open, he glanced up at the bard.

Ebra of Starn rested a finger against his cheek, tapping it lightly. "That's a good trick," he pronounced at last. "You truly surprised me, and that happens more rarely than you'd think." He turned to Aram, his brow pinching. "What's your name?"

"Aramon Raythe, sir."

"And what can you do, lad?"

Aram scratched at a flea in his hair. "I tie knots."

The bard spread his hands. "Well, what are you waiting for? Tie me a knot."

With a smile, Aram opened up his hand and pulled from it a length of round, three-stranded cord. Within two seconds, he produced a small but neat slipknot, which he offered to the bard.

But Ebra of Starn didn't take it, instead folding his arms. "What kind of knot is that?"

"It's a figure-eight knot, sir." Aram stood with his hand out, the knot dangling from his fingers.

Master Ebra looked like he was losing his patience. "What other knots can you tie?"

Aram retracted his hand uncertainly. "What kind of knot would you like?"

The bard's eyes narrowed to sharpened spikes. "How about a sling-stone hitch?"

With that, Aram's smile fell away, and his jaw sagged. Shoulders and head wilted, he stepped back into line. Markus could only gape at him in disbelief. Out of the one thousand two hundred and forty-three knots Aram had memorized, how had Ebra of Starn guessed the one he didn't know?

With a grunt, the bard turned away and walked to the middle of the line. Backing away slowly so that he could address every boy at the same time, he raised his voice and said, "You're all good lads, but I'm done here. There's no reason to continue. For my apprentice, I pick Aramon Raythe."

A collective gasp issued from the entire line of boys and the parents who stood behind them.

"And Markus Galliar!" shouted the bard over the outrage of the crowd.

Markus felt like he'd just been cut clean in half. Before he could process what was happening, a bellowing shout roared over the turmoil:

"Like hell you do!"

It was his father's voice.

Markus's stomach lurched, and his intestines froze to ice.

Baldur Galliar shoved his way to the front of the crowd, trudging forward with hard, drunken strides. Stopping at the end of the line of boys, he raised a finger and pointed it directly at Markus.

"That's my son! And he's not going anywhere with you!"

Ebra of Starn turned to look at him with a cool, professional gaze. "I'm sorry, sir. He's been selected."

With that, he turned his back on the wealthiest man on the North Coast. Taking Markus and Aram by the shoulders, the bard started leading them toward the inn's back door.

"Stop!" Baldur's voice thundered over the tense silence that had taken hold of the morning. "I forbid you from taking him!"

Ebra of Starn drew up and turned back to face him. "But you can't." He shrugged. "It's my privilege."

Markus could only gaze at the bard with his jaw slack and his heart resounding in his chest like a war drum. No one had ever stood up to his father. No one. He squeezed his eyes shut, for they were clouding with tears of panic. Any minute, his father was going to kill Ebra of Starn, and then he was going to take him home and beat him, perhaps, this time, to death.

It was then that Aram's mother burst out of the crowd and, running forward, scooped up her son in her arms, holding him close against her.

"Please! You don't want my boy, sir! He's simple! He can't take care of himself!" Tears streamed from her eyes, her hair billowing from under her headscarf in a cloud of disarray.

But the bard just smiled sadly. "Your boy's not simple, ma'am. Aram is very smart. He just sees the world a bit differently than the rest of us."

Sobbing, Aram's mother kissed her son on the forehead and hugged him harder before letting him go. As the bard walked them away, she sank to her knees in the grass, wailing and moaning piteously.

"Boy!" Markus's father roared, his voice hoarse with wrath. "If you take another step, I swear you'll get what's coming to you!"

Markus whimpered, his legs trembling. Tears, cold with fright, coursed down his cheeks, blurring his vision. He looked up at the bard with pleading eyes, shaking with a greater terror than he had ever known in his life.

Ebra of Starn shook his head. "No, Mister Galliar, he won't. Because you'll never lay another hand on this boy again."

Hollering profanities, Baldur Galliar lunged forward but was caught and held back by the other men in the crowd. As he raged and roared behind them, Ebra of Starn gently guided his new apprentices into the inn, closing the door mercifully behind them.

The bard guided them through the inn's dim and smoky interior to the stairs in the back by the kitchen, then led them up to the second floor, which was little more than a loft with a sloping ceiling. Flanters' only guestroom contained little by way of furniture: just a single bed with a straw-stuffed mattress, a rough-hewn table with a candlestick, a three-legged stool, and a strongbox. An unemptied waste bucket sat in the corner, its fragrance perfuming the room. The bard's rucksack was shoved up against the far wall, and his instrument case laid across the bed.

He hung his cloak from a peg on the wall then sat upon the stool and motioned for the boys to sit before him on the rough planks of the floor. Aram took a seat beside Markus, but Master Ebra motioned to him, so he scooted forward to sit on his knees in front of him.

"Let me see you," the bard said in a deep, baritone voice that had been trained to woo entire crowds.

Aram leaned forward, allowing Master Ebra to take his face in his big hands and examine his bruises closely. "Does this happen to you often?"

Scared and shaken by the events of the morning, Aram couldn't work up a voice, so he nodded in answer, then moved back to his seat as the bard motioned Markus forward. "Turn around and remove your shirt."

Markus froze with an expression that Aram had no trouble interpreting. The bard nodded. "Go ahead."

Looking ashamed, Markus pulled his shirt over his head, tossing it down on the floor.

"Turn around."

Red-faced, Markus did as instructed, revealing a back covered with deep purple bruising and swollen welts.

Master Ebra stared at him for a long moment without speaking. At length, he asked, "Did your father do this to you?"

Markus nodded.

The bard sat back on his stool, folding his arms. "You have my word, it won't happen again. That's going to take more than some ointment. Aram, go in my rucksack and retrieve the leather bag that's in there."

Aram did as he was bid, rummaging through the bard's large pack until he found a leather purse held closed by a drawstring. He returned to sit beside Markus on the floor and handed over the bag. From within, the bard produced a mortar and pestle, along with two small vials filled with amber liquid. He put a few leaves into the mortar then used the pestle to mash them, speaking as he worked.

"My name, as you are no doubt aware, is Ebra of Starn." His voice was calm and deliberate. "You may call me Master Ebra, or just Master, whichever you prefer. You are both now my apprentices, which means that your ties to this village and its people are now severed. From this day forth, you belong only to me."

Aram swallowed, not knowing how to feel about that. He knew he was supposed to be happy. But he wasn't happy. He was frightened, for he didn't know Master Ebra, and he didn't want to leave his mother, the one person in the world who understood him and defended him. All his life, he'd depended on her exclusively for his every need, and he didn't know how he would get on without her.

Adding fluid from the vials, Master Ebra continued mashing the leaves into a paste. "I will be performing tonight in the longhouse. It will be my last performance at this village. We will be leaving immediately on the morrow. I advise you both to say your goodbyes today to those that you love and who love you." He looked at Markus. "In my opinion, you shouldn't leave this inn, but if you decide to, I won't stop you. Now, turn around."

Markus did, wincing as the bard began applying salve and poultices to the weals on his back. When he was done, Markus replaced his shirt, looking pale but grateful.

Master Ebra cleaned the pestle and mortar with a cloth then tucked everything back in his sack. "Now. Do either of you have questions?"

"Why did you pick us?" Markus asked in a timid voice.

The bard drew in a deep breath. "I think you know why I picked Aram, since he is the reason why your rock floated in the air."

Markus nodded, looking humbled.

Master Ebra went on, "I picked you, Markus, for the opposite reason. Because, even though he tried, Aram was not able to make the rock float while it was still in your hand. It was only after you tossed it that he was able to arrest its flight."

Markus glanced at him in confusion. "What does that mean, Master Ebra?"

"It means that magic doesn't work on you, which is a rare talent, indeed."

Aram caught his breath. "That's why he doesn't have a color!"

The bard nodded. "That's right."

Markus's eyes widened in surprise. "You see in color too?"

Master Ebra cocked his head, scrunching his lips. "A little bit. Not as well as Aram. Aram is what we call a Savant. He sees things people like you and I can only imagine."

Aram felt a warm flush of humility. He had always known that his eyesight was different, though he had never understood why or what it meant. He had always kept it a secret, one of the many he was profoundly ashamed of, because it set him apart.

Markus looked skeptical. "How do you know he's a Savant?"

"Because of the color of his eyes. Only Auld Savants have that eye color."

Markus glanced sharply at Aram. "But he's not Auld!"

Aram exclaimed, "I thought all the Auld were gone!"

The bard leaned back on his stool. "When the Auld disappeared, they left something very important behind." He spread his arms. "Us. Every Vard has Aulden blood running through their veins. It's who we are."

"The Old Blood!" Aram gasped, remembering what Mistress Dayslin had told them.

"Old Blood, Auld Blood." Master Ebra shrugged. "It means the same. For most of us, the blood of our ancestors is so diluted that it's indistinguishable from the blood of any other man. But for a few of us—a *very* few of us—well, sometimes when a river branches, those branches merge back together downstream. That's how we get boys like Markus. And boys like you. You're what some would call a 'throwback.'"

Before Aram could respond, the bard slapped his knees with his hands. "That's all I'll say about the subject till you're older. Do not ask me again." He rose from his stool and moved to collect his cloak from the peg, pulling it over his shoulders. "Now. I'm going to go teach the children of this village who they are. Later tonight in the longhouse, I'll remind the elders of this village who they *were*. I'll be back late." He pulled on a pair of lambskin gloves and fetched his instrument from its case. "Go say goodbye to your mother, Aram. If you ever see her again, it won't be for a very long time."

"She already lost my father," Aram whispered. "How can she bear to lose me too?"

The bard looked at him sadly. "Do you know what happened to your father?"

"He left. People say he didn't want me."

The bard frowned, staring deeply into Aram's eyes. "Never think that, Aram. Not for one moment." He turned to Markus. "What about you? Is there anything you wish to say to your father?"

Markus lowered his gaze to the floor. "No. Nothing."

"Very well. Then get some rest. We'll leave before dawn."

With that, Master Ebra made his way toward the stairs. When he was gone, Aram shot up from the floor, quivering with a torrential mixture of excitement, sorrow, and fear. He looked down at Markus, who remained on the floor, staring at nothing, as though in shock. He didn't understand why Markus wasn't jumping up and down with excitement, for, against all odds, he'd gotten what he'd wanted all along.

As for himself, Aram was deeply conflicted. His dreams of being a sailor were extinguished. But at the same time, he felt a weak but wakening hope for the future, a future where he might be valued *because* he was different. It was probably too much to dare hope for, but he couldn't help hoping anyway.

"I'm going to go say goodbye," he said to Markus.

His friend moved from the floor to the bed and sat upon it, nodding. Aram felt bad for him because he thought he knew why Markus was so sad. Markus wasn't sad because he'd miss his father. He was sad because he *wouldn't* miss him. Aram wondered which was worse: a father who mistreated his son but cared enough to stay? Or a father who'd never cared enough to be there at all?

He walked down the stairs to the common room. As he passed the kitchen, he glimpsed Mistress Flanter stirring something in a heavy iron kettle that hung suspended over the fire. Her dark eyes met his, and they looked sad. He wondered why.

Outside, Aram found that the crowd had dispersed, for which he was grateful. He didn't want to chance running into Markus's father. As he walked through the streets of Anai, he noticed people staring at him. At first, he wasn't certain if it was all in his mind, but the longer he walked, the more it became obvious that people really *were* staring. The looks made him uncomfortable, so he walked with his gaze lowered, avoiding all chance of eye contact. It wasn't until he found himself at his mother's home that he finally dared look up.

He stood for a moment just staring at the old, cracked door of his cottage. As he did, a terrible sadness broke over him like a wave. At first, he couldn't bring himself to open the door, for he knew it would feel more like he was closing it. But from somewhere deep inside, he worked up enough courage to open it and step in.

His mother looked up at him from the table. With a cry, she surged out of the chair and dove toward him, scooping him up in her arms. Hugging him tight against her chest, she cried hard into his shoulder. He could feel her wet tears on his skin, and for some reason, she felt thinner and frailer than he remembered. It was minutes before she at last pulled back, kissing his cheek.

Her face was wet, her eyes red and glistening. Her dark brown hair fell in disarray, and there were black smudges on her cheeks from the ashes of the hearth. Her mouth tightened into a grimace and she shook her head slowly, her shoulders quaked by tears.

"Why Aram? *Why?*"

He didn't know what to say. He wanted desperately for her to stop crying, wanted to tell her he would stay and make it all better again, but he knew that he couldn't. Somehow, he knew that Anai didn't fit him anymore, if it truly ever had.

"I didn't mean to, Ma," he whimpered, wiping his nose with his sleeve. "I'm sorry, Ma. So sorry."

She hugged him again then sat him down at the table, taking the chair on the opposite side. She sank down into it and, struggling to compose herself, lifted her apron and used it to dab the tears from her eyes.

"When are you leaving?" she asked.

Aram hung his head. "Tomorrow morning."

"All right… All right. Let's get you packed."

Aram sat at the table while his mother rounded up the few possessions he owned in this life and stuffed them into a burlap sack: his soft felt blanket, the rough piece of linen he used to scrub his teeth in the mornings, and his wooden bowl, spoon, cup, and, last of all, his eating knife.

When she was done and he was all packed, she sat the sack down by the door and went to fetch him food, putting before him a plate of cheese and pickled herring. Aram ate in uncomfortable silence while his mother sat staring at him from the other side of the table, visibly holding back tears with a forced smile on her face. It was hard to eat with a lump in his throat and a boulder in his stomach. He had to work hard to swallow his food, each bite worming its way reluctantly down his throat. After a while, the silence started to bother him. He hated silence because it normally meant something had gone very wrong with a conversation. It was especially rare when his mother had nothing to say, and usually it was because she was angry with him.

These were, he realized, the last moments he would spend with his mother for a very long time, and they were just sitting there without speaking. That was wrong. It also might be the last chance he had to ask his ma about where his father had gone, and why he'd gone there. He didn't want to make her any sadder than she was, but he couldn't resist asking.

"Ma," he said in a creaky voice, "what color blood did Da have?"

She frowned slightly. "Brown. Just like yours."

"Can you tell me about the day he left us?"

His mother blinked once, the life and color fading from her face. It took her a moment to recover. She glanced down at her hands on the table, flexing her fingers slightly, making the wrinkles in them crease even deeper.

"There's not much to tell," she said carefully, still gazing at her hands. "He used to go into the city often. He was always gone for a week or so at a time, but then he'd return. Well, he'd just gotten back from a trip. He wasn't himself, but he wouldn't say why. He said he couldn't stay, that he had to go away again. He said he'd be back in another week." She bowed her head, shaking it sadly. "But he never came back."

Aram had stopped trying to eat. His throat had constricted to the point that even breathing was difficult.

"Did something happen to him?" he asked. "Maybe an accident?"

"No. Whatever happened to him was no accident."

"How do you know?"

"Because he left something behind."

Saying that, his mother reached inside her shirt and pulled out the necklace made of twine she always wore, the one his father had given her. On it a large knot was tied that took the shape of an intricate and perfect heart. Aram had seen it before many times, for his mother had worn it as long as he could remember. Not once had he ever seen her take it off. He had never stopped to wonder if it had some special significance, other than the gift of a husband to his wife.

She untied it from her neck and handed the twine necklace to him across the table. Aram held it up, admiring the artistry of the knot his father had tied. A small shiver went through him as the knowledge sank in that his father had also been a knotter. He'd never suspected it.

"It's an eternal heart knot," his mother told him.

"What does that mean?"

"It's an old Aulden tradition. It's a token their warriors used to give to their beloveds when they left for battle. If the man survived, the couple would burn the knot together as an offering of thanks. If he never returned, the woman would wear the knot around her neck as a reminder of his love."

Leaning forward, she took his hand in hers, closing his fingers around the heart-shaped knot. "I'm not sure why your father left us that night. But wherever he went, I think he knew he wouldn't be coming back. He left this for us. He wanted us to remember how much he loved us."

Lips trembling, Aram asked, "So it wasn't my fault?"

"Your fault?" His mother looked tormented by emotion. "How could you say such a thing? How could you ever think it was your fault?"

"I thought maybe he couldn't love me," Aram said. "Because of the way I am."

His mother scooted back her chair and hurried around the table, coming to kneel at his side. "No. Oh, gods, no." She took him into her arms, rocking him slowly as her tears mingled with his own. "Your father loved you more than anything in the world."

Hearing that made Aram cry harder. He clung to her with all the strength and conviction of a son's love for his mother. It was several minutes before she let him go, but even then, it was much too soon. His mother drew back and kissed him on the cheek. When he tried to return the necklace to her, she put up her hand.

"Take it," she whispered. Removing the necklace from his hand, she tied it around his neck. "Take it to remind you of your father's love. And mine, too."

Aram rose from the chair and picked up the sack with his things she had packed for him. Halfway out the door, he paused and turned back. "Goodbye Mama. I love you. I promise I'll be back."

His mother's smile was the most beautiful, saddest thing he had ever seen.

"I know you will," she said. "I love you too."

Aram stared fixedly ahead as he walked, unable to collect the darting thoughts that plagued his mind like a swarm of gnats. The emotions flitting around inside his head made him dizzy, and he didn't know whether to weep or laugh at the day's revelations. All his life, he'd thought that his father had abandoned them. Abandoned *him*.

But he hadn't.

Darand Raythe had left a token of love behind. As he walked, Aram clutched the twine necklace his ma had given him, squeezing the eternal heart knot with all his might. His father's blood had been brown, just like his. Old Blood. *Auld* Blood. The bard's words came back to haunt him like a condemning refrain: *Only Auld Savants have that eye color.*

Had his father, then, been some kind of ancient warrior?

The questions raged in his mind, each one spawning a dozen others. As Aram pondered them, he walked in a daze through the village without care for his destination and was surprised when he found that his feet had carried him all the way to the tide pools near the mouth of his cave.

Wishing to see it one, last time, he climbed across the rocks as the waves broke around him, raining him with spray. Inside the cave, he took up position atop the mound of rubble, where he always sat, and started knotting a thin cord while he contemplated the cave and his years of hard work amassed there. He sat there for hours, his mind slowly calming, taking comfort in the feel of the cord in his hands.

At length, he drew in a deep breath and snapped fully awake. He stood and gazed upon the stronghold he had built. In this cave, he had always felt safe. It was his domain, a place that he could make and mold into a shape that fit him, even when the rest of the world didn't. It was a place of refuge, of security, of escape.

Only, he no longer had a use for those things. What he needed now was answers, and he needed them before he left the village.

He took with him his favorite length of cord and then left the cave without looking back, knowing he'd outgrown it. As he walked, he fidgeted with the cord, bending and working it between his fingers as his mind chewed on the problem of where and why his father might have gone. The more he thought about it, the more certain he became that Ebra of Starn knew *something*, or at least had a suspicion.

Why, out of all the children in the village, had the bard spoken to him first? Why had Master Ebra come to *this* village, out of all the villages on the North Coast? And why didn't he want to speak of the Old Blood?

Too many questions; Aram's mind ached with them. He didn't want to wait until he was older to find out the answers. He wanted to find out *now*.

What was it, that Master Ebra had said? He'd be making one last performance tonight—and at that performance, he would be reminding the elders of *who they were.*

He would be talking about the Auld.

Auld Blood. Old Blood. His blood—and his father's blood too. Perhaps if he could somehow listen in on the bard's teachings, he would learn what Master Ebra didn't want him to hear. Perhaps he could even learn why his father had left a wife who loved him and a son who needed him more than anything in the world.

A tingling thrill traced over his skin, and his face lit up, his mood elevated by resolve. By the time he got back to the village gate, the sun had already set. The sky was black, the last glow of twilight already fleeing, a sky full of stars shimmering above him. How had the day gone by so fast?

He didn't have a lot of time.

Aram turned and walked as quickly as he could to the beach. In his hurry, he cut his feet more than once on sharp fragments of shells poking out of the sand. The tide was coming in. He made his way over the mudflats and up onto the sandy dunes, at last reaching the huts on the outskirts of the village. Few people were about, and no one noticed him as he skirted the village wall around to the south side, as far away from Flanters' Inn as one could get. There, he stopped, for on the other side of the wall was the longhouse where the adults gathered for special occasions, the place where Master Ebra would be performing.

Aram had no idea how he would get inside. He'd never been in the longhouse—only adults were allowed there. It was where the village elders met. Where adults liked to hold discussions without fear of children hearing.

Well, tonight, he needed to hear.

The windows were all too high to reach, so they wouldn't do him any good. And there were no doors except for the large one in front, so he couldn't steal in from the back or sides either. That left just one option.

Backing away from the wall, Aram gazed upward at the roof. The eaves weren't that far from the top of the wall, and there was a beam protruding from the gable above it. If he could get a rope over the beam…

A feverish excitement ignited in his veins, and he sprinted toward the docks. Cordage wasn't hard to find in a fishing village, after all, and it didn't take him long to secure himself a good length of rope. Carrying the heavy coil over his shoulder, he returned to the wall and there dropped the rope and squatted to make a throwing bundle to give the end of the rope some weight, so it would pass more easily over the beam. He made four arm-length loops then passed the rope around the loops a couple of times before pulling it through, giving the throwing bundle a nice handle.

Glancing around quickly to make sure no one was watching, he tossed the bundle up and over the gable beam, the bundle making him successful on the first try. Feeding more rope upward, Aram caught the end with the bundle as it came back down then quickly tied a running knot into it. This, he hoisted aloft, securing the rope to the beam. He gave it two good yanks, making sure it was snug.

That was the easy part.

The hard part was climbing.

He was strong enough. The days he'd spent hauling fish and freight off ships in exchange for a new knot or two had given him *some* muscles. But even with a decent amount of strength, there was still a certain technique to climbing a rope that Aram didn't know—he'd never tried it before.

"What in the hell are you doing?"

Aram flinched at the voice and nearly fell off the wall. If it hadn't been for his grip on the rope, he probably would have. Heart in his throat, he glanced down to see Markus staring up at him with a look that was either disbelief, anger, fear, or all three.

"I'm going up," Aram answered, though it sounded a lot more like a question.

Markus brought his hands up to cover his face, slowly shaking his head. Then, with a huge sigh, he climbed the wall himself. When he reached the top, Aram handed him the rope.

"What are you doing?" Markus whispered.

Aram wondered why he was asking him the same question when he'd already answered it. "I'm going up."

"That's not what I mean!" The irritation in Markus's voice was easy to understand, for he communicated it well. "I mean, *why* do you want to get on the roof?"

Aram wondered why Markus hadn't just asked that question in the first place. "I want to hear Master Ebra sing."

The look on Markus's face was indecipherable, so Aram elaborated, "He said he was going to remind the elders of who they were. I want to hear that."

Markus grimaced, glancing up at the beam overhead. "I'm sure he'll tell you, if you just wait!"

"He said he wouldn't tell me until I was older. He said don't ask again. I have to know, though! I need to know what it means that my blood is brown, and I want to know what happened to my father."

Markus's eyebrows raised in understanding. For a moment he stood with his face looking grim, staring down at the top of the wall. At length, he closed his eyes and breathed out a protracted sigh. "All right. Let me go first, then I'll haul you up."

At that moment, Aram felt more grateful to Markus than he'd ever been to anyone in his life. He scooted back and watched as Markus jumped onto the rope and pulled himself up. He didn't make it look easy, but it also didn't seem as hard as Aram thought it would be. Markus had a much harder time getting up and over the gable beam.

While he was climbing, Aram took the other end of the rope and tied a modified bowline around himself, stepping his legs through the loops. Standing on the roof, Markus hauled him up and helped him over the eaves.

"Thank you!" Aram gasped, stepping out of the rope harness onto the wood-shingled roof.

"What now?" Markus asked.

Aram pointed. About halfway down the length of the longhouse, a column of smoke was drifting up from below through a wide hole in the roof. Before Markus could react, he started toward it. When he reached the hole, he lay down on his stomach and peered down over the lip.

Three stories below, the floor of the longhouse was full of people gathered to hear the performance. The smoke pouring up through the hole came from a large hearth centered in the middle of the floor. Rows of long tables pushed together made long lines up the length of the room, where many people were seated, conversing over plates of food and cups of wine and mead. The bard wasn't in sight, for which Aram was grateful—that meant he hadn't missed the performance.

The smoke from the fire was making his eyes watery, and it was starting to sting his throat. Beside him, Markus gave a hacking cough. It was becoming quickly obvious that staying there on the roof wasn't going to work. They would have to find another way of spying on the gathering.

Looking down, Aram saw that there were many large beams that held the rafters of the ceiling, and one of those beams was just below the smoke hole. All around the inside of the walls ran a short ledge that they could drop down onto from the beam. It looked like a good spot to sit and watch the performance, provided no one looked up.

"You're not—"

Before Markus could finish, Aram swung his feet over the edge of the hole and dropped down onto the beam. It wasn't much of a drop—more of a long step, really. A few more long steps took him to the ledge that ran the length of the wall. There, he pulled back, tucking himself against the wall, his eyes scanning the gathered people below, making sure no one had seen him.

No one had.

There was a creaking sound, then suddenly Markus was there, scrambling across the beam to sit beside him. The look on his face was unmistakable.

"You're angry," Aram said.

Markus's eyes narrowed, but he didn't answer. Aram figured that probably meant he was *very* angry. He hoped his friend wasn't *too* angry. He had never had a best friend, and he cherished the thought that he had one now.

"Thank you," he whispered, to which Markus just nodded.

They sat against the wall, knees tucked against their chests, and waited.

Below, the sound of conversation echoed loudly throughout the long-house. There had to be fifty or sixty people gathered around the tables, representing most of the important families of the village and the outly-ing farms. Markus's father was seated at a table toward the front of the building, looking well into his cups. His own mother wasn't present, but he did recognize every other face, for they belonged to people he'd known and lived with all his life: merchants and craftsmen, bakers and fishermen, farmers and farriers—every cog in the village wheel, all gath-ered right below his feet.

The only piece missing was the bard.

A loud bang echoed through the longhouse, making Aram jump: the sound of the double doors slamming closed. The ambient light dimmed slowly as the dozens of candles in the hall were extinguished, and as the shadows lengthened across the room, the noise of conversation degraded to silence.

Aram glanced excitedly at Markus, who met his gaze. In that moment, something subtle and significant passed between the two of them, a shivering anticipation—not just for the imminent performance below, but also for the change that was coming to their lives. And in that brief moment, Aram felt more empowered than he had at any other time in his life, a sense of being on the cusp of a new beginning, one that had the potential to bring him everything he'd longed for. But before he left Anai for good, he knew he needed to tie up the loose ends of his childhood. He needed to know, once and for all, what had become of his father.

Below, stillness enshrouded the dim, wide hall. And into that stillness rose a voice. One, single note, stretched out and held, wordless and divine, at last falling into silence.

The bard entered the room, strumming on his eleven-string instrument that had a fretless neck and a wide, gourd-like body.

It was a sad, sweet melody he played, a hypnotic refrain, his fingers flitting up and down the neck like fireflies before slowing to return to the same minor chord that spanned an octave. As he played, he strolled down the length of the room between rows of tables, his fingers lightly brushing the strings, maintaining a consistent, droning keen reminiscent of bagpipes.

When he reached the front of the room, he paused and lowered his instrument.

"Tonight, I will sing to you 'The Ballad of Raginor' from the Fourteenth Tablet of the *Eyana Eman,* so that your blood will remember the greatness of its source…and the greatness of its loss."

With that, he threw back his head and let out a long, mournful note that quavered in the air before being joined by the haunting strains of melody that breathed from his instrument.

"In the Summer of Ages before the Sundering of yore
Before the Anchors of Heaven were wrought from ore
There were created gods to rule earth and sky;

Was there Lesya, earth-mother, whose loins begat man,
And Ahn, chaos-father, creator of theryl and wyrm
Brought forth Auld, born of aether and blessed with light,
And Man, born of mud and water, destined for death.
And over them, the fearless Raginor, beloved of Erok
Strong of countenance and full of grace was he,
Armed with argent bow only he could bend.
Long were his days, and abounding his wisdom,
Binding the earth with golden threads he had woven;
No rival had he, for within him, gods' blood did dwell;
The world was cast asunder the day Raginor fell.

For when Absulu, with regard to the Archons, did forewarn:
'O great Raginor, Lord of Eyries, heed my call!
The hearts of those who shelter us have turned to poison!
Swelled with pride are they, and filled with greed!
They have vipers and monsters and ravaging hounds!
No fear of the fight have they, for their anvils ring always,
Their weaponry is sharp, and their shields are strong.
Once glorious, their deeds now tarnished, their honor bespoilt.
Their way is evil, and their name is Betrayal.
The Disobedient! The Disavowed!
They did shirk the duties entrusted unto them!
They took up arms and embarked unto battle
All joined in war, furious and raging!'

Raginor clothed their armor in thunder and light
But Senestra clotted their blood and stoked their fear
And rendered their wyrms dull of fang and cold of breath.
They made war without rest, night and day unending.
Till the mighty Raginor gave the battle-call
And he led the host in glorious raiment and gathered unto him
A terrible light terrifying to behold!
Before him did fall thirteen viper-monsters

Till Draxel's sword did pierce his breast.
All wept and rent their garments, but none so much as Erok,
Whose beloved had fallen upon the field.
He laid him down and took up his sword
And uttered a curse unto Senestra and spake:
'Unto the last wyrm we fight, till our hearts cool to stone,
And our weapons grow dull and our blood runs red!'

Then did Erok and fierce Varanth bring the fight
And it seemed then that fate had turned,
For no weapon could pierce them and no serpent could poison.
Till Draxal, rallying his forces, struck Varanth a mortal blow
Which flung him from the sky and slew him upon the ground.
Grievously afflicted, Erok knelt in sorrow and lamentation,
His sword shattered but his spirit unbroken.
He stood again in defiance of the tempest
And unto Draxal took the fight.
Conceived of a hatred that had no fear of death
Erok cleaved the world in twain,
Casting Auld from Man and wyrm from theryl,
Light from Shade and Issia from Pyrial.
The Veil fell betwixt this world and its counter
Shredding Erok's spirit and body asunder.
The World Above will grieve the World Below,
Till the blood of Raginor is brought again from old."

As the bard's voice faded to silence, Aram sat leaning forward, sucked into the song like a boat caught in a vortex. He stared straight ahead, transfixed, heart thrumming wildly in his chest. So moved was he that he didn't react when the bard lifted his eyes to the rafters and locked his granite stare with Aram's own. The visions provoked by the lyrics had ensnared his mind, and nothing in the mundane world could break him away from that.

For within the strains of the ballad, Aram thought he'd found the answer to every mystery of his life. According to the song, Erok had cleaved the world in half, with Auld on one side and Men on the other, separated by some type of veil. It was the first Aram had ever heard of such a thing, and yet the concept resonated with all the authority of an epiphany. Perhaps that's what his gift showed him, what he could see with his opal eyes that no one else could see. All those glimmering lines and myriad colors that saturated the air—could they be the warp and weft of the Veil between worlds?

And that last line of the ballad: 'Till the blood of Auld is brought again from old...'

Old Blood. Auld blood. His blood.

His *father's* blood.

Suddenly, Aram was certain that's where his father had come from and where he'd returned to. He knew it in his gut, with a far greater conviction than he'd ever believed anything before in his life.

And if he could see that Veil, then maybe he could part it—maybe even find a way to bring his father home.

"Aram." Markus tugged at his arm. "It's over. Let's go!"

But Aram couldn't move. His gaze was focused on the threads that wove the fabric of the world, glimmering with color and complexity. Somewhere on the other side of them was his destiny.

Reaching out, Aram took hold of one of the aethereal threads and tugged at it, plucking it from the tapestry.

The Veil resonated, the world before him wavering, the air heating just a little bit. Cautiously, he plucked another thread, creating a fray.

"What are you doing?" Markus asked.

"Aram! Don't!" Master Ebra bellowed from below.

Ignoring them both, Aram plucked another thread and then another, creating a rent in the fabric just wide enough to get his hands through.

"Aram!"

With all the strength he could muster, he tore the rent open as wide as he could and peered through to the other side.

A light appeared before him, stunningly bright.

Aram gasped, for he didn't know what he was looking at, only that it was wondrous. It was like looking straight into the sun, though blindingly white instead of yellow. His eyesight filled with motes that floated across his vision. At first, he could make out nothing through the glare, for it was too painful to behold. He shut his eyes tight, seeing only red illuminate his eyelids. It took a moment before he dared crack them open enough to look again. When he did, he didn't immediately recognize what he was seeing.

Slowly, he realized that he was staring at clouds. He was floating within them, and they consumed the entire world. He could feel pinpoint pricks of mist, a heavy dampness in the air, and a frigid, high-altitude chill.

Then the clouds parted, and he looked down upon a world clothed in a single, infinite forest that sprawled to meet a sky more brilliant and bluer than any he had ever seen.

The clouds swirled back together, cloaking him in white. They gathered closer, and as they did, the world darkened, fading to the deep gray of thunderstorms. The air grew colder and the mist around him condensed on his skin, forming droplets that sucked the heat out of him and made him shiver.

The gray world around him faded to darkness.

He floated within a nothingness that went on forever, endless and unyielding. The clouds were gone, and he found himself doubting that they had ever been there. A terrible fear gripped him, and he glanced back the way he'd come. But he couldn't see the threads of the Veil he had ripped; the only thing behind him was eternal blackness.

Then he heard it: the shriek of a monster.

It was a cry that sounded like the mortal scream of a thousand deaths, a rasping wail unlike anything he'd ever heard. It carried through the darkness like a rogue wave, and he knew there was no place he could hide from it.

Somehow, he knew it was coming for him.

It had sensed his presence and was travelling this way across the vast distance between them. He had no idea what approached; he just knew it was something that wasn't supposed to exist in his world. He had to escape—only, there was nowhere to go. Another terrible cry sliced through the silence.

Then it came into view: a billowing form that fluttered toward him, gleaming from out of the darkness. It slithered with the ribboning body of a snake, long and sinuous, only flattened, like an eel. It had a dorsal fin that ran the length of its pale body and rippled as it swam through the dark. But unlike an eel, in place of gills, it had wings, long and spindly, insubstantial to move such a creature through either water or air. It had a long head full of teeth that looked like sharpened knives. The eyes that locked on him were vacant pools of emptiness.

Aram screamed as his body was jerked backward, and he spilled onto the wood planks of the ledge. With a cry, he scrambled like a crab away from the rent he had created in the Veil. It was still there, a black wound in the air the size of his body. The glittering fibers of the world were frayed around it, buffeted by a great wind that raced through the hole.

It was awful. Evil. Just the sight of it filled him with a visceral revulsion and a primal fear.

"What is it?" Markus shrieked above the howl of the wind racing through the hole.

Aram didn't know. All he knew was that he had to get away from it. That thing was in there somewhere, and it knew where he was. A brilliant light gushed out of the rent, flooding the rafters and the beams of the ceiling. Vaguely, he was aware of screams as the adults that filled the longhouse stampeded for the doors.

The ledge beneath him started shuddering like the bed of a wagon on a rough road, and dust rained down from above. A terrible grating noise filled the longhouse, as though every board and plank of its structure was on the verge of splitting.

And then he heard the shriek of the monster.

There was a sudden flash of blinding light accompanied by a scream that came from no human throat. And then the eel-like head appeared, lashing out at him like a whip. Its serrated teeth latched onto his leg and clamped down hard, stabbing all the way to the bone.

Aram screamed in agony as the monster dragged him back toward the rift.

Markus fell on top of him just as his legs disappeared into the hole, catching him around the chest and heaving him back. Aram screamed again as the monster's teeth sliced down the length of his leg, tearing him open as Markus dragged him further from the rupture.

"*Close it!*" Markus screamed. "Close it, Aram!"

Markus sprawled back, pulling Aram tight against his chest and clamping his arms around him. There was another violent flash, and the creature burst out of the rent again, mouth gaping. It lunged for them like a striking snake, but Markus got his leg up and kicked it away ferociously.

The thing recoiled with a defiant shriek then snaked back around, its hollow eyes riveted on Markus. Aram panicked. In desperation, he reached out and wove the threads of the air as quickly as he could, darning the hole in the Veil. As he wove, the monster struck out at them again, but his stitches held. The fabric poked and buckled, as though the thing on the other side were trying to scratch its way out. An enraged cry shrieked from the other side, sounding muffled and far away. Aram kept frantically weaving, tears of pain and rivulets of sweat streaming down his face. He wove and knotted as fast as he could while the monster threw its body against his mending over and over, shuddering the entire frame of the building. Frantic, Aram tied off the last stitch.

Then, as suddenly as it had appeared, the rupture was gone. The light disappeared and the longhouse went silent and still.

Panting, Aram collapsed back into Markus's lap, gazing up into his friend's face in shock, unable to blink. He was aware of Markus's panic breaths above him, but not much else.

"You're bleeding!" Markus gasped, laying him down on the planks and crawling around him.

He ripped a hole in Aram's trousers, tearing the fabric all the way down and exposing his leg. He pressed his hands against the wound, applying pressure, making Aram scream in agony. Struggling to free his belt, Markus wrapped it around Aram's leg, cinching it tight, as Aram whimpered and started shaking uncontrollably.

"Hang on!" Markus gasped. "I'll be right back!"

The planks beneath Aram's back vibrated as Markus moved away, leaving him alone with his agony. It seemed Markus was gone for a long time, but then he was back, dropping down at his side. Vaguely, Aram was aware of his friend wrapping rope around him, passing it behind his back and between his legs. Feeling suddenly lightheaded and cold, Aram whimpered harder. He raised himself up onto his elbows and looked down at himself. His leg was covered in dark brown blood that pooled beneath him on the ledge and saturated the front of Markus's shirt.

His strength gave out, and he collapsed back to the planks. The last thing he remembered was the rope around him drawing tight.

Markus heaved at the rope with all his might, lifting Aram off the ledge. He had gone up onto the roof and retrieved the rope from the gable beam, feeding it down through the smoke hole and over one of the rafters above them before securing it to Aram. With all his might, he heaved at the rope, lifting Aram off the ledge.

The boy was unconscious, and his body sagged in the makeshift harness, his arms dangling. He had already lost a lot of blood from the deep wounds in his thigh, and the tourniquet Markus had tied around him wasn't working as well as it needed to. Every pulse of Aram's heart sent fresh blood welling from his leg, splattering on the floor three stories below.

Feeding the rope slowly, Markus lowered Aram to the floor, where Master Ebra and a few other men received him and laid him out on the planks. Then Markus scrambled down the rope himself, hand over hand, dropping the final distance. There, he crouched beside the bard, who was already bent over Aram, examining his leg. He pressed his hands against the wound and didn't react at the color of the blood that gushed out to slick his skin.

"We have to stop the bleeding," Master Ebra said, his voice strangely calm.

He slid his own belt off and used it as a second tourniquet, pulling it tight, much tighter than Markus would have ever thought to do. He then ripped a shred of cloth off what was left of Aram's trousers, wadding it up and pressing it down deep into the largest of a series of wide gashes.

"Hold this as tightly as you can," he commanded Markus.

Markus did as he was asked, plunging his fingers into the wound, using the sodden rag to try to staunch the flow of blood gurgling out of it. His own breath came in sobbing gasps, and his hands were trembling violently. When he looked down and saw the amount of blood around them on the floor, it dawned on him that Aram was probably dying. The thought burned his throat and made his lips constrict against his teeth.

"Should we get his mother?" Markus asked, struggling against tears. He knew that if it were *him* dying, he would want his mother to be there.

"No." Master Ebra moved around to the other side of him. "Put more pressure on that cloth, as much as you can." He tore off his own shirt and started ripping the fabric into strips. "Has anyone gone for the healer?"

Markus noticed that a small crowd had gathered around them, the few adults brave enough to remain behind when the rest had panicked. Mister Rannel, the butcher, left immediately to find Mistress Dayslin, while another man, Jan Tubbard, crouched beside them.

"You've got to get his legs up higher," Mister Tubbard said, picking up Aram's legs himself and sliding a sack of potatoes under them. He then set two fingers on the boy's neck and checked his pulse, frowning.

To Markus, lifting Aram's legs seemed to be helping. His face looked a little less pale than it had, and there was less gray around his lips. Markus settled back on his haunches, keeping pressure on the artery while staring down at his bloody hands. It occurred to him then that no one in the room had mentioned the color of Aram's blood. Perhaps the elders had already known, or at least knew what it meant.

It seemed a great while before Mistress Dayslin arrived with a large bag. She set to work immediately with catgut and needle, cleaning the wounds with water and whiskey then stitching them closed. It took a long time to sew him up, for some of the gashes ran half the length of Aram's leg. While she worked, Markus stood and backed away, feeling weak and unsteady. He sat at one of the long plank tables and leaned forward, holding his head in his hands. When Master Ebra sat beside him, he didn't even know the man was there until he felt him patting his back.

"He'll be all right," the bard assured him. "What about yourself? Are you injured?"

"No." Markus shook his head. His thick leather boot had saved his foot when the creature attacked him. "What was that thing?"

Master Ebra's gaze drifted away and, for a moment, became haunted and distant. At first, Markus didn't think he was going to answer, but then the bard brought his hand up and, rubbing his eyes, admitted, "It was an aetherling. Though most people just call them therlings."

Markus stared at him hard a long moment before finally asking, "Where did it come from?"

"Aram did something very rash and very dangerous. He ripped a hole in the Veil, exposing our world to the void. Things could have gone a lot worse. If he hadn't closed the rupture when he did, it would have grown. Then we would have had a hoard of those things to contend with, not just one, and we would be begging for the Exilari. Aram was lucky."

"He doesn't look lucky." Markus watched as Mistress Dayslin

finished dressing Aram's leg. For the first time, he felt comfortably sure that his young friend wasn't going to die. "What's the void?"

The bard paused before answering, looking hesitant. "It's a long story. To make it short, our world was torn apart long ago in an event known as the Sundering. We live in the World Above, the world of Men. Most magical beings ended up in the World Below. Between these two worlds is only a vast emptiness we call the void, which is patrolled by therlings, like the one that attacked Aram."

"Will it come back?" Markus whispered.

The bard rose to his feet. "No. With the rupture sealed, it can't break through again. Not here, at least, although there will be echoes of what was done here further away. Unfortunately, now we have other worries."

Markus glanced at him sharply. "What kinds of other worries?"

Master Ebra's face turned grim, the lines of his brow deepening. "Exilari sorcerers can detect weaknesses in the Veil. If any are close enough, they will sense the rupture Aram made, and they'll know it didn't occur naturally. I'm afraid our young friend has drawn the wrong kind of attention to himself."

A new kind of fear grabbed Markus, making him shiver. His gaze darted to the boy on the floor before returning to Master Ebra. "Why would the Exilari care about Aram?"

The bard sucked in a cheek, looking away. It was obvious he was uncomfortable with the questions, and he was swiftly reaching the limit of how much he was willing to answer.

"Exilari sorcerers have little natural affinity for magic. They're like parasites, siphoning the ability from others to use for themselves. Unfortunately, over the centuries, they have bled the world dry of those who can provide what they need."

Markus pondered his words for a time. "Is that why the Auld disappeared?"

Master Ebra nodded. "The Auld in this world who survived the Sundering were hunted mercilessly by the Exilari. They kept them alive to harvest their essence. The Auld were a long-lived people. Many were tortured for centuries before they finally succumbed. But now the Auld are no more, and the Exilari have become desperate. They've been forced to prey upon the Auld's descendants. They comb the world looking for blood strong enough to give them the essence they need."

"The Old Blood," Markus whispered, his eyes going to Aram, who lay covered in blood dark as peat. A terrible foreboding filled him, making him shiver. "So, if their sorcerers sensed the rupture, they'll be coming here for Aram."

"Correct."

Markus stood from his seat. "Then we have to leave!"

Master Ebra held up a hand. "Not so fast. Aram is very weak. He would never survive a journey as he is. We'll have to remain here a few days, until he is strong enough to travel. We'll just have to pray their sorcerers are far enough away that we'll be gone before they arrive."

Someone had once told Sergan Parsigal that he bore a striking resemblance to a tarantula hawk wasp. The more he thought about it, the more Sergan agreed. The sting of the tarantula hawk was considered to be one of the most painful insect stings in the world. The finger-length wasp used its venom to paralyze its prey before dragging it back to its nest, where the tarantula was kept alive to feed the wasp's larva. Sergan knew he could be just as insidious as the wasp, and the people he preyed upon were just as unfortunate as the tarantula, for they were also kept alive and in torment the remainder of their days. He was very good at what he did, though he took no pleasure in it. Unfortunately, it had been years since he'd last had the opportunity to administer his sting, because those with the blood he hunted had become exceedingly few and far between.

Sergan dismounted stiffly then paused to stretch his legs before collecting his saddlebags and handing the reins of his black destrier to a stable boy. He tossed one of the bags over his shoulder and passed the other to his companion, Nahim a'Mahz, a burly Abadian man who had served as his Shield for the past six years. They had spent the entire day in the saddle, and it was well past nightfall by the time they had found the town's only inn. The roads through the lowlands had been wet and boggy, slowing their passage. His back ached from too many hours in the saddle, and he was in need of a good meal and a good bed.

The inn that awaited them was a two-story building made of river rock with a steeply sloped, wood-shingle roof. The glow of lanterns could be seen through windows covered with opaque slices of horn that were not as expensive as glass, yet thin enough to admit light. It looked like a decent establishment, perhaps owned by a well-to-do merchant or a local official. The odor of roasting meat drifting from the kitchen chimney smelled promising, at least.

Nahim at his side, Sergan crossed the yard and entered the inn's dim and smokey main hall. It was quiet, by all appearances a distinguished establishment. There were only a few people occupying the tables, all speaking in hushed voices. It was the kind of inn that drew a better clientele: merchants and government officials, perhaps even minor nobility. Good inns were far more than just a place for wayfarers to shelter overnight. They were places to do business, providing services and storage for merchants and travelers.

Approaching the innkeeper, Sergan nodded at Nahim, who withdrew a silver coin from his purse and moved forward.

"We will take two rooms," Sergan said without bothering to ask if the innkeeper had two rooms available. "One for myself and another for my companion. As well as food and stabling for our horses."

The bald innkeeper looked up, his eyes widening at the insignia on Sergan's silk tunic. "Of course, Exilar," he said with an exaggerated dip of his head.

"We will take our meals in our rooms," Sergan continued in a lowered voice. "Send up your best wine and a pretty face to serve it."

He waited while Nahim paid the innkeeper, then made his way across the common room toward the stairs. Out of the corner of his eye, he noticed the customers staring at him. He doubted that the citizens of this village saw many sorcerers. They were days out from Telibak, the largest city in the province, and the village of Bandin was off the major trade routes.

He entered the dim stairwell and mounted the steps. About halfway up the second flight, he stopped and stood still, every hair on his body suddenly standing on end.

The world jolted violently beneath his feet, forcing him to his knees right there on the stairs.

Gasping, Sergan brought his hands up to clutch his temples, his mind screaming. He felt Nahim's hands on his shoulders, steadying him, which was probably the only reason he didn't fall down the stairs. The inn rocked and lurched beneath him like a boat caught in a winter squall, and his head felt like a ball of lightning had ignited within it, searing his brain from the inside out.

Then it all just stopped.

With a gasp, Sergan fell forward, catching himself on the step above him.

"What is it?" Nahim asked, crouching at his side.

"A rupture…" He could scarcely get the words out. His hands scoured his temples, trying to scrub the pain out of his head.

"Where?"

"Somewhere close."

Pushing himself upright, Sergan regained his feet, though he had to lean against his companion for stability. His legs shook, and his whole body was weak. Quickly, he reached down and pulled out a small glass vial, one of many that were fixed to his belt. Unstoppering it, he raised the vial to his lips and took a sip of its contents. The potent liquid he swallowed immediately filled him with a euphoric bliss that even opium could not rival. It awakened every nerve in his body, sharpening them into acute focus. His vision squirmed, every aethereal fiber bleeding together before finally separating, revealing a world that looked very different than it had just moments before.

"Power," he gasped. "Whoever it is…*so much power.*"

It was overwhelming. Nothing had ever hit him with that much fury. Bringing the vial back up to his lips, he drank down a thirsty gulp. The feeling of euphoria intensified. The filaments that saturated his vision trembled like the threads of a spiderweb that had captured an insect.

His companion helped him climb the rest of the stairs to the second floor and find his guestroom. Anticipating his need, Nahim sat him down on the bed and brought him two cups filled with water from a pitcher on the nightstand. Sergan drank all the water in both cups then leaned forward over his knees, gasping to catch his breath.

"I've never felt that kind of strength in my life." He shook his head in astonishment. "I can hardly believe it."

"Can you tell who it was?" Nahim asked.

That was a good question. He *had* to know. Sergan raised the vial to his lips and took a few more sips of the liquid inside. Again, he could feel his mind and vision sharpen. This time, he cast his focus along the threads of aether in the direction of the rupture, applying all his great will to the effort.

"It was someone young," he said at last. "It feels like a boy."

It was hard to tell. Every person left a signature imprint on the world around them, which told a story about them. It was much easier to read that story standing in a room with the person, growing exponentially more difficult the further away they were. It was only because of the intensity of the soul in question that he could sense anything about him at all. Whoever this boy was, the strength of his imprint was far beyond anything in Sergan's vast range of experiences.

"He's a Savant."

"Are you sure?" Nahim asked, his eyebrows pressed together in disbelief.

"I'm sure." There was no other explanation for that kind of power—the kind of power that could tear the very fabric of the world.

"When was the last time we found a Savant?"

Sergan tossed the spent vial onto the bed. "Daymar Torian. Four centuries ago."

Torian had been the last Auld Champion the Exilari had defeated. It had taken a dozen sorcerers to bring him down, and even then, they had lost four of their own in the process. Torian's essence had been so potent that there were still vials of him left in the cellars when Sergan had begun his apprenticeship. Unfortunately, the last drops of Torian had been swallowed before he'd reached his own mastery of the craft, though he'd heard from others that Torian's essence had been divine, the purest and most potent soul to ever pass their lips.

"Can you tell where this boy is?" Nahim knelt in front of him, one hand on the hilt of his sword.

"Within a day's ride to the north." Sergan was certain he was right. His head still ached from the ferocity of the boy's assault on the fabric of the Veil.

"That close? The only village within a day's ride of here is Anai."

Sergan smiled, a faint thrill shivering down his nerves. If he was right, then this boy might be the next Daymar Torian. And with one so young, they could spend decades filling vials with his essence. Excitement coursed through his veins, for a find so rich might mean the salivation of his Order, a turn of fortune that couldn't have come at a more desperate time.

"Then I suppose we're going to Anai," he said. "There's a garrison in town. We'll stop there on the way out and ask for an escort. Go tell the innkeeper that we won't be needing his accommodations after all."

Nahim scowled. "I was really looking forward to that meal, you know. Not to mention the woman."

Sergan snorted. "I'm sure they have plenty of food and women in Anai."

Esmir Revin stood at the edge of his eyrie's terrace, which overlooked the Shar River above the falls where its waters plummeted thousands of feet into the Pyranthian Gorge. The roar of the falls was a constant thunder that he was used to, so much so that he rarely noticed it. The spray, borne by the wind, wet his face and dampened his thinning gray beard. He raised his liver-spotted hands before him, spreading fingers gnarled by arthritis and age. His skin, once a vigorous golden-brown, was now thin and translucent, knotted with veins. As his body slowed and his bones grew brittle, he felt an increasing sense of urgency. He had already seen twelve hundred summers, and he doubted he had another dozen left in him.

The wind blowing down off the mountains ruffled his hair, smelling of sulfur from the gorge and thick with the portent of rain. It was also too damn cold for old bones. Esmir tugged his fur overcoat tighter about himself and was about ready to start back inside, but then he paused, his gaze drawn to the unlit stone brazier perched like a gargoyle at the very tip of the terrace that jutted out from the cliffside. Such braziers had once been lit throughout the Heights, glowing from terraces all along the walls of the long canyon.

The eyrie where Esmir made his home was one of the highest in Skyhome, for he had come to live there with Daymar Torian and their dragons four hundred years before, when the Great Ones had ruled the sky. He lived there still, even though Daymar was long dead, and their dragons lost to the void, for no one had had the audacity to tell him to leave. Nor would he, for this was his home.

For three hundred years, Esmir had fought beside Daymar as his Warden. Together, they had defended Pyrial from enemies both Above and Below. Until Daymar had fallen, and so, too, had fallen hope. Daymar had been the last Auld Champion, and in the four hundred years since his passing, there hadn't been another born with the ability to succeed him.

Since Daymar Torian's passing, Pyrial's defenders had made do with far less. Through luck and innovation, they kept the Anchors of the Earth intact, despite Araghar's unceasing assault. But now they were losing ground. Recently, they had lost too many of their best. The Anchors were failing, and when the last Anchor fell, so too would their world come undone.

Esmir gazed sadly at his eyrie's unlit brazier, which had stood cold since his dragon had passed from the world. The lights of the eyries that once glimmered like stars in defiance of the night had been replaced by stillness and shadow. The great fires of the Heights had gone cold, for they had all died with their dragons, each and every one of them.

Down through the centuries, Esmir had maintained fresh wood in the beacon of his eyrie, feeding it with fuel and hope, on the off chance that Faranth or Agaroth would return to the world. Now, he questioned why he had. There would never be another Greater Dragon in the world, just as there would never be another Champion.

Esmir sighed bitterly, turning away from the edge. It was time to let the last of his hopes die, and himself along with them.

But as he started walking away, the entire mountain trembled.

Esmir staggered, every hair on his body standing on end. The eyrie's beacon fire sprang to life with a tentative, pale flame that looked feeble and sickly.

To Esmir, the color of the fire didn't matter. Something—no, *some-one*—had torn a rent in the fabric of the world. His arms dropped limply to his sides, and he gaped at the beacon whose faint, quivering light cast back the shadows of the eyrie for just heartbeats before succumbing.

Somewhere in the world, a Greater Dragon had made its presence known, if only for just a moment.

Esmir walked to the brazier and peered down at the smoldering kindling within, feeling his hopes rekindle for the first time in four hundred years.

After Mistress Dayslin finished bandaging him, they carried Aram back to their room at the Flanters' Inn and laid him on the bed. He was still pale and clammy, the shadows beneath his eyes darker and deeper than they should be. But he was alive, and for that, Markus was grateful. While he waited at Aram's bedside, the bard went downstairs and procured a meal from the kitchen. There was bone broth for Aram, served in a wooden bowl and heated with a hot stone from the fireplace. He also carried up two trenchers, round slices of bread soaked in sauce and covered with roasted pork.

Markus sat on the floor and ate hungrily, as he hadn't had a bite to eat all day. He even ate the trencher, which was stale and hard, though made more palatable by the sauce. Master Ebra, sitting on the room's only stool, chewed his food slowly, his eyes distant with thought. He hadn't spoken the whole time they ate, and he set the trencher aside without finishing it, as was customary, to save the stale bread for the poor.

When the bard was done eating, he sat upon the bed and propped Aram in his lap, waking him enough to spoon a little broth into him and get some water down his throat. The boy didn't open his eyes but swallowed the broth compliantly. After that, Master Ebra settled him back down in the bed, covering him with a wool blanket and tucking it in securely.

"I'm sorry," Aram whimpered, cracking his eyes open just a bit. "I was trying to find my father. I'm so sorry…"

Master Ebra pushed the boy's damp hair back from his face in a compassionate gesture. "Aram. The spirits of those we love go to a far better place. You will not find your father in the void."

"I thought… maybe…he might be still alive…"

The bard's eyebrows bunched together. "Beyond the Veil?"

Aram nodded weakly.

"What made you think that?"

"Your ballad," the boy whispered. "You sang of the Auld, and a world beyond the Veil. I thought maybe…"

"Ah. I understand now." The bard's lips pursed. "If your father truly were capable of such a journey, don't you think he would have returned home by now? I'm sorry, Aram, but your father isn't there either. Get some rest now, please."

Rising from the bed, Master Ebra returned to the stool and sat, looking deep in troubled thought, his gaze remote. Markus sat with his back against the brittle slats of the wall, his knees drawn up against his chest. He ran his finger over a circular knot in one of the floorboards that had cracks at the edges and seemed on the verge of popping out. He listened to the soft whisper of Aram's breath, the only sound in the room, thanking the gods he was still breathing. He had truly thought they would lose him. If it hadn't been for Master Ebra's quick intervention, he knew they would have. But Aram wasn't out of danger yet, and the threat of the Exilari nagged at his nerves.

"How long until we can leave here?" he asked the bard in a lowered voice.

"A couple of days," Master Ebra replied. "The therling opened an artery in Aram's leg, and I don't want it to start bleeding again. I'm also concerned about the wound festering if we move him too soon."

Markus was terribly worried about his friend. He didn't want the wound in Aram's leg to reopen, but he didn't want him taken by the Exilari, either. "What can we do to help him heal faster?"

"The bone broth will help. Cow or pig liver would do him good, I think, if we can scrounge up some tomorrow. And we need to change his bandages often to ward against infection."

Markus lay down on the floor with his head pillowed on his arm, wishing he had brought his cloak from home to wrap up in. The night was cold, and he couldn't stop shivering. He didn't think he could get to sleep, especially without a blanket or something to cover with. He lay there long minutes while the bard sat upon his stool, elbow on his knee, head cradled in his hand.

"Why do you think Aram's father is dead?" Markus whispered, rolling onto his back and staring up at the rafters of the ceiling. "Everyone in the village thinks he just ran away."

Master Ebra paused before answering. He leaned forward, studying Aram's face, probably making sure the boy was truly asleep. "After I met Aram, I made some discrete inquiries around the village. It seems that his father shared many of Aram's unique traits. And I think it's very possible that he shared some of his unique talents as well."

Markus sat up, leaning back against the wall. "Do you think Aram's father was a Savant?"

"Perhaps. At the very least, I think he had the affinity. Did you notice how no one who saw Aram's wounds questioned the color of his blood? It was almost as though they expected nothing different."

"That's true. So…what do you think happened to Aram's father?"

The bard's frown deepened, and his gaze flicked toward Aram again. But the sound of Aram's breathing was a soft and even whisper. "There is a good chance he was taken."

Markus stiffened. "By the Exilari?"

Master Ebra nodded.

"But…if he was taken by the Exilari…isn't there a chance he's still alive?"

The bard let out a heavy sigh, and the muscles in his jaw bunched. "Unfortunately, yes. I hope not, for Aram's sake." He rubbed his eyes wearily. "There is no reason to mention my suspicions to Aram. The knowledge would only bring him pain. I'm only telling you this because I think it's important that you have an understanding of the danger the Exilari present to Aram. In the coming days, I may be forced to make some difficult choices, and I can't have you questioning me. Understand that everything I do is in his best interest, no matter what it seems."

"I won't," Markus whispered, his heart aching with pity for his new friend. "What will the Exilari do to him, if they take him?"

Master Ebra replied in the thinnest whisper, "I won't let them take him. Not alive, at least."

Markus shivered, feeling a chill of revulsion. "What about me? Would the Exilari take me too?"

"They would, but for a different reason. You see, hunting those with the affinity is a dangerous task, so their sorcerers are always accompanied by people who are resistant to magic. They're called Shields. Exilari sorcerers take their Shields everywhere they go, to protect them from those they prey upon."

"Oh…"

Now Markus understood why Master Ebra had picked him along with Aram, for the Exilari would be interested in both of them. Markus wondered if the bard had selected him to protect him from the Exilari—or if, rather, his intention was to deny the sorcerers a potential Shield.

"Try to get some sleep now, lad," Master Ebra said.

Markus lay back down, rolling onto his side and bringing his legs up against his chest. The floor was hard, and the planks weren't laid precisely flat, so they gouged into his ribs uncomfortably. But he was exhausted, and he felt sleep creeping up on him, so he decided to close his eyes and try.

"Master Ebra," he whispered, "did Auld Champions also have Shields?"

There was a long pause.

"They did," the bard replied. "Only, a Champion's Shield was called a Warden."

"Master Ebra…are Aram and I really your apprentices?"

Another long pause. The bard's stool gave a slight creak.

"Yes. Only, I don't intend to teach you anything about music. Now, get some sleep. Tomorrow morning, we'll move Aram somewhere we can hide him, and I'll have things for you to do. You're going to need your rest."

Markus licked his lips. "If you want…I think I know of a good place."

Aram awoke in pain. The world was dark but scented with the nostalgic mixture of seawater and mildew he could never mistake. He knew immediately where he was before he opened his eyes to the surreal wonder of his cave. Wavering firelight played across the walls, making for a hypnotic dance of shadows and texture. When he turned to look, a shooting pain drove a spike of agony into his thigh, making him cry out. While his leg throbbed in time to his heartbeat, he lay still and tried not to whimper, clamping his jaw against the pain.

"Hey."

Aram squinted to see Markus kneeling at his side. His dark hair hung to his chin in damp strings, and his face looked filthy and haggard, more the face of a work-weary man than a teenage boy.

"How are you feeling?" Markus asked, concern shadowing his eyes.

"Hurts." Aram peered upward at him. "Why are we here?"

"Because it's safe."

Aram accepted the answer because Markus was right: his cave *was* safe, the safest place in all the world. What he didn't understand was why Markus thought he needed to be somewhere as safe and secure as his cave. Had something happened while he slept? Something that he didn't know about?

Opening his eyes wider, Aram saw Master Ebra seated on the other side of the small fire they had built on the mound in the center of the cave. Aram didn't know how he felt about the bard's presence here in his domain. He had never shown his cave to anyone but Markus, and he was afraid of what Master Ebra might think about it. Most people would look at his precious collection of knots and see only strangeness and eccentricity. Like any other boy would, he yearned for his new master's approval, and if the bard were to look in judgement upon him, then the pain of that humiliation would hurt worse than his leg.

Seeing him awake, Master Ebra stood and walked around the fire toward him, bending to press a hand against Aram's forehead. "No fever. That's good." He lowered himself to sit at his side. "Does your mother know about this cave?"

Aram shook his head. He had never told his mother about his cave, afraid she would forbid him from coming here. "No. No one knows."

"That's good." Master Ebra looked at Markus. "How old are you, boy?"

"Fourteen, sir," Markus responded.

"Do you know how to use a sword?"

Markus nodded. "My father hired a mercenary to teach me. He thought it was a skill I needed to know."

"I fear he was right." Master Ebra sighed, bringing a hand up to scratch his whiskered cheek. "I want you to return to the village and fetch supplies—enough to keep us here for a few days. And bring your sword back here too."

"It's not mine," Markus protested. "It's my father's. I can't—"

"We need it. We also need food and medicine for Aram. Blankets and fresh water."

Markus looked anything but pleased about the bard's directive, but he nodded. "I'll need coin."

"In my instrument case."

"Yes, sir." Markus rose and set about his task, retrieving a small but hefty-looking sack from the bard's case then paused, waiting for further direction.

Master Ebra said, "If you see anything out of sorts, come back here as fast as you can, but make damn certain no one is watching. Am I understood?"

"Understood," Markus assured him. Giving Aram a weak smile of encouragement, he dropped to his hands and knees and crawled into the low tunnel.

Aram closed his eyes, disappointed that Markus had to go. His leg felt better when Markus was there, and now it felt worse again. Besides, he was worried that the bard would be angry at him for ripping a hole in the world. He knew he deserved his anger, and the combination of guilt and pain was hard to bear. He must have let out a whimper, for Master Ebra took his hand.

"You're a strong lad," he said. "You'll make it through this."

Aram peered up at the old man, his jaw trembling with anxiety and pain. "Why did you bring me here, Master Ebra? Why did we leave your room at the inn?"

The old man patted his hand. "We're here because we're taking no chances."

Aram didn't understand. "I want Markus."

"Markus will be back shortly. Now, get some rest. Close your eyes, Aram."

He obeyed, nestling deeper into his blanket. "Will you sing me a song?"

"Later. I promise. For now, we must try to be as quiet as we can."

Aram didn't respond, for he was already fast asleep.

As Markus walked through the streets of Anai, he became gradually aware that the people of the village were staring at him, many with wariness or even fear in their eyes. He understood why. Whatever Aram had let into their small world, it wasn't natural, and it could have endangered everyone in the village. It still might, if the Exilari got wind of what happened and decided to come investigate. It was a good thing they were planning on leaving because, by the looks on people's faces, Markus felt certain they wouldn't be welcome here much longer.

He went first to Mister Dareau, who owned the bakery on the edge of the market. He found the baker out behind his shop, feeding dough into his brick oven with a long wooden paddle. Mister Dareau was a big man, one of the tallest in the village, and years of sampling his own goods had made him even bigger. He had a good nature, always quick with a laugh or an offer of help. But the moment he saw Markus, his face tightened with concern—a testament to the effectiveness of Anai's rumor mill.

"Markus." He set the paddle down and wiped the dough off his big arms with a rag, using the same rag to mop the sweat from his brow. "How is Aram?"

Markus felt his face redden. "Aram's doing well, sir, just in a lot of pain."

"I should imagine." The words were cordial, but much more guarded than they ever should be, coming from someone like Mister Dareau. The baker thrust his doughy hands into a pail of water, scrubbing them together. "What can I do for you, Master Galliar?"

Markus held up the bard's coin purse, stepping forward. "Master Ebra wants me to purchase supplies for our journey."

Mister Dareau lifted an eyebrow. "How long of a journey?"

Markus hesitated, for he'd never been a good liar. They weren't really going on a journey, at least not yet. "I...err...a week."

Mister Dareau dried his hands with a fresh rag. "Maybe you should confirm with Master Ebra before you purchase too much or too little of something. In the meantime, stay clear of your father. If you see him about the village, turn and walk in the opposite direction."

"Thank you, but—"

The sound of someone shouting broke Markus's attention from the conversation. Loud noises echoed from a distance, muffled by a consistent and growing thunder. Markus flashed a startled glance at Mister Dareau, who immediately dodged around him and made for the street. Markus followed, jogging after him.

They left the yard of the bakery and rounded the corner of the house, emerging into the market just as a band of mounted soldiers streamed in from the side streets, scattering villagers before their horses with startled cries.

The soldiers encircled the perimeter of the market before drawing their mounts up, their mounts stamping and snorting, lathered flanks heaving. The men on their backs wore the uniform of the Imperial Legions, a sleeveless scale mail tunic that left their arms and legs bared. Their horses wore tall saddles and elaborate barding that dripped with ornaments and tassels. Black and purple standards rippled above their heads, disturbed by the onshore breeze.

The soldiers dismounted in a clatter of armor and weapons and stood at the heads of their horses, training crossbows at the villagers. Two other men who had rode in behind them now slid from their horses' backs and walked forward, their eyes roving over the small crowd of frightened people. One of the two was a large Abadian man armored in a steel breastplate, carrying a longsword in one hand and a heater shield in the other. The man at his side was Cerylite, with an angular face and long blond hair tied back at the neck. His clothing was covered by a blue mantle, and his tunic bore the insignia of a winged serpent on the left panel. His disquieting gaze traveled over the frightened villagers, as though he were searching for something—or someone.

"Where's the bard?" he asked at length, glancing from face to face.

Only silence answered his question. Women drew their children protectively behind their skirts, and the village men stood shifting and trading nervous glances, but no one spoke. On the edge of the crowd, a babe started crying, and its mother cooed franticly in an effort to hush it.

Eman Tangreve, one of the village elders, stepped forward and bowed low. "Exilar, welcome to Anai. Allow me to—"

The blond man raised his hand. "Word has it that a bard was here last night reciting the Ballad of Raginor in your longhouse."

Markus stared wide-eyed at the man, realizing he was an Exilari sorcerer. His body stiffened, fear clouding his senses and numbing his brain, and he could do nothing but look on. The dark Abadian man with him must be the sorcerer's Shield. They were looking for Master Ebra— which meant they were really looking for Aram. They had to be.

People in the crowd shifted, but still no one spoke. The silence extended, tension compressing the air until it was almost too thick to breathe. The sorcerer's gaze swept over the crowd, coming to rest on Mora Haseleu, who stood in front of her father's salt shop.

The man stalked forward, crossing the street toward her. Mora shrieked when she saw him approaching, and Mister Haseleu lurched in front of her, shoving his daughter back, but the nearest soldier came forward and dragged him to the ground and kept him there at sword point.

Without thinking, Markus stepped into the street and blocked the sorcerer's advance.

The man halted and just stared at him, as though he couldn't believe someone would have the audacity to get in his way. For a long moment, the two of them just stood there, gazes locked on each other's face.

Markus's vision exploded as something struck him in the head from behind. He staggered, wavering for a moment before his legs gave out from under him. The next thing he knew, he was staring upward from the ground into the face of the sorcerer's Shield, who loomed over him like a menacing statue. The man looked to his companion, who nodded.

The Shield moved swiftly, catching Markus by the hair and dragging him upright. Wrenching his head back, he brought his dagger up to slice his throat.

"Stop!"

Wheezing panicked breaths, Markus glanced sideways to see his father threading his way toward them through the terrified crowd. Seeing the look on his father's face, Markus found himself fighting back tears. His captor held him locked against his chest in an iron grip, his sharp blade biting into the skin of his neck. Markus knew that if that knife moved at all, this one glimpse of his father would be the last he ever had.

Baldur Galliar halted in front of the sorcerer, hands raised. Even from feet away, Markus could smell the strong stench of alcohol roiling off him. His eyes were red, face oily and pallid, and he swayed unstably over his feet. Markus couldn't tell whether he was hungover from the night before or still drunk, but it didn't matter. He was *there*.

"I'm the bard," his father growled, eliciting a gasp from the crowd.

Markus gaped at him in dismay, wondering what he was thinking.

The sorcerer's eyes narrowed. "What is your name?"

"Ebra of Starn." The words came out badly slurred.

"Ebra of Starn," the sorcerer echoed, scrutinizing him with a frigid glare. "Last night you were witnessed performing a proscribed ballad before a gathered crowd."

"I apologize, Exilar. Please. Let the boy go."

The sorcerer took a step forward, slipping his hands out of his pristine white gloves. "You sang a forbidden song before a public gathering."

For the first time in Markus's life, he saw his father looking less than arrogant. Humbly, Baldur Galliar lowered his gaze, clasping his hands in front of him. "Do what you want with me, Exilar. Just please. Don't hurt the boy."

The sorcerer glanced at Markus then moved forward until he was but a nose-length from Baldur's face, grimacing at his foul breath. The surrounding crowd had gone rigid and silent, and Markus's own sharp, panicked breaths were the loudest sounds in the world.

"Do you enjoy singing, Master Bard?" the sorcerer whispered.

"I do." Markus's father averted his gaze, unable to meet the man's caustic stare. "Let the boy go, sir, and I'll sing whatever song you like."

The sorcerer gave his companion a wry smirk. "If this man's a bard, then I'm the Imperial privy boy. But apparently, he likes to sing." Shrugging, he took a step back. "So let's hear him sing."

The pressure of the blade left Markus's throat. In the same instant, the sorcerer's Shield struck out at his father with the speed of a viper.

Markus cried out and lunged forward, but a soldier caught hold of him, restraining him with his arms pinned behind his back as he kicked and struggled.

His father doubled over, clutching his middle as his intestines spilled wetly through his hands, slithering to the ground. Baldur Galliar fell forward, hollering in agony as he clawed at his guts, trying to rake them back inside.

"No!" Markus cried, his voice strangled by horror.

"He sings well, doesn't he?" remarked the sorcerer with a smirk.

His Shield struck out with a steel-toed boot, knocking Baldur the rest of the way to the ground. Then he kicked his head and started stomping on it, over and over, grunting as he put all his weight and effort into the blows. He stopped only when Baldur's head caved in, reduced to a bloody, flattened pulp. Then he dragged his boots through the dirt, one at a time, wiping off the gore with an expression of distaste.

Markus screamed, sobbing and struggling in the soldier's grasp. All his life, his father had mistreated him, sometimes terribly—but he didn't deserve this. Nobody deserved this. There were times he'd been good to him too. And, in the end, his father had been his only champion.

The soldier released him, and Markus collapsed to his knees, weeping openly into his palms.

The sorcerer raised his voice and addressed the gathered crowd, "You are all aware of the law, and you're all in violation of it. The bard wouldn't have sung a note if he didn't have an audience. By the order of God-Emperor Mirak, I declare the inhabitants of this village traitors to the Empire." He turned and gestured at the officers. "Burn it down."

The market collapsed into turmoil as people fled with wild cries of terror but were prevented from escaping by more soldiers streaming in from the side streets. Sobbing, Markus picked himself up off the ground and took two faltering steps toward the grotesque body of his father. But it was too much. He couldn't go another step, and his father wouldn't want him to anyway.

So he turned and sprinted up the street, past the bakery and the salt shop. He ran all the way to his home and barred the door behind him. Through the slatted windows, he could hear the terrified screams of the villagers and smelled the first traces of smoke.

He went immediately to his father's room and dragged the feather mattress off the bed. There, atop the wood slats that supported the mattress, was his father's unsheathed longsword. He pulled it off the bed and held it up, pausing to stare at it for a few seconds, incapable of doing anything else. A scream from outside made him flinch and, blinking, he shook his head to clear his mind, then dashed back to the front of the house.

He took his father's gutting knife off the table and thrust it into his belt under his shirt just as the door jolted. Another impact sent shards of wood flinging into the room and a third broke the frame entirely, the door bursting open. Two Imperial soldiers charged inside, weapons drawn.

Markus raised his father's sword in both hands, his arms shaking violently, his vision blurred by tears. One of the soldiers advanced toward him. Markus struck out at him with the sword, but the soldier simply batted the blade aside and rushed him. The weapon flew from his hands and Markus spilled to the floor.

A vambraced arm slid around him and dragged him backward toward the door. Markus beat his fists against the steel breastplate of the soldier holding him, but all he succeeded in doing was making a racket. The man moved like an iron golem, his grip indomitable. He never lost a stride as he hauled Markus out into the street and flung him down in the dirt, pinning him there with a boot driven into his back.

The man's weight made breathing almost impossible. Markus lay on his stomach gasping for air, his eyes trying to make sense of the madness that confronted him. Everywhere he looked, villagers—people he knew—lay sprawled in the street, dead or dying. Many were women. Children. Blood pooled in the dirt, leaking from the corpses of his friends and neighbors.

Up the street, soldiers with crossbows had collected a group of men in a small cluster, forcing them to kneel on the ground with their hands behind their heads. Further away, toward the market, women and children were being loaded into wagons. There were a few older boys amongst their number, none younger than ten.

He saw Mora's father among the group of captured men. Mister Haseleu knelt with his fingers laced behind his head, blood leaking down his face from a wound in his scalp. His lips were drawn back in a snarl, his teeth bared like a dog's, watching his daughter being loaded into a wagon full of other girls. Mora bucked and screamed, struggling as a soldier shoved her in and locked the tailboard of the wagon into place. There was a shout, then the wagon lurched forward.

The weight of the boot lifted off Markus's back. He tried to rise, but the stock of a crossbow knocked him back to the ground. He lay on his back, staring blearily upward as blood leaked from his scalp and tears drained from his eyes.

He heard the sound of slow footsteps approaching, and then a shadow fell over him. Markus looked up to find himself staring into the sorcerer's face, the man's crystalline blue eyes locked with his own. As Markus watched, the man raised a thin glass vial to his lips, taking a sip of its contents. He swallowed, seeming to savor the taste, and almost immediately, his eyes started changing. His pupils contracted, disappearing altogether, and his eyes filled with a haunting blue light that glowed from deep within, as though his very soul burned with ethereal fire.

The sorcerer's glowing eyes glared down at Markus, holding him captive in a way that no iron shackle ever could. The muscles of his face twitched. Then a puzzled expression creased his brow, and his face pinched in concentration. He stared at Markus harder, his eyes burning like angry blue coals. He drew back with a sharp gasp.

"Nahim!" he called, the sound of his voice ragged.

His Shield came jogging up, sword in hand.

The sorcerer nodded at Markus. "Bring him."

"Is that the one?"

"No." The sorcerer paused. "But he's Impervious."

The Abadian man's eyebrows flew up, and he glanced at Markus in astonishment as the sorcerer strode away. While he hesitated, Markus closed his hand around the hilt of the knife that he'd stashed under his shirt.

When the man bent to grab him, he struck out, stabbing the thin blade of the gutting knife into the man's eye socket, driving it deep, all the way to the hilt.

The sorcerer's Shield recoiled with a cry, his hands making it halfway to his face before his entire body started jerking spastically. He took a step backward then dropped to his knees. He folded forward, his body convulsing. His limbs flailed, feet drumming on the ground. His head jerked back and forth with the hilt of the knife still protruding from his face, white froth foaming from his mouth. Markus stared at the bizarre spectacle, transfixed, unable to look away.

"Run, boy!" Mister Haseleu bellowed at him.

That shocked him out of his daze.

Pushing himself to his feet, Markus sprang forward and pulled the knife out of the dying man's face then sprinted away.

A ram awoke to the sound of Markus shouting.

"They're burning the village! They're killing everyone!"

Markus's voice was so loud and echoing it made Aram's nerves scream. That, in combination with the things Markus was yelling, overwhelmed his ability to stay calm. He shot upright with a moan of pain and raised his hands to cover his ears, squeezing his eyes closed. He could still hear Markus shouting, so he moaned louder, trying to drown him out.

"Stop!" Master Ebra bellowed, springing to his feet and throwing his hands up. "Both of you, silence!"

The frantic yelling ceased.

The bard raised a finger at Markus. "Take a moment and collect your thoughts!"

Merciful silence settled in, broken only by the sound of Markus's sharp, rasping breaths.

"Now. Speak slowly."

"An Exilari sorcerer came to the village!" Markus said in a strained whisper that quaked with panic and despair. "He brought soldiers with him. They killed my father because they thought he was you!"

Hearing the misery in Markus's voice, Aram started whimpering. His thoughts drifted to his mother, but it scared him too much to think of her in danger, so he forced his mind away. He hugged himself and started rocking, his nails scratching at the soothing fabric of his shirt.

95

"They're killing people!" Markus sobbed, anguish in his voice. "They're burning the village. *We have to go!*"

"Did anyone see you?" Master Ebra asked, his tone careful and deliberate.

Markus wiped his tears with his sleeve. "The sorcerer saw me. He wanted to take me, so I killed his Shield."

There was a moment's pause. Then the bard whispered, "You killed a sorcerer's Shield?"

Aram's eyes shot open. He stared wide-eyed at his friend, his terror momentarily forgotten. His body relaxed, and his fingers stopped raking at his shirt. For reasons he couldn't fathom, he felt suddenly comforted.

"I'm sorry!" Markus gasped. "They were going to take me! I just reacted!"

Master Ebra heaved a great sigh. Lifting his hat, he ran a hand back through his hair. "They'll track you here," he said in a defeated voice. "We need to go."

The bard didn't sound convinced that leaving would do them any good. Aram was growing nervous again, and the look on Markus's face didn't help. His friend's eyes were red and haunted, his cheeks blotchy and glistening with fresh tears.

"Aram." The bard crouched at his side. "I need you to look at me."

Aram looked, though his vision was blurry, and his mind felt cold and fuzzy.

"That passage there." The bard pointed toward the back of the chamber. "Is that another way out?"

Aram turned to look in the direction Master Ebra pointed, to where there was a dark slit in the rock wall barely wide enough for a man to pass through. "It's a long tunnel. It has an opening, but you can't get out because it's too high up."

"How high is it?"

Aram frowned deeply, struggling to remember. It had been a while since he'd explored back there. "About as high as the roof of Markus's house."

The bard looked thoughtful. He glanced behind him, his eyes finally settling on the coils of rope Aram had collected in the cave. He rose to his feet. "Markus, bring some rope along."

"Can't we just go back out the front?" Markus asked.

"They'll be coming *in* through the front," the bard reminded him. He bent and lifted Aram in his arms, blanket and all. Aram gasped as his leg was jostled, but he gritted his teeth and didn't cry out. The bard carried him toward the back of the cave and set him down, leaning him up against the stone wall.

Master Ebra turned sideways and moved through the gap in the cave wall. It was a tight squeeze, Aram knew, but it did open up wider later on.

"Gather up a faggot of sticks!" The bard's voice echoed hollowly from the opening. "We need light!"

"What about your instrument?" Markus asked.

"To hell with my instrument!"

Aram couldn't believe Master Ebra would say such a thing. The oud he played was beautiful, and it seemed very special to the bard. That Master Ebra would let it go did more than anything else to drive home the reality of their danger. The bard wouldn't leave his instrument behind unless he had no choice.

He returned at length and picked up Aram. Markus walked toward them, carrying a bundle of flaming sticks that he had gathered from the fire.

"You walk ahead," Master Ebra directed him, and waited for Markus to go first.

The bard carried Aram in front of him at an angle as he edged his way back into the narrow gap. The passage curved abruptly, and as he shifted his posture to accommodate the turn, he scuffed Aram's leg against the wall. Aram clamped his jaw to stifle a scream, an action which left him tasting blood.

Eventually, the narrow passage opened up into a tunnel that seemed bored out of the rock, the ceiling high enough that they could walk fully upright. They followed the tunnel for a good distance, straight ahead, the fluttering firelight casting back the shadows around them. A light breeze stirred, coming from the tunnel ahead and guttering the flame of Markus's makeshift torch. Eventually, the passage widened into a small chamber with a perfect ring of sunlight streaming in from a hole overhead. Roots that looked like snakes dangled through the opening, none reaching far enough down to do them any good.

Master Ebra set Aram down on the floor then climbed onto the debris pile, shading his eyes from the brilliant sunlight, and looked upward through the hole.

"Do you think you can climb up there?" he asked Markus, indicating the roots.

"I don't think so." Markus's eyes shifted around the chamber. "Maybe if I stand on your shoulders."

"I couldn't support you." With a deep frown, the bard glanced at Aram. "If I hold your hands, do you think you could stand on my shoulders and reach those roots?"

Aram eyed the roots that were hanging well over his head. They were so far up, but he didn't have a choice, did he? He whispered, "I can try."

"We'll try it, then," the bard decided. To Markus, he said, "We'll tie the rope around Aram's waist, then you lift him onto my shoulders. I'll stabilize him."

Markus brought the rope over and helped steady Aram as the bard tied the rope around him. When Master Ebra tugged the knot tight, Aram nodded in appreciation of his choice of the bowline.

Master Ebra said, "Grab hold of the roots and pull yourself over the edge. Once you're up there, find something to tie that rope around and throw it down to us."

Aram nodded meekly, fearing the pain he knew was coming. If he fell… Even the thought brought a shiver. Just pulling himself over the edge was going to be excruciating. But he understood the stakes and knew they had no choice. They couldn't stay there forever, and they couldn't go back.

Markus grabbed him under the arms and lifted him onto the bard's broad shoulders. The pain was bad, and Aram had to bite his lip harder to keep from crying out. He tried not to put weight on his leg, but even with Master Ebra's hands clutching his own, he still had to put *some* weight on it. His body listed from side to side as the bard fought to stabilize him.

"All right, now," said Master Ebra. "I've got you. Try to stand still."

Aram tried, but his arms and legs were already shaking. Markus took hold of his ankles to help steady him.

"Can you reach the roots?" the bard asked.

Fear of falling almost made him balk. But Aram summoned his courage and, biting his lip, let go of one of Master Ebra's hands. He stretched up to grasp the nearest root, but it hung just out of reach. He would have to let go with his other hand and put weight on his leg.

"I think I hear something," Markus whispered.

Aram heard it too. The sound of voices echoed toward them through the tunnel. Fright electrified his nerves, making his stomach clench. Sweat broke out across his brow and needled the palms of his hands. But he didn't have time to be afraid.

He let go and lunged for the root, grasping it with both hands. Then, using every bit of strength he had, he pulled himself up, squeezing his eyes closed and groaning with pain. From out of the tunnel, the sounds and voices echoed louder, spurring him to go faster. Hand over hand, he pulled himself up the thick and rubbery root until he reached the break in the ceiling and climbed through the hole. His wounded leg raked over stone as he pulled it limply behind him. The pain was atrocious, and it was all he could do to keep from screaming. He clenched his jaw and covered his mouth with both hands, curling into a ball.

But he couldn't stay there like that. Not with Master Ebra and Markus still down there. Glancing around, Aram saw that he had emerged into the grove of trees north of the village. With dogged determination, he pushed himself to his feet and forced himself to hop on one leg toward the nearest tree. He fell down beside it and quickly untied the bowline the bard had applied, spilling the knot and releasing it from his waist. He wrapped the rope around the trunk of the tree, securing it tightly. Then he wriggled back to the hole on his belly and peered down, waving at his companions to hurry.

Markus stepped back from the rope and motioned for the bard to go ahead.

But Master Ebra shook his head. "You go first."

As Markus went for the rope, the bard's hand caught his arm.

"Protect him," Master Ebra said gruffly. "Keep him safe, no matter what. And if you can't…you know what to do."

Markus stared at the bard for a long moment before finally nodding. He couldn't argue, for he didn't have time. Hand over hand, he climbed the rope as fast as he could. Just as he got his legs over, the sound of shouts echoed up from below.

"Cut the rope!" Master Ebra called up to them. "Now!"

Markus lingered for a moment, feeling torn in half. He didn't want to leave the bard down there, but he knew he didn't have a choice. It was Aram they had to save, and Master Ebra knew it. Drawing the knife from his belt, he used it to saw through the rope, sealing the bard's fate by letting it fall, then he knelt to scoop Aram up in his arms. The boy was heavier than he looked, and Markus had to bounce him a bit to adjust his weight, but Aram didn't whine or cry.

Carrying him, Markus sprinted through the trees, the muscles of his jaw bunched with the strain of the effort.

"What about Master Ebra?" Aram asked in a pained and jostled voice.

"Don't worry!" Markus gasped. "He'll be along!"

He hated himself for the lie but couldn't tell Aram the truth—that they'd abandoned the old man to the Exilari. He struggled forward, grimacing with the strain of carrying Aram's weight, his lungs and muscles burning. He ran as hard and as fast as he could, north toward the river.

They hadn't gone far, not even a mile, when he started feeling nauseous, a cold sweat breaking out all over his body. He didn't know how much longer he could keep running without dropping the boy. A desperate fear clenched his chest, pressing him harder.

From the distance behind them came the sound of baying hounds.

"Dogs," Aram said.

Terrified, Markus glanced behind them. A few of the men in the village kept hounds that they used for hunting hares and foxes. Apparently, the soldiers had commandeered them. He redoubled his pace, sweat streaming from his brow, arms trembling with fatigue.

The noise of the hounds was getting louder. He ran faster, panting and hunched over from a cramp in his side, grimacing in pain. He made it maybe another league, but there came a point where his arms just gave out, and he collapsed, spilling Aram onto the ground. The boy cried out in pain, clutching his leg and writhing on the forest floor.

"I can't..." Markus gasped, panting for breath and grimacing in desperation. "Can't run anymore..." He tried to get his legs under him, but he just couldn't. His muscles simply wouldn't move.

"It's all right," Aram said weakly.

But it wasn't all right. Master Ebra had placed Aram's life in his hands, and he'd failed them both.

The hounds were almost upon them, and Markus didn't know what to do. He was shaking so hard, but he couldn't move, paralyzed as he was in both body and mind.

"Run, Markus," Aram urged him. "Just go."

Markus wept like a child, hugging Aram close. "I can't."

"You can!" the boy begged him. "Please, just go!"

Clenching his jaw, Markus shook his head. "I'm not going to leave you."

He couldn't. He remembered what Master Ebra had said. For Aram, capture meant a lifetime of agony. He couldn't let that happen.

He knew what he had to do. He just didn't know if he had it in him.

His hand moved to the knife at his belt. Hugging Aram with his other hand, he asked him, "What's your favorite memory?"

The boy's eyes grew distant. "The day Captain Holin took me sailing."

Weeping silently, Markus squeezed the knife until it shook in his grip. "I want you to remember that day. Close your eyes and try to see it."

"Why?" Aram whispered.

The baying of the hounds was louder.

"Just trust me." Markus ran a trembling hand through Aram's hair. "Can you see it?"

The boy nodded, his eyes squeezed closed.

Markus brought the knife closer. "What was it like?"

"It was a beautiful day," Aram said softly, his voice trembling. "The sky was so blue, with puffy white clouds. I can still feel the wind. The sails were full, and the ship was moving so fast!"

Markus stopped listening to his words, for he couldn't bear to hear them. He was only aware that Aram was still talking, and that's all that mattered. The boy's mind had gone to a beautiful place, and that's what Markus wanted. He wanted Aram to stay in that place, stay there forever.

"Keep talking," he whispered, groping within himself to find resolve. "Tell me about the rigging."

He would have to cut fast and deep, just like Mister Raynel did when he slaughtered goats. The goats didn't seem to feel much pain, so maybe Aram wouldn't either. Maybe he would just slip off to sea with his puffy clouds and his fast ship. Markus bit his lip, steadying his trembling hand. But when it came time to use the knife, his hand didn't move.

"I can't," he whispered, his voice giving way to sobs.

Dropping the knife, he gathered the boy in his arms.

And then the dogs were upon them.

But when the hounds lunged for their throats, someone yanked them back by their chains.

A net was thrown over him. Markus struggled to escape, but someone kicked him in the head, and he sank back to the dirt, stunned. He lay trembling as they bound his arms and legs. Then they left him there, lying on his side in the dirt and detritus. Tears washed his cheeks, and he couldn't bring himself to turn and see what they were doing to Aram.

After several minutes, he heard the soft crunching noise of approaching footsteps. He turned his head and looked up to see a man standing over him—a man he recognized. It was the sorcerer from the village. Markus felt an intense, visceral revulsion at the sight of him, and a fear that made his throat clench.

The man squatted down next to him and stared Markus keenly in the eyes with a sharpened glare. "You killed my Shield," he said softly. "I suppose you'll have to replace him."

He turned to his men. "Go get the wagon."

A ram's leg throbbed with a mountain of ache.

He lay blindfolded and bound on a pile of dead leaves and brittle and pokey twigs. He hadn't squirmed much as they tied him up; the soldiers were too strong, and his leg hurt too badly. He felt dizzy. The wet feeling on his leg meant that his wound was bleeding again.

He could hear Markus moaning and thrashing a short distance away. The noises were muffled, as though they'd shoved a rag in his mouth. Eventually, the thrashing stopped, and Markus was quiet. Then, all Aram could hear were the sounds of footsteps in the dirt and voices in the distance.

"Get him to the wagon," said someone close by.

Footsteps approached and paused right next to his head. A hand pressed against his leg, causing enough pain to rip a scream right out of his throat.

"Open your mouth."

It was a man's voice, even and calm, devoid of all emotion. Aram thought it a strange request, but he was frightened, so he did as he was asked. When a piece of wood was jammed between his teeth, hard, he bucked and cried out in surprise and fear. More feet rushed toward him, and strong hands held him down.

"I'm going to cauterize the wound," said the man with the cool and even voice. "It's going to hurt. A lot. Bite down on the stick."

Fear squeezed sweat from Aram's pores, but he bit down as hard as he could on the wood. He wouldn't cry out. He wouldn't. No matter what.

When it came, the pain was like a tidal wave that broke over him. Agony shot up his leg, tearing him open, burning and searing all the way to his skull. He screamed in spite of himself, howling until his throat burned raw. He bit the stick in his mouth clean in half. The pain was so intense, so awful, that it overwhelmed him quickly, grabbing hold of him like a rip current and jerking him away.

When Aram woke, he was in a wagon.

The floorboards beneath him shimmied and juddered, making his body shake. He lay bound and gagged on the splintery boards, curled up on his side, his leg stabbing pain all the way up his spine. He couldn't see, for they still had him blindfolded. He was miserable, his throat dusty and raw. And he was empty inside, an emptiness that ached worse than his leg.

The wagon rattled and shuddered along. His teeth rattled with it. He listened hard but couldn't hear the sound of anyone else in the bed of the wagon with him. Where was the terrible man who had burned his leg? He wished he could have seen the man's colors, but he was also glad he hadn't.

He wondered if Markus was there with him in the wagon. He didn't think his friend had gotten away. There was a small but awful part of him that hoped Markus was there with him, for he didn't want to be alone. He hated himself for thinking that way, so he stopped thinking altogether.

The emptiness inside ached harder.

His stomach roiled. His wound hurt terribly, irritated by the constant rattling of the wagon. The pain was making him nauseous. There was a growing lump in his throat that made him gag and soon had him fighting back bile. Which, with the cloth stuffed in his mouth, was terrifying. What would happen if he vomited? If it came out his nose, could he breathe?

Fear raked like claws down his back, making him squirm. He pumped his wrists against the bonds that held him, twisting his arms until the coarse rope fibers dug their way under his skin. Then he stopped and went limp.

Vomit surged into his throat. He gulped it back down.

Panic took hold of him. He bucked harder against the ropes.

"Hold still."

It was that same, cool voice, hollow and without emotion. He felt a hand on his forehead. It was cold to the touch, as if a piece of ice had been pressed against his skin. A light, tingling sensation fluttered down his face, startling him, and at first, he tensed. But the tingling felt good. It made his leg feel better. His eyelids grew heavy and his body grew warm. He slipped softly to sleep.

Markus sat in the bed of the wagon, his arms bound behind his back. He stared at Aram, who was unconscious again. The sorcerer had done something to him; he didn't know what. He watched the contemptable man lower the vial in his hand, tucking it into a leather strap on his belt. Then he turned to look at him.

"What's your name?" the sorcerer asked.

Markus didn't answer. He was still aching from the hole this man had carved out of his heart when he'd ordered his father killed. The sorcerer's men had sacked his village and taken many of the children captive. They rode in wagons behind them, mostly girls. A few boys. After hours of riding, many still hadn't stopped crying. He didn't know what had become of the bard. He'd seen Master Ebra being loaded, unconscious and bloodied, into the back of another wagon. He'd looked bad. Markus had no idea if he was even still alive.

The sorcerer stared at him flatly. He didn't seem to be bothered by Markus's lack of response. Nothing seemed to really affect him at all. He sat beside Aram, his blue mantle pulled around him like a cloak. His blond hair was tied back, though the shorter locks around his face had escaped the knot. His eyes drilled into Markus as though boring through his soul.

"You killed my Shield," he said. "That's inconvenient. Your friend created a rupture, so that means the Veil has been destabilized in this region. There might be more ruptures, kind of like aftershocks. And if any therlings come through, they'll be looking for him." He inclined his head toward Aram. Then he glanced back to Markus. "And I don't have a Shield."

Markus didn't know why the man was telling him that. He glanced away, looking back to Aram, taking in the sight of his unconscious face. So much had already happened to him. He wasn't sure how much more the boy's poor body could take. The sorcerer had done something to him, and it had helped a little. Not much, but at least he had gotten the bleeding to stop. But Aram still looked pale, his face clammy.

The man turned from him, his gaze drifting away.

Markus sat listening to the persistent creek of the wagon's wheels and the constant jingle of the horses' tack, though everything else seemed all blurred and muddled, as though the rest of the world had lost its relevance. He gazed blearily at the clouds of dust kicked up behind them. The road they followed was little more than two broad ruts where the passage of wagon wheels had scored furrows in the ground. To either side of them, wide, heathered meadows sprawled toward the flat horizons, broken in places by stands of maple and fir trees. Clumps of purple flowers mottled the pasturage, swaying slightly on a breeze.

He could feel the sorcerer's gaze on him again. Hard. Penetrating. He didn't dare look. Markus closed his eyes and focused on the sound of the wagon until it was the only noise in the world.

But even that didn't help.

He had to look. Had to see if the man was still staring at him.

He cracked his eyes open and saw that the sorcerer was looking at him. A slow smile spread across his face, an expression contradicted by the coldness of his eyes.

Markus froze, unable to break his gaze from that cold-as-steel glare.

He shivered harder.

Aram felt someone lifting him, and the movement of his leg ripped him out of sleep. He woke with a muffled cry, disoriented, his entire body hot with pain. He was lifted out of the wagon and settled on a mat. He lay there listening to the sounds of footsteps and voices around him, the noises of the children being unloaded from the wagons, and the general bustle of people setting up a campsite. He had no idea where they were, or even if they were still in the Vardlands. Shivering, he rolled onto his side, curling tight into a ball.

He lay there until someone came and removed the gag from his mouth. When the cloth was gone, he wheezed a great gasp, drawing in a huge chestful of air. He felt around his mouth with a tongue that felt parched and foreign. The absence of the rag had an immediate soothing effect. He could breathe easier now, but he couldn't relax completely.

"Aram."

It was Markus. He turned his head, but with the blindfold on, he couldn't see his friend. He was so grateful to hear the sound of Markus's voice that he wanted to weep, though at the same time, he hated himself for feeling that way. He should be sad that Markus was there, not glad for it. Feeling as fickle as a square knot, he curled up tighter.

"Aram, do you hear me?"

"I'm sorry you're here," he whispered, drowning in shame. "This is all my fault…"

"It's not—"

"Of course it's his fault," snapped a different voice.

It was the voice of the man who had burned his leg with fire.

"If it wasn't for him, you wouldn't be here," the voice went on, speaking to Markus. "None of you would be here. It doesn't make sense to lie to him."

The man was right. Everything was his fault. He had brought death to Anai. All his life, Aram had never understood why people treated him differently, why no one ever liked him. Now he knew why—because he brought destruction to everyone he loved.

Had his mother survived? He hoped she had.

Never rely on hope. Rely on yourself.

It was one of his father's old sayings. His father had always said little things like that. Clever things. Wise things. Aram missed them.

He wanted to cry, but he didn't let himself. He didn't want the man with the calm voice and the burning fire to see him weak.

He heard the noise of footsteps walking toward him. Aram stilled his breathing, for he was afraid to move so much as his chest. Behind his back, his fingers twitched. There was a gap of silence that seemed broader than all the sky. Around him, the sounds of the camp faded to obscurity.

"What's your name?" The man's voice was soft and smooth like velvet.

Aram didn't want to tell him his name. He felt a sudden pressure squeezing him on the inside. Like a giant, clawed fist that gripped his backbone. It didn't hurt, but it was the eeriest feeling he'd ever known.

"I'm going to remove your blindfold," the man said. "I want to see your eyes."

Aram didn't want him to see his eyes. They were an outward symbol of all that was wrong with him. But more than that, with the blindfold off, he would have to look at the man. He didn't want to. He was afraid to see his colors.

The man grasped him by the shoulders and raised him into a sitting position. Then he reached behind Aram's head and gently untied the knot, removing the strip of cloth bandage from around his head.

When the blindfold fell away, Aram gasped at the swirling colors that surrounded the blond man in a dizzying aura, so bright they were hard to look at.

Too many colors…

Leaning forward, the man inspected him closely, staring deeply into his eyes.

"Opal." He nodded as though confirming a suspicion.

Aram glanced from the man to Markus, who sat across from him against the trunk of a tree, his hands bound behind his back. Markus looked pale and terrified. His eyes were red and raw, and there was a mark on his cheek that had started swelling.

On the ground beside them, Master Ebra lay unconscious on a tarp. His face and head were covered in blood, and there was more blood on his clothes. His eyes were swollen shut, his lips split, and his nose had been badly broken.

Aram felt his stomach cringe with nausea. Master Ebra looked bad. He looked *very* bad. He looked like he was dying.

Aram shivered, feeling the blond man's eyes on him. He was afraid of him. Afraid of his colors.

The man sat hunched over, white-gloved hands resting on his knees. He gazed at Aram with piercing eyes, as though trying to peer deep inside him. He sat back, picking up a stick from the ground and resting it against his knee.

"My name is Sergan Parsigal. For now, you may call me Sergan." The many-colored man smiled a grim smile. He said nothing more for a moment, as though he were waiting for something to happen. Eventually, the smile slipped from his face. "I have told you my name. Now, I would like you to tell me yours." He raised his eyebrows, looking back and forth between Aram and Markus.

A long, uncomfortable minute dragged by, after which he let out a mirthless chuckle. "You don't like to talk much, do you?"

Fools always talk. Wise men listen.

That's what his father had always said.

"Fortunately, you don't have to tell me," said Sergan. "Someone already did."

Aram glanced down. When he looked back up, he found Sergan's gaze locked on his face. The colors around him stagnated, slowly running together like bleeding paint, growing darker as they mixed.

"Your name is Aramon Raythe," the man said. "And you are Markus Galliar."

Aram glanced at Markus, wondering how the many-colored man could know their names.

Sergan tapped the stick he was holding against his boot. "That's what the bard told me, anyway. The *real* bard." He cast a meaningful grin at Markus, whose face reddened. His eyebrows pinched and his eyes narrowed, glistening as they filled with tears.

"He isn't doing very well," Sergan said softly, sparing a glance for poor Master Ebra. "I'm afraid he doesn't like to talk much, either."

Aram understood why Master Ebra hadn't wanted to talk to this man. The bard could see auras too, just like him. He probably hadn't liked Sergan's colors either.

"You son of a bitch!" Markus growled, glaring at Sergan with hatred in his eyes.

Aram winced. He'd never heard Markus talk like that. He'd never heard *any* boy talk like that, especially not to an adult.

For some reason, Sergan seemed to find humor in the comment. "Why, yes, I am a son of a bitch. I have to be. It's my job, you see."

"What's your job?" Aram asked, honestly curious.

Sergan turned to him, and his smile finally warmed, if only just a bit. "I'm a sorcerer of the Exilari. A Rift Warden." He said it as easily as though admitting to being a wainwright or a blacksmith.

Aram's spine went rigid, hearing that. His hands were still tied behind his back, which was an awful feeling. A vulnerable feeling. He needed his hands, needed them badly. Whenever he was nervous or afraid, tying knots was the only thing that gave him comfort. Right now, more than ever, Aram needed that comfort, because he suddenly realized what Sergan's swirling colors meant.

He was gazing into the face of a predator.

The sorcerer smiled congenially. "Enough about me. I want to talk about you, for both of you are indeed special." He looked at Aram. "I have never felt the kind of power you used last night. No one has. No one alive, at any rate. You ruptured the Veil all by yourself. That's impressive." For the first time, he had real emotion in his voice, and a passionate excitement lit his eyes. "And you, Markus. You're a True Impervious, the only one I've ever met."

Aram glanced at Markus, wondering what 'Impervious' meant. It was a word he'd never heard before. Markus was staring hard at the ground, ignoring the sorcerer. If he was surprised by the man's statement, he didn't let on about it.

"What are you going to do with us?" Aram asked quietly.

"I'll be taking you to Karaqor," the sorcerer answered. "It's where we—the Exilari, that is—have our headquarters." He tossed the stick he was holding over his shoulder. "You, Markus, will be trained as a Shield. People like you aren't found every day, and your talents—or lack of them—are sorely needed. My superiors will also be very excited to meet Aram. No one like him has been discovered in generations."

Beside them, Master Ebra let out a groan. He moved a little bit, thrashing his head back and forth. He was still unconscious, though Aram could tell he was in great pain. He didn't like seeing that. Master Ebra was a good man, and he didn't deserve what had happened to him.

"Can't you help him?" he asked.

"No. I have little use for him, and he'll probably die anyway. He's not worth the essence."

To Aram, it sounded like the sorcerer *could* help Master Ebra, but was choosing not to. He wondered why he would do that. Even if he had little use for him, Master Ebra was still useful to other people. He wondered why Sergan would have gone through all that trouble to bring him along in the first place, just to watch him die.

His leg was starting to throb again. He wasn't sure what Sergan had done to it. The bleeding had stopped, though the pain seemed even worse than before. He was miserable in other ways too. The coarse hemp rope bit into his skin, and he hadn't had a sip of water since morning. His mouth was so dry it felt stuffed with sand.

Across the ring of wagons, the other children that had been carried away from the village were being unloaded. A weathered man with a dirt-encrusted face lowered the tailboard of the wagon the girls were in and motioned them out. They clung to each other, eyes wide and terrified.

The soldier made a growl and lunged for the nearest girl, catching her by the arm and yanking her forward with a screech. She came tumbling out of the back of the wagon, falling on her hands and knees. Picking herself up, she scurried away. The man caught hold of the next girl, tugging her forward. This one jumped out of the wagon on her own, dodged past him and scampered after the first girl toward the center of the camp.

"Let's go, all of you!" the man growled, standing back.

Across the campsite, the boys knelt in a long line, their heads bowed in defeat. Many were covered in bruises and dark, crusted blood. Aram knew all of them, though there were a couple he could hardly recognize. Jory and Kasry were among the bunch. Even though they had been mean to Aram, he still felt sorry for them. Jory looked particularly bad. His face was covered with blood and one of his eyes was missing.

"Here."

Sergan held a waterskin to Aram's mouth, and he gulped the contents down frantically, until the sorcerer took it away and held it up for Markus. The sun was setting around them, the sky taking on the deep color of the ocean. In the center of camp, the soldiers had cleared the ground and were building a bonfire. When they had it going, the crackling flames devoured the darkness but did little to warm him.

Aram was exhausted, so he rolled over and curled up on the ground, hoping to sleep. But as soon as he started drifting off, the world jolted.

Startled, Aram sat bolt upright. The ground heaved again, trying to buck him off.

All around them, the world was undulating, its vibrant fibers convulsing.

Aram cried out, and Sergan brought his hands up to clutch the sides of his head. Markus looked at them with an expression of incomprehension on his face, as though he had no idea what was happening and didn't understand why they were reacting the way they were. Eventually, the fibers of the world twisted back into place, though they still trembled as though afraid.

"Another rupture," Sergan gasped, his hand diving for the collection of finger-sized vials strapped to his belt. Unstoppering one, he sipped some of its contents then closed his eyes and appeared to be concentrating.

"It's not far," he said after a moment, his eyes squeezed shut, his brow wrinkled in concentration. He took another sip of the cloudy liquid that looked like watered-down milk.

"Some got through," he muttered. He opened his eyes, and there was fear in them. That terrified Aram. He wondered what kind of horror could scare a sorcerer.

"They'll be coming." Sergan surged to his feet. "We have to leave. Now." Turning, he shouted to the soldiers behind him, waving them over.

"*Who's* coming?" Markus asked.

But the sorcerer didn't respond. Within seconds, they were surrounded by armored men. Sergan shouted orders, rattling them off faster than Aram could keep track of them. The bard was lifted from the ground and placed back in the bed of the wagon, which was hastily loaded with provisions. From somewhere, Sergan produced parchment, quill, and an inkpot and stood hunched over the tailgate of the wagon, scribbling furiously. When he was done, he rolled the parchment up into a scroll and dribbled a few drops of his vial-liquid onto it. The scroll stayed rolled after that, even without a glob of wax to seal it.

Sergan handed the scroll to one of the soldiers. "Take this to the nearest regiment. Ride like hell through the night and don't stop." The man bowed and set off for the horse pickets while Sergan waved another soldier over, this one of slighter frame. Sergan stood looking him up and down critically, as though sizing him up. "Take off your armor and put it in the wagon."

The soldier gaped at him like he didn't understand the order. "My lord?"

"You heard me."

Looking both furious and fearful, the man pulled his armor off right there, removing his chain mail tunic and letting it fall to the ground along with his bracers and arming jacket, until he stood in front of them in only his undergarments.

"Your sword and shield," the sorcerer snapped. Looking dumbfounded, the man complied, retrieving his shield and setting it in the back of the wagon, piling his sword and armor on top of it.

Sergan drew a knife and started toward Aram. Aram tensed, for he thought the sorcerer intended to kill him. But instead, Sergan used the knife to saw through the bonds confining his legs.

"Get in the wagon," he ordered, moving to Markus.

But Aram couldn't move from the spot he sat in because it hurt too much to stand. He watched as the sorcerer freed Markus's legs, then Sergan lifted him and carried him to the wagon, setting him down next to Master Ebra, while Markus scooted onto the bed and sat next to him. Raising the tailgate into place, Sergan climbed into the driver's seat and waited there for the soldiers to finish harnessing the horses.

Twisting around, Sergan explained to them in a conversational tone, "They'll be coming for Aram. The therlings, I mean. They'll be coming through the rupture, and with his shine," he nodded at Aram, "he'll draw them like iron filings to a lodestone."

Aram was hardly listening to him. He sat gritting his teeth against the pain in his leg and staring down into Master Ebra's ruined face. When he looked up at Markus, he realized his friend was looking at him, fear and compassion in his eyes.

As soon as the horses were hitched, Sergan snapped the reins, and the wagon lurched forward, rattling away from the campsite and jolting back onto the rutted road. The sun had set completely, and the woods that surrounded their camp were dark and cold.

With his legs untied and his blindfold off, Aram wondered if he could do something—*anything*—to knock the sorcerer out of the driver's seat, so they could flee to safety and get help for Master Ebra. But when he tried to bend the strands of air around them, he couldn't grasp them. He tried for several minutes before finally giving up. Frustrated, he pondered the problem as the wagon lurched along. At first, he didn't understand why his magic wasn't working. It took him a few shuddering miles to realize that, for the moment at least, Sergan was trying to help them, so his mind didn't see him as the greatest threat.

With a sigh, Aram leaned back against the side of the wagon and stared at poor Master Ebra, wishing he'd wake up. Sergan didn't say another word to them, but drove the horses forward relentlessly until they were well away from the campsite before giving them a rest. Even then, he said nothing, but just sat staring into the darkness as though he expected an attack at any time.

When they started off again, the bard let out a low, heartrending moan. As the hours wore on, Master Ebra seemed to grow more and more uncomfortable. He moaned and thrashed often in his sleep, and eventually took to shouting out, moaning names of people that Aram didn't know. He wished he could do something for him, but he couldn't. He only knew how to tie knots in the air. He knew nothing about healing somebody that was broken.

Sometime past midnight, the bard's breathing became labored. His moaning continued, but he had stopped flailing about so much. His breaths took on wet and crackling sounds, and he let out a soft groan every time he exhaled. He looked so pitiful and uncomfortable that Aram couldn't bear it, and his eyes filled with tears. He wanted more than anything to help the poor man, for he knew that Master Ebra was dying.

Eventually, the bard's breathing slowed to the point that it took long, cruel seconds for the next breath to come. When his chest stopped moving altogether, Aram wept, for the bard had been kind to him. The only thing that gave him comfort was knowing that Master Ebra wasn't in pain anymore.

Sometime later, the wagon stopped, and Sergan jumped down from the driver's seat to check on them. He rolled Master Ebra's body out of the wagon and left him on the ground at the side of the road. Then he climbed back up into the driver's seat and lifted the reins.

"Aren't you going to bury him?" whimpered Aram.

"No." Sergan cracked the reins, sending the horses forward.

The wagon clattered on down the road. Aram's leg hurt terribly, and he was growing too tired to stay awake, so he curled up in the wagon bed. He lay there miserable for a long time, his heart and leg aching, until exhaustion finally got the better of him.

"Aram."

Somebody was shaking him awake. Aram rolled over, the action sending pain shooting from his leg into his groin. He moaned, sagging back. The pain was too great to sit up. His entire body was drenched in sweat, and he was cold and shivering. He didn't feel right.

"What's wrong with him?" Markus asked in a worried voice.

"He's feverish," came the sorcerer's response.

Sergan unwrapped the bandages on his leg, and Aram tried his best not to scream. When the cloth came away, a terrible odor rose from the wound. Markus made a strangling noise, recoiling. Even the sorcerer looked concerned.

"The wound's festering."

Aram tried to peer down at his leg, but it hurt too much to move even a little bit. Sergan sat for a minute rubbing his chin, frowning down at Aram's leg, while Markus leaned against the side of the wagon, staring at him with a stricken expression. Scowling, the sorcerer reached down and withdrew another vial from his belt.

"What is that?" Aram asked through clattering teeth.

"Essence."

Sergan took a sip from the vial, closing his eyes and appearing to savor the taste of the liquid. Then he bent forward and exhaled a great, steaming breath onto Aram's wound. Dropping the empty vial, he withdrew another and repeated the act, expelling the contents of the vial onto Aram's leg in one, long breath.

At first, Aram felt nothing. It took him a long moment to realize that his leg was no longer throbbing. It still hurt fiercely, just not as bad as before. His teeth had also stopped chattering, and he didn't feel so terribly cold. He looked up at the sorcerer in amazement.

Sergan stood, dusting the dirt of the wagon bed off his black tunic, his face still tight with concern. "That's all I can do for the moment. I'm running out of essence, and I need to save the rest in case the therlings catch up with us."

He drew his knife and held it threateningly before Markus's face. "I need you to understand something and understand it well. Your friend's life is in grave danger. If the therlings don't kill him, the infection will. Without me, he doesn't stand a chance."

Bending, he used the knife to cut the bonds from Markus's wrists. Then he turned to Aram and sawed through the rope lashed around his arms.

"I can feel them," Sergan said, climbing back into the driver's seat. "They're getting close. I sent riders for help, but I don't think it will arrive on time. There's a town ahead of us. Mardak. I'm not sure we'll reach it before they catch up with us."

He snapped the reins, and the horses started forward again. The wagon bucked as it skipped over deep ruts in the road, sending jagged lances of pain up Aram's back. He sucked in a sharp breath, balling his hand into a fist and smacking it several times against his good leg.

They traveled for several minutes before the pain finally started settling down. By then, the road had left the woods and now cut across a rolling lowland textured by shadows and scattered trees. Fog clung to the ground, swirling in the moonlight.

"What are they?" Markus asked.

Sergan glanced back over his shoulder, but not at Markus. Instead, he seemed to be watching for something behind them. "Aetherlings. Creatures that inhabit the void between worlds. There might be void walkers with them too. They'll be starving for essence, so they'll be drawn to Aram."

A high-pitched noise pierced the night, ripping across the lowlands toward them. It didn't sound like any animal Aram had ever heard. It wasn't a wolf's howl or the screech of an owl. It sounded mournful, like the wail of an injured beast. It sent tingles across his skin that started in the back of his neck and spread to his shoulders.

The wagon jolted hard as one of the wheels slipped into a rut. Aram stifled a cry. The pain was getting worse again, so much worse, and it had gone on too long. He didn't know how much longer he could stand it.

"Markus!" Sergan called over the clatter of the wagon. "Put the armor on!"

Markus stared at the sorcerer as though he didn't understand. But then another cry rose from out of the darkness behind them. He scrambled to the corner of the bed where the soldier had piled his armor and sword. He started pulling on items, first the leather tunic, then the chain mail, struggling to buckle the straps. Finally, he strapped on the bracers and buckled the sword belt around his hips.

The wagon bounced hard, and Aram bounced with it. He gave an agonized cry, for the pain was excruciating. He couldn't stand it any longer. He could also sense the therlings behind them, and they were coming closer. The fear provoked by their proximity was starting to strangle him.

"I see something," Markus gasped, looking behind them.

"See what?" Sergan called back, snapping the reins and urging the horses to a gallop. "What do you see?"

Markus stared behind them, hands gripping the tailgate of the wagon. Then he twisted back around, his eyes wide with terror.

"They're here!"

"You're going to be my Shield," the sorcerer called back to Markus. Aram thought Markus looked like he had just been stung by a jellyfish. His face had lost its color and his eyes had gone wide and round. Markus scrambled to where the soldier's shield lay clanking around in the corner of the wagon. He pulled it toward him, drawing the sword from its sheath. All the while, he kept his gaze fixed on the road behind them, his terrified eyes scanning the shadows. On his hands and knees, he crawled toward the front of the wagon, hanging on to the sideboard for stability.

"I don't know how to be a Shield!"

"It works like this!" the sorcerer shouted back over the clanking racket of the wagon. "You stand in front and take everything they throw at me!"

Markus looked terrified. "I'll die!"

"You're Impervious!" Sergan shouted back. "Magic can't harm you!" Cracking the reins as though they were whips, he hollered, *"Hah!"*

But the horses were tiring, their distended nostrils blowing steam, their coats lathered with sweat. They couldn't continue at that pace much longer.

Sergan told Markus, "They'll be coming for Aram, so we have to stand between them and him!"

"How do we kill them?" Markus asked, testing the weight of the sword in his hand.

"That's my job. I'll attack. You protect me. Do you understand?"

Markus looked like he didn't. "I think so."

Aram didn't know why Markus would lie about that. He glanced behind them and thought he saw a flicker of light far away, between the trees behind them, but it faded too quickly for him to be sure. He scanned the landscape for other lights, and soon, he saw them: dim white glows appearing from the shadows.

Sergan pulled back on the reins, bringing the horses to an abrupt halt. Picking up a leather pack, he bolted out of the driver's seat and slid down, setting the pack on the ground beside the wagon. Pausing, he removed his blue mantle and tossed it to Aram.

"Keep this over you, no matter what happens. It'll conceal your radiance." He stooped to rifle through the items in the pack. "Markus, get down here!"

Aram pulled the thick mantle over his head like a blanket, leaving only his face exposed, and peered out from under the fabric. His hands found the remains of the frayed rope Sergan had used to bind him, and he started fiddling with it nervously. The lights behind them were getting closer, approaching from different directions. Fear made his pulse thunder in his ears, the ache of his wounded leg all but forgotten.

Sergan rose, holding onto a green glass bottle that reminded Aram of the kind Kantimari sailors used to store their liquor. Unstoppering it, the sorcerer raised the container to his lips and, closing his eyes, drank deeply of its contents. Aram realized that the bottle was a bigger version of the small vials Sergan wore at his waist, just a much larger capacity. He was fascinated, knowing what the liquid inside those vials did—allowed the sorcerer to work his magic. He hoped the container was full. There were a lot of lights out there, and they were getting very close.

"Stand here," Sergan said to Markus, scraping an X into the dirt with his boot, "and don't move off that spot, no matter what. You are Impervious to any magic they use against you, so your goal isn't to keep them off *you*. It's to keep them off *me*. If you cower or run, I'll die and then Aram dies. Say you understand."

When Markus didn't respond, the sorcerer took him by the shoulders and shook him. "Say you understand!"

"I understand!" Markus moved to stand over the X as Sergan drew back behind him, standing with his back up against the side of the wagon.

The lights were closer now, growing in size and beginning to take form. As though confident, the creatures that trailed them had slowed their advance, spreading out to surround them in a wide but constricting ring. Gazing out at the lights, Aram's fear melted away, his mind growing strangely calm. As his fear ebbed, his thoughts and vision sharpened their focus, and the forms stalking them took on distinct shapes. They resembled creatures he knew: horses and wolves, long, thick snakes and pink-skinned panthers that looked like drowned farm cats. Each was corrupted in its own hideous and unique way, as though it had died and gone to rot, only to be resurrected by an incompetent god. Their bodies were pale and hairless, their limbs malformed and flailing. A terrible light gleamed from their eye sockets, as though their flesh was merely rotten clothing draped over the haunted souls of animals.

But not all were animals.

Walking in their midst were human shapes, equally twisted and bastardized. All were pale and misshapen, and their skin seemed to be nothing more than thin membranes webbed with veins stretched over gnarled bone. Each was clothed in rotted garments cut in styles Aram had never seen, as though they had come from a very far-away place— or a very ancient past.

Seeing them, Markus raised his sword and readied his shield. He looked prepared to fight, and also prepared to die. Aram was terrified for him. He knew Markus would try his best, but the sheer number of creatures that surrounded them was overwhelming, and he doubted even Markus's best would be enough to save them.

"Void walkers." Sergan swore. He took another great gulp from the bottle and settled into a fighting stance, even though he bore no sword.

"What's the difference?" asked Markus over his shoulder.

"It means they'll be even hungrier. And nastier."

Almost as one, the creatures halted. They stood frozen for a moment, like a predator before the pounce. Then, with a collective, otherworldly cry, they surged toward the wagon.

Sergan thrust out his arms, and as he did, his many-colored aura erupted with a blazing explosion of power. Creatures were lifted and hurled backward, others shredded to pieces where they stood. Bits of flesh and gore pattered down around Aram like rain, pelting the wagon bed and the mantle that covered him. Cringing, he reached up and tugged it all the way over his head to keep from getting splattered.

Guttural groans and shrieks alerted him to the fact that some of the creatures had survived the sorcerer's attack. He peeked out from the back of the wagon just in time to see three once-human monsters lunge toward him, angling wide of Sergan. The sorcerer stepped into their path and, thrusting out his hands, propelled them back with a brutal slap of dazzling light.

Aram held his breath, clutching the sideboard of the wagon with hands that, for some reason, refused to tremble. On the floor beside him, the length of cord his fingers and nerves had been relying on lay forgotten. His gaze was transfixed on Sergan, who stood with his arms outstretched, blazing with an eruption of many-colored light that overwhelmed both the darkness and their enemies. When the next wave of creatures swept toward them, Sergan picked the bottle up off the ground and, taking a quick gulp, swept his hands through the air in great arcs. Pale bodies ruptured, spewing ichor, and howls of mortal anguish filled the night air.

Two still got through: snarling creatures that look like rabid wolves with mange-ravaged hides charged at Sergan, flecks of froth spraying from their mouths. Markus stepped in front of the sorcerer at the last moment, raising his sword and striking out with his shield. The beasts broke off their attack and fell back out of range. Teeth bared and eyes glowing menacingly, they circled just out of reach. Within moments, they were joined by others of their kind that came racing out from the shadows. Soon, an entire pack was gathered around the wagon, taking turns rushing in and then dodging back again, seeming to be taunting both Sergan and Markus. As their numbers increased, their tactics evolved, with two or more creatures coordinating to attack from various angles. Markus held them off with his sword and shield, while Sergan stood panting, perhaps conserving his resources.

But then something changed. The creatures stopped attacking and backed away, snarling. Other human forms approached and ringed the wagon, gazing at its occupants with glowing dead eyes.

They raise their hands.

A deluge of light exploded from their palms and shot toward Markus and the sorcerer. With a cry, Markus brought his shield up just in time to deflect the light, scattering it in glowing rays that sliced like blades in every direction, brilliant enough to overwhelm Aram's vision.

Then the creatures attacked in earnest. More rushed forward from the shadows to stand with their fellows, adding their own brutal light to the offensive. Two came at Markus with swords, and even though he was strong, he was hard-pressed to repel them.

Markus dodged and fought, beating back the ones with weapons while deflecting a torrent of magic with his shield. But their numbers were too great. They were coming from too many directions at once, and there was only so many places Markus could be.

Sergan tilted his head back and shook the last drops from the bottle into his mouth before tossing it away. Then, with what looked like every last bit of magic he could summon, he swept his hands over his head in a great arc, producing a compressed band of light that shot out like a whiplash, slicing through the front ranks of bodies.

He raised his hands again to attack the creatures that remained. But then the color drained from his face and his arms fell to his sides, and Aram knew he was beaten.

The sorcerer was out of essence.

Apparently, Markus understood, too, for Aram could see the despair written on his face. Sword raised, Markus turned slowly in a circle as the remaining void walkers converged on them, growling and snarling.

"Stand next to me," Sergan said to Markus, his voice just as calm as it ever was, even in the face of death.

But something unexpected happened.

The creatures halted, their ears perking, heads tipped as though listening. For a long moment, they stood frozen. Then suddenly, inexplicably, they dashed away. Their glows faded in the distance, at last disappearing altogether. Watching them go, Aram heaved a sigh of relief, while Markus sagged to his knees. But Sergan's face hadn't changed. If anything, it had become grimmer.

Looking past Markus into the trees, Aram saw why.

The shadows of the night parted, and a new figure appeared, towering over all the others. It tucked its enormous wings close against its body as it emerged from behind a copse of tall pepper trees. Aram's breath caught in his throat and for a moment he couldn't move, couldn't swallow, couldn't even scream.

It was a dragon, and it was real.

The dragon's milky body was devoid of color, like that of a corpse, its wings tattered and scarred. Cold blue eyes glowed from within its skull. Reaching the road, it extended its massive wings, a display of strength that scattered any remaining creatures. Then it took to the air and glided toward them, letting out a terrible roar that shook the atmosphere. It landed right in front of them with earth-shuddering force, releasing gouts of crackling blue flames aimed straight for Markus and the sorcerer.

Cringing, Markus did the only thing he could do in the face of such an assault:

He raised his shield.

Roiling blue dragonfire poured over him, convulsing the air with broiling waves of heat. Aram cried out in horror, sure Markus's flesh would burn to char. But the blue flames were pure magic, and they were repulsed by his shield.

Its attack frustrated, the dragon thundered its outrage.

Emboldened, the other void creatures crept back out of the shadows, closing around them again. This time, they didn't hesitate, but swept right in, circling the dragon and ranging around to the other side of the wagon to come at them from behind. Terrified, Aram clung to Sergan's cloak, tugging it closer to his body, hiding the light of his gift beneath its shade. Every instinct within him screamed for him to throw it off and join the fight, but Sergan's warning echoed in his ears, and so he cowered in the wagon while his best friend stood braving a dragon's flames.

A roiling blue inferno gushed from the mouth of the great beast, and it was all Markus could do to stand before it. He couldn't do anything about the other void creatures coming at them from behind. He stood in defiance as long as he could, clinging to his shield, until the rage of the dragonfire drove him to his knees. And even then, he did not succumb. He raised his shield over his head and accepted the force of the searing blast even as the air around him heated to blistering. Behind him, Sergan knelt on the ground with his hands flung up to shield his face.

Markus squeezed his eyes closed and pushed back at the raging flames with all his might. The fire itself wasn't harming him, but the air it was heating did. It was starting to burn. He could smell his hair smoldering, and every breath he drew seared his throat. He didn't know how much longer he could stand it, but he knew that, if he fell, then Aram would die. And he was convinced that if Aram died, a small but wonderous part of the world would die with him.

So he stood in defiance of the flames as they ravaged the air around him, until he felt his skin start to scorch. And even then, he did not cower or falter.

Even in the face of death, he stood.

Aram looked on in horror as his friend's strength started to fail. He knew that even Markus's great courage couldn't last against such brutality, and he couldn't bear to watch him die. He knew there was nothing he could do. And yet, he knew that he couldn't let his best friend die alone. With that thought in mind, he threw off the thick wool mantle and climbed down from the back of the wagon. For some reason, his leg barely hurt as he slid to the ground and limped forward, determined to be there, at Markus's side, when his strength finally failed.

For some reason, he wasn't afraid.

He'd been frightened all his life, mostly of people. Not because they scared him, but because he didn't understand them, just as they didn't understand *him*. But the creatures they confronted on this night were different. He understood them well.

They were sick and ravenous, and every second they spent in this world took an enormous toll on them. That's why their skin was pale and decayed, why the lights of their souls were bared to the world. They were starving things. Dying things. And, like every other dying thing, they were desperate, especially the dragon. He could feel its overwhelming hunger, its need to kill them and feed upon their souls.

With that understanding, he knew that the only way to defeat the void creatures was to take pity on them. And, suddenly, he knew what he needed to do. Not only to save Markus, but to save *them*, to free the void walkers from their suffering.

With a resolve he'd never known before, Aram limped past Markus, inserting his own body between his friend and the dragon's breath. Spreading his hands, he limped forward.

He knew what they wanted, what they needed.

He raised his hands and a dazzling light gushed from his palms, streaming outward toward the creatures surrounding them. The light was not magic, but rather a substance far more fundamental. It was essence, and he was full to brimming with it. He drew it out of himself the way a spider spins a thread and cast it their way, then staggered as the agony of the act tore into him. He screamed in mortal pain, for it felt as though his soul itself were being stripped from his bones.

Hungering, the desperate void creatures soaked it in like lifeblood. The more he fed them, the greater their inner lights swelled, until they became an all-consuming brilliance that lit an area around them as though at high noon.

One by one, the twisted creatures disappeared. Having gotten what they needed, they were free to move on.

Whimpering in agony, Aram watched them go. He could feel his own strength waning. And yet he persisted, dispelling creature after creature, until only the void dragon remained.

The white dragon stared at him with glowing eyes that gleamed with voidfire, and Aram knew the dragon recognized him for what he was and understood what he was trying to do. Instead of draining him dry, the great beast exercised control and took only what it had to, sparing him. When it was done, it unfurled its massive wings, making a noise that, to Aram, sounded like gratitude.

And then it, too, departed, and darkness fell.

So did Aram.

His knees gave out from under him, and he collapsed to the ground.

Sergan bent over the unconscious boy, struggling to calm his racing thoughts enough to figure out how to properly deal with the situation. His brain was stuck somewhere in the gap between amazement, disbelief, and outright panic. The feat Aram had just performed far outstripped anything he had ever seen or ever heard of. By offering himself, the boy had satiated, then dispelled, a void dragon and its entire entourage. But now the most valuable life in all the world hung by a mere thread, and he couldn't let the boy die.

He had been right: Aram was a True Savant, the first that had been born in over four hundred years. Not only did his body produce vast amounts of essence, but he also knew how to instinctually use it. It had been years since Sergan had brought anyone back to the College with more than a vial or two's worth of essence in their bodies. The boy who lay dying in front of him was the windfall they needed to save the Exilari Order, and, by extension, the Empire itself.

He couldn't return to Karaqor with only a dead boy in his wagon.

Setting a hand on Aram's glistening brow, he grimaced, uttering a curse. "He's burning up, and I'm out of essence. We need to get him to the city, where there are specialized healers who can treat him."

But Karaqor was still three days away. Two, if they were lucky and the roads were clear. He paused, bowing his head in thought, and sifted through their options. "There's a garrison a few leagues up the road. We can get extra horses, so we can swap them out as they tire."

The boy Markus stood gazing down at his friend with dismal eyes. He had held his ground bravely—Sergan would give him that. Hell, he'd done far more than just hold his ground. Markus had taken the brunt of the dragon's attack, repulsing the voidfire. He doubted even a trained Shield could have withstood so much. Markus was far more than merely magic-resistant—he was a True Impervious.

Sergan had found two treasures, not just one. He would have to keep reminding himself of that.

Markus looked up at him with great sadness in his eyes. "Will he make it three days?"

Sergan scowled. "I don't know, but standing here isn't going to make him any better. Help me get him in the wagon."

The boy laid down his sword and shield and stooped to lift his young friend into his arms. Markus was a big lad, tall and broad of shoulder, and Sergan thought he looked around fourteen or fifteen. He climbed with him into the back of the wagon and pillowed Aram's head on his blue Exilari mantle.

"Make him as comfortable as you can." Sergan tossed the sword and shield into the back of the wagon and closed the tailgate. He swung himself up into the driver's seat then glanced back at Markus.

"I want you up here with me." He patted the seat next to him.

Markus stared at him but didn't move, so Sergan shot him a wry grin. "I thank you for saving me, but I still don't trust you behind me—especially not with that sword. No, thank you. Either you ride with me, or you ride with your hands tied behind your back. Your choice." He didn't care which the boy picked.

It took Markus a moment to decide. He gazed sadly down at his friend before nodding. He climbed over the front of the bed and slid into the driver's seat, scooting as far away from Sergan as the board would allow.

Snapping the reins, Sergan sent the horses forward. Despite the urgency, he didn't try to drive them faster than a walk. The poor beasts had been practically spent before the attack, and he was shocked he hadn't run them to death. He hoped they had another couple of miles left in them, at least.

Transferring the reins to one hand, he glanced at his young companion. "I'm not going to bite."

Markus glanced at him out of the corner of his eye, refusing to look at him directly. He sat with his fists clenched and his back rigid, looking ready to bolt.

Seeking to put him at ease, Sergan said, "You did well. *Very* well, actually. Not many trained Shields could have repulsed as much voidfire as you did without combusting. After you're properly trained, you're going to be the best."

Markus glanced at him hatefully. "I don't want to be a Shield."

The remark amused Sergan, for it revealed how naïve the boy was.

"I didn't want to be a sorcerer." He shrugged. "I wanted to be a nobleman and marry a fine young lady. I wanted to have four children and a dog. I really wanted that dog. I knew exactly which estate I would live in, and I knew exactly the woman I wanted to marry." He let slip a condescending grin. "But very seldom do we ever get what we want. I will never have the affluence or the family I wanted. Hell, I'll probably never get the damn dog. But that's just the way of things, especially for people like us. The world makes of us what it will, and it doesn't give a damn about what we want. If we're lucky, we'll look back from our deathbeds and find that our lives were lived for a purpose. But more often than not, all we'll see is a long list of missed opportunities."

He peered harder at the boy, studying him for a reaction. Part of him took no pleasure in squashing his young hopes, seeing his words as pure practicality. Another part of him *did* take pleasure in fracturing the boy's naivety, because he resented it. It was a luxury he had never been allowed, not since his father had disinherited him and given him over to the Exilari, where all traces of his childhood had been wrung out of him.

Markus sat like a stone, by all appearances ignoring him.

"You're one of the lucky ones." Sergan said. "Your life will serve a purpose, whether you want it to or not."

The boy turned to glare at him, defiance and resentment seething in his eyes. "What about Aram's life?"

Sergan could tell by the fire in his eyes that Markus already had a good idea of how bleak Aram's future would be, which was fine. He would find out soon enough anyway, when Aram was taken to the essence cellars. Markus could hate him as much as he wanted then, for it wouldn't matter. By the time he was done with his training, Markus would understand, and appreciate, why the sacrifice of the Gifted was necessary.

"Aram's life will serve a purpose too," Sergan said.

The boy's eyes narrowed. "What kind of purpose?"

Perhaps he was just fishing for confirmation. But if he truly didn't know, then Sergan wasn't ready to supply him with the information. Rather than lie, he chose to ignore the question. The wagon creaked down the road, the silence between them broken only by the sounds of their passage.

It was many minutes before Markus finally spoke. "I heard what you do to people like him. That's how you fill your flasks. With the spirits of the people you catch."

"Not their spirits," Sergan corrected him. "Their *essence*. If we took their spirits, they wouldn't live long, now, would they? We drain them of their soul's connection to magic."

After a long minute, Markus whispered, "Is it painful?"

"Yes."

There was no sense lying about it, for that would serve no purpose. Whether Markus learned the truth sooner or later didn't matter one bit, for what would happen to Aram was outside of the boy's control.

What he *didn't* have to know was that Aram would suffer more than any other. Because of the vast quantity of essence within him, the extraction procedure would be prolonged and merciless, and it could be repeated as often as the boy could replenish his body's supply. Which meant Aram was looking forward to a long lifetime spent in unbearable anguish.

Predictably, Markus's composure broke. His eyes teared up, and he cast Sergan a look of outright hatred. "Why would you do that to someone?"

Sergan answered without looking at him, "Because we don't have a choice. Whenever there's a rupture in the Veil, therlings spill through and people die. If it's a large rupture, entire cities could be overwhelmed. And we can't send people like Aram to seal them. The Gifted are like a beacon for those that are lost between worlds. It's like lighting a candle in the darkness, and every therling and void walker is drawn to the flame. You can't put someone that bright at the intersection of a rift. They'd be quickly overwhelmed and devoured. That's why this world needs sorcerers. I don't blaze the way Aram does. I don't glow at all, actually, not even a glimmer. That's what makes me effective. They don't see me coming until it's too late."

"Tonight, they did," challenged Markus.

"They didn't see me. They saw Aram. It was him they were drawn to."

Markus glared at him. "But Aram fought them off. When you ran out of essence, all you could do was cower. It was Aram that drove them away."

The boy was right. Aram was a treasure. A priceless treasure.

"And that's why we need him," Sergan explained. "With the amount of essence in him, Aram could fuel dozens of sorcerers for a hundred years or more. We wouldn't need anyone else—which is fortunate because we haven't *found* anyone else in a long time. The Old Blood has been running thin for a long while, and I fear it's run dry. Aram might be the last person we ever find who can provide us the essence we need." He glanced at Markus, looking to see if the boy was still listening to him.

He stopped talking, letting the logic sink in. He could tell by the look on his face that Markus understood the need. There was also a glimmer of boyish naivety, the kind that stubbornly clung to the narrative that just because something wasn't right then there had to be a way around it. But there *was* no other way, Sergan knew. For society to survive, some people had to be sacrificed.

"No one should have to suffer like that," Markus whispered.

"You're right. No one should. But if we don't seal ruptures as they happen and drive the therlings back into the void, then a lot more people will suffer. And we can't be having that, now, can we?"

The boy hung his head, looking defeated. Once again, his eyes brimmed with tears, but a stubborn streak within him wouldn't let them spill. Markus sat with his fists clenched at his sides, his jaw muscles bunching as he gritted his teeth. He muttered, "I don't care about anyone else. I won't let you have Aram."

Sergan could have chosen not to respond to that, but he decided to anyway. "Of course you will. Because there's nothing you can do about it."

The boy went silent, and to his credit, the tears dried in his eyes. He glanced into the back of the wagon, where his Gifted friend lay, struggling for life. Sergan didn't feel bad for him, for that wasn't his way. He never let emotions rule him. In fact, he often questioned whether he had any.

When Aram awoke, he was horrendously cold. His teeth clattered so hard that he thought they were going to chatter right out of his mouth. He lay beside a campfire that popped and crackled, shooting sparks into the air. It was dark, and the sky staring down at him was full of stars.

He had no idea where he was.

"Welcome back," said a calm voice beside him. "You've slept for an entire day and most of the next night."

The man beside him looked familiar, but it took a moment to place him. As soon as he recognized the sorcerer, a sharp lance of fear made Aram shiver harder. He saw Markus lying across the campfire from them, fast asleep.

"I want to know something," Sergan said in that ever-calm voice. "When you look at me, what color of aura do you see?"

Aram blinked, for he was surprised that the man knew of people's colors.

"Right now, you're blue," Aram said through shivering teeth.

The man frowned. "What was I before?"

"Many colors." The words trembled just as hard as his lips did. "Too many colors."

Sergan lifted an eyebrow. "And what color are you, Aram?"

Aram frowned. For the first time in his life, it occurred to him that he didn't know. He had never thought about it before.

"I can't see my own color."

The sorcerer scooted closer to him. "What color would you like to be?"

That was easy. "Yellow. Like Mora Haseleu." The thought brought sadness. The last time he had seen Mora, she had been in the back of one of the wagons with the other girls from his village.

"You'll never be yellow," Sergan said. "You're far more than just yellow. Tell me one last thing, for I'm curious. If you could be anything in the whole wide world, what would you be?"

Shivering, Aram hugged himself, desperate for warmth despite the thick blankets piled on him.

"I'd be a rope," he said through trembling teeth.

The sorcerer looked at him funny. "That's not what I meant, but all right. Why would you be a rope?"

Aram closed his eyes, growing tired. "Because ropes are the most useful things in the world. Ropes and threads and strings."

Sergan asked, "If you were the only rope in the whole world, would you rather stay one piece, or be untwisted into strands, so that you could help more people?"

Aram only had to think about it a moment. "I would rather stay one rope."

"Why is that?"

Aram squinted up at him. "Because once a rope is unlaid, it can't ever be strong again. I think one strong rope would do the world more good than a few weak ones."

The sorcerer nodded, a deep frown on his face. "Perhaps you're right. You've given me something to think about, at least."

He rose to kneel over Aram's leg and, very gently, started unwrapping the cloth. "This is going to hurt."

As the bandage came away, a terrible pain shot up Aram's leg that was more than he could bear. His eyes rolled back, and he went limp.

Sergan changed the dressing on Aram's leg, dismayed that the boy remained unconscious throughout the entire procedure. The wound was seeping again and had a foul odor, the skin around it red and inflamed. His hand went unconsciously to the vials at his waist, and he had to stop himself from removing one. They were all empty. He was out of essence and out of ideas.

Wearily, he rubbed his eyes. He was exhausted. The fight with the void dragon and its cadre had drained the hell out of him, and he hadn't slept in almost two days. Standing, he blew out a long sigh then made his way around the fire to where Markus lay.

Sergan sat beside him and scooped an acorn off the ground, tossing it into the fire. It popped sharply, startling Markus out of sleep. The boy shot upright, looking around for the cause of the noise.

"It's just me," Sergan assured him.

"Is he better?" Markus asked, looking at Aram.

Sergan yawned. "Not good. We'll be cutting it close. We'll arrive in Karaqor by evening tomorrow."

Markus looked at him with pleading eyes. "Can I ride in the back with him? In case he doesn't make it?"

Sergan lay down on his bedroll, pulling his mantle tight around him and closing his eyes. "If he doesn't make it, it's not going to matter if you're in the back with him or not."

"I don't want him to die alone."

He sounded miserable. It was enough to make Sergan conjure a scrap of pity for him, which surprised him, for he didn't have a lot of pity to go around.

"Fine." He rolled over and pillowed his head on his arm. "You can ride in the back. Just get some sleep. It's almost dawn."

Mile after mile, the wagon shimmied along. Markus sat in the bed, despairing as Aram clung to life. He had put up a good fight, a courageous fight, but the infection was now swiftly claiming him. His skin was burning, his breathing labored. Every so often, he thrashed and moaned before becoming very quiet again. It was like watching Master Ebra die, only much, much worse because Aram was his friend. He hadn't known how attached he'd become to Aram until the end. But now, after all they'd been through together, he felt as though he were losing a little brother. A very brave little brother, who had saved his life by putting his own body between him and dragonfire.

Markus wished he could give Aram more comfort to ease his passing. He held a damp cloth against the boy's brow. Every now and then, when it grew too warm from the heat of Aram's body, he would wring it out. But all the water in the world wouldn't quench the fire that burned inside his body, and it was consuming him quickly. Part of him knew it was better this way, much better than the fate Sergan had planned for him. It was just horrendous to watch.

Markus knew when Aram finally started slipping away. His breathing became irregular and sometimes he forgot to breathe altogether for long seconds, just as Master Ebra had done. Recognizing that his friend was at his end, Markus set the cloth down, for he knew it had ceased doing any good. He picked up Aram's limp hand and clung to it, fighting back tears.

"How is he?" Sergan called back from the driver's seat.

"He's dying," Markus shot back, making no attempt to hide the rancor in his voice. He blamed the sorcerer for everything. It was all Sergan's fault. He had brought destruction and death to everyone Markus loved.

"The city gate is just ahead," Sergan told him. "We're almost there. Try to keep him with us."

But Markus knew that Aram was too far gone for even the most experienced healers to save him. He held Aram's hand tight, and his lips kept mumbling, over and over, "It's going to be all right, it's going to be all right," even though he knew it wasn't.

Looking over the side of the wagon, he saw that they were traversing a road between fields of barley that looked ready for harvest. Ahead of them was an enormous city surrounded by high walls and bastions, with many clusters of houses huddled together outside the perimeter.

The wagon rattled over a drawbridge lowered over a moat and passed under the tall arch of the city gate, which was almost like a tunnel bored through the thick outer wall. On the other side of the gate, the smells and sounds of the city rose up around them. Hundreds of people filled the streets, moving everywhere, all talking and hollering at the same time. There was so much traffic. Crowds of people, carts and wagons, all jammed into narrow streets. The smell was hideous. The city stank of human and animal waste, body odor, and sweat. It made Markus want to retch. He gripped Aram's hand harder, saddened that the boy would have to draw his last breaths in the midst of such a stench.

Small houses made of dark stone were jammed haphazardly together to either side of the street, newer structures crammed between the old. Sergan turned the wagon onto a wider avenue that was paved with wooden logs: tree trunks that were split in half and laid down one aside the other. The sound of the horses' hooves made a racket on the wood. Aram let out a low moan, moving his head weakly from side to side.

Markus squeezed his hand, wishing he could take the pain away.

The street opened up into a large market full of merchants' stalls and lined with shops that were open to the elements. The marketplace was teeming with people, chickens, goats, and free-ranging pigs. On the side of the street, a shopkeeper displayed pairs of shoes on his counter, while dozens more pairs hung above his head, dangling from a long horizontal pole. Other shops offered meat and vegetables, bread and fish. The merchants' stalls were full of pots and pans, tubs and pails, and every assortment of household utensil.

Many of the people moving on the street were foreign. Dark-skinned Odessians who wore their hair in long braids, pale Cerylites with blue eyes, and veiled Free People swathed in bright colors and tinkling with bells. There were many ethnicities of people that Markus didn't recognize, for he had never seen anyone like them before. The marketplace was full of men and women haggling and arguing, often in languages he didn't understand. There were stone basins for washing meat and vegetables, along with tubs full of live fish and wicker cages stuffed with chickens and rabbits. He had never seen anything like it and wished Aram could see it too. When they passed by a rope maker's storefront, where cordage of a variety of weights and materials hung from poles and hooks, Markus's eyes grew moist again, for he knew how much that sight would have meant to Aram.

The road they traveled turned away from the market and ran adjacent to the city wall for many blocks, teeming with wagons and carts drawn by horses. Roving packs of dogs wove their way through the milling crowds. The smell of the sea filled Markus's nostrils, making him perk up just a little bit. The odor was comforting and nostalgic, reminding him of home.

The street turned into a neighborhood crowded with houses, narrow alleys winding between them. Here, the smell of human waste grew unbearable, until Markus could hardly stand to breathe. There were flies and insects everywhere, and the inhabitants walking along the sides of the streets looked unclean. People encrusted in filth passed by carrying baskets and heavy sacks, their clothing gray with ash or dust.

The lane ahead narrowed and became uneven as houses protruded at odd angles into the street. Overhead, laundry dangled from poles between houses, dispersed between drying meats and fish. Women called to each other from balconies, and hawkers roamed the neighborhood.

The sights, the smells, all of it, grew overwhelming. Markus huddled down in the wagon bed beside Aram, holding his hand, watching his chest rise and fall with each ragged, hard-won breath.

With a clatter, the wagon rolled off the boards onto cobble pavers. Markus looked to see that they were entering a wide plaza surrounded by multistory buildings with flat roofs and large porticos. In the center of the plaza was an enormous fountain where many women were gathered, washing laundry in the lowest basin. Other than the people around the fountain, the enormous square was thoroughly empty.

"*Yah!*" Sergan snapped the reins, driving the horses faster toward the far end of the plaza. As they approached the tall row of buildings ahead, Markus felt his nerves tingle. He didn't know what those buildings were, but they didn't look like any palace he had ever imagined. They were built out of tremendous light-colored blocks and stood many stories above the street, lined with columned walkways, stone bridges linking the upper floors.

Sergan drew the wagon up in front of the largest building. He vaulted down from the driver's seat and came around the bed, throwing open the tailgate. He hefted Aram into his arms and called for Markus to follow as he rushed up a flight of stairs into the building, past two armored sentries who scrambled to throw the door open before him.

Markus ran after him into the dim interior of the building and across a wide foyer lit by chandeliers glittering with scores of candles. Sergan rushed up flights of stairs to the fourth floor then sprinted down a hallway. Markus ran after him, rushing past two men conversing in the corridor, who moved quickly out of their way then stared after them as they passed. He followed Sergan all the way down the hallway to a door at the end.

The sorcerer kicked the door open and plunged inside. Markus followed him in, stepping into a dark room. In the light coming in from the hallway, he watched Sergan lay Aram out on the floor then scramble to a cabinet, retrieving a cloudy glass bottle filled with liquid.

Essence.

Kneeling beside Aram, Sergan raised the bottle and took a few gulps of the contents. Then he placed both hands on Aram's chest and, closing his eyes, appeared to concentrate.

At first, Markus didn't think anything was happening. But then he heard Aram moan. The boy stretched and tossed his head about, as though in pain. Sergan bent over him, moving his hands to Aram's wounded leg, his eyes squeezed shut, his face slack. Aram moaned again, louder this time. He brought his hands up, as though trying to push the sorcerer away.

"Hold him down," Sergan ordered.

His pulse racing, Markus rushed forward and did as he bid, taking Aram's thin wrists in his hands as the boy's moans turned to whimpering. Sergan's face was red, his jaw clenched, and a vein protruded from the middle of his brow.

Beneath his hands, a light bloomed out of the darkness, spreading up Aram's leg to his torso. It reminded Markus of the void creatures, the way they had glowed with that horrible inner light. He hoped this light was different. He didn't want Aram becoming one of them. Sergan's hands were shaking, and soon his whole body shook with them.

Suddenly, the sorcerer drew in a great, heaving gasp and threw himself back. He fell to the floor, where he lay panting, staring up at the ceiling with wide, unblinking eyes, sweat and spittle dampening his face.

On the floor, Aram lay still, the light within him fading. Terrified, Markus lay a hand on his forehead and found his skin cool to the touch.

"What did you do?" he asked.

Sergan rolled over onto his side, clutching his head and grimacing. "Light some candles."

Markus obeyed. Rising, he found a silver candlestick sitting atop a chest. He carried it to the hallway, where he lit the beeswax candle off the flame of another. Returning to the room, he used the candle to light others, until the room glowed with a warm, wavering light.

Only then did he realize where they were, and that this must be Sergan's private quarters. It was a large room with a table made of solid hardwood that had been either waxed or oiled. Sitting around the table were four carved chairs with high backs. There was a washtub in one corner and a chest in the other, and the entire back of the room was dominated by one massive bed enclosed by embroidered curtains. Tapestries covered the walls and the floor teemed with sumptuous rugs. Markus had never seen, or even imagined, such wealth, and it made him afraid.

With a groan, Sergan pushed himself off the floor and rose to his feet, bracing himself against the table until he caught his breath. Then he turned to look at Markus through stringy locks of hair that had fallen forward into his face.

"He's out of danger," he said in a ragged voice. "But he needs a healer."

"I thought you healed him." Markus frowned, confused.

"All I did was bring him back from the brink." Sergan sank into a chair and rested his elbows on the table, rubbing his forehead wearily. He motioned Markus over, indicating the chair next to him.

Feeling uncertain, Markus slid into it.

"I'm going to go find a healer," the sorcerer said, still breathless. "I'm not going to tie you up, because the guards will kill you if you try to leave, and you're not that stupid, are you?"

"No." Markus shook his head. He couldn't run away and leave Aram behind.

"I'll be back in a few minutes," said Sergan, rising. "Put him in the bed and fetch a bucket of water." He gestured toward the room's only window, which was shuttered with wood.

Looking at the window, Markus felt confused. "Where's a bucket? Is there a well anywhere nearby?"

The sorcerer gave a feeble grin. "Just open the damn window. I'll be right back."

With that, he left the room. After the door had shut behind him, Markus crossed the room to the window and opened the shutters. He was surprised to find that the window didn't look out upon the outdoors, but rather opened up into a shaft that ran all the way down to the ground floor of the building, perhaps further. There were two long ropes hanging in the shaft. When he realized the shaft led down to a well somewhere below the building, Markus gasped, for he never would have thought of such a marvelous idea.

Pulling on the nearest rope, he found it pleasingly heavy. He tugged down hard on it, which drew the rope through a pulley above. The pulley squealed and squeaked as he kept pulling the rope, hand over hand, until at last, a wooden pail arrived from below. He hooked it onto a metal bar sticking out of the wall just for the purpose, anchoring it there, then went searching for a water jug. He found one under the bed, next to a glazed ceramic chamber pot. He filled the jug with well water then lowered the pail back down the shaft.

Carefully, he moved Aram to the bed, tucking him in under the covers and checking him to make sure his fever wasn't coming back. The boy seemed to be sleeping peacefully, pale and clammy, but alive.

Relieved, Markus sat on the floor beside the bed, leaning back against the wall until the sorcerer returned with another man who carried a leather satchel at his side. Sergan motioned for Markus to come, but he didn't want to. He glanced at Aram, not wanting to leave him.

"He'll be fine," Sergan assured him.

Reluctantly, Markus followed him into the hallway, where five other men had gathered outside the sorcerer's door, all wearing blue mantles just like Sergan's. They were all sorcerers, Markus realized, feeling his mouth go dry. And they were all looking at him as though he were a horse at the market.

"Gentlemen, this is Markus Galliar." Sergan set a hand wearily on his shoulder.

Markus froze, looking from face to face. One Exilari sorcerer was too many, but five more…he wanted to crawl into Sergan's room and hide. At least with Sergan, he felt like he knew what he could expect by now. These men, though…he did *not* like the way they were staring at him at all. One with a hook nose and a receding hairline glowered at him with a pinched expression that made him look constipated.

"What do you think?" the hook-nosed man asked a dark-skinned Odessian, whose clothing was cut in a style that was different from the rest.

"He's too old to start the training," the Odessian man proclaimed in a deep, accented voice.

Sergan sniffed. "He repulsed the fire of a void dragon."

The men exchanged glances. Turning back to Markus, all five subjected him to even greater scrutiny, making him squirm under their combined attention.

"I suppose we can find a place for him," said the Odessian man at length.

The man with the hooked nose frowned harder, until the edges of his mouth practically sagged from his face. He gave a slight nod. "Take him, then."

The Odessian beckoned Markus forward and, grudgingly, he went with a glance back at the doorway.

Sergan waited in the hallway outside the chamber of the Synod. He was nervous, and that was unusual. It had always been his aspiration to become a member of the Synod himself, and in that way improve his status at the Imperial Court. With the delivery of the two unique boys, he could taste his ambitions coming to fruition. As a member of the Synod, he would have all the wealth and influence he could want, perhaps even access to the Emperor himself.

He paced nervously across the marble floor before the double mahogany doors of the Synod chamber, the sound of his boots ringing hollowly off the stark walls. He had broken a sweat despite the cool temperature. He fidgeted with his collar, which suddenly felt much tighter than it should.

With a creaking sound, one of the doors swung open, and a man appeared, dressed in formal white robes. Beyond him, the Synod chamber was dark, so much so that Sergan couldn't see any details within. Composing himself, he squared his shoulders and offered his hand to the man in the doorway, careful to press his thumb upon the second knuckle of the man's right hand, a secret handshake known only to members of the Exilari Brotherhood.

He walked into the dim room, his eyes adjusting just enough to make out silhouettes of men and women seated before him in a semi-circle. On the floor in front of them, the symbol of their Order was depicted in a tile medallion: a coiled serpent within a silver sun with curving rays. Light streamed down upon the medallion, the only light source in the room. Anyone who stood upon it would be bathed and blinded in a flood of light, while those looking on would remain anonymous, cloaked in shadow. Sergan walked forward to stand at the center of the medallion and there bent his knee, bowing his head deeply.

He heard a rustle of fabric behind him and the soft, metallic hiss of a sword being drawn. The sword's wielder came up behind him and slid the blade across him, the cutting edge kissing the skin of his neck. He couldn't see the sword, but he could hear the shiver of the nine rings that had been laced through the spine of the blade.

"Do you know the sacred watchword?"

It was a man's voice, loud and formal, ringing sharply off the cold marble walls of the chamber.

Sergan knew the ritual well, and he was ready to play his part. He responded, "Agaedian."

Behind him, the man's voice announced to those ringing the chamber, "The word is right and has been duly received."

"Who comes here?" asked a disembodied voice.

"Brother Sergan Parsigal, if it pleases the Synod," Sergan stated loudly. There was a brief pause, ripe with silence. He kept his eyes squeezed closed in an effort to acclimate his vision to the darkness more quickly.

"Brother Parsigal, why do you come?"

Keeping his head bowed, Sergan replied, "I have come to beg the Synod to receive my petition, as one who has bound himself to this Order as both serf and slave."

"Is it the will of this Synod that this petitioner might stand before us?" asked a woman.

"It is our will," many voices responded in unison.

There was a moment of pause. Then an old man asked, "Sergan Parsigal, do you come naked and humble before this Synod?"

"I do, Revered Master."

"Then rise and be heard."

The blade withdrew. Sergan let out a protracted breath, grateful that the ritual was finally over. He rose and stood with his hands clasped in front of him, gazing around at the silhouettes seated before him. His eyes were slightly more acclimated than they had been, and he was able to make out the features of some. The Revered Master sat in the center of the half-circle, an old man who had presided over the Synod for more years than Sergan had walked the earth. To his right was Master Exilar Sutto Maeor, a dark-haired man whose face and body seemed strangely elongated. He had the honor of being the Seneschal of the College. On his left was Master Exilar Saranda Cowler, a woman with unblemished skin and hair the color of nutmeg who currently held the position of Chamberlain.

Sergan raised his voice to address the gathering, so that it would ring off the walls of the chamber. "Thank you for receiving me, Revered Master, members of the Synod." He inclined his head in greeting. "I come before you today because I have brought two new boys into our fold. One, Markus Galliar, is a True Impervious. The other, a boy by the name of Aramon Raythe, is…" he drew a deep breath, "a True Savant."

His words provoked the expected exclamations of surprise. The silence was broken as several members of the Synod started speaking hurriedly, their voices cut off by the rapping of the Revered Master's wooden cane. When silence and order had at last been restored to the chamber, the Revered Master asked:

"Are you certain the boy is a Savant?"

"I am," Sergan replied, staring the Revered Master in the eyes. "He opened a rupture on his own, which is what alerted us to his Gift in the first place. In my own presence, he dispelled a void dragon along with its cadre. He sees the strands of the world in color and has the ability to bind them."

Once again, his words inspired quiet commotion among the men and women of the council. This time, the Revered Master let it go on for longer before silencing the voices with the butt of his cane.

"Where are these boys now?"

"I released Markus into the care of Brother Ando Nambe. Aram was afflicted with a wound that festered during our journey. He has been admitted to the infirmary, but I've been informed that he is expected to make a full recovery."

The Revered Master bestowed upon him a rare smile of approval. "This is excellent news. Brother Parsigal, it's entirely possible that you have just saved our noble Order. Today, you have taken a large step toward assuming your own place among this body…a step that has placed you on the very threshold of our doorstep."

Sergan's mind spun dizzily from the thrill of such lofty recognition. He bowed his head in gratitude, exhibiting the proper humility demanded by such high praise. For the first time since he had fallen from his noble father's graces, he could feel his dreams growing tangible once again.

"I humbly thank you, Revered Master," he said.

The old man swept his gaze around the seated members of the Synod. "Unless there is objection, I hereby order Markus Galliar's name entered into the sacred Roster of our Order, under the rank of Novice. I further order Aramon Raythe released into the care of the Extractors. Unless there is objection, of course."

Silence followed his words, during which Sergan's apprehension swelled. He could feel perspiration erupting across his skin, squeezed by anxiety from his pores. He almost let the opportunity to speak pass him by. It wasn't a matter of finding the courage. It was a matter of finding the resolve.

"Begging your pardon, Revered Master, but I do have an objection."

The Revered Master frowned at him with a look of great confusion. "What is the nature of your objection, Brother Parsigal?"

Sergan expelled a deep breath, struggling to gather his scattered thoughts into some type of order that might resemble logic. Paramount was the argument of the rope Aram had spoken of, an image which had moved him so much that it had motivated him to present the same argument before the Synod.

"I understand Aram's value in terms of essence production," Sergan said, speaking slowly and looking directly into the face of each of the twelve members of the council. "But I don't believe that relegating him to the cellars is the best use of him. Think about it—we might be able to extract a few dozen casks of essence from him before he dies—but what then? What's left? Will we ever find another with the ability? It's unlikely.

"Members of the Synod, I submit to you that Aramon Raythe's true value lies not in his body's production of essence, but in what he can *do* with it. As a True Savant, Aram is capable of performing bindings that are far beyond the abilities of any sorcerer. From what I have seen, he has vast potential. *Vast.* So much so, that I believe it possible that he may even be able to destroy the Anchors of the World themselves, and then we would never have to worry about a source of essence ever again.

"Revered Master, members of the Synod, I hereby move that Aramon Raythe be trained as a Rift Warden."

The ensuing uproar provoked by his words made Sergan regret having the audacity to propose such a notion.

"Order!" The Revered Master smacked his cane against the marble floor, raising his voice above the commotion. It took long moments of consistent banging before he was able to draw the Synod back into a semblance of decorum. Turning back to Sergan, he asked, "That's an intriguing proposition, Brother Parsigal. But never before has our Order admitted a Gifted student into our ranks. Even if we did decide to attempt this route, who would be his mentor? We have no one with the knowledge of teaching a Gifted how to bind."

Sergan smiled, spreading his hands. "Revered Father, Synod, I would ask you to reflect on exactly what it means to be Gifted. A nodomancer's talents are mostly innate; all he needs is a working knowledge of knots to teach himself how to bind. Mostly, he would just need a mentor to oversee his progress and indoctrinate him in our ways."

His gaze distant, the Revered Master nodded. "Thank you, Brother Parsigal. Your objection has been noted. You may go."

Sergan bowed low before the members of the Synod and departed the chamber, the large mahogany doors closing behind him with a resounding *thud.*

Once outside, he slumped against the cold wall of the hallway and struggled to catch his breath. He ran his fingers through his sweat-dampened hair, wishing he had a kerchief to blot his brow. He regretted proposing such an outlandish suggestion to the Synod, especially after they had bestowed upon him such high praise. He could tell by their reaction that his petition would be denied, which brought him disappointment. He had desperately wanted to be named Aram's mentor. He had convinced himself that the boy was the last steppingstone on his path to the Imperial Court.

Pushing himself off the wall, Sergan made his way down the hallway. He was exhausted from the journey, and he could smell his own body odor, which repulsed him. He had spent too many days without a bath.

He decided it was high time he found one. He had nothing better to do; it would take the rest of the night to get Markus processed and settled into Small House. The Extractors would be coming to claim Aram from the infirmary, to take him to the cellars where his body would be prepared for harvest.

Sergan let his feet carry him out of the fortress and into the Palazzo, where he summoned a carriage to take him to one of the more renowned bathhouses in the city. As the carriage rocked gently along the streets, he closed his eyes and leaned back into the soft cushions of the seat, struggling to relax.

Aram woke to a dull ache in his leg which, after the anguish he had suffered for so many days, was a joyous thing. Opening his eyes, he found that he was lying on a cot in a large room full of many other cots, some occupied, most not. He got the impression it was a place for sick people. He was covered in soft linens, his head resting on a pillow stuffed with goose down, the softest he had ever felt. He had no idea where he was or how he'd gotten there.

He didn't remember much of anything after the dragon. Just an ocean of agony worsened by the constant jolting of the wagon that had seemed to go on forever, every minute a different torture. He remembered feeling like he was burning and drowning at the same time. But he was better now. Much better.

A cold hand squeezed his. Turning his head, he took in the sight of an old man seated on a stool beside his bed. The hand that held his was bony, covered in thin, wrinkled flesh and mottled by liver spots. Turning his head further, Aram saw that the hand belonged to a frail old man with sparse white hair and a skeletal face. The man's dark eyes were sunken into their orbits, as though hollowed by the evils of what they had seen.

Noticing him awake, the man's thin lips gave a faint smile. "You are Aramon Raythe."

Aram nodded, looking up into the man's face, not sure whether to be glad or afraid of his presence.

"My name is Evanar Valeda, though few alive have ever heard it. I am more commonly called 'Revered Master.'" The smile slipped. "And you, child, are a True Savant."

It sounded like an accusation. Aram looked away, feeling suddenly ashamed. He didn't know what a Savant was; he'd never heard the term. By the way the man was looking at him, it sounded like something terrible. He didn't know what to say to that, so he said nothing. Besides, there was something about the old man that made him afraid.

In a gentle voice, the Revered Master continued, "I don't know who has the potential to be greater: you or me. But being great is not always a happy thing. I, certainly, have never enjoyed what I do. I have never considered myself evil, and yet, I can think of no man who has visited more evil upon this world than myself. My word alone has sent thousands to their graves: humans and Auld, dragons, therlings…you could say I have made a career out of plucking wings off of butterflies. I have stolen the lives and souls of countless innocents and sentenced scores of undeserving wretches to decades of torture."

The old man leaned forward, staring gravely into Aram's face. "So why is it that I balk at the life of one boy? I've been pondering that question for four days while you've lain here in this bed, and I've yet to find a satisfactory answer. I think that's because the answer doesn't lie within myself. It lies within you, Aramon."

Aram blinked, wondering what the old man was talking about. His words made no sense. He didn't know what kind of answer the old man was looking for, and he certainly didn't have one to give him, especially if he didn't know the question.

Still holding his hand, the old man said, "For some reason I can't fathom, I have decided to go against my better judgement where you are concerned—at least for a little while. Time will tell if my current derangement will persist, or if I will return to my senses and regret my mistake."

Aram just stared at him, thoroughly confused. The more the man talked, the less sense he was making.

"How old are you, boy?"

Aram managed to whisper, "Twelve, sir."

For a moment, the old man's eyes grew distant. "So young. Let's pray it's young enough." He patted Aram's hand. "For now, I will abstain from plucking your wings. But take my advice: live each day as though it were your last, for every day from now forward is a gift from me. Yet also understand that every gift in this world comes with a price. Someday, I will ask you to repay me for this mercy I have bestowed upon you."

With that, he stood and turned to a man whom Aram hadn't noticed, who had been standing behind him the whole while. "Enter Aramon Raythe's name into the sacred Roster of our Order, under the rank of Novice."

The man bowed slightly, then left. The old man lingered just a moment longer before rising to follow him. Aram let out a small, relieved sigh that the man was finally gone. He still had no idea what he'd been talking about, but he had a feeling that he'd narrowly avoided some dire fate, and for that, he was relieved. Feeling weary, he closed his eyes and settled back into his pillow. But before he could fall back to sleep, another voice addressed him.

"Aramon Raythe?"

Aram opened his eyes to see another man hovering over his bed, this one exceptionally large and muscular with dark skin. The man stood glowering down at him with his arms folded across his chest, scowling as though he had just eaten a piece of rotten fruit. Aram pushed himself upright despite the pain in his leg, wondering who this man was and what he wanted of him.

Without preamble, the man pushed Aram's covers back and lifted him out of bed. Aram started to struggle, but it was no use, for the man's muscular arms were thicker than both of Aram's legs put together. So he relaxed, feeling helpless, and let the man carry him out of the infirmary the way a mother carries a small child.

The man bore him down a long hallway and down several flights of marble stairs. Aram looked around at the building they were in, which was larger and far grander than any he had ever imagined. The man carried him outside and across an enormous courtyard filled with flowers and fountains, where he got a good view of the exterior of the building, which was one of three palace-looking structures arrayed in a U-shape around the enormous central courtyard.

They walked down a gravel path that bisected the yard, surrounded by geometrical flower beds and manicured boxwoods. Aram marveled at the fact that the man's arms didn't tire. He carried him to another building on the far side of the courtyard, this one only two stories, with a wood shingle roof and enormous eaves that extended well beyond the sides of the building. The big man carried him inside, setting him down on the floor of a narrow corridor lined with many doors. Leaving Aram there, he walked away.

Aram sat alone in the narrow hallway, perplexed, his leg throbbing. He was wearing only a linen chemise, which left his legs bare. It seemed like an inappropriate garment for sitting in a hallway. To his relief, the big man returned in short order with clothes.

Halting over Aram, he stated rigidly, "I am Ando Nambe. I am the Chief Eunuch of Small House, and you are my charge whilst you remain beneath my roof. Remove your garment."

Aram felt his cheeks flush. But he did as the man asked, pulling the chemise off over his head. He sat there, bare and cowering on the hallway floor, until the man held out the first article of clothing he carried, a pair of breeches. Aram tugged them on, biting his lip to get them on over the thick bandages that wrapped his leg. After that came a pair of trousers and a roughspun linen shirt.

Mercifully clothed again, Aram still felt naked under the harsh and unwavering gaze of Ando Nambe. The man loomed over him like a century-old oak and looked capable of wringing his neck with one hand. He wondered what a eunuch was, for he had never heard of one, and he figured it must be a very important position.

Ando Nambe informed him, "Whilst you remain at the College, you will live in Small House with the other students. There are normally three rules of Small House, but for you only, there are four. The first rule is: 'Obey the Masters.' The second rule is: 'Do not speak unless you are addressed.' The third rule is: 'Do not leave unless you are told to.' And, for you only, the fourth rule is: 'Work no magic unless you are asked.' You are expected to obey these rules at all times. Any failure to obey will result in punishment by flogging."

Aram winced, for he had seen a sailor flogged once. The young man had been stripped naked to the waist, his arms stretched above his head and bound to the rigging of his ship. The boatswain's mate had performed the lashing with a whip made from a wooden rod, to which many thick cords had been attached. The sailor's shrieks had been dreadful. The poor man had fainted after the first dozen or so lashes, but had received another six dozen after that, until the flesh was hanging in strips from his back. It was the single most terrible sight that Aram had ever seen, so brutal that it had made him vomit.

Ando Nambe pointed at the nearest door. "That is your cell. It is where you will live for the next few years until you graduate from Small House. Exactly how many years will depend on you, for it will be determined by how quickly you and your brother progress through the training regimen."

"My brother?" Aram asked.

Instead of replying, Ando Nambe moved around him and, removing a ring of iron keys from his belt, unlocked the door and opened it, motioning Aram forward. He stood gingerly, putting all of his weight on his good leg and propping himself against the wall. With hobbling steps that made him grimace, he moved to peer through the doorway.

He winced, the powerful stench of an unemptied waste pail hitting him in the face. Within, a youth rose to his feet from one of the two cots, his face frozen in shock. Recognizing Markus, Aram could only stare back at him with a dizzying thrill of joy and relief. A crooked grin spread across Markus's face that he would have laughed at if it hadn't been for the pain. Seeing his predicament, Markus came forward and supported him, helping Aram to one of the narrow cots.

Standing in the doorway, Ando Nambe said, "It is my understanding that the two of you know each other, so I will skip the introductions. Every initiate is paired with another, and the two are raised as siblings.

You will live together, eat together, and train together. Whenever one of you makes a mistake, the other will be punished for it. As brothers, you will succeed together or fail together. Is this understood?"

"Yes," both boys mumbled, exchanging a glance.

"Yes, *Ando Nambe*," the eunuch corrected.

"Yes, Ando Nambe," they said in unison.

The man nodded, looking somewhat satisfied. "Very well. This is your cell. For now, you will be locked within it every night. Every privilege in Small House must be earned, and you must earn the privilege of having your door unlocked at night so that you may socialize and use the public toilet. Is this understood?"

Aram glanced at the waste pail in the corner then looked at Markus. They said together, "Yes, Ando Nambe."

The eunuch pointed to Aram. "Until his leg is healed enough for him to walk on it, you," he pointed at Markus, "will bear his weight. You will wake each day before sunrise for combat training. After training, you will adjourn to the dining hall for breakfast. After breakfast, you will attend classes. After classes, you will eat lunch. After lunch, you will either return to the practice yard or return to class, and only afterword will you be served supper in the dining hall. This is understood?"

"Yes, Ando Nambe."

"You will remain here until morning, when I will come to prepare you for your initiation."

With that, he closed the door. The sound of the key turning in the lock made Aram flinch. He looked at Markus, suddenly uncertain. Markus didn't look mad at him, even though he had every right to be. It was his fault they were there, after all. But an enormous smile broke across the boy's face, putting Aram's fears to rest.

"I can't believe you're here!" Markus exclaimed, his eyes glistening with tears of joy. "I thought they took you to the cellars!"

"Why would they take me to the cellars?" Cellars were dark places where people stored food and dusty odds and ends, not other people.

Markus didn't answer immediately. The smile disappeared from his face and, to Aram, he suddenly looked sad.

"It's where they put people like you. You know. People with magic."
Then the smile sprang back to his face, though there was something odd
about it, almost like it didn't fit. "But don't worry about it!" He gave
Aram a quick hug. "You're here! And that's all that matters."

Aram smiled, for he was glad he was here with his friend and not in
someone's cellar.

"How's your leg?" asked Markus.

"It hurts." Aram reached down and touched the stiff bandages bound
tightly around his leg. "But it's better than it was." He would never forget the terrible pain of the journey. That, and the dragon. And Master
Ebra's dead face.

"The sorcerer saved you," said Markus. "I really thought you were
going to die."

"I thought I was too," Aram admitted. "Thanks for taking care of me."

"Of course!" Markus smiled back. "That's what friends are for."

No one had ever said that to him before, though he'd heard other
boys say it to each other. Overcome by emotion, Aram looked away.
For a moment, he didn't say anything, for he couldn't find the words.
He wasn't good at describing how he felt, and sometimes what he was
trying to say came out backwards. He didn't want to offend Markus.

"What's wrong?" Markus asked, peering at him with concern in his
eyes.

"I just...I've never had a friend before," Aram admitted, squeezing
his eyes closed, for it was too difficult to look at him. "Thank you for
being my friend."

Markus moved to sit next to him on the cot. "You don't have to thank
me for that. You saved my life."

Closing his eyes, Aram whispered, "You saved mine."

"Then we're even."

"No." Aram shook his head. "It's my fault this happened. If it wasn't
for me, you wouldn't be here. Your father would still be alive, and so
would Master Ebra and all the people in the village."

"You can't think that way," said Markus gently. "You didn't choose
this. None of this was your fault."

Aram thought of Master Ebra's pale, bloodied face. The bard had just tried to help him and had paid for that mistake with his life.

"It's not your fault," Markus insisted firmly. "It's *their* fault. Sergan Parsigal and the Exilari. They're all evil. But *you're* good. *You're* good, you understand?"

Aram wiped his eyes with the back of his hand. "They pluck butterfly wings," he whispered, thinking of the strange old man. He scrunched his eyebrows. "Is that what they do in the cellars?"

Markus swallowed, then nodded slightly. "Something like that."

"They're going to train us to be like them." Aram frowned. "Does that mean we'll be evil too?"

"Only if we let ourselves be," Markus assured him.

"I don't want to be evil."

"I won't let you be. Promise."

Aram smiled, feeling relieved. "I'm glad you're here," he said. But then it occurred to him that that was a horrible thing to say to a friend. "I-I mean, I'm not glad you're here. It's terrible that you're here. I mean…"

He shook his head in frustration, biting his lip. He didn't know how to say what he meant, and everything he said was wrong. His eyes searched the floor of the small room for a comforting length of string.

"I know what you mean," Markus said gently. "And I'm sad and glad that you're here too."

The cell they had been given was small, barely as wide as Aram was tall, with only two small cots made of straw pallets rolled out upon rigid wood frames, and they had each been supplied one wool blanket. Aram had a hard time sleeping because his leg ached, and it kept waking him up. Also, he hated wool. He wasn't sure which bothered him more. The blanket itched and scratched at his skin until he wanted to whimper, but when he threw it off, he shivered too hard to sleep.

Morning came too soon. He had just fallen into a peaceful slumber when the sound of the key turning in the lock awoke him. The door squeaked open and Ando Nambe stood in the doorway, an intense glower on his stony, round face. He wore a wide-sleeved robe over a long tunic, looking entirely different than he had the prior day, as though he had spent the evening preparing for a feast. Both boys jumped to their feet, trading nervous glances.

"Today you are to be brought before the Synod for your Reception," Ando Nambe announced in a terse, impatient voice. "There, you will join your hands and kneel before he who holds it. You will address this man as 'Great Lord.' He will have questions for you. You will respond in this manner: 'Yes, Lord,' or 'No, Lord.'

Thinking of the old man he had met, Aram hoped it wouldn't be him asking the questions. He felt quite certain the old man was just as evil as he claimed, and he had no wish to ever look at him again.

"You must request admittance into the Order," Ando Nambe went

159

on. "Speak the form exactly as I say it: 'Great Masters, we have come before you to request that you welcome us into your company as ones who wish to be bound to this mighty Order.'"

He glared back and forth between the two boys. "Will you remember the words exactly, or do you need me to repeat them?"

"No, Ando Nambe," said Markus quickly.

Aram shook his head. "No…no, Ando Nambe… But…"

"But?" The eunuch raised a menacing eyebrow.

Aram felt his brow tingle with perspiration. He licked his lips and squeezed his eyes closed, searching for the right words. Behind his back, his fingers fiddled with a lace he had pulled off one of his boots.

"What if we don't want to join the Order?" he asked.

Beside him, Markus gasped. Ando Nambe planted his hands on his hips and glared down at Aram with an incredulous expression. For a long moment, he didn't say anything. Then he threw back his head and issued a peal of bellowing laughter.

"To my knowledge, Aramon Raythe, no one has ever had the gall to say such to the Revered Master. If you wish my advice, I advise you to stick to the formula."

Aram nodded, disappointed. He glanced at Markus to find his friend staring at him with wide, fearful eyes. Aram understood. Markus apparently didn't want to join the Order either. He didn't blame him.

Ando Nambe gave a nod. "Very good. Now, come. Eyes to the ground. Markus, you be Aram's leg. And remember you are but wretched worms groveling before eagles!"

Gritting his teeth, Aram leaned heavily on Markus's shoulder and limped out of the cell, putting as little weight on his leg as he possibly could. He still had to put *some* weight on it, which brought him pain, but not agony. He hoped they didn't have far to walk. Ando Nambe led them out into the courtyard and set out toward the main buildings of the College. Aram was daunted by the distance but, leaning on Markus, attempted it gamely.

The courtyard of the College should have made for a pleasant walk. The hedges were in bloom, and the flowerbeds were full of blossoms.

Dogwoods and cherries bloomed along the shore of a long reflecting pool, and in the center, a large tiered fountain made splattering noises. Despite the beauty of the courtyard, Aram wasn't enjoying the walk. It was exhausting and painful, and since he had to lean so heavily on Markus for every step, he was sure his friend was tiring too.

At length, they finally gained the entrance of the tallest of the three buildings and entered a large, tiled room with a ceiling many stories overhead. To Aram's relief, Ando Nambe didn't lead them toward the towering staircase, instead motioning them toward a set of wide double doors.

"Do you remember the words exactly, or do you need me to repeat them?" Ando Nambe asked.

Both boys shook their heads. The eunuch looked at Aram. "Remember my advice. Now is *not* the time for candor."

Aram frowned, for he had never heard anyone say such a thing. *Peace of mind can't be purchased with a lie,* his father had always said, and he believed him. His father would have disapproved of Ando Nambe's advice.

One of the doors opened, and a man garbed in long robes appeared in the doorway. Ando Nambe moved forward and grasped his hand. The man inclined his head then motioned the boys forward while Ando Nambe stepped aside.

Markus and Aram walked together through the door, eyes lowered, just as the eunuch had directed them. Within, the room was dark, save for a dim light supplied by two candles that burned on some type of altar. To one side of the room, many people had gathered and were standing in straight lines. Aram could tell they were all garbed in the blue mantles of the Exilari, though it was too dark to make out their faces. On the other side of the room, before the altar, stood another man. Aram was relieved to see that it was not the old man he had feared.

Markus let go of him, and Aram forced himself to kneel in the center of the room. As he went down, a terrible fire shot up his leg, but he bit his lip to keep from whimpering, squeezing his hands into trembling fists.

Someone came up behind them and drew a sword, sweeping it down before their necks in a threatening gesture that made Aram go rigid with fear. His breath hitched, his eyes widening. Suddenly, the pain in his leg was forgotten.

"Who comes here?" asked a woman.

The first man responded, "Markus Galliar and Aramon Raythe, if it pleases the Synod."

Another voice rang off the harsh marble walls, "Why do they come?"

Silence.

None of the other voices responded. A bead of sweat rolled from Aram's brow, trickling down his temple. He wanted to look at Markus but didn't dare turn his head. He knelt there for long moments, his heart racing faster every second. It took him a long time to realize they were waiting for him to speak.

Raising his voice, Aram said, "Great Masters, we have come before you to request that you welcome us into your company as ones who wish to be bound to this mighty Order.'"

He said the words without faltering, his voice composed and steady. It was the first time in his life he remembered being able to speak without stuttering in front of a group of people, and he was so relieved, he felt like falling over backward.

The sword retracted. Behind him, he heard the rasp of the blade sliding back into its scabbard, then the door to the chamber closed with an echoing *thud.*

The man standing before the altar wore a look of severe authority. He was of middle years, with a thin, hawklike nose and dark hair that receded back to a high widow's peak. He stood facing them with his back to the altar.

Aram waited, gazing down at the smooth white marble of the floor, shivering in the dreadful cold of the chamber. He could feel all their eyes upon him, boring through the thin shirt he wore. Silence suffused the chamber, one moment bleeding into the next. He waited, dreading what was to come, all the while longing to just have it all done and over with.

The man before the altar spread his hands. "It is a grave thing you ask, for if you bind yourselves to this Order, know that it is for the duration of your lives. Do you wish to be, all the days of your life, a serf and slave of this Order?"

Aram wanted to follow his father's advice and tell them the truth: that he didn't want to join their Order because all he ever wanted was to become a sailor. But the words of Ando Nambe gave him pause. The memory of the evil old man he had met in the infirmary sealed his decision. He did not want his wings plucked.

"Yes, Lord," Aram said at the same time Markus did.

"And will you leave behind your own will and do what your masters order?"

"Yes, Lord," they answered together.

"Do you swear that, henceforth, all the days of your life, you will be obedient to the Revered Master of the Exilari and whatever masters be put over you?"

Aram drew in a deep breath and glanced at Markus. "Yes, Lord."

The man before the altar intoned, "Then we, the Eternal Order of the Exilari, welcome you both as brothers to our household. And we also promise you much pain and suffering."

The doors to the Synod chamber closed behind them. Aram stared straight ahead, sweat dripping from his forehead, holding onto Markus's arm like a drowning man clinging to a branch. His leg throbbed horribly from kneeling on it, almost as though it were festering again. He clenched his jaw and bore the pain in silence, though it took every scrap of willpower he had.

Ando Nambe stood before them. "You are now both servants and slaves of the Order. There are many things you must learn, and you have been assigned a mentor to teach you. Every moment of your life now belongs to him. Everything he tells you to do, you must do, no matter how taxing or repugnant the task. You will think only what he tells you to think and have no further thoughts of your own."

Aram was only vaguely listening, for his leg hurt too much to focus on anything else. It throbbed in time to his pulse, every other beat sending a spike of pain into his thigh bone. All he wanted in the whole world was to return to Small House and lay down in his cot. Or at the very least, sit on the cool tile floor.

"It is now time for lunch," Ando Nambe continued. "After lunch is training in the practice yard. After that, you shall work with your mentor."

"Who's our mentor?" asked Markus.

"I am," said a voice behind them.

Startled, Aram turned to find Sergan Parsigal standing behind them, and Aram's stomach twisted at the sight of him. The sorcerer was carrying a wooden crutch, which was little more than a knotty tree branch with a curved piece of wood fitted to one end. He walked toward them smiling one of his contemptuous grins.

Aram turned his face away, unable to look at him. Sergan stopped in front of them and set a finger under Aram's chin, directing his gaze up and into his own. Aram looked away, unable to tolerate the dizzying colors of his aura, which made his skin prickle.

"It's considered respectful to look someone in the eyes when they speak to you," admonished Sergan.

Aram groaned audibly, for the request gave him more discomfort than the pain in his leg. Nevertheless, he forced himself to stare straight ahead into the sorcerer's face—although he relaxed his eyes on purpose, letting his vision go blurry, which helped a little.

"That's better." Sergan nodded, stepping back. Crossing his arms, he appeared to be considering both boys. "Markus, I'd like to work alone with Aram today, so go ahead and start your classes. Go with Ando Nambe. Aram will catch up with you later."

"Yes, Sergan," Markus said, glancing worriedly at Aram before walking away.

"Stop," the sorcerer called after him.

Markus glanced back.

"I know I told you to call me Sergan, but that's not going to work anymore. Now that you're my apprentices, a certain amount of decorum is required. From now on, call me 'Lord Parsigal' or 'Exilar.' Either will suffice."

Markus gulped. "Yes, Lord Parsigal."

Sergan smiled. "That's better."

As Markus left with Ando Nambe, Aram felt his chest grow cold, for he didn't want to be left alone with the evil man. Stepping forward, Sergan offered him the crutch.

"Put this under your arm."

Aram obeyed, shifting his weight onto the crutch.

"Your *other* arm."

"Oh." Aram transferred the crutch to his other side and nearly fell over.

The sorcerer caught him quickly. "Now, try to walk."

With Sergan's help, Aram took a couple of unstable steps before realizing that he had to move his bad leg at the same time as the crutch. When he finally had it down, Sergan let go and motioned toward the hallway.

"Normally, I'll be conducting classes in my quarters, but since it would take too much effort to get you up three flights of stairs, for now, we'll meet down here in the study rooms. Follow me."

He set off down the tiled corridor. Aram came along behind, following him as quickly as he could, swinging his leg and leaning heavily on his new crutch. It didn't take too many steps before the piece of wood under his arm started to chafe. But the sorcerer didn't slow for him, instead making Aram push himself faster to keep up. Fortunately, they didn't have far to go. Sergan opened up a door halfway down the hallway and motioned him inside.

The room within was almost cozy, lined with bookcases and warmed by its own hearth. There were three chairs along the walls, and Sergan pulled two out into the middle of the room, motioning Aram to sit.

He went to a table beside the hearth, upon which two ceramic mugs and a plate of cheese awaited. Selecting one of the cups, he moved to the fireplace and removed a poker that had been resting within the spread of glowing coals. Without preamble, he plunged the red tip of the poker into the mug, holding it there until steam rose from the liquid within. Then, with a cavalier smile, he handed the steaming cup to Aram, repeating the act for a mug of his own before replacing the poker and sliding into the chair across from him.

Aram stared down at the frothy white mixture in his cup, considering the liquid dubiously. He lifted it to his lips and almost gagged from the sweetness of it.

"What is it?" he asked, screwing his face into a twisted grimace.

Seeing his expression, Sergan grinned. "Just drink it. It will help with the pain. Now. Let's get down to business. First, I want you to understand that you're lucky to be sitting here in front of me. Normally, the Order doesn't take in people like you. Instead, we use them for other purposes. Terrible purposes. And I don't think you'd like that. So. I need you to work harder than any other initiate has ever worked before and impress the hell out of everyone here. I need to prove to the Synod that you're worth more than your weight in essence. Understand?"

"Yes," Aram whispered.

"Yes, Lord Parsigal."

"Yes, Lord Parsigal," Aram muttered, staring deeply into the mug full of awfulness.

"Better." The sorcerer took a large gulp of his own beverage, as though to drive home a point. "Keep drinking. It's better while it's warm."

Aram lifted the cup to his lips, taking another sip of the toe-curling concoction. His gaze wandered around the walls of the room, which were softened with dark tapestries of battle scenes. The stones and ceiling above the hearth were darkened by soot, and the whole room had an aged smell to it that wasn't unpleasant, like a combination of dust and old leather.

"Let's talk about the dragon." Sergan sat back, draping one leg over the other. "It's what we call a void walker—or void *dragon*, in this case— because, at some point, it got trapped in the void between this world and its converse."

"The counter-world?" Aram asked, remembering a line from the bard's ballad.

Sergan nodded, his eyebrows rising as though he were surprised that Aram would know anything about it. "Yes. It's called the World Below. There are dragons down there. Real dragons. The one you encountered was just a memory of the real thing."

"It was hungry," Aram muttered.

Sergan's face took on a pinched look that Aram couldn't interpret.

"Yes," the sorcerer said carefully. "It was hungry. You gave those creatures what they needed, and that's why they went away."

Aram took another sip of his drink, more to avoid the sorcerer's eyes than any desire to taste the liquid.

"You have an exceptionally rare talent," Sergan went on. "You are what we call a True Savant. You have the natural ability to see the fibers that make up the world in color, and you can bend them to your will. The last person who could do that—that we know of—lived four centuries ago."

Aram realized he was trembling. He didn't know when he'd started, but the longer the sorcerer spoke, the harder he trembled. He'd known all along that most people couldn't see the colors he could, but he hadn't realized that *no one* could. No wonder he brought heartache to everyone he knew. He was born different—and it wasn't a good kind of different. It was a *dangerous* kind.

Sergan went on, "Usually, when we find a new initiate capable of becoming a sorcerer, we partner them with a mentor who can teach them what they need to know. Unfortunately, there's no one alive who can teach you magic, because you're not a sorcerer. You see, sorcerers can perceive the aether, but we lack our own essence, that necessary spark which makes touching it possible. You, on the other hand, have been Gifted with both sight *and* essence—and even more than that, you can see the threads of aether in color, which I cannot. You're a very rare thing, and that's why they gave you to me. I specialize in finding rare things. Like you, for instance. But also the information we need that might help you learn your craft."

Standing, he walked across the room to the small table in the corner. From there, he picked up a large leather-bound text with loose pages and a cover that had split from the rest of the binding. Sitting down with it in his lap, he took the worked leather cover off and gently set it aside.

"A long time ago, when I was studying in the College's libraries, I came across this old book. It's an excellent primer on nodomancy, which is what we call the type of magic you do—basically weaving the filaments of aether."

He opened the text to the first page, upon which was a masterful illumination depicting rows of interwoven knots. Every knot on the page was woven from one single gold strand, elaborately crossed to form swarming designs, each knot set against a panel of brilliant colors.

Aram's gaze traced the page, his eyes drinking in the beauty of it.

"To understand nodomancy, we need to understand the nature of a knot," explained Sergan. "It's simply a bend in a string. The more you bend the string, or cross the string over itself, the more complex the knot becomes. Theoretically, the power of a nodomancer is limitless, given that there are infinite knots, and each knot can have several permutations. The only thing that limits a nodomancer is his vocabulary of knots and his fluency at tying them."

Sergan gestured at the decrepit tome in his hand, its parchment riddled with worm traces. "This book is a study of the only other Savant we have good records of. His name was Daymar Torian, and he lived four hundred years ago. We captured him and kept him confined here at the College for over a hundred years. Some of the members of our Order found him a fascinating subject. This manuscript was the result of their 'conversations.'"

He turned the heavy book around in his lap and tilted it so that Aram could study the handwritten manuscript. "It says here that the fibers of the world—Torian called them 'strands'—can be distorted by stretching, twisting, crumbling, and bending."

He scooted his chair around so that Aram could look on as he traced the strange, elaborate script with his finger. "It's a lot like tying knots with cord. There's always one, best knot for every job. Same thing for magical knots."

Hearing that, Aram sat forward, his mind spinning. He felt a profound stirring inside, for everything Sergan said was hitting home. For the first time in his life, he had an inkling as to why he was the way he was…and it was a powerful revelation. A *vindicating* revelation.

Sergan turned the page, pointing to a large, artfully-penned diagram of many different types of knots. Aram leaned forward, entranced, staring at the diagram with a growing feeling of exhilaration that tingled his skin. The parchment that had been used was not the best, for it still retained dark hair follicles from whatever animal it had been cut from. It made the delicate ink strokes harder to read. But even still, that diagram of knots was the most beautiful piece of art that Aram had ever seen.

"This is a table of knots," Sergan went on. "It categorizes aethereal knots by function, likening them to knots made with cord. This first picture shows knots that are like rope hitches. Like this one here"—he pointed at one of the tediously composed diagrams.

"An anchor bend," said Aram, his eyes swimming with joy. The book had classified the knot correctly for, technically, it *was* a hitch and not a bend. His stomach twinged with excitement.

Sergan smiled. "That's right. Only, it's not made with string. It's made with filaments of aether. But it accomplishes a similar purpose: it anchors something to something else." He leafed through the next several pages. "From there, it goes on to classify different knots and breaks them down by purpose."

He looked at Aram and smiled. Then, closing the book, he handed it to him. "I'm going to leave you in this room for an hour with this book and a ball of twine." He smiled mirthlessly. "Do you have any questions before I leave?"

Aram stared down at the poor, dilapidated book in his hands, wishing he could mend the worm traces. "No, Lord Parsigal."

Sergan smiled and produced a handful of twine from a pouch at his belt. He handed it to Aram. "Oh—do you know how to read?"

Aram shook his head.

Looking disappointed, Sergan said, "We'll add that to our list of studies, then."

He rose to leave, moving the chair back to its former position against the wall. "I'll be back in an hour. In the meantime, I want you to tie as many different types of knots from that book as you can." He nodded at the plate of cheese. "And eat something."

When he left, Aram heard the sound of the door locking behind him. But rather than the noise making him feel frightened, it made him feel relieved. He was alone. Smiling, he took the length of cord in his hand and started leafing through the text. He had a burning tingling in his stomach, the way he always got whenever a new ship tied up to the wharf with a crew of sailors he'd never met before—men of great knowledge, who might show him types of knots he'd never learned.

New knots.

An entire *book* of new knots.

If the book in his lap were food, then he would be salivating.

Tingling with anticipation, he scanned the pages, looking for knots he didn't know, his fingers itching to bend the twine in his hands.

22

Markus followed Ando Nambe down a long hallway to the dining hall, which was filled with people eating on long trellis tables covered with expensive linens. Markus stood in the doorway, looking around, and saw that many of the people in the room were staring at him. He glanced at Ando Nambe, uncertain. The eunuch motioned him toward the front of the hall, where there was a short line of people waiting for food.

Markus walked across the room and got in line, glancing nervously around. For the most part, people had turned their attention back to their meals, though he was still the object of a few curious stares. The line inched forward, and it took a few minutes to reach the man serving barley porridge out of an iron kettle. Markus received his bowl then looked around for a place to sit, at last spotting an open seat at the end of a long bench.

He sat beside a small man wearing a brown mantle, who gave him a disdainful look before turning to ignore him. Markus was starving, so he lifted the bowl with both hands and downed all the porridge in a few gulps. When he set it down, he saw that many of the people around him had stopped eating and were staring at him.

After that, he sat with his gaze pegged on the table for the remainder of the meal, until a loud bell tolled somewhere else in the compound. At the sound of the bell, everyone rose and filed out, and Markus followed. Once in the hallway, though, he was unsure where to go.

A tugging on his sleeve caught his attention, and he turned to find a youth standing next to him who was about the same age as himself, with freckled skin and flushed cheeks, an apologetic smile on his face.

"Are you Markus Galliar?"

"I am," Markus said.

The boy stuck out his hand. "My name's Podarius Lucan. Everyone just calls me Poda. I'm supposed to show you where the practice yard is."

"Thank you! I was feeling a bit lost," Markus admitted, relieved. He shook Poda's hand then followed him down the hallway back in the direction of the large staircase.

"Welcome to the Order," Poda said with a smile. "Do you have the affinity? Or are you resistant?"

"What's the affinity?" Markus asked.

Poda explained, "People with the affinity can see the aether, at least a little bit. They're basically people who can be trained to be sorcerers. If you're resistant to magic, then you can become a Shield."

"Oh." Markus scratched his cheek. "Then, I guess I'm resistant." Sergan had used the word 'impervious,' but he supposed it probably meant the same thing.

"Me too!" exclaimed Poda. "Who's your mentor?"

"Sergan Parsigal. Do you know anything about him?"

Poda shrugged. "Only that he's a sorcerer, and he's not around very much. Everyone says he's an ass." He gestured at the door. "After lunch we always go out to the practice yard for afternoon training. You missed morning classes and exercise."

"How many hours a day do we train?"

"That depends. For Shields like you and me, two hours before breakfast and four hours in the afternoon."

"*Six hours?*" Markus exclaimed. "What could we possibly do for *six hours?*"

"Lots of things, unfortunately," Poda said. "Physical training runs on a four-day cycle. The first day is for short exercises that are pretty intense. The second day is the worst. We push our bodies as hard as we can, all day long. The third day is just light exercise, and we learn different skills, like how to fletch arrows or how to read maps. Then, on the fourth day, we train hard again but not as hard as we do on the second day. Does that make sense?"

"I think so." Markus didn't think he was going to like that routine. "What day's today?"

"Second day." Poda smiled apologetically.

Markus groaned. "Of course."

They started out across the yard but stopped when Markus saw Aram hobbling after them with his new crutch. They waited for him to catch up, and he lurched toward them excitedly, an enormous smile on his face.

"He had a knot book!" Aram exclaimed when he reached them, face glowing in delight. "You wouldn't believe—"

"Don't trip, gimp!" shouted a boy, likely another student, as he walked past them.

Aram paled, all sign of his former joy washed from his face. Markus felt sorry for him. Aram already had his challenges, and the crutch just made him stick out more. It didn't seem Aram was destined to fit in anywhere.

"This is Poda," he said, introducing his companion, hoping Aram would feel better meeting at least one friendly face.

But Aram just nodded at Poda with a half-hearted smile and remained silent as they crossed the courtyard and walked past Small House. The practice yard was a wide, cleared yard surrounded by a grove of trees, and it was full of wooden frames and poles, bales of hay, and rocks that looked purposefully spaced. Markus wondered what all that equipment was used for—it looked more than a little intimidating.

They were immediately introduced to their instructor, Sword Brother Davir, an Abadian man with an excessive amount of body hair, his face and neck covered in tattoos. He wore an arming jacket and an iron breastplate, leather bracers strapped to his arms. Surrounding him were the other students of the class, four boys and two girls, standing in pairs.

"Initiate Galliar. Initiate Raythe. Stand here."

Markus and Aram moved forward to stand in front of him. The man considered them for a moment, a long frown on his face. He reached out and grasped Aram's arm, encircling it with his fingers. With a disgusted sigh and a shake of his head, he motioned them back into line with the other students.

"We will start with warm-ups," he announced. "After that, we will carry stones"—a proclamation that was met by groans up and down the line of students— "then we will climb ropes and then…"

He went on for a while, listing various tortures that made Markus break into a sweat just hearing them.

Davir pointed at Aram. "You cannot train with your peers, but you will train, all the same. You will start with lying on your back and lifting each of your legs a handspan off the ground, one at a time. Begin now."

With a hopeless expression, Aram set his crutch down and lay on his back, closing his eyes and gritting his teeth. His face went pale as he attempted to lift his bad leg, and Markus could tell he was in a lot of pain.

"Galliar!"

Markus flinched, returning his attention to Davir.

"Get moving!"

It was only then that Markus realized the other students had already set out on a run of the perimeter of the College, and he was already behind. With one, last glance at Aram, he set off after them.

Aram lay in the dirt, clutching a warm cloth to his leg, which throbbed terribly. He had spent the last hour doing small but excruciating exercises under the direction of Sword Brother Davir, who insisted that the only way his leg would get better was by using it. He'd done exactly what the Sword Brother asked, putting his heart into the exercises, comforted in knowing that the other initiates were training much harder than he was.

As he sat there, he watched Markus and the others running back and forth to the stream carrying large stones, which they stacked into a pile in the center of the practice yard. Once Davir was satisfied with the collection, he set them to the task of carrying all the heavy stones back again. After that, the students were made to wrestle, even the girls. Markus was actually better than the other boys at wrestling, probably because of his greater age and size.

After wrestling, the students were made to hang from beams of wood above a large mud puddle. They hung there until their strength finally gave way, and they fell to the mud. After that, they were ordered back up the rope to hang until their arms gave out again.

After watching Markus struggle through that, Aram was glad for his simplified exercises. Even the two girls were made to do everything the boys did. They didn't stack as many rocks as the others, nor did they dangle for quite as long as the boys, but Aram could tell that they put more effort into the regimen than all the boys combined, and the short-haired girl had won the foot race.

After the intense workout, the students were made to walk the perimeter of the College to cool down. Then the more adept students were released to attend their afternoon classes, while the others remained behind in the practice yard for more exercise. Aram followed the students heading back to class, casting a look of sympathy at Markus, who stared after him with a disheartened look on his face.

He walked with the group of his peers across the courtyard toward the same building they had been in earlier. The girl with short red hair had come with them, along with a small, emaciated-looking boy with wide eyes. There were also two larger youths, one a brown-skinned boy with curly black hair and a muddled aura the color of pine pitch. The other was the boy who had called him a gimp earlier, a blond-haired Nesian who had a chaotic blue aura.

Aram had a hard time keeping up with them. His leg screamed in protest with every step, and he wasn't used to how the crutch chafed his armpit. But he hobbled along gamely, determined not to be left behind.

The blond boy turned back to regard him with a scoundrel's grin on his face. "Hey, gimp. What's your name?"

Aram sagged. A familiar weight fell over his heart, squashing his feelings like a heavy boot. He'd hoped things would be better here, that there would be other people like him...people who were different. But he'd been wrong.

The blond-haired boy stopped, the others stopping with him. The tall youth with a shock of curly dark hair regarded Aram with a smug grin on his face, while the other boy and the girl just stood off to the side, looking on.

"I said, what's your name?" the blond boy repeated, his lip curled into a sneer.

"Aram Raythe," he whispered, averting his gaze, face heating with embarrassment.

"Why did they let a gimp in here?"

The tall boy sniggered. "Someone must have left the door open."

"Knock it off, Obriem!" The girl came forward, looking as though she'd had enough. Throwing a contemptuous glare at her companions, she stalked over to where Aram stood contemplating the patterns of the flagstones.

"Just ignore them," she said. "They're jackasses. This whole Exilari-thing has gone to their heads."

Aram couldn't look at her, for he was quivering with shame. It was all he could do to stand there without fleeing. The two older boys were still smirking at him like jackals grinning at a piece of meat.

The girl brushed a lock of damp red hair off her brow. "I'm Peshka. The tall loudmouth is Obriem, and his idiot friend is Rehaan. And that's Babalo." She nodded at the small, gangly boy who stood apart from the others, looking like someone had stenciled a smile on his face.

"Adababalo Sarefelaprida," the boy corrected her. He lifted his sharp chin proudly. "Prince of Kantimar!"

Aram looked up to gaze at him wide-eyed. "You're a *prince?*"

Peshka waved her hand. "He keeps saying he's a prince. That doesn't mean he is one."

Babalo stamped one foot on the ground, lifting his chin higher. "I *am* a prince!"

"Prince of Bullshit!" Obriem chortled, while Rehaan wheezed laughter.

Peshka glared at them both but didn't say anything. Maybe they were incorrigible, Aram thought. That's what his mother always called boys like that. He didn't know what it meant, exactly, but it sounded like some kind of condition.

"Do you need help?" Peshka asked, glancing at the carved piece of wood he was leaning on.

"Uh-uh." He gathered the crutch close to him, feeling his cheeks flush a deeper shade of red.

"How did that happen to you?"

Aram bit his lip. He didn't want to admit how he'd gotten the injury. It had been stupid, and he didn't want them to think that *he* was stupid. But they were all staring at him with gazes that demanded an explanation, and he was no good at lying.

He whispered, "A therling bit me."

His admission was met by silence.

Then all three boys burst out in a fit of laughter, Obriem and Rehaan clutching their middles.

"A *therling* bit you?" Rehaan guffawed. "Ladies and gentlemen, I believe Babalo has finally met his match! I hereby crown Aram Raythe, King of Bullshit!"

Aram's vision blurred with tears as the heat in his cheeks boiled over. He started hobbling away on his crutch as fast as he could, fleeing the group of clapping and hollering teenagers. With a sharp glare at the others, Peshka bolted after him. She caught up in just a couple of steps, clutching his arm and slowing his pace.

"Walk with me," she said.

Feeling bolstered, Aram let Peshka guide him into the tall building and through the narrow halls to a small room with desks. At the front of the room stood a maple lectern, currently unoccupied. The boys took their seats and sat snickering into their fists, throwing derisive glances Aram's way. Obriem kept mouthing "King Bullshit," his eyes glinting with amusement.

The sound of a throat being cleared behind them brought instant order to the room and snapped Aram's attention back to the doorway. An older man wearing a blue mantle emblazoned with the insignia of the

Exilari stepped into the classroom. His eyes scanned the faces of the other children before coming to rest on Aram.

"Ah." His eyebrows flew up. "We have a new student. What is your name?"

"King Aram the Bullshitter," Obriem whispered to Rehaan, who threw back his head in silent laughter.

"I heard that, Obriem." Their instructor raised an accusatory finger. He strolled past the desks and assumed his place at the lectern, his hands moving to clutch the edges of the slanted top.

"You must be Aramon Raythe, Sergan's new boy," the instructor said with a kindly smile. "Your legend precedes you. As far as I'm aware, you are the only twelve-year-old in history to dispel a void dragon."

Obriem's sneer melted. Jaw going slack, he exchanged looks with Rehaan. Peshka opened her mouth to say something but then closed it again. Babalo sat slouched in his seat, blinking slowly.

Smiling, their jovial instructor addressed the class. "Initiate Raythe is Gifted—something that you, Obriem, and you, Rehaan, will never be. Welcome, Aram Raythe, to the study of Natural Science. I am Professor Kalasko. It's my hope that you and I can learn from each other."

By the time Professor Kalasko finished speaking, Aram had sunken so low in his chair that he was almost ready to slide under the desk. Everyone in the class was looking at him, and he could not read their expressions. He was mortified, as though the professor had stripped him naked and called him up to stand in the front of the room.

He spent the rest of the hour wallowing in embarrassment and self-pity. Eventually, Professor Kalasko left, and another instructor came to take his place, welcoming Aram to the study of Philosophy and Rhetoric, which proved to be just as tedious as it sounded. All throughout the next hour, the other three students kept shooting glances back his way. The expression on Obriem's face had evolved from mocking to hostile, and his eyes had lost their sparkle, darkening.

The hour of Philosophy seemed like the longest in Aram's life, and when the other students finally left, Peshka clapped him on the shoulder on her way out. Aram sighed heavily and gathered his crutch then hobbled out the door. In the hallway, he drew up, startled. Sergan stood waiting for him, a filthy and sweat-drenched Markus standing at his side, cheeks and lips flushed red from exertion. Seeing him, Markus gave an exhausted smile.

Sergan looked back and forth between the two of them. "I see you both survived your first day as initiates of the Order. I'm supposed to spend the last two hours before supper with both of you, but I don't think I can tolerate Initiate Galliar's smell." He crinkled his nose. "Markus, every day when you come in from the practice yard, you are to bathe before entering my presence. Do you know where the baths are?"

"No, Lord Parsigal." Markus shook his head, looking dejected.

"Then go find Ando Nambe and ask him," Sergan snapped. "Aram, come with me. Markus, use soap!"

When Markus had gone, Sergan led Aram back into the room where the classes had been conducted, pulling together two desks. After Aram took a seat, the Exilar leaned forward, knitting his fingers on the desk.

"What we're going to do every day in here is take what you learn about knots from that book and other books I give you and apply that knowledge to the world around you. In other words, you're going to learn to practice magic."

Hearing that, Aram went cold. He muttered, "I can't."

Sergan scoffed. "What do you mean, you can't? I've already seen you do it."

"I can only do magic when someone else is in danger," Aram admitted.

The sorcerer regarded him for a moment before leaning back and folding his arms. "Well, now. That's inconvenient. Why is that?"

"I don't know. I can see the threads, but I can't touch them unless I have to."

Sergan nodded slowly. "So you need a catalyst, then. Interesting."

Aram frowned at him in incomprehension "Lord Parsigal, what's a catalyst?"

"A catalyst is something that helps something else get started. Like how every fire needs a spark. Essence is my catalyst. Without it, I can't touch the threads either. But this is damn inconvenient. We can't put someone in danger every time I need you to study your art." He sat silent for a time, seeming to be pondering the problem. At length, he asked, "What if *you're* in danger?"

Aram shook his head. "That doesn't work."

"Just because it hasn't worked before, doesn't mean it won't. We'll try it. In the meantime, either you do magic, or I'll order Markus tied to the post every night after supper to receive ten lashes." Sergan smiled pleasantly.

"What?" Aram gasped when he understood what his mentor had just said. "Please, no!"

"'Please, no,' *Lord Parsigal.*"

"No, Lord Parsigal! Please! It's not fair!"

Sergan waved his hand. "Nothing in this world is fair. So... Now that Markus's skin is well and duly threatened, it's time to practice some magic. I want you to snuff out that candle." He nodded at one of the beeswax candles burning in sconces on each wall of the room.

Aram looked at the nearest one, considering its wavering flame dismally. "All right. I'll try."

He reached out with his mind and strummed the strands of aether that crossed the room like harp strings, summoning a raging gust of wind that slammed into him like a hurricane, practically knocking him out of his chair and lashing his hair against his face. It swept every flame in the room off its wick and knocked the fire in the hearth off the logs. Within an instant, the room went dark, the only light the orange glow of the coals in the fireplace.

Sergan sat in the shadows for a moment, hair in disarray, contemplating Aram with a thoughtful expression. Quietly, he muttered, "I suppose Markus's skin will remain intact for another day." He rose from his chair, patting Aram on the head as he moved toward the door.

"Tonight, I want you to hit the books. And keep tying those knots."

Aram frowned, staring at him in incomprehension. "What good is hitting books? Can't I just study the diagrams?"

Sergan's lips parted, and he stared sideways at Aram with a funny look on his face. He started to leave but halted, turning back. "Has anyone ever told you that you're a very, very peculiar boy?"

Aram breathed a heavy sigh. Even coming from Sergan, the words hurt.

"Yes, Lord Parsigal. Everyone."

Sergan sat across the desk from the empty chair that belonged to his immediate superior, Lord Exilar Tobias Ganith. He had been waiting alone in the Lord Exilar's office for almost an hour. At first, when the wait seemed longer than it should, he had grown irritated. But as the minutes compounded, Sergan was starting to sweat. Something was wrong. The Lord Exilar wouldn't keep him waiting *this* long unless he were trying to make a statement.

Minutes later, the office door finally opened, and Lord Ganith made his appearance, hanging his mantle on a peg on the wall before situating himself behind his desk. Folding his hands on the desk's surface, he regarded Sergan without expression. Sergan settled back in his seat, folding his hands in a facsimile of his superior.

"The Revered Master desires an update on your charge," Ganith informed him.

Sergan brought a hand up and fidgeted with his collar, which suddenly seemed entirely too tight. "We've made some progress," he reported. "I have Aram working on knots from Daymar Torian's notes. So far, he's managed to blow out a few candles and extinguish the fire in the hearth. I'd say he's doing well."

Lord Ganith's expression did not change. "Let me be frank," he stated blandly. "The Revered Master allowed you to take Aramon Raythe into your tutelage with the understanding that his abilities would be exceptional. If all he can do is extinguish a few candles, then he is worth far more to us as a source of essence."

Sergan thought the man was being premature in his judgement, but he knew better than to contradict him. The problem was, if Aram couldn't find a way to summon magic at will, then it wouldn't matter how exceptional he was. "Then I'll push him harder. He has the ability, but there's a block in his way."

"What kind of block?"

Reluctantly, Sergan explained, "He claims he needs a catalyst, but I don't believe it. The boy's a Savant, after all. I have a feeling it's just a crutch, so we're going to be working on getting past it."

"And what is the boy's catalyst?"

"Aram needs to feel that someone other than himself is in danger. Only then does the aether become tangible to him."

A troubled frown etched itself deeply into the Lord Exilar's face. "Then perhaps you are wrong. Perhaps he is not a True Savant."

Sergan's mind scrambled for recourses. He couldn't let Aram be taken away; the boy was too important to his plans. He had to find some way to stall them.

"Give me a week," he said. "I'm certain I can get him past his block. I just need to find the right motivation to get him over the hump."

The Lord Exilar's lips compressed into a fine line. "A week is too long. I will inform the Revered Master that I have allowed you a period of three days to prove to the Synod that Aramon Raythe is worth his weight in essence. However, if he has made no progress after three days, I will recommend that he be remanded to the cellars."

Sergan grimaced in disappointment, for he had no idea if he could deliver on his part of the bargain. Three days was not a lot of time. He would have to be much harder on the boy. *Much* harder.

He rose to leave with a mutter of thanks, wiping the sweat from his brow.

Their second day at the College went better than the first. Aram awoke before dawn and followed the other students out to the practice yard, where he performed the small but excruciating exercises prescribed by Sword Brother Davir. When he was done, he watched the others practicing footwork in the pre-dawn darkness. It was Day Three of the training cycle, the day of rest, which the students spent performing light exercise and honing skills.

After morning combat training was breakfast, which consisted of dried figs, bread, and cheese. Aram sat beside Markus on a long bench and took his time about arranging his food on his plate, as he did every meal, since he hated anything that was disorderly. There were two figs, which was good, for he liked symmetry. But that left just the small slice of bread and the smaller wedge of cheese, and he couldn't find a good way to arrange them. With a sigh of disappointment, he broke them into smaller pieces and dispersed them in an alternating pattern around his plate.

Satisfied, he picked up a fig and started chewing, only to find Markus staring at him. And not just Markus. Most of the students at the table were staring at him, too, with perplexed expressions on their faces. Aram stopped chewing, a terrible feeling of anxiety creeping over him, for he didn't know what he'd done to make them all look. Did he have something in his teeth? Something on his face? Ashamed, he lowered his gaze to his plate, hiding his panic as best he could, while Markus glared everyone back into minding their own business.

After breakfast, Aram attended Grammar class with Professor Callain. By the end of the class, he was able to write his own name with quill and ink. Callain had him practice writing small letters over and over, scribing them across a strip of discolored parchment. It turned out that scribing was more difficult than it looked. Because of the angle the nib was cut, the quill could only make downward strokes, so each letter couldn't be made all at once and had to be broken up into a series of multiple strokes. It took him many trials before he finally produced a rendering of his name that Callain deemed acceptable.

Markus didn't fare as well. His attention kept drifting from his work. His gaze wandered the room, studying the other students who were his new peers. His quill would go still in his hand, making a widening stain in the parchment.

"Initiate Galliar!"

"Yes?" Markus exclaimed, his back snapping straight.

"I asked, name the first four letters of the Abadian alphabet."

Every face in the classroom was pinned on him.

"I'm sorry. I wasn't paying attention."

Callain awarded him a frown of disapproval. "Not a good start, Galliar. Not a good start."

One of the students in the front of the class giggled, though Aram couldn't tell which one. Markus focused harder after that, and by the end of class, could scribe every consonant in the Abadian alphabet.

When the hour was up, Professor Callain bid them good day and left the room, to be replaced by Professor Greeling, an exhausted-looking man with sagging eyelids that never seemed to blink. Professor Greeling taught Arithmetic. It turned out that Professor Greeling wasn't well-respected by his students, and there were a lot of gestures and eye-rolling whenever he turned his back.

Aram decided he liked Arithmetic better than Grammar, for he discovered that he had a knack for it. With little instruction, he was multiplying and dividing numbers in his head, though he found he had an easier time of it with his eyes closed. Unfortunately, Professor Greeling must have seen him with his eyes shut and thought he'd caught him sleeping, for he came up and rapped his knuckles on Aram's desk.

"What are you doing, Initiate Raythe? Unless you can tell us the quotient of," he glanced at the problem on the slate board in the front of the room, "ten thousand four hundred fifty-two multiplied by forty-two thousand five hundred twenty-one off the top of your head, I suggest you pay attention to the process." With that, he turned and strolled back toward the front of the classroom, hands clasped behind his back.

Aram frowned down at his desk for a moment with his eyes scrunched, at last saying, "Four hundred forty-four million four hundred twenty-nine thousand four hundred ninety-two."

The professor stopped midstride and turned slowly toward him. So did the rest of the class.

"What was that you said?"

Realizing that every gaze in the room was pegged on him, Aram froze rigid in his seat, petrified he'd gotten the quotient wrong. Swallowing heavily, he repeated the number in a trembling voice, "Four hundred forty-four million four hundred twenty-nine thousand four hundred ninety-two. Sir."

Professor Greeling's eyebrows shot up, and he strode to the podium with more animation than Aram thought him capable of. There, the old man picked up a piece of chalk and started scribbling rapidly across a slate board on his podium while the class looked back and forth between Greeling and Aram, wide-eyed. With a final, adamant jerk of his chalk, the professor took a step back, gazing down at the slate, his face going slack.

"Class dismissed," he muttered.

Despite his crutch, Aram was the first out the door. Markus came bolting after him, catching his arm and pulling him to the side of the hallway.

"How did you do that?"

Aram shrugged. "Arithmetic is easy."

Markus shook his head vigorously. "No. Arithmetic is not *that* easy. At least, not for the rest of us."

"I'm sorry," Aram whispered.

The other students leaving the classroom streamed past them, Obriem muttering "freak" as he walked by. Aram closed his eyes and turned away, making his way toward the entrance to the building. He hobbled on his crutch to the courtyard, where he found a bench and sat upon it, dropping the crutch, and leaned forward with his head in his hands. He sat there for a while feeling miserable, hating everything and everyone at the College. His fellow students were mean, the training wicked, his quarters filled with the overwhelming reek of the waste pail that they were only allowed to empty once a day. He even hated his clothes. His trousers were too tight and the roughspun shirt was itchy on his skin. He found himself scratching at the fabric a lot, hoping his fingernails would soften the fibers a bit over time.

"Hey."

Aram looked up to find Peshka hovering over him, but since she had been one of the people staring at him in the classroom, he looked away. She sat next to him, leaning forward and staring into his face until he burned with embarrassment and squeezed his eyes closed.

"Are you all right?" she asked.

Aram nodded. He sat with his arms wrapped around himself, rocking slightly. She was looking at him so intensely that he wanted to squirm right out of his skin and escape.

"Professor Sabrien sent me," she said gently. "She wants to know why you're missing class."

Aram shook his head. He didn't want to go to another class.

"You've got to come," Peshka insisted. "You'll get in trouble."

Trouble. He couldn't afford to get in trouble because Markus would take the beating. He started trembling because walking back into the classroom would be the most embarrassing thing he could think of doing. Everyone would stare at him in ridicule again and mouth insulting words in his direction. At least back in his village, when people treated him like that, he could escape to his cave, which always made him feel better. But there was no escape at the College—his tormentors went everywhere he went.

"You can sit by me," Peshka said, laying a hand on his back. "Come on."

Drawing in a deep, deep breath, Aram bit his lip and grabbed his crutch, standing to follow her.

Aram suffered through Professor Sabrien's class as best he could, trying hard to ignore the other students. Peshka sat next to him, as she promised. Markus was already there, seated next to a beautiful Odessian girl with the softest skin Aram had ever seen. But her colors were so chaotic that her aura seemed almost damaged—just like most of the other colors in the room. Out of the entire bunch, Aram decided that only Peshka and Poda could be trusted to be kind. Their auras were green and clear and put Aram at ease. The others, though... Of course, considering the students were all in training to be Exilari, it made sense that they'd be chaotic.

Their instructor, Professor Sabrien, was a striking woman with long, black hair and green eyes that sliced through nonsense and distraction. While Professor Sabrien stood in command of the class, every student sat with their backs rigid in their seats, hands folded on the desks in front of them. No one coughed or fidgeted, and there was certainly none of the disrespect that had gone on the previous hour.

After class was supposed to be lunch, but as they walked toward the dining room, they were intercepted by Sergan. The sorcerer came striding from around a corner with an intense frown on his face, halting in front of them and physically blocking their path. Aram looked at Markus, who glanced back at him.

"I'm going to need Aram for the rest of the day," the sorcerer snapped, sounding even more terse than he did normally.

Aram's stomach rumbled its disappointment. And even though he was eager to work on more knots, the look on Sergan's face made him fearful.

"Let's go," the sorcerer said, already striding away.

With a sigh, Aram hobbled after him. Instead of leading him back to the study room where they'd met the previous day, Sergan made for the stairs, mounting the mahogany steps. Aram halted at the base of the wide staircase, gazing upward at the many flights of stairs, feeling daunted. Gripping the handrail and his crutch at the same time, he followed his mentor up the stairs, taking one step carefully at a time, his bad leg jabbing pain into him every time he accidentally put weight on it. It took him many minutes and a lot of pain, but at last, he arrived at the fourth floor. There, he found the hallway empty, and he had no idea behind which door his mentor had disappeared through. He wandered down the hallway until he found a half-open door. There, he paused and knocked on the frame, staring past the door at the opulent quarters within.

"Come in," Sergan commanded.

There was a strain in his voice that hadn't been there the previous day. Aram felt the tension palpably, and he wondered why it was there. Something had changed. Changed for the worse.

Sergan motioned him toward a chair then sat across from him. Aram sank nervously into his seat, leaning his crutch up against the armrest. His gaze wandered the room, lingering on a large, walnut bureau with many tiny drawers. He wondered if Sergan kept his socks in those drawers. They didn't look big enough to store much else. All around the room glowed an assortment of tapers. They were everywhere, at least a dozen, perched on every surface in the room.

Leaning forward and clasping his hands over his knees, Sergan said ominously, "Today, we'll be getting through your block. I've been informed that we're running out of time. If I don't get you practicing magic without a catalyst in three days, they'll take you away from me, and I can't be having that."

"Who would be my mentor?" Aram asked.

"I'd rather not say. Just be assured they won't be as nice as me. Now. We have to get you using magic without having to threaten someone else. So, this is what we're going to do. I'm going to threaten *you* instead. That would be progress, at least."

Aram shook his head roughly. "It doesn't work that way. I've been in danger before, and it didn't work for me."

"What was the most dangerous situation you've ever been in?" Sergan asked.

It didn't take Aram long to think about it. "When I was eight years old, I fell into a well. I had to tread water for an hour before anyone heard me yelling for help. I was sure I was going to drown, but there was nothing I could do about it. I couldn't use magic to help myself, even when I thought I was going to die."

Sergan sat back, knuckling his chin. "That was four years ago. Maybe things have changed."

The sorcerer's eyes drifted to the fire crackling in the hearth. He sat staring at the flames for a while, his eyes thoughtful and distant. At length, he let out a grunt and rose from his seat and walked across the room to a window set into the rear wall, hidden by wood shutters. He paused in front of the window and glanced back at Aram. Then he opened the shutters.

The window that was revealed didn't look down upon a street or the courtyard behind the building. Instead, it stared out at another dark wall only an arm's length away. In the space between walls hung two thick, plain-laid ropes made of course fibers.

Aram rose from his chair, a cold feeling of dread crawling through his insides. He didn't like the look of that little space between walls. He had no idea what Sergan Parsigal had in mind, but whatever it was, he was already frightened.

"What's down there?" he asked.

"A well," the sorcerer responded, staring down the shaft. "Five stories down. The water's very cold, and the well is very deep. It leads to an aquifer beneath the College."

Sergan motioned toward the shaft. "Blow out a candle, or that's where you're going."

Aram's breath stopped, and he froze rigid. The hour he had spent in the well had been the most terrifying in his life. Ever since then, he'd had a bad fear of wells. And Sergan's well wasn't just deep. It was *five stories down.*

"I can't..." he gasped, taking a step back, his stomach heavy with ice. "Lord Parsigal, please don't make me do that. Don't make me go in the well."

"Then blow out the candles," the sorcerer said calmly, gesturing around the room. "Just like you did yesterday."

Aram's breath came fast, panicky, his pulse racing. His impulse was to turn and flee, to pick up his crutch and hobble out the door. He shook his head, his desperate hands fiddling with the thin lace he'd taken from his boot.

Frantic, he turned his attention to the nearest candle, willing it to snuff itself out. The candle flame wavered blissfully, ignorant of his need. Aram narrowed his eyes, concentrating on the colorful threads that flickered around it, and reached out with his mind to touch them. But, just like they always did when no one was in danger, the filaments parted like vapor and wouldn't let him grasp them.

He shook his head. "Please. I can't. Please...."

"Then down you go."

"No." Aram's tears spilled down his face. "Please. I'll try again."

But he knew he couldn't. One last time, he held his breath and reached out desperately for the threads of aether.

Once again, his attempt failed.

He blew out a heavy sigh, wilting with despair. "Please don't put me in the well."

Sergan gestured to the shaft. "Climb onto the bucket, or I'll have Markus flogged."

Hope flared. At last, someone else was at stake. Aram turned to the nearest candle and pinched his brow in concentration, knowing that now he could put it out.

But nothing happened.

It was just a dirty trick, he realized with despair. Sergan had made it clear that Markus's punishment didn't hinge on his use of magic. The only way Markus would be hurt was if Aram didn't obey and let the sorcerer lower him into the well.

Sniffing back his tears, he drew himself upright and turned to Sergan. "You won't have to hurt Markus. I'll go."

Aram leaned over the opening of the window and peered down the well shaft. There was no light down there, so he couldn't see the bottom. The rope disappeared into bottomless shadows, and anything could be down there. Anything at all. Aram drew back, feeling his courage start to slip.

"Let me by," Sergan snapped.

Aram stepped back to let the sorcerer take his place at the window. Sergan grabbed hold of the rope and started hauling. From somewhere above came the sound of a pully creaking as it turned. Hand over hand, Sergan pulled the rope through the pully, which screeched in protest every time he yanked. Aram stood rigid, his hands and feet tingling, his heart thrumming with wild abandon. A slick sweat had broken out across his forehead and on his palms.

At last, a wooden pail appeared. Sergan stopped pulling and grabbed the pail, tossing the water out of it and hooking it on a metal rod that had been put there for that purpose.

Sergan said with unbearable calmness, "Go fetch a candle."

Aram's body reacted automatically without his mind willing it to. He went and fetched a taper off the wall, handing it to Sergan. The sorcerer blew it out, then broke it in half before handing top part back to Aram.

"You'll keep this candle on you the whole way down, and you better not drop it. When you manage to light it, I'll haul you back up. Not before."

"What if I can't?" Aram asked, his voice wavering. His jaw was beginning to tremble as he stared straight ahead at the shaft.

"Then you will spend the rest of your life in agony," the sorcerer responded with the same, implacable calm.

"What?" Aram whispered, hoping he'd heard him wrong.

Sergan turned to fix him with a frigid glare.

"If I fail to teach you to use magic at will, then my superiors will hand you over to the Extractors, who will take you down to the essence cellars. There, they will bind you and stab a hot poker into your eyes to prevent you from using magic ever again. After your eyes are burned out of your head, they will strap you to a table, where they will extract what's inside you to be distilled like liquor. It's an excruciating process that involves inflicting a tremendous amount of mental pain, enough so that your body responds by secreting essence in a desperate attempt to stop the anguish. As the essence leaks from you, it's harvested and stored for people like me to consume."

Aram could only stare at him, slack-jawed and numb, stunned by the horror of it. Part of him wanted to deny Sergan's words, deny that anyone could possibly be that evil. But another part of him knew that Sergan *was* that evil. And everyone like him.

"What would you do to Markus?"

The sorcerer shrugged. "Markus is in no danger. He will be trained as a Shield, and eventually, he'll be awarded to me."

Aram backed away from the man, slowly shaking his head. There were a hundred things he wanted to say, and all of them started with 'I can't believe you would…'

But that was the problem. He knew Sergan would do everything he promised. Which was why he had to go into the well.

"Then move, so I can get over." Strangely, his voice sounded just as calm and even as the sorcerer's.

When Sergan stepped aside, Aram limped to the window and placed the candle in the bucket. Swinging his bad leg over the sill, he waited for the sorcerer to take hold of the rope before closing his eyes and swinging his other leg over to straddle the pail.

"Go ahead," Aram whispered, trying not to stare straight down into the dark shaft.

Without a word, Sergan complied, lowering the bucket down the shaft in jarring increments. Aram clutched the rope, which creaked overhead as the pail beneath him swung in a pendulous arc. Every time Sergan let the rope slip, a rain of dust from the rope's fibers fell into his eyes. Nevertheless, Aram kept his head craned back, preferring to look up instead of down.

Slowly, the light faded in the shaft and shadows closed in around him. Still, the pail continued its relentless journey downward as the light above drew further away. The air of the shaft was cool, and it smelled wetly of old mildew. From somewhere down below, he could hear the slow, consistent noise of dripping water. Little by little, the pail lowered until the light overhead was just a distant glow, barely more than a memory.

His feet touched water.

Startled, Aram reached down and grabbed the candle from the pail before it could float away. Then with a splash, the rest of him went in, and his head plunged under. He clung to the rope, using it to pull himself back to the surface and then keep himself there, so that he wouldn't have to tread water.

"I can't see!" he shouted up the shaft. "I can't light the candle if I can't see it!"

A light blossomed directly above him like a silvery mist.

"Light the candle." Sergan's voice echoed from above, reverberating hollowly off the walls of the shaft.

But Aram couldn't. It was all he could do to keep the taper out of the water and cling to the rope at the same time.

He was starting to panic. His breath came in gasps that made him dizzy. The rope had stopped moving and creaking. He was trembling. Shaking. His fingers ached, screaming to open up and let go.

Fear is your enemy. Don't surrender to it.

It was his father's voice, echoing in his mind. The sound of it comforted him. Strengthened him. Soothed the exhausted muscles of his hands and calmed his brain so that he could think.

The water lapped at him, wanting to slurp him down. He couldn't let it. There had to be some way to light the candle, some way to convince himself that Markus would be in danger without him. But the sorcerer had deliberately chased that possibility from his mind.

He was shivering, and he couldn't tell whether it was from cold or fear or both rolled up into one.

He concentrated on the candle, applying all of his mind to it. It would take so little effort to create a spark, just enough to make a flame. All he had to do was sever one thread of aether and release the energy stored within it.

But to sever a thread, he had to touch it first, and the aether around him remained as intangible as the air. His tears came back, and this time he didn't try to stop them.

They would be coming for him, to take him away. They would burn out his eyes and strap him to a table. He didn't want to spend the rest of his life screaming in agony.

But then he realized he didn't have to.

He could simply let go.

"Light the candle, Aram," came Sergan's voice, echoing distantly. "Don't make me hand you over to them. Just light the candle."

Aram glanced down at the cold, dark water, feeling empowered by it. He didn't have to spend the rest of his life in the cellars. He had a choice.

Growing up in a seaside village, he had seen people drown. He had also listened to the accounts of survivors who had been revived after drowning. They all said the same thing: that after the fight leaves you and the water fills your lungs, all that is left is a great sense of peace.

That's what he wanted.

Peace.

Aram opened his hand and dropped the candle, letting it fall into the black water.

Then he let go of the rope.

He slipped beneath the surface and bobbed back up, treading water while resisting the impulse to climb onto the rope. He knew that rope would become a problem later on. When the panic set in, he didn't think he could stop himself from reaching out for it. He would have to swim down as deep as he could, deep enough that he wouldn't be able to fight his way back up.

"Aram!" Sergan's voice echoed down the shaft. "Did you let go?"

I did.

"Climb back onto the bucket, Aram. I'll haul you up."

No.

"Climb up, Aram. I won't give you to them. I promise. Just climb back up."

But he wasn't going to climb back up. He had to go, now, before he started believing the sorcerer's lies.

"Aram! Take the rope!"

No.

With a last breath of air, he let himself sink beneath the surface. He turned and swam downward toward the bottom of the well, kicking hard and taking long, steady strokes. It was difficult. Swimming into that cold darkness went against every instinct of self-preservation. He forced himself to swim deeper and deeper, until his lungs started burning. Then the anxiety set in, making him doubt himself.

Fear is your enemy. Don't surrender to it.

His father's voice helped a bit. It strengthened his resolve, allowing him to continue, to push himself deeper, until he was past the point of no return.

He swam as hard as he could, until his lungs burned for air and panic overcame his courage, snatching away his control. Suddenly desperate, he turned and started back, kicking and clawing for the surface. He wanted out of the water, he wanted to breathe again, he wanted to go home.

Soon the urge to breathe became unbearable. He clenched his jaw to keep from inhaling, struggling to go faster, fighting as hard as he could. He could see the light of the shaft so very far above, so far out of reach.

The burning pressure in his lungs made him feel like his insides were on fire. He couldn't bear it any longer. The pain was excruciating. He didn't have the strength to endure.

Giving in, Aram opened his mouth and sucked in a great, great, gasp.

Cold water filled him. He could feel the weight of it dragging him down. The water made his lungs burn worse…so much worse. It hurt so badly. So very, very badly.

The darkness around him receded, glittering with innumerable sparkling lights.

A great calmness descended upon him. It cradled him like a mother's embrace, bringing him comfort and peace. He stopped kicking and just floated there, letting the gentle water rock him to sleep.

See you soon, papa…

He felt his father's strong arms wrap around him, holding him tight. Pulling him upward toward the surface.

26

Markus sat next to Poda at one of the long tables in the dining hall, sore from the day's exercises in the practice yard. He'd spent half the day sprinting back and forth to the river and the other half of the day swimming in it. His muscles felt like limp rags of cloth with all the strength wrung out of them. He kept glancing at the doorway, wondering where Aram was.

"Next time, I won't let Obriem beat me," grumbled Poda. "I thought I'd had him, but my foot slipped."

"Oh, your foot slipped?" Peshka asked with a taunting grin on her face. "Like it does when it goes in your mouth?"

Poda chuckled. "Yeah. Like that."

Earlier, Poda had, in so many words, called Sword Brother Davir old. He hadn't meant to, but Poda was shy and sometimes he got things twisted around in his mouth. Davir probably knew what he meant but chose to make a big deal of it anyway. He'd challenged Poda to a wrestling match, which hadn't ended well. Poda's lip had been split right down the middle, and he limped a little when he walked, which was why Obriem had beat him in the footrace.

Markus glanced at the door and frowned. It was getting late. Supper was just about over, and Aram still hadn't returned from his lessons with Sergan. Markus couldn't imagine what was keeping him. The sorcerer had kept him to himself all day—he had even missed afternoon exercises.

199

"Hey, where's your friend?" asked Poda.

"I don't know." Markus tore off a bite of bread and chewed on it, his eyes darting back to the dining hall door.

Peshka said, "That was incredible what he did in class. I can't believe how smart he is."

"Yeah. Aram's smart, all right."

Halfway down the table, Babalo erupted in a fit of shrill laughter and hand clapping. His partner, the Odessian girl named Enari, stood up from the table and fled toward the door in tears. Seeing the way Enari could handle a sword, Markus was sure he wouldn't want to be Babalo tonight.

The bell rang and everyone in the hall rose from their tables and headed for the door, leaving their empty plates behind for the servants to pick up. Markus followed the flow of the crowd out into the court-yard then stopped and turned back, hoping to see Aram. He waited in the twilight, watching people making their way back to the dormitories, until the last person drifted past him and the door shut. He stood in the courtyard a moment longer, alone, before finally turning and heading back toward Small House.

As he walked, he gazed out at the fading sunset that was already waning to purple on the horizon. The courtyard's braziers had been lit, drawing bats that fluttered by overhead in search of insects attracted by the light. It was a pleasant evening, warmer than the past two had been. The nights in Small House could get cold, and there was no hearth to warm their beds.

Markus was hoping to find Aram in the cell they shared but was disappointed to find that his friend hadn't returned yet. When Ando Nambe came along to lock the door for the night, the big eunuch peeked his head in and frowned heavily, scrunching up his face.

"Where is Initiate Raythe?"

"I don't know." Markus couldn't keep the apprehension he felt out of his voice. "He was with Lord Parsigal...but it's been hours."

Ando Nambe nodded slightly. "I will check."

He closed the door, shutting out the light of the hallway. As complete darkness fell over him, Markus heard the sound of the key turning the lock. He lay down on his cot and drew his blanket over him. He wondered if Ando Nambe would stay to let Aram in when he arrived. He lay there for a long while, waiting, his mind torn between exhaustion and anxiety.

Eventually, exhaustion won out.

The lock turned, and the cell door opened.

Markus jerked upright, throwing off sleep and squinting into the glare of the light. Holding his hand up to shield his eyes, he made out the shape of Ando Nambe silhouetted in the doorway. With a glance at Aram's cot, he noted that it was still empty.

"Where's Aram?"

"Initiate Raythe took ill," the eunuch informed him. "He is in the infirmary."

Ando Nambe stepped back from the doorway, using his key to unlock another cell door. Markus stood and followed after him, alarmed by the news.

"Took ill with what?"

Ando Nambe didn't look at him, "Lord Parsigal did not say."

"Is he all right?"

The big man finally turned to frown at him. "Worry less about Initiate Raythe and more about your physical training. Sword Brother Davir says you are not giving enough effort."

A sleepy Babalo wandered out of his cell, rubbing his eyes. Markus stepped past him, trailing after the eunuch. Apprehension screamed at him that something was wrong. He didn't trust these people, didn't trust them with Aram especially. He had no reason to believe them and every reason not to.

He demanded, "I want to see Aram."

Ando Nambe continued down the hallway toward the door. "I'm afraid that's impossible. Initiate Raythe will return when he is well."

That wasn't good enough for Markus, but he could tell by the eunuch's dismissive indifference that he would get no further information from him. Reluctantly, he followed the other students out to the practice yard through the gray light of early morning. There, they met Sword Brother Davir, who stood before them in a padded arming jacket, holding a wooden practice sword and carrying a wooden shield. Spread out on rugs before him were eight other practice swords and shields.

Markus came forward and selected a sword and shield and was shocked by how heavy they were. The sword was easily twice as heavy as any metal sword he had ever held, as though it had been weighted, its insides hollowed out and filled with iron. The shield was similarly weighted, not quite as outrageously as the sword, but enough to make him realize that the day's lessons would be exhausting.

"Who can tell me why we train with wooden swords?" Davir asked.

"So we don't get injured fighting with real ones," Obriem responded.

"There is that. What else?"

"So we don't hurt real swords?" Enari asked.

"There is that also. Now. Why do we train with *weighted* swords?"

"To make us stronger and faster," Markus responded.

"Yes." Davir smiled. "We train with weighted swords and shields so when it becomes necessary for us to wield real weapons, they will feel light and agile in our hands. You may set your shields down. Markus, come here. Bring your sword with you."

Markus set his shield down and moved forward to stand in front of the other students.

"Hold your sword out," Davir instructed.

Markus complied, and Davir grasped his sword's wooden blade, encircling his fingers around the midpoint. Pointing at the wider half of the blade, he said, "This half is called 'the strength.'" Pointing at the thinner end of the blade, he said, "This half is called 'the weakness.'"

He stepped back and crossed his own sword with Markus's in such a way that the thin part of his blade was touching the wider half of Markus's.

Davir said, "Right now, the weakness of my sword is bound to the strength of Markus's sword. If I wanted to push his blade aside, I would have to push very hard, because in this position, he has the advantage of leverage. But if Markus wants to push my blade aside, all he has to do is twist his wrist."

He nodded to Markus, and Markus performed the motion. That slight rotation of his blade was enough to push Davir's sword to the side.

"Do you understand now why the halves of the blade are called the strength and the weakness?"

"Yes, Sword Brother!" the students responded together.

Davir dismissed Markus and called Peshka forward.

"It is possible to use a blade's strength and the weakness at the same time. Here is an example." Reaching out, he raised Peshka's sword, crossing his blade with hers. "If Peshka strikes at me, I am forced to defend. I can accept her blow on the strong part of my blade, while at the same time" — he jabbed the tip of his sword out, stopping just shy of her neck — "stab her with the weak part of my blade. With one sword, I can both defend and counterattack at the same time."

Nodding at Peshka, he dismissed her too. As she walked back to join her fellows, Davir asked, "What is the most dangerous part of the sword?"

"The strength!" shouted Babalo.

"The point!" shouted Enari.

"The weakness!" shouted Poda.

"All of it," said Markus, and Davir nodded.

Holding up his sword, Damir touched the tip. "I can stab you with the point." He trailed his finger down the length of the blade. "I can slice you with the edge." He moved his hand back to the hilt. "Or I can bludgeon you with the crossguard or with the pommel. It does not matter what piece of the sword I use to kill you, you will be dead. Now. We will begin today with the high guards."

The lesson progressed for another hour, the students moving through the first tedious steps of a dance that always started with the left foot forward. By the time they were ready to break for breakfast, Markus's face was slick with sweat, his tunic sticking to his skin. His belly had moved past complaining to demanding.

At the dining hall, he ate breakfast in silence, his thoughts drifting to Aram, wondering what had happened to him and hoping he was all right. He was growing terribly concerned. Unless Aram had been badly hurt, he should have been out of the infirmary by now.

After breakfast, he suffered through his morning classes without really paying attention, his fingers drumming the tabletop. His professors didn't say anything about his distraction, which surprised him. No one questioned the empty chair at the table beside him, which also surprised him.

But when it was time for afternoon exercises in the practice yard, all thoughts of Aram slipped from his mind. Sword Brother Davir had built an obstacle course for them out of different sized barrels that they would have to either jump or climb over. That occupied all of his concentration and endurance for the rest of the daylight hours.

Before Markus realized it, it was evening, and Sergan hadn't summoned him for his afternoon lessons. He walked absently back across the courtyard toward Small House, watching the bats zipping by overhead with high-pitched squeaks. When Ando Nambe came to lock his cell for the night, Markus didn't ask about Aram, for he knew he wouldn't get an answer.

When morning came, Aram's cot was still empty.

He went to morning training with the others, but he barely paid attention, going through the motions, his mind elsewhere. A terrible, cold fear had taken root in him, starting out in his middle then expanding until all of his insides were ice. He didn't trust Sergan Parsigal. He didn't trust anyone at the College. What if they had decided that Aram was worth more for his essence than he was for his abilities?

By the time afternoon training ended, Markus was beside himself with worry. The sorcerer had ordered him to the baths before seeking him out, but Markus didn't bother. He was sweating so badly that he could smell his own stench, but he didn't care how much his odor offended. He wanted answers, and he was determined to get them.

When he returned to the classroom, Sergan was not there. Markus waited for a time, but then he became impatient. First Aram had disappeared and now Sergan. It was too much of a coincidence. There was more to the story, and no one was telling him.

If Sergan wasn't going to come looking for him, then he was going to go looking for the sorcerer.

He remembered where Sergan's quarters were from the night they had first arrived in Karaqor. He doubted Sergan would be there, but it was someplace to start. He took the stairs up to the fourth floor and found the right door, pausing in front of it to collect his emotions before he knocked.

No one answered.

Markus stood for a while, waiting, apprehension sawing into him like a serrated knife, cutting a little deeper every second. Lifting his hand, he knocked harder.

Nothing.

He tested the doorknob and found it unlocked. Taking in a deep, steadying breath, he turned the knob as quietly as he could. He let the door swing open just a crack then rushed it the rest of the way, so it wouldn't screech on its hinges.

The door screeched anyway.

Markus stood in the doorway, expecting a storm of retaliation. But instead, he discovered that Sergan's chamber was dark and empty. Quietly, he moved inside, leaving the door open just a crack to admit a little bit of light. He looked the room over carefully but saw nothing, no clue that would tell him where Aram or the sorcerer had disappeared to. He was about ready to turn and go but then something caught his eye.

A small piece of cord lay on the floor. Frowning, Markus walked over to it and bent to pick it up. Fingering the cord in his hand, he confirmed that it was Aram's, the one he was always fiddling with, especially when he was nervous. But the presence of the cord really didn't tell him anything, other than that Aram had been with Sergan, but he had already known that. With a sigh, he turned back toward the door.

And saw Sergan Parsigal standing in the doorway with an irate look on his face.

"Why are you in my quarters?" he asked very slowly, his voice just as calm and composed as ever. The more Markus heard it, the more dangerous that composure seemed.

"I...I came looking for Aram."

Sergan moved into the room, closing the door quietly behind him. "He's not here."

Markus took a step backward. "Where is he?"

"Aram had an accident," Sergan answered. "He was taken to the infirmary."

Markus stared hard at Sergan's face, looking for some sign that he might be lying. He had every reason to doubt him and no reason to believe him. At best, something terrible had to have happened to keep Aram in the infirmary so long.

"I want to see him."

The sorcerer shook his head, taking another step toward him. "No. First, we need to address the problem of you entering my personal quarters without an invitation."

Markus looked down at the cord trembling in his hands. "He's not there, is he?"

Sergan frowned. "Now, why would you say that?"

Markus backed up another step. Unable to look at the sorcerer, he accused, "You gave him to *them*, didn't you?"

Sergan shook his head. "No."

"Then let me see him."

"You can't." His expression changed, becoming almost compassionate. "I'm told his situation is very precarious. He's not allowed any visitors. Why don't you go back to the practice yard? I'll check with the infirmarers. When they feel Aram is out of danger, I'll send for you."

Markus caught his breath in fear. "What's wrong with him? What did you do?" Stepping around Sergan, he started backing toward the door.

"I didn't do anything," Sergan responded. "It was an accident. Now, go. As soon as Aram is allowed visitors, you may see him."

Markus turned and left, knowing he didn't have a choice but to obey. He didn't know whether or not Sergan was telling the truth; all he knew was that Aram needed him. With a heavy heart, he slinked out of the

sorcerer's quarters and headed down the stairs and out into the courtyard, where he sat on a bench holding his head in his hands. A cool
breeze wafted his hair and chilled his skin. Overhead, two ravens circled
in the air, wheeling slowly.

"He's not back yet?"

Markus looked up to find Poda standing over him. Behind him were
the rest of the students in his class, half with expressions of concern, and
half with expressions of disdain. He ignored the mean ones, hoping they
would go away. He didn't have the emotional energy to waste on them.

"Sergan said he had some type of accident," he said. "But I think he's
lying."

Frowning, Peshka came over to stand next to Poda. "Why would
Lord Parsigal lie to you?"

Markus was afraid of voicing his suspicion. For a few reasons. They
might think him paranoid, and even if they didn't, none of them knew
that Aram was a True Savant, and he didn't think he should arm them
with that information. In the end, he decided it really didn't matter. If he
was right, then he would need all the help he could get. And so would
Aram.

He admitted, "I think they took him to the cellars."

Peshka sat next to him, peering into his face with a look of intense
confusion. "Why would they do that?"

"Because Aram's not like you and me. He's special..."

"Special," chortled Obriem. "That's one word for it."

With a growl, Markus leapt up and lunged at him. His fist connected
with Obriem's temple and sent him reeling back. Before he could recover, Markus bowled into him, knocking him to the ground, then started
pummeling Obriem's face.

"Stop it!" Peshka shrieked. "Stop it! You're going to send him to the
infirmary!"

Hearing that word, Markus froze, Obriem cowering beneath him.

The infirmary.

He didn't want to send anyone to the infirmary—he wanted to go
there himself. Reaching down, he offered Obriem his hand. "Here's your

opportunity," he said with an insolent grin. "I want you to hurt me."

"Gladly!" the boy snarled, letting Markus hauled him to his feet. But then he paused, collecting himself, and glared at Markus suspiciously. "What are you up to, Galliar?"

"What are you doing?" asked Peshka.

Rubbing his bruised knuckles, Markus told her, "I want to make sure Aram really *is* in the infirmary. There's only one way they'll let me in." He looked at Obriem. "Will you do it?"

Obriem stood rubbing his jaw, looking undecided. Blood leaked from one of his nostrils, and his cheek looked like it was going to swell. At last, he waved Markus off, snarling, "You're not worth the whipping."

"Please." Markus forced the word out, hating the sound of it. "Do it for Aram."

"I don't give a shit about Aram."

Peshka came to stand next to Poda, her arms crossed. "Help him, Obriem. You're going to get a thrashing anyway."

"Aram's one of us," said Poda.

The other students nodded their agreement.

Obriem spat a wad of pink spittle on the ground then glared sideways at Markus. "You're going to duck."

"I won't."

Obriem snorted. "Yeah, you will."

Markus raised his chin. "Come find out."

Obriem's eyes narrowed. Then his fist went flying.

The daylight fractured into shards of red. Markus didn't remember falling, but suddenly he was on the ground and Obriem was kicking his head over and over.

"Obriem, no!" Peshka shrieked

As Obriem brought his leg back for one last kick, all Markus could think of was his father's head collapsing, of the final crunch of bone and the spray of bloody pulp. Then Obriem's boot connected with his face, exploding that thought.

"**W**hat's going on here?"

Someone was shaking him hard. Markus's head hurt, and he felt terribly nauseous. He thought he was going to vomit. He groaned, pushing himself into a sitting position.

"Obriem broke Markus's nose," said Babalo.

"It looks like he broke his head." That sounded like Professor Callain's voice.

Markus tried opening his eyes, but the light of the sun was too bright. He let out a groan.

"Don't just let him sit there bleeding," Callain snapped. "Someone get him to the infirmary. Obriem, *come with me.*"

With Poda's help, Markus managed to stand and take a few wobbly steps forward. Obriem had done a better job than he'd expected. He'd asked for it, but that still didn't make it right. Obriem was a bully and, more than anything else in the world, he hated bullies.

"I'll walk you there," offered Poda, and Markus let him, holding onto Poda's arm for stability.

"You really don't look good," the boy said as he led him toward the wide double doors. "I can't believe you let him do that to you."

"I can't either."

He had a hard time moving his jaw. His face was already starting to swell. Poda opened up the door for him and led him inside, guiding him past people who gawked at him as he fumbled by. He was glad Poda was leading him, for he had no idea where the infirmary was. Eventually they found it, down a long flight of stairs and through a twisting maze of corridors.

"Good luck," said Poda when they reached the door. He patted him on the back. "I hope you find him."

Markus did too. He opened the door and walked in, leaving Poda in the hallway. The infirmary was just one large room with many beds. Only a few of the beds were occupied, and he did a quick scan of the room, looking for Aram. But just as soon as the door closed behind him, a man with the obligatory scowl of a healer stood from a chair and blocked his view.

"What happened to you?" the man asked, taking Markus's jaw and turning his head, first one way then the other.

"I think I broke my nose."

"Humph." The infirmarer pointed to a stool. "Sit there and don't move. I'll be right back."

Markus watched him walking away but ignored the command to sit. Instead, he quickly made a survey of the beds, his eyes falling on one occupied by a boy who looked the same size as Aram. Markus hurried over to it, walking faster with every stride, all thought of pain forgotten. By the time he made it halfway across the room, he knew for sure it was Aram.

And he also knew for sure that there was something very wrong with him.

He paused at Aram's bedside, sorrow clutching his throat. Aram was sleeping, but his skin was pale and bloodless, his lips and eyes ringed with gray. Markus reached out to touch his hand.

"I told you to sit over there."

He startled, glancing back to find the infirmarer standing right behind him, his scowl deepened to a glower.

"What happened to him?" Markus whispered, staring down at Aram's lifeless body.

"He drowned," said another voice.

Markus whirled. Sergan Parsigal had come up to stand beside him so silently that he hadn't noticed. Markus gazed down at Aram, tears of despair clouding his eyes. It didn't seem possible. How could Aram drown? He was a strong swimmer—he wanted to be a sailor!

"How?" he croaked, his throat constricting.

"He fell into a well," Sergan said gently. "I jumped in after him, but by the time I got him out..." He shrugged.

"But he's alive..." Markus shook his head adamantly. Aram was still breathing. He was just asleep.

Sergan glanced at the healer, who stood with his mouth narrowed to a grim line that confirmed all of Markus's fears.

"It's unlikely he'll wake up," Sergan said. "I'm sorry."

Tears spilled from Markus's eyes. "I don't understand—he could swim! How did this happen?"

"He hit his head on the way down," Sergan said gently.

The healer moved forward, inserting his body between Markus and the bed. "I need to have a look at you, son. Go sit on the stool."

Markus backed away, staring at Aram's pale face. He wanted to lash out at Sergan, at the healer, scoop Aram up in his arms and carry him away to safety. But there was nowhere safe. They had been brought to a nest of vipers. He was supposed to be protecting Aram from these monsters, but he had failed.

Heaving a sob, he turned and fled the infirmary.

It was dark when Aram opened his eyes.

He was disoriented and, at first, he didn't know where he was. The room he was in was large and cloaked in shadow. The only light came from a single candle burning at the far end, timid and wavering. He tried to lift his head, but he was too weak, and his head was too heavy. Instead, he relaxed into the pillow, feeling the weight of weariness pulling him back under. He fought it, forcing his eyes open, and stared up into the shadows.

A motion beside him made him turn.

Through vision that was slightly doubled, he saw the form of an old man sitting at his bedside. At first, Aram was confused, for he couldn't place him. The man looked familiar, though he didn't remember seeing anyone like him in the village. He narrowed his eyes, trying to merge the two images into one. His vision squirmed into focus, and he remembered.

It was the Revered Master who sat beside his bed, calmly gazing down at him. Aram remembered then that he was no longer in the village. He remembered the well. He remembered drowning.

"How did I…"

The old man patted his hand. "Exilar Parsigal dove into the well after you and pulled you up. But he didn't save you."

Aram scrunched his eyebrows, not understanding what the Revered Master meant. He was still alive. So, what did he mean, that he wasn't saved?

The Revered Master went on, "I told you to live each day as though it were your last. Tell me, young Aram, did you heed my advice?"

"No."

He hadn't taken that advice. In truth, he'd forgotten all about it. Aram grew cold, now remembering the context of that conversation. He also remembered why he had chosen to drown himself in the well. Suddenly, he deeply regretted that he hadn't succeeded.

The old man squeezed his hand. "I was sincerely hoping things would turn out differently for you. Alas."

The cold feeling within Aram froze solid. His breathing sharpened, his pulse racing, even though he was too weak to do anything but lie there.

The Revered Master turned his head and said to someone behind him, "Go ahead and tell the Extractors they can have him. Only…let him keep his eyes."

Aram stared in horror into the man's face, his mouth working in silent denial. His body had gone limp and numb. All he could feel was white-cold panic.

The Revered Master stood and smiled down at him regretfully. "It is possible that the pain will help you find your spark. If you do, I will set you free. If not, then…" He gave a soft sigh. "I hear it's easier if you don't fight it."

Markus sat in his cell, legs drawn up against his chest, gazing at Aram's empty cot. He'd returned to Small House after fleeing the infirmary, skipping supper. His head hurt so badly it made him ill, though not half as much as his heart. That was a raw and open sore, and it felt like it was starting to fester.

Someone knocked on his door. Apparently, Ando Nambe hadn't locked it, for Markus glanced up to find Poda and Peshka in the doorway, both looking just as miserable as he felt. Peshka's eyes were red and watery, and Poda stood with his gaze trained on the floor.

"What is it?" Markus asked, his voice low and gravelly.

Peshka grimaced, fresh tears spilling down her cheeks. "Aram's dead. Professor Callain just made the announcement."

"What?" He shot bolt upright, hoping he'd heard her wrong.

"I'm so sorry," she whispered.

Markus squeezed his eyes closed, throttled by grief. He collapsed back against the wall and covered his face with his hands, shoulders lurching in silent sobs.

PART II

THE WORLD BELOW

Even though four years had passed, Markus still looked back on Aram's death with a profound sense of shame.

As the days went by, his grief became easier, but the shame never lost its hold on him. It lingered with him, always shadowing him like a footpad, darkening his dreams and dispelling his happiness. He hadn't known Aram long, but he had come to think of him as a little brother, one he had vowed to protect. One that he had failed.

Markus would never forgive himself for leaving Aram's bedside that day. And he would never forgive Sergan Parsigal for making him go.

His hand clenched into a trembling ball, the way it always did whenever he thought of the sorcerer who was his mentor. It was an involuntary reaction that he'd never been able to shake, even after spending hundreds of hours with the man.

Markus leaned back in his chair, kicking his legs up on the desk and rubbing his eyes wearily. He sat in his room on the second floor of the dormitory where he and the others had lived since graduating from Small House. Peshka and Poda had rooms down the hall, along with Obriem and Enari. Rehaan had been expelled after failing too many classes, and Babalo had left too. Apparently, he really *had* been a prince. His older brother had died, and Babalo had become heir to some throne.

Markus looked down at the length of string between his fingers. He had been absently fiddling with the thin cord, tying and untying a succession of overhand knots, just as Aram used to do. It was the same piece of string he had found on the floor in Sergan's quarters, the one Aram had been holding before he fell into the well. Markus always kept it on him, usually wearing it loose around his wrist like a bracelet.

He rose from his chair and wandered over to the window, still fingering the string. The shutters were open, admitting a cool breeze from the bay. It was summer, and the days were mild but humid. His room was warm, even with the window open. It was a modest space dominated by a bed with a straw-stuffed mattress and curtains that kept the drafts and the insects out. There was also a small table and one spindly-legged chair. There was no waste pail; instead, he had his own private latrine that emptied into the moat.

Against the foot of the bed was a cedar chest where he stored all of his worldly possessions, mostly clothes. He had also graduated from the unbleached tunics of an initiate, and now wore the black tunic of an Exilar—though without the blue mantle, for he had yet to pass his final tests.

A knock at the door broke his attention away from the string. He opened it to find Mistress Amrie, one of the maids who served in the dormitory. She was an older woman whose children were all grown, and to replace them, she had taken to adopting the occasional student under her wing. For some reason, this year, she had chosen Markus to lavish attention on. He was grateful for the small treats and snacks she left him, especially when he returned hungry from the practice yard. But Mistress Amrie could be too attentive, and whenever his mood slipped toward melancholy, she had a habit of coming around too often.

"Master Galliar," she said with one of her infinitely maternal smiles. "My, but you seem to have grown three inches in a week!" Her smile became a critical frown. "You haven't been taking care of yourself again. When's the last time you shaved?"

His hand went absently to his face and stroked the long stubble on his cheeks. It had been a while. He supposed he should either shave or grow it out, one of the two.

Managing a forced smile, he asked, "How can I help you today, Mistress Amrie?"

"I just came to check if you had any laundry."

Markus peered behind her and saw the basket of clothing she had set down in the hallway. Among her other duties, Mistress Amrie cared for all the students' laundry and changed out the straw in his mattress when it needed it.

"Thanks, but nothing this week."

He probably could have given her the outfit he was wearing, but it could go a couple more days and he wanted to save her the work. When she was gone, he shut the door and leaned back against it, feeling relieved. He needed fresh air, more than just what was blowing in through the window.

He tied Aram's string around his wrist, the way he always wore it. Then he left the room, starting down the hallway in the opposite direction Mistress Amrie had gone. He managed to slip out of the dormitory without any of the other students seeing him, for which he was grateful, because he wasn't in the mood to have to stop to talk to people.

He really didn't know where he was going until he found himself by the lake at the far end of the College. It was a peaceful place, and he like to go there to be alone. The lake was surrounded by willows, and occasionally geese and swans plied its smooth water or roosted on the shore. There was a tree he liked to sit under with weeping branches that encased him like a deer blind. He could sit there for hours when he wanted to be alone, and no one would ever know he was there.

That's what he wanted. To be alone. That's why his feet had carried him here.

Sitting under the tree, he leaned back and savored the scent of the willow leaves. On the shore, two geese and a swan were getting into a head-bobbing, wing-flapping row. Watching them made him smile, for it was the kind of remedy he needed. He let his mind wander, thinking that a nap might be in order.

Just when he was about to drift off, he heard two voices approaching. He couldn't see who it was with the branches in the way, which was fine, because that meant they couldn't see him either. The last thing he wanted was to be bothered. Whoever they were, they were laughing and carrying on. As they drew near, he realized that he recognized one of them.

Sergan Parsigal.

Immediately, Markus froze, his heart jolting to a stop. Even after all the years he'd spent studying under the sorcerer, his body always seemed to have that reaction whenever Sergan came near. Deep down, Markus loathed him. Which was unfortunate, considering Sergan had already earmarked him to be his new Shield, an honor Markus did not want.

As Sergan came into view between the branches of the willow, Markus drew back behind the trunk. He couldn't see the face of the woman who accompanied the sorcerer, for she had her back to him, staring out at the lake. Whoever she was, she wore the blue mantle of the Exilari, so Markus was sure it was someone he knew.

"Why did you bring me all the way out here?" she asked.

Sergan smiled. "Oh, I think you know."

The woman laughed, turning just a bit, enough for Markus to get a good look at her. It was Ciana Chandary, a young sorceress who had graduated with last year's class. To Markus's knowledge, she hadn't even left the College yet on her first assignment.

"I've had my eye on you for a while now," Sergan said. Reaching out, he took Ciana's hand and kissed it tenderly.

"I know."

"And?"

"I'm here, aren't I?"

"Aren't you," Sergan whispered. Wrapping his arms around her, he drew her close and kissed her slowly, lovingly. When the kiss ended, he pulled back, still gazing into Ciana's eyes.

Markus thought then about bolting but knew he would be seen. So instead, he hunkered down with his back against the tree, hoping to the gods the two of them would leave.

They didn't.

He closed his eyes and didn't watch as Sergan and Ciana made love beside the lake. When they finished and lay together cuddling, Markus stayed hidden and frozen like a rabbit. It seemed like hours before they finally stood and helped each other into their clothes.

"I hope you'll agree to come on more walks with me," Sergan said, kissing his lover's cheek.

"If you'll have me." Ciana smiled.

"Oh, I'll have you, all right." With a devilish grin, Sergan drew a vial from his belt, raising it to his lips for a taste. He closed his eyes, the expression on his face turning to outright bliss. Lowering the vial, he passed it to Ciana.

"What's this?" the young woman asked, holding the container under her nose.

"Just taste," Sergan prompted. "I promise nothing sweeter will ever pass your lips."

The woman brought the vial to her mouth and took a sip. Lowering it, she closed her eyes and breathed out a long, satisfied sigh.

"What is that?" she gasped. "It's like ambrosia for the soul!"

Sergan tossed back another swallow with an indulgent moan. "I always wondered what a Savant would taste like."

Markus's chest froze, and his eyes shot wide open, his breath hitching in his throat.

"Savant? Do you mean—"

"Aramon Raythe," Sergan confirmed with a smile. "But don't tell anyone. The Revered Master wants his essence saved for...more *necessary* exercises." He chuckled.

"Oh, I don't know." Ciana grinned. "I'd say this exercise was very necessary."

Sergan trailed a finger down her cheek. "Still. Let's keep this between the two of us, shall we?"

"Of course."

They strolled away hand-in-hand, leaving Markus shuddering beneath the tree, his hand gripping his throat to keep from screaming. Hot tears scorched his eyes, and his blood boiled in his veins. It was all he could do not to vomit.

Aram was alive.

Alive.

For four *years*, he'd been kept alive and in agony.

Everything they'd told him, everything Markus thought he knew, it was all just lies to keep him in line, to keep Aram suffering…

He'd spent the last four years doing everything these bastards had told him, grieving for a friend he should have been saving.

He'd let Aram suffer down there for four years.

Four.

Years.

He stayed there, shaking, until the sun set behind the trees and the cool silence of twilight fell around him. Then he stood and stumbled back toward the dormitory, his mind too strangled for thought.

He found the second floor empty, for the others had already gone to supper. He trudged down the hallway in a daze, vision blurred by tears. He dove into his own quarters, slamming the door behind him, and threw himself down on the bed, where he lay in a trembling mass.

He didn't know how long he'd been there when Peshka found him. He hadn't heard her enter; she seemed to just appear beside his bed.

"Hey," she said, kneeling next to him with an expression of concern. "What's wrong?"

Markus only shook his head, for the truth was too painful to bear, much less voice.

"What's wrong with him?" asked Poda from the doorway.

"He's alive," Markus said raggedly. "They lied to us. He's alive."

"Who's alive?" asked Peshka. She moved to sit beside him, placing a hand on his back.

"Aram."

"What?" Poda surged into the room. "How do you know?"

"I overheard Sergan talking to Ciana down by the lake," Markus said miserably. "They were sharing a vial of his essence." Grimacing, he shook his head. The truth was unendurable. "He's been alive all this time…they've been torturing him for *years!"*

Rage took hold of him, severing his control. With a growl, he sprang to his feet and strode across the room to where his sword was propped against the wall. Grabbing the hilt, he turned toward the door.

Poda stepped in front of him. "Where are you going?"

Markus glared at him, not in the right mind to explain himself. "I'm going to get him out of there. Now, move."

Peshka shook her head, glancing at Poda for help. "You can't do that. The cellars are protected by magic."

"Then it's a damn good thing I'm Impervious."

He tried stepping around Poda, but the young man spread his hands, blocking the doorway. "You can't go there. They'll kill you."

"Let them try," Markus growled. "I failed Aram once. I won't fail him again." Reaching out, he tried pushing Poda out of his way.

But Poda had grown too much in the past four years to be pushed casually aside. He stood a hand taller than Markus now, and his wiry muscles held a deceptive amount of strength. He caught Markus's hand.

"Stop," he said. "You can't be rash about this. At least think it out. Plan. If you're going to do something, then give yourself the best chance. Give *Aram* the best chance."

Markus sucked in a deep breath then heaved it out in a great sigh. Poda was right. Just rushing mindlessly into the cellars wasn't the answer.

"All right." He turned and strode back toward the bed, sitting down on it heavily and laying his sword across his lap. "What kind of plan?"

Poda bit his lip, his gaze sliding to the side in thought. Out of all the older students, Poda was the smartest. If anyone could figure out a way to rescue Aram, it was him.

He stood in the doorway for minutes, arms crossed, his face pinched into lines of thought. At last, he sighed and shook his head, his shoulders sagging. "It's not going to work."

"Don't say that," Markus growled menacingly.

Poda spread his hands. "Think about it. Not only do you have to get him out of the cellars, but you also have to get him out of Karaqor. And then what? Every sorcerer in the Exilari will be looking for him. And they'll find him—he'll shine like a beacon. There's no chance you could hide him. They'll just track you down and kill you, then they'll take him right back."

Exasperated, Markus punched his fist into the mattress. "He's already been down there *four years!* I'm not leaving him there another day!"

Poda licked his lips, looking suddenly grim. "You don't have to leave him there. But you can't rescue him either—they'll just take him back."

Markus gaped at him. "Don't leave him and don't rescue him? What the hell, Poda? That makes no sense!"

Peshka gave a soft gasp of understanding. She glanced at Markus, her eyes shadowing. "He's right. It's the only way. You can probably get *to* him, but you'll never get him out."

Poda's cheeks glowed red as though ashamed. "It's what Aram would want. It's what *I* would want, if I were him."

Only then did Markus realize what his friends were trying to say. "You want me to break in there and *kill him?*"

He opened his mouth to say something in protest but only silence came out. He couldn't force words past the knot in his throat, for he knew Poda was right. No matter how much it hurt, he was right.

Hanging his head, Markus whispered, "Whatever it takes."

Peshka took him in her arms and hugged him, her tears wetting his cheek. Then Poda was there, too, kneeling next to them, hugging them both.

Markus tore off a bite from the slice of bread Peshka had smuggled him from the larder. He wasn't hungry, but she had insisted that he eat. He sat on the floor with his back against the wall, watching Poda pace up and down the length of the room. Poda's scraggly hair hung in his face in greasy clumps, and his cheeks were a more splotchy red than usual.

"Isn't Obriem assigned to watch the entrance to the cellars some nights?" he asked.

"I think he is," replied Peshka.

Poda nodded, biting his lip. He paced the floor a few more times before suggesting, "We can ask him to look the other way."

Markus shook his head. Obriem had become more agreeable over the years, but he was still an arrogant, self-centered ass. "He won't do it."

"He might," Poda differed. "Obriem felt really bad about Aram after the way he treated him. We can at least ask him. He should be up in the rookery right now."

Markus didn't like the idea. He didn't trust Obriem. "What if he turns us in?"

"I don't think he would," said Peshka. She tugged at her shoulder-length red hair, looking annoyed by it. It was the longest Markus had ever seen her wear it.

While Peshka fiddled with her hair, Markus drummed his fingers on his leg, tired of watching Poda pace. He was getting impatient. It was past the night bell, and according to the rules, his candles should have been snuffed out already. If someone noticed the light, there would be explaining to do.

Poda stopped his pacing and bit his lip. "All right. I'll go get him."

Markus sat straight upright. "No. We can't risk it."

"Do you want to get inside or not?" Poda asked. "Because I can't think of another way."

Markus heaved a sigh, standing up. Reluctantly, he nodded.

"Wait here," said Poda, and left the room.

Markus glanced at Peshka, fingering his string bracelet and shifting uncomfortably. She hadn't stopped looking at him since the moment she had entered his room, and the compassion on her face was touching. He gave her a halfhearted smile, not sure whether he was trying to reassure her or reassure himself.

"They'll kill you," she said.

Markus shrugged, for she was likely right. If he succeeded in depriving the Exilari of their most prized source of essence, he had no doubt they would take their anger out on him. The fact that he was the most Impervious Shield in the Order might save him from the gallows, but he knew it wouldn't save him from the whipping post. And flogging might be the easiest part of his punishment.

"I can't leave him there," Markus said.

He hoped she understood. He thought she did, for she nodded and looked away. Peshka had to understand that no amount of pain he could possibly suffer would be close to what Aram had been forced to endure. Since coming to the College, Markus had learned a lot, not just about the specifics of being a Shield, but also about the sorcerers they protected. He knew exactly what it took to extract essence from a victim. And by now, he knew the procedure was far more terrible than even the bard had described.

No matter what they did to him, he vowed he would not leave Aram in the cellars another day.

It didn't take long for Poda to return, Obriem following in his wake with an irked expression on his face. He stood by the door with his arms crossed, glaring at Markus derisively. "You honestly think you can break into the cellars? You're a fool, Galliar. And soon you'll be a dead fool."

"Thanks for coming," Markus muttered. "Means a lot."

"Look, the only reason I'm here is to talk you out of it."

"Then go back to the rookery."

Markus turned his back on Obriem and walked toward the window, which had been shuttered to hide the candlelight from view of the courtyard below. He peered through a gap in the shutters, waiting for Obriem to leave. But instead of leaving, Obriem approached and set his hand on Markus's shoulder, and the gratitude Markus felt washed away all the bad feelings that had ever come between them.

"I want to help," Obriem said in the gentlest tone Markus had ever heard him use. "But what I'm not going to do is risk my neck just to help you get yourself killed."

Markus's shoulders sagged in disappointment.

"But there is another way…" Obriem added quickly.

Markus turned to look at him, his interest piqued. "What way?"

Obriem shifted his weight uneasily. "They let them out for sun and exercise once a day. They're allowed to walk around a cloister on the far side of the compound. They're not under heavy guard because there's no need for it…they're not a threat."

"How do *you* know about this?" Markus asked, glaring at Obriem suspiciously.

Obriem grimaced, lowering his gaze. "Because I'm one of the guards who watch over them."

"What? You've seen him?"

Obriem nodded, looking ashamed. "I didn't want to tell you. I figured you were better off not knowing."

Markus lunged for him, knocking Obriem back against the wall and punching him in the face. It took both Peshka and Poda to pull him off.

"You son of a whore!" Markus growled. "How long have you known?"

"A while," Obriem answered. "Look, I'm sorry."

Markus groaned, throwing his head back. He pointed at the door. *"Get out."*

"Wait." Obriem ran his hand over the red spot on his cheek where Markus had slugged him. "I said I wanted to help you, and I do." He drew in a deep breath. "The place I'm talking about isn't that far from the lagoon. If we could have a boat ready, there's a possibility they wouldn't miss him for a while."

Real hope surged into Markus for the first time. His breath caught, and he felt a flood of relief that made him dizzy. Turning to Peshka, he asked, "Could you get ahold of a boat?"

Peshka worked at the stables, which wasn't too far from the boathouse. She shrugged. "I suppose. But where would you go? The lagoon's the first place they'll look."

"Maybe not," said Poda. "Not if we give them reason to look somewhere else."

Markus looked from one friend to the other, marveling that they were all willing to risk their futures in the Order to help Aram. Even Obriem. For a long time after he'd first gotten there, he'd thought that everyone at the College was evil, and there could be no such thing as a decent Exilari. His fellow students had made him reevaluate that idea.

Of course, they weren't Exilari yet. And there was a good chance, after tonight, they might never be. Markus looked around the room, his eyes wandering over the furniture as his mind grappled with doubts. He weighed each of their fates against the plight of one boy whose mind and spirit were most likely long broken. The more Markus thought about it, the more wrong their involvement seemed.

"I can't ask any of you to help me," he said.

Poda looked from Obriem to Peshka, then firmly crossed his arms. "This is about Aram, and we're going to help."

Markus's eyes blurred, for he knew at that moment that he and Aram had the best friends in the world.

"Thank you."

They stayed up half the night planning. By morning, it was decided that they would wait two more days, until Obriem's next watch. Obriem assured them there would be no more than four guards, all regular men on the Exilari payroll. Peshka and Poda had volunteered to create a distraction on the other side of the College. There was an old wooden shack over there, surrounded by a grove of trees. It wouldn't take more than a spark to burn the shack to the ground, and if the fire spread to the grove, it would threaten the rest of the College. The plan sounded too good to be true. Which probably meant it was, but it was the only plan they had.

The next two days went by in a bleary haze of anxiety, misgivings, and indigestion. When the morning of their attempt finally arrived, Markus felt like a quivering mess. He was frankly surprised that no one suspected anything, from the way he'd been acting. More than one professor had chastised him for not applying himself to his work, and he'd received far more blows in the practice yard than he normally would have, simply because he was too distracted to react fast enough.

He went to eat the midday meal with the others, his heart pounding as though he'd spent all morning running laps around the compound. He couldn't stomach swallowing even one bite, which was frustrating, for he knew this meal might be his last. After lunch, the older students were rewarded with an hour of rest before afternoon drills. They returned to the dormitory without rest in mind, instead meeting in Poda's room for a last-minute review of their plans.

Poda and Peshka shook his hand before slipping out the door to carry out their part in the mission. Markus tried to express his gratitude, but the words failed him. After they departed, he was left alone with Obriem.

"It's time for my watch," said Obriem. "When the two o'clock bell rings, I'll walk away. I'll leave the door to the cloister unlocked behind me."

"I don't know what to say." Markus spread his hands.

Obriem just smiled. "That's because there's nothing *to* say. Just remember: when this is all over, you will owe me, Galliar."

Markus chuckled. "How about I just let you beat me up again?"

Obriem grinned. "I'll take it."

Markus remained behind in his room, giving Obriem time to assume his post. When the chimes in the bell tower sounded half-past one, he took Aram's string off his wrist and, gripping it tightly, muttered a prayer to Ahn, a deity no Vard had prayed to for centuries. But all the other gods had already failed him, so Markus decided to give the Fallen God a chance. Replacing the knotted string back on his wrist, Markus picked up his sword and set out to either rescue or murder his best friend.

He'd seldom been to the side of the compound where the cellars were located, for there was nothing much over that way, so he had no reason to go there. Obriem had described to him where the door to the cloister was located. He crossed the yard to a long windbreak of sycamores that separated the east side of the compound from the lagoon. There, he stopped, hidden by the trees, and gazed out across a wide, clipped lawn to find Obriem standing beside the door to a decrepit-looking stone structure that looked like it might once have been part of some larger type of fortification. He waited in his hiding spot until the bell struck. Then, exactly as planned, Obriem walked away from his post.

Markus paused a moment longer, grappling with fear. His palms were sweaty, and his hands were trembling, his pulse a chaotic frenzy in his ears. He closed his eyes and whispered one last prayer then, clutching his sword, walked out of the trees and strode across the lawn toward the heavy wooden door.

Fortunately, no one saw him crossing the wide swath of grass, which was a miracle, for he had no way of explaining why he was there if he got caught. By the time he arrived on the door's threshold, his breath was coming in ragged gasps and his trembling had turned to outright shaking. He tested the door and found that Obriem was as good as his word: it was unlocked. Taking one last glance around, he opened the door and let himself in.

He stood within a covered walkway lined with robust stone columns. Markus stepped quickly behind the nearest column, hoping that no one had glimpsed him. There, he stood with his back pressed against the stone, clutching his sword against his chest. He waited there for several pounding heartbeats until he was sure he hadn't been seen, then chanced a peek into the interior courtyard.

A handful of people were gathered in the small, confined area. None were speaking. All looked emaciated, the spark of life snuffed from their eyes. Some stood still as statues, while others lay curled on the ground. A woman in a linen shift paced restlessly back and forth in a deep furrow that looked worn into the ground by her own feet. On the far side of the courtyard, a young man sat hugging his knees tight against his chest, rocking slightly.

Aram.

The sight of his old friend brought tears to Markus's eyes. He never would have recognized him, had he not been looking for him specifically. Aram was dressed only in a pair of filthy trousers, the rest of his body naked. His ribs protruded sharply from his back, and his skin was stretched over his features, pale and paper-thin. His hair was matted and so greasy that it looked wet, and his thighs looked thinner than Markus's forearms. Seeing him like that provoked a stab of fury deep in his gut sharper than anything Markus had ever felt before.

He wanted to kill someone. Anyone.

He retained just enough reason to stop himself from rushing the two guards. Fighting for control, Markus forced himself to turn his attention from the pitiful scene in the courtyard. He looked around the arcaded walkways that bordered the yard, looking for the third guard Obriem had warned him would be there. He couldn't see him, at least not where he stood, and he couldn't move away from the pillar, or he'd be spotted...but maybe that wouldn't be a problem. He wore the tunic of an Exilar, if not the mantle. It should at least give them reason to hesitate.

Sheathing his sword, he stepped away from the pillar and walked toward the nearest guard, nodding in greeting the moment their eyes met. The guard tensed, his hand going to the hilt of his sword. But then he recognized the uniform, and though he frowned, he drew his hand away.

"You're not supposed to be in here," the guard said, taking a step toward Markus.

"I'm here to relieve you," Markus said. "You're wanted back at the College."

The man's frown deepened. "What? Why's that?"

Markus moved as though to step around him, but then twisted and caught the man in a chokehold, pressing the edge of his knife against the guard's throat. There was a shout from the man across the courtyard, who brought a crossbow up and trained it on him.

Markus swung his prisoner around, using his body as a shield. "Drop it, or he dies!"

The man in his arms started to struggle, so Markus increased the pressure of the blade against his neck, drawing blood. The guard went still.

"Put it down!" Markus yelled at his companion. "Or I'll cut his throat!"

A prisoner in the courtyard started making loud, huffing grunts that sounded like a bear. One of the women had scampered to the wall, where she stood whimpering and clawing at her face. The guard with the crossbow bent to put his weapon down but then turned and bolted for the door.

"*Stop!*" Markus cried, but it was too late.

He shoved the guard he was holding head-first into the wall. The man went limp, sagging to the ground.

Many of the prisoners had fled to a door on the far side of the small courtyard and were howling and banging on it. Aram wasn't among them. He sat where he'd been, clutching his head and rocking frantically.

Markus sprinted toward him, catching him up in his arms and turning his head to look at him. "Aram! *Aram!*"

Aram started to struggle. He opened his mouth and let out a horrible wail. Markus squeezed him against his chest in a bear hug and held him tight as Aram bucked and fought against him. Chafing Aram's back, he said into his ear, "It's me. Markus. It's me. *It's me…*"

Aram continued to wail, his fists pounding against Markus's chest. Growing frantic, Markus pulled back, taking Aram's face in his hands and forcing him to look into his eyes. "Aram! You know me! It's Markus! I'm going to get you out of here!"

Aram's fists stopped. He collapsed against Markus's chest and started sobbing. Not knowing what else to do, Markus scooped him up in his arms and was horrified to discover that Aram didn't weigh more than a child. He didn't fight as Markus carried him through the far door of the cloister. Hearing shouts behind them, he sprinted for the trees. On the other side of them was the lagoon where the boat would be.

In his arms, Aram started struggling again.

"Easy," Markus gasped. "I've got you! I've got you!"

Something whistled past his ear, and an arrow struck the ground in front of them, followed by another. Markus sped his pace, plunging into the line of trees. He sprinted faster, ducking tree limbs as someone shouted at his back and another arrow *thunked* into a tree next to him.

They burst out of the trees onto the shore of the lagoon.

But the boat wasn't there.

Markus staggered to a halt. Looking up and down the shoreline, he searched frantically for the boat Peshka had promised would be there.

He screamed in rage and despair. Cradling Aram, he raced down the shore in the direction of the city. Ahead, more guards emerged from the trees, blocking their path.

There was nowhere to go. They were out of options.

With a sob, Markus sank to the ground, hugging Aram against him, his hand moving to the knife at his belt.

Something *punched* him in the back, and he cried out.

The knife fell from his hand and he slumped backward. Markus turned his head to see Aram kneeling next to him, tears washing his face. He was making motions in the air with his hands, beautiful strands of color appearing between his fingers. *Magic.* Aram was weaving magic, Markus realized.

And then Aram made a slicing motion.

Behind him, the air ripped open, light pouring from the slice. The wound grew bigger, yawning open between them and the onrushing guards. Like a tear in the fabric of the world, it kept ripping, racing across the shoreline and out across the surface of the lake, tearing an enormous gash across the water. The shoreline disappeared, and all Markus could see was dazzling white light.

A thundering roar trembled the earth.

Out of the light emerged the enormous body of a void dragon, pale and wretched as a ghoul, its scales loose and rotten, its wings tattered and laced with holes. It bounded out of the light and reared above them on the shore, wings outstretched, steam belching from its nostrils.

The dragon came down, jarring the earth, and struck out at them with fangs that were long and sharp as daggers. The great jaws closed, latching onto him, and suddenly Markus was flying through the air. His body slammed hard against the ground in an explosion of pain that tore up his insides.

Lying on his side and moaning with agony, he watched helplessly as Aram moved to stand between him and the dragon, his arms spread out at his sides. A blinding radiance gushed from his hands, just as it had that night in the forest, all those years ago. The dragon seemed to be soaking it in, spreading its wings and throwing its head back.

As Markus looked on in horror, the dragon's pale and ravaged body started mending. The bare patches of skin were enclosed in fresh scales, the tears in the membranes of its wings closing. The deathly paleness of its flesh started warming with a flush of color.

Then Aram wavered, and the light faltered. His eyes rolled back, and he collapsed to the ground.

The void dragon emitted a piercing shriek that shook Markus's insides. Lashing out with its tail at the guards, it lowered its head and closed its jaws around Aram, lifting him bodily from the ground. Then the dragon turned and sprang back into the rupture, disappearing in an explosion of light.

Consciousness crept back to Aram only slowly. He floated toward it like a feather lofted by a gentle breeze. He was coming back from somewhere deep, somewhere safe and secure, a feeling all but lost to him until now. His body rocked gently, listing to and fro, as though he floated on the gentle surface of a lake. Cool mist collected on his face, and he could feel gusts of air rushing past him.

His eyes opened slowly to a dazzling brilliance unlike anything he had ever known. It moved beneath him like millions of shimmering diamonds, all gleaming and sparkling, all racing by faster than the wind. As his eyes adjusted to the light, he realized that he was looking down upon the sparkling radiance of sunlight reflected off the surface of an ocean, and he was suspended in the air above it.

Fear gripped him, for he realized that the void dragon still had hold of him, grasping him in its talons like an eagle carrying its prey.

An enormous, milk-colored wing dipped in the air next to him, and he felt his body roll. The talons tightened their grip on him, tucking him close against an enormous torso. The great wings beat again, propelling them higher. Far below, the ocean darkened as its waters receded into the distance.

The dragon pierced a thick bank of clouds, misting Aram's face with millions of tiny droplets that chilled his body and refreshed his spirit. With a great downstroke of wings, the clouds fell away, becoming a flat, soft surface that expanded beneath them to the horizons.

A golden brightness broke over his face, so intense that Aram was forced to squint against it: the light of the first sunrise his eyes had looked upon in four long years of darkness. The sight was so arresting, so heart-breaking, that he let out a great, strangled sob of gratitude and grief.

Before sorrow could take hold of him, images of sunrises filled his mind, one after another, each more breathtaking than the last. Every sun-rise his eyes had missed while he was locked in the cellars flashed across his mind. He closed his eyes and sighed, savoring the visions, reveling in the comfort of knowing that every sunrise he had ever lost had just been given back to him.

The dragon clutched him tighter against its body. Then it tucked its wings and dove toward the cloudbank. The frigid wind chafed Aram's cheeks, and his stomach plunged. He squeezed his eyes tight in fear, only daring to open them when he felt the dragon level off.

Below, the ocean transitioned to land, and a great swath of lush for-est appeared, stretching into the distance. The dragon dipped a wing and banked, changing direction toward a marching line of snow-capped mountains. It gave a cry that reminded Aram of the shriek of a hawk, though far deeper and more resonant. The sound made him smile, though weakly, for his body and mind had reached the limit of what he was capable of after so many years of isolation and torment.

As he felt his consciousness ebbing, Aram allowed himself to feel something he'd thought he would never experience again:

Hope.

The startled cries of dragons drew Esmir Revin to the edge of his ter-race. He arrived just as a whole flock of them took to the air, pushing off from their perches on the cliffs with a turmoil of wings. All along the ey-ries that lined the canyon walls, startled people surged to their feet and raised their hands to shield their faces from the sun, eyes searching the cliffs above the chasm for the source of the disturbance.

Esmir rushed to the edge of the terrace, leaning over it to peer out over the abyssal gorge below, but saw nothing to merit such a commotion. He was just about to turn away when he heard a tremendous *whoosh whoosh whoosh* accompanied by a great gust of air.

Esmir threw himself backward just in time as an enormous void dragon spilled half-onto the terrace in a tangle of tattered wings, its talons gripping the lip of the cliff to keep from falling. It balanced there for just a moment, its milky-white chest heaving for breath. Then its ravaged wings went limp, and the golden fire dimmed in its eyes. With a soft moan, the dragon let go and slipped backward into the chasm.

Aghast, Esmir rushed to the edge and watched the dragon vanish into the abyss in mute horror and disbelief, for he had once known that particular dragon well. It must have given what was left of its ravaged life to leave the void and fly all the way to his eyrie.

Then Esmir's eyes fell on the reason why.

A limp, emaciated figure lay on the stone of the terrace, a mere handspan away from the edge. Esmir rushed forward, pulling the boy away from the cliff. Taking the limp form in his arms, he rose and carried him off the terrace into his quarters, laying him down on his own bed. Only then did he pause to see what the void dragon had spent the last of its strength to deliver him.

It was a youth in his mid-teens, and he looked on the verge of death. His features were drawn and pale, his limbs frail and thin. Esmir checked him for a pulse and was unsettled to find it weak and racing—the boy was clinging to life by a thin fingernail. Like the dragon who had delivered him, the boy had been drained of essence almost to the point of death.

There was little Esmir could do, for essence was something he had been born without. Hurrying to a table, he picked up a crystalline decanter of Wellspring water and unstoppered it. Sloshing some of the bottle's potent contents into a cup, he returned to the boy's bedside and lifted him into his arms, holding the cup to his lips.

Praying the youth retained enough of his faculties to swallow, he tilted the cup. The boy sputtered and coughed weakly, but then his throat worked, and he swallowed the liquid down. Encouraged, Esmir poured a little more of the sacred water past his lips. This time, the boy didn't choke. Taking his time, Esmir held him until he'd finished the entire cup and his pulse slowed its feverish pace. Then he laid him back down in the soft bed and rose with a shuddering sigh of relief.

Esmir rubbed his face wearily and sat on the edge of the bed to consider the young man whose life he had just saved.

The boy was Auld, by the look of him, though Esmir suspected he might be a mix. It was hard to tell—his skin was pale and discolored, but it retained the golden flush of the brown blood that flowed only through Aulden veins. His features were sharper than most, but that could be due to emaciation. It was obvious this boy had been subjected to tremendous hardships over a long period of time that had taken an awful toll on him.

Curious if he was fully Auld or something in between, Esmir used his thumb to peel open an eyelid, checking to see if the boy's eyes were as turquoise blue as his own.

What he saw made him gasp.

Esmir's mouth opened, and his heart skipped a beat. Disbelieving his own vision, he checked both of the boy's eyes, gaping at the inordinately rare color.

Opal.

Esmir drew in a long, quivering breath, his mind reeling dizzily. No wonder the void dragon had brought him here.

Scrubbing at his hair, he turned and went to the wooden pole where he kept what few garments he owned hanging beside various herbs and dried meats. Tugging off his filthy robe, he donned in its place baggy pants and a thigh-length vest. He stood for a long moment, running his hands over his clothes, softening the wrinkles creased into the fabric by years of disuse.

Head spinning, Esmir left the unconscious boy to his rest and exited his eyrie. He walked down a long tunnel bored into the sandstone cliff and illuminated by narrow shafts placed at intervals that admitted a surprising amount of sunlight. There were hundreds of such corridors that formed an enormous labyrinth within the cliffs, linking the homes, shops, and eyries of Skyhome like the warren of an ant nest.

It took him a long time to reach the level where the Dedicant Mother of his people made her home, for his legs were over a thousand years old and were far less agile than they used to be. He hesitated outside her door, trying to remember how many centuries it had been since he had last stood on Luvana's threshold. It took a while to bring himself to knock. It took even longer for the door to open.

Luvana Elegar greeted Esmir with a sour look, which was an improvement over the normal scowl of derision he usually received from her. Her long gray hair was captured in a thick braid that trailed out from beneath the beaded blue headscarf that marked her as a sage. The wrinkles on her face ran deep—deeper even than his own—one for each year of life she had been forced to suffer his existence, or so she claimed.

"Esmir!" she exclaimed with a scornful smile. "What catastrophe has occurred to bring you down from your lofty perch?"

He scowled but bit his tongue against the taunt he wanted to let fly. "Let me in, Luvana. It's urgent."

"Urgent?" She lifted her eyebrows but stepped back from the doorway, her gaze trailing over him. "Whatever's wrong, it must be quite serious, indeed. Nothing less would make you put on real clothes. Isn't that your best outfit?"

Esmir moved past her with an angry grunt. She motioned him deeper into the room, a spacious chamber with a curved ceiling carved out of rock, the starkness of its walls softened by colored rugs and tapestries. A hearth was built into the center of the room, its smoke drawn upward through a hole in the ceiling that was only partially effective, as the chamber smelled strongly of woodsmoke mingled with spice.

"I suppose you didn't come to socialize." Luvana picked up a cup of honeywine she had left on a table.

"I have news," Esmir growled.

"Obviously." Luvana chortled. "Otherwise you wouldn't be here. Very well. Spit it out."

Esmir blew out an exasperated puff of air. "A void dragon smashed into my terrace a few minutes ago, disgorging a dying boy before plummeting into the gorge."

Luvana's expression froze. "That's...unusual."

"Unusual?" Esmir barked a rancorous laugh. "The boy was drained to his last drop of essence—sucked dry! I brought him back from the brink, at least for now. Luvana…he has opal eyes."

The woman lurched, choking on her wine. Sputtering, she set her cup down on the table and wiped her mouth. "You're not drunk, are you?"

"The hell with you!" Esmir bellowed. "Luvana! I'm telling you that for the first time in four hundred years, a boy with opal eyes has returned to the eyries. And you ask me if I'm drunk?"

"Bah!" Luvana raised her hand. "After all you've failed at, do you really need to ask me why I'm skeptical?"

Esmir hung his head, shaking it slowly. There were so many things in his life he regretted, but now wasn't the time to start dissecting them. The boy needed help and needed it quickly.

"Listen to me, Luvana. I think he's been tortured, probably over a long period of time. I need a skilled healer. I need a dragon. And, more than anything else, I need your trust."

"My trust!" The old woman issued a contemptuous laugh. "I'd have better luck trusting a vulture around carrion. But all right, I'll summon a healer. Why do you need a dragon?"

Esmir sighed. "Because if this boy's been through half of what I think he has, it's going to take more than a healer to save him."

Luvana's smile faded. "And what kind of torture do you think he's been subjected to?"

"The void dragon came through a rupture, so I think the boy did too. He had to come from the World Above. And to be drained as much as he is…it stinks like the Exilari."

"Rubbish!" Luvana batted her hand dismissively.

"Then come look at him!" Esmir spat. He'd had enough. "Set aside your contempt for me for one moment and come see him for yourself!"

Luvana's eyes narrowed, and she stared at him hard for a long moment. At last, she nodded. "Very well. I'll summon a healer."

Fuming, he waited in her quarters as she went out. When she returned several minutes later, he stormed out of her room and made his way down the corridor without turning to make sure she was following.

He could hear her footsteps dogging him as he made his way back up the stairs to the Heights. By the time he reached the level of his own quarters, he was huffing for breath like a new windrider after a first flight.

He held his door open for Luvana, who appeared untroubled by the climb. Once inside, he motioned her toward the bed, where his young charge still lay unconscious. Her face suddenly serious, the Dedicant Mother approached the boy cautiously and hovered over him a moment before sitting on the edge of the bed. Just as Esmir had done, she lifted one of the boy's eyelids and peered inside. Bowing her head, she murmured a soft prayer only the gods could hear.

Then she turned back to Esmir. "What else do you need from me?"

He moved forward to stand at her side. "If he's spent any time in the cellars, then he's endured enough pain to drive a grown man insane. The Mother only knows what that kind of pain would do to a boy. We're going to have to bring him back slowly, not all at once. More than anything else, he'll need reassurance and a profound sense of security."

"You need an empath." Luvana lifted an eyebrow. "Why can't we just carry him down to the dragons?"

Esmir knew what she meant: *away from you.* He wanted to strangle her. But more than anything, he wanted to strangle himself, for he knew he deserved all the rancor she could heap upon him. He took a moment to collect himself, letting his anger cool and gathering his thoughts enough to speak.

"You need me, Luvana. *He* needs me. I'm the only Warden left alive who has ever trained a Champion."

Luvana wrenched her eyes from him and gazed down into the boy's ashen face. Lifting a hand, she smoothed his matted hair back with the tenderness of a mother.

"There's one more thing," Esmir said slowly. "The void dragon that brought him here…" He drew in a deep breath. "It was Agaroth."

Luvana blinked, her gaze darting from the boy to Esmir. Face suddenly grave, Luvana gave a slight nod. "I'm sorry, Esmir. I am. All right. You'll have your healer, your dragon, and your boy. Just don't fail him the way you failed Daymar Torian."

31

Calise Andar knocked on the Dedicant Mother's door and then stood fidgeting, shifting her weight and fiddling with her brown hair, pushing it back behind her ears before pulling it forward again. She tugged at her linen skirt, only then realizing it didn't match her leather shirt. She cursed under her breath, for she never thought about the clothes she wore until it mattered. And, right now, it mattered.

Luvana answered the door with a welcoming smile that put to rest Calise's fidgeting. As Calise entered, she couldn't help staring at the walls as she crossed the room. She had never been inside the Dedicant Mother's quarters before and had never seen the rich tapestries Luvana owned, which told the story of the world—not the history of it but, rather, the wonder.

Each tapestry depicted one of the sacred Wellsprings, locations of extraordinary natural beauty imbued with the power of the Mother's blood. Once, there had been seven Wellsprings, but now there were only five, for two had been corrupted. The tapestry behind Luvana depicted the most potent Wellspring of all: the Heart of the Mother, a heart-shaped pool of blood-red water that lapped at the feet of an enormous statue of the goddess.

Luvana motioned Calise to have a seat on the floor by the hearth upon furs and pillows arranged around it. She took a seat next to her, scooting closer and smiling warmly. "Calise. Thank you so much for coming. I've heard so much about the work you've been doing with the injured. You really have quite a Talent."

Calise blushed under the praise, averting her eyes to the tapestry behind Luvana.

Luvana offered her a cup of mulled honeywine, which she accepted gratefully. Taking a sip of the hot liquid, she said, "I've had a hard time fitting in, Mother. But I love it."

It's not that people didn't treat her well—they did—but Auld ways weren't always comfortable for humans, like an elegant shoe cobbled for another's foot. But she loved healing, and the Dedicant Mother was right; she had a Talent for it. It was the same Talent that had rescued her from a life of servitude in Eldinor, at the hands of the Kal-Kalath.

"And how is Zandril?" Luvana asked.

The mention of Zandril brought a smile to Calise's lips, for she couldn't help smiling every time she thought of her beautiful dragon. Zandril had bound her only six months before, and she still hadn't stopped thanking the Mother every day for that blessing. Though she could already carry Calise on her back, among dragonkind, Zandril was still considered an adolescent, and had years to go before reaching full maturity.

"She's growing," Calise smiled. "A lot."

"Wingmaster Vandra says Zandril is very good-natured, as are you." Luvana used a metal hook to remove the pot of honeywine from an iron rack above the hearth. Grasping the handle with a towel, she refilled her own mug then topped off Calise's mug before replacing the pot.

"Thank you, Mother."

Luvana sat forward, her eyes capturing and holding Calise's gaze. "I called you here to ask a favor. It would entail spending time away from the infirmary, but I believe it's important."

Calise didn't like the sound of that, for she had patients that needed her attention. Whenever she wasn't flying with Zandril to offer her services to the nearby towns, she was in the infirmary, for healing was her duty and her passion.

"What is the favor, Mother?" she asked.

Luvana sighed, setting her cup down at her side. "Esmir found a boy…or perhaps the boy found Esmir—who can say? Alas, he's starved and near death and has been very traumatized. We believe that some emotional support might go a long way toward helping him mend."

Calise frowned, uncertain what Luvana was asking of her. A wounded boy, she would gladly tend. It was the 'emotional support' part that gave her pause. She wasn't very good at emotion. Emotions hurt, and she didn't like hurting. She'd done enough of it.

"That's terrible to hear," Calise said, "but I'm not sure what I could—"

"You and Zandril," Luvana corrected. "We need you both. What the boy needs most right now is a healer's touch and a dragon's empathy. You can find him in Esmir's eyrie."

Calise sat blinking, taken aback by what had just happened. Luvana had just shut the conversation down prematurely, before she had a chance to agree to anything—or disagree. She glanced uncomfortably at Luvana and found the Dedicant Mother staring at her as though daring her to protest. Her stomach scrunched. Calise had always heard that Luvana had the personality of a battle axe, but this was the first she'd had a chance to experience it.

"Why is the boy with Esmir?" she asked. "Wouldn't it make better sense to bring him to the infirmary?"

"Esmir seems to think the boy might have what it takes to be a Champion," Luvana stated casually, as though speaking of a piece of furniture or the ingredients of a dish. "He wants to keep him close."

Calise's confusion deepened. "But, Mother, I thought you forbid training any more Gifted."

"I did. But this boy is not merely Gifted."

Calise's jaw dropped. "The boy's a Savant?"

Luvana nodded gravely. "We believe so. Will you help him?"

Calise was speechless. She sat staring straight ahead, blinking slowly, as she pondered the implications. A True Savant hadn't been born in hundreds of years. If this boy could pass the Trials and become a Champion, then they still had hope of defeating Araghar.

"Of course," she whispered absently, the mug of honeywine forgotten in her hand.

Luvana removed it from her grip, then stood, motioning her toward the door. "Thank you very much, my dear. Do you know your way to the Heights?"

Calise nodded, drifting toward the door in a daze.

She left Luvana's quarters and mounted the steps to the Heights, the abandoned cliffs of Skyhome where the eyries that had once housed the Greater Dragons were located. Of all the eyries in the Heights, only one was still occupied, and that was Esmir's. Even though his dragon had been lost centuries before, the old man had remained behind, the lone survivor of a lost heritage.

As Calise arrived before Esmir Revin's eyrie, tendrils of anxiety squirmed across her skin. For a moment, she paused, staring at the humble-looking oaken door in front of her that led to the eyrie that had once belonged to Daymar Torian and his dragon, Agaroth the Red, two names right out of legend. Esmir had been Torian's Warden, his friend, his partner in life. But Esmir had failed his Champion—a failure that had resulted in the loss of Araghar...and the loss of Daymar Torian.

Calise shuddered, thinking of the boy, and raised her hand to knock. It took some time before she heard the sound of shuffling footsteps on the other side. The door cracked open, and out peered an old man with a greasy gray beard and a red nose much too big for his face, which was beleaguered by a perpetual frown. Without preamble, Esmir pulled the door open wider and beckoned her inside, gesturing toward a large alcove at the far end of the cavern.

Nervous, Calise muttered a greeting and stepped inside the ancient eyrie. She paused, her eyes taking in the enormous chamber that had once housed Greater Dragons. A pool of clear water gurgled in the center of the chamber, fed by the Wellspring that existed deep beneath Skyhome. There were two room-sized alcoves carved out of the walls on either side of the main cavern, for the eyrie was meant to house two large dragons and their riders. The cavity on the right stood dark and empty. The alcove on the left, partially hidden by a wicker partition, contained a bed and several other items of furniture, as well as its own hearth, and was exceedingly cluttered with what looked like a lifetime's worth of items that had never once been gone through and sorted.

Esmir pulled back the partition and led her through the cluttered alcove to the bed, upon which lay the boy beneath a mound of covers. A chair had been pulled up next to the bed, and Calise sat down upon it, leaning forward to take in the boy's features.

He was older than she'd thought he'd be. With all of Luvana's talk of a boy, she wasn't expecting a youth of fifteen or sixteen years. His skin was waxy, stretched tight over a face that might have been handsome if it wasn't so thin and mottled. Matted, reddish-brown hair clung to his forehead, and his breathing was weak and shallow. Apparently, the Dedicant Mother hadn't overstated his condition.

She glanced up at Esmir. "What happened to him?"

The old man stared down at the youth through scraggly strands of white-streaked hair. "He was tortured and reaped of essence."

Calise sucked in a breath, looking back at the boy with profound sympathy. No wonder his face looked so haggard and drawn. He was too young to experience such horror.

"Where did he come from?" she asked.

Esmir pursed his lips. "The Abadian Empire, I believe."

"Where is that?" She had never heard of the place.

"The World Above."

Calise glanced at Esmir, thinking he was being sarcastic. When she realized he wasn't, she stared harder at the young man on the bed. He appeared to be Auld, though it was hard to tell. Were there still Auld in the World Above?

"Who would do such things to a boy?" She placed a hand on his brow and was shocked by the lack of warmth in his skin.

"There are a great many people who would." Esmir sighed heavily. "We have our work cut out for us. His muscles are atrophied, and he's obviously suffered from hunger, so whoever did this had him for a long while. There's much damage here that needs undoing."

Calise nodded, understanding. "I'll do what I can for him."

She felt a strong presence behind them and turned toward the mouth of the eyrie. "Here's Zandril."

Esmir hurried across the cavern to the wicker partition and slid it back, exposing the mouth of the cavern. A shadow passed over the wide terrace beyond the opening as something outside blocked the sunlight. Seconds later, a small golden dragon alighted on the end of the terrace with elegant precision and folded her graceful wings. Noticing Esmir, she froze, her delicate head slightly tilted, the round pupils of her eyes contracting to slits. But then she relaxed and slinked forward, moving with the grace of a stalking leopard, the firm muscles of her shoulders rippling beneath her glistening skin.

Smiling, Calise rose and crossed the alcove to meet her soul-bound companion, thankful she was here. She hugged Zandril's sinuous neck, the dragon returning the gesture by drawing her close. Zandril was a beautiful creature, with a long, tapered head that ended in a beak-like snout. She had twin horns that looked carved from jasper, and her eyes were a burnished gold, large and expressive. Darker, soft spines ran the length of her back, all the way to the end of her serpentine tail. Releasing Calise, the dragon turned to consider the man standing next to her with a look of reproach that was impossible to mistake.

"It's just Esmir," Calise said, scratching Zandril under the chin. "Come, love. There's a boy I want you to meet."

Calise turned and walked back into the alcove. Zandril followed her with a side-eyed glare of distrust for the old Warden when she passed. Calise worked hurriedly to move odds and ends out of the dragon's way, while Esmir scooted furniture. When the area in the center of the floor was cleared, Zandril crept forward, pausing before the bed and tilting her head like a hawk. Tentatively, she extended her neck and sniffed the boy's face, her eye ridges constricting in an expression that looked very much like human concern.

"What do you think?" asked Calise.

She felt Zandril's response in her head, an upwelling of sympathy for the broken creature on the bed. The dragon settled to the floor, curling her body on the rug as she did for sleep. But instead of tucking her head beneath her wing, as was her custom, Zandril rested it instead across the boy's legs.

Calise smiled at Esmir. "I think she's adopted him."

Aram opened his eyes to find himself encased by the same darkness that gripped him every night in his narrow cell. Fear had woken him from sleep, as it always did. He was cold and shivering, and he could feel the panic already setting in. He didn't know what time it was, but he was terrified it was morning. That's when they came. Every other morning, without fail. Terrified, he gave a whimpering moan, tears of panic coursing down his face. He had lost the will to fight a long time ago. Now, deprived of all semblance of courage and dignity, all he could do was cower.

When he heard the metallic ring of keys, he shrieked and scampered to the corner, tucking his body against the cold, filth-greased wall of his prison. He squatted there in the dark, shaking and hyperventilating, whimpering in fear, completely naked, for he wasn't allowed to wear clothing in his cell, lest he try to strangle himself.

The door opened with a metallic shriek, and a dark form stood silhouetted in the doorway. Aram curled up, covering his face and pressing his trembling body back against the wall, shaking his head frantically.

When the man stepped forward to claim him, he started screaming.

"No!" Aram shrieked. *"No more! Please! No more!"*

The man reached out to haul him from the cell.

But then the man evaporated, as did the cell around him.

The shadows receded.

A soothing tranquility settled over him like an invisible embrace filled with warmth and compassion. A strong, protective presence entered his mind, pressing its soul against his and lending him a sense of comfort and security he hadn't felt in a very long time.

He felt a soothing hand stroke his hair.

"It's all right...It's all right...we're here. You're safe."

A calm, feminine voice uttered words in an accent he'd never heard before. Yet the profound sense of serenity that voice brought him made him sigh in relief, and he could feel the tension leaving his body, draining

right away.

For the first time in years, he felt content.

Opening his eyes, Aram gazed upward into a face he didn't recognize. It belonged to a teenage girl, close to his own age, with brown, shoulder-length hair and freckles, and a nose that looked slightly askew. Her compassionate smile was the most beautiful thing he had ever seen. She had a yellow aura like Mora Haseleu, though richer and far more golden.

"Who are you?" he tried to whisper, but the words came out raspy and barely audible.

"I'm Calise," the girl said. "I'm a friend."

Her accent was thick but beautiful. Some of the consonants were softened, the vowels drawn out in a way that made her words sound almost like a foreign language, though he understood her. "Where's Markus?"

She shook her head. "I don't know who that is."

Aram closed his heavy eyelids and slipped toward sleep. But then her voice brought him back.

"Here. Drink."

She propped his head up and held a cup to his lips. The water that entered his mouth was the purest he had ever tasted. Aram drank as much as he could, until he was too tired to swallow any more. Then he closed his eyes and relaxed, letting go.

"Sleep, my friend."

The comforting presence was back, enfolding him, and he knew he wasn't alone. It was like another mind pressed against his in an embrace that was warm and soothing, and he understood that he was protected and secure. The strength of that presence was almost overwhelming, and he knew it would never let anything harm him ever again. With a smile on his lips, Aram faded back to sleep.

He slept a long time.

Sometime in the night, the shadows started slipping back again, and he felt the cold darkness of his cell encase him once more. He started shivering in anticipation of the pain.

His door creaked metallically, making him tremble and whimper.

"No... Please, no..."

But then the presence inserted itself between him and the doorway, denying entry to those who wanted to claim him.

The door closed and locked.

The shadows receded.

Later that night, when that door tried opening again, the protective presence was back, shielding him, making the shadows go away. Each time that door tried to open, it closed quickly, until finally, it stayed closed and locked.

"You're all right," whispered the feminine voice. "You're safe. Sleep, my friend."

He slept.

And for once, it was a peaceful sleep.

When Aram awoke, the girl was gone.

In her place was a dragon.

Aram screamed, cringing back from the powerful figure that loomed over him like a sentinel pine. The dragon tilted its head and peered down at him intently, as though contemplating how best to eat him. Aram curled into a ball, but that was all he could do to protect himself. He didn't have the strength to squirm away from the beast. His limbs felt like they were weighted down with lead.

The dragon extended its head toward him and sniffed. As it did, a peaceful sense of comfort filled his mind and, at that moment, Aram recognized that this was the guardian who had been watching over him, the fierce presence standing between him and the man in the doorway of his nightmares.

Aram's eyes filled with tears of gratitude, and he reached his hand toward the dragon's face. He touched his fingers to the soft muzzle, which was covered in smooth scales that felt like satin. Movement beside him caught his attention, and he turned to see the face of the girl that had appeared in his dreams. What she was still doing here, outside of the dream, he didn't know, but her very presence was comforting.

"Thank you," he whispered, filled with a strong sense of certainty that he would have died without this girl and her dragon's intervention. "Thank you both."

"You're welcome," the girl responded with a smile.

Aram frowned at her voice, which sounded so familiar and yet so foreign. Something about her speech reminded him of the way some of the old farmers talked. Perhaps her people were some distant relation.

"How do you feel?" she asked.

Aram smiled weakly. "I'm better. Thank you."

"Are you hungry?"

Aram's smile grew bigger. "Yes. I'm hungry."

She patted his shoulder then stood and walked away, leaving him with the dragon, which he regarded with curiosity. It was far smaller than the void dragon who had carried him here, wherever *here* was. It was only then that he realized he was in a bed, the softest bed he had ever lain on, within some kind of cave that had been converted to a home. He looked around at the stone walls and the dilapidated furniture, wondering if this was the dragon's den, though it looked more like the cave of a hermit.

The girl returned a minute later, carrying a bowl and spoon. Settling into a chair at his side, she set the bowl down then arranged the pillows behind his head, propping him up, then brought a spoonful of golden liquid to his lips.

"Open."

"What is it?" Aram asked.

"Broth."

Aram sipped the spoonful of broth, which was rich and delicious, the best he'd ever swallowed in his life. He closed his eyes, savoring the taste and texture of fresh food, something he hadn't had in a long, long time.

"More broth?"

He nodded and let her spoon him another mouthful. The broth felt good and warm in his stomach. He drank as much as he could, but then his eyes started feeling heavy again.

"Better?"

"Yes…" Aram whispered. "Better."

She smiled, setting down the bowl. "Sleep, my friend."

With a smile, he obeyed.

32

Markus lay on his stomach in the infirmary, every breath he drew an excruciating labor. He didn't know how long he'd been there, and it took him some time to remember how he'd ended up there. He heard the squeak of a chair next to him and then winced at the sight of an Exilari mantle. He couldn't see who it belonged to because he was too weak to turn his head.

"There's an arrow in you." He recognized Sergan's voice. "It went through your ribs and into your lung, and that's where it got stuck."

Markus knew the sorcerer was right, for he could feel the arrowhead there, wearing at his tissues every time he drew a breath. His lung was heavy with fluid, either infection or blood, and his chest gurgled and popped with every inhalation.

Sergan's voice went on, "Now, we have two options: either pull it out of you or push it through. The arrow's barbed, and it's held onto the shaft with sinew, which softens when it gets wet. So, it's unlikely we could pull it out with the arrowhead still attached. Which means we're pushing it through." He leaned closer to Markus's ear. "Regretting your actions yet?"

He was not. Aram was out of the dungeons and wouldn't have to suffer there another day. His own suffering was acute, but it wouldn't last forever.

Sergan drew back. "I think it's rather ironic that your attempt to save your friend actually killed him. Aram's dead, by the way, in case you didn't know. Void dragon."

He'd already known that. Markus had seen the void dragon snatch Aram up in its deadly jaws. He was glad for him, for he knew his friend was now beyond the sorcerers' reach, and they couldn't hurt him anymore. He just wished he could join him, but he knew that Sergan Parsigal didn't have the mercy to execute him. He drew in another excruciating breath that popped and wheezed, and he had to clamp his jaw to keep from coughing. The arrow was agony, and he wanted it out, one way or another.

He found the strength to look up and saw Sergan rise and move his chair back, a chirurgeon coming to stand behind him. The man held some type of metal instrument that looked twisted and brutal.

"Awake or unconscious?" the chirurgeon asked.

Sergan appeared to think about it a moment, his face squirming through expressions as though tormented by the decision, at last muttering reluctantly, "Put him out."

The chirurgeon came forward. "Probably for the best."

Markus didn't protest as the chirurgeon pulled out a flask of amber liquid and uncorked it, spilling some onto a cloth.

Markus awoke in pain, but not nearly as much as before. The arrowhead was out, which was a source of heady relief. He could take all but the deepest breaths without experiencing too much pain. His lungs no longer sounded like he was breathing through a froth of soap bubbles, and the air was much easier to move.

Opening his eyes, he saw that he still lay in the infirmary. All of the other beds were empty, including the one Aram had occupied when they said he had drowned. Looking at that bed, Markus's eyes started to water. He hoped that, wherever he was, his young friend forgave him and understood.

He lay there for a long time, staring at the ceiling and drifting in and out of sleep. He had no idea how much time had passed since his ill-fated rescue attempt. It seemed like only hours but judging by the amount of pain he was in, it was more likely days.

He recognized the sound of Sergan's footsteps when the sorcerer entered the room. There was something about them that was unmistakable, as though Sergan's arrogance affected even the sound of his stride. Markus didn't want to look at him but was forced to when the man arrived at his bedside. He was dressed in his formal robes, his hair pulled back and neatly tied. In his hands, he carried a sack of wine.

"I brought you a gift," he said and set the wine sack down on a table by the bed. "It's fresh from the vineyard. I'm happy to see you're feeling better."

Markus couldn't stand to look at him, so he directed his stare back up at the ceiling.

"I came to let you know that I've forgiven you," Sergan went on. "You paid the price for your mistake. You killed your friend and nearly killed yourself. All for nothing, really. Aram was so weak, he wouldn't have survived the rescue, I'm told."

Markus glared at him hatefully.

"I'll be leaving for a year," Sergan told him. "While I'm gone, do everything your betters tell you to do. I'm told that when you graduate, you will be awarded to me. I'm sure we'll make a very effective partnership. Our talents have already been commissioned by the Emperor. You'll have the chance to save thousands of lives from monsters like the one that killed Aram. I'll leave you with the wine."

Sergan started to turn away but then paused. His hand went to his side, withdrawing a flask of Aram's essence from his pouch. "I really hope that we can let bygones be bygones. Try to understand that this" — he waggled the flask in front of Markus's face—"is what's going to save those thousands of lives."

Then he turned and walked away, the sounds of his arrogant stride echoing off the walls of the infirmary.

A ram awoke groggy from the most peaceful sleep he remembered
ever experiencing.

The girl and the dragon were gone. He was alone in a large cave that
reminded him of the one he'd had when he was a boy, where he'd kept
his knot collection. Only, instead of mold and seawater, this cave smelled
of cloves and roasting meat.

He tested his limbs and found that they had more life in them.
Gathering his strength, he pushed himself upright and sat looking
around the cave. It was bigger than he'd thought, for the area he was in
was just a niche carved into the wall of an even larger cavern. There was
a fire pit in the middle of the room that served as a hearth, with a kettle
suspended over the flames. Whatever was in the kettle was filling the
room with a mouth-watering aroma. Dozens of rugs covered the floor,
all looking decades old. In fact, the entire living space looked well-used
and yet entirely neglected. Every aspect of it seemed foreign, from the
interlaced designs of the tapestries to the sinuous shapes of the furniture.

He heard the screech of a scooting chair and turned to see an old man
rise from a desk and amble toward him with an arthritic stride. The man
looked like he had been tall once, before his back had become stooped
with age, though if he had ever had a waistline, it had long ago been
consumed by his gut. His complexion was muddied brown, and his eyes
were brilliant turquoise, a color Aram had never seen on a person. He
wore a thick wool coat darkened by years of soot and body oil, and his

hair and beard looked like they had never seen a bath.

"Where am I?" Aram asked.

"Pyrial," the old man answered matter-of-factly. "Some call it the World Below."

Aram believed him, for the bard's ballad had mentioned such a place. "How did I get here?"

The old man cocked an overgrown eyebrow. "You don't remember?"

Aram thought about it. His memories were dim, though he remembered Markus rescuing him from the cloister very vividly. After that... an image flashed in his mind of flying among the clouds with the ocean beneath him, milky-white wings bearing him higher into the sky.

"I think a dragon brought me."

"That's right. A dragon did bring you, but that was several weeks ago.

"Several weeks?" Aram didn't understand. Had he been asleep all that time?

The old man nodded. "You've been gravely ill. The void dragon used the last of its strength to bring you to me. Do you know why?"

"No." The news saddened Aram, for the dragon had saved his life.

"I think I do." With a pained grimace, the old man lowered himself to sit beside him on the bed. "You see in color, don't you?"

The question provoked a stab of fear, for nothing good had ever come from a mention of his Gift. Aram whispered, "Everyone sees in color."

The old man scowled. "You know what I mean. You see the threads of the aether in color. Only True Savants have that ability."

Aram cringed at the words, a jolt of panic shooting through his body, for those were the same words that had condemned him to the cellars. A panicky sweat broke out on his forehead. But though the old man looked gruff and stern, he didn't *seem* like he was there to do him harm.

"My friend..." Aram said. "Markus... Did the dragon bring him too?"

"No." The old man shook his head. "No one else. Just you."

"He was injured trying to help me. He was hurt bad." A great sadness filled him. "I have to go back for him."

The old man swiped his hand in a dismissive gesture. "You can't go back. They would find you and throw you right back in their cellars. I don't think that's what your friend would want."

Aram clenched his fists in despair. Markus had been shot with an arrow in the back. At the very least, he was seriously injured. He could even be dead. But Aram knew that if he did try to go back, there was nothing he could do to help his friend. He couldn't go anywhere near the College. The Exilari would sense him immediately. He couldn't hide his shine, not from Sergan or those like him.

He lifted his eyes to the old man, studying the quilting of wrinkles that creased his cheeks. He saw that the man was looking at him just as intensely, as though he were studying him too.

"What's your name, son?"

"Aram."

The old man nodded. "My name is Esmir Revin."

"Nice to meet you, sir."

Esmir leaned forward, his gaze hardening. "Understand something, Aram. Your job for now is to recuperate in body, mind, and spirit. You will stay here with me and eat every morsel of food you can stuff down your gullet. I also want you up walking as much as possible. Your muscles are weak from disuse. We need to get you well and strong as quickly as possible."

"Why is that?" Aram asked.

"Because this world needs a Champion."

Aram stared at the man sideways, blinking in confusion. It took him a full second to realize what he meant and, when he did, he shook his head adamantly. "I can't be a Champion. I can't even help Markus."

Esmir looked him up and down with an appraising eye. "If they let me train you to pass the Trials, believe me, you will be able to help far more people than just Markus."

Aram continued to stare at him in confusion. "What do you mean, 'if they let you?'"

The old man shifted position, grimacing as he transferred his weight from one hip to the other. "Every apprentice needs to be approved by the Council of Elders. I will put forth your petition."

Aram frowned. "If I have as much potential as you say I do, then why would they not let you train me?"

"It's less of a problem with you," said the old man. "And more of a problem with me." Aram waited for him to elaborate, but he didn't. Instead, the old man changed the subject. "I didn't know there were any Auld left in the World Above."

Aram realized he was talking about him. "I'm not Auld."

"Well, you certainly have Auld in you." The way the man's eyes raked over him made Aram uncomfortable.

"I'm a Vard," Aram explained. "It's said we have Auld blood in our veins, but it's diluted."

The old man let out a grunt. "Well, your own bloodline can't be very diluted, because you look like you could be my nephew."

Aram frowned. "What if I don't want to be a Champion?"

The man looked offended by the question. "What would you rather be? A milkmaid?"

Dismayed and embarrassed, Aram said quietly, "All I ever wanted to be was a sailor. That's all."

Esmir looked perplexed. "Why a sailor?"

"I love rope. I love knots. I'm very good at them. I'm not very good at anything else."

The old man spread his hands. "But don't you see? Auld magic is based on knots—it's all about tying and breaking threads of aether. That's why you love knots. It's your mind trying to master what comes to you naturally: magic."

Aram just stared at him, for the explanation frightened him as much as it excited him. For the first time in his life, he understood why he was driven to spend so much time practicing an activity that everyone around him had always considered a waste of time. His mother had always claimed that his knots were what he did with his hands when he got nervous or upset, but there had always been more to it than that. He'd always had an obsession with knots, and there were never enough knots in the world to quench his thirst for them. Now, he understood why. But that reason terrified him.

Feeling weak, Aram lay back in bed, resting his head on the over-stuffed pillow. The old man leaned forward and patted his arm then rose to his feet with a grimace.

"I'm too damn old for this," he grumbled. "You rest. There are some people I have to talk to."

Aram felt suddenly guilty, for he knew that this man, along with the girl and her dragon, were the reason he was still alive.

"Thank you for saving me," he said.

The old man paused, his face looking suddenly regretful. "How long did they have you, boy?"

Aram swallowed, for he wasn't sure. "I honestly don't know," he said softly with a shiver. "Years, I think."

"And how did you gain their attention in the first place?"

Ashamed, Aram hung his head. "I caused a rupture in the Veil."

For some reason, the old man looked startled by the answer. With a grunt, he walked away.

Esmir left his young charge to rest and made straight for the stairway. Earlier, he had noticed a thin line of white smoke rising from the terrace below, so he knew that the Council was meeting. They would probably just throw him out, should he push his way in there, but he had to try. He was old enough to know that miracles didn't fall out of the sky every day, and when they did, they usually went unrecognized—even by the people who desperately needed them.

When he reached the council chamber, Esmir paused just long enough to run his hands through his hair. He should have taken more time to clean up, but he'd been flustered by the boy's reluctance. Drawing a deep breath, he puffed out his cheeks. Then, without knocking, he swept open the door that had been barred to him for over four hundred years, letting himself in.

Within, the members of the Council were gathered on rugs arranged around a small fire pit. There were twelve members in all, including Luvana, who, as Dedicant Mother, guided the Council, the ruling body of Skyhome. Four of the people gathered around the fire were respected windriders, true warriors of the air. There was also the head cook and the head steward, as well as representatives from the powerful craft halls. One wall of the chamber was open to the elements, revealing the bottomless chasm of the Pyranthian Gorge below them. The opening provided a mercifully swift end for those the Council convicted of crimes meriting execution and had always made Esmir nervous.

As soon as he entered the room, Luvana stopped talking in midsentence. "Warden Revin! To what do we owe the pleasure?" Her voice dripped caustic acid. "It's been years since you've graced our hall."

"It's been years since I've had reason," Esmir grumbled, limping forward.

"And what reason have you now?"

As if she didn't know. Coming to stand across the fire pit from her, Esmir snapped, "Don't fence with me, Luvana. You know why I'm here. I want to train the boy." He folded his arms, not caring that every person in the room was staring at him with expressions of disgust.

Luvana flashed him a condescending smile. "That's exactly what we convened to discuss. Please join us, Warden. Many of us have quite a few questions."

"What questions?" Esmir grimaced as he lowered himself to the ground, his hips and knees popping in arthritic protest.

Luvana poured him a cup of tea from the pot over the fire. "For one thing, this boy is not from our world. Our war is not even his to fight."

Wingmaster Vandra, a muscular woman with long black hair and brown skin that was thicker and rougher than cow leather, turned to regard him with a thoughtful expression. "We are told this boy fell into the hands of the Exilari, who are thralls of an Archon," she pointed out. "How do we know he's not in league with them?"

"He's not a boy," Esmir barked. "Aram is a young man. A young man they tortured for *years* to extract his essence. That doesn't smack of cooperation."

"And then there's the matter of who would train him, should we decide to go that route," Luvana said quietly, in the act of refilling her mug.

"We've been down this road before, Luvana." Esmir raised a finger. "And I'm *still* the only person in Skyhome who's ever *successfully* trained a Champion."

The Dedicant Mother's face heated at the barb, but at least she had the wisdom to hold her silence. Pushing himself painfully off the floor, Esmir swept his gaze over the gathering. "Do what's right," he growled. "For us and for Aram."

With that, he turned and made his way toward the door. But before he could reach it, Luvana called to his back:

"One last thing."

Esmir turned around.

Luvana asked, "Do you think he can survive the Trials?"

Esmir spread his hands, for who could say? Aram was as frail and thin as a wraith, and the Exilari had surely dealt his spirit a devastating blow.

"Now, that, I'm not sure about," he admitted. "But if you won't let him train, then we'll never know. Now, good day to you."

That night, Aram dreamt of Markus carrying him once again out of the hell that had been his prison for so many years. In his dream, they stumbled together along a shoreline, and when Markus went down with an arrow through his heart, Aram held him in his arms and watched him die. He awoke gasping ragged breaths, his body chilled by fear and grief. He fought tears from his eyes for, even though he hadn't seen Markus die in real life, he feared for him. He lay in bed for a long time, unable to return to sleep, until he heard the sounds of Esmir moving about.

He rolled over and opened his eyes, finding the old man stirring the morning coals awake. He asked in a scratchy voice, "What did they say?"

Esmir turned to look at him. "They said they would think about it."

Aram took in the answer, not sure how he felt about it. Should he be happy or disappointed? He didn't know. There was a lot he didn't know, and that bothered him. The old man wasn't pleased, he could tell. Esmir went about preparing the fire with a dark glower on his face.

Feeling guilty, Aram decided to test his strength and rose from the bed, steadying himself against a bedpost. He stood there hanging onto the bed until a wave of dizziness passed, then walked unsteadily to the woodpile on the other side of the cave. He picked up a log, which was all that he could carry at one time, and delivered it to the fire. Esmir shot him a look that Aram ignored, and he returned to the woodpile to fetch another. Esmir didn't say anything, just watched him like a mother hen while Aram fed the hearth until its fire was burning lively.

Aram watched in silence as Esmir prepared a breakfast of goose eggs and some kind of fried flatbread. Aram accepted his plate with a word of gratitude and stared down at it for a moment, trying to figure out how best to arrange it. He settled on tearing the bread into four pieces that he spaced evenly around the plate, with the egg yolk in the center like a rising sun. Satisfied, he dug in, eating as much as he could, until his stomach felt like bursting. When he was done, he set his plate on the floor and leaned forward to warm his hands over the fire.

Esmir nodded at the plate. "You didn't eat very much."

"I'm sorry. I'm full." His stomach just wasn't the size it once was. He noticed the old man staring at him from out of the corner of his eye, and it made him feel uncomfortable. Esmir seemed to stare a lot, and he wished he knew why.

Esmir grunted. "Calise is on her way. Do you remember her?"

"Yes." Aram liked Calise and her dragon. They had both been very kind to him.

Esmir took Aram's plate and set it aside before pushing himself up off the floor. "I asked her to take you for a walk today." His voice was raspy with effort. Ambling stiffly toward the table, he added, "It will do you good to get some fresh air."

Aram glanced around the room. "What's wrong with the air in here?"

The old man paused in the action of lowering himself into a chair.

"It's fresh enough," Esmir muttered with an affectionate smile, and settled into his seat. He opened a text that had been lying on the table and started reading, skimming a finger across the page. He sat like that in silence as Aram scanned the room, mesmerized by the elaborate designs of the tapestries that reminded him of the heart knot he wore about his neck, the only item he retained that anchored him to his roots.

It was another hour before Calise arrived, and by the time she did, Aram had grown so uncomfortable with the silence of the cavern that he was overjoyed to see her. She looked just as he remembered from his dreams, which seemed surreal. The girl and her dragon had rescued him from the dark confines of his prison, just as surely as Markus had.

She smiled cheerfully and made straight toward him, but Esmir rose to intercept her. He tossed her a leather pouch, which Calise caught in one hand.

"Take him down to the bath," Esmir ordered, his voice grating like a dull plow. "When he's clean, get him some clothes that fit."

Aram glanced down at himself, and for the first time noticed that he was wearing threadbare trousers and a shirt that must have belonged to Esmir, which was far too big for him. He felt his embarrassment sink to new depths. When Calise started toward him, he tucked his legs against his chest and ducked his head.

She crouched next to him, her arm resting on her knees. "Hello. Remember me?"

Aram was too ashamed to respond. He kept his eyes pinned on the stone floor, wishing desperately he could hide.

"Let's get you to the bath. You'll feel much better, I promise."

She held her hand out and Aram looked at it, petrified with anxiety. He glanced at her face, and her calm and easy smile reassured him. Hesitantly, he raised his hand, and the sight of it shamed him. His hand was dark with filth, every crease and crevice in his skin lined with grime.

"I'm sorry," he muttered, retracting his hand.

"For what?"

He didn't answer her, for humiliation had a stranglehold on his throat. Still, he didn't resist as Calise took his hand and helped him up. Like an obedient lapdog, he followed her toward the door on legs that felt weak and spongy. He glanced at Esmir, who just waved him on and turned back to his book.

Calise led him out the door, where he found himself in a hallway carved out of sandstone rock. Seeing the walls of the tunnel, he paused, for they were etched in intricate, interlaced knot patterns, leaving no patch of stone unadorned. Calise stopped and waited for him while Aram stood staring in awe at the designs. She smiled at his reaction.

"I always forget about them." She ran her fingers across the textured surface of the nearest wall. "They're remarkable, when you stop and really look at them. But when you see them all the time…" She shrugged.

The designs were more than just remarkable. They were *knots*. Or rather, just *one* knot—one, large, interlaced cord that ran all along the entire length of the corridor. Aram could not keep his eyes off it as they started forward, his gaze filled with wonder as he took in the plaited knotwork with myriad crossings. He had never seen anything so beautiful in his life. The pattern continued as Calise led him down a flight of stairs to a lower level, where there was another long hallway with walls graced with a different pattern that rivaled the first in beauty and complexity.

Unable to keep his eyes off the walls, Aram practically ran into Calise when she halted in front of a doorway.

"Here's the bath," she told him. "Take your time. I'll wait here."

But instead of going inside the room, he wandered along the wall, studying its intricacies closer. "Who made the designs?"

Calise shrugged. "I have no idea. I assume they've been here almost as long as Skyhome. Perhaps you can ask the Dedicant Mother. She might know."

With one last glance at the etched knotwork, Aram reluctantly left her in the corridor and entered the bath. The lighting was dim, provided by oil lanterns set on marble pedestals, the air warm and muggy. It had a foul smell to it, like rotten eggs, though it wasn't overpowering. Before him were three circular pools of water that bubbled and steamed. No one was using them, thankfully. He didn't think he could have gone in with anyone there.

Moving to the nearest steaming pool, he removed his clothes and lowered himself into the water. It was hot, but not too hot, not so much that he couldn't stand it. The water was far more soothing than he would have imagined. He lay there soaking for a time, but he didn't want to stay too long, because he knew that Calise was waiting for him, and he didn't want to leave her in the hallway. Finding some soap, he scrubbed himself as hard as he could, until his skin felt raw and the water around him turned a murky brown. When he felt reasonably clean, he climbed out of the pool—and sank immediately to his knees, overcome by dizziness.

He sat there on the ground at the edge of the pool, holding his head until the world stopped rocking and spinning. Then he found a towel to dry off with. But when he held it up to himself, he froze and just stood there.

For the first time, he took in the emaciated condition of his body, and what he saw repulsed him. Across his chest, every rib was visible, his collar bones protruding from sunken skin. His arms were so thin that he could wrap two fingers all the way around his bicep. His knees and elbows looked huge and knobby, and the bones of his pelvis jutted out from his waist. An intense shame overwhelmed him, and it was all he could do to move the towel over the ruin of his body with trembling fingers, a body that looked much older than he remembered it. How many years of his childhood had been stolen from him? A great sadness overcame him, and he found himself battling back tears.

When he was dry, Aram thrust his arms into the sleeves of his shirt and pulled up his trousers, regretting that he had to put dirty clothes back on over clean skin. He had no shoes, so he walked barefoot out of the bath and found Calise in the hallway, sitting on the ground with her back against the knotwork wall.

At the sight of him, she rose lithely to her feet, her smile blossoming. "You look like a different person!" she exclaimed. "Who would have guessed there was a young man under all that filth. How old are you?"

Aram stared at her speechless for a moment, groping through his agonized memories for a sense of time. In the cellars, one week had blurred into the next, just a constant cycle of torture followed by periods of rest.

"I don't know," he murmured with a sense of shame.

Calise peered closer at him, scrunching her brow. "You look a little younger than me," she said, her eyes thoughtful. "Sixteen, maybe?" But then her smile came back. "Esmir asked me to get you some new clothes. I bet that will make a big difference."

"I bet it will," Aram said, though he knew nothing could make *that* big of a difference. Only time and food would fix what was wrong with him, though fitting clothes might hide some of the damage. He had a hard time believing that Calise was still smiling when she spoke to him.

He thought most girls would be repulsed.

"I'm going to take you to Tailor's Row down in Hearth Home," Calise said. "We'll get you some clothes that fit and maybe some other things."

"I don't have any money."

Calise swiped her hand dismissively. "You don't have to worry about payment. Esmir gets anything he wants. Besides," she held up the leather purse the old man had flung at her. "It feels like there's enough here to outfit twenty of you."

"Twenty?" Aram asked in amazement.

She gave him the funniest look. "Well, almost twenty." The look turned into a grin. "It doesn't matter. Come on!"

Aram hurried after her, struggling hard to keep his gaze off the walls. She led him down the corridor to a stairwell that spiraled downward for what looked like forever. Aram halted and stared down the shaft, certain his weakened legs couldn't take that many stairs.

"How far down?" he asked.

Calise gave him an apologetic smile. "All the way. Think you can make it?"

Aram shook his head adamantly. "Uh-uh."

She paused, looking thoughtful, then said at length, "I think it'll be good for you. We'll just take a lot of rest breaks."

Aram gazed at the staircase dubiously, but Calise had been so nice to him, and he wanted to please her, so he conceded. They took the stairs slowly as faster people dodged around them. It took a long time, and quite a few breaks, but eventually they made it to the bottom. It wasn't until they were halfway down that Aram started wondering how he was going to make it back up again.

At the bottom of the stairs, Calise led him out onto a wide outdoor terrace. At first, Aram's attention was drawn to the small town that rose up around them—until his gaze was drawn upward to the cliffs above it. His eyes widened, and his head tilted back, his jaw opening. For before them, across a wide chasm, was a landscape of cliffs that towered over them all the way to the sky, made of thousands of layers of sandstone streaked with wide bands of red and gold. The terrace they stood upon protruded from another soaring wall. The sky above could be seen as only a sinuous strip of blue between pairs of soaring walls. To the east rose an enormous bell-shaped mountain peak that towered over the cliffs, ringed by a halo of golden light.

The village below the cliffs had a contrasting air of normalcy. It looked like the sort of community that wouldn't have been too out of place in the Vardlands, containing workshops and houses, people and animals, arrayed in a succession of long terraces.

"This is Hearth Home," said Calise. "It's where the craft halls and the kitchens are located, along with everything else that goes into supporting the eyries—the caverns where the dragons live. There's stables, laundries, pantries, stables…whatever you can think of, really."

Aram nodded, feeling daunted by the looming cliffs, for they looked ready to come crashing down on top of them. He followed Calise into the village, which was comfortingly familiar. Many of the sights and smells reminded him of home. The biggest difference was in the construction of the buildings, which were tall and lean, built of thin bricks the same color as the sandstone bluffs, with lead roofs and angular gables.

Aram followed Calise along Hearth Home's excruciatingly narrow streets that weren't much more than walkways between houses. Yet, they were cleaner than any streets he had ever seen. People going about their business stared at him as he walked by, which made him anxious. He found himself looking up at the walls or down at the ground, consciously avoiding eye contact.

It was odd, how it all seemed so foreign, and yet so familiar. Bakers here still toiled at the daily business of transforming wheat into bread, though their ovens were rounded and made of clay. The blacksmiths still hammered at their forges, though their bellows looked like boxes instead of accordions. They passed a butcher's shop, where the carcasses of whole pigs, sheep, and chickens hung from beams projecting from the eaves. Across from the butcher's was a large chandlery, where an entire family labored together to produce hundreds of candles at a time, dipping racks draped with long wicks into vats of heated tallow.

They stopped to let Aram rest on one of the wider streets. He sat on a barrel and massaged his legs, which were burning and shaking, while Calise looked on with an expression of pity. People and animals passed them by, along with two-wheeled carts with wooden wheels studded with nails, carrying casks of wine and bushels of fruit. All the people that passed looked very similar to his own, though their features were more rounded and their eyes brilliant turquoise. The clothing they wore was very different. Men and women alike wore loose-fitting tunics, the women's longer than the men's, and women wore their hair free or in braids, not done up under headscarves.

A shadow passed over him, and Aram glanced up to see a dragon skimming by overhead. Others soared in the narrow space between cliffs, while dozens more lined terraces that ribbed the canyon walls above them. Glancing further up, he saw that the cliff directly above them was honeycombed with what could only be dragon caves. He sucked in a breath that he held on to, too amazed to let it back out again.

"They're beautiful, aren't they?" Calise asked.

Aram could only nod. He sat gazing upward at the dragons until his legs didn't hurt so much, then set off down the street again. They walked until they reached a one-story brick building attached to a taller structure.

"Here we are," said Calise.

The shop in front of them had a long counter that faced the street, upon which a variety of clothing items and materials were spread. A tailor's workshop, Aram realized, noticing the tidy displays of expensive-looking wools and linens. Inside, they found three apprentices working on a large rectangle of fabric laid out on a long trellis table. One apprentice was marking the fabric with a measuring stick and chalk, another cutting it with hand-forged scissors, while the third stitched along behind him.

Seeing Calise and Aram standing at the counter, the master tailor broke himself off from an inventory of his fabrics and came toward them with a smile that quickly wilted when he saw the state of Aram's clothes. Aram flushed, wishing he could walk away.

"What do we have here?" the tailor asked, a forced smile returning to his face. He looked from Aram to Calise, eyebrows raised.

"A foundling," Calise said with a grin. "This is Aram, Warden Revin's new charge. He needs clothing."

"I'd say he does," the tailor muttered. His eyes narrowed, and he scanned Aram up and down critically, then motioned with his hand for him to turn around.

"Retainer?" he asked.

"Apprentice."

Aram shot her a questioning look, for he didn't remember apprenticing himself to anyone. But before he could protest, the tailor waved him inside, standing back to let him pass, giving him an exceptionally wide berth. He led Aram to a corner, where a cloth had been draped from the ceiling as a privacy screen. He undressed down to his breeches, which were just as filthy as the rest of his clothes, then stood with his arms out as the tailor took his measurements swiftly with a length of string, writing them down on a wax tablet. Aram was grateful for the drape of cloth, because Calise lingered on the other side of it, and he would be mortified if she saw the state of him undressed. At last satisfied, the tailor retreated to the interior of the workshop then returned a few minutes later with a stack of garments in hand.

"You'll be difficult to fit. Try these on, then I'll have to make adjustments." To Calise, he added, "There's not much to him."

Aram lifted the first garment, a pair of breeches so short they may as well have been a loincloth. He put them on then worked his legs into a pair of loose pants of undyed linen. The next item was a brown tunic that fell past his waist, over which he strapped a leather belt with a large brass buckle.

Emerging from behind the drape, Aram balked when he saw Calise's reaction to his new clothes. Her expression went slack, her eyes going wide. He couldn't figure out whether it was shock or horror that registered on her face, but whatever it was, he blushed bright crimson and almost fled.

She motioned for him to turn around, and Aram did as she asked, acutely aware of her eyes on him and wanting to die and melt into the ground. The tailor checked the fit of the clothes, finding plenty of slack in the tunic. If it weren't for the drawcord that he'd knotted extra tight, the pants probably would have fallen right off.

The tailor gave Calise a woeful look. "I can take them in if you leave them here a couple of days."

Calise scratched her freckled cheek, face tight with thought. "Let's let him wear what he's got on. Could you alter another outfit for him, one we can pick up later? Then he'll have an outfit for now and one to grow into."

"He has a lot of growing to do," the tailor grumbled. "Tell Warden Revin to feed him occasionally."

Calise laughed good-naturedly then turned to Aram. "I would have never guessed you'd clean up so well. You're quite handsome!"

Aram's eyes narrowed in anger and shame, for he hadn't taken Calise as the type of person to make sport of him like that. He dodged around her and headed out of the shop, weaving through the flow of foot traffic in the street. He heard her footsteps rushing to catch up with him and quickened his pace.

"What happened?" she cried, drawing abreast of him and catching his arm. "Did I offend you?"

He kept walking, face heated to scalding. "No."

"I did, I can tell. I didn't mean to!" she insisted. "What did I do?"

Aram stopped to look at her. One glance at her face sent him into a spiral of confusion. She really did look upset.

"You weren't mocking me?" he asked.

She shook her head. "No! Why would I do that?"

Aram drew in a deep breath, so frustrated with himself that he wanted to bang his head against something. He never understood people, and they never understood him. It was like a sinkhole he could never crawl out of. Not for the first time, he wished he could be anyone—*anyone*—else in the whole wide world.

"I'm sorry," he said, unable to look at her. "It's just that…people don't say those kinds of things to me unless they're trying to be cruel. I mean, most people. Not you." He stared at the ground, burning in frustration.

He couldn't even get an apology out of his mouth without stumbling over his own words.

Calise's face was a study in bewilderment. "I can't understand why anyone would treat you like that. There's nothing wrong with you."

Aram gave a bitter laugh. "There's plenty wrong with me. I'm just glad you don't see it."

"Well, I certainly don't!" Calise smiled as though she meant it then glanced up the street with a worried expression. "We really need to get to the cobblers, so we can be getting back. It's a long way up. Will you walk with me?"

Aram nodded, then followed her meekly, feeling mortified. Calise was the nicest person he'd ever met—nicer, even, than Mora Haseleu. He should have trusted her aura instead of making assumptions and acting like a fool.

"I really am sorry," he said, feeling glum. "I won't mistake you again."

Calise wrinkled her mouth, looking perplexed. "I just can't believe people would say such things to you. You're really nice."

Aram couldn't help but smile. "You think so?"

Calise grinned back. "Yes. I think so."

By the time Aram made it to the top of the stairs, it was evening, and his legs were burning and shaking so hard that he could barely stand. Calise was patient and talked the whole way up the stairs, through all of the long rest stops on the landings. By the time they reached the top, Aram knew a lot about her. And the more he knew, the more he liked her.

Calise was only half Auld, as he should have guessed by her lighter skin and freckles. She'd been born in one of the human settlements, which were apparently spread thinly across the land. But her parents had died when she was little. When it was discovered that she had the affinity for magic, she'd been shuffled from place to place—not always good places—until, eventually, she had come to live at Skyhome. Her Talent was healing, which Aram could attest to. She couldn't see in color like him, but apparently, she could *feel* things he couldn't feel—things inside a person, which, to him, sounded extraordinary.

When they reached Esmir's door, the Warden opened it but then stood in the doorway, physically blocking their entrance to his eyrie. He loomed over them with his arms crossed, narrowed gaze shifting between the two of them as though they were children who had done something wrong.

"You had to put him in the brown," he remarked, stepping out of the doorway and barking a snide laugh. "Luvana's going to crack an iron cask."

275

Aram didn't understand why the Warden was so upset. He glanced at Calise, seeking clarification.

"He's going to be an apprentice, isn't he?" Calise asked, striding after Esmir into the eyrie. "I wasn't going to buy him clothes that he could only wear for a day or two."

Esmir settled into one of the chairs at the table, leaning back heavily and staring up at them through the big, baggy pouches that rimmed his eyes.

"Damn the wind and all it blows," he muttered, lifting a heavy ceramic mug to his lips. "You did fine. It's not your fault that Eraine Vandra's an unreasonable codstick."

Calise leaned close and whispered in Aram's ear, "I pity you, you know."

Aram suppressed a grin as Calise departed, leaving him alone with the cross old man. Not knowing what else to do, he headed toward the pallet Esmir had been sleeping on, determined to give the old man his bed back.

"Where are you going?" Esmir demanded. "Sit down!" He lifted a foot and kicked an empty chair out from the table, sending it skittering backward across the floor. Startled, Aram scooted the chair back and sat down, trying not to squirm under Esmir's overbearing gaze.

"What's wrong, Mister Revin?" Aram asked.

"*Warden* Revin," the old man corrected. "Or just Esmir. I'm not much of a Warden anymore, if I ever was. How are your legs?"

"They burn," Aram admitted. "I'm not used to stairs."

The old man grunted. "Which means you need to be trotting up and down those stairs six times a day. I want you out and moving every moment you're not eating or sleeping."

Aram nodded, knowing he had a long way to go if he wanted to get his strength back.

Esmir took a drink from his mug then wiped his mouth dry. "Now, let's talk about you. While the Council is lollygagging, we're going to assume that they're going to approve your training, because it would be unthinkable for them not to."

"But I haven't decided—"

"Bah!" Esmir barked. "Like the Council, you'll do it precisely because it would be unthinkable for you not to."

Aram squirmed, not liking this man's logic. For the first time in years, he felt hope for a future he'd never thought he'd have. And after visiting Hearth Home, he realized he was much more comfortable down there than up here.

"Tell me why," he said. "Why do I have to be a Champion?"

"Because this world hasn't had a Champion in four hundred years, and we need one now more than ever before." Esmir pushed back his chair with a nerve-grating shriek. "Come with me, boy."

Aram did as he asked, rising to follow the old Warden toward the mouth of his cave. Esmir led him through the cavern and out onto the terrace, a wide, triangular piece of hewn rock that projected from the cliff face. To the right, a waterfall plunged from the top of the cliff into the gorge below, its spray misting them. A cool breeze tossed Aram's hair as he followed Esmir to the edge, where they stood looking out over a great gorge so deep that he couldn't see the bottom. Immediately, his stomach plunged, and his palms started sweating. He started backing away from the edge, but Esmir caught him by the arm and held him steady.

"Welcome to Pyrial," he rumbled and, with a sweep of his hand, indicated the whole of the landscape that surrounded them: the soaring cliffs of the gorge and the mountains beyond.

"Skyhome exists to defend this land from its ancient foes: the Seven Archons. Do you know what an Archon is, boy?"

Aram's mind went back to the night he had hidden in the rafters of the longhouse and listened to the bard's performance. The ballad Master Ebra had recited had spoken of Pyrial, the World Below, and the Archons. He didn't know exactly what an Archon was, but he knew they must be powerful, because Erok had Sundered the world in an attempt to defeat them.

"'Their way is evil, and their name is Betrayal,'" he whispered.

Esmir lifted an eyebrow. "You know the Ballad of Raginor?"

"Yes." Aram had only heard the Ballad once, yet he could recite it from memory, just like anything else he'd ever heard. He was good at remembering things, which was how he kept track of so many knots.

"If you know about the Archons, then you know about the Sundering," Esmir said. "For millennia, our Champions kept the Archons at bay. But within the last few hundred years, we started running out of Champions. We were being culled, you see. As the strongest of us were defeated, only the weakest endured. After generations of this culling, those who had the strength to pass the Trials became few and far between. The last was Daymar Torian." A profound sadness filled Esmir's eyes. "He fell fighting the Archon Logarin in your world. The Exilari took him to their cellars and subjected him to the same horrors you endured."

Aram felt a shiver pass over him. Daymar Torian was the Savant Sergan had told him about, the one the Exilari had questioned under torture to produce the book of knots. Suddenly, he felt dirty and tainted for studying the diagrams in that book.

Esmir set a hand on his shoulder, turning him away from the edge and leading him back inside. "Since Daymar's death, the Archons both here and in the World Above have been running rampant. In the last hundred years, two regions of Pyrial have fallen to the armies of Kathrax. At the same time, Mirak has been expanding the Abadian Empire in the World Above."

Aram gasped. "The Abadian Empire is ruled by an Archon?"

"Yes," the old Warden confirmed. "And his brother Logarin is the Revered Master of the Exilari."

Aram's jaw drooped, and suddenly, he couldn't breathe. He stopped in his tracks, for a long moment staring straight ahead into nothing. "I met him," he whispered. "He's the man who put me in the cellars."

"And he's the man who brought down Daymar Torian," said Esmir softly. "With my help."

Aram glanced at him sharply. "What do you mean?"

Esmir bit his lip, his eyes dark with self-loathing. "I was Daymar's husband, and also his Warden." He gestured around them at the walls of the cave. "This was our eyrie, where we lived with our dragons, Agaroth and Faranth. For three hundred years, we were successful at keeping

Kathrax and his horde at bay, but then his brothers moved against us too. Mirak and Logarin created the Exilari for the sole purpose of breaking down the Veil, for reuniting our two worlds has ever been the Archons' goal."

He went to his table and took a seat, Aram following him. There, Esmir replenished his mug with liquid from a pitcher then poured Aram a mug of his own, sliding it toward him. Aram lifted it and took a sip. The liquid burned his throat, and he coughed and sputtered, setting the mug down. Whatever kind of liquor was in there, it was strong.

Esmir heaved a deep sigh, rubbing his brow. "Logarin lured us through the Veil with the offer of a treaty. Daymar didn't want to go, but I talked him into it. We were fighting a losing battle, and I was desperate and terrified for him. At the time, we didn't know what the Exilari were capable of. I underestimated their sorcerers. Badly."

He took a large gulp from his mug. "Logarin set a trap for us. He met us at the rupture with a dozen Exilari sorcerers. They beat Agaroth and Faranth back into the rift. Daymar opened another rupture and pushed me through, right before the sorcerers set upon him. I tried to go back for him, but he closed the rift before I could get through."

He took a heavy sip of his drink, looking haggard and pale. Aram regarded the old Warden sadly, for he understood the man's pain. Like Esmir, he had left his best friend behind in another world, at the hands of the Exilari.

Esmir drew in a deep breath, visibly collecting himself. "Since Daymar fell, the Archons have been moving almost unchecked. Kathrax and his forces are advancing across Pyrial. In Issia, Mirak and Logarin have been gathering the resources to tear through the Veil. Do you understand, now, why the world needs a Champion?"

Aram did, which was why he felt so wretched. The world really *did* need a Champion. Esmir was right. But he wasn't one, and he could never *be* one. He couldn't even work magic to save himself. He shook his head, for he knew Esmir was wrong to pin his hopes on him.

"I can't be a Champion," he muttered, casting his gaze downward in shame. "Don't you understand? I've already failed everyone I know.

Because of me, my village was sacked, and my best friend was captured by the Exilari. I'm just as much a failure as you."

Esmir stared at him over the rim of his mug. At last, he grimaced, tilting his head back and taking a heavy gulp.

"Then that's perfect," he said, setting the mug down firmly. "You're a failed Savant and I'm a failed Warden. Perhaps two wrongs can't make a right, but it's possible two failures can make a Champion. Will you try with me?"

Aram sat staring at the table for a long time, feeling terribly unsettled. The more he thought about it, the more he knew he had no choice. Esmir was right: he would do it because it would be unthinkable not to. But it was more than that. Far more. This was his one chance to prove to the world and himself that everything that seemed wrong with him was actually right, that his peculiarities were his strengths and not his weaknesses. This was who he was, what he was built for, and he couldn't deny this duty without denying himself. Reluctantly, he nodded.

"Then it's settled." The Warden clapped an enormous hand on the table, jolting his mug. "Get over there and make us some supper, boy. While you're doing that, I'm going to try to figure out how many goats I have to sacrifice to get you the Council's approval."

Aram bedded down that night on the pallet in the corner of the alcove, while Esmir returned to his own bed, snoring atrociously. The old Warden had been into his cups all night, and he'd gone to sleep on his back, mouth gaping, sawing a racket. Every once in a while, his snoring would stop completely, often for seconds at a time, before starting up again with a good deal of hacking and sputtering. Once, Aram was so convinced the man had died in his sleep, he was on the verge of going to shake him.

He couldn't sleep, though he'd tried for hours. Not just because of the snoring, but because of all the thoughts that were spinning in his head, making him feel anxious and even slightly ill. Trying not to disturb Esmir, he drew on his new clothes and let himself out. He was curious to see more of the hallways and their knotted etchings. He made his way down the stairs, wandering through corridors, studying the beautiful interlaced knotwork that seemed to be one enormous, plaited braid. He ran his hand along the walls as he walked, as though touching the textured surface would make it more real.

Climbing down another stairwell, he came to a hallway that led to an enormous cave. Even before he walked into it, a peculiar odor made him aware that there was something in there he wasn't used to. He walked inside a few steps, and the odor became much stronger, though not unpleasant, like a strong combination of brimstone and animal, though it was like no animal he knew. He moved forward, eyes scanning the enormous empty chamber that was strewn with rushes and lit by many braziers, its tall roof supported by thick columns of stone.

All around the cavern, spaced at intervals, were alcoves just like Esmir's, enclosed by wicker screens. In the center of the cavern was a wide pool of water and, before it, the rock of the floor was smeared with blood, most dry, but some of it recent. It looked like a murder had happened there or, at the very least, a slaughter.

"What are you doing here?"

Aram startled. Turning, he found himself confronted by a tall, muscular woman with a long braid of raven hair and a proud, angular face. She was dressed in a tunic similar to the one he was wearing, though hers was black and sleeveless and made of a much finer material. She had the look of a soldier, though she was lacking a uniform. The aura that surrounded her was a greenish shade of blue, not chaotic enough to scare him, but enough to give him pause.

"I...I was just looking around," he stuttered as the woman approached him with a long scowl on her face.

"Who are you?" she demanded. "Who put you in those clothes?"

Aram brought a hand up to his chest, feeling at the brown fabric of his new tunic. "My name's Aram, Mistress. Warden Revin gave me the clothes."

The woman's eyes narrowed at his use of the word 'mistress.' She crossed her arms and eyeballed him up and down with a disgusted expression. "You're Esmir's foundling?"

"Yes…"

The woman snorted. "And he put you in the clothes of an apprentice without the endorsement of the Council?"

"Yes…" Aram barely stopped himself from calling her 'mistress' again.

The woman looked like she was about to snarl. "Then this is what you're going to do. You're going to turn around and march out of this eyrie. Go back to Esmir and inform him that he just lost my vote."

Feeling horrible, Aram nodded. Shoulders slumped, he turned and started away. But when he got halfway to the door, an idea struck him, and he turned back around.

"What if I help you find it?" he asked.

"Excuse me?" The woman shot him an incredulous glare.

Aram swallowed heavily. "You said that Warden Revin lost your vote. What if I help you find it?"

The warrior-woman stared at him for a long, speechless moment. Then she threw back her head and burst out with a fit of laughter that echoed off the stone walls of the cavern. Humiliated, Aram fled toward the door, moving as quickly as his weakened legs would carry him.

"Stop!"

He halted, turning reluctantly back around to find the woman standing with a wry smile on her face, hands planted firmly on her hips.

"You have a lot of audacity, boy," she said, not unkindly. "Almost as much as Esmir. Tell you what. Come down to the training grounds tomorrow and you can start looking for my vote." She frowned heavily. "There's not much to you, is there?"

"Not much," Aram agreed.

The woman approached, putting her hand out. "Give me your arm."

Aram did, feeling ashamed. She grasped his forearm, her strong fingers easily encircling it.

"I've never felt a weaker arm." She let go with a disgusted sigh. "What the hell did they do to you?"

Aram opened his mouth to answer, but the woman waved him silent.

"Look at me."

Aram had a hard time meeting the woman's steel-hard gaze. The feeling of her eyes locked on his made his bones squirm. He forced himself to keep his gaze fixed on hers, though the act made his skin crawl and took every last scrap of his will. She was hard and cold as old granite, inside and out.

Holding his gaze, the woman asked sternly, "How much mettle do you have, boy, because you better not waste my time."

"I was tortured in a dungeon every day for years," Aram answered. "They didn't break me."

The woman nodded slightly, her expression thoughtful. "Then you have more mettle than I do. You're going to need every drop of it. See you tomorrow. Go tell Esmir you found the vote he lost."

"Thank you," Aram said, then turned and hurried back toward the hallway. If his legs were stronger, he would have run, for he was buoyed by his encounter. He walked as quickly as he could, his heart thudding happily.

A ram reported to the training grounds the next morning. It took him
a bit to get there; the place where the apprentices trained was on
the same level as Hearth Home. He was winded and limping by the time
he reached the bottom of the stairs, his legs burning from both yesterday's abuses and the morning's.

The woman-warrior he'd met the night before was there ahead of
him, standing beside a man just as big as Sword Master Davir, but much
ornerier-looking, for half his face was ravaged by burn scars. The two
adults stood in the midst of a group of boys and girls who looked between the ages of eight and twelve. Aram paused in confusion, glancing
from face to face.

"Did I come to the wrong class?" he asked.

The woman smirked, and some of the children snickered.

"You're in the right class," she assured him. "You're too old to be put
with the little ones, so I'm going to have you train with the novices." She
gestured at the children as her words sank into Aram like a knife.

Too old to train with the little ones… Dear gods. They would put him in
with the babes if they could!

"I'm Wingmaster Eraine Vandra, in case Esmir didn't tell you," the
intimidating woman said. "This is your instructor, Master Grayson
Henrik, whom I have tasked with the impossible job of bringing both
your constitution and skillset up to speed. I'm going to stay here today
to see what you're made of. Have a seat."

Embarrassed and humiliated, Aram sat in the back of the small group of six boys and five girls who all turned to gawk at him. He tried not to look at them, for it wasn't the first time he felt like the object of ridicule, and he found that pretending he didn't notice was the easiest way to handle it.

Vandra took a seat on a nearby boulder and leaned back with one knee up, while Master Henrik took up position at the front of the class, his hand resting on the sword at his side. He launched into giving the students a set of detailed instructions that Aram didn't pay attention to. He was too busy avoiding the stares that kept shooting back to nettle him. When Henrik was done, every student jumped up with a loud *"Ha!"* and took off at a run. Caught off guard, Aram pushed himself to his feet and started limping after them.

"Not you." Vandra pointed at her side. "Over here."

Aram approached her, feeling chagrinned. "They're children."

Vandra shrugged dismissively. "These 'children' have been training to be warriors since they were old enough to hold a spear. Any one of them could beat the snot out of you."

The information made Aram feel even more out of place. "Why am I even here? I've never had that kind of training!"

"You begin today." Vandra drew a long knife from her belt and used it to scrape the dirt out from under her fingernails. "Do you know how to swim?"

"Yes…" Aram shivered, his mind going instantly back to the well. He felt his pulse speed up.

"Good." Vandra blew the dust off her nails and, flipping the knife, dropped it back into its sheath at her waist. "I want you to start by swimming back and forth across that pond as many times as you can." She pointed behind him.

Turning, Aram saw a wide pond behind them that was almost the size of a small lake. It was buried beneath the shadows of the cliff, under a great lip of rock. It didn't look terribly wide or deep, but just the sight of it made Aram's stomach tighten. His experience in the well had made him afraid of water, and his legs were burning and weak from the walk down to the training grounds.

But Vandra didn't look like she was willing to argue.

Blowing a sigh, Aram stripped down to his breeches and started toward the pond. The water was a lot colder than it looked, and he shivered and clutched himself as he waded in deeper, until he could no longer touch the bottom. He treaded water for a minute, squeezing his eyes shut, trying to ward off the fear of drowning. It took a great effort of will to force himself deeper.

He swam out into the pond, kicking as little as possible and using his arms to carry him forward. When he reached the middle, he glanced back over his shoulder at the shore. When he saw how far away it was, he felt a sharp stab of panic lance through him. He lingered for a moment, treading water, fighting to steady himself. When at last he got his breathing under control, he started forward again.

As Aram swam, he fought back memories of the well, of the burning need of his lungs for air, of the outright panic that had seized him as he struggled for the surface. Of the great gasp of water he had taken in, and the horrendous pain that had swallowed him whole.

By the time he reached the opposite shore, he was shaking so hard that he couldn't stand, both from the fatigue and the fear. Teeth chattering, he sat hugging himself in the cold mud. He looked back across the pond at Vandra, flushed with shame.

"Swim back!" the Wingmaster called to him.

Balling his fists, Aram forced himself back into the water. His arms hurt terribly, and he found himself having to kick more than he wanted to. He kept his gaze fixed on the shoreline, taking comfort in the fact that every stroke carried him a little closer to it. Once, he broke his rhythm and came up sputtering, terror seizing his breath. Somehow, he got his fear under control and managed to make it to the center of the pond. He squeezed his eyes closed, trembling in frustration and despair. He pulled himself forward through the water, jaw locked and groaning with every stroke.

Before he reached the shore, his strength failed.

He tried not to panic, for he knew how to float. And it worked, at first, but after a few seconds, he was sinking. The water of the pond simply wasn't as buoyant as seawater.

Desperate, Aram turned over and started dog paddling. He was having a hard time keeping his head above water, and he started taking in mouthfuls of it. He floundered, coughing and sputtering. At last, he came to the end of his strength.

He wanted to shout for help, but he didn't have the breath.

He was drowning again.

The knowledge made him want to weep, but he was too tired to be sad or scared. He closed his eyes and gave in, letting the water carry him under.

Just as his lungs started burning, an arm slipped around him and hauled him upward. He broke the surface with a great gasp and let his body go limp as Vandra towed him back to shore. There, he curled up on his side in the sand, panting and shaking, coughing the water out of his lungs.

He didn't know how long he laid there. He must have passed out, for the next thing he knew, someone was shaking him awake. Opening his eyes, Aram found himself looking up into the face of a wiry boy who looked to be the oldest student of the bunch, standing shirtless over him.

"Get up!" the boy ordered. "You're my partner, and I'm not going to let you make me look bad!"

Groggy, Aram climbed to his feet on legs that felt like jelly. Glancing around, he saw that the other children had divided into pairs for sparring. He had never sparred in his life and had no idea what to do.

The boy he was paired with immediately dropped into a fighting stance and brought his fists up, his left foot forward, his weight balanced between his feet. Aram tried his best to copy the stance, bringing his arms up and centering his gravity over his squishy legs. But before he got his feet into place, the boy struck out with a lightning-quick jab that cracked Aram on the cheek.

Crying out, he lurched back, cupping his face. He glanced at Vandra in confusion, for he didn't understand why the woman was doing this to him. Didn't she understand that he'd almost just died in the water?

Didn't she understand he had no idea how to fight and was too exhaust-ed to react in time?

Before he could recover, the boy swung again, landing a solid punch on the side of his head and sending him reeling. Aram rubbed his ach-ing temple and looked up from the dirt, only then realizing he'd been knocked to the ground. Rolling over with a groan, he pushed himself back to his feet.

"Again," the Wingmaster ordered, clapping her hands.

Aram's opponent dropped into his stance more, bobbing up and down on the balls of his feet. Aram barely got his arms up before the boy struck out with a left hook. When Aram moved to block, he received a head-stupefying punch from the boy's right fist.

He fell, moaning, to roll back and forth on the ground. His opponent stood over him, arms still up and ready to land another blow.

"Again," said Vandra.

Shaking and dizzy, Aram pushed himself to his feet, swiping the sweat out of his eyes. His ears were ringing, and his vision was fuzzy. His opponent waited for him to find his balance before bringing his hand back.

Aram threw himself forward, pawing at the boy like a cat goading a rat. The boy stepped sideways and struck out with a combination of punches that took him in the nose and the eye before sending him solid-ly to the ground.

Aram knelt in the sand, clutching his face as blood leaked through his fingers from his nose. The pain was white-hot, though it was a pain he could tolerate, for he'd endured far worse every day in the cellars.

Peering groggily up, Aram saw that all of the other children had stopped fighting and were gathered around, staring at him with either concern or contempt—he couldn't tell. His opponent dropped his hands and backed up, turning to look at Vandra for direction.

"Again," the Wingmaster said, hands on her hips.

The boy looked down at Aram, hesitating. He licked his lips then glanced back at Vandra. "I think he's had enough."

Vandra shook her head. "I'll tell you when it's enough."

Hearing that, Aram felt defeated. Vandra didn't want him—that was easy enough to tell. He figured the Wingmaster was trying to make him give up, to make him quit. He ground his teeth, the bloody taste of failure on his tongue.

No.

He wasn't going to give up. If all it took was a nosebleed to defeat him, what hope did he have against an Archon?

Wiping the blood from his face, he stood and brought his hands up.

His opponent swept out with a jab that took Aram in the ribs. The next punch hit him in the jaw. Aram staggered back, his head spinning. But he didn't go down. Spitting blood, he straightened and brought his hands up again.

"I'm ready," he said.

The boy glanced at Vandra, who nodded.

He struck out with a heavy blow that Aram somehow blocked. But the next punch slugged him in the gut, doubling him over and knocking the wind out of him. Aram bent, clutching his middle and groaning. Vandra came forward to stand behind him, arms crossed. Her presence incited him. Clenching his jaw, Aram drew himself upright and brought his fists up.

"Come on," he said.

His opponent nodded and dove at him with an uppercut that snapped Aram's head back, then he followed up with a punch that drove him straight to the ground. Aram stayed down, dark, syrupy blood draining in a thick rope from his face, his vision darkening.

"I'm sorry," his opponent whispered.

Aram shook his head. This boy wasn't his true adversary. It was Vandra, and he wasn't going to let her win.

Summoning his resolve, he pushed himself off the ground and stood wavering, bringing his fists up.

"Enough."

All eyes turned to Vandra, who laid a hand on Aram's shoulder.

"Everyone gather around!" the Wingmaster called. "Let's welcome our newest student..." Her voice trailed off and she frowned. "What's your full name, son?"

"Aramon Raythe."

The woman's face went slack. Her lips parted, her eyes widening. She whispered, *"Raythe?"*

Aram nodded, then turned to spit a mouthful of blood on the sand. "Yes. Why?"

The woman stood studying his face intensely as he stared back at her in confusion and growing dismay.

"It's a common name here," she said at last. "You must have Auld roots." Gathering her composure around her like a cloak, she turned her back on him. "Class dismissed."

Aram stood, dizzy, while the other students filed past him, clapping him on the shoulder. When the last boy left the training yard, Aram limped after him, leaving Vandra behind, staring at his back.

Esmir paused before the door to the Council chamber long enough to start fussing with his tunic before giving up on it. Taking a deep breath, he thrust the door open and entered, striding forward to stand before the members of the Council with as much failed dignity as he could muster. Luvana greeted him with a sardonic smile.

"Warden Revin, thank you for coming."

Esmir scowled. "Always a pleasure."

Gesturing around at her fellow council members, Luvana informed him, "We have decided, with two noted abstentions, to allow your foundling to be trained. Wingmaster Vandra has vouched for his charac-ter. Though, to be honest, I'm not sure whether we are doing the young man a favor or handing him a death sentence, for it seems unlikely he will survive the Trials."

Esmir inclined his head in gratitude. "Thank you, Dedicant Mother, for giving Aram the opportunity to prove you wrong."

Before he could turn to leave, Luvana's voice stopped him. "One last thing. Why didn't you bring Aram's family name to our attention?"

Esmir frowned in confusion. "I didn't think to ask him his family name. Why?"

Wingmaster Vandra's eyes stabbed him like a cold spear. "Well, I *did* think to ask him. He introduced himself as Aramon Raythe."

Esmir glanced from Vandra to Luvana, an avalanche of thoughts cascading through his head. "Raythe? Are you saying that he might be Darand's boy?"

"He'd be the right age," Vandra mused. "Have you looked at his face?"

Esmir exhaled, his shoulders wilting, for he hadn't looked hard enough, apparently.

He said quickly to Luvana, "Don't tell him."

Vandra broke in, "If he really is the son of Darand Raythe, then he needs to know about his father."

Esmir strode forward, positioning himself directly in front of the Dedicant Mother. "He's been through enough, Luvana," he said firmly. "Give Aram time to mend."

Luvana and Vandra exchanged critical glances.

"Talk to him," Luvana ordered. "Let's make sure we're right."

Esmir nodded. Mind spinning, he left the council chamber and hurried back to his quarters. Opening the door, he noticed that his young charge had arrived home before him. Aram was sitting hunched beside the fire pit, his head cradled in his hands. Upon hearing him enter, the boy turned around.

At the sight of his face, Esmir drew in a cursing breath. If the young man really did resemble his father, it would take him at least a week to find out, because Aram looked like he'd been set upon by a band of brigands. His face was cut and bruised, his lip split, and both eyes were purple and swollen. Dried blood crusted his nostrils, and his pupils looked bleary and out of focus.

Esmir motioned him forward. Aram rose and approached, walking as though in a drunken stupor. When he halted before him, Esmir took him by the chin and lifted his swollen face to examine it. The boy was really a piece of work. He felt a sharp flash of anger, then shoved the feeling aside. Despite the fact that he'd taken a beating, Aram had managed to impress Vandra, and that was no easy thing to do.

"Next time try ducking." He released Aram's chin and moved toward the table, where a decanter of whiskey sat waiting for him. "I have good news. The Council has decided to approve your training. I want you to work with Henrik during the day, and I'll work with you in the evenings."

"Work with me on what?" asked Aram, sliding into the chair next to him.

"Magic, of course."

Esmir uncorked the decanter and poured himself a healthy cup. Taking another glance at Aram's face, he poured the young man one as well.

"I can't do magic," said Aram, staring down into the cup. "Not unless someone is in danger."

Esmir nodded. "That's how Auld magic works."

Aram's head snapped up. "What do you mean?"

"It's thought to be some type of safeguard."

Aram's breath caught, and he sat looking straight ahead with an expression of profound shock. Esmir nudged Aram's cup. "Here. Drink. Believe me, you need it."

Aram lifted the cup to his lips, wincing at the bite of the alcohol. But he persevered and got down a few sips. Esmir topped off his own cup then sprawled back in his chair, rubbing his eyes.

"Keep drinking while I'm talking," he ordered. "Auld were created by Ahn the Father, or so the story goes. He didn't want his children to be seduced by power, so Ahn put a block within us: we are unable to use magic for our own gain, even to save our own lives. We can only use magic as an act of altruism."

Frowning, Aram asked, "Then how do Champions fight?"

Esmir took a heavy sip of his drink. "That's the reason for the Trials. Supposedly, it's to prove to the gods that a candidate's abilities and character justify having their magic unlocked." Esmir downed another swallow of whiskey. "That's what a Champion is: a person whose block has been removed. Take another sip."

Scrunching his nose, Aram did as he bid.

"You're a good lad," Esmir said, staring hard into Aram's bruised face. "I bet your father is very proud of you."

Aram shook his head, staring vacantly at his cup with his swollen eyes. "My father left us when I was small."

The answer made the hairs on the back of Esmir's neck rise. "So sorry to hear that. Do you know why he left?"

"No. My mother said she guesses he went off to fight some war somewhere. Only, he wasn't a soldier, so I don't understand why she would think that. He left this behind."

Reaching into his shirt, Aram pulled out a necklace made out of knotted twine. He untied it from his neck and handed it across the table. Esmir stared down at the necklace's pendant, which was simply a large, intricate knot in the shape of a heart. At the sight of that knot, Esmir sighed heavily.

He held up the necklace. "Do you know what this is?"

"It's an eternal heart knot," replied Aram.

And so it was. There was a lot of symbolism in such a knot. Esmir wondered if the young man knew any of the stories that knot could tell him.

"What was your father's name?" he asked, handing the necklace back.

"Darand Raythe."

Esmir took another sip of his whiskey. "Well." He did his best to smile. "I'm sure that, wherever he is, Darand Raythe is very proud of you."

The next morning, Aram returned to the training grounds, though getting there was even more of a challenge than the previous day, for his muscles burned terribly. His aching body had kept him awake most of the night, and he'd tossed and turned on his pallet. He was sure his nose was broken, and he thought he might have a bruised rib. The headache was the worst. He didn't know if it was from the blows to the head or from all the whiskey Esmir had made him drink, but it hurt just to hold his swollen eyes open, and every candle he looked at had a shimmering halo around it that had nothing to do with magical auras.

By the time he got down to the level of the training grounds, all of the students were already there, sitting cross-legged on the ground around Master Henrik, who sat on a boulder above them. Upon seeing that the class had started without him, Aram froze, his stomach taking a plunge into a dark vortex. Anxiety got ahold of him, for after yesterday's failures, he feared that his classmates wouldn't want anything to do with him. Interactions with people had always made him uneasy, and this situation was so much worse because he knew nothing about these people or their world.

Trying to be as quiet as he could, Aram crept up behind the rest of the students and sat well back from them in the lee of the wall. He tried to make himself as small as possible, hoping to all the gods they wouldn't notice him coming in late. When Henrik's eyes fell upon him, Aram ducked his head to hide his face.

"Ah, Aram. Good of you to show up."

Aram slumped, looking up at Henrik through a lock of ruddy brown hair. He didn't know what to say—or even if he was supposed to say anything at all—so he kept his mouth shut and sat frozen, like a hare confronted by a lion.

"Tomorrow, try to arrive on time," Henrik advised, his voice mild, then returned to his lecture.

Unable to listen, Aram sat steeped in feelings of worthlessness and self-pity. Humiliation filled him, and he wanted to weep, but weeping would be even more humiliating, so he didn't.

To his dismay, the boy who had given him a licking the day before stood and walked toward him, probably to torment him some more. Aram tried pretending like he didn't notice him, even when the boy came up next to him.

"Can I sit with you?" the boy whispered.

Aram glanced at him, confused. No one ever wanted to sit with him. He didn't know what this boy's purpose was, but he feared it was malicious. He'd come to expect terrible things from people, and he didn't see any reason for this boy to be different from anyone else who had mistreated him.

"I'm Kye. You're Aram, right?"

Aram nodded, unable to look at him.

"I just wanted to say I'm sorry for yesterday. I think you're very brave."

Now Aram knew Kye was there to torment him, for there was no way Kye could think that after the beating he had given him. Feeling a profound sadness, Aram gazed down at the sand in front of him.

"What's wrong?" Kye whispered.

Aram shook his head.

There was a long silence as Kye stared at him and Henrik went on lecturing about something that probably was important. At last, Kye turned away.

"Sorry," he whispered, and started to rise.

"Wait," Aram said.

Kye sat back down, gazing at him quizzically.

"Do you really mean that?" Aram didn't think it was possible, but just in case it was—on the slightest sliver of a chance it could be possible—he wanted to make sure.

"I do." Kye nodded. "You kept getting up. Even after you knew you were beaten. You kept getting up."

Hearing that kind of praise coming from someone younger than himself made a knot form in Aram's throat. "Thank you."

"I'm sorry I busted your nose," said Kye. "And your lip."

"And my ribs," Aram added factually.

Kye giggled, earning him a glare from Henrik.

"Do you have something to add?" their instructor demanded with an irritated glare.

"Nuh-uh!" Kye's face reddened, and Aram couldn't blame him.

Henrik's eyes narrowed, but he returned to his lecture. "As I was saying, there's an art to defensive fighting. Think of it as the art of not getting hit. Too many people think that the best defense is a good offense. They focus on hurting their opponent, while oblivious of the fact that they are taking damage themselves. Let's take Aram yesterday."

Hearing his name, Aram wanted to melt into the ground.

"Aram. What was the biggest mistake you made?"

What was it that Esmir had said? Oh, yeah. "I didn't duck."

The students laughed, but Henrik nodded. "That's right. Not once did you try to dodge a blow. While you were so focused on hitting Kye, he was tearing your face up."

Aram nodded glumly, for it was true. Kye ribbed him with an elbow, sending a jolt of pain through his side that made him wince.

"Sorry!" Kye gulped.

"So, if you're so focused on defense, when is it time to strike?" Henrik rose from his rock and walked toward the nearest boy. "Stand up and hit me."

The boy, a wiry youth with a prominent nose, rose to his feet and adopted a fighting stance. For seconds, he just stood there. Then, without warning, he lashed out.

There were two sharp *thunks,* and the boy was on the ground.

Henrik stepped back, looking at the class as he offered his hand to the boy to help him up. "Don't attack. *Counterattack.* Every time you defend, attack at the same time or immediately after. Don't passively defend— *aggressively* defend. Make your opponent pay in blood for every attack they make. Any questions?"

There were none.

"All right. Sparring pairs. Practice aggressive defense. Not you two." He motioned for Aram and Kye. When they came forward, Henrik told them, "Aram's head looks like it needs a day off." He raised a finger at Aram. "But you still need to build your muscles. Kye, take him up to the Henge. Show him what he's in for. On the way back, get him some food."

"I already ate—" Aram protested.

"Eat again."

"The Henge?" Kye asked. "But that's for—"

"People like Aram," Henrik finished.

Kye's eyes grew huge.

The boy trotted toward the stairs, and Aram followed him with a glance back at Henrik. He wondered what the instructor had meant by 'people like' him. The names he used to be called came immediately to mind—words like 'moron' and 'idiot.' He didn't want to be called those names here too.

But as they started up the dim stairwell, Kye turned to him with burning eyes. "You're training to be a *Champion?*"

Embarrassed, Aram could only nod.

"That's...wow. I mean...*wow.*"

Aram hoped he meant it in a good way.

Kye glanced down at Aram's body, his eyebrows knitting together. At last, he smiled. "You've sure got a long way to go."

Aram's face reddened, but then Kye laughed. At first, Aram thought he was laughing at him, but then he realized Kye was joking good-naturedly.

"A *long* way," he agreed, doing his best to smile, despite his swollen lips. He was already having a hard time with the stairs, and he wondered how far up the cliff they had to climb. He didn't want Kye to have to wait through all the rest breaks he would need if they had to climb to the level of Esmir's quarters.

"What's this Henge?" Aram asked, already winded.

"It's where Champions used to train." Kye glanced at him. "Are trained." He frowned hard. "Seriously? Are you really training to be a Champion? I mean, no offense, but…you really *do* have a long way to go."

Aram didn't have the breath to spare on a response because he was already panting.

"Do you need to stop and rest?" asked Kye with a look of concern.

"No," Aram gasped, gritting his teeth against the pain in his legs as he forced himself up another switchback of stairs.

Kye was right—he was horribly behind. He had to catch up to the other students—not just the students in Kye's class, but the students his own age, whom he hadn't even met yet. He didn't have time to stop and rest. He never would.

"Only really special people can be Champions," said Kye. "Are you like that?"

"I see in color," Aram admitted, hoping Kye knew what that meant.

"Oh. Oh! That means…you're a True Savant?"

"I guess so."

"You *guess* so? Do you have any idea how many years it's been since the last Champion passed the Trials? Like, centuries!"

Aram clenched his jaw and tried to narrow his focus to the step immediately ahead. Sweat streamed down his face, and his legs and lungs felt like they'd been lit on fire. He took another step and felt his muscles turn to liquid. He collapsed on his rump and glanced up to find Kye hovering over him with a look of shock and concern.

"I'm fine," Aram panted. "Fine." Using his hands, he started pushing himself back to his feet.

Kye stared at him, shaking his head. "You don't stop, do you?"

"I can't," Aram gasped.

Kye glanced back up the stairway, his finger ticking the air, as though trying to count how many flights they still had left to go. Frowning, he sat down on a step. "Well, you'll have to stop, because I need a rest."

Aram dropped back down beside him, heady with relief. He brought his legs up and rested his head against his knees. They sat there for minutes until, at last, Kye rose and helped him to his feet.

"We're almost there," Kye said, trying to sound cheerful. "Only a dozen flights more to go." He managed a weak smile, which was stillborn, as he seemed to think better of it.

He started forward, Aram climbing doggedly after him. By the time they reached the top of the steps, Aram figured he'd probably feel better if they amputated his legs. But he'd made it, and that's what mattered. He felt a small amount of pride in that.

They stepped out of the stairwell onto the summit of a high bluff at the top of the gorge. Aram found himself standing in a circle paved in fine white sand, and at its center rose a dark obelisk made of one enormous chunk of obsidian. The square was ringed by massive dolomite monoliths, the outer ring free-standing, the inner ring consisting of four structures that resembled doorways, with two vertical stones capped by another stone laid across the top of them.

"What are they?" Aram asked, turning slowly to take in the imposing structures.

"Portal Stones," said Kye, swiping his hair out of his eyes. "They're ancient. No one knows who built them."

Aram stared in wonder and trepidation at the monuments, filled with a burning curiosity. "Why are they here?"

Kye gestured around them. "This place is called the Henge. It's where people training to be Champions are tested."

Aram stared at the dark monoliths, a cold feeling slithering over his skin. "What if a person doesn't pass the Trials?"

Kye peered at him with a look of dismayed confusion. "You don't know?"

Aram shook his head. "No."

Kye frowned deeply, licking his lips. He looked like he didn't want to tell him. But then he pointed at the nearest trio of standing stones. "You go in, and either you come out or you don't. If you do come out, you're either a Champion or your mind is broken…there's nothing in between."

Aram stared at the standing stones, a cold feeling of dread coiling in the pit of his stomach. The dark monoliths suddenly looked like doorways to nightmares, even though he could see right through them to the other side. There was a slight shimmering between the stones, like air heated by the ground. But there was something else too. A sinister feeling, like the promise of pain. He wondered if Kye felt it, or if it was only for him.

"What's inside?" he asked.

"What you take in with you," said a woman's voice.

Startled, Aram turned to see Wingmaster Vandra striding toward them across the circle of sand. This was the first time he had seen her wearing her hair loose, and it fell down her back in a snarly mess. She was wearing black leathers made from some animal Aram was unfamiliar with, covered by a fur-lined cloak that billowed behind her, tossed by the wind blowing across the gorge.

"The Trials are the measure of a man," Vandra explained, coming to stand before him. "These are portals to the Shadow Realm. There are creatures in there that are not men. We call them the Overseers, and it is they who administer the Trials. No one knows whether it's these creatures' intent to forge a Champion, or whether they serve their own purpose, and only Champions can win their way back out, despite them."

She turned slowly, her gaze traveling from stone to stone in the wide circle. "Most who enter, don't come back. Whatever the Overseers are, they are powerful enough, and sinister enough, to break the minds of most who enter, by using your own thoughts and weapons against you."

She turned back to Aram, her face hard and implacable. "Now you understand why I will spare you no blow and show you no mercy. It is my responsibility to give you the best chance of returning from those stones with your mind intact."

Aram met her gaze. "Do you think I'll fail?"

The woman hesitated, at last nodding. "Most likely. But I promise I'll do everything I can to keep you alive."

38

"I spoke to Eraine Vandra," said Esmir, plopping his considerable weight into the chair across the table from Aram. "Tomorrow, she wants you to move into the dormitory with the other students."

Hearing that made Aram sad. He had just begun to get used to Esmir's abrasive company. He nodded, his eyes fixed on the table while his fingers fiddled with the drawstring of his pants, tying and untying it over and over again.

"I don't want to move to the dormitory," he said softly. "I want to stay here with you."

Esmir snorted. "You'd rather be around a flatulent old man than children your own age?"

Aram looked up sharply. "They're not my age. I'm a lot older than they are, which makes me look like an idiot. And I'm not near as good as any of them at anything, which makes me look even more like an idiot." Just thinking about living with the boys in his class was a prospect that terrified Aram, for he knew that he wouldn't be accepted. He glanced at Esmir with pleading eyes.

Esmir waved his hand dismissively. "They know you're not an idiot. You're Gifted, which puts you on a level that none of them could ever approach. Maybe you're not as physically strong as they are, or as skilled with weapons, but they have been training their entire lives to be windriders, while you have not. And they know that."

Aram sighed, his shoulders sagging, for he saw that there was no

301

way he was going to be able to change Esmir's mind. He would be relegated to the dormitory, where he'd likely spend every evening being either ignored or ridiculed by boys four years his junior.

"You need to make a friend or two."

Aram looked at him plaintively. "I'm not good at making friends."

"Well, maybe you just need practice." Esmir spread his hands. "That's what we do when we're not good at something, isn't it? Practice?"

Aram puzzled over the idea for a long moment. He didn't think Esmir was right, because he'd practiced making friends his entire childhood—had even invented imaginary friends to practice with—and yet, that practice had never helped him make real friends.

Until Markus. And now Calise.

Aram frowned, realizing that maybe Esmir was right. Maybe all that practice was finally paying off. Kye seemed friendly enough.

"Maybe there's one boy…I guess I can try," Aram allowed.

"Excellent." Esmir clapped his hand on the table. "Now, let's eat! I know I'm hungry, so you must be starving."

Standing, the old Warden went to the hearth, where a kettle hung over the fire. There, he ladled peas onto two plates. He then retrieved a potato that had been roasting down in the coals, dividing it between the two plates, then added slices of buttered beef. Replacing the pea ladle, he crossed the room back to the table, where he set Aram's plate down before him.

Seeing that some of his peas had run into his potatoes, Aram picked up a wooden spoon and started separating them, scooping the peas to one side of the plate and the potatoes to the other, with a perfectly straight line running between.

"Stop."

Lowering his spoon, Aram glanced at Esmir.

"Every night at supper, you always eat the same way," the old man pointed out. "You push everything around your plate until you have an arrangement that satisfies you. Then, you only eat one thing at a time and never alternate. Is there a reason why you do this?"

Aram frowned at Esmir, uncertain why the old man suddenly cared about how he arranged the food on his plate. He said with a shrug, "I like eating one thing at a time."

Esmir peered at him hard. "Why?"

"I don't like to mix the flavors."

"Why not?"

Aram made a face. "It's gross."

Esmir stared at him sideways. "So, if you mixed everything together on your plate, you would find that gross?"

Aram was repulsed by the notion. "That would be *disgusting.*"

As soon as he said it, Esmir picked up his own plate and started mixing his peas together with his potatoes, mashing it all up with animated motions, adding insult to injury. Aram stared in horror at the travesty of a perfectly good meal, now destroyed. Even the slice of beef hadn't been spared but was coated with mashed-together peas and potatoes.

"This bothers you?" Esmir asked, still stirring. "Just looking at me doing this?"

Aram nodded, feeling queasy.

"Why?"

Aram stared at him in incomprehension, wondering how it could be that Esmir didn't understand. "It's like…how would you feel if someone licked a chamber pot in front of you?"

Esmir chuckled. "I supposed I'd feel disgusted, but this is food, not a chamber pot." With one last, explicative mash, he set the spoon down. "What other kinds of things bother you like this?"

Aram thought about it. "Scratchy wool. Ticks."

"Ticks don't count," dismissed Esmir. "What else?"

"Really loud noises. Certain sounds…"

"What kinds of sounds?"

"I don't like it when people scratch," Aram admitted.

"Like this?" Esmir scratched at his arm vigorously, the noise sending a nerve-abrading shiver down Aram's spine.

"Yes!" Aram winced, cringing and squirming in his seat.

Esmir smiled kindly. "Daymar was the same way. There were certain things that annoyed the hell out of him. Being touched was one. Heat was another—made him anxious and cranky. And food. For him, it was texture. He couldn't eat beans of any kind, even though he said he liked the flavor—it was just the texture that bothered him. Want to know what he did about it?"

Aram didn't want to know.

"He forced himself to eat beans every day for two years. Even after that, he ate them at least once a week. Every time we came home, he'd go sit in the sweat bath for hours. He did everything he could to desensitize himself to the things that troubled him most. Until they didn't trouble him anymore." He smiled sadly.

"Why would he go through the bother?" Aram asked. "Why does it matter that I don't like peas mixed with potatoes?"

"Because it's a weakness," Esmir explained. "And weaknesses are something you can't afford."

"Everyone has weaknesses."

"You're not everyone."

While Aram contemplated this, Esmir picked up his chair and scooted it closer. "It's true that there are some weaknesses that are outside of our control. But even with those, we can usually find ways to adapt. As for weaknesses that we *can* control…well, life is about conquering our weaknesses and turning them into strengths. It's how we grow as individuals. We can't let our weaknesses limit our potential. We want to be defined by our strengths, not our shortcomings."

Aram mulled those words over, deciding, at last, that they sounded like wisdom. Reluctantly, he nodded.

Esmir's face grew hard. "I want you to take your plate and stir everything together, just as I did."

Aram's eyes went wide, and he shook his head adamantly. Just the thought made his stomach clench. He could feel seeds of nausea starting to take root in his gut.

He glanced down at his plate, feeling a growing panic. "I can't…"

"You have to."

He didn't think he could. It was unimaginable. The flavors, the textures. *No, no, no…*

He sighed, closing his eyes. If he couldn't mix a pea with a potato, how could he become a Champion?

Reluctantly, he picked up his spoon and started mixing everything together on his plate, mushing up the peas with the potatoes and smearing everything over the meat until it was all just a lumpy catastrophe. Staring down at it, he felt his stomach roil.

"Give it a try," prompted Esmir.

Aram looked at him dispiritedly. Then, dipping just the tip of his spoon into the mixture, he stuck out his tongue to give it a taste.

"Bah!" Esmir slapped his hand on the table, jolting Aram's plate. "That's ridiculous. Take a whole bite! Just shovel it in!"

Aram plunged the spoon into the hateful mixture, scooping up a heaping portion and lifting it to his lips. Squeezing his eyes closed, he did as Esmir bade, plunging the whole thing into his mouth. The moment it landed on his tongue, his throat locked up tight and his stomach convulsed. It was all he could do to swallow the mouthful of pea-paste, and the awful taste and texture remained behind even after the lump went down.

"Keep going," ordered Esmir. "I don't care if you puke it all up. But you *will* get every bit of food on that plate down your gullet."

Aram forced down a second bite, though it made him retch. With one last, despairing glance at Esmir, he dug into the rest, holding his nose and shoveling it in as fast as he could, trying hard not to chew. By the time the plate was empty, he was shaking with the urge to vomit. Tears streamed down his cheeks, and his mouth was filled with slimy mucous.

"You did it!" Esmir exclaimed as Aram pushed his empty plate away. "And that's how you'll eat every meal from now on. Understand?"

Aram slumped in defeat, thinking he'd rather hammer his hand flat three times a day. But he also knew that Esmir was right—it was a weakness, so it would have to be dealt with.

"Will it taste better over time?" he asked.

"No," Esmir said. "What will change is your ability to cope with the experience."

While Aram regained control over his stomach, Esmir cleaned their plates and removed the kettle from the heat. When he was done, he returned to the table with a small, loose-leaf book, its pages held together by whip stitching. He set the book down on the table, turning it toward Aram. "Here are some of Daymar's notes that I collected and bound. I want you to read a few pages every day, and every evening we'll talk about what you read the previous day."

"I can't read," Aram admitted with an apologetic smile.

The old man sighed and rolled his eyes. "Yet *another* weakness we will have to turn into a strength. All right, then, starting tomorrow, you will wake an hour before dawn and report here to learn your letters before going down to breakfast with your classmates."

It just kept getting worse and worse.

"For now, *I'll* read." Esmir snatched the book back, then paused. He closed the cover. "Never mind. I'll just talk. There are two basic types of magic: active and passive. Passive magic is born of the earth. No one makes it—it's just there. An example is this Wellspring water." He held up a glass bottle and sloshed its contents around before returning it to the table.

"Auld and humans perform what's known as active magic. They make things happen that are unlikely to happen on their own. They can do this by manipulating strands of aether. Strands can also be read, because many things influence the aether around them. Events that have large impacts on the threads of the world can be felt and read from a great distance. And a very long time after."

The concept intrigued Aram, for he had always wondered how Sergan had found him when he'd opened the rupture. Maybe that's how he'd done it.

"And there is yet another type of active magic," Esmir went on, "one that takes a great deal of skill. It's about using the aether to store energy and then release it by degrees in specific patterns. That's where your love of knots comes in. Think of a knot as a complication. The greater the complication, the more energy it can store, the same way a compressed spring stores energy."

"What does the energy do?" asked Aram.

Esmir shrugged. "Just as different kinds of knots have different functions, different aethereal bindings have different purposes. And the more improbable the occurrence, the more complex the knot has to be to accomplish it."

"What does essence have to do with it?" Aram wondered.

"Essence is our soul's connection with the aether. The souls of some beings are entirely essence, for they are aether incarnate. People have the capacity for more or less, depending on the person. Some people produce no essence at all." He smiled. "Like me. The more essence a soul produces, the greater that soul's affinity for magic."

His own soul produced a lot of essence, Aram knew. Enough to fill barrels. "So, why do Exilari sorcerers need essence? And why aren't they blocked from using magic like me?"

"They're not blocked because they are not Auld, and they're not even supposed to have magic," Esmir said. "Sorcerers are human—they're not born with the affinity. Because they don't have essence of their own, they have to steal it from other people." He leaned back in his chair. "That's enough for tonight. Do you know where the dormitory is?"

"Down by the training grounds," Aram muttered, still thinking of the essence cellars and all the oak barrels he had personally filled.

"You'll be moving in after tomorrow's exercises." Esmir rose from the table with a grimace. He gave a great yawn, stretching his arms toward the ceiling of the eyrie. When Aram stood to move to his cot, the old Warden handed him the book. "There's pictures too."

Aram took it with a smile of gratitude.

The next morning, Esmir woke Aram before dawn and sat him down on the cold stone floor of the eyrie next to an oil lamp whose flame guttered in a breeze coming in through the cave mouth. He gave Aram a piece of chalk along with a parchment with lines of letters and numerals, then cleared a space on the floor large enough for him to work on.

"Pay attention, because I'm only going to do this once," Esmir growled. Then he pointed at the first row of letters on the page. "These are vowels. They represent sounds made with an open throat. This one is 'a,' this one is 'e'…" He continued on through all the vowels and consonants, down to the bottom of the page. "Now, practice writing the characters on the floor. Every time you write one, say the sound out loud. I want to hear you."

Aram nodded and got busy. He found it easy to remember which character made which sound because, once he thought about it, every letter looked very similar to the sound it made. 'O' was an open sound, and the character that represented it looked open as well. 'P' was a very sharp sound, and to Aram, the character that represented it looked like a sharp blade.

At first, Esmir stood over him, arms folded, nodding whenever he got a letter right. Within short order, he stopped nodding, for he looked like a woodpecker. He walked across the room and plopped into his chair at the table, resting his chin in his hand.

When Aram had copied the letters as best he could, he stood up to admire his work and was disappointed to find that his chalkmanship was not very neat. Unlike the beautiful lines and curves Esmir had inked upon the parchment, Aram's writing looked like wet beach sand after a flock of seagulls had scratched at it. Dispirited, he knelt back down, deciding to practice more and try to make his characters neater.

A knock at the door interrupted him. Esmir opened it to admit Wingmaster Vandra into the room. Seeing her, Aram sighed regretfully, for he knew his writing lesson was over. He *hated* being interrupted from a task once he started, something that bugged him just as badly as mixing peas with potatoes.

"I need to borrow Aram," Vandra said without preamble, her voice lacking its characteristic abrasiveness.

Esmir's eyebrows drew together. "Why?"

The woman strode forward into the room, her gaze wandering over the cluttered items stacked along the walls. "Something's happened in the Winmarch. I need someone to read the strands. I can ask Luvana… but I think Aram might have a better chance at discerning the details."

Hearing that, Aram set down his chalk, frustrated, hoping Esmir would tell the woman that he was busy and to go away, but one look at Esmir's face told him that wasn't going to happen. The old Warden had gone from looking obstinate to looking intensely concerned.

"What happened?" Esmir asked.

Vandra glanced at Aram. "Three Elesium were found slaughtered."

Hearing that, Esmir's face crumpled. He stood shaking his head slowly, staring at Vandra as though the woman had just confessed to committing a murder. The Wingmaster looked equally stricken, though there was fire and an unmistakable thirst for vengeance in her gaze.

"What are Elesium?" asked Aram, rising from the floor.

Esmir turned to regard him. "The great horses of the Winmarch, creatures very strong and pure of spirit." He turned back to Vandra. "Minions of Kathrax? So far south?"

"That's what we fear," Vandra admitted. "There are rumors from the Eldenwood that they've taken wing, though there's only one way to know for sure. I need Aram to read the strands."

Aram walked forward, confused. "I don't know anything about reading strands."

Esmir assured him, "Yes, you do. What color aura does Vandra have?"

"The same color as her eyes," Aram answered warily. Turquoise was an unsettling color, though not so bad as blue or purple.

"And what color of aura do I have?"

"You don't have one."

Esmir was a Warden, just like Markus.

"And what does that say about me?"

Aram thought about it. He had never tried to assign words or descriptions to the colors of a person. To him, colors were just a feeling, like the emotions conveyed by a song. It took him a moment to figure out the right word to describe what he felt when looking at Esmir. "You are...empty."

The old man gave a fragile smile. "Daymar used to tell me it meant I was boring."

"That's a better word," Aram agreed. "Boring."

Esmir exchanged glances with Vandra, and the Wingmaster's lip curled slightly.

"You just read the strands," Esmir assured Aram with a pat on the shoulder. "Go with Vandra. Do what she tells you."

Aram let out a long sigh, for he would have to leave his letters and chalk behind. But he did as he was bid and went with Vandra, following her out into the hallway. The Wingmaster walked at a quick pace, her footfalls sharp. Aram found himself hurrying to keep up with her. His legs were still tired from the long walk up the stairs to the Henge.

"How far away is it?" he asked, hoping the place they were going wasn't too far. He didn't want to appear weak in front of Vandra, but he didn't think he could take another long flight of stairs so soon.

The Wingmaster answered, "On the other side of the mountains. Winhome is in the middle of the grasslands."

Aram almost choked. "How long a journey is *that?*"

Vandra glanced at him with amusement glinting in her turquoise eyes. "Less than an hour. We're going by dragon."

Hearing that, a thrill of excitement gushed into Aram's body, kicking his pulse up. Though the memory of his flight with the void dragon was hazy, he could still remember the rush of air against his face, the glittering ocean so far below, and that consummate feeling of peace. The chance of experiencing such bliss again made him shiver in anticipation.

"I'm going to fly on a dragon?"

"If she'll have you," Vandra said. "I'm hoping Zandril will condescend to carry you."

At the mention of Zandril, Aram's enthusiasm bubbled over. Calise was one of the two nicest people in the world, and just the thought of spending a day with her and her beautiful dragon made Aram smile. Walking fast to keep up with Vandra's long strides, he followed the Wingmaster down the stairs to the level of the big eyrie.

As they entered the great cavern, Aram halted in the doorway and stared in wonder at a space filled with dragons. The eyrie looked so much different in the daylight than it had when he'd first visited it at night. The screens of the alcoves were drawn back, revealing the homes of dragons and their riders. There was a bustle of activity as people went about the business of the day. Beyond the enormous cave mouth, many dragons sunned on a wide terrace, while others soaked in the large pond in the center of the cavern.

"This is the Southern Eyrie," Vandra told him, directing him forward with a hand on his shoulder. "It's my eyrie. There're three others: The Northern, the Western, and the Lower Eyries."

"Do all the dragons live in these caves together?" Aram asked. "Or do any of them have their own eyries, like Esmir's?"

"Only the Greater Dragons lived alone. They preferred their solitude. Lesser Dragons are far more social. That's why we live all together. Our dragons would be too lonely apart."

Each alcove looked furnished and cozy, Aram saw, with beds for the riders and a straw-strewn area where their dragons nested. Many dragons were sleeping, curled with their heads tucked under their wings. To Aram, each dragon-alcove resembled a smaller version of Esmir's cave, just less cluttered and homier. The eyrie had to be the size of Hearth

Home, perhaps larger, and amidst the alcoves and recesses, wood and brick structures had been built.

Following Vandra through the eyrie, Aram found himself gaping in wonder at the dragons surrounding him, his spirit stirred by their very presence. Though they were not large, they were creatures of surpassing power and beauty. Their intelligent eyes, their imposing countenance, all painted a portrait of creatures that were far more than just animals and greater than humans…they were something apart, something esoteric and extraordinary. The dragons were a wide variety of colors: browns and golds, oranges and reds, some darker, though none were particularly vibrant. Each had its own aura, just as people did, though theirs seemed far more intricate. The dragons looked at him as he passed, and he could feel them pressing against his mind: curious, questioning, as though they saw in him something more remembered than recognized and didn't quite know quite what to make of it.

"Aram!"

He turned to find Calise hurrying toward them across the eyrie. Excited to see her, Aram started toward her with a smile, but then realized that Calise was not smiling back. Her face was compressed in sorrow, and her eyes were red and glistening with tears. When she reached him, she greeted him with a hug then pulled back to look at him, shaking her head.

"What kind of monster would kill Elesium?" she whispered.

Aram didn't know, for he had no real understanding of what Elesium were.

Calise turned to Vandra. "You have to find who did this!"

"We'll do everything we can," Vandra assured her. "Aram sees in color. He'll be able to read the strands and hopefully give us some idea of what happened."

Calise glanced at Aram with a startled look in her eyes. "You can do something like that? I mean…I didn't know you could…already…"

"We have to fly to Winhome," Vandra said. "Do you think Zandril would mind carrying Aram?"

"Oh!" Calise looked surprised by the question but recovered quickly.

Her eyes went vacant for a moment, as though she were deep in thought, but at last she blinked and nodded sharply.

"She will take you," she said to Aram.

"That's very kind of her," Aram muttered, wondering what that look in Calise's eyes had been. It had only been there for a second, but he didn't know if it was good or bad.

"It's more than kind," said Vandra. "It's rare that a dragon will carry someone other than its own rider."

"Isn't Calise coming with us?" Aram asked.

"I can't," Calise said. "Zandril's not big enough to carry us both."

Feeling disappointed, Aram followed Calise as she led them back across the eyrie toward the alcove where she and Zandril made their home. As they approached, the dragon rose and stretched, the spines on her back raising. Then she stalked toward them, her golden eyes catching and holding Aram's.

In the back of Aram's mind, he felt a familiar stirring, one he remembered from his tortured dreams. Here again was the comforting presence, the guardian who had stood between him and his nightmares day after day. It was this dragon's presence in his mind that had brought him back from the hell that had imprisoned him.

"I can feel her," he said wonderingly, knowing that the stirring he felt was Zandril's soul touching his.

Immediately, he felt the dragon's surprise, and he got the impression that she recognized in him a strength that surpassed anything she had ever sensed before in a human. Suddenly self-conscious, Aram pulled his mind back from the dragon's touch, an action that left him feeling dizzy. He closed his eyes and stood quietly for a moment with his hand on his brow, collecting himself. When he opened them again, he realized that every dragon in the eyrie was looking at him, every great, golden eye staring at him with a mixture of respect and curiosity.

Looking bewildered by the dragons' behavior, Vandra contemplated Aram with a thoughtful frown. She stood for a moment staring at him, at last nodding slightly, as though in answer to an unspoken question.

"Let's get you in the air," she said.

Aram felt a moment of panic. "I don't know how to ride a dragon."

Calise took his arm, guiding him toward Zandril's back. "She won't let you fall. All you need to do is trust her."

Once again, Aram could feel Zandril's presence in his mind, seeking to reassure him. Aram paused before her, hesitant. She crouched, lowering her body to the ground in an effort to make her back more accessible to mount. Her chest and belly were encircled by leather straps that formed some kind of harness, though there was no saddle.

"You need this," Calise said, and unbuckled the belt she wore, which was dripping with other straps attached to it. She buckled it around his waist then helped him with the other straps that girthed his thighs. "This keeps you on her back. When you get up there, just buckle yourself to her harness straps." She smiled, stepping back.

"Let's go." Vandra motioned him forward. "We're wasting time."

Aram started toward Zandril but paused, quickly realizing that mounting a dragon was a lot different from mounting a horse. Zandril offered her leg, which he used to help pull himself over her back, gritting his teeth as the motion jostled his bruised rib. Once up, he sat for a moment, feeling somewhat light-headed, before searching for the straps to buckle himself into her harness. Zandril lurched as she rose, a motion that send Aram's stomach into a plunge.

"Hang on to her spine," Calise suggested.

Heart pounding, Aram caught a hold of one of the stiff brown spines on the crest of the dragon's neck, tightening his legs around her body the way he would if riding a horse. He could feel her muscles rippling beneath him, the even tide of her breath, and the warmth of her internal fire. The moment he was stable, Zandril moved forward, stalking like a panther toward the mouth of the eyrie.

Vandra turned and jogged across the cavern to where a large brown dragon waited. Without pause, she climbed onto its back, and the dragon rose and sprang forward, bounding toward the mouth of the cave.

Zandril halted, letting the brown dragon surge past them and take a running leap off the end of the terrace. Aram gasped as the dragon unfolded its wings and caught the air, soaring upward above the cliffs.

As soon as Vandra's dragon took flight, Zandril sprang after it. Aram panicked, not ready to be cast off the edge of the cliff, terrified he would fall from the dragon's back. But then he felt a calming presence in his mind as Zandril sensed his fear and tried to reassure him, filling him with the certitude that she would never let him fall.

Reaching the end of the terrace, she cast herself off and dropped downward into the gorge. Aram felt his stomach plunge, icy wind whipping his face and clawing tears from his eyes. Reflexively, he gripped the dragon's back with his legs, hands locked on Zandril's spine. But his terror lasted only a second, for Zandril unfolded her graceful wings and caught the air, breaking from the dive and soaring upward. Within seconds, all of Aram's fear had melted away, leaving him breathless.

He was flying.

Aram smiled in thrilled wonder as they sailed out over the abyss of the gorge, a great fissure between the mountains that ran for miles, opening into a dark crack that looked to have no bottom. Ahead, Vandra's brown dragon soared with neck and wings outstretched, riding the updrafts of air above the canyon. Vandra rode with her body leaned forward, pressed against her dragon's neck. Aram imitated her posture, crouching low. Fear forgotten, he closed his eyes and reveled in the exhilaration of dragonflight.

Dipping a wing, Zandril banked, following the rolling foothills of the mountains and soaring out over a verdant grassland beyond. Below, their shadows raced over the ground beneath them, perfect silhouettes against the waves of tall grass. They followed Vandra's dragon as it dipped lower, until they skimmed the ground, Zandril's wingtips almost parting the grass.

Startled, a flock of large white birds took wing beneath them, flushed by the shadows of the dragons, which must have looked like two great eagles stooping upon them from above. They continued for miles, soaring over the prairie, which unfolded before them like a great, rolling expanse of ocean.

Vandra's dragon slowed its flight, angling toward the ground. Right before they collided with the grass, it reared in the air with a mighty

backstroke of its wings, Zandril following suit. Together, the two dragons alighted on the ground in the middle of the open grassland.

As soon as they landed, people gathered around them, seeming to
appear right out of the grass. It took Aram a moment to realize that what
he had thought were rolling hills were actually sod houses, their walls
and roofs green with new sprouts. The sight made him think of his old
home in the fishing village of Anai, with its sod roof and the goat that
was always getting up there, the one he had to catch practically every
day and bring back down.

Sliding off Zandril's back, Aram paused to stroke her neck, silently
thanking her for the exhilarating flight, an experience he knew he would
treasure amongst his most precious memories. Seeing that Vandra was
already on the ground, greeting the small group of villagers, he hurried
to catch up with her.

The people who came out of the huts to gather around them appeared
to be in mourning. More than a few stood off to the side, clutching each
other with consoling hugs. The two men who approached them first had
faces set with lines of rage, their eyes red with emotion. Vandra brought
her hand up to her brow in greeting, the others returning the gesture.

"Wingmaster Vandra," said the taller of the two, a man with a red
scar on his face and long, unbound hair. "Thank you for coming. It's
awful."

"Who would do such a thing?" demanded an old woman who stood
behind him, her voice cracking with sorrow.

"Find them!" said another man who clutched a tall spear. "No matter
what you have to do. Find the sick bastards who did this!"

"We'll do everything in our power," Vandra assured them, her voice
somehow firm and consoling at the same time. She glanced around at
the small crowd that had gathered around them, raising her hands in
reassurance. "Such a crime will not be tolerated. Whoever did this will
be brought to justice."

To Aram, the magnitude of grief the people of this village displayed
seemed disproportionate, as though their own children had been slain.
He sympathized with them, for he'd been very attached to a few of the

horses about town, especially the old gray carthorse that had belonged to Mister Hanary. But yet, these were still *horses* that had been slain, not people. He did not understand the depths of grief in the eyes of the villagers, and he wondered if there was something he was missing.

He felt Vandra's hand come to rest on his shoulder.

When he glanced up, Vandra nodded in the direction of something behind him, and Aram turned to look.

And froze, his breath hitching in his throat.

Behind him stood two large horses the color of truest gold, their manes and tails impossibly long and lush, the color of spun platinum. A silvery aura shone from their bodies, and in their eyes, Aram saw something truly arresting to behold:

Majesty.

These were not mere horses.

They were Elesium.

The two Elesium stood a distance away and simply regarded them. At the sight of the great horses, the people of the village stopped and stood still, bowing their heads in deference. Even Vandra inclined her head and brought a hand to her chest, her face sad and solemn. Aram followed suit, for he saw how the Elesium transcended the mundane. They were not mere animals, but creatures of purest spirit, just as Esmir had said.

The larger of the two horses, a mighty stallion, tossed its head and started forward, approaching them at a stately pace. The stallion was roughly the size of a destrier, though far more striking. Its graceful neck was proudly arched, and its dark eyes were somber and sorrowful. The Elesium stopped before Vandra and Aram, regarding them intensely through thick strands of its long forelock, which spilled between its ears and fell forward over its face. The stallion stood before them for a long moment, then lowered its head and pressed its forehead against Aram's chest.

Awestruck, Aram stroked the stallion's silken head. As he did, he felt a profound stirring deep within his soul. As with the dragon, he felt an immediate connection with this great animal, and he could feel the magnitude of the Elesium's anger and grief as though they were his own. An image came to his mind, one of dark, sinister creatures swooping out of the night with riders that leapt from their backs. The vision faded, leaving Aram with a choking sadness. The stallion pulled away, turning to

318

stride back toward its companion.

Aram whispered, "They came on dragons. They came from the north."

Exclamations of anger and surprise rose from the people surrounding them. The man who had spoken to Vandra frowned deeply, staring at Aram in dismay. *"Who is he?"*

The Wingmaster set a hand on Aram shoulder. "Dedicant Mandrel, I would like you to meet Aram. I brought him with me to read the strands. Aram is a True Savant."

There was a collective cry from the people surrounding them.

Mandrel exclaimed, "Father of Horses! Will he be a Champion?"

"Only time will tell." Vandra removed her hand from Aram shoulder, gazing down at him thoughtfully. In her eyes, Aram thought he detected a heavy weight of doubt.

Mandrel came toward him and took Aram by the shoulders. His eyes burned fierce, and his face contained the feverish intensity of a zealot. His strong fingers gripped Aram with all the ferocity of grief, and he rasped, "Find them! Find who did this!"

Aram swallowed, not sure how to respond. He glanced at Vandra for direction. When none came, he whispered, "I'll try, sir."

Mandrel nodded, letting go of him. "Come. They will lead us there."

Aram followed Vandra and the old man to the far side of the village, where a small herd of rugged brown horses stood grazing. These looked the same as any other horses Aram had ever seen, though all had long white blazes on their faces and four white socks on their feet. They looked exceptionally well cared for, their manes braided and tied with ribbons, their coats clean and glossy, as though curried regularly.

Without pause, Mandrel leapt onto the back of a stallion that stood bareback and bridleless. Vandra pulled herself onto the back of a grazing horse whose only reaction to its new rider was an irritated swish of its tail. Aram picked out a small mare that seemed gentle enough. Even so, it took him several attempts and much embarrassment to climb onto her back.

Without prompting, their mounts raised their heads and started forward in a single line, trotting past the sod huts of the village, toward where the golden Elesium awaited, silver manes and tails rippling in the wind. As they approached, the two great horses turned and waded into the tall prairie grass. Aram's horse fell in behind Vandra's, while Mandrel's stallion brought up the rear. Aram thought that odd. He would have expected Mandrel to lead, for he knew the way and seemed to have great status among his people. But, apparently, a Wingmaster of the Eyries had more.

They rode for a few leagues out into the open prairie, the breeze waving the tides of grass around them like the swells of an ocean. Large eagles with enormous wingspans wheeled overhead, and every once in a while, a grazing antelope would shoot its head up and freeze at the sight of them.

Eventually, their mounts slowed and lowered their heads. Their gait became laborious, as though some great weight bore down upon them. Ahead, Aram made out the golden forms of six Elesium, all standing together in a circle, each facing the center of the ring.

Vandra's horse stopped well back from them, and she dismounted and stood waiting for Aram and Mandrel. Aram slid off his horse and approached Vandra cautiously. The two great horses who had led them to this place walked forward, heads lowered, to join the others of their kind. Only then did Aram notice that the breeze had stopped and even the sounds of birds had ceased. The air around them was still, suffused with a profound sense of solemnity.

As he walked at Vandra's side toward the circle of Elesium, Aram found himself holding his breath in fearful anticipation of what they would find. When they neared, Vandra drew up with a gasp, her body stiffening. Aram's heart froze, stunned by the horror of the sight that confronted them.

Three Elesium lay slaughtered upon the grass: two adults and a foal. Their brown blood drenched the ground, their bodies ravaged and dismembered. All three had been gutted and the meat stripped from their bones—not by animals, but by the knives of men.

Aram gazed upon the scene with a tremendous sense of loss and dismay, for he understood the terrible significance of what had occurred here. This was far more than the slaying of a few horses; a grave insult had been dealt to the wonder and dignity of the world. This was far more than just murder. This was a travesty, a crime against nature itself.

He sank to the ground and knelt there, head bowed, hands sunken into the blood-wet grass. A desperate impulse came over him, the need to understand what had happened here. It spurred him forward, and he could do nothing but obey. On hands and knees, he crawled forward through the filth and the blood, until he knelt beside the body of the slain stallion. Eyes moist with tears, he leaned forward and hugged the stallion's great, muscular neck. As he did, something deep within him stirred awake.

All around him, the strands of the world came alive and filled his vision like the vibrant threads of a tapestry. He was used to feeling the subtle vibrations in the strands, the kind made by every creature in the world and every circumstance, so elusive that they usually passed beneath his notice. But what had happened here had been like punching a hole through the pattern of the web, ripping the strands right out of it. The magnitude of horror dealt here had left an indelible mark upon the warp and weft of the world.

As Aram stroked the stallion's blood-matted hair, bits of visions started coming to him. Closing his eyes, he looked out upon the moon-fed prairie as though through the eyes of another. What he saw made him cry out in grief and dismay. He clenched his hands into fists around the stallion's mane, forcing himself to suffer the visions without pulling away. For a moment, it was as though he saw through the eyes of the dead stallion, experiencing the last brutal moments of its life as it lay bleeding out in the grass, watching the two creatures it loved more than life murdered before its eyes. Overcome with anguish, Aram threw back his head and let out a wailing moan.

He didn't hear Vandra coming up behind him, but suddenly the Wingmaster was there, crouching at his side. In a trembling voice, he told her, "There were two men. And something else—I don't know what to call it. They came on dragons. They captured one of the foals..."

His voice faltered as a part of him that had slept all his life came fiercely, violently awake. "'Their name is Betrayal!'" he gasped. "They did this! The Disavowed!"

With a sob, he bowed forward over the neck of the stallion, weeping like a child. He barely felt Vandra's hand on his back, the gesture giving him little comfort.

"Thank you, Aram," she said softly. "That's what we needed to know." Standing, she turned to Mandrel. "Ask the Elesium if they would move into the mouth of the gorge for now, where our Wings can watch over them."

Cheeks moistened by grief, Mandrel looked around at the circle of mourning horses. "They will not go. They are proud."

"Try to convince them," Vandra said.

Taking Aram by the arm, she drew him upright. Aram stood with his head bowed, feeling hollow and broken. He wished he could say some words of condolence to the Elesium surrounding them, but he knew that any expression of sympathy would be grossly inadequate. There was only one thing he could say that would make any difference to the great souls gathered there in mourning.

"If I survive the Trials, I'll find them," he swore, though he didn't know how he could fulfill such a promise. He was weak and unskilled, and he knew very little of the world he found himself in. Nevertheless, he was profoundly moved, and he knew he had to do something.

Mandrel came forward and took Aram into his arms, embracing him tightly. "Thank you," he whispered. "You have the heart and spirit of a Champion. I can only pray that you have the strength to match."

Wiping his eyes, Aram muttered, "I hope so too."

The man kissed him on the cheek, then drew away. As Aram stood collecting himself, one of the great horses came forward and pressed its head up against him. He could feel its gratitude and its faith in him, a faith he knew he didn't deserve. When the stallion withdrew, the entire herd turned and walked away, wading back into the tall grass of the prairie.

Aram stared after them, stricken by wonder and horror and quivering in trepidation over the commitment he had just made.

Vandra ordered Aram to return to the training yard that afternoon, despite the deep melancholy that infected him. He wanted to do nothing more than retreat to his bed and lie there the rest of the day.

"It will do you good to be active," Vandra told him sternly, and that was that.

So Aram found himself once again with Master Henrik in the training yard, running laps and hauling buckets of water until his muscles burned. Just when he was so exhausted that he doubted he could lift another pail, Henrik called the students over to gather for a lesson.

Feeling awkward because he had missed the morning training, Aram sat beside Kye, the only one of his classmates he had ever spoken to. He sat uncomfortably, a rock digging into his bottom that he couldn't squirm away from because his classmates had packed so tightly around him. The boy on his right had breath that smelled like sausage, and he couldn't get away from that either. He tried holding his own breath so he wouldn't smell it, but that didn't work very well, so he sat suffering through it the way Esmir had taught him to suffer through peas and potatoes all mashed together.

Master Henrik stood over them, arms crossed, looking fierce and imposing. "When you go into battle, you carry two swords in your belt," he pronounced. "The first sword, you hold in your hands. The second sword you hold here." He bent to prod the chest of one of the boys standing at the edge of the crowd. "It is called resolve. You must be a master of both these weapons, for if you have mastery of one without the other, your enemy will crush you. When you take up a sword, do so with the intent to kill. If you are hesitant, then your grip will be hesitant, and that will be your undoing. When you attack, try to kill with one blow. If your first blow fails to kill, then kill with your second blow. Contrary to what most people think, a swordfight is not a dance. It should be brief, and it should be brutal. And that is all it should be. Who can summarize what I just said?"

Henrik picked a dark-haired girl in the front who shot her hand up quicker than the rest.

"When you fight, fight to win, and hit as hard as you can!" she answered.

Henrik lifted his eyebrows. "Is that what I said?"

There were mutters of no and many shaking heads. The dark-haired girl looked down, face reddening.

"Certainly, you should always fight to win," Henrik explained. "But never try to defeat your opponent by relying on strength. If you rely on strength, you will hit too hard, and then your momentum will carry you off-balance. You'll have to recover, but by the time you do, you'll be dead. Whenever you cross swords, never think about hitting hard—just think about killing. Now, pair up. We're going to spend some time sparring today. After each bout is over, you will trade partners."

Aram looked at Kye, who smiled apologetically. The other students had already been training with weapons for years, while Aram was thoroughly unskilled. What made matters worse was that everyone knew it.

When he stood to collect his practice sword and raised it to defend, Henrik's admonition about resolve flashed through his mind. He knew he didn't have any, so Aram expected to get crushed.

And of course, since that was his expectation, that's exactly what happened. Kye easily pushed his blade aside with the first attack, scoring a hit. Aram reeled back, knowing that if Kye's sword had been sharp, he would be breathing through a hole in his chest.

His next opponent, a large, muscular boy close to his own height, simply reached out and grabbed Aram's sword, ripping it right out of his hands as he stood there in shock. The third boy he was paired with took a little pity on him. When Aram lifted his sword to guard, his foe lowered his own weapon and spent a moment adjusting Aram's posture and grip before driving home a killing blow—or what would have been, had the boy not softened it.

Miserable, Aram left the training ground with his head bowed and shoulders stooped. It had been a horrible day, and all he wanted to do was return to Esmir's quarters and spend the evening quietly studying. Unfortunately, that wasn't to be, for when he arrived at the old man's eyrie, he found that his pallet had already been removed.

"You're moving into the dormitory," Esmir informed him, handing over the extra outfit the tailor had altered for him. "I'll expect you back here in the morning to work on your letters. And don't forget to study," he reminded him, adding Torian's book to the top of the pile of clothing in Aram's hands.

Feeling dejected, Aram left the eyrie and followed corridors carved in intricate stone knotwork back down to the level of the training grounds and found the dormitory where the other novices lived. As he approached the door, a terrible feeling of anxiety came over him. What if his new roommates rejected him? After his performance in the yard, he expected they would. He had no idea where to go or what to do, or even how to find a bed—what if he chose one that was already taken? He paused in front of the door, trying to summon the courage to open it. Before he could, the door opened and a young man his own age nearly careened into him, eyes widening in surprise.

"Oh!"

When Aram didn't react, the young man peered at him in confusion. "What are you doing here?"

"Moving in," Aram said uneasily, unable to look at him. When he seemed even more confused, Aram clarified, "I'm new."

Understanding dawned on the young man's face. "You're the one training to be a Champion, aren't you?"

Embarrassed, Aram nodded wordlessly. The youth's gaze travelled over Aram's gaunt body, and the expression of bewilderment returned.

Aram knew what he must be thinking—the same as everyone else who met him.

"I know," Aram said dejectedly. "I've got a long way to go."

For some reason, the statement caused the youth to laugh—and not in a bad, scornful way, like everyone else who had always laughed at him. To Aram's shock, it was a good laugh, one that lifted his spirits and set him aglow in the realization that he had somehow, unknowingly, said something funny.

"You'll fit right in," the young man said with a grin. "My name's Jeran Hanmere. Come on, I'll show you around. Do you know if you're bunking with the novices or the apprentices?"

"I have no idea," Aram admitted.

Jeran paused for a moment in thought then gave a slight shrug. "I doubt you'll be a novice long. They'll want to confirm you quickly, so you may as well come bunk with us. What's your name?"

"Aram."

He didn't know whether to be happy or terrified at the notion of bunking with youths his own age. On one hand, it was possible he could make new friends. Far more likely, his new roommates would be so far ahead of him in skill that they would think him inept. But the matter was settled, for Jeran was already waving him to follow. Carrying his belongings, Aram traipsed after him down a hallway past boys and girls of various ages—all staring at him—to a room that contained two rows of bunk beds and was occupied by young men his own age, who all stopped what they were doing and looked at him.

Aram halted in the doorway, frozen like a deer staring down the shaft of an arrow. He could feel every gaze drilling into him, leaving wounds that bled his courage dry. He didn't move as a few of the apprentices came forward, appearing to size him up.

"Who's this?" asked a shirtless youth whose cheeks were fuzzy with a premature attempt at a beard.

"This is Aram," Jeran announced. "He's the one training to be a Champion."

Eyebrows flew up, making Aram's spirits drop proportionately.

A dark-haired youth with bold and penetrating eyes came forward with his arms folded across his chest. *"That's a Champion?"*

"Shut up, Iver," Jeran snapped.

Mortified, Aram couldn't even summon a reply. Jeran clapped him on the back, propelling him forward into the room.

"The bunk below mine's empty," he said. "You can take it."

Giving Iver a side-eyed glance, Aram followed Jeran down the nearest line of bunks. At the foot of the beds were two iron-shod chests. With a sheepish grin, Jeran removed his belongings from one chest and stuffed it all into the one next to it—which was already full—and sat on the top to close it. "I kind of took advantage of yours being empty."

Aram stuffed his clothes and Torian's book into the empty chest then turned to face the young men gathering around him. A youth with short auburn hair came forward and shook his hand. "I'm Eugan. They say Calise's dragon let you ride her alone. That's pretty unbelievable."

Aram finally managed a nod, his mood lifting just a bit.

"Is it true you can see in color?" asked a strong youth with a thick shock of hair much lighter than his skin.

Aram nodded. There were mutters, and he looked around to see a few of his new roommates staring at him with fascination in their turquoise eyes.

"That's why they're training him to be a Champion," Jeran said.

"Yeah, well, he'll never survive the Trials," remarked Iver, stripping off his tunic and tossing it onto his bed.

"Shut up, Iver!" Jeran snapped. "You don't know that!"

"Well, it's true." The dark-haired youth gestured at Aram. "Look at him. The wind can blow him over. The last person who entered the Henge came back broken, and from what I heard, he was one of the strongest Wingmasters we've ever had." He looked at Aram with unsympathetic eyes. "I don't understand why Vandra agreed to train him. Either she's damn desperate or damn cruel."

With that, he jerked down a towel that was hanging from his bunk and headed for the door.

"I'm sorry," Jeran said to Aram after Iver had gone. "Don't pay him any mind. He's an ass."

"Iver *is* an ass," agreed Eugan, sitting down on his own bunk. "But he's also right." Looking at Aram, he said, "I don't know what Vandra's game is, but she's not doing you any favors."

Aram saw that the remaining young men in the room were staring at him with looks of concern. He knew that he should be more worried, for Vandra had already told him that his chances of surviving the Trials weren't great, but he figured if the Wingmaster thought he stood no chance at all, she wouldn't have agreed to train him.

"I really don't have a choice," Aram explained, looking at the ground. "Kathrax is winning. He's killing Elesium..."

There was a collective gasp from the group, the young men exchanging glances of dismay and disbelief.

Jeran asked, "Who told you that?"

"I was at Winhome this morning," Aram said. "I promised them I would help. Somehow..."

He could see the flames of ire and the ice of vengeance in the eyes of each of the young men surrounding him, and he knew that every one of them would have made the same promise in his place. Only, they all knew that he had no way of keeping it.

Softly, Jeran asked, "How old are you, exactly?"

"I don't know." Aram shrugged apologetically.

Eugan blew out an exasperated sigh, rolling his eyes.

Jeran let his gaze travel around the circle of young men surrounding them. "What do you say we all pitch in to help him? Maybe together, we can get him up to speed."

"I'm in," said the youth with peach fuzz on his face. When the others gaped at him, he spread his hands. "Somebody's got to do something."

"It's a lost cause, Corley," said Eugan. At Jeran's look of outrage, he snapped, "You all know there's only one way this is going to end. If you really want to help him, then convince him to quit." To Aram, he added, "I'm sorry, but you don't have what it takes to be a Champion." With that, he turned and walked out the door after Iver.

"That's two," muttered Corley.

Jeran stroked his chin. "Are you sure you won't quit?" When Aram shook his head, he nodded, face resolute. "All right, then. I'll help you. How about the rest of you?"

Aram looked around the circle of youths. As his gaze passed over each of them, they all looked away, and not one of them spoke up in answer.

Disheartened, Aram looked at Jeran and tried his best to smile. "Thanks for wanting to help me." Then he bent and started retrieving the possessions he'd stuffed in the chest.

"What are you doing?" asked Jeran.

"I'm going to go bunk with the novices."

"Why?"

Aram didn't answer. He didn't know how to admit that it would be too awkward to live with a group of young men who just wanted to see him quit. At least none of the novices had said anything like that to him.

But as he reached the door, Corley stepped forward and blocked him. "Wait. I'll help you too."

Aram paused.

"I will too," said another apprentice.

"And me."

"Me too."

Aram paused in the doorway, overcome by emotion. Swallowing heavily, he turned around to face the group of youths who, each and every one, had just volunteered to help him. For a boy who had grown up without any friends, to suddenly have an entire room full of friends was overwhelming. Not trusting his own voice, he swallowed heavily and gave a weak smile of gratitude. As he walked back to replace his items in the chest, a few of the young men clapped him on the back.

He spent the rest of the afternoon getting to know his new roommates—all but Iver and Eugan, who didn't return until just before the supper bell rang. When they all filed out of the dormitory, Aram followed them down a long corridor that led into the outskirts of Hearth Home, where there was a large building made of clay bricks surrounded by kitchens. The building contained long rows of tables where the students, younger and older, all sat together for a hearty meal of meat, bread, and vegetables.

Aram picked up the bread and tore a piece off. He was about to start arranging his plate the way he usually did, but then he paused and thought better of it. Resigned, he tore the bread up into pieces and stirred it all together with his vegetables, then smeared the entire mixture on top of his meat. Swallowing his nausea, he dug into the meal, heedless of the stares that were aimed at him.

The next four months went by in a furious jumble of mental and physical training. Aram spent the mornings and evenings with Esmir, learning to read and write and studying an endless series of knots. Then, in the evenings, his new friends took turns working with him in the practice yard with various weapons and fighting techniques. Every day he was stronger and faster than the day before, and eventually Vandra relented and told Henrik to move him out of the class with the novices to join the students his own age. Aram was overjoyed. He was still years behind the rest of his classmates, though not so far behind as before.

When the day came for him to be called before the Council to be confirmed as a member of the fighting Wing—if only a junior member— his friends helped him ready himself for the occasion. They fed him the scripted phrases he'd have to say and taught him the basic manners of standing before such an austere body. Never in his life was Aram so grateful to have friends. Even Iver and Eugan were nice enough to him, though neither would take part in his training, claiming that it went against their morals to help someone commit suicide. Aram didn't like hearing them say that, for it hurt, and he didn't like to think that's what he was doing, but he respected their decisions.

On the day of his Confirmation, he stood in the brown vest the tailor had altered just for him, with a long red sash tied over it, symbolic of the pledge he would make. The way the vest was tied together, with the left flap drawn across the right and clasped at the side, created a space above the belt that was like a large pocket, in which he had tucked the five items his friends had told him he must have in his possession: a small knife, a short willow switch, a piece of bread, a flower, and a folded letter he had been told to write to one of his parents, and he had chosen to address it to his father.

The doors were opened, and Aram swallowed nervously before walking into the chamber, where the members of the Council sat upon rugs arranged in a wide ring. All he could think of was his reception into the Order of Exilari, and that memory continued to haunt him. Strangely, he found it much easier to walk before the Council than it had been to walk into the dormitory for the first time. He felt the gazes of the Council members drilling into him, which made him nervous, but it didn't inspire the visceral fear and embarrassment he felt when singled out before his peers.

"Young Master Aram," said an older woman with a thick braid of gray hair. "So happy to finally make your acquaintance." She gestured him forward. "I'm Luvana, the Dedicant Mother of Skyhome. Come stand before me."

Aram did as she bid, walking between Vandra and another woman to assume his place in the center of the ring. He stood gazing around the circle of people sitting around him, feeling a little like a fish caught in a net. Again, his mind went back to his initiation into the Exilari. This felt like a similar occasion, though far less terrifying. For the most part, the people gathered around him regarded him with looks of casual interest. There were only a couple of adults who fixed him with a less-than-welcoming stare.

"What brings you before this Council, Aram?" the old woman asked.

Just as his friends had instructed him, Aram responded, "I have come to pledge my life and soul to the defense of all that is pure and beautiful."

"And just how do you intend to defend all that is pure and beautiful?" growled a man to his right. "You seem to have a hard enough time defending yourself."

There was a pause of silence, during which even the air seemed to compress.

Shaken by such a malicious opening question, Aram turned toward the brusque man who had challenged him. "You're right. I can't defend myself. But I will give all that I am to defend others."

The man grunted, looking skeptical. Another woman asked, "And how do you intend to survive the Trials?"

Aram had anticipated that question and was prepared to answer it. "I'm already working every waking moment and applying every effort I can."

"And what if your every effort isn't enough?"

Recognizing Vandra's voice behind him, Aram turned to look at her. "Then I guess I'll fail the Trials. But that's not going to stop me from attempting them."

Vandra nodded gravely. "You brought the tokens?"

Aram thrust his hand into the pocket of his vest and removed the three items he had brought with him. There were five bowls set in the center of the circle, one for each item. Into the first bowl, Aram placed the small willow switch. Into the second bowl, he placed the small knife. He placed the remaining items into the last three bowls in no particular order.

"These tokens symbolize the faith that is being placed in you," the Dedicant Mother explained. "The offering of a weapon represents your willingness to fight for our cause. The offering of bread represents your willingness to give back to the world what the world has given to you. The offering of a flower represents the honor you show the Earthmother. The offering of a switch represents your pledge of obedience to your superiors. And the offering of the letter represents your gratitude to your parents, for raising you to be a son of the world."

When all five bowls contained their respective items, they were collected and, one by one, fed to the fire, all except the knife. Aram felt weak as he watched the letter he had written his father blacken and curl, eventually deforming into a gray piece of ash. When the fire had consumed all of his offerings, Vandra rose and retrieved his knife from the bowl, handing it back to him.

"This offering we return to you," Vandra said, "to remind you of the commitments you made here tonight. Wear it always, so that you never forget your purpose."

Accepting the knife back, Aram bowed.

Taking him by the arm, Vandra turned him to face the Council and stated formally, "Your pledge of service has been accepted. Go forth as a Confirmed member of the fighting Wing."

A year and a half had passed since the ill-fated rescue attempt, but Markus still found himself sore in the mornings from the arrow he had taken. As he stood in the yard beside the stables, he worked his shoulder around, trying to stretch some of the stiffness out of it. With his other hand, he stroked the neck of his horse, a dappled gray ambler that was probably worth more than the entire village of Anai. Behind it was tied a pack horse that was loaded with all the supplies he and Sergan would need for their journey to the capital. The stallion kept rubbing its muzzle against him, probably looking for carrots. He didn't have any; all the supplies were loaded in bags on the back of the pack horse.

The sun was hot, for summer was well underway, and even though the bay kept the air at a moderate temperature, the stable yard was hot and dry. He'd been waiting there a half-hour already, with no sign of his traveling companion. Reaching up, Markus gave the stallion a good scratch behind the ear. With nothing better to do, he checked the ropes on the pack horse one more time, making sure the load was secure.

Sergan's laughter echoed across the yard before the man came into view, walking beside his most recent lover, an exceptionally beautiful young woman who worked in the College library. Seeing Markus, Sergan gave his companion a lingering kiss goodbye then made straight for his black courser. Hoisting himself into the saddle, he donned a felted travelling hat and riding gloves.

"Are you coming?" he asked Markus, turning his horse toward the road.

Gritting his teeth, Markus put his foot in the stirrup and swung himself over the back of his horse. He waited for Sergan to go ahead before falling in behind him. The horse he rode eagerly picked up its feet, clopping out of the yard in a swaying, four-beat gait. Sergan said nothing to him as they rode out of the College grounds and into the streets of Karaqor, which bustled with people and carts, loose animals and dirty children. It took another hour to clear the city gates and pass over the ancient stone bridge into the lowlands beyond. There, they headed southward along the edge of the Bosphian Sea past fields of lavender and grain.

The road they followed was known as the Amber Road, an ancient stone-paved Haddian highway that had persisted for centuries as one of the main trade arteries that connected the northern Empire with the southern provinces of Felora and Kartak. The road ran straight through vast swaths of flat lowlands that had been reclaimed from the sea, bordered by sluices and dikes. Every so often, they passed numbered mile markers, tall stones that had been erected alongside the road by the ancient Haddians. They passed other travelers, sometimes in wagons or carts drawn by teams of horses, though most people simply went on foot, clutching walking-sticks and wearing large packs on their backs.

Markus rode in silence throughout the morning, staring at the black horse ahead of him and the swollen saddlebags it carried. The longer he stared at those bags, the angrier he got, for he knew what was in them. Sergan never went anywhere without a good supply of essence and, by the bulge of his saddlebags, he had brought enough to level a city. Markus wondered how much of that essence had been harvested from Aram and came to the conclusion that probably most of it had been. Sergan had kept the reason for their journey to himself but had let slip something about the importance and difficulty of their mission. Which meant that he'd brought along a trove of "the good stuff," as he called it.

The knowledge that Sergan carried bottles of essence distilled from his best friend made Markus physically ill. If he hadn't been convinced of the necessity of the work they did, and convinced of Sergan's importance in it, he would have run the sorcerer through with his sword a long time ago. He rode in silence, eyes pinned on those swelled saddlebags, every mile gouging dull spikes of guilt and hatred a little deeper into his soul.

Eventually, they came to a forested region. There, they turned off the Haddian road and followed a narrow ridgeway along the hilltops. The ridegeway was dry and afforded a commanding view of the area around them, which was probably why Sergan had decided upon that route, for they would have due warning if any brigands intended to waylay them.

Markus's body rocked with his horse's hypnotic gait, his head nodding in time to the creak of his saddle. He found that his eyelids kept slipping lower and lower, and he was starting to have a hard time holding them open. The cool breeze was peaceful, the sun warm and gentle on his skin.

"Do you intend to ignore me the entire trip?"

Markus jerked upright in his saddle, shocked to find Sergan riding beside him. He must have fallen asleep without realizing it.

"If I can," he said.

The sorcerer pursed his lips. "We're going to have to learn to work together. We are partners now, and we're likely to be together for a very long time."

Markus scowled, for he didn't have the words to say how much that bothered him. "That doesn't mean I have to like you."

"No. It doesn't mean you have to like me," Sergan agreed. "As long as you keep me alive, you can despise me all you want. And you will keep me alive, won't you?"

Markus swallowed a bitter lump of anger, for the sorcerer was right. He would fight to the death to preserve Sergan Parsigal's life, because to do any different would put too many other lives in jeopardy.

"Why are we going to Ababad?" Markus asked. "Doesn't the Emperor have Exilari at his disposal?"

Sergan waved an insect out of his face. "He does. But none like us."

"What do you mean, 'like us?'"

"You are the most Impervious Shield the world has seen in a few hundred years, and I'm the most talented sorcerer." Sergan smiled.

"Together, we make one hell of a team. It appears our talents are needed."

"What for?" Markus asked.

"I'm not entirely sure," Sergan admitted. "Something secret. But I'm told that if we're successful with this mission, then there's a good chance I'll be appointed to the Imperial Court."

"And what about me?"

"As my Shield, you'd accompany me to Court. Of course, you'll have to dress the part and look respectable every day. No more letting your whiskers go days between shavings." Sergan smiled sardonically.

Markus grimaced, looking away. The last thing he needed was the sorcerer presiding over his grooming habits. With a laugh, Sergan kicked his horse forward, resuming his place at the front of their small column.

Markus rode, fuming, his stomach roiling from the same oily sickness he felt whenever he was forced to interact with Sergan. It was starting to sink in that he might very well be forced to serve a life sentence at this man's side. The more he thought about it, the more nauseous he became. It was a dilemma that occupied his mind throughout the whole of the afternoon, until evening finally descended upon them.

The shadows were lengthening as they approached Maran's Ferry, a small town on the banks of the Namsby that was the only river crossing in a hundred miles, so it saw a fair amount of trade. Because of that, the town offered a few good inns, including one that catered to a higher class of traveler.

Even though it was after sunset, the guards at the town gate let them by without question, for they took note of the Exilari insignias on their mantles. The streets of Maran's Ferry were narrow and muddy and smelled heavily of smoke. By the time they drew to a halt in the inn's yard, Markus was ready for a bed. He dismounted and waited while Sergan paid a stable boy to put their horses and baggage up for the night. Then he followed Sergan across the yard and up the wooden steps to the inn, a river rock structure with soda-lime glass windows and a wood shingle roof. After such a long ride, his legs felt spongy and foreign, but he was grateful to be able to stretch them after so many hours in the saddle.

Sergan opened the door for him, letting him into the inn's great room, which had several long tables arranged on a rush-strewn floor. They found the proprietor in the back, bringing up fresh potatoes from the cellar. All it took was one look at Sergan's mantle to have the man fawning over them, promising his best cheese and beer and mattresses filled with fresh straw.

"One or two rooms?" the innkeeper asked.

"Two rooms," Sergan said, passing the man a silver Exilari coin.

Markus fled up the wooden stairs to the second floor, where he found his own room, which was outfitted with a strongbox and a bed. He slipped his coin purse into the strongbox then flopped his exhausted body down on the bed. For long minutes, he just lay there, staring up at the wooden rafters of the ceiling and scratching at the fleas that crawled up out of the mattress to bite him. He figured he could go downstairs and get a meal at any time, but he would wait as late as he could in hopes of avoiding Sergan.

He stared at the bedroom door longingly, wishing he could open it and run. No one would stop him if he did. Sergan wouldn't know he was gone till morning and, since he was Impervious, there was no way he could track him down and bring him back.

But Markus knew he couldn't do that.

Wherever there was a rupture, people died. Sometimes many people. That's why they needed the Exilari. And that's why the Exilari needed him.

He despised his life and he despised himself for living it.

Regardless, it was his duty to endure.

Markus slept restlessly, for the hay in the mattress wasn't fresh and was filled with vermin. There were rats in the rafters. He could hear them scratching and gnawing all night. He rose early and went downstairs, hoping to get the packhorse loaded before Sergan came out.

As he crossed the yard, his attention was drawn to a young woman operating a sweep to draw water from the inn's well. The sweep was made from a tall post to which a horizontal pole was fixed, one end weighted. The woman lowered the bucket down into the well, using the counterweight on the sweep to help draw it back up. When she had filled two large pails, she picked them both up and started lugging them across the yard toward the inn's back door.

Markus jogged up to her, bending to relieve her of the weight of her burden.

She let him take the buckets with a grateful smile. "Thank you so much!"

The woman led him into the inn and across the great room to the kitchen in the back. There, he set the pails down.

"That was very nice of you," the woman said. "I didn't think Exilars stooped to hauling water."

Markus grinned, amused by her statement. "The day I think I'm above hauling water is the day I should probably quit the Order."

Looking at her face, he realized she was much younger than he had first thought, perhaps even younger than himself. Her eyes had a mischievous glint in them that caught and held his attention.

She smiled, motioning for him to follow her out the door. "What's your name, Exilar?"

"Markus. Markus Galliar."

Leading him back out into the great room, she offered him her hand. "Lyra. Pleasure to meet you."

He shook her hand awkwardly, the action bringing a smile to her lips.

"So, what exactly does an Exilar do, other than hunt people?" she asked.

Markus's buoyed mood sank deeper than the ground. Suddenly, he wanted to be somewhere else. Anywhere else.

"We try to keep people safe," he muttered. "From…things."

He turned to go, desiring nothing more than a hasty exit.

"Things?"

He turned back around, nodding glumly. "Things."

He wanted to explain to her that he wasn't a child-torturing monster. But he was forbidden from talking about the Order, so people like this girl were left to think about him what they would.

"Can you elaborate on these 'things' you keep me safe from?" she asked.

Markus shook his head. "Unfortunately, no. I can't. It's kind of ridiculous, but there it is."

"Galliar!"

Markus winced at the sound of Sergan's voice.

"Time to go!" the Sorcerer called across the great room.

Lyra looked from Markus to Sergan then back to Markus with a grin.

"Well, it was a pleasure meeting you, miss," Markus said sheepishly.

"And it was a pleasure meeting you, Exilar. Look for me the next time you come through this way. You've managed to spark my curiosity."

Markus grinned. "I will."

Now he didn't want to go. Hating Sergan and the Exilari and the entire Abadian Empire, Markus walked across the room, glancing back for one last look at Lyra before the door closed behind him. Feet crunching on the gravel of the yard, he followed Sergan toward the stables.

"Well, it seems you're already turning out to be an improvement over my last Shield," Sergan commented. "If you can get the women to come to you, I'll spend less money on whores."

"All I did was haul water for her," Markus said defensively.

Sergan chuckled as he opened the stable door. "That's the problem with women. They all want men to do something for them."

A ram took the cloth Jeran tossed him and used it to wipe the sweat
off his face. Looking over the edge of the cliff, he could see the rooftops of Hearth Home far below. They had run half the Gambit, but they
still had the other half to go, and his legs and lungs were already burning. It was heartening to see that Jeran was just as exhausted as he was.
The youth was bent over with his hands on his knees, panting hard to
recover his breath. After a year and a half of climbing the long staircase
from Hearth Home to the Henge, Aram could finally keep pace with the
other apprentices in his class.

"Ready?" Jeran panted.

Aram took a gulp from his waterskin. "Ready."

They started up the second half of the long staircase. Aram took the
stairs two at a time, his hamstrings screaming in protest. He knew he
would be worthless tomorrow, but at the moment, he didn't care. The
only thing he could focus on was reaching the top of the Heights.

"Almost there," Jeran gasped.

There were still a couple hundred more stairs ahead of them. Gritting
his teeth, Aram did his best to ignore the pain, determined not to fall
behind. The world seemed to narrow around him, compressing until it
encompassed only the next step above him. He was just about to give in
to his body's aching need for rest when a conical marker on the edge of
the staircase told him there were only fifty more steps to go. Summoning
the last of his endurance, he pushed on, at last crossing the threshold at

the top of the stairs and there collapsing to the ground in a gasping ball of jelly.

"We made it," he panted, rolling onto his back and staring straight up into the sky.

He wanted to whoop with joy, but he was too tired, so he closed his eyes and smiled. Eventually, Jeran rose to his feet and offered his hand to help him up. Grateful, Aram accepted the help and stood swaying on legs that felt insubstantial.

"Now to get down." Jeran wheezed a laugh.

Aram groaned. He glanced around and saw the Portal Stones of the Henge across from them. The sight solidified his resolve. He couldn't give up. He had to push himself as hard as he could, and then press further. He had no choice.

"Let's go," he said with fresh determination, and started toward the stairs that would lead them back down to Hearth Home.

"Wait for me!" Jeran gulped and rushed to catch up.

The journey down wasn't as bad as the race up the cliff had been, but it was still brutal. By the time they arrived at the bottom of the long staircase, Aram's clothing was drenched with sweat—literally dripping. He stumbled into the bath after Jeran, leaving a trail of clothes behind him on the floor. He lay in the heated water until his muscles felt some-what capable of supporting his weight again, then picked up his soggy garments and retreated to the dormitory to find fresh clothes.

The only shirt he had clean was a sleeveless vest, which he pulled on over his head, then scrubbed his fingers through his shoulder-length hair. Figuring he was somewhat presentable, he made for the door, in-tent on going up to Esmir's eyrie for another look at an illuminated text on knots that the old man had salvaged from some dark corner.

As he passed by Jeran, the youth clapped him on the back. "You're getting there!"

Aram smiled and nodded, for he was. At least in some ways. He still had a long way to go with wrestling and weapons, although he was proving to have some skill at archery. He could read as well as any, and he was blessed with a memory for words and facts, so studying was not something he really had to apply himself to. If anything was going to hold him back, it was his lack of martial skills—or lack of confidence, although even that was improving.

Walking down the corridor, Aram stopped at the sound of his name. Turning, he found Calise behind him, rushing to catch up. He couldn't help grinning when he saw her face. He didn't get to see her much, but whenever he did, he could feel his spirits lift.

"You look exhausted!" she said, catching up to him.

"I am," he admitted. "Henrik's been running us ragged. What are you doing down here?"

He hardly ever saw Calise on the lower levels. She spent most of her time in the infirmary when she wasn't flying with Zandril to the various towns on her healing circuit. She was carrying a leather satchel that hung from her shoulder by a long strap that looked heavy. She patted it, grinning.

"Books," she said. "For Esmir." Then she thought about it. "Actually, they're probably for you."

"Really?" Aram asked excitedly. Since he'd started studying with Esmir, he had developed a love of books. "Want me to take them to him? I'm heading up there right now."

"Sure, you can take them. But how about I walk with you?"

Glad to have her there, he relieved Calise of the satchel, which proved to be heavier than it looked. Aram wondered what kind of books it contained—they felt more like stone tablets.

"Is that *muscle* I see?" Laughing, Calise reached out and squeezed his arm.

"I guess it is." Aram grinned sheepishly as he walked with her down the hallway. In truth, his body had filled out so much that he had grown out of several sets of clothes since the first ones she had helped him purchase.

"You look really different from the first time I saw you," Calise told him with a cursory glance. "You're like a different person. You've really come out of your shell."

Aram frowned, not understanding. "I've never had a shell."

Calise laughed and clapped him on the arm. "You're so funny, Aram! I love your sense of humor. So, how's training going?"

"Exhausting. And frustrating," he admitted. "I'm working as hard as I can, but I'm still not sure it's enough."

Calise gave him a smile of encouragement. "It will come. You still have time."

"Let's hope it's enough." He had been working so hard, but he still wasn't at the level of his classmates. And to succeed at the Trials, he would have to surpass them. By far.

Calise's face grew serious, and they walked in silence for a while. At length, she asked, "Do you ever get scared that you'll fail the Trials?"

"I do," Aram admitted. "I'm terrified of letting everyone down."

For just a second, her lips compressed, but then she raised her chin and gave him a reassuring smile. "You won't let anyone down. There's no way you're going to fail. I know it."

"How can you know it?" Aram asked.

"I just do."

He nodded absently, wondering how she could be so sure when he wasn't. Maybe it was part of her Talent, like healing. Maybe she could read the strands around him. He hoped so. It made him feel better that Calise thought he had a chance.

From ahead down the corridor came the sound of shouts.

Aram glanced at Calise, but before he could react, a group of people rushed past them down the corridor, dodging around them. Alarmed, Aram pressed his back up against the wall and turned to Calise.

"What's going on?" he gasped.

"I don't know."

Taking him by the arm, she hurried him down the corridor in the direction of the stairs. He jogged up the stairs behind her despite his legs' screaming protest, all the way up to the Southern Eyrie. There, they crested the staircase into a bedlam of windriders scrambling into their armor and gear as the Wings prepared to take flight.

Calise gasped, "I'm sorry, I have to go!"

Aram understood. Whatever was happening couldn't be good. It looked like Skyhome was preparing for war.

"Stay safe," he muttered, though she was already gone, rushing across the eyrie to the alcove she shared with Zandril. He wondered what was happening but didn't dare stop anyone to ask.

"Aram!"

He turned to see Vandra coming toward him, her face grave. "Where the hell have you been?"

Aram opened his mouth to respond, but the Wingmaster talked right over him. "There's an army from Araghar headed south, and the Eldenwood's on fire. I need you to come with us."

"Me? Why?" Aram gasped.

"Because there might be people who need defending in a way that only you can defend them."

Aram froze, feeling suddenly stunned. He wasn't ready for something like this. He had no idea how to use magic, not really, at least not at this level. He wanted to tell Vandra he couldn't do it, but he was too afraid to say the words. One look at the Wingmaster's implacable face sealed his silence. They both knew that if others were in danger he may—just *may*—be able to do *something*. And that scared him too.

"You'll ride on Narath, if he'll have you," Vandra said, propelling Aram forward with a hand on his back. "His rider's taken ill and can't fly."

Aram followed Vandra, having a hard time keeping up with the Wingmaster's long strides. She led him toward a large alcove on the far wall, where a dark gray dragon lingered protectively over a young man who lay sweating on a cot. When they neared, the man lifted his head, looking pale and flustered. The dragon glowered at them, its dark pupils contracting.

"This is Osgan and Narath," said Vandra.

The rider nodded a weary greeting.

The dragon tilted its head, peering down at Aram with a reticent look. Uncertain, Aram moved forward, extending his hand toward the dragon's glistening snout. Narath lowered his head, accepting his touch, allowing Aram to set his palm upon the smooth scales of his face. When he felt the dragon's mind meet his own, Aram stiffened, for Narath was a much stronger presence than Zandril, instantly commanding his awe and attention. He stood for a moment locked in an acknowledgment of mutual evaluation as the dragon accustomed itself to him, and him to it. He could feel its wary hesitance give way to curiosity. He opened himself further and let Narath probe his mind, feeling the dragon's curiosity yield to a deep and solemn respect.

Aram lowered his hand slowly, staring up into the dragon's face in startled wonder. For a moment only, he had seen himself through the dragon's eyes. Instead of a weakling, Narath recognized in him an ancient and eldritch strength, greater than any he had ever sensed in a mortal. Aram took a step back, feeling overwhelmed and humbled.

"He'll carry me," he whispered.

The Wingmaster lifted Osgan's arming jacket off the floor and held it up for Aram. "Turn around."

Aram did as she bid with a glance at Narath. He put out his arms to his sides, allowing Vandra to draw the padded jacket around him, securing it with laces. It was followed by a brigandine breastplate and a scaled skirt, which Vandra buckled in place with silent efficiency. Aram looked down at himself then glanced at Osgan to thank him, but the young rider had fallen asleep.

Vandra thrust Osgan's sword into Aram's hands. "Stay on my wing," she ordered, handing him an iron helm. "Understand?"

Aram nodded, knowing that he could trust Narath to obey the Wingmaster's command. Watching Vandra stride hurriedly away, he pulled the helm over his head and buckled the chinstrap. Then he looked up at the dragon.

Responding to his silent question, Narath knelt and swept a wing back for him to mount. Aram accomplished the act much easier than he had with Zandril, for his body was much stronger now. As soon as he strapped himself into the riding harness, Narath lurched upright and stalked forward toward the mouth of the eyrie. He spread his dark wings, shaking them slightly, as though stretching from sleep. They waited on the terrace for Vandra's Ragath to take wing, then Narath kicked off from the edge and dove after them into the canyon.

Startled, Aram clung to the dragon's spines as they plunged straight down the cliff before leveling off seconds later. Soaring steadily above the abyss, the dragon drew abreast of Ragath, while the rest of the Wing took up position behind them, two dozen dragons flying in branching formations.

Aram rode leaning forward over Narath's neck, thrilled and terrified at the same time. They crested the rim of the canyon and climbed higher, sweeping over the ridges of the surrounding mountains. They were flying northward, toward the opposite side of the continental divide with the grasslands at their back. Ahead, Aram made out a brown haze on the horizon, though it took him seconds to realize that the haze was actually smoke spread out in a thick, dark layer, reinforcing his sense of urgency. He didn't know what kind of land lay ahead of them but, somehow, he could sense its need.

As they soared over the flanks of the mountains, a great, dense forest appeared in front of them, stretching into the distance until it was veiled by smoke. Aram let his eyes rove over the deep green of the canopy as they flew over it. Converging on their position were flights of dragons that had set out ahead of them from Skyhome's other eyries, flying in elongated, V-shaped formations.

Ahead of them, from out of the forest canopy, rose an enormous tree, taller than all the rest, its branches stretching over the surrounding grove like a protective mother. It was toward that tree that Vandra angled her dragon, the rest of the Wing following. Aram wondered if Vandra aimed to land near the tree, though he didn't know how they could possibly find a landing place amidst such dense growth. But as soon as his mind formed the question, it was answered. On the other side of the great tree was a ridge of rocky hills that rose above the surrounding forest.

Vandra's brown dragon banked toward it, spreading his wings and arresting his flight, coming to land on the crest of the hill. Narath alighted next to him, the others setting down along the ridgeline. Vandra slid immediately from Ragath's back, and Aram followed her to the ground, striding forward as the other members of the Wing collected around them.

Within seconds, a group of men and women emerged from the forest, clothed in leather and suede, their garments ornamented by feathers. They had the proud look of the Auld, brown-skinned and brown of hair, though they were not as stout as their mountain-bred kinsmen, and more willowy than even the people of the grassland.

Vandra strode toward them as they approached, greeting the first man who came toward them by raising her fingers to her brow. "Harak! What's the situation?"

Harak stopped and regarded them with the haunted eyes of a man who had looked upon the face of death. The sight of him set Aram instantly on edge. He swept his gaze down the line of people who had come to stand before them and saw the same look in many of their eyes.

"An army from Araghar descended upon us, thousands strong," said Harak. "They brought fire to the forest! Void walkers and therlings supplement their ranks."

Hearing that, Vandra's glower deepened. Her gaze turned to the north, where thick gray smoke billowed from the forest in the distance. She stared at the churning smoke for a long while, her gaze seemingly lost in it.

"Darman! Fax!" she called in a ringing voice, sending two scale-armored warriors scrambling toward her. "Get the Wings in the air. Don't attack head-on. Come in high and fast from the north." As the men sprinted back to their dragons, Vandra turned to Aram.

"Go with them." She pointed at the forest folk.

"And do what?" Aram asked.

"The Great Tree's an Anchor. Don't let it burn."

Aram glanced toward the enormous tree that dominated the forest, rising far higher than any other tree around it. It was so big...it towered hundreds of feet like a colossal sentinel, its trunk a dark contortion of burls and furrows. Like the Elesium, it had a pure, silvery aura that was so vibrant it took his breath away.

"That's an Anchor?" he asked, staring in awe at the Tree. "I don't understand."

Vandra gave him a sideways glance, as though she couldn't believe he was so ignorant. "The Anchors uphold the Veil. We can't let it fall."

Aram glanced back at the Tree. It looked strong, certainly, but strong enough to hold up the entire Veil? He didn't know exactly what that meant, only that it sounded a lot like holding up the sky. He pressed his lips together, his mind grappling with the logic of it.

Vandra turned and started away, but Aram called after her, "I don't know what to do—"

"Do everything you can!"

Then she was gone, and Aram brought his hands up to shield his face from the powerful gust of wind created by Ragath's wings as the dragon vaulted into the air. The rest of the Wing rose after them into the sky, climbing steeply and angling toward the north. Aram watched them go, feeling smaller and weaker as the dragons diminished in the distance, leaving him alone with an impossible task. He glanced at Harak, who regarded him with a withering look. Then he turned in panic to Narath and felt the dragon's mind press against his.

He felt helpless. He was just a weakling boy with a love of knots. Nothing more.

The look in the dragon's eyes seemed to disagree. *No*, it seemed to be saying. *You are far more.*

A ram stood on the rocky outcrop, watching Vandra and her flight of dragons take to the sky. To the north, a great swath of the forest burned. He could see the orange glow of the fire, for its flames leaped high over the canopy. Ash rained down around them like snow, coating the ground in gray powder, and the smoke was so thick, it burned his throat. Even though the fire was still in the distance, it looked like it was advancing quickly.

Feeling confused and overwhelmed, Aram turned to Harak. "I don't know what I'm supposed to do."

The man did not appear to hear him. He was staring at the fire, eyes distant and sorrowful. His hair was long, worn in thick ropes reminiscent of the limbs of the Great Tree. The skin of his face reminded Aram of tree bark, and his visage was both grave and resolute.

Turning away from the fire, he waved Aram forward. "Come."

Aram left Narath with a last, regretful glance and followed Harak back toward his waiting people. Together, they turned and headed down the rocky hill. Entering the forest, Aram found himself suddenly transported to a different world. The air darkened and cooled dramatically, filling with moisture and a thick, verdant aroma. A fine mist sprinkled his face, and motes of dust circulated in the angled rays of light streaming down to dapple the forest floor.

The footpath they followed was little more than a deer trail, and Harak's people followed it in silence. The air thickened the further they went into the grove, taking on a musty odor that spoke of patience and age. It was almost as though he could sense the presence of the grove through his feet, as though the trees themselves had souls that stirred around him. It was a surreal feeling that would have normally set him at ease, had he not realized the danger that loomed ahead of them, threatening all that was wondrous about this place.

They reached an overgrown thicket completely sheltered from the sun by overhanging branches. The canopy solidified above them, soaring upward and vaulting overhead, until they walked beneath an enormous dome created by interlaced branches and leaves. Thousands of lanterns dangled from above, lighting the bowl of the dome, which was dominated by the enormous trunk of the Great Tree that rose from its center, its roots radiating outward like sprawled legs. All around the rim of the dome were masses of huts that looked to have been built of mud and woven vines. Each hut was covered in foliage, with warm light glowing from within. People were about, mostly gathered along the shore of a pond that ringed the enormous trunk of the Tree.

Aram stared upward at the verdant dome, at the lanterns casting a restful, whimsical light over the hollow, and realized that their glow was not produced by oil or candle flame. Instead, they emitted a steady cool light that didn't waver or gutter. Glancing around the dome, Aram saw that the same cool light emanated from deep within the waters of the pond, the mud around it glistening as though coated with silver dust.

There was magic here. The kind of passive magic that Esmir had spoken of, born of the earth itself. It was an ancient and potent magic, different than the kind he knew. It had nothing to do with knots or threads in air, and everything to do with the ageless spirits of the trees and the nourishing vitality of the forest loam. It was the same kind of magic he had sensed in the Elesium, and it permeated the entire forest and the ground beneath it.

"What is this place?" he breathed, lost in a daze of wonderment.

"It is Edylwylde," answered Harak. "The Heart of the Grove."

Walking to the edge of the pond, Aram bent and scooped up a handful of water. The water shimmered in his hand, casting its silvery light in thin ripples over his flesh.

"What kind of magic is this?" he asked.

"The pool is a Wellspring, the lifeblood of the earth," Harak answered in a sad, strained voice, gazing down at the water in Aram's palm. "It has great healing properties."

Aram tilted his hand and let the water spill back into the pond then glanced around at the people gathered around its shore: mostly women and children. They were working feverishly to fill pitch-lined cannisters and ceramic amphorae with the water from the pool.

"You're going to carry it all out?" asked Aram in disbelief.

"No. We are gathering the sacred water to fight the fire. Every drop is equal to ten pails of mundane water. Even so, our efforts are not likely to be enough."

"Why don't you evacuate?"

Harak looked at Aram as though he voiced blasphemy. "We are Servants of the Grove. We cannot abandon our duty. We are linked indelibly to this place. If the Heart of the Grove perishes, then so do we."

Aram turned slowly, taking in the ephemeral dome that sheltered the forest's Heart. This was a sacred place. He could feel the nearness of the Mother, her essence suffusing everything around him. Raising his hand, he saw that his palm still glimmered faintly from the touch of the Wellspring water.

"I won't let it burn," he whispered then realized what he had just done. Once again, he had made a promise that he doubted he could keep. He had made such a promise to the Elesium, and in doing so had done them a great disservice. If the water of the Wellspring wasn't enough to hold the fire at bay, then there was little his knots of aether could do.

A woman approached them, walking around the perimeter of the pool, carrying a wooden pail. Her hair was worn in ropes similar to Harak's, though they were longer and ornamented, hanging down her back in a shimmering waterfall of tinkling rings and medallions. She was older, but as Harak's skin resembled the bark of the ancient Tree, hers was more mottled, reminiscent of a sycamore. She had a strong aura that shimmered like the light of the Wellspring.

"This is Shinota." Harak indicated her with his hand. "She is our Dedicant Mother, the wisest of us all."

Aram bowed before her, unsure whether that was the proper greeting. She came forward and, setting down her pail, took his face in her hands. Leaning very close, she peered directly into his eyes. The strength of her presence set him off-balance, and he wanted desperately to look away, but she held his gaze firmly. He was forced to look directly into her eyes, unable to break away.

Releasing him, she stepped back with a slight gasp. "Yours is an elder soul," she muttered. "What color am I?"

"Silver," Aram whispered. "Like the Wellspring."

She smiled deeply, proudly. Turning to the others, she proclaimed:

"To us has come one who sees in color, a son of Raginor. Tell me, what is your name, and why are you here?"

Aram thought of the vow he had so rashly sworn. Licking his lips, he glanced at the sacred Tree. "My name is Aram Raythe, and I'm here to do everything I can."

Shinota nodded, looking satisfied. She bent, reclaiming her pail, then returned to the pool to continue filling amphorae with water from the sacred spring.

Aram looked around, feeling suddenly lost. Looking from Shinota back to Harak, he asked, "Do you have a pail for me, so I can help?"

The old man smiled and nodded.

Aram worked with the people of the Grove throughout the remainder of the day, filling cannisters with water and using them to soak the earth in the area surrounding the Heart of the Grove. He lugged heavy amphorae most of the day, thanking the gods for all the effort he had put into his physical training. Eventually, when the forest around the Heart had been drenched with Wellspring water, the people of the Grove turned their energies to stockpiling it instead. He left them then, returning to the rocky hill to check on Narath.

He emerged from the Grove into a world whipped by wind and

smothered by smoke and falling ash. Long before he reached the crest of the hill, he was coughing so hard, he could barely breathe. He found Narath agitated, his wings mantled, the light of fires blazing in his eyes. Seeing him, Aram broke into a run and clambered onto the rocks, where he stopped at the dragon's side and stared down at the horror that confronted them on the other side of the hill.

What he saw was a world engulfed by hell.

Wind-scourged flames flared into the sky as thick gray smoke poured from the forest nearby. Glowing embers rained down around them, hot enough to hurt when they landed on his skin. The forest beyond the hill had been decimated—the flames were almost to the bottom of the cliff, and everything behind them had been reduced to smoldering char and glowing embers. In the distance, Aram could make out the silhouettes of dragons against the darkening sky, adding dragonfire to the carnage as they engaged the army of the enemy. He searched the sky for Vandra and Ragath, but at that distance, it was impossible to tell one dragon from the other.

Beside him, Narath snarled in pain as a large ember fell upon his wing.

"Go!" Aram ordered, stepping back and giving him room to take flight.

But the dragon didn't budge, instead lowering his body for Aram to mount.

"No." He shook his head. "You have to go! I'm staying here."

He could feel the dragon's forceful protest, and he knew that, under no condition, would Narath leave him behind. Frustrated, Aram didn't know what to do, or if it was even possible to argue with a dragon. He moved forward until he was standing at Narath's side and, reaching out, set his hand on his long, sinuous neck.

Immediately, the dragon's feelings came into acute focus, almost as though they shared one mind. Aram thought back to his experience within the Heart, of his pledge to do everything he could. He tried to assure Narath that he was not defenseless, though the dragon could feel his self-doubt. In the end, an agreement was struck between the two of them, one that seemed more like a stalemate. Narath would take to the skies to avoid the flames but would linger in the area above the forest.

When Aram withdrew his hand and stepped back, Narath lowered his head, fixing Aram with his commanding gaze.

"I know," Aram said. "I'll be careful."

Seemingly satisfied, the dragon pushed off from the outcrop and took to the air, spiraling upward into the sky, wings glowing red and translucent in the light of the flames. Coughing into his sleeve, Aram sprinted back down the hill, taking the narrow path back through the trees toward the forest's Heart.

He arrived to bedlam. The people of the Grove were rushing to the defense of the perimeter they had established, for they knew the flames were advancing quickly. Aram stood watching on the margin of the turmoil, unsure of what he should be doing—or if there was anything he *could* do.

As the shadows deepened and night fell, the only light was the cool glow of the lanterns overhead and the silvery blue light of the Wellspring that wandered in sinuous ripples over the interior of the dome. A deep silence settled over the hollow as the air filled with smoke.

Aram stood beside the glowing pool, staring in the direction of the oncoming blaze, his pulse thrumming in his ears. His body was locked rigid, his mind was scrambling to figure out how a few diagrams of knots in an old book could save a people and their forest from death by burning. Shivers of desperation trembled his skin, for no matter how hard he grappled with the problem, he did not understand the power within him. It was one thing to tie a slingstone hitch around a rock and make it float. It was another to stop a wildfire goaded by the wind.

When the crackling roar of the flames howled in his ears, and the orange light of the blaze overcame the glow of the lanterns, he knew it was time to act, to do *something*, even though he knew little more of magic than he'd known when he lifted Markus's rock. As Aram looked around at the people he was failing, desperation took hold of him. He had told them he would do everything he could. But, in the end, he feared that the only thing he could do was die with them.

"It's time."

He turned to find Shinota standing behind him.

"I don't know what to do," he whispered, his lips trembling.

"No one does, in times such as these. Just do what you can."

He nodded and clenched his fists, watching her walk away through a shower of glowing embers.

And then the fire was upon them, spreading over the vault of the dome.

Flaming leaves and tendrils of vine rained from the canopy. The fire roared like a ferocious beast and the sounds of screams filled Aram's ears. He stood paralyzed, gazing upward as the fire devoured the dome, watching the world turn to flames around him. Within moments, the entire dome was engulfed, heating the air around him to broiling.

As Aram gazed upward at the sight of his impending doom, the sound of the fire suddenly quieted in his ears and the air around him seemed to lose its heat. He looked upon the devastation around him as though from a distance, feeling aloof and apart from it. A calmness crept over him, releasing the stranglehold terror had on him. When he looked back up at the flaming dome, it wasn't the fire he saw…it was the beautiful tendrils of aether surrounding the flames.

He knew what to do.

Raising his hands, Aram started weaving the air. He pulled two long threads of aether out of the fabric of the world and started forming an intricate knot, passing the working end through the bight of another thread, tucking it under, then weaving it together with the next knot, which he used to anchor his creation to the trunk of the Great Tree. Then he formed more knots in quick succession, each coming faster and easier, until he was working dozens at a time, each shimmering and glowing before him in an expanding network of filaments. When he was done, he pulled the last knot tight and let the enormous web of aether rise and seal itself to the interior of the dome.

Then he spilled every knot at once, creating an enormous tangle that sucked all that energy away, draining the heat from the surrounding fire and funneling it back—toward himself. With a cry, he diverted all that furious heat into the Wellspring, which spattered and hissed, its waters churning violently for only a moment before returning to its previous, silver calm. Above, the canopy steamed as though doused with water, damaged but intact.

But it wasn't enough. He had protected the dome, but the fire still raged around it, consuming the Grove, a hungering monster that could never be satiated. Even from where he stood, Aram could feel the intensity of the inferno.

Before he knew what he was doing, he was running across the dome and plunging into the forest beyond, pressing forward into the blaze consuming the thicket. He staggered as far as he could go, shielding his face from the roiling heat, until the intensity of the blaze was too great to stand. The inferno around him howled like a ravaging monster, breathing terrible gusts of searing wind that assaulted him from all sides, savaging the canopy and boring into the great hearts of the trees, reducing them to coals. With a motion of his hands, Aram wove a dense blanket of aether, slamming it down over the canopy of the Grove. The glowing fabric smothered the flames beneath it and drank in their heat. But he didn't know where to channel all that energy, how to dissipate it, for the Wellspring was behind him. He needed a place to put it all; the heat had to go somewhere. Not knowing what else to do, he released it into the air.

He sliced every crossing at once, releasing all the rage of the fire into the air above the forest, where his skein unraveled in violent streaks of light that threaded the night sky like a murderous aurora.

Watching the light slowly dwindle in fading sparks, Aram started forward but then staggered, a heady dizziness overcoming him. The amount of magic he had just woven had its price, and it was taking a toll on him. He was very familiar with the sensation of being depleted of essence. Weakened, he stumbled forward, nevertheless, walking the perimeter of the Grove, tearing the flames from their roots and flinging them into the sky until the night glowed as though it were dawn.

The further he walked, the weaker he became, until his body quaked and the flaming forest with its vicious heat seemed to writhe and lurch around him. Sweat ran like rainwater into his eyes, and his body felt terribly cold, as though he were adrift in a frozen sea. Still, he pressed forward, even as his vision dimmed, and every step he took turned into a stagger. At last, he stumbled and collapsed, falling to his knees and roughing the palms of his hands.

"Here! Drink this!"

Looking up through watery eyes, Aram saw Shinota crouched beside him. She took him in her arms and cradled him against her, bringing to his lips a container filled with liquid that glowed with a silvery light. He tilted his head back and gulped the Wellspring water as though it were lifeblood. When he had drained the container, he felt a warm, tingling sensation wash over his body, clearing his vision and steadying his hands.

Gasping his thanks, Aram pushed himself to his feet and started forward again. The water had invigorated him, pulled him back from the brink, but he was still exhausted, body and mind. When he stumbled, Shinota caught him and held him up, taking his arm and walking him forward, stabilizing him as he knotted the air and calmed the rage of the fire. He wove his net before him, casting it out like a fisherman, reaping a harvest of flames.

At some point, he must have fainted, for he found himself lying on his back and staring straight up into a sky heated to glowing. When he tried to rise, hands clasped him and held him down. He was vaguely aware of being carried, but then that sensation, too, faded. The last thing he remembered was a cold wash of water moving over him, as though he floated on a calm and patient sea that filled him with a soothing comfort, bearing him away on gentle tides of slumber.

Markus looked out from the second-story balcony of the villa he shared with Sergan upon the shadowy rooftops of Ababad. From where he stood, he had a view of the high towers of the Imperial Palace and the dark waters of the Bosphian Sea. From the distance came the faint sound of music of a kind he had never heard before, played on flutes and strings, with a droning and atonal quality that was both haunting and lonely. He breathed deeply, savoring the air, which carried the sweet scent of jasmine and lacked the stench of sewage that was ubiquitous in the North.

It was a clean city. A *fresh* city, for the old Elrysian city that had existed in this place had been razed to its foundations. Kavanosa had fallen to the Abadian army after a sixty-three-day siege, and Ababad had grown from its bones, the ancient stone blocks of its palaces and monuments cannibalized for new construction. In the following years, everything Elrysian had been systematically expunged from Kavanosa and its environs, for the Elrysians had celebrated the magical philosophies of the ancients, practices no longer tolerated by the new Imperium. Kavanosa's temples had been vandalized, the statues of its gods and heroes beheaded and dismembered.

The persecution of the Elryisans had gone beyond the mutilation of their cities and monuments. Black-robed Imperialists armed with caustic mixtures carried out acid attacks against citizens of the Old Empire slow to disavow their ways and religion. Elrysian scholars had scrambled to hide their books, and cellars were converted into secret places of study and worship. It had taken generations, but eventually the last vestiges of Elrysian culture succumbed to centuries of relentless suppression. Now, all that was left of Kavanosa was scattered blocks of stone that could be distinguished from the rest of the city's masonry because of the superiority of craft employed by the ancient stone carvers.

With one last glance at the harbor, Markus left the balcony and strode across the main room of the villa toward a walnut table. Next to the table was an austere-looking cabinet that consisted of a chest sustained by a trestle stand, with a front panel that opened to reveal rows and rows of little drawers inside, where Sergan kept his vials of essence.

Pouring himself a splash of wine from a pewter flagon, Markus drank it down and was about to help himself to another but thought better of it. Instead, he let down the front panel of the cabinet and let his gaze wander the rows of drawers within. Each drawer was richly sculped and inlaid with mother of pearl, a sight that made Markus wince, for that was the color Aram's eyes had been, and he knew that within many of those tiny drawers were vials of essence that had been drawn from the body of his friend.

Staring at the cabinet, a cold and throbbing ache came over him. With a finger, he nudged out a drawer, revealing its collection of vials filled with milky fluid. He picked one up and cradled it in his palm, reflecting upon it sadly. Aram had left no grave for him to mourn over, only thousands of tiny vials, each filled with a small but significant part of him. Markus's vision blurred, and he squeezed his fingers closed around the vial in his hand, fighting back an intense hatred of Sergan, the Exilari, and himself. With a sad heart, he returned the little vial to the drawer and shut the cabinet, regretting opening it in the first place.

Swallowing his grief, he picked up the wine bottle and filled his cup to the brim, chasing down his self-loathing with watered-down wine—not very effective, but better than nothing. Cup finished, he went to where his formal tunic and mantle hung from a pole on the far side of the room. He had an engagement to get to, and had to make himself look the part, even though he'd much rather remain in the villa, drinking wine alone on the balcony while listening to the babble of the courtyard fountain. He donned his black silk tunic with its embroidered symbol of a coiled serpent within a golden sun, pulling his blue mantle over his shoulders. Checking the small, foggy mirror mounted over the wash basin, he confirmed that his dark hair was just as unruly as he'd feared. It took some water from the ewer and a good amount of finger-combing before he was satisfied.

Strapping his sword belt over his tunic, he left the villa and headed down the street in the direction of the palace, past Andrazi Fortress, which contained the largest library in the Northern world. He followed a procession of stone buildings, patios, gardens, and fountains down streets that were well-paved and well-lit by oil lamps, passing schools and bathhouses, shops and conservatories. Ababad itself stood in stark contrast to Karaqor, one a well-bred and cultured lady, the other, a dirty and low-born whore. The one thing that struck him as odd was the lack of windows in the tall buildings; Abadian life centered around the central courtyards within the buildings themselves, keeping household goings-on hidden from the street.

The Imperial Palace was situated on a low hill above the harbor. It was dark by the time Markus reached the main gate, and the streets had all but emptied, for the people of Ababad retired early. The guards who warded the gate didn't stop to question him, but stood back and bowed as he passed, for the blue mantle he wore was invitation enough.

Inside the garden courtyard, a large crowd had gathered. Markus paused and stood to the side, gauging the terrain, uncertain where to go or whom he was supposed to be interacting with. Sergan had told him to show up, and that's all the direction he had offered. Markus scanned the crowd for the sorcerer's face—not that he sought his company, but because he wanted to be seen. As soon as his presence was noted, he intended to leave as expeditiously as possible. He threaded his way through the crowd in the courtyard, drawn by the smell of roasting meat toward the entrance to the hall.

"Markus!"

He turned at the sound of his name to see Peshka and Poda coming toward him.

"Peshka!" he managed, just before she careened into him, sweeping him up in an exuberant hug that practically lifted him off his feet. Poda stood off to the side, grinning broadly, one hand resting on the pommel of his sword.

"I didn't know you were here!" Markus exclaimed.

Peshka gave him one last squeeze before releasing him and stepping back. Her dark auburn hair was longer than she used to wear it when they were in training, hanging well past her shoulders. She was a sorceress now, and Poda was her Shield. Markus had a hard time with that, for he had a deep loathing of sorcerers. But Peshka had never been anything but good to him, and deeply loyal, so he found himself perpetually confused in her presence.

A grinning Poda stepped forward to embrace him. "By all the lands! I don't believe it! We've been worried about you!" He, too, had changed since Markus had last seen him, his face weathered and thinner, as though he had aged years.

"I'm doing better." Markus smiled. "I'd be a *lot* better if I didn't have to put up with Sergan every day. I've been cooling my heels at our villa while he's been out rubbing elbows and smoking hashish with every minor noble in the city."

"I never understood how he affords his tastes." Poda rolled his eyes. "So, what are you doing here?"

Markus spread his hands. "We were summoned by the Emperor for something big. I still don't know the particulars. Sergan's being tight-lipped about it."

Next to them, a woman in a brocaded gown let out a peel of laughter. Taking Markus and Poda by the arms, Peshka led them away toward a quieter corner of the courtyard. Soft music drifted from the hall, and the smell of the banquet was making Markus's mouth water.

"What about you?" he asked. "Why did they send you here?"

"We don't know," answered Peshka. "We were told to come to the city and wait for further instruction. Well, we've been here a solid month and, so far, there's been no 'further instruction.' It's all very mysterious."

She stabbed an amused glance at Poda, as though it were some kind of inside joke.

Markus frowned in confusion. "That is…amazingly peculiar. Have you seen anyone else around here from the College?"

"Poda thought he caught a glimpse of Obriem when we first got here."

"I might have been wrong," said Poda.

Peshka crossed her arms. "Well, right or wrong, we haven't seen anyone else."

"Interesting," Markus muttered, although he thought it far more troubling than interesting. Why would the Order send three sorcerers and their Shields all to the same city? It would have to be something big. Something *very* big, and apparently secret, as well. "Where are you staying?"

Peshka said, "We're staying at an inn on the other side of the city. It's called the Blue Lantern."

"I'll try to come by tomorrow. Right now I—"

"I see you've found some old friends."

Markus turned to find Sergan approaching through the shadows of the courtyard, carrying a tall leather cup. His face was skewed by his signature smirk, and his pale eyes glistened. Arriving at Markus's side, he took Peshka's hand and kissed it.

"I'm happy to see that you found each other. I hope the four of us can get together sometime in the next couple of days." Releasing Peshka's hand, he took a sip of his drink and turned to Markus. "I came to apologize. It turns out that I have an unexpected meeting, and I won't be able to introduce you around as I'd planned. Go ahead and enjoy yourself without me. Eat the food—it's delectable. You *must* try the peahen."

Feeling relieved that he wouldn't have to suffer Sergan's company, Markus did his best to smile. "I'll find my way around. Enjoy your meeting."

Raising his cup, Sergan gave Peshka an abbreviated bow then walked back across the courtyard, long mantle fluttering behind him. Watching him go, Markus let out a protracted sigh.

"Want to go find the food?" asked Peshka. "I've never tried peahen before."

She offered Markus her arm, and he took it gladly. She really did look lovely with her hair longer. If not for the vials of essence she wore on her belt, she might have even been beautiful. Then a thought hit him, and Peshka's attractiveness dissolved before his eyes.

He knew whose essence she wore at her waist. How could she do it? How could she *drink* his best friend's soul? Aram had been her friend too. Markus swallowed heavily, lowering his gaze to the sword he wore at his side, knowing he was complicit.

"What's wrong?" Peshka asked.

"I'm just thinking I need a drink," he said, forcing a smile.

Sergan was sweating by the time he arrived at the office of the Grand Vizier, which was under a small dome beside the palace's interior gate. The building was guarded by sentries, who stepped in front of him to block his entrance but moved aside when he produced a scroll with the Imperial Seal.

The room he entered beneath the dome was dark, illuminated by the light of a single taper perched atop a silver candlestick. It was silent and shadowed and hauntingly empty. There was only one place to go, and that was through a wooden door on the far wall.

Crossing the floor, Sergan knocked hesitantly on the door then waited, feeling a bead of sweat roll down his temple. The Grand Vizier was the highest-ranked noble in the Empire, who had the capacity to convene the council of all other viziers and was entrusted with the Imperial Seal. The only way Sergan could possibly feel more nervous was if he were meeting with the God-Emperor himself.

The door opened, and a stoic man in a tall, cylindrical hat looked upon him expressionlessly, then moved aside to admit him. Within, Grand Vizier Amselmi was seated behind an ornate desk veneered with panels inlayed with ivory. Behind him on the wall was a sumptuous tapestry depicting the execution of Oraphen, who had led the Slave Revolt a hundred years before. Sergan knew the choice of tapestry was intentional: a reminder to all who came before the Imperial Court of the price of insurrection.

The Grand Vizier was a bearded Abadian man wearing a bulky white turban. He had a slender nose that ended in a sharp point and dark, penetrating eyes. The wide-sleeved kaftan he wore was woven of damask with gold embroidery, a thread reserved for nobility. He regarded Sergan a long, searching moment before motioning him forward.

Hesitant, Sergan moved to stand across the desk from him, for there was no chair in which to sit. The vizier held out his hand, and Sergan relinquished the scroll of invitation, which Amselmi glanced over, as though reminding himself of who stood before him.

"Exilar Sergan Parsigal," he said in a deep voice rich with a Bosphian accent.

"At your service, Your Excellency."

The man extended his hand, and Sergan bowed forward to kiss the vizier's signet ring, a gesture of obeisance and submission to Imperial authority.

"I've heard many stories about you," Amselmi acknowledged in a flat, emotionless tone. "Some speak well for you. Others don't."

Sergan felt pinpricks of perspiration tingle his brow. He gave a forced smile in an attempt to disguise his apprehension. "I hope the good stories outnumber the bad."

"There is only one story that interests me at the moment, and that is the story we shall write together."

"And what story is that?"

Vizier Amselmi knitted his hands together upon the desktop. "As you are aware, the Emperor's personal Exilari have been trying, unsuccessfully, for years to create a stable rupture through the Veil. Recently, they have discovered a way to do so, and the Emperor has made new alliances on the other side whose goals align with our own: to break the Anchors of Heaven and tear down the Veil entirely. We need sorcerers willing to journey to Pyrial in support of our new allies there. Of course, you will be well-compensated, for in exchange for our assistance, our allies there have promised us every drop of essence we can reap."

Sergan stood rigid, staring straight ahead as his mind grappled with the vizier's statements. The World Below was the world of plenty, the source of all essence. With the Emperor's mandate, he could infuse himself with enough raw power to perform real miracles.

"How is that possible?" he whispered. "The Anchors are protected by impenetrable wards. No human sorcerer could ever break them."

Holding his gaze firmly, the vizier answered, "They are not impenetrable. It is possible, especially if they are already weakened. What we need is a strong enough sorcerer with the right kind of essence." His eyes went to the vials Sergan wore on his belt.

Sergan's eyebrows flew up, and his hand reflexively moved to his waist.

"The Anchor will sense the essence of an Auld Savant and interpret the wielder as an ally. Its wards will not activate."

Sergan wished there was a chair he could slip into. His head was spinning. For the first time, they had the capacity to break the Anchors of Heaven themselves. If the God-Emperor willed it, they could smash the two worlds back together, uniting the World Above and the World Below—in effect, reverse the Sundering.

They could return true magic to the world.

"What about the therlings?" he asked. "With a permanent rupture, they will be pouring continuously from the void."

Face as menacing as a gargoyle's, the vizier responded, "The Emperor's allies in the World Below have been successful at taming them. They have created an entire army of therlings and void walkers, though there are only so many they can control at once. We will need to act swiftly and decisively."

"There's not enough essence left," Sergan muttered. Aram Raythe had been the last person found in the world with the Gift. It would seem the very last drop of the Old Blood had finally been wrung from the world.

"The World Below is the source of all essence," the vizier reminded him, "and now we'll have unlimited access to it. Only...there is a catch."

Sergan frowned. "What's the catch, Your Excellence?"

"There has been a stirring in the Web of Ages. Something has awakened—a presence that has long been slumbering. A great power is stirring, the kind that hasn't been felt in the world since the Sundering."

"A Champion?" asked Sergan skeptically.

"This soul is stronger, but it is only just now awakening, and its power hasn't had time to fully mature. We must excise this soul from the Web before it does."

Sergan screwed his face into a frown. So the Emperor wanted him to destroy an Anchor and defeat a waking power as old as the Sundering? He was skilled, but not *that* skilled. "Your Excellence, I doubt I can—"

"Of course you can," snapped the vizier. "You have already defeated this soul once. It was the other members of your Order who let him slip through your fingers."

Sergan's mind flinched. The entire world felt like it was ready to capsize.

"Aramon Raythe?"

"Is that his name in this life?" The vizier had a distant look in his eyes.

Sergan let out a held breath, feeling engulfed in a maelstrom of bewilderment. His customary self-assurance had been stripped away, and he felt shaken and very far out of his depth. "Exactly what would you have of me, Your Excellence?"

"The Emperor's allies in Pyrial are very powerful and very capable," said the vizier. "You are to help them break the Anchors before we run out of essence in this world. And bring the son of Raginor to his knees."

Sergan bowed his head gravely. "It will be as you say, Your Excellence."

Aram opened his eyes to the cool glow of Edylwylde's hundreds of lanterns. At first, he thought he had just dreamt of the fire, that it had all been just some terrible nightmare. But then he smelled the overwhelming stench of the burned forest surrounding him, and he knew it was far too terrible to be a mere nightmare.

With a groan, he pushed himself upright and was immediately rewarded with an acute feeling of vertigo that made him collapse back again. He lay on his back, staring upward at the roof of the dome, and he saw with a sense of enormous relief that it was still whole. A large part of the north side had been blackened by the fire, but it held. Many of the interwoven vines and branches of the canopy still bore leaves, which gave him hope that the part that had taken damage might someday be made whole again.

"How are you feeling?"

Squinting, Aram turned his head and saw Wingmaster Vandra crouched next to him, her arms resting on her thighs. Her face was blackened by soot that had been eroded by sweat. Dried blood encrusted her forehead from a gash on her scalp, but otherwise she seemed hale. The look in her eyes was intense and full of defiance.

"I feel fine," Aram replied, rubbing his eyes. "Just dizzy."

With Vandra's help, he pushed himself upright. Once the world stabilized, he took in the sight of dozens of people bent on the task of repairing the homes they had almost lost in the night. The ground of the hollow was covered with a thick layer of gray ash speckled with dark flecks of debris. Miraculously, only a couple of the woven huts looked as though they had been damaged by the flames.

He frowned at Vandra. "How did you know I could...?"

"Esmir knew," Vandra replied. "I took a gamble and placed my trust in him. And in you."

"How did he know?"

Vandra lifted her eyebrows. "Esmir knows better than anyone the Gift of a True Savant. He figured that all you needed was a reason, and that your mind would do the rest."

"It did." Aram thought back to the previous night and found he didn't have a good recollection of it. Everything seemed foggy and muddled together. He remembered a few details, but all else was just a jumbled blur.

"I remember starting the first knot in the aether...then suddenly I was working thousands of knots at once. It was like I just knew what to do. Only...I don't remember how I did any of it." He gazed sadly at the damaged dome. "I wish I could have done more."

"You did enough." Vandra patted Aram's arm. "The forest has suffered grave injury, but it will heal. The Great Tree survived, as did those who tend it. They survived, because of you."

Aram stared at her as the shock of what she'd said gradually settled into him. She was right. What he had done was nothing short of extraordinary, and he didn't know how to feel about that, for there was a host of conflicting feelings churning inside him all at once. He felt a small sense of empowerment and even a stir of vindication. But both those feelings were trampled by a profound sense of shame or perhaps embarrassment, and he had no idea where those feelings came from.

Standing, Vandra bent to dust the ash off the scale skirt that covered her thighs. She offered her hand and helped Aram to his feet, steadying him with a firm grip on his arm that felt like an iron manacle.

"We must go," she said, her tone suddenly stern. "The Wings took casualties."

Upon hearing that, a cold fear swept through Aram. "Calise—?"

"She's tending the injured. Come."

With Vandra's support, Aram walked unstably toward the path that led out of the dome. Before he got halfway across the hollow, Shinota emerged from a hut and came toward them, sweeping Aram up in an emotional embrace. Shocked, Aram hugged her back. She held him a long time, gently rocking him, like a grandmother cuddling a long-absent grandson.

Kissing his cheek, Shinota drew back. "Thank you."

There were tears in her eyes. Aram didn't know how to react. Embarrassed, he bit his lip and stared hard at the ground. When he looked up, he saw that all the members of the village had stopped what they were doing and had turned toward him. Almost as one, they touched their hands to their foreheads.

Never in his life had Aram experienced gratitude directed toward him. Overwhelmed, he returned the gesture then allowed Vandra to escort him out of the dome, glad to be leaving a situation that caused him intense discomfort because he had no idea how to act.

Markus swung down from his horse's back and stared out across lowlands shrouded by a thin white mist. The sight ahead was unexpected and somewhat chilling. Imperial legions were arrayed across the field ahead of them, along with what looked like several divisions of auxiliary. Many of the soldiers carried unlit torches in their hands, and all stood looking ready to go into battle against an unseen enemy.

Markus shot a questioning look at Sergan, who was looping the reins of his horse around the pommel of his saddle. The sorcerer still hadn't told him the nature of their mission, had in fact ordered him not to ask him about it. But looking out upon the disturbing sight ahead, Markus felt he couldn't hold his tongue any longer. He was an Exilar, not part of the military. His enemy was void walkers and therlings, not people. He was just about ready to demand an explanation when he saw four riders approaching—and he recognized all of them.

Poda and Peshka drew their mounts up beside himself and Sergan.

Behind them were Obriem and Emar, the sorcerer he had been paired with. They all stared out at the gathered army with looks of confusion on their faces.

Obriem dismounted and approached first, his face grave. He had grown a wiry, straw-colored beard, his hair cut short over his ears. His body was a solid burl of tangled muscle. There was very little of the boy left in him that Markus had met when he had first entered the College.

Unlike Markus, Obriem had been disciplined severely for his part in Aram's failed rescue. He had been tied to a post and mercilessly flogged, nearly to death, and his back would bear the scars for the remainder of his life. He had never forgiven Markus.

Slipping his leather gloves off his hands, Obriem came to stand in front of them with an intense glower. "What are we doing here, Sergan?"

The sorcerer didn't respond. Instead, he motioned for them to accompany him into the mist, away from the fielded army. Peshka shot Markus a questioning glance, to which he responded only with a shrug, for he was just as confused as she was. They followed Sergan as the mist swirled around them, at last parting to reveal a circle of tall standing stones. Sergan walked into the circle of stones, all the way to the center of the ring. There, he halted and waited for them.

Markus let his gaze slip over the ring of monoliths as he entered the circle. They were like nothing he had ever seen, and they seemed to radiate a subtle and eerie power of their own. The entire place was ghostly, the feel of it giving him goosebumps. He didn't know what the purpose of the stones was, but he knew he didn't like it. When the five of them had gathered in front of Sergan, the sorcerer raised his hands and gestured at the stones looming around them like eldritch sentinels.

"This is a place of power." His gaze slid from face to face, lingering on each of them in turn. There was none of his usual, characteristic acidity in his tone, only a grave solemnity that prickled the back of Markus's neck even more than the ominous stones surrounding them.

"Circles of standing stones in this world mark the placement of Anchors in the World Below," said Sergan. "Together, the Circles and the Anchors uphold the Veil that keeps the two worlds apart. But they are not perfect. As you well know, there are ruptures in the Veil. And wherever there are ruptures, therlings and void walkers pour through the rent, seeking the one thing they desperately desire above all else: the restoration of their essence.

"Our Order was founded to protect our world from the ravages of these beings. In order to accomplish this, we have always relied on sorcerers armed with essence. But every year, the number of people in this world able to provide that essence has decreased exponentially, until we have finally arrived at a crossroads. The vials of essence we wear on our persons are likely all we'll ever have, for it would seem that magic has finally gone extinct in this world."

Obriem mumbled something under his breath to Peshka that Markus couldn't make out. His own mind grappled to understand what Sergan was telling them. Was it truly possible that this long legacy of magic could ever come to an end? That there could be no other people like Aram ever born to the world? He couldn't fathom it, nor could he sort through all the possible ramifications.

"Without magic, we have no way to combat the therlings or seal the ruptures," Sergan went on, his tone grave. "After the last of our essence runs out, it's predicted that within just a score of years, most of this continent will be overrun, and most of the population slain.

"But it doesn't have to be that way. Magic still exists in the World Below, a land that bleeds essence from its pores. It lies just on the other side of the Veil, a mere stone's throw away. All we have to do is open a stable rupture and go through."

"What about therlings?" Markus asked.

Sergan leveled his gaze at him. "We have allies on the other side who have found a way to tame them. But they cannot tame them all. We must break the Anchors that uphold the Veil. And we must do so quickly."

"What kind of allies?" Markus asked warily.

"The kind we need," Sergan assured him. "Those who share our values and our goals and are committed to helping our cause."

Obriem reached up and scratched his beard. "So, what, exactly, are we here for?"

Sergan paused before answering, as though for dramatic effect. "Peshka and Eman will open and maintain a rupture. Obriem and Poda will defend them long enough for us to go through—along with the legions the God-Emperor has seen fit to supply us with."

Markus felt the blood drain from his face. "We're going to the World Below?"

Sergan nodded, sucking in a cheek. "We have to destroy the Anchor beneath these stones in order to make the rupture permanent."

Before anyone could state an objection or press him with questions Sergan snapped, "You have an hour to prepare," and walked away from them, out of the circle of stones.

Narath landed on the eyrie's terrace with a lithe grace that belied his formidable countenance. The moment Aram was off his back, the dragon went immediately in search of his rider. Weary, Aram made his way off the terrace as the rest of the Wing landed around him. Walking under the vault of the cavern, he headed across the enormous chamber in the direction of the stairs, shoulders slumped and eyelids drooping. But before he reached the exit, his gaze was drawn to a commotion outside one of the alcoves.

There, several people had gathered around an injured rider, who was laid out on the floor, his dragon hovering behind him, clearly agitated. Aram determined to pass by the poignant scene without stopping to look, for though he felt sympathy for the rider, he knew his presence would be an intrusion. But then he caught a glimpse of Calise kneeling next to the injured man, her hands pressed against his bloody chest.

Aram couldn't help but stop and stare. Calise's aura blazed golden like the sun, streaming rays into the air around her. The light traveled down her arms, suffusing the injured man. He watched in concern as she appeared to struggle, her face strained with the effort of keeping the man alive. With the exception of Sergan's, Aram had never seen such an outright display of magic.

And it was beautiful.

He could see that Calise's magic worked in a way entirely different from his own. Her magic came from within and had nothing to do with knots or aether and everything to do with the strength of the compassion that existed within her. It wasn't the kind of magic that could be used in battle, but it was the kind that could mend the wounds after.

Only, the wound she was working on was beyond what even her great heart could heal. When the glow of her magic faded, so did the dying man's aura fade with it, and Aram knew that, despite Calise's efforts, her patient was gone.

A thunderous shriek echoed through the cavern unlike anything he'd ever heard before, or ever wanted to hear again: the keening grief of a dragon.

People scrambled backward as the dead rider's dragon reared back, spreading its wings and gushing fiery breath at the high ceiling of the eyrie. With mindless ferocity, it lashed out with its tail, dashing the screen of the alcove behind it and sending a stack of crates flying.

People screamed and fled as the dragon shrieked its rage across the eyrie, spewing dragonfire everywhere in a great arc.

And Calise was in the way of it.

Rushing forward, Aram wove a shield of glisten aether between Calise and the dragon's fury. White-hot flames, roiling with heat, gushed against the shield as Calise threw her hands up.

But the heat did not touch her. Aram wouldn't let it.

Walking around her, he inserted himself between the rampaging dragon and Calise, and when the dragon's gaze fell upon him, he felt the full force of the creature's soul-rending grief. Their minds met, and it was all Aram could do not to scream.

He understood.

Never had he felt a greater sadness, a terrible, mindless ache. The dragon's love for its rider went beyond any love Aram had ever experienced, far beyond even the love he bore for his parents. It was unbearable, as bad or worse than the tortures he had suffered in the cellars of the Exilari.

He knew then that the dragon would not survive its rider's death.

The bond between them was too strong to be defeated. Their souls were intertwined and could not be separated, even in death.

But underneath the weight of all that terrible grief, Aram felt another stirring of emotion, one he hadn't expected: deep inside its great weeping heart, the dragon clung to a piece of knowledge that gave it some measure of comfort. The dragon believed with a certainty that its soul would be reunited with his beloved in the World Beyond, and that together they would continue the bond they had forged down through the great expanse of eternity.

It was the way of things.

"Go ahead," Aram said. "Take him. But don't hurt anyone."

The dragon bowed its head, and Aram could sense its shame. It had never meant to be a danger but had lost its mind to grief.

Aram moved backward just in time as the creature extended its mighty wings. Then, with one great leap, it scooped up the body of the dead man and, tucking him close against its breast, leaped for the cave mouth and plunged into the yawning crevasse.

Shaken, Aram stood looking after them for a moment, his vision blurring. He felt a hand on his arm and turned to find himself staring into Calise's stricken face. She was smeared with blood and grime, and she, too, had tears in her eyes.

"They'll be all right," he whispered, his voice shaking.

She nodded, wiping her eyes. Then her hand left his arm, and he felt her fingers intertwine with his. It was the most compassionate gesture he had ever felt in his life. He turned to look at her, his body trembling.

"Aram!"

Vandra's harsh voice made him jump, and he tore his hand away from Calise. He gaped with startled eyes at the Wingmaster, who stood looking at him with a peculiar expression on her face, one too complex for Aram too decipher.

Bringing a hand up to her brow, Vandra shook her head wearily. "Go get some sleep. That's an order!"

Feeling empty, Aram started immediately toward the door.

"Wait!" Calise called after him. He halted and looked back.

She opened her mouth to say something but then appeared to think better of it and shook her head instead. "Never mind."

Aram smiled at her sadly then walked toward the stairs.

Markus stood beside Poda within the ring of standing stones, one hand gripping the hilt of his sword, the other clasped around the handle of his shield. Sergan stood before them, a thumb hooked in a leather baldric that crossed his chest that was ribbed with finger-length vials of essence held in place by woven straps. Behind them, the first four cohorts of the Imperial legions had drawn up close and were waiting just to the other side of the standing stones.

Sergan scraped at the ground with his boot, kicking up a divot of grass. Gazing down at it, he said calmly. "When the rift opens, therlings and walkers will spill out quickly. Be ready." He looked up at them, his eyes boring into each of them with a dark intensity. "At all times, you must remember what we are dealing with. These were creatures ripped from this earth and flung into the void. Many used to be Auld or human. But it doesn't matter what they once were—things that go into the void are no longer what they seem. It doesn't matter if they are man or beast or even a child—they want to kill you. You must not hesitate. Void walkers don't bleed, and they don't feel pain. Remember: these are creatures that will never know the peace of death unless you bring it to them. Keep that in mind. It makes it easier."

As Markus looked on, the sorcerer withdrew one of the glass vials from the baldric. He stood holding it in his hand as his eyes surveyed the soggy, mist-laden ground in the center of the ring. Markus couldn't take his eyes from the vial, feeling his stomach tighten in revulsion. Sergan used his thumb to pop the cork and raised the vial to his lips, closing his eyes and tilting his head back. Markus watched the sorcerer's throat move as Sergan swallowed the essence down, at last lowering the vial with a slight smile and a contented sigh. Then he popped open another container, downed its contents, then drank another, tossing the spent vials over his shoulder.

At his side, Peshka and Eman were doing the same. When they had each saturated themselves with essence to the point that the very air shimmered around them, Sergan raised his hand.

No matter how many times Markus witnessed the sorcerer use stolen magic to amplify his own pathetic affinity, the sight still took him off guard. Like an opium addict, Sergan's pupils constricted to pinpricks then disappeared altogether, swallowed by a haunting blue light that glowed from deep within his eye sockets. Beside him, Peshka's eyes took on a similar glow, as everything that was beautiful about her fell away like a veneer. Eman, his eyes glowing with unholy light, walked forward to stand at the side of the two other sorcerers, all three of them together linking hands.

A brilliant flash of voidfire lit the circle of stones for just an instant, overwhelming Markus's vision and sending motes dancing before his eyes. Then a powerful white flame burst upward from the ground, burning back the mist and crackling into the sky.

"Get back!" Sergan ordered in a voice that didn't sound anything like him, resembling the creaking moan of an ancient corpse.

Together, the six of them retreated backward through the ring of stones as the brilliant intensity of the magic before them took on a golden sheen and expanded, dominating the circle, crackling like a bonfire.

"Be ready!" Sergan shouted.

When the first therling emerged from the rift, Markus stepped in front of Sergan, dampening the light of his shine. Filled with essence to the point that it leaked from his body in visible waves, Sergan would stand out like a beacon of flame to any therling coming through the rupture and, in their hunger, they would seek him desperately. This was the primary reason sorcerers had Shields: to make them less of a target.

Then there was also the other reason, seldom spoken of: to protect their sorcerer from other Shields.

He interlocked his shield with Poda's and Obriem's, forming a solid wall that blocked the magical auras of the three sorcerers behind them. The first therling, an eel-like creature, made it only half out of the rupture before it was sliced in half by a ray of magic that cleaved down upon it like a guillotine. The second, a hairless horse with a milky-pink body, came charging out of the rupture. It stumbled and fell only feet away, rolling once before sliding through the dirt, coming to a halt at Markus's feet.

Then, people emerged.

They spilled from the blazing glare of the rupture, twisted silhouettes, walking toward them with purpose in their strides. As they neared, the shadows folded back enough to reveal their features. Most looked like decomposing corpses. Some had hair; others didn't. Some retained their clothes, garments of a style unlike any Markus had ever seen. One of the walkers seemed whole and healthy, and Markus could imagine meeting him on the street. A more recent victim of the void, perhaps.

All in a line, they pressed forward toward the lure of the essence they could sense but could not locate, for the glow of the sorcerers who wielded it was cut off by the impregnable character of their Shields. One by one, the undead walkers were cut down, some sliced in half, others exploding in clouds of raining flesh. Some simply slumped to the ground and lay dead, while others thrashed in their death throes.

Then the dragon came.

It was smaller than the void dragon that had taken Aram; nevertheless, the sight of it filled Markus with an anger and hatred almost as great as his contempt for Sergan. When the dragon bore down upon them, disgorging voidfire, Markus stood before it, shield raised, repulsing the roiling flames that heated the air around him. The force of it nearly drove him to the ground, but he lowered his center of gravity, refusing to go down. The air around him heated to blistering, and he could smell the odor of his hair starting to singe.

Right before the might of the dragon could overwhelm him, all three sorcerers struck out with an attack that cleaved through the dragon's neck like an executioner's sword.

Spewing fire, the dragon's neck flopped on the ground like a headless snake, its spasms gradually subsiding before halting completely. Then, to Markus's surprise, the corpse of the dragon began to harden, turning to stone before his eyes. The stone began to age, cracking and rupturing. Pieces sloughed off, raining down in brittle chips of rock until, at last, the stone dragon collapsed and crumbled to dust. Panting, Markus looked back over his shoulder to take in the sight of Sergan's glowing eyes.

"That's it," the sorcerer said. "Let the soldiers through."

The six Exilari retreated, relinquishing their position as Sergan signaled the officers of the army behind them. As one, the first cohort of foot soldiers advanced toward the rift, swords drawn and shields interlinked.

"What happens now?" Markus asked, donning his helm.

Sergan looked at him with his glowing blue eyes. "Now we destroy the Anchor."

A terrible feeling of foreboding made Shinota glance up from the injury she was tending. Dropping the bloody cloth, she rose to her feet and took a step forward, gaze fixed on a charred section of the dome. The strands of aether around her flinched as though wounded—though she could not see them in color, her turquoise eyes could see the threads vibrating like a spider's web that had trapped an insect.

She took another hesitant step. Then the entire fabric of the world recoiled as though a knife had been thrust through the weave of it, severing thousands of threads at once.

"A rupture!" she cried.

Before the words were even out of her mouth, the canopy above her started to shudder. Leaves and charred branches rained down from above, and there was an ear-splitting drone, like a million cicadas all screeching at once. As she watched in horror, the dome overhead eroded. A large branch collapsed just in front of her, raining leaves and flowers. A war cry rose from hundreds of throats, and then uniformed soldiers were pouring toward them.

She rushed toward where one of their warriors stood with a bow, but she didn't make it to him in time. He was quickly overwhelmed, cut down where he stood. All around, the screams and shrieks of her people assaulted her ears.

Shinota raised her hand and started weaving the air.

She wasn't a True Savant, but she knew enough to be deadly. Calling for her people to flee, she wove a wall of flames that engulfed a group of soldiers advancing toward the huts. Then she struck out at another group of men hacking their way through a cluster of her people. Shrieking a cry, she walked forward, weaving the threads of air as quickly as she could, using what skill she had. But very soon exhaustion set in, and she started dropping threads.

She wasn't a Champion.

She had done all she could.

But the soldiers from the world of Men kept coming, and there was no way she could keep them out.

When she felt the sword pierce her chest, her last regret was not for the people of her village. Her sacred duty was to protect the Anchor.

And in that duty, she had catastrophically failed.

"Wake up!"

Aram awoke to someone shaking him violently. He opened his eyes and stared groggily into the inky darkness of the dormitory. Someone shook him again, and he shot upright so quickly that he banged his head on the bottom of Jeran's cot.

"What is it?" he gasped, rubbing his forehead and ducking out from under the cot.

"There's been a rupture!" Calise's panic-stricken voice sliced through the darkness. "The Heart of the Grove is under attack! Vandra needs you!"

"What?" Aram gasped, but Calise was already moving away.

He donned his pants and scooped up his sword. Pulling his tunic around him, he struggled to tie the laces while jogging after Calise down the corridor. They took the stairwell up to the eyrie, where Vandra waved him toward Narath, who welcomed him with a mental meeting of minds. Nodding his thanks at Narath's rider, Aram climbed onto the dragon's back and strapped himself in. The big dragon surged forward without hesitation and, in just a few strides, cleared the mouth of the eyrie and vaulted into the air.

Aram felt nothing of the thrill of flight he had the first two times he'd ridden dragonback. Now, his nerves were screaming with panic, and his stomach felt sickened with dread. The people of the Grove hadn't had time to recover from the last attack. He shouldn't have come back with Vandra. He should have stayed.

They flew on Ragath's wing as the flight of dragons soared over the white peaks of the Kemeri Mountains. Even before they were over the forest, Aram could see a dark plume of smoke rising from the Grove. A great section of the forest had already been burned from the last fire—miles and miles of black and flattened earth—but this was a new fire, and he could see the tongues of flame snapping at the air even at a distance.

When they were close enough to make out detail, Aram felt his stomach lurch.

The Great Tree was engulfed by flames that gnawed at its trunk and consumed its branches. Beneath it, the domed canopy of Shinota's people was ablaze.

Staring at the burning Tree, Aram felt a scream rise and then die in his throat, for he knew that they were already too late. Ahead, he saw the dragons of the Wing swooping down to land on the granite outcrop, dropping off their riders before vaulting back into the sky.

Narath brought him down with a great gush of displaced air. Before the dragon touched the rocks, Aram slid off his back, landing hard and drawing his sword as he ran after Vandra.

Markus gazed upward at the burning tree that rose higher than any tree he had ever imagined, tongues of flame ravaging its branches and scorching the air. All around him fires burned, some lit by sorcerers, others by the Imperial forces who accompanied them. He stood in a world he had never really believed existed, and that world was on fire.

It was appalling.

He caught movement from the corner of his eye and raised his shield just in time to deflect an arrow that was meant for Sergan.

From out of the burning forest poured warriors who ran at them with swords and spears, others loosing arrows from recurve bows. They looked to Markus like Vards, his own kinfolk, and yet they were clothed in garments that looked completely foreign. Whoever they were, they were not therlings. The men and women assaulting them were clothed in living flesh. And like all living things, they died easily when met with Exilari magic.

As soon as they broke into the clearing, the warriors started dropping. The Imperial footmen simply formed a shield wall and let them break themselves against it until there was nothing left to kill. The sight of the carnage turned Markus's stomach, the screams of dying men polluting his ears. He stared across the glade at Peshka, who stood with eyes that blazed with sorcerous power, her arms working swiftly in graceful motions as they bound the aether. The sight of her was ghastly, an adulteration of the kind person she was meant to be. Never again would he look upon her in the same light. In her own way, she was just as corrupted as he.

Aram ran headlong through the forest following Vandra, sword drawn, heart pounding in his throat. He could smell the smoke and hear the crackling of the blaze even though he couldn't see the Great Tree through the thick canopy. His heart ached, for he could feel its deep sorrow and anguish.

He heard the sound of fighting ahead, and he readied himself, pulling at strands of aether and gathering them around him. He was ready to fight. He was ready to die if he had to.

What he was not ready for was the sight of Shinota lying dead on the ground, her beautiful heart cut from her chest.

This was wrong, Markus realized, feeling ill. These people had no chance against six Exilari and an army of Imperials. He stood sweating, fighting nausea until his stomach revolted on him and twisted, emptying itself upon his boots. When he was done puking, he straightened and, as though in a dream, disengaged himself physically and mentally from the fighting. He lowered his sword and simply walked away.

"*Markus!*" Sergan called after him. "*Get back here!*"

Markus ignored him and kept walking.

Rushing footsteps made him turn.

He got his shield up just in time to block a spear coming at him. Then two warriors set upon him. With one, brisk motion of his blade, he had the first one down. Then he spun toward the second one and froze.

Aram stood in front of him.

Impossible.

It couldn't be.

Markus gasped, his body and mind locking rigid.

Aram was dead. He'd gone into the void.

His heart wrenched, and his weapon sagged in his grasp.

Seeing his hesitation, the thing that looked like Aram sliced out with its sword. Markus brought his blade up just in time to block the strike. When he swept out with a counterattack, his opponent dodged backward.

Markus froze, gaping in horror at the face that haunted him, both sleeping and awake.

But the youth that stood before him couldn't be his friend. It was as Sergan had warned him: things that went into the void came back corrupted. The creature in front of him might once have been Aram, but it wasn't anymore. Aram was now a void walker, and the kindest thing Markus could do for him was bring him the mercy and peace of death.

With a cry of despair, Markus charged his best friend.

The thing that was no longer Aram brought its sword up just in time, deflecting the cut Markus threw at him.

Desperate, Markus arced his sword around, determined to deliver Aram to the afterlife he deserved.

Somehow, the void-Aram dodged his blade but lost its footing and fell.

He didn't have time to recover before Markus raised his sword for a killing blow.

And froze.

Syrup-covered blood streamed from a cut on Aram's brow. Markus gaped at him, halting the blade even as it fell.

Therlings don't bleed.

Aghast, Markus dropped his shield and released his helm, revealing his face.

"Markus?" whispered Aram, only his lips moving, as though every other part of him was paralyzed.

Markus could only stare at him, mouth open, tears clouding his eyes.

"You're alive..." he whispered.

The youth on the ground gazed up at him, eyes wide and lips quivering.

"What have you done...?"

A ram blinked slowly as he stared up into Markus's face, unable to believe what he was seeing. His heart had beat into his throat, and his stomach had capsized. He was reunited with the best friend he'd ever had—only to find him taking part in the slaughter of innocents.

Repulsed, he scrambled away from him.

"Aram!"

Markus rushed forward, holding out his hand. But Aram shot to his feet and edged backward.

"You killed them!" he cried, tears of heartbreak streaming down his face. *"Why did you kill them?"*

Markus shook his head. "I didn't! I swear, I didn't! Please believe me—I didn't kill anyone!"

"You were part of it! They were good people!"

"I didn't know!"

Aram stared hard into Markus's eyes, wanting desperately to believe him. But the dead that littered the ground made believing hard. He glanced back and forth between Markus and Shinota's body, trembling in despair and indecision.

"Markus!"

Looking up, Aram saw Sergan Parsigal storming toward them, a terrible light in his eyes. The sight of that horrible man filled his gut with cold revulsion. Before he could think, he was dodging around Markus with his sword raised, vision red with hatred.

"No!"

Markus caught Aram by the shoulder, pulling him back behind him and shielding him with his own body. Raising his sword, Markus shouted at Sergan, "Don't come any closer!"

Behind Sergan appeared a line of Imperial foot soldiers, weapons poised. The sorcerer stopped and a small smile blossomed on his lips, eerily disturbing when combined with the haunting blue fire in his eyes.

"You have one decision to make, Markus Galliar. Do you want Aram to die quickly? Or atrociously? I'll give you ten seconds to think about it."

Aram glanced from Sergan to the soldiers. He could use magic to defend them, but there were dozens of soldiers, each holding a weapon. There wasn't much he could do against so many. And then there was Sergan, a sorcerer of renowned capability.

"Five," said Sergan. "Four, three, two—"

"Be my Shield!" Aram gasped, sheathing his sword and wrapping his fists around handfuls of aethereal strands.

Tying them into a form that resembled a cat o' nine tails, he lashed out at the soldiers, multiplying the tails as they whipped through the air. Armor shattered as tongues of air connected with the front line of footmen, and men and weapons went flying.

Sergan uttered a growl and threw his hands up, summoning a crackling blue sphere that sizzled in his palm. With all his might, he flung it toward them, but Markus merely raised his shield, deflecting the magic easily.

The remaining soldiers charged them and, at the same time, Sergan conjured a lightning-fast torrent of projectiles that riddled the air around them. Markus dropped to one knee, bracing against the oncoming charge, and raised his shield in defense of Aram.

But just before the first soldiers reached them, a raging wind howled over the glade, forcing the men back and beating Sergan to his knees.

Aram drew his sword and sprang forward, determined to take advantage of his adversary's weakness. As he did, someone lunged toward him and caught his arm. Aram struggled, bringing his sword up to belt the man in the face with his pommel, but the man caught it easily. Grappling for control of his blade, Aram lifted his fist to bash him in the face.

It wasn't a man.

It was Vandra.

All around them, dragons were landing, the gusts of air displaced by their wings keeping the soldiers at bay. Aram turned back to see Sergan's face lose its color all at once, the light of the unholy fire dimming in his eyes.

"Come with me!" Vandra shouted, taking his arm and pulling Aram after her as she retreated toward Ragath.

But Aram twisted out of her grasp and darted back to where Markus stood, staring slack-jawed at the flight of dragons dropping from the sky.

Aram clutched his shoulders, shaking him. "Did you kill anyone? *Anyone?"*

Markus shook his head vigorously, tears raining from his eyes. "No!"

Aram believed him.

He turned and shouted at Vandra, "I'm not leaving without Markus!"

Vandra's face darkened in confusion that gave way quickly to anger. "Get on Narath!" she commanded, striding toward him. "That's an order!"

"No." Aram shook his head. "Not without Markus!"

"Narath can't take you both!" Vandra growled, then her eyes widened at something behind Aram.

Aram glanced back to see more soldiers advancing toward them, a pair of Exilari in front. Sergan sprinted to join them, tilting his head to quaff a mouthful of essence as he ran. Aram felt a powerful dread creep over him, realizing that their situation was quickly becoming dire. Glancing around desperately, he noticed a woman lying dead beside a green dragon that still hovered over her, shedding its grief in gouts of flame.

Aram released Markus and ran toward the dragon, practically careening into it with the force of his desperation. The meeting of minds was brief and anguishing: the shattered heart of a creature begging for release and the pleading of a young man desperate to save his best friend. The dragon moaned a low, keening groan, lowering her head.

An accord had been reached.

Loranth would set aside her grief to take one last flight before returning to die at her rider's side.

Motioning for Markus, Aram called, "She'll take you! Hurry!"

Looking horrified, Markus stood as though rooted, licking his lips and looking ready to run the other direction. He glanced back over his shoulder just in time to see a ball of magic arc toward them. Lifting his shield, he deflected it. Then he scrambled toward Aram and climbed onto Loranth's back.

The green dragon barely gave him a chance to grip its harness before vaulting into the sky in a gust of wind and swirling dust. Then Narath swept in, alighting to pick up Aram.

As soon as he pulled his leg over the dragon's back, someone shouted. He glanced up to see a crackling lance of magic streaking his way, and there was nothing he could do about it, for he couldn't lift a hand to defend himself.

At the last instant, Narath vaulted into the air and, with one great stroke of his wings, lifted them clear of the attack. Taken by surprise, Aram was almost flung from the dragon's back. He fell forward, holding on desperately with his arms wrapped around Narath's neck. Ahead of him, Vandra's brown dragon angled sharply upward into the sky, Markus and Loranth flying at her wing. Looking back, Aram took a last glimpse of the Great Tree burning behind them before it was lost in a black cloud of billowing smoke.

As they flew, his thoughts returned to Loranth and the rider she had lost. Part of him wanted desperately to try to intervene, to do something to convince her that her life didn't have to be over. But he had glimpsed the mind of the dragon, and he knew that Loranth could not stay. He would respect that. For this was the way it was meant to be.

When they landed, Loranth waited only as long as it took Markus to slide down from her back before taking wing. Aram watched her go with a heavy heart, wishing her godspeed. But then his gaze fell on Markus, and he couldn't restrain the joy he felt at seeing him here. Seeing him *alive.* Running toward him, Aram crashed into Markus with a great, euphoric hug.

"I thought you were dead!" Markus cried, stepping back to look at him with eyes wide and incredulous.

Aram opened his mouth to say the same thing, but his voice broke, so he laughed instead. He wiped tears of joy from his eyes and hugged Markus again, thanking the gods for returning his best friend to him.

He shook his head. "I can't believe—"

The sounds of running footsteps cut off his words. Turning, Aram put his hands up at the sight of a dozen men with swords and spears spilling forward to encircle them. Before he could react, Vandra swept past him, tackling Markus and knocking him to the ground. One of Vandra's men kicked Markus's sword away from him and pressed his spear against his neck.

"*Stop!*" Aram cried. "He's my friend!"

"He's one of their sorcerers!" Vandra snarled.

She straddled Markus's back, pinning him down with her weight and the strength of her thighs while one of her men tossed her a rope to bind Markus's arms behind his back. Standing, she hauled Markus to his feet and shoved him toward two of her men, who caught him by the arms.

"He's not a sorcerer!" Aram shouted. "He's a Shield! *He's my friend!*"

In two forceful steps, Vandra was in his face, shoving him backward with all of her weight. Aram staggered, but before he could fall, Vandra clamped a muscular arm around his neck and grabbed a fistful of his hair.

"Take him!" she snarled at her men, who led Markus away while Vandra restrained Aram with arms that felt like pillars of marble.

There was nothing he could do. He couldn't even turn his head and watch Markus go.

Vandra hung on to him for minutes after they were gone, the rest of her men dispersing, going back to tend their wounded and their dragons. At last, Vandra released him, flinging Aram away from her with such force that he fell onto his stomach.

"Report to Esmir!" she shouted.

"Please..." Aram begged, eyes welling with tears. "You don't understand!"

Vandra pointed at the stairwell. "Get the hell out of my eyrie! NOW!"

Picking himself up, Aram retreated. He fled the eyrie at a run and took the stairs up to Esmir's quarters.

He found the old Warden on the floor, leaning against a wall of his cave, legs splayed in front of him, a text folded open in his lap. His mouth was open, and he was snoring loudly.

Aram threw himself down at the table and buried his head in his hands, tears wetting his cheeks. He could not bear it. Markus had risked his own life to save him more than once, and yet there was nothing Aram could do to save *him.* He had no idea what Vandra intended to do with him, but he feared for Markus's life.

With nowhere else to go, he went to Esmir and shook the old man awake.

"What!" Esmir rasped, opening his baggy eyes.

"I need you!" Aram gasped. "Please! Wake up!"

"What is it?" The old man set the book down on the floor and sat up, wiping a trickle of saliva off his jowl. His eyes were watery and almost as red as his nose. Aram suspected he'd been in his cups again.

"My friend—the friend I told you about! Markus!" He had a hard time getting the words out. "I need your help!"

It took a long time to explain to Esmir about Markus, about the Heart of the Grove, about the torching of the Great Tree. By the end, Esmir sat staring straight ahead, as though incapable of processing all he had just heard.

At Esmir's lack of reaction, Aram bit his lip, fighting back tears of despair. "You don't understand!"

"I *do* understand," Esmir barked. "I was Daymar's husband as well as his Warden. I doubt there were ever two men closer than we were."

Aram hung his head. "What will happen to him, Esmir?"

"They will try him before the Council. They will likely find him guilty."

Terror lanced through Aram's heart, and he shot to his feet. "Then I need to talk to them! Right now!"

Esmir shook his head heavily. "You have no right to speak to the Council."

"I don't care!" Aram gulped, already heading for the door of the eyrie.

Bursting into the corridor, he took the stairs down to the level of the Council room and, without bothering to knock, thrust the door open and strode in. Within, the Council was already convened. Every person in the room turned to look at him as Aram forced himself into their midst. Expressions ranging from shock to outright hostility greeted him, but he paid them no mind. He strode right to the center of their circle and stopped beside the fire. Rage flaring in her eyes, Vandra started to rise, but the Dedicant Mother waved her down.

Looking at Aram with a stare of chiseled ice, Luvana said, "This is a closed meeting, Apprentice. We have heavy matters to weigh, not the least of which is the destruction of the Grove. Now, remove yourself! Turn around and walk back out that door."

Aram shook his head, his fists balled at his sides. His eyes felt red and raw, but at least they were dry. Desperation fueled his courage and trampled his prudence.

"I've come to beg for the release of Markus Galliar," he said. "He is my friend from my village. He was captured by the Exilari at the same time I was. He's been—"

"Exilar Galliar has been sentenced to death," interrupted Luvana flatly. "Now, go."

The world stopped.

"No," Aram gasped, shaking his head emphatically. "No! You can't do that! He's my best friend! He's like my brother! He's risked his life for me—"

Eyes flashing in ire, the Dedicant Mother rose to her feet and pointed at the doorway. "Leave here now, before I charge you with insubordination!"

Taking a menacing step toward her, Aram shouted, "I will not leave here until you release Markus!"

"Vandra," Luvana said quietly.

The Wingmaster surged to her feet and started toward him. But Aram evaded her, backing away toward the open wall of the chamber, maintaining his distance.

"Talk to him!" Aram pleaded. "Markus wouldn't kill innocents! He didn't hurt anyone!"

Vandra stalked toward him relentlessly. Aram backed away from her, mindful that he was being cornered against the cliff's edge. "Please! Just talk to him!"

Vandra hesitated, and Aram swung to glare his rage and defiance at Luvana. "If you execute Markus, you may as well kill me too!"

Scowling, Luvana waved Vandra forward. "Get him out of here."

The Wingmaster swiped out to catch him, but Aram dodged sideways, positioning himself right at the edge of the opening that looked out over the gaping chasm. Vandra drew up immediately, raising her hands, her eyes peering deeply into Aram's as though gauging his resolve.

To the Council, Aram proclaimed, "Markus Galliar is innocent. Either agree to hear his side of the story, or I'll take a long step backward."

"Wait!" One of the old men seated before the fire rose to his feet. "Would you believe the word of a Champion, Luvana?"

The Dedicant Mother kept her eyes on Aram as she answered, "He's not a Champion yet, Barom, and he'll likely never be."

"Nevertheless." The old man spread his hands. "If this young man passes the Trials, then a Champion is exactly what he will be. But he will never pass the Trials if he flings himself off the cliff. That this boy feels strongly enough to threaten his own life gives me pause. I wish to speak with this Markus Galliar before we condemn both these young men to death."

Luvana's lip curled, her eyes full of reproach. "Very well." To Aram, she ordered, "Move away from the edge."

But Aram shook his head. "No. Not until you talk to Markus."

There was a long, tense moment during which no one in the chamber moved. At last, Vandra turned and strode toward the door with a spitted curse. "I'll get him."

Aram remained at the edge of the chasm, feeling the wind of the gorge at his back. Every member of the Council was staring at him, but he didn't care. All his life, he'd wished desperately for a best friend, and he had found such a friend in Markus. He couldn't abandon him—he couldn't live with himself if he did. Compared to the pain of knowing he'd failed his friend, a plunge into oblivion would be a welcome alternative.

It took many minutes before Vandra returned with two men leading Markus, who came behind them in chains. He had been stripped of his armor and was brought forth before the Council shirtless and bruised, a cut on his cheek, his bottom lip split. As he entered, his gaze went straight to Aram and, seeing his position at the edge of a cliff, his eyes widened in fear. He shook his head vigorously.

"Markus Galliar." The Dedicant Mother rose to her feet, her eyes cold as death. "You stand accused of aiding the massacre of the people of the Grove. What do you have to say in your defense?"

Markus tried to spread his hands, but the chains binding his wrists denied him the motion.

"I didn't know!" he swore. "The army went through first. I didn't know they were killing villagers until I got there!"

Luvana's eyes narrowed. "What did you know, and when did you know it?"

Markus glanced around desperately at the members of the Council. "I knew we were breaking an Anchor to create a stable rupture. I didn't really know what that meant. I never heard anything about it before today, and I didn't know anything about a village. The moment I stepped through the rupture, all I knew was that we were under attack. I defended the sorcerer assigned to me until I saw the bodies, and when I realized what was happening…I abandoned my sorcerer…"

"And then what?"

"Then I saw Aram."

"By all reports, you attacked him too," the Dedicant Mother said coldly.

"I thought he was a void walker." Markus glanced at Aram with a look full of profound sorrow. "Please believe me—I would never kill civilians. I didn't know. I didn't …" His voice collapsed into sobs. His strong shoulders shook, and he raised his chained hands to his face.

"Did anyone see him abandon the fighting?" asked Luvana.

"I did!" snapped Aram. "He broke off from the fight and came to me!"

"And I," said Vandra. "I saw him lower his guard and walk away from the sorcerer he was protecting." She glanced at Aram, nodding slightly, and he smiled back with heartfelt gratitude.

Luvana's gaze went from Vandra to Markus, who stood bowed beneath the weight of his guilt. Tears glistened on his cheeks, his face red and tormented.

To Aram, she asked, "Will you vouch for him with your life?"

"With my life," Aram answered, for the first time daring to hope. "He's Impervious. If I pass the Trials, he can be my Warden."

The Dedicant Mother raised her hand, rubbing her eyes as though exhausted by the decision before her. "Very well. Are there any who disagree?"

Three hands went up around the fire, but they were outnumbered by the hands that didn't. Aram sagged in relief, feeling a heady dizziness. He moved forward, relinquishing his position at the edge of the chasm.

Luvana asked Markus, "Will you foreswear your allegiance to the Exilari and seal your cause to ours?"

Markus hesitated. "What exactly is your cause?"

"The defense of our world," Luvana answered. She added acidly, "From people like you."

Markus glanced back at Aram. "Do you support this?"

Aram smiled through tears of gratitude. "With all my heart."

"Then I will do the same."

"Very well." Raising her voice, the Dedicant Mother pronounced, "Let Markus Galliar be assigned to the fighting Wing as an apprentice. Wingmaster Vandra, he is now your charge. Have Esmir begin his training as a Warden."

As the two young men departed the Council chamber, Eraine Vandra watched them leave with a long, considering gaze. In truth, she was surprised that Luvana had conceded to halting the execution. She had grave misgivings about her own support, but it was a gamble she felt she had to take, because she felt deeply that Aram's only chance of success might lie with his Impervious friend. When Aram had first arrived at Skyhome, Vandra had held out little hope for him. She had doubted he would survive the training, much less the Trials of a Champion.

But now, each day a little more, she felt her mind changing. Aram was improving faster than she had ever imagined, and the magic he could summon was no less than miraculous. After his defense of the Grove, Vandra had allowed a tenuous hope to take root. But that hope depended on two grave uncertainties. First, every Champion needed a Warden, and the only trained Warden they had was Esmir, who was far past his prime. Which was why Vandra had voted to save Galliar's life, though only time would tell whether the young man's training as an Exilar hadn't poisoned his core.

It was the second uncertainty that was the source of many more sleepless nights.

Regarding Luvana with a long and searching gaze, Vandra asked, "When do you intend to tell Aram about his father?"

"Not until I have to."

Vandra nodded gravely, for she hoped Aram wasn't destined for the same calamity.

PART III

APPRENTICE

Markus spent the remainder of the day getting reacquainted with Aram. He couldn't believe how healthy his old friend was and how much he had grown. Aram had changed so much from the twelve-year-old boy he had rescued from Jory Kannet and his friends back in Anai. And not only physically—Aram was much more animated when he spoke, and he seemed to have a passion for life that had been lacking when he was younger, perhaps learned from his experience in the cellars. His face had lost a lot of its severity, so his rigid gaze wasn't as unsettling as it used to be.

Markus was also amazed by the world he found himself in. He had known dragons existed, for he had seen and fought the ones that had come through ruptures. But he could have never imagined what a real, living dragon would look like. His experience on the back of one had been the most breathtaking minutes of his life. The people who lived among them reminded him of his own people, the Vards, though many of their customs were different. They had the same brown skin and hair, and any one of them could have passed for a citizen of Anai. It was the accents that threw him off the most. They rolled their *r* sounds instead of softening them, and accented different syllables.

Markus followed Aram back to his dormitory and, once there, set him up in his own bunk, moving his things to the one beneath it. He then introduced himself to the other apprentices who would be his roommates. They seemed nice enough, except for Iver and Eugan, who seemed a little hesitant, not sure what to make of him or his past with the Exilari, and both had an obvious dislike of Aram.

They stayed awake long into the deep hours of the night, whispering about home and their experience with the Exilari and Aram's experiences in this new world. When Markus tried questioning Aram about the cellars, though, he wouldn't talk about it. He grew quiet and clammed up. Markus understood, so he stopped asking, feeling horrible for him, wishing he could have gotten him out of there years before he did. He was just happy that whatever horrors the Extractors had inflicted upon Aram hadn't caused irreparable damage. It was almost unbelievable, really. He had seen the other people in that courtyard with him, and their minds had been broken, one and all.

Of course, none of them were Aram, and that made a big difference.

When they blew out the small candle and lay down to sleep, Markus pulled his covers up and gazed at the shadows of the ceiling, beyond grateful for this chance to start over—to become a person he wasn't ashamed of being.

In the morning, they ate breakfast with the other apprentices. Aram was excited for the day—excited to show Markus around his new home and show him how much he had learned with the aid of his new friends, hoping more than anything that Markus would be proud of him.

But as soon as they arrived at the training grounds, Master Henrik told them they would no longer be training with the other students. From now on, they would be reporting to the Henge every day. Hearing that filled Aram with not just disappointment but a dark feeling of foreboding. He didn't like looking at the ring of standing stones, knowing what they meant for him. He didn't know why he and Markus had to train there. There wasn't even any equipment up there. Besides, who was going to instruct them?

He led Markus up the many long flights of steps to the top of the cliffs. There, Aram started across the sand-paved circle to the center of the stone ring, but when he got there, he saw that Markus hadn't followed him. Instead, his friend had walked toward the edge of the bluff and was looking down into the great fissure of the gorge. Aram could only imagine what Markus was thinking—probably the same thing *he* had been thinking when he'd first seen the bottomless rent in the earth: wondering what kind of evils could be spawned down there.

Eventually, Markus turned away from the edge and walked toward him across the circle. There, they stood in silence, peering at the stone monuments: Aram, with feelings of anxiety and dismay, and Markus, with a look of wary speculation.

To Aram's surprise, they were joined by Esmir, who came out from behind one of the perimeter buildings, panting from the climb and limping toward them with the aid of a cane.

Drawing up in front of them, the old man bobbed his head at Markus and said, "I'm Esmir Revin. I'm what you Exilari call a Shield. I was a Champion's Shield, so I'm called a Warden. I'll be making you unlearn everything those imbeciles taught you." To both of them, he said, "From now on, you will report here, to me. Our goal is to make Aram into a Champion." He poked his cane into Markus's chest. "And you into his Warden. How many years did you study with the Exilari?"

"Five and a half," answered Markus.

"Well, you can throw out most of what you learned from them." Esmir swiped his hand through the air with a disgusted look. "Shielding a Champion is very different from Shielding one of their sorcerers. Even with all the essence they can drink, an Exilari sorcerer still can't see in color. Which means they can only do one thing at a time, and they have to focus on the details. True Savants, on the other hand, see in color, but it's more than just that. Daymar described it as weaving an entire loom of threads all at the same time. Which means that Aram can weave an entire tapestry of magic in seconds, so you're going to have to learn to react a lot faster."

Markus glanced at Aram with a look of new appreciation.

Esmir continued, "So all of those cumbersome forms and exercises they taught you will have to be forgotten. You will have to learn to be fluid on your feet. You can't use a bulky shield, so you'll have to learn how to use your own body to Shield him. It's all about positioning. But, more than that, it's about teamwork. The two of you will have to train together until you can anticipate every move the other makes. You're going to have to move as one body controlled by the same brain—and that's going to take a hell of a lot of coordination and practice." He rammed the butt of his cane into the sand. "Which means we need to start *now.*"

As he was speaking to Markus, Aram was gazing around the square, looking at the ominous standing stones surrounding it, each a door to a terrifying unknown. The longer he stood there, the deeper anxiety's sharp claws dug into him.

He looked at Esmir in concern. "How will any of this help me prepare for the Trials? Won't I have to go in alone?"

"You're ready to move on to a new phase in your training," Esmir told him. "But it's taxing, so you can only spend so much time at it. And you'll need Markus the moment you come back out of those stones, so you need to start working together."

"Will there be any Trials for me?" asked Markus.

Esmir gave him a sad, knowing smile. "Every day of your life will be a trial. It's a heavy burden, knowing that the life of a Champion depends upon you exclusively."

Markus frowned, a worried and distant expression on his face. "That's…intimidating."

"It is. Everything you do from this moment forward should be done with that thought in mind." The old Warden clapped his hands. "Now, for the first order of business! We have to get both of you sized for armor. You'll also need swords. *Real* swords," he added, lifting his eyebrows at the worn blade Aram wore at his side.

"I've got armor," said Markus.

"Bah!" Esmir crinkled his face. "You can throw that armor off the cliff. It's too damn heavy, and it will slow you down too much. A Warden needs special armor, so he can be light on his feet. The same for a Champion." He pointed a finger at Aram. "You need armor that can take a beating in case Markus goes down. And it needs to be made of a material that's highly conductive. So that's going to be our first order of business. Now, to the armorer!"

With that, he headed toward the stairs.

When Aram and Markus just stood looking at each other in confusion, Esmir turned back and demanded, "Unless you'd rather fight naked?"

The trip down the cliff took much longer than it should have, for Esmir had to be loaded into a series of wooden elevators and lowered down by winch. But eventually, they made it all the way down to the level of Hearth Home and entered the town. Aram couldn't help smiling at the way Markus walked with his eyes drawn upward instead of watching where he was going, narrowly avoiding running into several people. It reminded him of his own reaction when he'd first seen the spectacle of the cliffs and the flights of dragons in the sky.

They followed Esmir through the town's busy streets, passing people and carts and goats and chickens fluttering by. They came at last to one of the broader streets, where the larger craft houses were located. There, Esmir led them to a two-story building with a large workshop behind it.

When they entered the shop, a small bell mounted to the top of the door tinkled, announcing their presence. An old man wearing a leather bib apron appeared. Seeing Esmir, the armorer broke into a smile and came forward, hugging the old Warden and clapping him on the back.

"Adric!" Esmir all but bellowed. "I've brought you two young waifs. This here is Aram Raythe, Champion-in-Training. And this is Markus Galliar, who might someday be his Warden, if the gods hate him enough."

"This is Adric Krommer," Esmir told the boys. "He has been Master Armorer for the eyries longer than I've been alive."

Knowing how old Esmir was, Aram exclaimed in awe, "Wow, you're *old!*"

The armorer's eyebrows shot up, and he exchanged looks with Esmir. Aram felt Markus's hand on his back. There was a short but awkward moment of silence, then Master Krommer chuckled and patted him on the shoulder.

"Let's take your measurements, son." He directed Aram toward the back of the room where another door opened into the workshop. Esmir and the armorer went through first, and when Aram started after them,

Markus caught his shoulder.

"Don't point out to people that they're old. You can hurt their feelings."

Aram flushed, mortified that he might have hurt Master Krommer's feelings. He'd said the wrong thing again, just as he always did. He could kick himself.

"Should I say I'm sorry?"

"Maybe." Markus frowned. "Actually, don't. It might make it worse."

Cheeks flushed, Aram hurried through the door into the back of the workshop. There, six apprentices were hard at work, tooling and stitching leather, shaping metal plates, and riveting chain links. One of the younger boys came toward them, bowing to Esmir.

"Get their measurements." Master Krommer motioned at Aram and Markus.

The boy produced a length of knotted string and went right to work, starting with Markus.

While Aram waited his turn, Esmir explained, "Each piece of armor crafted in Master Krommer's workshop is fitted specifically for the wearer, taking into account his abilities and style of fighting."

"Why does it matter?" asked Aram.

"Because the armor has to move with you, not against you. You want it to fit you perfectly in every situation, so you're not encumbered. The armor crafted in this workshop is the finest in the world—*either* world. No other could approach it."

Aram considered the Master Armorer with a newfound respect and felt suddenly wretched. Hanging his head, he mumbled, "I'm sorry I hurt your feelings by pointing out that you're old."

Hearing that, Master Krommer closed his eyes and brought a hand up to his face. Then he threw his head back in a fit of hearty laughter. Clapping Aram on the back, he said to Esmir, "He's just like Darand, isn't he?"

Hearing that, Aram said, "My father's name was Darand."

Esmir blinked. With a forced smile, he muttered, "Well, isn't that a coincidence," then guided Aram quickly toward a full suit of scale mail hanging from a rack. "Here's an example of the kind of armor Master

Krommer's workshop is capable of turning out."

Aram reached out and touched one of the red lacquered scales of the cuirass. It had a satin sheen and seemed as fragile as glass. Each scale was etched with fine patterns that were almost invisible to the eye. "What kind of material is this?"

"Dragon scale," Master Krommer answered with a smile. "It makes for the lightest and strongest armor."

Aram tensed, retracting his hand. "You slaughter dragons?"

The old armorer smiled. "Not at all. Most dragons petrify when they die. But sometimes—no one knows why—that doesn't happen. In that case, a dragon's remains are never wasted. The hideheight is used for armor, the meat is fed to the ill and injured, and the bones are made into weapons, among other things."

Finished with Markus, the young apprentice came over to take Aram's measurements. When he was finished, Master Krommer explained that they would have to return in four months so that he could check the fit and make any necessary adjustments.

"Four *months?*" Aram was stunned. It seemed like such a long time for a workshop with that many apprentices.

Esmir explained, "Because it's so resistant, dragon scale is the most difficult material to work with. Making a suit of armor out of it is a very long and detailed process."

"How is it made?" Aram asked.

"Each cuirass has about a thousand scales. The scales have to go through a lengthy curing process that can take up to two months. After that, we lace them together then lay them out in rows to be tooled and lacquered. It takes a couple of weeks to tool them all, and each scale receives ten coats of lacquer. Each layer must dry and be sanded before the next can be applied. After lacquering, we tie them all together."

Aram stared at the suit of scale mail with a greater appreciation. He wondered if his armor would look similar

"What about swords?" Markus asked.

Esmir smiled a mischievous grin. "That's where we're headed to next."

"Where are we going now?" Aram asked.

"To the Brausa family workshop," Esmir answered. "They own the only forge hot enough to produce a star-steel blade. It's been in their family for generations. And by generations, I mean thousands of years."

Aram followed Esmir down the street into the main market square, his eyes roving over the tower houses surrounding it. Each house was several stories tall with an entrance on the second floor. Bronze placards were mounted to the sides of the buildings, many of which bore the symbols of the trade practiced by each workshop. Some were etched with the craft master's personal trademark, usually the stylized picture of an animal or craft item.

They arrived at a building marked by a bronze placard featuring a sword crossed with a feather. Flagstone steps led from the street to a large oaken door, which Esmir held open for them. Within, they found themselves in a long, thin room with many swords mounted on the walls. Aram was drawn to the nearest wall, which contained blades of various types, some familiar, others not. His eyes roved over the weapons, which all looked to be made of superior workmanship.

The rear wall of the shop contained only a single, elegant sword mounted horizontally. Walking closer to view it, Aram saw that the blade was single-edged, long and thin with a graceful curve, the point tapered slightly upward. The hilt, carved of bone and wrapped with cord, canted in the opposite direction and had a disk-shaped guard. Aram had never seen any sword like it. The metal of the blade had a satiny sheen and seemed to lack any imperfection.

"What kind of sword is this?" Aram asked.

Coming up behind him, Esmir answered, "That is a star-steel blade. It is the sword of a Champion."

Aram reached out slowly, gripping the hilt and testing the feel of it in his palm. "Why do Champions need special swords?"

"Because a Champion's sword must be able to withstand blows that would shatter normal steel. A Champion strikes with the strength of his soul, not the strength of his muscles." A strange smile slipped to Esmir's lips. "Tell me, Aram, how strong is your soul?"

Aram frowned, thinking hard, for it was a novel and intriguing concept. "I don't know. I've never measured it."

"Yes, you have," said Markus. "You survived four years in the cellars of the Exilari—and you can still smile. That says something." He turned to Esmir. "Do you think they can make a blade that strong?"

The old man raised his eyebrows thoughtfully. "We'll see."

They turned at the sound of a door opening behind them, admitting the swordsmith who owned the workshop. He was the antithesis of every blacksmith Aram had ever met, a small man with delicate features. His dark hair was worn tied back from a round face that was glistening with sweat and yet somehow without a trace of soot. Esmir immediately strode forward, greeting him warmly.

"Onsel! Good to see you again. This is Aram and Markus." He motioned them over. "Markus will be needing a Warden's sword. Aram will be needing a star-steel blade."

At that, the swordsmith frowned, and he looked at Aram with acute speculation. Walking forward, he went to Markus first, taking him by the shoulders and running his gaze over him, turning him slightly first one way, then the other. Then he moved to Aram and did the same.

"Let's go in the back," he said, motioning with his head toward the door.

The two young men followed him into an enormous workshop.

Many apprentices were working at different stations around the room, attending to their various tasks with acute attention. There were three live forges in the center of the room, heating the air of the workshop to an uncomfortable temperature, even though the walls were set with many windows that let in the cool breeze from the gorge. Only a couple of apprentices looked up upon their entry, their eyes going right back to their work. Seeing them, a thin man slightly taller than Onsel rose from where he'd been crouched by one of the forges and approached them.

"This is my brother, Gadan Brausa," Onsel said. "He will see to the construction of the Warden's sword."

Gadan Brausa greeted them with a meek smile and a nod, then drew Markus aside and started questioning him.

"I will be constructing the star-steel blade," said the smaller brother, and bade Aram follow him to the other side of the workshop, to a cold forge set into the back corner. There, he produced a wax tablet and told Aram to stand up as straight as he could, correcting his posture and examining him from various angles while Aram stood rigid, feeling intensely uncomfortable. At length, the swordsmith stepped back to look at him, knuckling his chin, a grave frown on his face. With a grunt, he started the whole process over again. Occasionally, he would motion for Aram to turn slightly, taking more notes on his tablet. At one point, he produced a string and started measuring everything about him, from the length of his forearms to the diameter of his legs. Aram glanced across the workshop and saw that Markus was receiving a similar treatment by Onsel's brother, which made him feel mollified.

"The creation of a Champion's blade is a monumental undertaking," the swordsmith explained in a soft voice as he worked. "Each blade is forged from iron mined from a fallen star. But more importantly, the source of carbon in the steel is dragon bone, which allows the steel to be heated far beyond what normal steel could ever endure."

Aram had seen plenty of falling stars, but he had never heard of anyone actually catching one. "How long will it take?"

The swordsmith answered, "Six months."

Aram winced, casting a questioning glance at Esmir. "Will it be ready in time for my Trials?"

"You won't need it for your Trials," Esmir answered. "You'll need it after."

"In the meantime, I will loan you a similar blade, though of far less quality," Onsel Brausa said. "You must understand, a star-steel blade is crafted specifically for its wielder. The materials are very rare, and the work that goes into it is great. It takes time to smelt the iron from the meteorite to make the steel, but then I will need you present to begin the forging process. Return here a month from now, before dawn."

Aram nodded, his eyes wandering over the tools in the workshop and the glowing coals of the forges. "One month."

Seeming satisfied, the swordsmith turned back to his forge. When Markus was done with Onsel's brother, they were loaned blades that would resemble the ones that had been commissioned for them. Though dulled and made of mundane steel, they were still of excellent craftsmanship.

After that, Esmir led them back to his eyrie then spent the rest of the afternoon working with Markus while assigning Aram to the task of scrubbing his floor. They remained with Esmir the rest of the day, at last going down to supper with the other apprentices.

After supper, they returned to the dormitory, where Markus had a chance to become better acquainted with their roommates. He and Jeran found they had much in common, for they both came from families of fishermen. Although Jeran's family had grown up fishing the shoals of southern Pyrial, he had led a similar life, with an overbearing father and an absent mother. Even Iver showed Markus a wary respect, clasping his hand in greeting before probing him about his training as an Exilar, which seemed to intrigue him greatly. The conversation was hampered by Markus's difficulty with their accents, but in the end, that just seemed to make it more fun.

Aram sat on his cot, watching Markus with his new friends, feeling a little lonelier every second. Many of them were closer to Markus's age than his own, and he began to fear Markus would enjoy their company more than his. But it turned out that his fears were misplaced for, seeing him sitting on his bunk, staring at the floor, Markus called Aram over and included him in the conversation. In that moment, Aram realized that, for the first time in his life, he was surrounded by a group of people he could call true friends.

That night when he went to sleep, it was with that thought in his mind and a smile on his face, feeling more content than ever in his life.

The next month passed agonizingly slow.

In the mornings, they trained in the Henge with the new weapons the Brausa brothers had lent them. The weighted broadsword they had loaned Markus had a long, double-edged blade attached to a hilt with a sturdy crossguard and a disk-shaped pommel. Aram had been given a dulled sword that resembled the beautiful star-steel weapon on the wall of the Brausas' workshop.

In the afternoons, while Esmir worked with Markus on fundamentals he would need if he was ever to be a Warden, Aram returned to the never-ending supply of books Esmir was always providing him. They ranged in topic from anything to do with knots to mathematics to music and history. He applied himself to their study with an obsessive fixation, for he found them fascinating. Every day on the way to Esmir's, he could feel his heartbeat pick up in anticipation of what he might find within a leather binding. Books, he was finding out, could be just as much of an adventure as knots, and equally rewarding.

So caught up was he in his studies that he began neglecting other things. His friends started chiding him that he was always occupied, and they started searching for ways to pry him from his studies. They also started getting on him about his appearance, teasingly at first, then with increasing concern. It was true that he found it increasingly hard to tear himself away from his studies to do things as boring and unnecessary as folding his bedsheets or scrubbing the stains out of his clothes. Both were an enormous waste of time, and, really, who could tell if he was a couple days late on changing his breeches?

"Look," Markus said to him one night, pulling Aram aside. "I know you love your knots and books, but if you want to have any friends left, you'd better learn to break yourself away and spend more time with them. And start taking better care of yourself. You're not a boy anymore."

Red-faced, Aram glanced down at his rumpled, sweat-stained tunic, the same one he'd been wearing for the past few days.

"And you need to start shaving," Markus insisted, prompting Aram to raise a hand to his face.

Feeling around, he discovered that he had somehow managed to grow patches of scraggly whiskers on his cheeks. He didn't know where they'd come from or when they'd gotten there. He'd been sporting peach fuzz on his chin for months, but at some point, it had given way to the real beginnings of a beard—and he hadn't even noticed.

"I don't know how to shave," he whispered.

So commenced his first shaving lesson, when he received his first-ever gift from Markus: a bone-handled razor.

After that, Aram became scrupulous about spending more time with his friends and making sure his clothes were always clean and his face recently shaven. He recognized that, while obsessing over things like knots and books might be a strength, it could also be another weakness. He could learn a lot by applying himself so obsessively—but he could lose a lot of friends doing that too. There was a delicate art to balance that he needed to find, and he vowed to strive for it.

A month went by.

He hardly noticed.

But one day, Aram found himself waking before dawn to take the first of many walks down the long stairs to Hearth Home, to knock on the door of the Brausas' workshop.

The door opened, and he was met by Onsel, who motioned him inside without speaking. He led Aram to the smithy in the back of the workshop, which was empty, save for two apprentices. Both boys bowed formally to him when Aram entered. One came forward and handed him a black apron, which he tied on before following Onsel to the forge.

"A star-steel blade is a work of art," Onsel Brausa informed him. "But more than anything, it is an extension of its wielder. Because of that, you must be present during critical moments of the forging of your blade, and you must also put your own effort into it, so the blade knows you as its master. From time to time, I will ask you to return here to participate in different steps of the process."

Aram nodded excitedly, his eyes wandering over the tools that lined the walls of the shop. There were various types of long-handled grasping tools and tongs, and a vast assortment of hammers, ranging from very small ones to sledgehammers with handles longer than he was tall. There were files, chisels, and clamps of all sizes, along with troughs of water and large, floor-mounted whetstones and anvils.

"The strength of a star-steel blade lies in its composition," the delicate swordsmith said quietly. "Each sword possesses a destiny. To achieve that destiny, it must perform its duties without breaking or bending. So, inside, we give it a core of soft and flexible steel. Then we cover the core with a jacket of harder steel. This makes the blade strong and allows it to hold a fine edge."

Motioning for Aram to follow, he guided him toward the cold forge in the back corner of the workshop. On the left side of the forge was the bellows, which was operated by a piston pulled with a long handle. The forge itself was long and narrow, simply a trench cut into the floor and filled with charcoal, covered by a large hood to vent the smoke.

Squatting beside his forge, Onsel motioned Aram to crouch next to him. "This is the forge where the blades of Champions are created."

Opening a container at his side, he selected an irregular chunk of bright steel roughly the size of his palm and handed it to Aram. "This is special steel mined from a fallen star."

Aram gazed down at the heavy chunk of steel in his hand, marveling at it. To think, he was holding an actual piece of a star, something that had fallen from the heavens. It was irregular, reminiscent of pumice, and glistened with flecks of many different colors, just like his own eyes.

Taking the piece of steel back, Onsel handed Aram a thin metal rod as long as his forearm. "The first step to creating a star-steel blade is to light the forge. This is a task only you can perform. To light the forge, hammer this rod to a sharp point. If you strike it hard and fast enough, the point will produce heat."

He gave Aram a small hammer then motioned him toward an anvil set into the floor. Aram held the rod at an angle and struck the tip of it with the hammer.

"That's good!" said Onsel. "Now, just like that—flatten it!"

Aram did as instructed, striking the metal rod with his hammer several times, making a *tink-tinking* sound. When the end was flat, he turned it over and struck the other side.

"Keep turning it," Onsel directed. "Strike faster!"

Aram did as he said, turning the rod over and over while striking it with the hammer, lengthening the end and sharpening it to a point.

"Faster!"

He could feel his forehead start to sweat. Pressing his tongue against his upper lip, Aram concentrated harder, putting all his vast focus into the precision of the act, striking the rod faster until the tip started heating up.

At that point, Onsel handed him a strip of parchment, which he held to the heated tip, and watched as it started smoldering, then blackening, at last producing a flame.

"Quick! Light the forge!" Onsel urged.

Moving quickly but carefully, Aram scrambled past him, shielding the tiny flame with his hand, and used the lit piece of parchment to ignite the kindling within the forge.

Instantly, the star-steel forge blazed to life.

"Good!" Onsel cried.

Grabbing a shovel, he added fuel to the forge. "This is special charcoal made from crushed dragon bone!" he said loud enough to be heard over the scraping of the shovel and the crackling of the flames. "It produces far more heat than regular charcoal and will add carbon to the steel without letting it burn!"

The forge flared, casting sparks upward toward the hood. As the forge heated, Onsel stirred the coals with an iron rod, working the piston of the bellows with his other hand.

"The color of the flame tells us the temperature of the forge," he explained, pumping the bellows. "If we want a hotter flame, we add air to the forge."

With that, he stopped pumping and let the flames cool, fading from pink to orange. Fascinated, Aram watched the flames of the forge gradually dwindle, leaving the coals glowing red. At that point, Onsel grabbed a pair of tongs and placed one of the large steel ingots directly into the coals. "We start out with four times more steel than we actually need, because most of the impurities will be removed during the forging."

Aram crouched on the floor, watching in silence as the piece of star steel gradually heated until it was red-hot. When it reached the right color, Onsel motioned his apprentices forward then removed the chunk of steel with a pair of tongs. He set the glowing steel on an anvil and held it there with the tongs while his apprentices used sledgehammers to beat the glowing steel flat, hitting it in turns while Onsel held it to the anvil.

After it was flattened, the glowing ingot was returned to the forge to reheat. Then it was removed and placed on the anvil again. This time, Onsel picked up a small hammer and started tapping out a rhythm on the anvil. His apprentices stood on wood boxes to add to their height. They took turns beating the steel with their sledges while Onsel tapped with his hammer as though drumming a cadence. It took Aram a moment to realize that Onsel was using his hammer to communicate, giving directions to his apprentices by varying the patterns of his tapping. When the steel was flat, he doused it in a water bath, which steamed and gurgled.

"This pulls out the impurities then peels them off the surface." Setting the cooled steel wafer back on the anvil, Onsel rose to his feet. "This is as far as we go today," he said with a gentle smile. "You did well. I will call you back in a week to move on to the next step."

Aram nodded absently, gazing down at the steel that would someday be his sword. He felt no small amount of pride that he was allowed to participate in his sword's forging. Thanking the master swordsmith, he removed the apron and left the workshop.

The stench of the burned forest permeated everything: the air, the soil, the food, the water...even his hair and clothing. For the hundredth time that day, Sergan spit the taste of ashes out of his mouth, gnashing his teeth. Smoke was still thick in the air, and in many places, the Grove was still smoldering. He had to be careful wherever he walked to avoid stepping on the charcoaled remains of both people and animals.

He waited in front of the pavilion that had been erected beside the new gateway they had established between worlds. Scores of soldiers had been flooding in from the Imperial side of the gateway, more every day. An entire army was gathering, ready to defend their freshly gained territory. They brought with them many miners and Extractors to harvest the wealth of essence they had secured.

The Extractors were already busy filling jugs and carts with water from the Wellspring. Others had set about the task of butchering the great Tree, harvesting its wood, which was rich in essence and had other arcane properties. Even the soil around the Wellspring was being mined. After the battle, the soldiers had figured out that the loam possessed healing properties, and many had slathered it on their wounds.

"Exilar."

Sergan turned to regard the soldier who stood awaiting his attention. "Yes, Corporal?"

The soldier, a gaunt man with pale skin splattered with freckles, reported, "A woman claiming to be an emissary wishes to speak with you."

"Interesting," Sergan muttered under his breath. The Grand Vizier had warned him he'd be contacted by their allies in this world. Sergan assumed those allies were the ones responsible for torching the forest, although he had seen no evidence of them yet. "Bring her here."

"At once, Exilar."

He watched the man walking away, a tingling sensation crawling over his skin. A frown crossed his lips, then his gaze drifted to Obriem, who stood apart from him, intent upon the rape of the Wellspring. He had never liked Obriem, but since Markus had defected, he had no choice but to work with him. The sorcerer Obriem had been paired with had died during the battle for the Anchor, which was an unfortunate convenience. Sergan lacked a Shield and Obriem lacked a sorcerer, so he'd taken him on. It was either him or Poda, and Poda's nature was too gentle for the task at hand. Obriem had a coarser side to him, a grit that would be necessary for what they faced ahead.

He called Obriem over with a sharp whistle.

"Some type of emissary's coming to speak with us," Sergan informed him. "I want you here with me."

Obriem wiped the sweat out of his eyes, creating a smear of sooty grime across his brow. "Do you suspect treachery?"

"I always suspect treachery." Sergan trained an accusatory smile on Obriem.

The young man scowled, not missing the expression nor the intent. Sergan enjoyed irritating him, for Obriem irritated *him.*

He cut the smile short, though, as he caught sight of a small party riding toward them around the perimeter of the Wellspring. At their head rode an albino woman with long, lustrous white hair, and though her skin and eyes were wincingly pale, her facial features were striking. She drew her horse up in front of them, looped her reins around the pommel of her saddle, then lowered herself lithely to the ground. Stepping forward, she bent at the waist, presenting herself with a formal but masculine bow.

Sergan plied her with a gallant smile. "Welcome to my encampment, Mistress…?"

The woman returned his smile. "Greetings, Exilar. My name is Lazair Saliste. My master, Kathrax, has sent me here to speak with you regarding our mutual interests."

Sergan ran his gaze over her, taking in her silken robes, which were strangely unaffected by the environment of ash and soot she had traversed reaching him. She must not have come from far away, he decided.

"Exilar Sergan Parsigal. So honored to make your acquaintance, My Lady Lazair." He mimicked her bow. "Please join me inside?"

Holding back the tent flap, he waited for her to enter the pavilion before following her, Obriem having to duck to enter behind them. Inside, the tent was large enough that they could both stand upright, covered in rugs and appointed with elegant furniture. Sergan motioned his visitor to have a seat at a long walnut table, pouring her a cup of wine before taking one of the chairs across from her.

Folding his hands, he invited her, "Please enlighten me about our 'mutual interests.'"

The pale woman took a sip of her wine, capturing and holding his gaze. He couldn't help but stare at her, for he found her intensely fascinating. As the seconds went by, and his initial shock subsided, he found himself reassessing her appearance, his appreciation of her looks swelling enormously.

Her skin was chalky white with undertones of pink, in some places all but translucent. The woman's eyes were her most arresting feature, for they were a shivering purple-blue, framed by long eyelashes that appeared frosted with ice. Her face seemed chiseled from crystal, all sharp edges and angular planes, and there was a subtle sheen to her cheeks that made them glisten in the candlelight. By the time she opened her mouth to speak, Sergan was convinced that he sat across the table from the most striking woman in the world.

She smiled at him with full lips that were naturally pink. "In the land where I come from, there are four great tribes who are ruled by four great thanes who are, in turn, guided by prophets of the Divine Archon Kathrax."

Sergan grunted. "There are many gods of men, my lady, but I've never met one I'd consider divine."

The woman's brows compressed slightly in what might have been irritation. "The Divine Archons are far greater than mortals and yet less than gods. Once, before the Sundering, there were seven. Seven brothers, the Scions of Senestra."

Sergan knew that name, for in the ancient myths, Senestra had been a human sorceress seduced by the Earth-Father, spreading her legs in exchange for divinity. Ahn had sired on her seven sons, the Seven Archons, who had been entrusted with the protection of the Auld, their father's mortal children. But when Senestra received the gift of divinity, she turned against her lover, sparking the War of Desolation that had been fought between the gods of Auld and the gods of Men. The Archons of Senestra had betrayed their vows and turned against the Auld. In response, the first Champions arose to oppose them, and the ensuing battle had eventually ended in the Sundering, stranding most of the Archons in the World of Men—the World Above. Of course, all of that was just mythology—just ancient man's pathetic attempt to explain the cataclysm that had broken their world.

So, this woman and her people worshipped a demigod who, if mythology was to be believed, was committed to the annihilation of the Auld and the defeat of their Champions.

Interesting.

They had achieved that goal in the World Above, it would seem. And now this Archon Kathrax was moving against the Auld in the World Below, conceivably to end the race forever.

Perhaps there was something to mythology, after all.

"And what would the Divine Archon have of me?" Sergan poured a cup of wine for himself.

The woman gave him a wan smile. "The Archons of both our worlds have been working for centuries to reverse the Sundering. Your God-Emperor has pledged you to the service of his brother, Kathrax, to aid us in this task."

Sergan stared at her vacantly, his mind working as swiftly as it could to connect all the dots she had just strewn before him like breadcrumbs.

God-Emperor Mirak ruled the Abadian Empire supposedly by divine right and was regarded by most of his subjects as truly divine. Mirak was also called the Never-Dying for, according to legend, that same man had ruled the Abadian Empire for hundreds of years. Since no one except his servants were allowed to see the Emperor, this claim had never been proven nor disproven. Most people of reason tossed the notion aside, assuming that the births and deaths of Emperors were cloaked in secrecy so that the illusion of divinity could be maintained.

But if mythology could be believed, then perhaps there was something to legend, as well.

Sergan's eyes narrowed. "You're saying that the Emperor of the Abadian Empire is an Archon?"

Lazair nodded, smiling coyly. She took a sip of her drink, smoothing her crystalline hair back from her face. "Your Emperor is one of the three Archons that exist in your world."

Sergan reminded himself of how much he hated religious fanatics. It was too bad this woman was one of them. She was almost beautiful enough for him to want to attempt a dalliance.

"Who are the others?" he asked.

"One is the ruler of your own Order." She smiled grandly.

"Valeda?" He could not suspend his disbelief any longer and let out a hearty chuckle. "The wine must be too strong for you, my dear. Maybe you should leave off."

"You believe I lie?" She scoffed, as though it were *he* that was the fool.

"I'm not calling you a liar. I'm calling you delusional," Sergan corrected. "Either that, or you think I am."

Setting down her cup of wine, Lazair gave him an enigmatic smile then rose gracefully to her feet. "Come with me, then. Let me prove my sanity."

Intrigued, Sergan rose after her. Setting down his wine, he followed her out of the tent and let her lead him back to the rest of her entourage, who had remained behind with their mounts.

"I invite you to ride with me out a short distance from this camp," Lazair said, untying her reins from her saddle.

Sergan looked at her sidelong, wondering just how far he dared trust this mysterious and exotic creature. "May I bring my Shield along?"

"Of course."

He licked his lips, pausing in indecision. Then he summoned Obriem with a jerk of his head. Lazair waited for them to procure mounts, then motioned for him to take a place behind her black horse.

Clucking his stallion forward, Sergan motioned for Obriem to ride abreast of him. Together, the three of them rode away from the defiled Wellspring into the smoldering devastation of the forest. A white haze of smoke hung low to the ground, rising from hot spots that still seethed beneath a thick layer of ash. The Grove was thoroughly denuded, reduced to a charcoaled wasteland. Sparse, blackened snags were the only evidence that there was ever a forest here in the first place. Ash drifted like snowflakes from the sky, dusting the shoulders of his mantle.

Sergan kept his gaze fixed on Lazair's back as they rode. She sat her horse straight, fully at ease in the saddle. Every so often, she glanced back at him, flashing him a knowing smile before turning back around.

Eventually, they came to a place where the ground sloped downward toward a dry riverbed. There, Sergan's eyes fell on a good-sized encampment that all of his scouts either hadn't noticed or had somehow forgotten to inform him about. Sergan traded looks with Obriem, who sat his horse rigidly with an ever-deepening scowl. Apparently, his new Shield didn't like the situation either.

They started down the blackened hill toward the riverbed. His horse shied when a rock turned under its hoof. The beast was already ill at ease, made anxious by the sights and smells of the surrounding terrain. Beside him, Obriem's mount tossed its head and chomped nervously on the bit.

Before they reached the bottom of the slope, Sergan's attention was captured by the sound of low, inhuman moans. He rode leaning forward, scanning the ground ahead, but could see nothing through the hundreds of tents that blocked his sight. Whatever was making the noises, it sounded like a wounded monster wallowing in pain.

Lazair drew her mount up on the outskirts of the camp. There, they were met by warriors wearing some type of tribal costumes who walked out from the encampment to intercept them. There were three men: two younger and one older. The older one's face and body were covered in intricate tattoos. The younger men's bodies were also inked, although far less elaborately. Perhaps the tattoos served a symbolic function.

Lazair dismounted, and Sergan followed suit. He attempted to greet her men, but they ignored him. In silence, they relieved them of their horses. Sergan stood for a moment surveying the camp, his gaze lingering on the dark rows of felt tents. Judging by the amount of ash that had been churned to gray sludge on the ground, Lazair's people had been there for some time. Which meant that, somehow, they had managed to keep their presence hidden from his own scouts.

"Are you a sorceress, my lady?" he asked.

The crystal-white woman turned to look at him with her shimmering purple gaze. "Of a kind."

That didn't explain it, but it was something.

She led him forward, down one of the main roads that cut through the center of the encampment. The fog clung heavily to the ground here, as did the silence. Even the air felt heavy and haunted. The camp was mostly empty and unnaturally quiet, with only a few people within sight.

Which made the low, inhuman moans coming from the far end of the encampment all the more unsettling.

"Do you know of the three gifts Senestra bestowed upon each of her children? The Three Signs of an Archon?" Lazair asked.

Sergan had to think about it. It had been a while since he had studied any type of religious tracts. "The Crow's Foot Mark. The Obsidian Signet..." He squinted, straining hard to remember. "...and the Baelsword."

"That's right." She paused next to a tent. "Wait here."

He glanced at Obriem, who rolled his eyes. Sergan couldn't contain his smile, for this woman really *was* delusional.

Lazair emerged from the tent carrying a long, thin object wrapped in black silk that could only be a sword. She brought it forward and laid it down upon a rug in front of the tent, and there folded the fabric back to reveal the weapon beneath. The sword's hilt was made of bone, the pommel carved in the image of a panther's head. It was encased in a lacquered scabbard that lacked any ornamentation, although the workmanship looked exquisite. Sergan put his hand out, desiring to draw the weapon from its sheath, but Lazair pulled it away from him, glancing at him with a sharp look of fury.

"Only I have permission to handle it."

"Of course." Sergan stepped back with a glance at Obriem, his irritation running rampant. "I assume this is one of the Baelswords you're talking about?"

"It is. Come." Apparently, Lazair was done smiling. She walked away from him, cradling the sword in her arms like a new mother.

He followed her through the camp in the direction of the awful noises. As they strode between the neat rows of empty tents, he could feel his skin prickle, his nerves stretching thinner by the moment. The quiet was unnatural, as was the lack of people. Even soldiers on campaign left followers behind in camp to see to the necessary tasks.

But, as they cleared the last row of tents, all of his doubts and worries about the camp fled completely from his mind. Sergan stopped between footsteps, catching his breath.

Tied to the ground by thick iron chains was a dragon that groaned and thrashed, straining against its bonds. Its wings were held splayed and flattened by hooks that had been embedded in its flesh, caught around the slender wing bones. Its long neck was held straight by a series of U-shaped anchors driven into the ground. Dark brown blood wept from wounds covering its body, and the pupils of its eyes were contracted in agony. Seeing them walking toward it, the dragon let out a long, ghastly moan.

The sight of a creature so fierce, so magnificent, reduced to such a pathetic state filled Sergan with awe. He glanced at the white sorceress in amazed wonder.

"You captured a dragon. What are you going to do with it?"

Glancing back at him, Lazair's smile returned. But instead of answering, she walked on, leading them past the dragon to where another prisoner was staked to the ground. This one was Auld. Like the dragon, the man was bleeding from numerous wounds, his syrupy blood drenching the sand. As they drew nearer, he tilted his head, glaring up at them in hatred and defiance.

"My master desires dragons," Lazair explained. "The problem is, dragons are soul-bound to their riders. So when the rider of a dragon dies, so does the beast, unless the bond is severed first."

Sergan paced slowly around the man and his tormented dragon, surveying the scene with morbid curiosity. He'd always envisioned dragons as proud beasts, but this one moaned and whimpered like a beaten cur. Perhaps it sensed something of Lazair's plans for it. Or for the rider it was bound to.

"What are you going to do to it?" he asked.

Walking closer to the dragon, Lazair knelt to stroke its sleek, gray neck. "The bond pairs two souls in death as well as life. The only way it can be broken is through the complete destruction of one of those souls."

Rising, she slid the Baelsword from its sheath.

Seeing the naked blade revealed, Sergan sucked in a gasp at the same time as the dragon's rider issued a heartrending moan. The Baelsword glowed with a terrible, dark power that scintillated over the blade. Sergan could feel it even from where he stood, filling him with a stark loathing that hollowed his insides.

Perhaps if myths and legends could be believed, then so could Lazair.

"This is the sword of Draxal that delivered Raginor a mortal blow." She rotated the weapon, letting its dark fire undulate over the steel. "A Baelsword claims more than just the life of its victim. It also claims the soul." Moving slowly, she knelt beside the man staked out on the ground. Just as she had with the dragon, she caressed his skin, trailing her hand across his bared chest.

Compelled by dark interest, Sergan moved closer, squatting beside her. He peered intently into the man's eyes, wondering if the sight of the blade would melt his defiance. To his satisfaction, he saw that it had. Panic now filled the warrior's eyes as he gazed upward at the malevolent sword.

"Please," he whispered, his voice dry and raw. "I beg you…"

"Yes." Lazair smiled indulgently. "I want you to beg me. I want to hear terror in your voice. Plead with me. Promise me everything."

To Sergan's disgust, the man began to weep. He remained at the man's side, fascinated by the spectacle of his terror, listening to the frenzied wailing of the dragon as the woman rose to her feet and raised the sword.

"Please…" the man whimpered.

His dragon thrashed and shrieked piteously, bucking against its chains with all its incredible might. Sergan wondered why it didn't smother them with flame then realized that every movement Lazair had made put its rider between the dragon and themselves. Realizing her tactic, Sergan stood and backed away, for once the rider was dead, there would be nothing stopping the dragon from slaying them all.

"Don't worry," Lazair said, stroking the Baelsword. "We are protected."

With an abrupt motion, she thrust the sword deep into the man's chest. He howled and shrieked piteously as the dark energy from the sword poured into the wound, snaking over his body, slithering into every orifice. His chest caved in, and his eyeballs melted to gore in their sockets. Black ichor ran from his mouth and nose, cutting short his mortal scream.

The dragon's keening shrieks went on long after its rider's ended.

Lazair moved to kneel beside the pathetic beast, bending to stroke its great, muscular neck even as it strained against its bonds. Reaching up, she removed the necklace she was wearing. Sergan walked forward, wanting to get a closer look at it. What he thought was a pendant was actually a signet ring.

The second sign.

Slipping the ring onto her finger, Lazair pressed it against the dragon's flesh and started mumbling words he couldn't hear as the signet seared the beast's hide with a sizzling sound. The dragon's thrashing slowed, it's snarling quieted. The creature's body stiffened and then went limp, its great, golden eyes closing. For a long moment it lay there as though dead, even its breath arrested in its chest.

Lazair whispered a word, and beneath her hand, the dragon stirred. Its eyes opened slowly, making Sergan's breath hitch.

The dragon's eyes were liquid pools of shadow, dark reflections of the Baelsword's power.

Sergan glanced up in wonder, staring wide-eyed at Lazair.

"Now I have a dragon," she said as she rose, replacing the necklace with its ring back around her neck. "I understand your master is having problems with a Gifted boy. Fortunately, these artifacts work equally well on all things imbued with essence." She smiled as sweetly as a courtesan. "Boys included."

Leaving the smithy, Aram decided to grab a bite to eat from the kitchen before heading up to the Henge. Today was the first day Esmir was going to have him train simultaneously with Markus, and he was nervous. Markus had spent five years training to be a Shield, while Aram had worked only a year and a half honing his skills, and much of that effort had been focused on strengthening his body. He did not want Markus to see him as incompetent or weak, but he feared that was exactly how he would look.

By the time he took the steps up to the Henge, Aram arrived breathless and anxious. Stepping into the circle of sand enclosed by the Portal Stones, he saw that Markus and Esmir were already working together. Both had practice swords in their hands and were circling each other slowly. As he watched, Esmir advanced and struck out with a diagonal slice that Markus deflected before replying with a counterattack.

Aram stopped and watched the bout, marveling. With the way Esmir was always limping around, he would never have credited the Warden with the ability to move like that. There was another sharp *clang* of steel meeting steel, then Markus's sword was on the ground. Aram looked on in disbelief.

"Aram! Just in time," Esmir called, waving him over.

Aram jogged over to find the old man panting, sweat rolling down his face, yet nevertheless victorious.

"Fetch your sword and get behind Markus," Esmir directed.

As Aram did as he asked, the old Warden moved to stand in front of Markus. "Everything I do, you do. This is Prime."

With that, he stepped forward with his right foot, raising his blade to mid-guard as Markus emulated him. Bringing his feet together, he raised his sword over his head and switched to a two-handed grip, rotating it slowly downward while stepping forward again. Keeping his feet stable, he swept his sword upward, then, twisting the hilt, stabbed straight out, ending with the tip pointed downward. Aram watched Markus follow Esmir's motions then took his own place behind him, copying their movements with his practice sword.

Setting his sword down, Esmir clapped his hands. "Practice that until I tell you to stop."

The first couple times were rough. But after a few repetitions, Aram and Markus moved fluidly together through the forms. After that, Esmir guided them through another five choreographed maneuvers, having them repeat the forms over and over until they moved as one.

"You must practice these movements until your bodies perform them as automatically as breathing. Markus, when Aram lifts his blade, you must be able to anticipate exactly where he will be on the next beat of the rhythm. It is essential that you move step for step with him. Which isn't as easy as it sounds since you'll be standing in front of him."

Esmir watched them with a long face, massaging his beard with his hand until, at last, he shook his head until his jowls waggled.

"Again! This time clear your minds. You should be thinking of nothing—the movements must come from your body, not your head! If you try to think, you hesitate. The only thing your head will do is slow you down and get you killed. It has no business in a fight. Now! This time, I want you to try to make your movements crisp and precise. Ready, begin!"

As they flowed through the prescribed motions, Esmir barked out directives:

"Each movement needs to be sharp! Snap your sword up, Aram! Better! Wrong way, Markus! Stop, stop, *stop!* Back to Prime! We're doing this again!"

And so the morning went.

They practiced until the odor drifting up the cliff from Hearth Home told them it was time for lunch. At last, Esmir released them, and two sweaty youths raced down the thousand stairs to Hearth Home.

After lunch, they retired to the dormitory for an hour's rest, then returned to the Henge and continued working until twilight fell and the smell of supper called them back down the cliff again. When at last he retired for the night, fed and bathed, Aram collapsed into his bunk as though all his strength had been bled out of him. But no sooner had he fallen asleep than Jeran and the other apprentices came in, laughing and talking boisterously. Irritated, Aram turned over onto his stomach, pulling his pillow over his head to muffle the sounds.

"Oh, no, you don't!" said Corley, jerking the pillow off him. "You're coming with us! Both of you!"

"Where are we going?" asked Markus groggily as he slid down from the top bunk.

"Where *are* we going?" asked Eugan, entering the room on the heels of the others.

"It's a secret!"

Aram sat up, suddenly curious. It sounded like they were going on an adventure, which was something he had always wanted to do. But you needed friends to adventure with, and he hadn't had any till now. Excited and grateful, he sat up and pulled on his boots. The moment he had them on, Iver burst out laughing.

"Um… You might want to put on pants," Jeran suggested with a grin.

Aram was so exhausted, he'd forgotten he wasn't wearing any trousers. Embarrassed, he tossed off his boots and pulled his clothes on rapidly. When Markus was dressed, they gathered together in a closely packed circle, formulating their plans.

"All right," said Iver in a sharp whisper. "I overheard Vandra saying that there's a dragon clutch in the Southern Eyrie that's close to hatching. She didn't come out and say it, but—"

"Why are we whispering?" interrupted Aram.

Everyone turned to look at him with blank faces. Then they started laughing. Aram didn't understand why, but he laughed with them, then stopped laughing when they did. He cast a confused glance at Markus, who just smiled and patted his back.

"Anyway," Iver continued in a normal voice, "since Vandra was telling this to Henrik, I got the impression the eggs might be meant for us. Which would make sense. She said there are seven eggs in the clutch, and there are seven of us. So I think we need to go check them out for ourselves and maybe figure out which egg each of us wants."

"Count me out," said Eugan, earning himself looks of outrage. "If Vandra finds out, none of us will be getting a dragon. We may as well pack our things and head back down the mountain."

Corley waved his hand dismissively. "Do you really think they would spend years training us just to throw us out over an *egg?*"

"A *dragon* egg," emphasized Eugan. "You guys are nuts. What happens if you're caught handling the eggs and then one ends up not hatching?"

"Don't get caught!" said Iver. "Look, this is something we *have* to do! If we wait for these eggs to hatch, there's a chance the hatchlings might reject us. But if we each pick an egg and spend some time holding it, maybe the hatchlings will remember us when they come out!"

"What happens if a hatchling rejects you?" asked Aram.

"Then it becomes feral and it flies off," Jeran answered. "And that doesn't do anyone any good. Iver's right. We *need* to do this."

Markus reached up and scratched the back of his head, a troubled look on his face. "I don't know. I just got here. I don't think it's a good idea for me to start breaking the rules already."

Jeran frowned heavily. "He's right. It wouldn't be a good idea for him. But our Champion needs a dragon!"

Iver's face turned to stone. "He's not a Champion. He's never going to *be* a Champion. I say he stays with Markus. There's no sense wasting a dragon on him anyway."

Hearing that, Aram felt every sliver of excitement in him die a sudden death. Struggling to hold back tears, he returned to his bunk and flopped down upon it.

"What the *hell*, Iver?" exclaimed Corley, probably too loudly.

"Yeah, what the hell?" echoed Markus.

Feeling dejected, Aram lay back in bed, pulling his legs up. "Why don't you guys go on? I'll stay with Markus."

"No." Glaring at Iver, Jeran strode toward him. "You're coming with us, whether you want to or not!" Bending, he grabbed Aram's arm and hauled him upright. "Iver's just being an ass. As usual."

Iver snorted, crossing his arms. "Fine, he can come. But I still don't think he should touch a dragon egg."

Aram didn't want to go anymore. He saw that Markus didn't look like he wanted him to go either. But Jeran and Corley looked insistent, and he wanted desperately to go on an adventure with his new friends.

"So, where are the eggs, exactly, and how do we get there?" asked Jeran.

Iver's mood broken, he responded with a harsh glance at Aram, "Vandra didn't say where they are, but there's really only one place they can be, and that's in the steam room."

"Why the steam room?" asked Corley.

"Because. They have to stay warm and moist."

"How do we get to the steam room?"

The apprentices looked at each other.

"I think I know," said Eugan, and everyone turned to look at him. "It's in the back of the eyrie on the other side of the soaking pool."

Iver scrunched his face. "Hmm… This might take more planning than I thought. I'll go scout it out tonight. Then maybe tomorrow we can go together."

"Are you kidding?" Jeran exclaimed. "You'll get caught, for sure! You can't lie with a straight face."

"Hey, that's not—!"

"You know I'm right." Corley looked thoughtful. "We need someone with a face everyone trusts. Preferably someone with a reason to be in the eyrie."

There was a short interval of silence, during which Aram stared at the floor, tying and untying little knots into the drawstring of his pants.

When he glanced up to see what they were all waiting for, he saw that everyone was looking at him.

"No." Markus shook his head rapidly. "Uh-uh."

"But he's perfect!" exclaimed Corley. "Look at that face! Besides, everyone knows Vandra's sweet on him. If Aram's seen in the eyrie, people will just think he's supposed to be there."

"I like it," said Iver, nodding slowly.

"Of course you do," snapped Jeran. "You just want him to get caught!"

Iver snorted. "That's not true. Well, maybe a little true. But still." Noticing Markus glaring at him, he gave a frustrated sigh. "Look, I like Aram as much as anyone." He spread his hands. "That's why I don't want him to get killed. In fact, I'm surprised you do."

"What do you mean, you don't want him to get killed?" Markus asked.

Iver flashed him an incredulous look. "He didn't tell you? People who fail the Trials don't come back alive. Or at least not sane."

Markus's face slackened. Then he swung to Aram. "Why didn't you tell me?"

Aram shrugged. "I didn't think it mattered."

"You didn't think it *mattered?*" Markus turned back to Iver as the rest of the boys edged away. "What are his chances?"

"Almost none." Iver glared at his friends. "That's what I keep trying to tell everyone!"

Markus looked around the ring of other apprentices. "Is it true? Is he right?"

There was a long pause followed by a general consensus of nods. Markus threw his hands up. He stalked to the side of the room, where he stood glaring at the wall and scrubbing his hands through his hair.

"I'm not supporting this," he said at last. He swung back around, face red with anger. "Tomorrow, we'll talk to Esmir and tell him we quit. We'll find a way to get back home—"

"No." Aram strode toward him, hands clenched into fists. "I'm needed here."

"Not if you can't pass the Trials!"

Aram pointed at Iver. "He doesn't know me! But you do. *You do!*"

Markus went quiet, closing his eyes. For long moments, he stood stiff and still as a scarecrow. At last, his shoulders slumped, and he let out a protracted sigh.

Opening his eyes, Markus glared defiantly at Iver. "He'll pass the Trials."

Hearing the confidence in his best friend's voice made Aram want to hug him.

Iver held Markus's gaze for a long time without looking away, as if the two of them were locked in some contest of wills, where the winner would decide Aram's fate. In the end, it was Iver who backed down.

"All right," he said. "If you feel that strongly, then I'll give him the benefit of the doubt. But mark my words"—he lifted a finger—"if he goes into those portals and doesn't come back out, don't blame me. Understand? Don't. Blame. Me." Each word was punctuated by a finger-shake.

"I won't," Markus said in a gruff voice, looking down. "I'll blame myself."

Aram shook his head. "No. If I don't pass the Trials, then I'm the only one to blame. Just me. This is my life, and I'm the only one who's going to say what I'm going to do with it."

Markus licked his lips, at last nodding. He glanced around the room. "Then I guess it's settled."

"Good!" Corley smacked his hands together. "Now, Aram's going to go scout us out some dragon eggs! Right, Aram?"

"That's right." Aram started toward the door.

"Just don't prove me wrong!" Iver called to his back. "And don't give us up if you get caught!"

Feeling vindicated, Aram smiled. He went and fetched a candlestick then left the dormitory. The hallways at night were very different than during the day. There was no light from the shafts, so the only illumination was the faint glow of the taper in his hand. He walked with his hand cupped, shielding the candle's delicate flame, watching the strange knotwork on the walls squirm in the shadows as he passed.

Taking the steps up to the eyrie, he paused outside the door, wondering if he should snuff out the candle. He wasn't sure which would be worse: announcing his presence with the light or being caught sneaking around in the dark. In the end, he decided that being sneaky just wasn't right. If he got caught, he'd rather get caught out in the open.

Keeping the candle shielded, he opened the door and stepped into the Southern Eyrie. It was cold inside, far colder than the dormitory or even Esmir's eyrie at night, which was better shielded and had a smaller opening. The enormous cavern was dark, except for a few lights that glowed from behind the privacy screens that had been drawn across the alcoves.

Aram stood by the door for a moment, surveying the room, considering his chances. There were still a couple of people moving around, and he was pretty sure he would get caught. He almost turned back and retreated down the stairs, but then a terrible fear stopped him. For the first time in his life, he had friends who believed in him. If he turned back now, he would prove their faith unjustified.

Holding the taper near his chest, he pondered the problem. Should he go ahead and risk Vandra's wrath? Or turn back and face the disappointment of his friends? It was a terrible decision. He stood for long moments licking his lips, toes squirming in his boots, his stomach tied into knots.

At last, he made up his mind. Girding his courage, he started forward, walking purposefully as though he had every right to be there. He hadn't gone far when a screen opened, and a man appeared in front of him. His heart leapt into his throat. Aram fought it down and nodded a greeting at the dragon rider then continued on his way. He could see his objective clearly in front of him: the soaking pool. All the big eyries had one. This pool was large, extending all the way from the center of the cavern toward one of the shadowy back corners.

He set his course toward it, his gaze scanning the walls, searching for the opening to the steam room. It took him a moment, but he finally saw it: a dark oaken door in the shadows behind the pool. Aram paused for a moment and glanced behind him, making sure no one was looking.

Then he hurried around the pool and tested the door to see if it was locked.

It wasn't.

Opening the door, he stepped inside.

The air within was sweltering and humid, fed by steam rising from a small pool of bubbling water in the center of the floor. A hazy, golden light filtered down from above, though Aram couldn't see its source. He took a step forward, his boot sinking into deep sand that covered the floor. And then he saw it: a hollow dug out of the sand, filled with eggs. Sucking in a breath, he froze, his eyes going wide.

He had never seen a dragon egg before, and he found himself mesmerized. They were different shades of tan and speckled with dark brown flecks like a wren's egg, though instead of a shell, they were covered with a soft, leathery membrane. Each egg was as large as a good-sized melon, irregularly shaped.

Moving to the clutch, he sank to his knees and twisted the candlestick into the sand to prop it upright. Eyes wide with wonder, he ran his gaze over the seven eggs that sat tilted at various angles inside the nest. Hesitantly, he reached his hand toward the nearest one.

"Don't!"

Aram flinched, jerking his hand back.

Glancing behind him, he met Vandra's eyes and froze, his heart growing cold with shame.

53

Vandra sprang forward and caught Aram by the arm, dragging him roughly away from the eggs and hauling him to his feet. She caught hold of his face and jerked his head toward her, forcing him to look her in the eyes. There was such fire there, enough to set a wet haystack ablaze.

"What are you doing here?" she snarled, tightening her grip until her fingers dug into his cheeks.

Aram opened his mouth to answer but panic ripped the words right out of his throat. He froze, not knowing what to say. He didn't want to get the others in trouble, but his father had raised him not to lie.

Lies breed like rats and gnaw at you just the same.

Drowning in shame, Aram whispered through trembling teeth, "I wanted to see them."

That was true at least, even if it was just part of the truth. Yet the explanation seemed to exasperate Vandra, and her fingers dug deeper into his cheeks. Aram clamped his eyes shut.

"How did you know the eggs were here?"

He couldn't tell her. Then Iver would get in trouble—just when he'd won his friendship and trust. If he admitted the truth then that tentative bond would be severed, and Aram couldn't bear to sacrifice even one of his new friends.

Swallowing, Aram found his resolve. He wouldn't lie to Vandra, nor would he give up Iver. "I'm sorry."

"I asked you a question," Vandra growled. "Who told you the eggs were here?"

"I can't say."

The words took every scrap of courage he could summon, for he feared the Wingmaster's wrath. He didn't know what the woman would do—punish him, maybe dismiss him altogether. Whichever, he had to accept it. The truth was, whatever happened, he deserved it. What he couldn't do was confess the others' involvement. Not even Iver's. Aram's desperation for acceptance from his peers overrode even his fear of Vandra's disappointment.

Vandra hauled him outside the door, closing it behind them. She softened her grip on him. "Understand something." Her voice was suddenly even, which somehow made it worse. "If you had touched one of those eggs, it wouldn't hatch. Because whoever touches a dragon egg makes a soul-bond with the dragon inside. No Lesser Dragon could survive a bond with you—your touch would have killed it."

"Just my *touch?*" Aram asked in horror. "Why? Am I that terrible?"

"You're that *powerful.*" Vandra's eyes flared in contempt. "Now, who put you up to this? This is no small thing."

"I can't say." Aram felt thoroughly defeated. Vandra was going to take him to task, and he knew he deserved everything he got.

"Aram," Vandra said in a kinder voice. "Whoever told you to do this knew you would get caught. No matter what you think, they're not your friend, so there's no reason for you to protect them. Tell me who it was. They're just as guilty as you are, and you don't owe them a thing."

He could feel the burden of Vandra's disappointment settling around his shoulders like an ox collar. Perhaps Vandra was right. Perhaps Iver was lying and had set him up to get caught. Even still, Aram hesitated. On the chance that Iver *did* have faith in him, he would have to keep that faith. His newfound friendships were much too valuable to risk.

"I'm sorry." He hung his head. "I'm not going to tell you."

Vandra raised her eyebrows. "You realize you'll have to take the punishment for both of you, then?"

Aram nodded, his eyes filling with tears of shame, his lips trembling.

"Very well." Vandra let go of his arm, taking him instead by the collar of his tunic. "Whoever it is you're protecting, they don't deserve your friendship."

With that, she hauled Aram forward by the collar, walking him swiftly back across the eyrie. People had gathered in the open space of the cavern, drawn by the commotion. They looked on curiously as Vandra marched Aram through their midst. He glanced at Calise as they walked by Zandril's alcove. He saw the dismay in her eyes, and his shame bit deeper. He couldn't keep the tears back. He could feel them wetting his cheeks as Vandra shoved him out onto the terrace in front of the eyrie, propelling him toward the edge of the cliff.

Seeing where she was taking him, Aram began to struggle, but Vandra caught him in a headlock, and no amount of fighting was going to do any good. She was a big woman, taller and stronger than him.

More riders helped her restrain him. Together, they forced him all the way to the lip of the terrace, until the tips of his toes touched the very edge of the cliff. Panicked, Aram went limp, terrified of struggling and knocking them all off the cliff. One glance downward filled him with a heaving vertigo. He sagged, trembling in Vandra's arms, staring into the gaping maw of the chasm.

He could feel Vandra's hot breath against his ear. "One last time. Who told you the eggs were there?"

He was going to die.

But if he named Iver, he would lose his friends. All his life, he had known only the pain and despair of isolation. The self-doubt, the feelings of worthlessness—he couldn't bear to live like that again. He'd rather die.

Clenching his jaw, Aram squeezed his eyes shut and silently shook his head.

"Very well."

Vandra jerked him by the hair. Aram cried out in anticipation of the fall. But instead of pushing him forward, the Wingmaster dragged him backward.

"Toss me the rope!" she called to someone behind her.

As Aram stood staring at the cliff, held forcibly by strong, stout men,

Vandra tied the rope about his torso, pulling the knot tight, then proceeded to tie his wrists in front of him with a thinner cord. Another man lashed the other end of the rope to a metal bar driven into the rock of the terrace.

Then, they hauled him forward.

This time, when Vandra shoved him to the edge, she leaned him out over it.

Aram screamed, recoiling.

With a heave, she shoved him forward.

He was falling.

The rope jerked taut, nearly cutting him in half. He slapped hard against the cliff, the impact stunning him instantly. He went limp as his body moved in a pendulous swing, spinning and swaying at the end of the rope as Vandra lowered him, foot by foot, down onto a ledge that was just wide enough for him to sit upon. For several minutes, all he could do was lie there, pressing his body as close as he could against the rock. The icy breath of the abyss ghosted past him, and the world rocked and spun beneath him.

Desperate, he sat up and tugged hard on the rope, but his hands were tied, so he couldn't climb it. He saw Vandra peering over the edge at him, her long hair whipped by the wind. There was sadness and disappointment on her face, and something else that Aram had a hard time reading.

"We'll bring you up in the morning!" Vandra called down to him.

Before he could plead for mercy, she disappeared.

Aram brought his knees up to his chest, his bound hands clutching the rope with all their strength.

He felt more secure like that, but it still took a while for the motion of the world to stabilize. There was some measure of comfort in knowing that the rope anchored him somewhat. If he did fall from the ledge, he wouldn't fall far. But then, he would end up dangling over the bottomless gorge all night, and he could think of few worse fates. And he was cold. So cold.

He sat there, gripping the rope as the night lengthened, waiting for the terror he felt to lessen. It never did. Instead, he just got colder as the shadows grew longer. He started shivering violently, and he had to fight a growing terror that he was going to pass out from the cold and fall from the ledge. He curled up as tightly as he could, squeezing himself against the cliff, and sat quivering in panic as the minutes wore on to eternities.

The night deepened.

He could hear sounds coming from above as the eyrie went on about its life without him. Occasionally, a dragon would launch from the terrace overhead, startling him mercilessly. Every time he thought the sky to the east was warming, it turned out to be his imagination.

Eventually, either exhaustion or the cold got to him, and he started nodding off. He didn't fight it, even though he didn't know whether he was drifting toward death or sleep. Instead, he gave in to the mercy of oblivion and let it carry him away.

Aram woke to sunlight and the tugging of the rope. It took him a panicked second to realize that he was being hauled back up the cliff. But when he finally felt solid ground beneath him, he didn't have the strength to rise. He lay there shivering in the sunlight, flat on his belly on the terrace. He couldn't feel his hands or legs. He was shivering too hard to move, and the terrace beneath him didn't feel stable, but rocked and bobbed like a bark tossed by waves.

He hardly noticed when someone wrapped a blanket around him and coaxed him to rise. He was led back inside the eyrie and tucked into bed, warm covers piled atop him. All he could think of was how cold he was, how desperate he was for heat. He didn't know or care who the person was that helped him. He felt a soothing hand caress his hair.

"Sleep, my friend. Sleep."

He did.

Vandra never mentioned the incident again. Not once.

She treated Aram no differently, as though it had never happened. After he woke, Aram returned to the dormitory, to his normal life. Shivering on the ledge overnight had given him a cold, but otherwise, he was no worse for wear. And to his surprise, he was greeted with hugs and apologies from his friends. Even Iver looked humbled, hardly able to meet his gaze.

"I can't believe you didn't give me up," Iver said.

Aram just shrugged. "You had faith in me," he said, thinking that would explain everything.

But apparently, it didn't. The young men of his dorm kept staring at him all day—all but Markus, who for some reason, became exceptionally quiet. He sat on his bed most of the evening, shooting hateful glances at Iver whenever he wasn't looking, until it was time to snuff out the candles.

When Aram closed his eyes, he heard a quiet and beautiful voice echo through his mind: *Sleep, my friend.*

Calise's voice.

It took a few days for Aram to truly feel like the cliff was behind him, and even then, he still occasionally felt like the world was tumbling out from beneath him. He continued to train in the Henge with Markus, but there was a little less sureness in his step. His self-confidence had taken a blow—not that it had ever been strong in the first place. As the days went by, he caught Markus and Esmir exchanging worried glances more and more frequently.

Before he knew it, it was the day he was supposed to head back down to the Brausas' workshop for the next stage of his sword's manufacture. He had been looking forward to it all week, and he felt his spirits lift as he descended the long stairs to Hearth Home. When he entered the smithy, the heat and the odor of the forge hit him in the face, a smell like fire and earth all rolled into one, combined with the odor of sweat from the men who worked there. The star-steel forge was already lit, the coals glowing orange. Seeing Aram, Onsel waved him over. He tossed him an apron and wound a strip of cloth around Aram's head to keep the sweat out of his eyes.

"Ready for the next stage?" he asked.

The swordsmith had a glint of anticipation in his eyes. Aram wondered how the smith could feel excited about a day's work, when every day at the forge seemed to be exactly the same, just heating and cooling steel and banging hammers.

"Here, sit down!" Onsel sat on the floor before the forge and patted the space next to him.

Aram noticed Onsel had bits of steel spread out on an anvil. He sat next to him and watched the swordsmith stir the pieces with a finger. He selected one and held it up in his palm, showing it to Aram.

"We have to separate the hard steel from the soft steel," he explained. "The soft steel is going to become the core of your sword, and the hard steel is going to become the outer jacket." He pointed to the chunk of steel in his hand. "See how this one is broken clean? This is harder steel. So, we're going to set it aside and save it for the jacket."

The smith picked up a piece with rough, jagged edges. "This is softer steel. We're going to use it for the core. It makes the blade more flexible, so it can bend without breaking."

Aram helped the smith sort through the pieces, separating those that had broken cleanly from those that had jagged edges. After the steel was separated, Onsel had him work the piston to operate the bellows. Together, they heated the forge, increasing the airflow until the flames glowed cherry-red.

"Where's your apprentice?" Aram asked.

"Today, you are my apprentice," Onsel informed him with a smile.

Hearing that, Aram felt hesitant. He didn't know anything about forging a sword, and he was terrified he'd get it wrong. He was just about to object when Onsel handed him a long-handled sledgehammer then selected a metal rod from a pile of rods, along with a thin steel plate about the size of a brick.

"I'll tap out commands to you with my hammer." Onsel looked up at Aram, his face glistening with sweat from the heat of the forge. "You need to strike with even force and rhythm. Pay close attention to my hammer. If I tap faster, then you strike faster. If I tap slower, then you strike slower. When you hear my hammer drag across the anvil, you stop. Understand?"

Aram nodded, for he was fascinated, and paying extra-close attention. If he was paying good attention, he never had to be told anything twice. He climbed onto the crate he had seen the apprentices stand on and leaned on the sledgehammer with its head resting against the floor. He glanced at Onsel, who gave him a smile of encouragement.

The swordsmith shoved his iron rod into the forge alongside a plate made of star steel, keeping them both submerged in the coals until they glowed a vivid orange. Removing them, he set the glowing plate on the anvil and, touching the heated rod to it, welded them together with firm strikes of his mallet.

"Tap your hammer against the anvil," Onsel directed. "That means you're ready."

Aram hefted the heavy sledge in both hands, getting a feel for it, then tapped the face of the hammer against the anvil. Onsel lifted his small hammer and struck the anvil twice—the signal to begin. Lifting the hammer, Aram brought it down with all his might.

Bang!

"Too hard!" the swordsmith shouted. "Don't swing it! Just let it fall!"

Aram lifted the sledgehammer again, this time letting it fall with its own weight onto the hot steel.

Bang!

"Good!" Onsel struck his small hammer on the anvil: *Tap-tap.*

Bang!

Tap-tap.

Bang!

Tap-tap.

Bang!

Tap.

Bang!

Tap-drag.

Aram lowered the hammer, panting, a sheen of sweat slicking his forehead. He rested the sledgehammer on the floor, leaning against it.

"Good!" Onsel said.

He returned the plate to the forge, and they repeated the process, heating the plate and striking it, first one direction then the other, several times as the morning wore away. At last, Onsel moved the steel plate to a vat of clay, which he ladled onto the plate's surface, the clay steaming and hissing.

"What's that for?" asked Aram.

"The clay prevents the steel from overheating," Onsel said, then smiled up at him. "You did good! That's all for today, son. Come back tomorrow for the next step."

Aram wiped the sweat from his brow with his arm, still breathing hard. His ears were ringing, and his cheeks felt raw from the heat of the forge, but he was smiling, and he looked with no small amount of pride at the iron plate he had helped flatten.

Thanking Onsel, he headed back to the dormitory. But halfway up the stairs, he heard Markus shouting his name.

"Where have you been?" Markus gasped, running up to him, winded from the descent. "We've been waiting for you!"

"I thought we weren't practicing today!" Aram gulped.

"*We're* not practicing. You are!" Markus looked flustered, perhaps even angry.

Aram frowned in confusion. "Just me? Why? No one told me!"

"Because." Markus took his arm and directed him up the hill. "Esmir wants you to go into one of the portals. And he says I can't go in with you."

"What do you mean?" Aram asked, feeling like a bucket of cold water had been thrown over him. "I'm not ready for my Trials!"

"It's not the Trials," said Markus. "It's different. You'll have to ask Esmir when we get up there. Let's go! He's getting cranky, and you know what that means."

That was enough to prompt him. Aram followed Markus back up the stairs, jogging as fast as he could, until the long climb finally made him moderate his pace. Just a couple of months ago, he couldn't have made it to the top without stopping to rest a few times, but his legs were stronger now. A *lot* stronger, as was the rest of him.

When they arrived at the top of the bluff, he discovered that Markus had been right—Esmir *was* in a cranky mood, which meant they would be working doubly hard. As soon as the old Warden saw them, he gestured for them to hurry, a deep scowl making his face look like bad-quality parchment.

"Where have you been?"

"I was at the Brausas' workshop!" Aram gulped.

Esmir drew his lips back from his teeth, looking like he was about ready to start spitting. "Next time tell me when you're going down there! I've been waiting here for two hours!"

Aram doubted that. Esmir was usually late to their practices. *Very* late. And he typically hauled himself up the stairs with last night's liquor on his breath. Aram glanced at Markus for confirmation. His friend just smirked and rolled his eyes. It was all Aram could do to keep from smiling.

"Let's get to work." Esmir raised a hand, pointing at the Portal Stone behind them. "That's the first of the Four Portals. It's the only one you can enter multiple times. It's also the least dangerous, because it doesn't submerse you fully into the Shadow Realm—you just touch the surface of it. It's used by students to practice magic."

"How's that?" Aram asked, looking at the stones. There was something about their dark, rough-hewn appearance that set him on edge. The dolomite stone on the right was slightly taller than its counterpart on the left, making the portal look like a dilapidated doorway.

Aram glanced at Esmir nervously, feeling every hair on his body stand upright. "Why haven't I gone in before?"

"You weren't ready," Esmir answered.

Aram frowned, glancing back at the dark portal that beckoned like a hungering gateway he didn't want to walk through.

"And I'm ready now?"

The furrows in Esmir's brow deepened. "I think so."

"You *think* so?" Aram licked his lips.

Esmir gestured at the portal with the butt of his cane. "You're going to start practicing in there as often as you can. When you go in, you'll be given everything you need, including the ability to use magic without a catalyst."

Aram gasped, feeling a thrill of excitement tingle his fingertips. He had always dreamt of being able to touch the strands at will. He shot a grin at Markus, for suddenly the Portal Stone was looking less like an ominous mouth and more like a doorway to adventure.

"What should I take in?" he asked excitedly.

"Nothing." Esmir walked toward the portal, leaning heavily on his cane. "In the Shadow Realm, everything you take in can be used against you. Even your clothes."

Aram glanced down at the long tunic and pants he was wearing, struggling to imagine how they could be used to harm him. The first thing that came to mind was strangulation. Then an image came to him of his own clothes attacking him as though they were filled with an invisible body, a thought that made him grin.

He looked at Esmir dubiously. "So...I'm supposed to go in naked?"

The old Warden nodded. "Unless you want your own boot kicking you in the groin. Don't worry. If you need to be clothed, they'll clothe you."

Aram thought about it. Whoever the Overseers were that lived inside the portal, they had to be good; otherwise, how would they be good judges of a person's character?

"I'll go naked." He decided to put his faith in the process. When Markus shot him a funny look, Aram raised a finger. "Just don't laugh at me."

Markus gave a nervous chuckle, though by his face, he wasn't convinced that going into the portal at all was a good idea. "You're braver than me."

Aram turned to Esmir. "Do you want me to go in now?"

The Warden waved him toward the portal. Aram hesitated only for a second, weighing the ominous specter of the portal against his excitement over finally being able to practice binding without a block. In the end, his excitement won out, and he trotted across the sand to the stones, pausing beside them to undress. He took everything off, including his breeches. He even removed the heart knot necklace his mother had given him. He could feel his pulse racing—not in fear, but in anticipation.

Shooting a grin at Markus, he entered the imposing arch of standing stones.

It was night.

The same ring of standing stones surrounded him, though here, they were much taller, looming over him and canting slightly inward. Each monolith glowed with its own muted light, and the obelisk at the center of the circle bore sets of carved runes upon its face that hadn't been there before. It hummed softly, a low and constant drone that was almost outside the range of his hearing. Beyond the ring of stones, there was only darkness, as though the world ceased to exist outside them.

Looking down, Aram saw that he was clothed in a plain gray cloak worn over a tunic of the same color. He brushed his hand across the fabric, assuring himself that it was real, and discovered that it was smoother and softer than any linen he had ever felt.

He paused, looking warily around the circle of glowing stones.

Not knowing what he was supposed to do, Aram walked toward the obelisk.

As he approached, the humming noise grew louder and became discordant, a sound that did to his ears what wool did to his skin. He gritted his teeth, wishing he could scratch the sound out of his head. Pausing beside the obelisk, he reached toward it cautiously. As his hand drew near, he felt a tingling sensation in the tips of his fingers, as though the circulation had been cut off and was just now returning. He withdrew his hand quickly, and the tingling faded.

Frowning, he stared at the carved runes on the obelisk, which looked utterly foreign. Summoning his courage, he placed both palms flat on the cold, smooth surface of the obsidian stone.

The runes came to life, glowing softly with an azure light. There was a grinding sound, and the obelisk vibrated as though shaken by a tremor.

Aram flinched, retracting his hands, his pulse suddenly racing. This wasn't right. Nothing about any of this was right.

The light of the standing stones dimmed, the world around him darkening, until all that was left was the light of the glowing runes, which seemed to float before him in the darkness.

Aram turned in a slow circle, glancing warily around. There was another grating sound, and then the light of the stones increased slightly, shedding a muted glow across the square.

Aram froze.

In the opening of every portal stood a person.

No—they were not people. They were something else. Something older.

Aram didn't know how he knew that, only that he did. Each had a smooth, ageless face with features that seemed somehow washed out. They were not human or Auld, but something that existed apart, or perhaps something that was no longer. Perhaps they were gods or the children of gods, or something far more sinister. They were all staring at him with whiteless eyes the color of squid ink.

Fear seeped into him, chilling his insides and drowning his courage. He didn't know what those things beneath the Portal Stones were, but he knew that he wanted nothing to do with them.

Their faces seemed almost serpentine, with slitted nostrils and long, thin lips. Their bodies were twice the height of a man and hairless, though their gray skin was subtly striped.

They stared at him and did nothing.

Aram could feel himself starting to sweat, although the air around him was cool. If this was a test, then he didn't understand the nature of it. These things had given him clothes and light to see by, but nothing else. There didn't seem to be any challenge he needed to overcome, no puzzles to solve. Unless the test lay in these ancient creatures themselves. He assumed they were the Overseers, though perhaps that was a naïve assumption to make.

Maybe they were waiting for him to make the first move. He walked forward warily toward the nearest of the stone doorways, where one of the gray beings stood beneath the horizontal slab of rock. He couldn't tell if its glassy eyes were tracking him. When he stopped in front of it, the being did not react.

For a moment, they simply regarded each other, each staring into the eyes of the other. He was almost certain that the being nodded slightly.

The attack came without warning.

Bolts of blue lightning streaked down from the top of the obelisk, tearing into him with raking claws and pounding him to his knees. Aram screamed as crackling energy coruscated over his body, searing his skin like wrathful flames. He rolled and thrashed on the ground like a man on fire, but the sorcerous energy stuck to him like tar, and all his writhing didn't make it go away.

He could smell the stench of his own burning flesh. The pain was intolerable, ripping screams from his mouth. The onslaught continued, forked spears of energy clawing at him, biting deeply into his skin.

In a last, frantic bid for life, Aram reached out and caught hold of the ethereal strands and began to weave, wrapping the aether into a complex knot of energy that sucked the heat right out of the air, quenching the searing net with a steaming hiss.

Panting, he collapsed back on the sand in infinite relief as the agony slowly faded. He rolled onto his side and looked down at his body, expecting it to be badly charred from the heat of the assault. But it wasn't. His clothes were scorched and smoldering, but his flesh remained intact, as though he had just imagined his skin burning. He sagged back with a relieved sigh, closing his eyes.

"Aram! Can you hear me? *Aram!*"

Aram opened his eyes to find someone standing over him. His first thought was that it was one of the creatures from the portal. Terrified, he recoiled, scrambling back then cringing into a ball.

"It's just me!"

Lowering his trembling hands, Aram looked up to see Markus standing over him. He sat down next to him, his face intense with concern, and set a hand on Aram's shoulder to steady him. It took Aram a long moment to stop trembling, and when he did, he looked into Markus's face with a slight, wistful smile.

"I did it," he whispered, his voice shaking. "I saved myself."

He glanced down at his body and found that he was still wearing the cloak and tunic the Overseers had given him. The garments were riddled with blackened holes and, in places, were still smoldering, but his body was unharmed. Markus stood and helped him to his feet, his gaze running over him.

"Are you injured?"

"No." Aram couldn't believe it. He didn't know whether the crackling energy was real, or whether it had all been just in his mind.

Fingering the burned sleeve of Aram's tunic, Markus shook his head with a grin. "Next time, wear Iver's clothes."

Aram looked down at the burned cloak he was wearing. "I don't think so. I wouldn't want to be attacked by Iver's clothes."

The sound of Markus's laughter made Aram realize he'd made a joke. He started laughing too, which made Markus laugh harder.

"You survived your first experience within the portals," Esmir said, inspecting him with a critical gaze. "Was it difficult?"

Aram nodded. "Those things in there…they're powerful. I don't know if they're necessarily evil, but they weren't right either. The lightning they made was…it was *really* bad. But then I stopped it. I stopped the lightning. Esmir, how come I can defend myself in there but not out here?"

"That's a good question, and I don't have an answer," the old man said. "There's been much speculation, but no one knows for sure. Some believe it's a different world, where our rules don't operate. Others think the creatures in the portals exert some kind of power or control over Auld magic. All we know is that they give a candidate everything they need to be successful. Including defensive magic."

"But how did I know what to do? It was just like at the Grove—it just happened. I don't know what I did!"

Esmir grunted. "You know the fundamentals—you've been studying them all your life."

"Knots," Aram said.

"That's right. And you're a True Savant, which means that you know instinctually how to bind them into something of great complexity. You can see the details of the threads, and you can also see the tapestry."

"But *how* does it work? That's what I don't understand. I don't know what I can do and what I can't do. I don't know my limits."

"Limits," Esmir mumbled. "Well, it's all about essence and energy. Every strand you weave spends essence, and when you exhaust what you have, you're done, at least until you replenish what you've lost. Beyond that, it's just confidence in yourself. You must practice every day until it's second-nature."

"I don't have much confidence in myself," Aram said thoughtfully, remembering all the years he'd spent being told he was different and odd. After you hear something so many times, it starts to define you, and it eventually becomes a prison. He had been confined by that prison all his life, and now he feared the world outside its walls.

"What am I going to do?" he whispered. For the first time since he had started down this path, he felt real, sincere doubt.

"What you need, you won't find out here." Esmir gestured at the portal. "You'll find it in there. We'll give you a rest for a couple of days. But then you're going back in. And every day after, until you find your confidence."

Staring at the portal, Aram asked, "What if I don't find it before the Trials?"

Esmir's lips constricted. "Then you won't come back out."

Sergan watched Lazair winding toward him through the Imperial encampment that was growing bigger as the days went by, fed by a
constant influx of men and supplies through the permanent rent in the
Veil created by the destruction of the Great Tree. As Lazair approached,
he nodded in her direction, bringing the sorceress to Obriem's attention.

Lazair smiled warmly when she noticed their eyes on her. Sergan was
surprised she'd be without escort in a military encampment, something
many would consider unwise for a woman of Lazair's unique beauty.
But Sergan had no fear for her safety. Any woman who could wrest a
dragon from its rider had no need of protection from men.

Today she wore a wide-sleeve gown of rich crimson velvet that fell in
elegant folds about her sinuous frame. Her face was powdery white, her
lips, cheeks, and eyelids tinted with red pigment. Besides accentuating
her features, the makeup also begged the question: what kind of woman
took time to apply rouge in the midst of a military campaign? The more
Sergan saw of Lazair, the more fascinated by her he became.

She stopped in front of him and presented her hand for him to kiss,
and he did, his eyes locked on hers. Beside him, Obriem tensed, and
Sergan couldn't blame him. Lazair's presence was disquieting, to say the
least. Ally or not, he would not be letting his guard down around her,
even for an instant. He didn't trust any woman who owned a Baelsword.

"And to what do I owe the honor, my lady?" Sergan asked.

"Your skills are requested by my master," Lazair replied, ignoring

Obriem's presence, as though he didn't exist in her version of the world. "He is pleased with the stability of the rupture you managed to create here, and he wishes us to continue destabilizing the Veil. We've been ordered to advance toward the Winmarch. That's where the Mother's Heart is located, which is the keystone anchor that supports all others. Along the way, we will assault the Altier Highlands, destroying the Anchor there."

"Sounds like we've got our work cut out for us," Sergan muttered with a smile. "Kathrax truly intends to unite the two worlds." He shook his head in disbelief. "It's almost unimaginable."

"All it takes is the right combination of Talents. And the right source of essence."

She glanced down to his waist, at the belt he wore that was ribbed with small vials. Half had been used to create the breach and bring down the Tree, but the other vials were still filled with Aram Raythe's essence. Once it ran out, he would have to return to the College to replenish his stores. But there was another way to acquire more.

From its source.

The guardians of this forsaken world had used Aram to defend the Great Tree, probably because they knew that his essence would enhance the Anchor's defenses. Sergan was willing to bet that, if they attacked another Anchor, the dragon men would feel pressured to use him once again.

How predictable they were.

It was perfect. Not only would his allies crack the Veil open a little further, but he may even be able to secure a prize beyond any other: the essence of a True Savant.

Sergan beamed a wide smile. "I look forward to it, my lady."

Supper was an extravagance. Apparently, one of the cooks had heard about Aram's punishment on the cliff and had taken pity on him, baking him a fresh barley loaf hollowed out and filled with mutton stew. When Iver started to say something, Markus reminded him that all he had to do was confess his part in the egg-incident if he desired a bowl. Aram shared his loaf with his friends, passing it around the table, because he didn't feel right about enjoying the meal without them.

After supper, the apprentices went back to the dormitory. They were all in high spirits, for that afternoon it had been confirmed that they were all candidates for the dragon eggs when they hatched. They were almost done with their training. Aram wondered if Markus would also be a candidate for a dragon egg, since he was new. But he was actually the oldest of all of them, so Aram figured that improved his chances.

When they opened the door to their dorm, Aram was surprised to find it already occupied. Kye was standing in the middle of the room with a rucksack, looking lost. Aram was overjoyed to see him, for he hadn't spoken to Kye since he'd left the novice classes. Seeing him enter, Kye erupted into a smile.

"What are you doing here?" Aram asked, excited.

"Moving in! I turned fifteen yesterday."

"Finally!" Corley barked a laugh, sweeping forward to clap Kye on the back.

Kye grinned. "I know. It took forever! Hey, where's an empty bunk?"

"You can have the one under my bed." Corley thumbed his hand toward his corner of the room.

While Kye got settled, the other apprentices didn't waste the opportunity to plan another adventure, one to make Kye feel included in their midst. They gathered together in the center of the room, Iver with his hands on his hips, Jeran on his bunk, leaning back with one leg up, while Eugan stood with his arms crossed, looking exceptionally unconvinced that another adventure was a good idea.

"Are you kidding me?" Eugan threw his hands up. "You saw what Vandra did to Aram. I don't want to end up hanging off a cliff."

"Not even for mutton stew?" Jeran asked, then ducked quickly as Eugan swiped out at him.

"What if it's only just a *little* trouble?" Corley had a mischievous glint in his eyes.

"Or a little cliff?" Jeran interjected.

Finished with unpacking his belongings, Kye inserted himself into the ring of friends, seamlessly joining the conversation. Aram envied him, for he didn't know how Kye could walk into a room and within minutes feel at home with the people there. It was a skill that had always eluded him, one of the great mysteries of social interaction that everyone else in the world seemed to know instinctively—everyone but him.

"Hey, I overheard Nathrey Kant mention the eggs are almost ready to hatch," said Corley. "Maybe this time—"

"No. Just no." Markus shook his head adamantly. "No more dragon eggs!"

Aram wished that everyone would just forget his shameful experience with the eggs, but tonight's bread bowl stew was a good indicator that it was still on people's minds. And it wasn't just the apprentices in his dorm, but he'd caught other people staring at him in the hallways when he walked by.

"I know what I'd like to do," said Corley. "You know the abandoned eyries in the Heights? I heard there's all kinds of ancient weapons and relics up there."

The idea sparked a chorus of support from everyone but Iver. Aram's curiosity was piqued. He had seen the doorways that led to the empty chambers up on the level of Esmir's quarters, but he had never had the courage to open any of them.

"Why are they abandoned?" asked Markus.

"No more Champions." Eugan shrugged. Reaching into a leather pouch at his belt, he withdrew a ripe pear and bit into it, juice dribbling down his chin. Talking as he chewed, he added, "And no Greater Dragons."

"What's a Greater Dragon?" asked Markus.

Aram shivered, recalling his experience with one. "Remember the void dragon? Like that." He didn't remember it very well, other than its milky-white coloration and its impressive size. Esmir said the void dragon had slipped into the abyss after delivering him to Skyhome. Aram still didn't know whether the dragon had been alive or dead at that point, but its loss made him sad.

Markus asked, "What happened to all of them?"

Eugan took another bite of pear. "There weren't that many to begin with. The last died in the war. As we lost more Champions, we lost their dragons. Esmir's and Torian's were the last."

His words were followed by an uncomfortable silence. For a few seconds, no one spoke or so much as fidgeted, their gazes turned downward to the floor. Aram wondered if it was the dragons that they mourned, or rather something more enduring, like the passing of an era. Looking up, he saw that all of their gazes had turned to him. He didn't know why.

"Wow," Markus said, breaking the silence.

"So, now all that's left of them is empty eyries," Corley said. "No one lives there, except Esmir."

"I want to see them," whispered Aram. Markus shot him a concerned glance, but Aram paid him no mind. He knew nothing of Champions or their lives, and the way he figured it, he had the right to be curious, more than any of them.

Markus asked, "Are the abandoned eyries off-limits?"

"Not really," Corley replied. "I mean, no one's ever told us we *can't* go there."

"So, why don't people go?"

"They're kind of haunted." Eugan finished the pear and tossed the pit over his shoulder. Jeran shot him an annoyed glance, to which Eugan just shrugged.

"That's bullshit, Eugan," said Iver. "No one ever said they're haunted."

"I meant, it's like a graveyard up there. It would be, I don't know, disrespectful or something."

"Then I don't want to do it," said Markus.

"I want to," Aram insisted. "I want to see what it was like. The way they lived. I want to know."

Understanding dawned on Markus's face, and he nodded slowly.

"Imagine it," said Jeran. "Not just people with the affinity, but actual Champions. Like Aram is going to be."

He flashed Aram a confident smile, which Aram appreciated more than anything in the world. So many people didn't think he had a chance; he got tired of hearing it. It was nice to know that he had friends who believed in him.

"All right," Markus conceded, "as long as we don't get in trouble."

"We won't," Jeran assured him. "The worst thing that can happen is we get a long lecture about honoring the past."

Aram just hoped it wouldn't be a stern lecture, for he really didn't want to earn any more of Vandra's disappointment. But the curiosity to see what was up there in those empty eyries burned him far more than the lure of the dragon eggs had.

Corley rubbed his hands together in excitement. "All right, then. It's decided. Let's go tomorrow night, after everyone's in bed."

"I can't," said Jeran. "I've got scullery duty."

"The next night, then." Corley beamed.

And it was settled.

Jeran's constant snoring woke Aram before dawn. Which was fortunate, because he had forgotten that he was expected back at the Brausas' workshop. He dressed quickly then made his way down the stairs to Hearth Home. Only the first blush of dawn was apparent in the east as he wound his way through the quiet streets in the direction of the smithy. He could smell the scent of the morning dough on the air, one of his favorite smells in the world. It made his mouth water and his stomach rumble.

He found Onsel waiting for him by the forge. This time, the swordsmith had an apprentice with him, a young man Aram had never seen before with a shock of reddish-brown hair that drooped limply over his face. When Aram entered the workshop, the apprentice's gaze fell on him and just stuck there, as though he were some kind of anomaly. Feeling uncomfortable, Aram managed a weak smile in his direction, which went either unnoticed or ignored.

"This is Becht," Onsel motioned at the young man. "He is a journeyman who is working toward creating his masterpiece. I invited him here today to observe the process of folding star steel."

Aram nodded at the young man, who was still staring at him. At last, the apprentice blinked, looking embarrassed.

"Sorry," Becht said, attempting a smile. "It's just that I've never met a Champion before."

"I'm not a Champion yet," Aram said, answering his smile with one of his own. "Hopefully, you're not wasting all this work on me."

"Gods forfend!" Onsel erupted, throwing his head back and laughing heartily. "Young man, if you don't pass your Trials, your ghost will be indentured to me for the rest of eternity in repayment for this sword!"

Aram gulped, for he understood what a risk the smith was taking on him, and he was genuinely terrified that the blade he was helping forge might go to waste. But before he could launch into apologies, Onsel called him over, and the three of them gathered beside the forge.

"Today and tomorrow will be the last days you'll spend here," Master Onsel informed him. "After this step, I'll hammer out the blade's shape then send the sword out to different experts who will finish it. A master polisher will spend weeks polishing the blade. Then it goes to the master hilt maker, then to someone else who will make the scabbard, then yet another master craftsman who will finish the edge. It's quite a process."

Aram's jaw went slack, and his mind spun, for he had never imagined so much work could go into the making of just one sword. Master Onsel was right: if he didn't pass his Trials, he really *would* owe the swordsmith an eternity of servitude, for the sword was made specific to him, and could be sold to no one else.

Moving around him, the smith knelt beside the anvil. There, he had placed the steel plate they had forged during Aram's last visit. On top of the plate, Onsel had arranged thin wafers of broken star steel, piled in many perfectly fitting layers, until he had accumulated a mass of dozens of wafers roughly the size and shape of a brick.

"Today we will fold the steel," Onsel announced. "It must be consistent all the way through the length of the blade. Think of the folding process as like making bread. All the pieces of steel must be mixed together so they are uniform, just like kneading dough. Only, we cannot knead steel. So, we fold it instead. During this step, it's crucial that the steel remains at a much lower temperature."

Standing, he moved to a stack of straw that had been placed beside the forge. "This straw is one of the secrets of forging star steel," he explained with a stern look at both Aram and Becht. "So you are not to talk about this outside this smithy."

Holding a piece of straw over the forge, he lit it on fire, then dropped it onto the heap of straw to set the rest alight. Watching the straw burn to black ashes, he said, "We will wrap the burned straw around the steel, so it doesn't overheat in the forge and become too soft."

He then bent and collected a piece of parchment. This, he dipped in water then wrapped it around the brick of steel wafers. Picking the bundle up, he rolled the brick in the straw ashes, thoroughly coating it, then covered the whole thing with watery clay.

"Heat the forge!" he commanded Becht, who immediately started working the piston to move the bellows, bringing the forge to life. Onsel placed the bundle of steel in the forge, raking charcoal over it.

"More!" Onsel ordered his apprentice, spurring him to work the piston faster, heating the flames to a hungry, pinkish-red. Then he stood, waiting, as the brick of steel heated, every so often moving aside the charcoal to check its color.

Aram stared at the orange-glowing brick of steel in the forge, transfixed, hardly noticing as time wore on. This was *his* sword they were making, and every minute that he spent at the Brausas' workshop drove home the point that this was no ordinary blade they were forging. This was the star-steel blade of a Champion. No conventional sword could compare.

Eventually, the brick of steel wafers reached the right temperature. With a pair of long tongs, Onsel removed it from the flames and placed it on the anvil.

"Hammers!" he ordered, and both Aram and Becht scrambled for the long-handled sledges and climbed onto the crates. Onsel grabbed his small hammer and started tapping out instructions. Lifting his sledge, Aram let it fall, striking the first blow.

"Take turns!" Onsel commanded, tapping with his hammer to set the pace. Aram and Becht took turns hitting the steel brick with their sledges, listening to the *tap-tapping* of Onsel's commands. When they were done, the brick of steel had been compacted, the individual wafers crushed together.

Onsel then beat a deep groove into the center of the block with a chisel, all but cutting it in half. He then folded the steel block back over itself and directed Aram and Becht to beat it again with the sledgehammers.

"This is how we fold the steel," he explained as he beat another groove into the brick, this one running counter to the first. "First, we fold it one way, then the other, over and over. Every time the steel is folded, it loses impurities and becomes more uniform."

Each time the brick was folded, they repeated the process, covering it in straw and clay and placing it back into the forge to heat.

"We do this a dozen times. Every time we fold the steel, the number of layers doubles. When we are done folding, the steel will consist of over a thousand layers."

Aram glanced at Becht, amazement in his eyes. The journeyman smith just smiled and nodded, thumbs hooked in his thick apron.

Aram spent the rest of the morning at the forge folding steel then spent the afternoon in the Henge with Markus and Esmir. Esmir didn't make him go back into the portal, but instead worked with them both on timing, making them repeat the same forms over and over until Aram's arms felt like they would fall off, especially after using the sledgehammer all morning. At the end of the day, when Esmir let them go, two very sweaty youths practically fell over each other to escape down the stairs to the baths.

Halfway down the stairs, someone called Aram's name. He stopped and looked back, panting. It was Calise, rushing down the steps toward them. Seeing her, his spirits lifted, for he hadn't spoken to her in days and days.

"Aram! I haven't seen you in so long!"

Suddenly realizing how terrible he must look, Aram felt an instant of panic. He was so covered in sweat and soot, people across the canyon could probably smell him.

"I've been really busy," he said, fighting to contain his embarrassment. "How... How have you been?"

"I've been busy too. The enemy's marching across the Altier Highlands, sacking towns and villages as they go. It's not looking good. There's been a lot of skirmishes. They're getting reinforcements from somewhere. A *lot* of reinforcements."

"Will there be another battle?" asked Markus, nervous excitement in his voice.

"This is Markus," Aram said, realizing that the two had never met.

Calise turned to Markus, her gaze wandering over him with a look of...something...in her eyes. Something that made Aram's stomach clench in jealousy.

"Probably," she said.

"I hope not," Aram said, feeling suddenly disheartened. "Battles are dangerous. I don't want you getting hurt."

His words made her smile, and she turned her attention back to him. It was a beautiful smile that lifted his spirits, making him forget the brief moment of jealousy.

"Zandril will keep me safe," she said.

"Still."

Suddenly, Aram's eyes widened as a thought occurred to him. "We're going on an adventure to the abandoned eyries tomorrow. Want to come?"

"Really?" Calise gasped. "Esmir is letting you?"

"Esmir doesn't—"

"*Mind.*" Markus stated firmly, his stare locking on Aram's. "Esmir doesn't mind."

Aram frowned, trying to figure out what he had done to earn such a look from his best friend. Calise glanced back and forth between the two of them, at last asking suspiciously, "Esmir doesn't know, does he?" Before either of them could respond, she said, "That's all right. I'd still love to go!"

"Better ask the others first," Markus warned. "What if they say no?"

Calise snorted. "Then I'll come anyway. When are we going?"

"Tomorrow after supper."

"I'll be there." With a smile, she headed back up the stairs, leaving both Markus and Aram looking after her in consternation.

"She likes you," Markus said, laughing as they started down again.

Aram shook his head. "She doesn't like me. She just wants to go on an adventure."

"And risk Vandra finding out? No way! She must like you a *lot.*"

The statement made Aram's hopes soar higher than the cliffs. But then reality brought them crashing back down.

"No." The weight of disappointment crushed the word. "Girls don't like me."

Markus grinned. "Maybe girls didn't *used* to like you. But you've changed *a lot.* Come on."

"Do you really think I've changed?" Aram asked, hurrying to keep up with him.

"Yeah, I think you've changed," Markus said. "I mean, look at you."

Maybe he was right, but Aram just didn't *feel* any different. Especially when he was around Calise. For some reason, she made him nervous.

Maybe it was because she was so pretty.

"You've really got to get better about the way you think about your-self," Markus chided, looking back at him. Suddenly, he halted, turning to peer at Aram closely. "Why are you smiling?"

Aram realized he'd been thinking of Calise and forced the expression off his face. "I'm not smiling."

"Yes, you are. You're smiling!"

"No, I'm not!" Aram insisted. When Markus started laughing, his face turned burning red.

"Don't worry." Markus patted him on the back. "She likes you too."

"She doesn't!"

"She does."

"She doesn't!"

Markus chortled. "Yes. She does."

That night when Aram lay down to sleep, his thoughts drifted to Calise. He felt just a tinge of envy, though he didn't understand why. Calise was older than he was—somewhere between him and Markus in age. She was sweet and yet strong, with a casual confidence and grace. Someone like her would want someone like Markus, who was intelligent and handsome and self-assured. As Aram closed his eyes and drifted off to sleep, he decided that Markus would be better for her, and that thought made him sad. Sad, but glad because, more than anything, he just wanted his two best friends to be happy.

The next morning was the last that Aram spent helping Onsel Brausa forge his blade. They spent all morning folding steel, working up to the point that the blade was ready to be shaped. But that was all Aram could do. The remainder of the work would have to be finished by much more capable hands than his own. When he left the brothers' shop, Aram thanked Onsel profusely for giving him an opportunity to be a part of the making of his own blade. He was actually sad the work had ended, for he found it gratifying, and he enjoyed learning new things. He left the Brausas' shop feeling bittersweet, anxious to see how the final blade would look.

After that, he returned with Esmir and Markus to the Henge again, to stand in front of the Portal Stone that had given Aram nightmares half the night, for he knew Esmir would be wanting him to go back through it today. The old Warden stood at his side, long strands of his thinning gray hair tossing about in the wind coming up from the canyon. He leaned heavily on his cane, looking a hundred years older than the twelve hundred he actually was.

Lifting his cane, Esmir pointed at the portal. "They went easy on you last time. Today, they'll know you, so they'll be better prepared."

Aram gaped at him, wondering exactly what the old man would define as 'hard.' He had no wish to go back into the Shadow Realm, to face those strange creatures again. Last time, he'd barely gotten away with his life. If the Overseers knew him better now, as Esmir claimed, they'd sense every weakness he had and exploit it. He shivered even though the wind wasn't cold. Reluctantly, Aram set down his practice sword and undressed down to his breeches.

"Are you sure you want to go in there wearing those?" Esmir asked.

Aram glanced down at his cotton undershorts and started to untie the drawstring, but then he paused. They didn't look very deadly. Not wanting to go naked again, he decided to leave them on.

With a wry smile, Aram responded, "If they want my breeches, they can have them. It's been a week since I washed them last."

"*Again?*" Markus feigned disgust, while Esmir rolled his eyes.

"My other pair fell apart." Aram shrugged with a smirk, then turned and walked toward the portal.

"Wait," Markus called, making Aram turn back to him. For a moment, Markus looked like he didn't know what to say, but then he summoned a halfhearted smile. "Be careful."

Aram smiled back. Then, squaring his shoulders, he drew a deep breath then entered the portal.

He was back in the world of darkness, only, this time, he was in a different place. The standing stones were gone, as was the obelisk. Instead, he stood on a flat surface that seemed to go on forever in every direction. There was nothing else around, as though the world consisted of just a level plain. Wherever he was, it existed in a mute twilight that seemed to come from everywhere and nowhere, barely enough to ease the darkness just a little.

Turning in a slow circle, he scanned the flat terrain, looking for the Overseers but not finding them. He didn't trust their absence any more than he would have trusted their presence. He knew they were there somewhere, scheming against him.

He was fully clothed again in a different tunic and cloak. Or maybe it was the same one, just without the burns. No, that couldn't be. Esmir had kept the outfit he'd emerged with the last time he'd gone in. His breeches were missing, he discovered. In their place, he wore a loincloth, his legs bare beneath the long tunic.

He was holding a sword of a type he had never seen before. It wasn't like the elegant, curved blade Onsel was making for him. Nor was it anything like the heavier, double-edged blades carried by the soldiers of his own world. This sword was slender and slightly tapered, possessing a single edge. There was no crossguard, just a copper disk attached to the tang. He held it up and tested its weight, finding it light and perfectly balanced. He wondered if it was a sword from the realm of the Overseers.

For the moment, there didn't seem to be anyone to use it against.

The thought of his missing breeches returning to attack him made Aram smile. Holding the sword ready, he walked forward. There was really no place to go, for what lay ahead of him was exactly like what lay behind, the same as in every other direction. But he couldn't just stand there waiting for something to attack him, and forward seemed just as good a place as backward.

As he walked, Aram noticed that there was no sound to his footsteps. In fact, there was no sound at all to the world. Neither was there any movement of the air or even scent. It was as though all of his senses had been stripped from him. The farther he walked, the more he came to question the existence of this place. Perhaps he was just imagining it, and this place didn't exist at all. Maybe none of it did. Maybe the Overseers were all just part of his imagination. But a nagging fear that this place was very real and very dangerous continued to nettle him, and he decided to take it seriously.

Lost in thought, he wasn't expecting the attack when it came.

A rupture appeared in the air before him and a shadow stepped out of it. Before he could bring his sword up, the shadow fell upon him, striking out at him with a blade of its own. Aram twisted back out of reach, blocking the next strike that came for him. The sword connected with his own with a solid hit that rattled his bones.

Before he could recover, the shadow came at him again. Once more, Aram barely dodged the slice. The shadow was *fast*. Every time it attacked, he was always an instant behind it.

Perhaps the shadow-man wasn't real, but his fear was. All he could think about was Master Henrik saying that a swordfight was not a dance, that it should be brief and brutal. Already, this dance had gone on too long. The skill of his faceless opponent surpassed his own, and he knew he couldn't keep dodging and retreating the whole length of the forever-plane.

Don't attack. Counterattack.

Henrik had said that too. That's what he was doing wrong, Aram realized—he was passively defending. He needed to start *aggressively* defending.

He parried the next thrust, turning the shadow-sword aside with the strength of his blade, at the same time slicing out with the blade's weakness.

For the first time, his faceless opponent was forced to defend. Without hesitation, Aram stepped forward to press his advantage. It was as though his body suddenly remembered all the long hours it had spent training and finally realized that it knew what to do. With an empty mind, Aram let his body take over, dealing a rapid succession of blows that drove the shadow-man backward. With a final thrust, his blade pierced his opponent's chest.

But the shadow-man did not go down. Instead, he cleaved in half.

Suddenly, Aram found himself facing two shadowy opponents that separated and then came at him from both sides. The acute panic Aram felt was over in an instant, for he couldn't afford the distraction. Once again, his mind turned off, and his body moved of its own accord, his sword defending and attacking at the same time as he danced backward in an effort to put both of his opponents in front of him.

There was a deafening thunder and a brilliant flash of light. He closed his eyes, the scorching light glaring red through his eyelids.

When he opened his eyes, he saw that both his opponents had disappeared, and that he was once again alone on the flat, expansive plain. Panting, Aram lowered his sword slowly, turning in a circle as he glanced about. It was too much to believe that the Overseers would let him off so easily when they almost had him defeated.

When one of the Overseers appeared before him, he skittered backward with a cry.

Aram's sword flew from his hands and something wound around his neck and started strangling him. He tried to slip his fingers under it, but it was already too late—a thin length of string was cutting into his skin like a garrote.

Just when he started to panic, one thought occurred to him: string had always been his ally, and he refused to be killed by it.

Reaching out with his mind, Aram sliced the cord around his neck with a knife of sharpened aether.

The Overseer made a pushing motion, and suddenly Aram was sliding backward. He slid faster and faster across the nothingness, until he was flying.

Then the Portal Stone appeared behind him, swallowing him whole and spitting him out the other side.

Aram stared up at Esmir, who was gazing down at him with the midday sun haloing his head. When he saw that the old man was chuckling, Aram glanced down at himself. The clothes the Overseers had garbed him in were gone, and so were his breeches. When he saw that he was lying naked on the ground, his cheeks glowed red-hot with embarrassment.

Reaching down, Esmir removed a length of cord from around Aram's neck, holding it up before his eyes. "Seems to look familiar."

Aram gaped at the dangling cord that had almost strangled him, at last recognizing it for what it was: the drawstring of his breeches. He threw a hand up, smacking his forehead. Esmir stepped away and Markus tossed his tunic at him. When he was decently clothed again, Aram reached a hand up and groped at his neck, realizing that the ligature mark from the cord was still there, a thin indentation that encircled his neck. It hadn't healed like his burns had the previous day.

"Why didn't they heal me like they did before?" he asked Esmir as the old man led them toward the stairs.

"Because you weren't really burned, I imagine," Esmir answered.

"Maybe next time, you'll think twice before taking anything in there with you."

"I won't think about it at all! I'd be stupid to take anything in there!"

Markus clapped him on the back. "You're just lucky they didn't strangle you with your dirty breeches."

Aram grimaced at the image, but then he winced, his eyes going wide as a thought occurred to him. "That was my last pair of breeches!"

At that, both Markus and Esmir started laughing.

The rest of the day dragged by at a glacier's pace. Aram sat sprawled against the wall in Esmir's quarters, a book open and unread in his lap. He had spent more time watching the candle burning down than he had reading, convinced that the taper was made of special wax that burned at an impossibly slow rate.

Perhaps sensing their restlessness, Esmir dismissed them early. Aram raced Markus out the door. They took the stairs down to the baths and made it to Hearth Home in time for supper. When they reached the table they shared with the other young men from their dorm, all eyes went to Aram, and jaws dropped. Aram glanced from face to face, wondering what he could have possibly done now. Slowly, it dawned on him, and his hand went to his throat, which was covered in dark bruises from the drawcord.

"*What happened?*" gasped Corley. "I know Esmir said he wanted to strangle you, but I thought he was joking!"

Setting his plate on the table, Aram glanced at Markus. "Go ahead. Tell them," he muttered, staring at his plate.

"Aram strangled himself," Markus announced, trying but unable to keep a straight face. "With his own breeches!"

Aram hid his face in his hands as the table erupted around him.

"What?"

"*What?*"

"No shit!"

"Are you serious?"

Pretty soon, the whole table was roiling with laughter, especially after the full story came out. The inevitable jokes that followed continued even after supper on the long walk back up the stairs to the dormatory. At first, Aram was scared they were making fun of him—until he realized it was nothing of the sort. He had mysteriously found himself in a position he'd never expected to be in: the center of attention in a *good* way.

The last of the Underwear Head jokes were still coming in when they burst through the door of their room to find Calise there, waiting inside.

Aram felt his cheeks go from blotchy to brazen red in the span of a heartbeat.

"*Underwear* Head?" Calise arched her eyebrows.

Mortified, Aram turned and made for the door, but Markus thrust his arm out, blocking any hope of escape. Squeezing his eyes closed, Aram turned around slowly to face a grinning Calise.

After Markus had recounted the tale, Calise reassured Aram, "It's all right! I'm sure it happens to everyone." But then she saw the ligature marks around his neck. "Oh, that looks bad. Are you sure your breeches did this to you?"

"It was the drawcord," Aram admitted, making Markus smirk.

"Uh-huh…" Calise looked around at the young men in the room. "So, are we going on an adventure, or what?"

"Why, yes, we are!" exclaimed Corley, clapping his hands together. "You're coming along too?" When Calise nodded, he raised his hands. "All right. Everyone get a sack!"

"What's the sack for?" asked Jeran.

"For things we find that we want to take with us."

"Wouldn't that be stealing?" asked Markus.

"Nah. Nothing up there belongs to anyone, at least no one alive."

"I don't know," Markus frowned. "It sounds like grave robbery."

"There aren't any graves up there," said Iver.

"Still."

"Well, I, for one, am taking a sack. You don't have to." With that, Corley walked across the room and pulled a soft felt bag out of his chest.

Markus shrugged. "Fair enough."

Eugan grunted something, then went to fetch a sack of his own. In the end, it was only Corley, Iver, and Eugan that ended up with sacks, while the rest of them decided that looting the eyries would be pushing their luck and morals too far. They waited a bit longer, to make sure that most of Skyhome's inhabitants would be in bed. Then Kye picked up a candlestick and they all followed Corley out into the dark hallway and took the stairs upward toward the Heights, seeing by the light of Kye's tiny flame. When they reached the level above Esmir's eyrie, they exited the stairwell and turned down a long, black corridor.

"Where are we?" asked Kye.

"These levels were where the Greater Dragons were kept," explained Corley. "I figured we'd start on this one so we wouldn't have to take the risk of running into Esmir."

"What if we run into someone else?" asked Aram, rubbing his scored neck.

"We won't. He's the only one left who lives up here."

"Why's that?" asked Markus.

"Because. He's the only one still alive who ever had a Greater Dragon."

"Where's Esmir's dragon now?" Aram asked.

The boys stopped and stood staring at each other for a long moment before turning to look at Calise, who spread her hands. When no one came up with an answer to that question, Corley just shrugged and continued on with their adventure. He led them down the hallway by the light of Kye's taper, eventually stopping at one of the doorways. He waited until the others were gathered around then opened the door, which shrieked ghoulishly as it swung inward.

Even though there was only darkness all around them, Aram could tell they were entering a large, open space. The air turned cool, and there was a slight breeze coming from what could only be the mouth of an eyrie. He could imagine them standing in the middle of Esmir's quarters, or at least another cavern just like it.

"It's too dark to see anything," complained Calise. "How are we supposed to know what's here?"

"With this." From out of his burlap sack, Iver produced a cloth-wrapped torch.

There was a general muttering of appreciation as Iver ignited the torch off the flame of Kye's taper. As the torch blazed eagerly to life, its flames cast back the shadows, revealing an entire cavern before them, the light of the torch casting ghostly shadows across the walls.

"Whoa," several of the apprentices muttered at once.

Before them, in the middle of the chamber, was the stone carving of a dragon, curled around itself the way a snake wraps into a coil. It was massive, far larger than any dragon in the eyries below. Aram thought it was the size of the void dragon that had carried him, but it was hard to tell. It was a haunting sight, made even more so by the fact that it looked so incredibly real.

"Maybe we should go," whispered Kye, backing away.

"Why?" asked Aram, staring up at the dragon statue in awe.

"Because this is a grave, and we shouldn't be here," whispered Calise.

"A grave?" Markus peered at her then turned to stare at the stone dragon in the center of the cavern. "Are you telling me that's *real?*"

Aram's jaw went slack as he realized that's why the stone dragon contained so much detail. At one time, it had been a living dragon, but now it was petrified. Driven by a compulsion he couldn't ignore, Aram crept forward until he stood beside the dragon's long neck. Reaching out, he trailed his hand over the smooth texture of its scales. A great sadness filled him. This had once been a living monarch of the skies, now immortalized in cold stone.

"That's what happens when dragons die," whispered Kye. "They turn to stone."

"It's called a dragon cairn," said Calise, coming to stand beside Aram, setting her hand next to his upon the stone. "There's two bodies here: the dragon and its rider." In answer to Aram's confused look, she explained, "If a rider dies before their dragon, the dragon carries their body off somewhere, usually to a beautiful place, and wraps around them just like this. Then the dragon dies and becomes stone. That way, they're together forever. I'm not sure why this one stayed here. Maybe it didn't have the strength to fly elsewhere."

Aram asked in a trembling voice, "Why do dragons turn to stone?"

"Because that's what happens. When they're alive, it's like the fire inside them warms their flesh and keeps them living. But when they die, that fire goes out, and their flesh cools to stone."

Aram took a step back and gazed at the sad monument that confronted them: the last embrace of two souls united in death. He couldn't imagine a love so pure and so enduring, or what it would be like to be loved like that by another.

Suddenly, he felt an intense urge to leave. He didn't want to be here any longer because he knew he *shouldn't* be here. Cast before them in stone was a last, tender moment, and it should remain private. Their very presence here was an intrusion that disturbed the austerity of this place.

Turning, he hastened toward the door and retreated back out into the shadowed corridor. Unable to find his way in the dark, he stopped and leaned back against the wall as he waited for the others. He felt overwhelmed and ashamed, and he'd had enough of adventures.

When the others came out, he looked at Corley and demanded, "Did you know we were going to find this?"

"No." Corley looked intensely regretful. "I mean, it makes sense that some of them might have died here, but I just didn't think…"

"Let's just go find another eyrie," said Iver. "One that's unoccupied."

"No." Aram locked his gaze with Iver's and firmly shook his head. "We're going back."

"What?" Iver gasped. "Don't tell me that scared you?"

"It didn't scare me." Aram looked from Iver to Corley, then turned to take in the others. How could they not understand? "This isn't right. What *we're* doing isn't right. We're not supposed to be here. This is *their* place. Not our place. We need to go."

"Aram's right," said Markus, licking his lips.

"You always agree with him," snapped Iver. "Look—"

"I always agree with him because he's always *right.*" Markus's eyes flared angrily. For a moment, he looked like he was getting ready to punch Iver.

"We're leaving," said Calise, taking Aram's arm. "The rest of you can stay here if you want, but you shouldn't."

Crossing the hallway, Aram drew the eyrie's door shut, closing it quietly so as not to disturb the repose of its occupants. He shot Iver one last, hard, glare, then let Calise pull him away. The rest of the apprentices followed them back toward the stairs, leaving only Iver and Eugan behind, standing in the hallway with their sacks. Aram felt bad, worried that he might have lost two friends. But then he thought of what Markus would say if he asked: if that's the way Iver and Eugan were going to act, then they didn't deserve his friendship.

58

Sergan watched Lazair slide from the back of her dragon, drawing the Baelsword from its sheath. With the grace of a panther, she stalked across the coarse moorland grasses toward him, nodding a greeting. Today she wore a white gown that was divided for riding, slit up the front and back so high that it came damn close to compromising her virtues—if she had any.

Her gaze traveled to the woman who lay in front of him on the ground, weeping and quivering from terrible burns that covered half her body, inflicted by his sorcery. Or perhaps she whimpered because of the imminent threat to her dragon, which a single lance of lightning had knocked out of the sky.

Sergan looked on in fascination as Lazair crouched next to the woman and stared down at her, as though enjoying her anguish. She looked almost disappointed when the woman didn't acknowledge her presence. It wasn't an act of defiance—which Sergan would have applauded—but, rather, his victim was in too much pain to notice much of anything.

Rising, Lazair glanced at him. Then she raised the Baelsword and pressed it down against the woman's chest, not stabbing her with it, but just poking a bit. She leaned her weight against the sword, slowly at first, making the woman beneath her wail and thrash piteously. Sergan stopped the thrashing, binding the woman's limbs with invisible ropes of aether. He watched Lazair's face as the sorceress pressed more of her weight down against the hilt, at last succeeding in piercing the woman's

477

skin, grinding it slowly deeper into her chest.

At some point, the screams stopped. The woman's dragon did not react to the death of its beloved, for Sergan's lightning had stunned it cold.

Rising, Lazair motioned one of her officers forward, bidding him kneel beside the great beast. Apparently, this creature was meant for him.

Looking around the battlefield, Sergan realized how one-sided their victory had been. Nine out of every ten corpses he counted belonged to the defenders. Their own forces had suffered almost no casualties.

He left Lazair and strolled toward the twisted body of one of the natives he had personally killed. It was a man with the gold-brown skin of the Auld, his turquoise eyes fixed upward in the infinite stare of death. He had fought bravely, protecting his family. Their corpses all smoldered in the blackened ash behind him that had once been their hut.

Obriem came forward to stand at his side. Sergan could feel the weight of his judgment. He was too young to understand.

"Is there any reason why you're being unnecessarily ruthless?" Obriem asked, not even attempting to hide the disgust in his voice. "I mean, this was bad, even for you."

Sergan shrugged, prodding the corpse of the father with the toe of his boot. "The logic is simple. If we threaten what they love, they will have no choice but to defend it."

Obriem dragged his blade across the thatch that covered the ground, wiping blood from his sword. "And what if they send more dragons?"

"Then I'll enjoy knocking them out of the sky."

Lazair walked over and grasped the dead father by his hair, tilting his head to stare into his eyes. The lines of horror etched into his face made her smile.

"I see you're enjoying yourself," she said.

"You do provide rousing entertainment." Sergan inclined his head, applauding her cruelty.

He glanced up at the sky, scanning for anything on wing. But the sky was clear and cloudless, absent any sign of dragons. After the violence of the battle, the only things moving overhead were the ravens. Those had arrived before the fighting had even begun, drawn to the sight of impending carnage as though they had some type of prescience for bloodshed.

"Don't worry. They'll send the boy," Lazair said, following his gaze. "Probably when we threaten the caverns."

They had been making good progress since leaving the Eldenwood. Another two- or three-days' march across the stony moorland would see them at the Caverns of Eld Elan, which was their objective. Like the Great Tree, there was an Anchor there, though Sergan was having a hard time visualizing it.

"What exactly is this Anchor?" he asked. "It's not a tree, obviously."

Lazair glanced behind her, to where her men were dragging the bodies into piles to be burned. "The caverns themselves are the Anchor. Deep within their heart is a Wellspring called the Tears of the Mother. If consumed by the dying, it will cause the afflicted to fall into a deep, blissful sleep. Sometimes, they awaken with their wounds healed. If not, they die painlessly, knowing only a great sense of peace."

"Hmph." Sergan was still hoping to find a Wellspring with essence concentrated enough to distill. "Sounds like I should try bottling some of those tears."

Lazair smiled and let out a soft chortle. "Unlike other Wellsprings, the Tears don't keep well. Otherwise, there would be vats of it everywhere. The Caverns of Eld Elan are a place of pilgrimage. The dying need to be brought *to* the water, not the other way around."

A place of pilgrimage. That did indeed sound promising, for it sounded like a place very sacred to the people of this land. Sacred enough to fight for. Perhaps even sacred enough to risk the life of a half-trained and would-be Champion to defend.

Sergan hoped so.

He wanted to get ahold of Aram Raythe before Lazair did.

Vandra stroked the dark scales of Ragath's horned head. They perched upon a rocky crest that looked down upon the dark, pockmarked moorland of the Altier Highlands. The army of Araghar was on the move, marching south across the rugged heath known as the Bloodmire. It was dark, but the campfires of the enemy were visible and easily quantifiable. Vandra figured there were at least twenty thousand, which was more than problematic. The enemy had been receiving reinforcements ever since capturing the Eldenwood, and their ranks had swelled considerably. Apparently, defeating one Anchor was not enough. They were marching in the direction of the Caverns of Eld Elan, where the Altier Anchor was located.

Their objective bothered Vandra more than she wished to acknowledge, for it was a pattern that was truly terrifying. One by one, the Anchors of Heaven were falling beneath Araghar's might, and the Veil was eroding. She knew what would happen when the last Anchor fell: the two worlds would align, merging into one. Such a collision would cause devastation of a magnitude not seen since the Sundering, uniting the power of the Archons and sealing the fate of all things magical.

No. The armies of Araghar must be stopped here, on this plain, before their cancer could spread further. It would be a hard fight, though not impossible. After all, they had dragons that could rain fire from the sky, and their Gifted warriors were worth any ten of the enemy's soldiers. She just hoped the enemy could be stopped before they reached the town of Inuine, which stood between the army of Araghar and the caverns.

Vandra heard the crunching noise of footsteps coming up behind her and turned to see one of her captains, Garam Kade, approaching, his plumed helm tucked in the crook of his arm. Kade's pox-cratered face was grim, his lips stretched thin.

"It doesn't look good." He spat on the ground. "They're just a couple of miles from Inuine."

"Their objective isn't Inuine." Vandra stroked her cheek absently, eyes distant in thought. "It's the Anchor."

Kade grunted, which was the closest he ever got to voicing agreement. Raising her hand, she pointed toward the dark outline of distant hills that looked like the serrated edge of a knife blade.

"The caverns are on the other side of those hills. But we have to stop them before they reach Inuine. The town walls won't stand up against such an assault."

"What about their sorcerers?" Kade grumbled. "We've already lost three dragons this week."

Vandra nodded absently. It was possible that the Exilari sorcerers who accompanied Araghar's army were responsible for slaying the three dragons they had lost. But there were also natural occurrences that could bring dragons down from the skies, such as lightning or severe downdrafts. Still, they had to find a way to counter a magical attack, should it come.

Kade's frown deepened until it looked like another scar on his face. His eyes lifted to scan the sky above them, which was mottled by just a few scattered clouds.

"We need cloud cover," Vandra muttered, following his gaze.

"It feels like a Northerner is coming," he said.

He was right. The clouds did appear to be moving quickly across the sky, especially when compared against the reference point of the distant hills. The moorland got its share of wind, especially this time of year. The northern gusts were especially brutal, which was why the scrub-like trees that peppered the Highlands grew at an angle. Such a wind usually brought clouds along with it.

"It might bring a storm," said Kade.

He usually only acknowledged Vandra's strategies with tacit approval. Often, Vandra wondered why Kade hadn't accepted the position of Wingmaster when it was offered to him by the Council. Kade had never explained why he had refused the position, leaving it to Vandra, who had been the Council's second choice.

Nodding at Kade, she turned away from the view and mounted her dragon. Without Altier's infantry to support them, even dragon-fire wouldn't be enough. She would have to dispatch riders to alert the fortress of Shenmore. But if they wanted the clouds on their side, they would have to act quickly.

Three days had passed since their ill-conceived adventure to the eyries of the Heights, and Aram still couldn't get the image of the dragon cairn out of his mind. It haunted him throughout the day and troubled his dreams, eliciting every kind of emotion. It was such a sad and yet beautiful thing, that two souls could be so intertwined, even in death. He could never imagine being loved like that. All his life he had craved acceptance and, deep inside, he wondered what it would be like to share such emotional intimacy. It took him three days of sorting through his feelings to realize that what he longed for most was a dragon's unconditional love.

But he could never experience that. Vandra had said no Lesser Dragon could survive being soul-bound to him because his mind was too powerful. Aram didn't understand why that would be. He could communicate with Zandril and Narath easily enough, and it hadn't seemed to bother them one bit. He didn't understand how a soul-bond could be so much different than that meeting of minds.

He had awakened before dawn, unable to sleep. He had dreamt of the void dragon, the only Greater Dragon he would ever see, for all the others of its kind were no more. That he had brought about that dragon's end was a nearly unbearable thought, and he couldn't get the vision of that selfless creature out of his mind.

Things that came from the void weren't truly alive. That's what Esmir said.

But, to him, that void dragon had been alive. It had been *his*, if just for one moment in time. How could a soul-bond be so much different from that? He wondered if, somewhere deep down in the chasm below the cliffs, lay the petrified remains of a creature who had been meant to love him.

Aram left the dormitory and took the stairs up to the Henge. He hadn't intended to end up there, but he hadn't intended not to, either, and that's where his feet carried him. It was cold up there, high on the bluffs. The sun had only just awakened and hadn't quite had a chance to crest the horizon.

Aram walked toward the edge of the cliff, coming as close to it as he dared, and stood for a while looking down. The canyon was so deep and so narrow that he couldn't see the bottom. It just disappeared into a great, dark emptiness. Somewhere deep down inside was the body of a dragon that, in a better world, should have been his.

"You're up early."

Aram glanced behind him to see Esmir, who came to stand at his side. He wished he could confide in the old Warden, but that line of conversation would inevitably lead to their misadventure in the Heights. He didn't want to get his friends in trouble, so he kept his emotions tucked inside.

"I couldn't sleep." Nodding at the gorge, Aram asked, "What's down there? At the bottom?"

Esmir shrugged. "Nothing good. Over the years, many people have tried to climb it, and some even tried to fly their dragons down into the abyss. But there's a point where it becomes too hot for people, even for dragons. Some say the crack goes all the way to the heart of the earth." He shrugged. "Who knows. I certainly do not."

Aram continued to stare down into the fissure, trying to envision what the bottom of it might look like. Another sound behind him made him turn, and he saw Markus crossing the Henge toward them, out of breath from the long climb up. He flopped his arms at Aram in a gesture of frustration.

"I was looking all over for you!"

"I'm sorry," Aram said. "I left early. I didn't think."

"Well, it's time to start thinking." Esmir ruffled Aram's hair. "Now that you're both here, let's get to work!"

"I haven't eaten," Aram protested.

"And whose fault is that?"

He supposed Esmir was right. Aram flashed Markus an apologetic grin then walked toward the chest where they kept their practice weapons.

"Stop," commanded Esmir. He turned and pointed at Markus. "Start going through the Willow Forms. This time, try not to look like a *weeping willow*." Turning to Aram, he ordered, "Back into the portal."

Aram groaned. He *hated* the Shadow Realm. Every time he went there, it seemed to get worse. Shoulders slumped, he walked over to the first Portal Stone and started wriggling out of his clothes. He stared at the portal warily, his chest filling with a cold dread.

"Go on," prodded Esmir.

Swallowing, Aram glanced back at Markus one last time then gathered his courage and stepped inside.

He stood on a sandy beach. It was twilight, and the sky was a deep, dark gray that faded to pink on the horizon. A languid wave broke against the shoreline, rushing toward him, only to slow and retreat, leaving behind a ribbon of white froth. Glancing down at his clothes, he saw that he was wearing one of the outfits his mother had made for him when he was a boy. His feet were bare, and when he flexed his toes, they dug deep into the cool, wet sand. The gritty texture of the sand felt exquisite, a nostalgic pleasure he had all but forgotten. He walked forward, feeling the sea breeze lift his hair, the thick odor of salt heavy in his nostrils. Almost, he could imagine that he was back in Anai.

Aram's hand went to his neck, and he realized with a shiver of fear that he still wore the heart knot necklace his mother had given him. He had forgotten to take it off. His breath caught. All he could think about was the garroting drawstring of his breeches. Only, the necklace was already around his neck, and wasn't constricting yet. If the Overseers intended to use it against him, they had planned a different trap.

The light of sunset had all but faded, now only a streak of gray over the black expanse of ocean. Ahead in the shadows, he could see the faint lights of a village glistening through a thin grove of trees. Aram hesitated, for there was something about those lights...

The lights, the trees, the ocean.

Looking behind him, he saw the rock.

It jutted out of the surf, just as it always had. During the summer, it was a sunning spot for fat, lazy seals. At high tide, it was almost always swallowed by the sea. He'd climbed on that rock more than once, and each time had received enough scratches on the bottom of his feet from its jagged surface to make him regret the attempt.

So, this was how they intended to use the heart knot against him. Not a physical weapon, but an emotional one. Aram wasn't sure he was up to the challenge.

Markus had told him of how the Imperial soldiers had sacked the village, setting fire to many of the structures and slaughtering the townspeople, carrying others away. Aram had always feared for his own mother, although Markus had assured him that he hadn't seen her harmed.

So, was this the test? Was he supposed to walk into the village and find out his mother was dead? He didn't know if he could bear that. His ma was the kindest, most loving soul, even when she didn't show it. Whenever it seemed that life itself had rejected him, she had always made him believe that he still mattered. His mother's words were both comfort and armor. They gave him worth when he felt worthless and forbade him hatred when he felt self-pity. She always let him fight his own battles yet was always there to bandage his wounds. She was everything to him, for he had been everything to her.

If she was gone, he didn't know what he'd do.

The tide had retreated, leaving him alone and shivering on the sand. The lights of the village beckoned, and he could no longer ignore them.

They called to his soul.

Aram left the sand and the waves behind and climbed the sand-drift dike that bordered the seashore. The further he walked, the faster his feet carried him, until he was practically running. He jogged past the burned remains of the widow's hut, all the way to the village gate, which was already closed and barred for the night. Aram lifted both hands and pounded on the gate, but it didn't budge. No one came to answer his knocking. Frustrated, he gave the gate a good kick then turned and leaned with his back against it, struggling to think.

The goat hill.

Excitement jolted down his nerves. Sprinting, he followed the rise of the land to the summit of the little hill behind his cottage, the one the goat always used to climb to gain access to their turf roof. But when he approached the crest of the hill, Aram was afraid, so much so that his joints locked up, and he couldn't move.

What if their home was a burnt-out husk like Mistress Dayslin's had been? What if his ma wasn't there? What if she was dead or carried off by the soldiers? He squeezed his eyes shut, clenching his hands into fists, steeling himself for whatever he would find on the other side of that hill. Crouching, he got down on his hands and knees and crept forward to the edge of the hill and looked down.

He almost cried when he saw the familiar turf roof below. Smoke from the hearth puffed from the chimney, and there was a thin glow of light squinting through the shutters.

Just like the goat, he dropped down from the hill onto the roof. Then he slid from the roof onto the wall and jumped from there to the ground. He landed on all fours and popped up like a ground squirrel, rushing for the door.

Just as soon as he reached it, the door opened, and he froze.

"Aram?"

V andra hunched low over Ragath's neck as the dragon tucked its wings and dove into a stomach-plunging stoop, dropping straight down from the sky upon the army spread out across the plain below them. Frigid wind screamed past her face as the ground rose toward them. Small details became large within seconds, then veered as Ragath pulled up at the last moment, blasting the enemy encampment with ground-charring flames.

All across the Bloodmire, the other dragons of the fighting Wing engaged, igniting soldiers and supply wagons, fortifications and horse pickets. As Ragath's great wings pumped them back toward the sky, Vandra turned to assess the swath of destruction behind them. Ragath's body rolled as he banked sharply, maneuvering into position for another run.

Suddenly, the day around them darkened.

Startled, Ragath stopped abruptly with a strong backstroke then remained hovering as Vandra scanned the skies for the cause of the change. Dark clouds had converged overhead in a sky that, just moments ago, had been all but cleared by the wind. At first, she felt elated, for the clouds would mean cover, should they need it. But then, far across the plain, a thin fork of lightning jabbed down from the sky, followed by a crackling rip of thunder.

A chill went through her.

It was sorcery.

And not just any sorcery, but of a magnitude she had never experienced or even imagined. How much raw power would it take to affect the weather across an entire expanse of sky, enough to command even the clouds? And what horrors could that kind of power inflict if directed at living things?

Another streak of lightning speared downward from the clouds, impaling a dragon in mid-flight. Vandra screamed, reaching out for Garanth as jagged ropes of energy clawed over his body for just an instant before he tumbled from the sky. The dragon crashed hard into the ground, plowing through the topsoil until he finally came to rest in a broken tangle of wings.

Cold horror braced Vandra, for she knew both Garanth and his rider well.

Another bolt of lightning stabbed down, and another dragon fell to the earth.

"Flee!" Vandra cried to Ragath. "Get to ground!"

Ragath wheeled on wing, pumping hard to clear the battlefield as the rest of the Wing followed him. Vandra crouched low on her dragon's back, feeling the great muscles strain beneath her as a lightning storm descended upon them to riddle their formations. Her heart pounded, and her body trembled in terror and grief, her gaze scanning the clouds above for the flare of light that would end them both. Glancing back, she saw the others following and willed them to go faster, hoping to fly clear of the sorcerer's range. But then another dragon right next to them fell in a ball of crackling energy.

"Down there!" she shouted, pointing toward the serrated hills that ran the length of the Bloodmire.

Ragath obeyed, landing at the base of a steep defile out of line of sight from the plain. There was a torrent of displaced air as the other dragons of the Wing alighted around them, all wild-eyed, their neck-spines raised like hackles. Riders leapt from their backs, rushing to care for their injured.

Vandra slid from Ragath's back and rushed through the three-dozen or so dragons that had managed to flee the battlefield, taking quick survey of the casualties. Several riders had been laid out on the rocks, some being tended to, while a couple looked already beyond aid. Moans turned to wails and screams of grief as riders and dragons alike succumbed to their injuries. Vandra stopped and stared at the prone body of Lisia, her friend of many years, lying dead on the rocks, her emerald dragon sprawled at her side, its flesh steaming as it moaned in agony.

Rushing forward, Vandra knelt beside the suffering dragon, tears spilling from her eyes. She trailed her hands along his face. Then she pulled her long dagger from its scabbard and ended his misery.

Never before had Vandra experienced such devastating power as had just been inflicted upon them by the enemy. She couldn't explain it. It was as though the forces of Araghar had birthed or corrupted a Champion of their own. No single sorcerer could have filled the sky with so much lightning, each bolt perfectly timed and perfectly directed to inflict the most injury.

Garam Kade came up to stand at her side, gazing down with pity upon the dead dragon. "We can't stay here," he said. "They'll be coming to finish us off."

Vandra knew he was right. They were in an untenable situation. All the enemy sorcerers needed to do was get within line of sight. The Wings would be vulnerable if they stayed here.

"How many casualties?" Vandra asked, rising.

"Twelve pairs."

"By the wind," Vandra breathed. So many.

They had to do *something*. The enemy would be advancing upon the town of Inuine. They couldn't simply retreat and abandon it—or the Anchor. They would have to stay and find a way to fight.

A ridiculous notion struck her.

Vandra paused for a moment to think it through, at last deciding upon it, for even a ridiculous plan was better than no plan at all.

She turned to Kade. "Find Calise and send her back to Skyhome. See if one of the dragons who's lost a rider will be willing to fly with her. Tell her to fly far wide of the battlefield, above the clouds. Have her bring both Aram and Markus."

Sergan stared at Lazair with a mixture of fear and wonder. Just moments before, she had summoned a thunderstorm and had single-handedly cleared the sky of every dragon. It was an astonishing feat that he could not imagine replicating. And she had done it all without one drop of stolen essence.

Which meant she didn't need it.

"You're Gifted," he said, unable to believe he hadn't seen it sooner. Somehow, Lazair was able to hide her shine, even from him. He'd never heard of such a thing.

The woman smiled as though he had given her a compliment. Her unbound silver hair whipped around her face, tossed by the wind. It didn't hide her eyes, though—eyes that glowed with the cold light of sorcery.

But being Gifted still didn't explain the amount of devastation she had single-handedly wrought. He doubted even Daymar Torian could have reaped such a harvest on the battlefield.

"Not just Gifted," he decided. "You're a Champion. *How…?*"

Lazair drew the Baelsword from its sheath, and he saw that it seethed with a terrible darkness. She raised the sword and stared at it, turning the hilt to make the tongues of dark flame writhe around it. "Animals weren't the only things lost to the void during the Sundering. Humans were too. Even Champions."

Sergan actually took a step away from her, his stomach tightening in dread. "You're a void walker."

Lazair lowered the sword but held it at mid-guard, its power coruscating up the length of her arms. "I was born fifty thousand years ago, when the world was still whole. I and others like me were flung into the void when Erok Sundered the world. For countless centuries, I existed in torment. Until my master rescued me and returned to me the lifeblood I had been denied."

"Essence," Sergan guessed.

Lazair sheathed her blade in one brisk motion. "Yes."

"Are there others like you?"

"A few." She smiled indulgently. "Perhaps you will get to meet them one day."

Unnerved, Sergan glanced to where Obriem stood standing some distance away, scanning the sky for dragons. He made a mental note to talk to him about staying closer, just in case he needed Shielding.

"If you have Champions of your own, then why do you need me?" he asked.

"Because the essence within me is tainted. I cannot unlock the Anchor's wards."

Sergan frowned. "So you don't really need me. Just what's in my vials."

"Don't worry, Exilar." Lazair smiled coyly. "Your life is safe. Not only are you the servant of an Archon, but I can't channel the essence in your vials."

Sergan found that ironic. The magic he could summon was like a candle flame compared to the inferno that was Lazair. But even with all her might, she could not channel the essence of a Savant.

He felt his tension ease, his muscles physically relaxing.

Thank every god he was still needed.

Aram wanted to weep at the feeling of his mother's arms enfolding him. In the end, he couldn't keep the tears back and neither could she, so they sobbed together on the threshold of their cottage. His ma held him crushingly tight, and her shoulders shook as she cried against him. He could feel her wet tears on his cheek, mingling with his own. She rocked him slowly, just like she'd always done when he was little, only, now, he was taller than she was.

"Oh, Aram." She released him, stepping back, and took his face in her hands. "They said you were dead..." She wiped the tears from his cheeks with her thumbs. "Oh, gods. Look at you! You're all grown up!"

His ma pulled him inside and closed the door. Aram stood for a moment, gazing around the dim little cottage in shock. He had forgotten how small it was. His ma's bed was just the same as he remembered it, and the floor was still strewn with its comfortable rushes. He recognized all the bowls and pots set beside the hearth, but there was a man-sized coat hanging from a peg on the wall that seemed an intrusion into their private world. He glanced at his ma in disbelief. Had she remarried? Staring hard at the coat, he thought maybe she had. He didn't want to ask because he wasn't sure how he'd feel about the answer.

She took his hands. "Let me look at you."

He felt her gaze running over him, examining him the way a buyer might inspect a horse for purchase. Reaching up, she brushed a lock of his hair back, but of course, it just fell forward again. She fingered the shirt he was wearing, frowning at it as though the cut looked foreign, even though she'd made it with her own hands.

Wait.

His ma hadn't stitched these clothes. These were the clothes the Overseers had put him in.

This was all a test.

The thought arrested his breath. Aram gazed at his mother through eyes shadowed by confusion. Was none of this real? Was it all just a scenario crafted to examine his reactions? Or had the Overseers somehow transported him to Anai? Was it possible that he was here physically? He stared at his mother hard, trying to figure out whether she was real or not. It was impossible to tell.

He frowned at the man's coat on the wall. He thought it unlikely the Overseers would have placed another man's coat inside his mother's home if they wanted to convince him that a made-up place was real. It was an odd detail.

Which meant that, more than likely, he really was home.

Somehow, the portal had transported him back across the Veil to Anai. Was that the test, then? To make him not want to go back? Perhaps that's what happened to all the people who entered the Portal Stones and never came out again. Maybe they were all taken to places they loved and simply chose to stay. Gazing into his mother's watery eyes, he understood how easy it would be to fail such a test.

Calise vaulted onto Zandril's back then sat there for a moment, trying to slow the spread of panic through her veins. So many dead...so many priceless souls. And she was needed *here*, with the injured. Why did Vandra have to send *her?* Leaning forward over Zandril's sleek neck, she caressed her dragon soothingly.

"I need to ask a favor, my love," she whispered.

Closing her eyes, she conveyed to Zandril their need and, even though dragons do not speak the language of men, she knew the concept had been understood. The conversation that took place between them was more a collection of emotions bundled with mental images. It produced feelings of dismay and agitation. Nevertheless, Zandril relayed her request to those dragons who had lost their human companions in the battle, seeking one willing to make one last flight.

It was a horrendous thing to ask of a creature grieving for its beloved, but their need was dire. Even so, Calise released a held breath when Zandril returned her answer.

Siroth would come.

The courage of that dragon made her vision blur and took away any fear she may have felt for herself. With fresh resolve, she willed Zandril into the sky, awed at the sight of a large black dragon following them into the air. Heading almost straight up into the sky, Zandril raced toward the protection of the clouds with Siroth on her wing. Calise squeezed her eyes closed, her heart thudding so hard she could hear it pounding in her ears. Her body trembled as she waited for the bolt of lightning to knock them from the sky.

Somehow, they made it.

Hidden by the cloud cover, they crossed the expanse of moorland back in the direction of the mountains. Throughout the long flight, Calise couldn't stop thinking of the great sacrifice Siroth was making. Every moment without the human he mourned would be excruciating, and yet, somehow, he bore it. He was a strong dragon, one of the biggest in the fighting Wing.

Even still, she could feel his anguish, and she hated herself for inflicting it.

Markus stared at the Portal Stone, feeling his nerves tightening little by little. He cast a worried glance at Esmir, one of several he had given the Warden in the last hour. He had finished practicing his forms only to find that Aram had not returned yet from the stone archway. He was long overdue, and Markus could tell by the look in Esmir's eyes that the old Warden was worried too.

"Do you think he's in trouble?" he asked.

But Esmir didn't respond. He stood with his arms crossed, glowering fiercely into the space between stones. Frustrated, Markus scrubbed a hand through his hair and paced away, glancing around the ring of monoliths. It had been too long. Something must have gone wrong.

The sound of running footsteps made him turn.

He watched as an exhausted Calise burst over the top of the stairs. She careened toward them in lurching strides, stopping only when she stood in front of them. Panting, she glanced around frantically.

"Where's Aram?" she gasped. "We need him!"

The desperation in her voice was alarming. Esmir hurried toward them, demanding, "What is it? What's going on?"

Calise was panting hard. Sweat streamed from her brow, carving runnels into the grime that stained her face. Markus could practically feel the dismay roiling off her.

"There's been a battle!" she gasped. "The enemy is using sorcery! Vandra needs you both!" She straightened, her brow furrowing. "Where's Aram?"

Markus lifted his arm and pointed at the Portal Stone. "In there."

Calise's face darkened. "What's he doing in there?"

"Training," Markus answered with a questioning glance at Esmir. "But he's been in there an awfully long time."

The old man licked his lips. Esmir's gaze had returned to the Portal Stone, and he was glowering so hard, it looked like he was trying to bore a tunnel through it with his eyes.

Markus had passed the point of frustration and was now feeling afraid. "I'm going in after him."

"No." Esmir scowled and shook his head. "It won't work for you. You're Impervious to magic."

"Then what do we do?" Markus was starting to panic.

A muscle in Esmir's face twitched. "We wait."

"But Vandra needs him *now!*" exclaimed Calise, despair sharpening her voice. "It's urgent! Truly urgent!"

Esmir took a deep breath then looked to Markus. "You go. I'll stay here."

"What about Aram?" Markus demanded.

Calise paused. "You can go by yourself—Siroth knows the way. I'll wait for Aram."

Markus glanced at the Portal Stone, grinding his teeth in anxiety. "What if he doesn't come out?"

Esmir sighed. "Then there's nothing we can do about it."

Aram gave his mother another hug. "How've you been, Ma?"

She looked a lot older than he remembered. There was far more gray threading her hair, the lines around her eyes carved deeper. There was also something about her demeanor that seemed different, though he couldn't tell what it was.

"I've been better," she said with a weak attempt at a smile. "It hurt so much when I thought I'd lost you. But you're here now." She looked like she was going to start crying again. "They said the Exilari took you to their cellars, but you're alive. *You're alive.*"

He didn't know what to say, because he didn't want her to know the truth. Seeing his ma so close to tears tore at his throat. "Markus rescued me," Aram whispered. "I'm all right now."

She closed her eyes in relief. "I was so worried. I cried every day. The thought of you in their cellars…"

He didn't want to lie to her, but she also didn't need to know all the painful details. She didn't need to know about the terrible wagon ride to Karaqor, or about Sergan and the well, or the four long years he had spent in agony.

"It's all right, Ma. Markus got me away from them. I'm just fine now."

For some reason, his words made her cry again. He hugged her close, just like she'd always hugged him whenever he cried like that. He rubbed her back and kissed her cheek, tasting her salty tears.

"It's all right. Don't cry, Ma. I'm alive, and I'm here."

Eventually, her tears dried up. She blotted her eyes with her apron, a sad smile appearing on her face. "Look at you. You're a young man now." She shook her head in wonder. "You look just like your father."

Did he? Aram couldn't remember what his father looked like, at least not more than just a vague image. His da had been tall and broad of shoulder, and he'd had a wiry beard that used to scratch whenever he kissed him. His arms had been big and strong, able to pick him up with one hand, but he'd also had a gentle way about him. Aram couldn't imagine resembling a man as powerful as his da. He'd always been small and weak for his age, and he still was, in comparison to his friends. Maybe his ma was just trying to make him feel better.

"Let's see," she muttered, looking around the cramped room. "You can sleep here for now. I, oh...." She grimaced, her gaze flitting away like a timid butterfly. "Aram...I remarried."

That explained the coat. He couldn't imagine his mother being married to anyone but Da. Aram's mind sifted quickly through all the men of the village that he remembered, and he couldn't think of one that was good enough for her.

"Do you remember Mister Haldon?" she asked.

At the sound of the name, Aram stiffened. He remembered Mister Haldon well. He'd worked for Markus's father hauling supplies and cartloads of fish to and from the curing houses. He'd been a mean-tempered man who used to beat his mules whenever his cart got stuck in the mud. Hearing that his mother had married such a wretch made his stomach clench and his hands curl into fists.

His ma hung her head and stood clutching her hands in front of her. "I was pretty...shaken...after all that happened," she admitted. "Manny helped me. Without him..." She shook her head, her mouth twisting. "I don't know what I would've done. I hope you understand."

He didn't understand. Why would his mother stoop to marrying someone like Manny Haldon? No amount of grief could justify that. "Does he treat you right, Ma?"

Instead of answering, she glanced away, then walked across the room to a wooden crate with a few cups and chipped plates set atop it. "You must be thirsty! Let me make you some tea!"

"I don't want any tea, Ma." Aram shot toward her, his pulse racing and mind throbbing. "Why did you marry Mister Haldon? He's not a nice—"

"You can sleep here for now," his ma cut him off. She picked up a small kettle off the floor and poured water into it, determined to make the tea anyway. "We'll make a bed for you. Tomorrow we should start looking to find you an apprenticeship. You're too old now to—"

The door swept open, and the shadow of a man filled the doorway. His ma flinched, stepping away from Aram. For a long moment, the man in the doorway stood without moving, his gaze going back and forth between Aram and his ma.

"Where did he come from?" growled Haldon.

Just the sight of Manny Haldon heated Aram's blood. This man had no business in his home, and certainly no business with his mother. Haldon was even uglier and meaner-looking than he remembered. He'd put on a lot of weight, and his nose had become bulbous and tomato-red. He was dirty, and Aram could smell the stink of him from across the small room, a noxious mixture of fish and body odor.

His mother moved to hover behind Aram protectively, clutching his shoulders. "He's alive, Manny! They were wrong!"

Haldon stood staring at Aram with a look of belligerent confusion, his mouth working as though chewing a cud. He sputtered something unintelligible. Then, with a grimace, he spat, "He can't stay here!"

"He's my son! What would you have me do, turn him out?"

"Damn right!" Haldon leaned forward, pointing a meaty finger at Aram. "Haven't you caused enough problems, you little moron? It's your fault half the damn village was burned down! I lost my home, and I lost my trade! If I hadn't married your fucking mother, I'd be a beggar!"

His words snapped something inside Aram. Hatred filled him, and his vision went red. Deep inside, he felt a powerful stirring as something within him ignited. Vaguely, he was aware of his mother crying. But it hardly registered, for all of his concentration was bent on the oily details of Manny Haldon's face.

"Don't talk about my ma like that."

The words didn't sound like his own, for they came from a place no words of his had ever come from. He wasn't small and weak anymore, but capable and powerful.

Stepping forward, Haldon poked his finger hard into Aram's chest. "Who the hell do you think you are? Nobody tells me how to talk to my wife in my own house! Get the fuck out, you little shit!" Grasping Aram's arm, he jerked him toward the door. "Get the fuck out!"

With a shriek, Aram's mother started forward, hands outstretched. She caught Haldon by the arm, trying to hold him back. With a growl, the big man turned his fury on her, shoving her forcefully backward to the floor.

The cauldron of anger inside Aram boiled over, and a geyser of blue flames erupted beneath Manny Haldon.

Markus sprinted down the long flights of stairs to the Southern Eyrie, where he stopped, eyes scanning the situation. The eyrie was unusually empty, for most of the fighting Wing had flown with Vandra. Only two dragons remained behind: Zandril, and a large black dragon that had to be Siroth.

He paused only long enough to round up some armor and borrow a sword from the armory, then turned toward the two waiting dragons. The sight of Siroth drew him up short, for he wouldn't have imagined that a reptilian face could be capable of displaying such depths of pain. Siroth once might have been magnificent, with glimmering scales that looked like cut obsidian. But the dragon's luster was already starting to dull and fade. Markus could almost sense the fire of life within him growing dim and cooling.

He approached Siroth cautiously and stopped at his side. He placed his hand on the cold neck, caressing the dragon as he would a horse. Instantly, he felt a connection: the dragon's presence in his mind. Without words, and in a matter of heartbeats, Siroth communicated to him everything that mattered.

Siroth's rider, a beautiful woman named Faril, had been killed by some kind of magical strike. Siroth had also been injured. He could feel the dragon's pain, which emanated from a large burn that scorched his side. But that pain was nothing compared to the anguish Siroth felt over Faril's loss, for she had been violently ripped away from him. She had been a kind, intelligent person, and a ferocious fighter. Siroth was eager to get back to her and had only agreed to come to avenge her loss.

Markus introduced himself to the dragon hesitantly, using feelings and thoughts instead of words. He tried to reassure Siroth that he would help him in his quest for vengeance, and though he wasn't as fierce a fighter as Faril had been, he would try his best.

For an instant, he saw himself through the dragon's eyes, and what he saw shocked him. To Siroth, he was a strong warrior with a determined spirit, a man Faril would have been proud to fight alongside of.

To Markus's astonishment, Siroth lifted his head, the life rekindling in his eyes. He lowered himself so that Markus could climb onto his back, his grief giving way to hope and bloodlust.

Crackling blue flames enveloped Manny Haldon, crawling over him like writhing snakes. After several seconds, they faded, relinquishing their victim. Haldon wasn't moving. He lay lifeless on the floor of the room, his body sizzling and popping like frying bacon. For a long time, Aram just looked at him and couldn't move, frozen rigid in the grip of horror. His mother lay on the floor, sobbing and hugging herself, and the cottage was filled with smoke and the stomach-turning odor of roasted meat.

"What did you do?" his ma shrieked.

Aram shook his head mutely, taking a step backward. Somehow, he'd killed Haldon, even though he had no idea how. He'd made a couple of complicated knots in the air and then sliced through them all at once. The result had been a sorcerous assault that had quickly gotten away from him. He'd lost control.

He backed toward the door.

He'd killed a man.

Actually *killed* a man.

He had to go before someone found him here. Before they blamed his mother.

His hand found the door. "Tell them I did it, Ma. Tell them I ran."

His voice shook so hard the words were barely intelligible.

"Wait!" his mother screamed, rising from the floor.

He caught her and crushed her against him. "I'm sorry! I'm sorry!"

He couldn't hold back the tears. Lips trembling, he kissed her cheek. "I love you, Mama."

He fled through the door into the dark night, sprinting for the village gate. He slowed to a walk after only a block, afraid to attract notice. Behind him, he heard the sound of shouts as people ran from their homes, drawn by the commotion. Aram kept his head down and walked faster, shaking in fear and self-loathing.

He had killed a man.

Killed a man, in cold blood.

Did that make him a monster? He figured it did.

"Hey!" someone shouted.

Aram glanced back and saw a man he recognized, an old fisherman who lived by the wharf. Seeing his face, the man pointed at him. "You..."

The village bell began tolling.

Aram bolted for the gate. Realizing he was being chased, he scrambled into a narrow alley between two houses, a space barely wide enough to squeeze into. There, he huddled in the darkness with his back pressed against a wall that cut off the alley. He waited until the footsteps passed before starting back toward the street.

Someone stepped in front of him, blocking his path.

Aram gasped, staggering backward.

The man who blocked the alley's mouth wore the blue mantle of the Exilari.

Calise paced anxiously around the ring of stone monoliths, her emotions gyrating from worry to anger to outright desperation. She clenched and unclenched her fists at her sides, casting furtive glances every few seconds at the portal, but none of her pacing and glancing sped time or made Aram reappear.

"Where could he be?"

Esmir didn't answer. He stood in the center of the circle beside the obelisk, staring hard at the ground.

Calise was beginning to fear the worst, and that fear was starting to strangle. Aram was sweet and innocent, and if anything happened to him, it would be like losing a beautiful part of the world. Aram had grown on her more than she'd realized. His peculiar ways were so endearing, and he had a way about him, a calm and powerful strength that was comforting. What if he was in trouble? What if he needed help?

"There has to be something we can do to get him out!" she cried.

The old Warden glanced at the portal. "You have the affinity, so I suppose you could try going in after him. Only, it's unlikely you'll end up in the same place he is."

Calise thought about that. "Maybe I can beg these Overseers to tell me where he is."

Esmir's bushy eyebrows lifted, but otherwise, he didn't respond. Calise took that as tacit approval.

"I'm going in," she said. "If I find one of the Overseers, I'll try to make them listen to me. What do we have to lose?"

Esmir's heavy gaze settled on her. "You. That's what. If those beings chewed up Aram and spat him out, what do you think they will do to you?"

Calise shrugged. "Probably nothing. I'm not trying to be a Champion."

He nodded slowly.

A triumphant smile curled her lips, and Calise walked immediately toward the portal arch. She would find Aram. She didn't know how, but she would.

Markus clung to Siroth's back, shivering from the cold air that sped by them faster with every beat of the dragon's wings. Below them, clouds stretched dark and rolling like the swells of an ocean. He didn't know where they were, only that they were somewhere over mountains. Every time he thought about how high they were and how long it would take to fall from such a height, he felt the dragon's mind press against his own, reassuring him. Siroth would never let him fall. Even when his beloved Faril had died on his back, Siroth had borne her body safely to the ground.

As they flew, Markus's other fears became more tangible. He wondered if Aram had ever made it out of the Portal Stones, and he feared he hadn't. Markus didn't know what good he could do anyone without Aram. He couldn't protect them all. His immunity to magic didn't extend beyond himself. The best he could do was jump in front of an object under magical attack. He had no idea if that even extended to protecting the dragon he rode.

As if sensing his doubt, Siroth pressed upon him a feeling of faith that was both unearned and undeserved. Markus didn't understand where that misplaced faith could have come from, for the dragon did not know him. In response to that thought, Siroth seemed to take offense. Apparently, he considered himself a fine judge of character.

But how did Siroth know anything about him? Had he somehow inherited the bond from Faril? As soon as Markus's mind formed the question, the dragon summarily dismissed it. Even though he respected Markus, Faril had been his beloved, his soul's companion. Markus understood and felt embarrassed for even thinking that a dragon as great as Siroth would ever form any kind of bond with him. But Siroth dismissed that idea too. An image of Markus riding a dragon even larger than Siroth flashed briefly in his mind, and he took that as assurance that he was worthy enough to someday form a dragon-bond.

If he could.

He was Impervious to magic, so was such a bond even possible? For that matter, how was Siroth able to communicate with him at all? He thought of Esmir. The old Warden had bound a dragon, so somehow, it must be possible. Perhaps because it was a connection of the soul and not a connection made by magic. He would have to ask Esmir about it.

Siroth adjusted his wings and began his descent. They slipped into the clouds and the world became engulfed in a blanket of mist. But that didn't last long, for with one stroke of the dragon's wings, they broke through the other side, bursting out of the clouds.

All at once, Markus had a clear view of the battlefield, and what he saw was terrifying. Thousands upon thousands of enemy soldiers had amassed upon a pockmarked plain and were advancing toward a good-sized town surrounded by earthen walls that looked inadequate.

The sky around them lit up in a blinding flash of light.

A jagged spear of lightning streaked down from the clouds, spiking toward them. Markus didn't have time to scream before it hit.

Nothing happened.

Terrified and shaking, he clung to Siroth's back with all of his might. The dragon was just as unnerved as he was. An image came to mind that was startlingly painful, and he knew this was how Faril had died. When the lightning struck, Siroth had been certain Markus would be killed, too, and was astonished that he wasn't. The dragon's heart swelled with vast relief, and also vast appreciation, for he now understood Markus's true value.

And so did Markus himself.

Siroth landed amidst a gathering of dragons that were protected from the battlefield by a low ridgeline. The moment he leapt from Siroth's back, Markus found himself swallowed by a bedlam of confusion. Dragon riders converged on him, cheering and slapping him on the back. At first, he didn't understand why, but then Siroth reminded him of the lightning strike that should have killed them both.

Vandra rushed up to them, demanding, "Where's Aram?"

The Wingmaster's face was covered in grime, and she stood gripping the hilt of her sword. There was a wildness to her eyes that Markus had never seen before. Her gaze didn't stay in one place, but kept shifting, as though distrustful of the ridgelines behind them.

"Aram is…" He swallowed, not knowing what to say. "Right now, he's…lost." He winced, knowing how bad that sounded. "I mean, hopefully he'll be on the way."

Vandra peered at him with a hard and probing gaze. "What do you mean, *lost?*"

Markus glanced back at the ridge. "He went into one of the Portal Stones in the Henge. He hasn't come back out yet."

"And how long has he been in there?" Vandra asked, brow furrowing in concern.

Markus wasn't sure. "He went in there right after sunup."

Vandra recoiled. "It's late afternoon!"

What?

It was already?

"Maybe he came back out," he whispered, feeling weak.

Vandra scrubbed her hair in frustration. "Damn the wind and all it blows! Why did Esmir send him in there if he wasn't ready for it?"

Markus didn't have an answer to that. Vandra shot him an exasperated look then flung her hands up. "Then you're it! You're all we've got." She looked like she wanted to kill someone, maybe even him. "This is the situation. Their sorcerers have magic, and we don't—at least, we don't anymore, thanks to Esmir. All we have is you. Obviously, you can't take on the entire Aragharian army by yourself, so I will have to find another way to use you."

Had she seriously thought that Aram could take on an entire army? And what could *he* do, without Aram?

"Their objective is the Caverns of Eld Elan," Vandra went on, pacing back and forth. "They'll have to cut through the town of Inuine to get there, and that will slow them down. But after the town falls, there will be nothing between them and Eld Elan."

An entire town was going to fall…and she was worried about a cavern?

"Why do we care about a bunch of caves?" Markus asked.

Vandra shot him an exasperated look. "The Altier Anchor is located in a cave system. That's where you're going."

"Me?" Markus balked. "Just *me?"*

"We don't have anyone else!" Vandra snapped. "I can't even send anyone with you, because they'll just be knocked out of the sky!"

A wave of dizziness convulsed the ground, and Markus extended his hands to steady himself. Where was Aram? He needed him here. He couldn't defend an entire Anchor alone. "What am I supposed to do? I don't have magic!"

"They do, and that's the point. Prevent them from using it! Fly to the cave system and guard the Anchor there with your life. We'll try to find a way to meet you there but, honestly, I don't know how we will. You need to kill their sorcerers, and you'll need to do it alone."

"How will I find them?"

"They'll find you. Go to Eld Elan. Stay there and don't leave the Wellspring, no matter what. And when they come, kill them. It's as simple as that."

Calise considered the arch before her that was formed by three enormous monoliths. Just looking at it, there was no way of telling that it was a portal. She could see right through to the other side, where the sand of the Henge extended to the cliff wall. There was no doorway or shadow, nothing that looked out of the ordinary.

And yet, she could feel it.

The Portal Stone didn't feel right. Even from a distance, there was a discordance to it that just seemed out of step with the rest of the world. It took her a long moment to put a finger on exactly what it was, to pick out the individual strands of aether with her limited vision. Beneath the arch, the threads were rotated at an angle, as though the warp and weft of the world had become inverted. That's all she could see with her limited mind-sight, but it was enough to give her a moment's pause. Wherever that doorway led, it was at odds with the rest of the world.

She glanced at Esmir for reassurance but found none in the old Warden's stony face. He stood with his arms crossed, glowering at her from beneath a protruding ridge of eyebrows, every line and wrinkle of his face mustered to intensify the expression. Frustrated, she turned back toward the portal. No matter what lay on the other side of that archway, she had to go in. Whatever it was, Aram was facing it alone. And if she didn't bring him out, there was far more at risk than just his life.

Squaring her shoulders and lifting her chin, Calise walked into the portal.

She stepped out into the Southern Eyrie. It was dark, as though nighttime had settled over the mountains. And there were other inconsistencies. For one thing, she was alone. There were no other people about, which would never happen in the real eyrie, even at night. The screens had been pulled over the individual alcoves, so she couldn't tell whether or not they were occupied. The scent of dragons that she found so comfortingly familiar was absent from the air, as though the eyrie stood long abandoned.

She turned slowly, considering the strange situation around her, trying to decide whether it was real or not. Was this all part of a hallucination? Or had she been transported to the future or past somehow, to a time where the eyries stood empty? She was reminded of the night she'd gone with the apprentices to explore the Heights, when they had found the dragon cairn. This place had a similar feeling, though this was eerier because it hit closer to home.

She heard a sound behind her and turned.

Standing behind her was a being unlike any other she'd ever seen. It wasn't human, but rather something that looked at least partially reptilian. It was much taller than a man, and extremely slender, clothed in black robes. Calise sucked in a sharp breath. The creature before her was so inhuman, she had no way of guessing what its intentions were, for its face contained no comprehensible expression.

Summoning every scrap of courage she had, Calise took a step toward it. "Are you an Overseer?"

She wasn't surprised when the thing did not respond. It seemed aloof and hadn't moved at all, as though its only purpose in life was to observe.

"I'm looking for someone," Calise said. "His name is Aram Raythe. He's in here somewhere."

Again, no response. She couldn't tell if the creature even heard her. Her eyes darted around the large cavern that was so familiar and yet so utterly foreign. Like the being in front of her, the eyrie seemed frozen in time. She was beginning to get the feeling that she stood in a world where she was the only thing alive.

"Please," she whispered. "Wherever he is, we need Aram back. Something bad has happened. Please return him to us."

The thing continued to stare at her with its liquid black eyes, unblinking. Calise felt herself starting to sweat despite the cold temperature in the lifeless eyrie. She had a prickling feeling on her palms, and the little hairs on the back of her neck stood upright.

"Please." She spread her hands. "At least show me where he is."

Nothing.

She clenched her fists in desperation, struggling to come up with some way to appeal to this detestable creature—if it even understood her at all. She thought back to what she knew of the Overseers, which was very little. They supposedly administered the Trials for those who would be Champions, culling those with the Gift who did not meet some standard of character.

If that were true, then there was no way Aram would ever fail such a test. His character was flawless.

Or maybe it wasn't.

Was it possible to be *too* kind? Calise felt her heart sink. Perhaps Aram didn't have the fortitude to be a Champion. He didn't have much confidence in himself. The more she thought about it, the more she feared for him.

Markus collected some wood for torches then buckled himself into the harness on Siroth's back, feeling the muscles beneath him bunch. Pushing off from the ground with his strong legs, the dragon pulled himself into the air with a powerful stroke of his wings. They gained altitude quickly, and as they rose, Markus had a good view of the moorlands below. The army of Araghar had been met by the defenders of the Highlands, a small garrison that had been deployed to protect the nearby town.

The Highlanders were enveloped by Kathrax's forces, fighting a losing battle. Markus had no idea who these people were, and he could see none of their faces, for which he was glad. Otherwise, he didn't think he could pass by overhead and leave them to their fate.

There was nothing he could do for them. His own mission was crucial, and there was nobody else that could do it. He understood enough about the Anchors to know that they were like rivets, only they held the world apart instead of together. Kathrax was trying to destroy those rivets, and if he did, the world of magic would fall prey to the world of men. All that was good and wholesome in this world would be consumed by those who longed to despoil it.

He couldn't let that happen. But he didn't know how he could possibly defend the Anchor by himself, not against sorcerers capable of grounding an entire dragon Wing. Even if he had Aram with him, he didn't think it would matter. Nevertheless, he had to try.

He had no idea where the caverns were but, fortunately, Siroth did. The dragon flew straight toward them, untroubled by the lances of lightning hurled at them by the sorcerers on the ground.

Ahead, the rolling moorland tumbled into a broken karst region that looked like a stone forest. Small streams threaded around sculpted rocks that loomed like craggy sentinels over the surrounding landscape. A fine mist clung in a layer above the trees, looking almost like smoke. Somewhere down there was their destination. The dragon banked slowly over a thicket of riddled stone monuments, at last alighting atop a ribbon-like ridge of hills.

Shivering, Markus slid from the dragon's back, his boots slipping before finding purchase on the rocky hillside. He stood for a moment taking his bearings, uncertain where to go. Immediately, a vision sprang to mind of a dark cave gaping from within the shadow of the canyon below. In the vision, a slender path meandered through a forest of enormous, sculpted rocks, some of which he recognized, for they were standing in front of him. He started toward the path then paused, turning back.

"Will you be here when I come out?" he asked the dragon.

There was a heavy pause, stretched and burdened by the weight of unendurable grief. A muddled mixture of emotions was the only answer he received, and it took him a while to interpret it. Yes, Siroth would wait. His beloved rider was dead, and the dragon feared that Markus's death was imminent too. He had no desire to witness the fall of another courageous soul and would much rather flee this world than bear another loss.

Nevertheless, he would remain. If Markus survived, he would need wings to carry him away.

Feeling a humbling gratitude more poignant than any he had experienced, Markus raised his sword in salute to the dragon's courage. Then he held his weapon close and started down the trail toward the cavern.

Aram froze, trembling in fear. The Exilari sorcerer who blocked the entrance to the alley was no one he recognized, but that didn't help, for one sorcerer was just as dangerous as another. Cold revulsion broke over him like an icy wave and, all of a sudden, he was drowning in it. His thoughts had frozen to a standstill, and his body locked rigid. Sharp, jagged breaths hissed from his chest, his pulse thrumming his veins. He took a slow step backward, followed by another.

"Stop."

The word snapped around his neck like a collar, and he halted without meaning to. The sorcerer raised his hand, extending it toward him slowly. Rooted by terror, Aram stared at him, unable to react. Inside, he struggled against a mindless, feral panic.

He wouldn't go back to the cellars. He wouldn't.

Opening himself, he sought the same violent power he had used to save his mother from Haldor. But no matter how much he struggled to grasp it, his command of the aether eluded him completely. He couldn't touch it, couldn't summon magic to defend himself.

The realization was chilling.

His magic was unlocked in the Shadow Realm, but not in this place. The fact that he was once again bound by the rules of his own world could only mean one thing.

This wasn't a test.

Somehow, this was real.

He wanted to call for help or scream or flee, but he was too terrified to do any of those things. So, instead, Aram stood still, frozen raw.

The young sorcerer motioned him forward. "If you surrender without a fight, I'll let your mother live."

The man knew who his mother was, which meant that he knew who *he* was.

Aram felt physically torn in half. Could he go back to the cellars to save his mother's life? Did he have that kind of courage? He tried to swallow, but his throat was too dry to accomplish the act.

Despair claimed him. In front of him was a decision he didn't have the strength to make.

64

Sergan wound his way across the battlefield, his mind muddled in a strange, surreal haze. Obriem trailed behind him, sword and shield in hand, looking fiercely disappointed that he hadn't had the chance to kill anything. Most of the battle had been waged in the sky, not on the ground. What was left of the Inuine garrison had been routed, the men fleeing toward the hills, and Lazair's general had dispatched riders to give chase. There was nothing between their own forces and the Caverns of Eld Elan.

Killing was thirsty work, and Sergan could've downed an entire flagon of wine. His throat was crusted with dust, his mouth achingly dry. He didn't understand why that was, considering he hadn't broken a sweat throughout the entire battle. Not once had he looked even one of his victims in the eye. The dragons and the riders he had brought down with conjured lightning hadn't been given a chance to fight back. They simply dropped from the sky.

This was not the first battlefield he had ever walked across, and the sight of severed limbs and spilled guts didn't bother him. But his nose was filled with the stench of blood, and the odor made him ill. Even Obriem seemed affected, for the young man kept hawking up mouthfuls of either bile or phlegm, which he spat upon the ground.

The soldiers of Lazair's army went about their business with admirable efficiency, as though mopping up after a battle was just part of their daily routine. They were an ugly, brutish mob, armored only in furs and boiled leather, their lard-greased braids and beards clinking with rings and ornaments. Yet they were damn good at what they did, so Sergan applauded them. He had never seen better fighters, for each had the spirit and strength of an ogre, born and bred for the purpose of war. They waded through piles of corpses, scavenging weapons and armor and slitting the throats of those unfortunates still alive. Even their own were not spared, if they were too injured to continue the fight.

Sergan took a quick look around, checking his location. He was trying to find Lazair, but the last he had seen of the woman, she was streaking across the sky on her dragon in pursuit of another that had apparently eluded her.

He waded on through the carnage before at last giving up and returning to the hill where her officers had gathered and were engaged in conversation, no doubt planning their next massacre. There, he found a wagon loaded with provisions and helped himself to some wine that had mostly gone to vinegar.

He lowered the tailgate of the wagon and climbed aboard, leaning back against a crate. He closed his eyes and relaxed, covering his nose with a kerchief in an attempt to ward off the smell. Obriem lingered beside the wagon, crunching on an apple, of all things. Sergan couldn't imagine how he could work up an appetite.

It was another hour before he caught sight of Lazair's dragon gliding across the sky, returning to land just shy of the hill. She caught sight of him almost immediately and, leaving the dragon to feed on the dead, walked toward him with a smile.

"Exilar, you look like you could use a bath."

Sergan gave her a weak smile, finding no humor in her observation. Her own pale, skeletal face was absent any sign of blood or grime, quite remarkable for a woman who had personally killed dozens of the enemy.

"A bath is definitely in order," he said, removing the kerchief from his face. "Point me in the direction of some hot water and send a pretty maid to lather me up."

"Unfortunately, you don't have time for a bath. Did you see that dragon flying over just now?"

He took a glance at the sky, which was empty of everything but clouds. "Did one get by you?"

She snorted, bringing out a cotton rag to blot the dew from her cheeks. "It would have gotten by you too. The rider is a True Impervious."

That was unexpected. So far, they had met with little magical resistance during their campaign—which surprised him. He had assumed that more of the Auld would be Gifted, but it seemed that the ability had been culled from Auld bloodlines even here. He hadn't spared a thought for those resistant to magic, though he should have. The news made him wary. He would much rather encounter another sorcerer than a True Impervious.

He also couldn't help wondering if Lazair's Impervious rider might be Markus.

"The dragon was headed to the Caverns," Lazair continued, "which means they'll arrive ahead of us. You need to confront them now, while they're alone."

Sergan frowned, not liking that idea. All he had was Obriem, and Lazair didn't have a Shield of her own. A single Impervious was more of a threat to them than an entire division of soldiers. "Then what's the point of the army, if you think I can destroy this Anchor alone?"

"The Anchor isn't the only thing we're here for," she reminded him. "My master desires lands and resources and slaves. He is especially interested in subjugating those who oppose him."

"Your master sounds like he has a lot in common with my Emperor."

"Of course. They are brothers, born of the same seed." She scrubbed her hand wearily across her brow. "You need to go. Follow me, and I'll introduce you to your new mounts."

"Our new mounts?" Sergan repeated as Obriem glanced at him sideways.

They followed Lazair toward the rocky crest of the hill, to where two dragons perched like eagles. The larger was a deep bronze with a wide wingspan, and the smaller was a sleek-looking green. The eyes of both shone with the same dark energy that radiated from the Baelsword.

"The bronze is Martax," Lazair told him. "The green is Yuron. They were both recently parted from their riders."

Sergan cocked an eyebrow in her direction. "You're giving us dragons?"

Lazair smirked. "Unless you'd rather go on horseback? Through the canyons, the trip will take at least a day."

Sergan looked up at the mighty Martax, who turned his head to consider him with eyes that glowed with the oily light of corruption. He wondered if any part of the creature still remembered the rider that had been severed from its soul.

"He doesn't look very friendly," he observed. "Will he carry me, or eat me?"

"Martax is now a thrall of my master. He will carry you because it is my will."

Sergan grunted. He followed Lazair up the rocks to where the two dragons waited. Tentatively, he reached his hand up and stroked the dark armor of Martax's neck. The scales were far smoother than they looked and almost iridescent. The dragon's face looked both ferocious and wizened, his teeth curved like the talons of a raptor. Truly, this was an intimidating monster.

"What do I do?" he asked. "I have no idea how to ride a dragon."

"There's not much to it." Lazair trailed her hand along the dragon's back. "You strap yourself into the harness and tell Martax where to go."

"How does that work, exactly?"

"He will open himself to you, for I have commanded it," Lazair answered. "Dragons do not speak in words, but he will understand you, nevertheless. Try it. Close your eyes and invite him in."

Sergan wasn't sure he liked the idea of inviting a ferocious beast into his head, though he supposed he didn't have a choice. Closing his eyes, he reached out toward the dragon with his mind and found his invitation accepted. At once, his awareness was saturated by the dragon's presence, which was so brutal and powerful that he drew in a sharp gasp.

Images flooded his mind, and he became aware of Martax's agreement to carry him. The dragon had taken his measure and deemed him worthy. He felt stripped naked, every nuance of him exposed to this great beast and yet, somehow, it felt right.

"This will work," he whispered, glancing back to grin at Obriem. "I think we might actually enjoy this."

Aram stood frozen in the cold grip of terror. The Exilari sorcerer blocking the mouth of the alley beckoned with an outstretched hand, motioning him forward.

"Come, now," the sorcerer said. "You don't want your mother harmed. I promise you, she won't be, if you come quietly."

Aram's body quaked, his breath coming in sharp gasps. He couldn't go back to the cellars. He'd rather die a thousand deaths. Images of his time there flashed through his mind as he stared in horror at the Exilar's white-gloved hand.

Every other day they would wake him from sleep and haul him from his cell. They would drag him to the table, where they would bind him down with leather straps and thick iron manacles. He always bucked and screamed and tried to wriggle out of their grasp, but the Extractors knew what they were about, and one struggling boy couldn't give them much of a problem, no matter how hard he fought.

Then they would leave him there in the dark, shivering in terror, fear-sweat collecting on his face. He would lie there, strapped to the table, sometimes for hours before they began. He never knew what they were doing during that time. Perhaps they were preparing the tortures they would subject him to or getting the flasks ready to fill with the essence they would extract from him. Or maybe they just left him there to wallow in fear, to marinate in the anticipation of what he knew was coming.

He remembered the first time they had strapped him to the table. As he waited in the dark, sobbing and trembling, one of the Extractors came forward, a younger man with guilt in his eyes. The young Exilar had looked down upon him with compassion and placed a comforting hand upon him.

"It's easier if you don't fight it," he'd said.

Then he left.

And then the pain came, horrid and brutal. It ripped screams of agony right out of his throat. And it only intensified, until his screams turned to shrieks, and he writhed and bucked uncontrollably. He could never identify the source of the pain; it attacked his entire body all at once, burning him on the inside and flaying him on the outside. It went on and on as he fought against his bonds, jerking his hands against the manacles until his wrists bled. When the pain at last diminished, hours later, he would lay quivering, wracked with sobs, pleading for death and crying for his mother. Then they unstrapped him and took him to the surface to recover before dragging him back down to his dark cell. He was always allowed a day of rest, but no more.

The next day, they carried him back to the extraction room and subjected him to the same treatment in a horrific cycle that would continue for years, until the pain nearly drove him insane.

He couldn't go back there.

He couldn't.

Aram glanced frantically behind him, but there was no way out. The alley ended at the back wall of a house. He turned back to the young Exilar, struggling to think. Maybe he could rush him and knock him out of his way. If he hit him hard enough, he might get enough of a lead to make it to his mother's house and warn her before they could catch him.

But that wouldn't work, he realized. The sorcerer had to have a Shield. Even if he could get by him, he wouldn't be able to evade them both.

"It's time to decide," the man said calmly. "Are you coming out? Or am I going in after you?"

Mutely, Aram shook his head. He wanted to wail in despair. His legs were trembling so hard he could barely stand. And yet, his mother's face filled his thoughts, and her warmth filled his heart.

In the end, love won out.

Somehow, he found the courage to walk toward the sorcerer.

Toward the pain.

Calise stood looking at the alien form of the Overseer, her fear and frustration mounting. The creature stood impassive, simply staring at her, unmoved by the urgency of her pleas. She was out of ideas. Wherever this place was, Aram wasn't here. And, without this creature's help, she had no hope of finding him.

"Please!" she begged. "We need him! *We* need him, and you don't. Let him go! Let him go *right now!*"

In a fit of rage, she drew the dagger she wore at her belt and lashed out at the Overseer. No sooner did she move than her body hit a solid wall of air. The dagger flew from her hand and she tumbled to the floor. She lay there for a moment, fighting to get her wind back, at last wedging herself up on her elbows.

"Aram!" she screamed. *"Aram!* Where are you? We need you! *Aram!"*

Only silence answered her.

She scrambled to her knees and crawled forward to reclaim her dagger, glaring in hatred at the appalling creature. "If you've killed him…" she whispered, her voice trembling. She couldn't finish the threat. There was nothing she could do that would affect these entities. Sheathing the dagger, she screamed, *"Aram!"*

Something made Aram halt.

It was the sound of a voice, thin and weak, coming from a far distance.

He heard his name again, and at last, he recognized Calise's voice.

The sorcerer held out his hand. "Come now or your mother dies."

Aram almost obeyed, but then he heard Calise cry out his name again.

"Is this your choice, then?"

Trembling, Aram shook his head. He didn't know what Calise was doing here, but she had entered the Portal Stone, and there was only one reason why she would've done that.

She needed him badly.

But his mother needed him too.

Torn between his mother and Calise, he made the decision he felt he had to, one that he was certain he would never forgive himself for.

Fixing his gaze on the Exilari sorcerer, he shook his head.
"No."

Instantly, the alley faded, and he tumbled into darkness.

Vandra looked out upon the battlefield from her position on the ridge, growing more disturbed and desperate by the second. The defenders of Inuine, vastly outnumbered, had been routed, and a host of light cavalry had been dispatched to run them down. She knew many of those men and women, for she had grown up on the moors. Some were probably members of her own clan, though she had no way of knowing.

She couldn't just cower and watch them be cut down. Neither could she endanger the dragons by ordering them to the sky. Too many had already fallen, and the loss of each dragon was also the loss of its rider, a double tragedy.

But maybe…maybe they could still put the dragons to use.

Raising her hand, she called her captains over. Kade and Somlan jogged to her side, looking grim and careworn.

She motioned down the slope at the fleeing warriors. "Find a volunteer to fly down there and direct any allies back in this direction. If we can bring them here, to the hills, we can defend them from the high ground."

Kade exchanged glances with Somlan. "It's a suicide mission. Whoever goes isn't likely to even reach them, much less round them up."

"It's that or leave them to their deaths," Vandra spat. "How many are down there? A hundred? I'll risk the life of one man to save a hundred of our brethren."

Kade nodded, caressing the overgrown whiskers that covered his pockmarked cheeks. "I'll go."

Somlan's mouth opened in surprise, and Vandra shook her head. "I can't spare you. Find someone else."

But Kade fixed her with a rigid stare, the set of his face telling Vandra she wasn't going to win that argument.

"I can't ask my men to do something I wouldn't do myself," he said roughly. "I said I'll go. Promote Calver to my place. He's a good man."

Vandra squeezed her eyes closed with a grimace. "All right, Kade. All right. You just better damn well make it back."

Kade grimaced. "I'm too damn ugly to kill."

Vandra stared at him a long moment, her emotions almost getting the best of her. Collecting herself, she whispered, "May the wind carry you, Kade."

When he was gone, she issued orders to have the men and dragons stand ready to receive the enemy. Then she lingered on the ridge as the two men departed. Kade made his way to his green dragon, Taranth, a beast just as old and cross as its rider. Without hesitation, Kade vaulted onto Taranth's back and the two of them took to the air.

As Markus descended the trail into the canyon, it started raining. The trail was steep and narrow, and it twisted between enormous rocks chiseled from the hillside by the scouring action of water. It was almost like walking through a forest of narrow columns that loomed over him. In places, the grade was so steep, he did more sliding than walking downhill. In other places, the trail disappeared altogether for a ways, and he had to forge his own path. By the time he was halfway down, the rain was coming faster and harder, giving him misgivings. Gullies and ravines were not good places to be in a thunderstorm.

Eventually, he came to the bottom of the canyon. Here, there was only a thin stream that looked completely insufficient for the task of causing the amount of devastation that had been inflicted upon the landscape. He followed the stream as it meandered through the canyon, eventually arriving at a grotto hollowed out of the cliff. Deep within it, almost hidden by the shadows of the cliff, was the cave Siroth had shown him in the vision.

Drawing his blade, Markus removed his sword belt and tossed the scabbard on the ground, not wanting to be burdened by it. Then he turned slowly, eyes scanning the surrounding cliffs, but he didn't see any signs that the enemy had arrived at the grotto ahead of him. Reassured, he moved under the shadow of the overhang, seeking cover from the rain. There, beneath the cliff, a shallow pool of water had collected. Behind it, on the back wall of the grotto, yawned the dark opening that was the entrance to the Caverns of Eld Elan.

Markus hesitated, considering the opening carefully. It reminded him of Aram's cave back home, the one that housed his extensive collection of knots. Only, this cave appeared far more intimidating. Aram's cave hadn't been very deep, and he had been well-acquainted with it.

Slinging his pack down, Markus found that the torches he'd strapped to it had gotten drenched by the rain. Flinging them aside, he had to stop himself from shouting in frustration. Now, he had no way to make fire. He couldn't enter the cave itself unless he wanted to stumble around in the dark.

He didn't know what to do. He supposed he could stand outside the cavern's entrance and guard the grotto. It was either that or brave the darkness in hopes that the Wellspring wasn't too far from the entrance.

He stood for a moment considering his options, at last deciding he didn't like any of them. One man could hold the entrance, even against many, but he would much rather do so with a spear instead of a sword, which he wouldn't be able to swing in such a narrow passage. There were no trees around that he could fashion a spear from, so he would have to make do with what he had. That being the case, he decided to go at least a short way into the cave, to get an idea of where he could retreat to if he had to. He would need to be careful. Caves could be unpredictable, and he didn't want to fall to his death.

Walking to the opening, he hesitated in front of it and peered inside, which was like looking into a dark, yawning throat. Cold air moved past him, as though the cave itself were alive and breathing. He turned back, glancing back up the canyon, nearly overcome by feelings of helplessness and futility. The task Vandra had given him was impossible. There was no way he could defend this cave alone.

But he didn't have a choice. Drawing a deep breath, he pushed his fears to the edge of his mind and entered the passage, using his sword to prod at the ground in front of him like a walking stick. Determined, he inched forward into the darkness, which encased him immediately.

A few more steps and a bend in the cave eliminated even the memory of sunlight. Very seldom had Markus experienced total darkness, and it was disorienting. He reached out and trailed his hand along the cave wall, as much to stabilize himself as to guide his passage. The temperature plunged as soon as the light gave out, taking on a damp chill as cold as the high mountain passes. His wet hair made it worse, and he immediately started shivering.

The further he went, the more unnerved he became. It would be very easy to get lost in the darkness if he broke contact with the wall, even for a second. The breath of air moving past him told him there were other entrances ahead, somewhere in the darkness. This wasn't just a cave, but an entire cave system, and if he became lost within it, he might never find his way back out.

He almost turned back. After all, he'd just meant to go in a little ways, to make sure he could take refuge within if he needed to. But the air moving past him changed his mind about going back. It was coming from somewhere, which meant the caverns had at least one other entrance. Those who meant harm to the Wellspring wouldn't necessarily enter the caverns through the grotto.

Feeling conflicted and more than a little claustrophobic, Markus paused for a moment, gathering his thoughts and fighting back feelings of helplessness. Just when he was ready to give up and head back, he noticed the faintest light on the cave wall just ahead.

Relieved, he moved toward it. The glow came from a side passage up ahead. Markus walked forward, his pulse quickening, for he had no idea what the source of the light could be.

Turning into the side passage, he followed it only a short distance before it opened into a wide cavern filled with stalactites illuminated by a soft, rippling light. He paused before entering the chamber, letting his gaze move carefully over the obstacles in his path. There didn't seem to be anyone lying in wait for him, though it was hard to tell. Some of the cave decorations had grown into wide columns, behind which a man could easily be hidden.

When Markus was as certain as he could be that he wasn't walking into an ambush, he started forward, winding his way along a path between stalagmites that were reminiscent of sharpened teeth. He found himself having to duck in places, as glistening spikes jabbed down from the ceiling overhead. Pieces of stalactites littered the floor, broken off from their bases.

The light seemed to be coming from an opening in the far wall ahead between folded stone decorations that look like marble draperies. Markus lifted his sword and adjusted his grip on the hilt then moved toward the opening. In the entrance, he paused.

Ahead was a smaller chamber that encased a circular pool. It was from the pool's smooth surface that the blue light emanated, swirling over the rocks and ribboning the walls with scintillating tendrils of light. The shore of the pool sparkled as though coated with silver dust.

It was a Wellspring.

Edging forward, Markus knelt on the shore of the pool and dipped his fingers into the glowing blue water. Shocked, he retracted his hand. The water was warm, much warmer than it had any right to be, surrounded by the frigid air of the cave. And yet, no steam rose from its surface.

It was so unnatural.

He rose and backed away, glancing around. For the first time, he saw signs that other humans had come to this place. He could see their footprints in the silvery dust that clung to the ground. There was another opening on the other side of the chamber. Another entrance, more heavily travelled, judging by the prints.

Staring at the Wellspring, a powerful sense of awe crept over him. This was what he was here for, what he had come to protect. This place was hallowed. He could feel the solemnity of the cavern seeping into him as though exuded from the surrounding rocks. He had the strong sense that there was something here far greater than himself, something profound, something essential to the earth.

Markus tightened his grip on his sword, feeling his resolve solidify. No matter what was coming, he would stand against it to his last breath.

Aram tumbled out of the portal, rolling across the sand and smacking his head on the ground. Feebly, he pushed himself upright, just as Esmir came rushing toward him. The old man caught him by the arms and hauled Aram to his feet, bracing him by the shoulders as he raked his gaze over him with a menacing expression.

"What happened to you?" Esmir demanded. Then he waved his hand through the air. "Tell me later! Calise is in the portal, looking for you. Get your clothes on! You're needed!"

Aram sprang for his clothes, but only had time to get his breeches up before Calise came staggering out of the portal. For a moment, she stood blinking as if stunned, but then her eyes fixed on him. She threw her head back and sagged visibly in relief before rushing toward him and sweeping him up in a hug.

"Thank the wind!" she gasped, pulling back. "I thought you were dead! Are you all right? Did they hurt you?"

Shaking with apprehension, Aram struggled into his pants and pulled his tunic over his head. "I'm fine. Nothing's wrong. It's just… what happened?"

"There's been a battle!" Calise exclaimed. "Their sorcerers called lightning and killed twelve of our dragons! Vandra needs you to protect the Anchor because we can't stop them!"

Aram glanced around, feeling disoriented. "Where's Markus?"

"I sent him ahead," Esmir growled. "Now, get going!"

Aram hesitated, his mind reeling from too many shocks too close together.

Casting his emotions aside, he sprinted after Calise toward the stairs.

Vandra screamed as the spear-thrust of lightning impaled Kade's dragon. She watched them fall, crackling energy clawing over the dragon's body, streaming a trail of smoke. Taranth hit the ground and rolled, mowing down a line of footmen. It was seconds before he tumbled to a rest against a rocky scree. Vandra spat upon the ground, shaking in fury, for there was nothing she could do.

She brought her hand up, fingers splayed, commanding her warriors to hold. Below them, the defenders of Inuine fled toward them, chased by a large group of cavalry that were swiftly overtaking them. The fleeing Highlanders were outnumbered and exhausted, losing ground with every stride. It wouldn't be very long before they were overrun, and Vandra was starting to fear that they wouldn't be able to gain the slopes in time. Every instinct she had screamed at her to order her dragons to their defense. But she had to let the enemy come to them. Somewhere down there was a sorcerer—or sorcer*ers*—and they had to keep their dragons out of range.

Beside her, Somlan growled, "Are we just going to wait for them to be slaughtered?"

"We can't risk more dragons." Vandra glanced at the sky, praying for a miracle to descend. But there were no miracles to be had. The enemy had superior numbers and superior capabilities. And magic.

There was a cry from her warriors on the adjacent ridge, directing Vandra's attention to the ravine behind them. Hundreds of soldiers on horseback were pouring into the ravine, flanking their position. Beside her, Somlan cursed and drew his sword, starting forward.

A bolt of lightning arced down, and a dragon behind them fell over and convulsed.

Sorcerers had entered the ravine.

"To the air!" Vandra screamed.

Within seconds, the ridge was abandoned as the surviving members of her Wing raced to their dragons. Vandra sprinted to Ragath, a terrible fear gripping her as she watched the first group of dragons take flight. As she climbed onto his back, the sky lit up above them with an iridescent flash that was followed by a reverberating clap of thunder. A jagged net of crackling energy appeared, clawing at the air.

Five dead dragons fell from the sky, trailing lines of smoke all the way to the ground.

Ragath reared back with a roar of fury, nearly dislodging her.

"Gods be damned!" Vandra cried and jumped from her dragon's back, drawing her sword.

The men and women of the Wing gathered around her, forming a line behind their dragons, preparing to receive the enemy charge while waiting for the lightning to descend.

A shadow streaked by overhead, and then the ridge before them erupted in flames. Startled, Vandra glanced at the sky to see a small golden dragon sweeping by overhead. When it reached the end of the ravine, it banked sharply, turning back toward them.

"No!" she screamed as a streak of lightning speared down from the clouds.

But instead of stabbing through the dragon, the lightning exploded in the air, erupting into a shower of sparks.

The gold dragon dove toward the ground, spewing flames that carved a fiery path right through the heart of the charging cavalry, enveloping men and horses alike. The rest of the enemy horsemen wheeled to retreat.

Defying another lance of lightning, the gold dragon swept low over the ravine, laying down a path of fire that consumed dozens more. This time, when the dragon passed over, it came close enough for Vandra to identify Zandril. And when she saw who rode upon Zandril's back, she almost sank to her knees in relief.

Aramon Raythe.

More spears of lightning streaked down from the clouds, this time aimed at the dragons on the ground. Every bolt died a violent death as they smacked into an invisible barrier that had been woven in the air above them. The sky above the hills lit up with showers of sparks and arcing forks of electricity. On the ground, her warriors rallied, streaming forward to attack the remaining horsemen who hadn't succumbed to the flames.

Vandra heard a shout and whirled, sword already raised, just in time to block a ringing strike from an enemy warrior who had managed to circle around and come up behind her. The leather-clad warrior was as large as an oak tree and fell upon Vandra with an oak's weight of inertia. She crumpled beneath him, her sword arm pinned to the ground.

Vandra struggled, but the warrior butted her in the face with his iron helm. For a moment her consciousness ebbed, but then the clamor of the battle came rushing back. With her left hand, she drew her dagger from its sheath and drove it deep into the warrior's back. There was a grunt of pain, and then the pressure on her eased. Vandra took the opportunity to stick him twice more, just to make sure, before throwing him off.

She struggled out from under her dying opponent, kicking him in the head for good measure. Then she staggered back, hauling her sword up with both hands. Next to her, Somlan was engaged in a brutal struggle with an enormous warrior who had him overpowered. Bringing her sword back over her shoulder, Vandra swung the blade with all her weight behind it, lopping the man's head off.

Somlan nodded his gratitude. He dodged behind her to fight at her back as more enemy warriors swarmed around them. They were massive, armored in leather and fur, wielding monstrous weapons. It took all of her strength to block their swings, and she couldn't just rain down mindless blows against them but had to be smart about her footwork and attacks.

Exhausted, she lost her footing and almost lost her life, but some-one thrust a sword through her opponent from behind, and the man crumpled.

Turning, she looked for someone else to fight, but there wasn't any-one. Panting, Vandra scanned the ravine, realizing that the battle was over. Somehow, they had won.

She glanced up to thank the man who had just saved her life and found herself looking into the youthful face of Aram Raythe, who stood in front of her with burning eyes, his sword sheathed in blood.

"You came," she gasped. She lowered her guard slowly, taken aback by the look on his face.

The eyes she looked into were not the eyes of a boy.

A man stood before her, his gaze burning with magic and fury. It took Vandra a moment to understand. This is what Auld magic looked like when it blazed within a man, and it was a powerful and eerie sight.

Slowly, the burning fire dimmed in Aram's eyes, and the boy she knew stood before her once again. Vandra took him by the shoulder, drawing him close in an embrace, for she couldn't be prouder.

"You have to go," she said gruffly, panting from exhaustion. "I sent Markus ahead to the Anchor. He's going to need you."

Aram pulled back, nodding, then stooped to wipe his blade clean on the back of the man he had killed.

Markus stood beside the glowing Wellspring, watching its light ripple across the walls and ceiling of the cavern. Here, the cave decorations seemed sculpted from white marble, and they were finer and much more numerous than in the larger chamber he had passed through. One of the stalagmites across the room reminded him of the silhouette of a woman. The wall behind it was ribbed in dripstone, looking as though it housed a pipe organ. The chamber of the Wellspring was a beautiful place. A hallowed place, of a kind he never could have imagined seeing in the World Above.

As he stood there, his thoughts turned to Aram, wondering if his friend had made it out of the portal. A great sadness filled him, for he feared that he hadn't. Why had Esmir sent him in there when he wasn't ready, when he knew there was a chance he wouldn't come back out?

He paced back and forth along the shore, struggling to push those thoughts aside. Right now, worry wouldn't serve him, so he forced himself to turn his attention back to the cavern surrounding him. He could feel the power of the Anchor throbbing the air around him. He still didn't have a good sense of exactly what an Anchor was or how it worked. No matter how long his gaze roved over the walls, he didn't see anything that stood out to him. Nothing about the cavern seemed capable of standing in defiance of nature, of holding two halves of one world forever apart.

He also wanted to understand the relationship between the Anchors and the Wellsprings, for it couldn't be coincidence that one always occurred beside the other. Perhaps the Wellsprings provided some kind of lifeblood to the Anchors. Or perhaps life-magic…

A sharp sound made him startle.

Snatching his sword off the ground, Markus stepped sideways to put a wide stalagmite at his back. He stood with his gaze fixed on the opening in the wall that led to the large chamber, feeling his mouth go dry and his insides squirm. Slowly, he edged toward the opening.

There, he halted, staring out into the looming darkness.

For a long time, he saw and heard nothing.

But then a light appeared at the far end of the wide cavern, coming from the passage where he'd seen the footprints. He readied himself, adjusting his grip on his sword, watching the orange light of a flame spread across the cavern wall.

A figure stepped into the chamber, eclipsing the light. Another followed, this one holding a torch. Markus wished he could see their faces, but all he could see was the dark silhouettes of their bodies, as undulating shadows obscured their faces. They crossed the chamber toward him, winding through the forest of stalagmites. It wasn't until they stepped into the pool of light cast by the Wellspring that he made out who it was, and his stomach twisted.

Sergan and Obriem.

The sorcerer flashed him a smile and nodded in greeting. Markus froze, taken off guard by the look in Sergan's eyes. At first, he wasn't sure what to label it. Was it disappointment? Hurt? It couldn't be. Whatever it was, it was quickly replaced by anger. Sergan's face went rigid, his smile faltering.

Markus's gaze dropped, and he noticed that Sergan was holding a vial of essence in his hand, which he made a point of slowly drinking. He swallowed, squeezing his eyes shut and smacking his lips.

Markus understood. It was Aram's essence in those vials.

Standing beside Sergan, Obriem looked unsettled, as though dismayed by the prospect of fighting an acquaintance. And even though he and Obriem had never seen eye to eye, Markus bore him no ill will.

"Why, Markus." Sergan smiled congenially, his eyes blazing with the cold light of sorcery. "What an absolute pleasure to find you here. Are you alone, or did you bring Aram with you?"

Markus didn't speak, for he couldn't decide which answer would give him the best advantage. For all Sergan knew, Aram could be hiding in the cave behind them, which might give the sorcerer pause. Or maybe it would embolden him; it was hard to say. So he kept his mouth shut and met Sergan's eyes.

The sorcerer chuckled. He glanced at Obriem. "I guess we've scared him speechless."

Markus felt his ire rise, and his grip tightened on his sword.

Sergan tossed the empty essence vial away. There was a small tinkling sound as it shattered against the stone. "You're alone, then. That's too bad. Or maybe it's good."

He took a step forward.

"Let's talk about how this is going to play out. You're Impervious to magic, but not to Obriem's steel. And, to my recollection, he was always better than you in the practice yard."

Another step forward.

"Meanwhile, while you're distracted by Obriem, I'll be kicking over stalagmites."

A smile. Another step.

Markus licked his lips, settling deeper into his stance.

"Maybe I can't attack you with sorcery, but I can toss anything in this cave at you. Things around here look pretty sharp." Sergan drew to a stop just out of range as Obriem came up to stand at his side.

"Or, you can surrender." Sergan shrugged. "Up to you."

Markus felt cold sweat collecting on his brow. He had very little chance of beating them both. The sorcerer was poison; he'd always known that. The man was a scorpion, and during the time Markus had known him, Sergan's sting had only become more deadly.

"Where is Aram?" the sorcerer asked.

"Maybe he's behind you."

Obriem glanced back, but Sergan's smile only broadened. "If he were here, I'd sense him. So, where is he?"

Markus shook his head. "He's safe. He'll never be yours."

"Why not?" Sergan asked, but then he frowned, and true concern shadowed his face. "You've got to be kidding me. Fate hands you a Savant, and you get him killed before there's even a battle?"

Markus's face turned red, as all the worry and doubt he'd been holding in clawed to get out. Fury encased him, and he had to restrain himself from lunging at Sergan. It was only the prudence and patience drilled into him by multiple instructors that stayed his hand.

"That's too damn bad," Sergan muttered, shaking his head. "What a waste."

With a growl, he swept his hand out as if throwing something. At the same time, Obriem lunged forward. When Markus swept out at him with his blade, a narrow stalactite broke off the roof and hurled at him. He swiveled quickly to deflect it, breaking off his attack.

Obriem's weight crashed into him, driving Markus backward as another stalactite came flying at him like a lance. This one hit him in the shoulder, and would have penetrated, had it not been for his leather cuirass.

Before he could recover, Obriem clubbed him with the edge of his shield, at the same time thrusting out with his sword. Markus barely managed to dodge the strike. He tried to bring his sword around to counterattack, but the blade caught on the boss of Obriem's shield, and he couldn't get it around in time.

A heavy stalactite cracked hard against his helm.

Reeling, Markus disengaged and staggered backward, giving himself room.

Seeing him floundering, Obriem cast a questioning glance at Sergan, who nodded him forward. When Obriem turned back to Markus, there was regret in his eyes. He blew out a deep breath, puffing his cheeks. Then he advanced.

Seeing him coming, Markus lunged with his sword, turning Obriem's shield to the side and striking his chest. But Obriem's steel breastplate held, and all the blade did was clang against it. Obriem moved sideways, slicing out and catching Markus in the shoulder. The strike didn't penetrate, but it hurt like hell.

Cursing, Markus retreated further, positioning himself with a stalagmite on his left, making defensive use of the cave's decorations. Blood ran down his face and a numbing pain filled his shoulder.

He blocked Obriem's next strike with the strength of his blade, at the same time slicing out with the tip. A grunt of pain told him that his blade had connected.

When Markus drew his sword back for a follow-up, another shard of stalactite slammed into his head.

Dazed, he didn't react in time to avoid Obriem's shield, which swiped up and struck his jaw. His head whipped back, his vision exploding. His foot lodged in a lattice of calcite, and he fell to his haunches, reflexively raising his sword to ward off the next three blows that Obriem battered down on him.

Defiant, Markus struck out with his leg, sweeping Obriem's feet out from under him and toppling him over with a cry of pain. Markus rolled away and, somehow, they both ended up on their feet. Obriem was grimacing, badly favoring his left knee. Markus knew it was time to press his advantage, but for some reason, he hesitated.

This was Obriem, who had helped him rescue Aram from the cellars and had taken a beating for it. He'd always been an ass, but he'd also always been there whenever he was truly needed.

"We don't have to do this!" Markus shouted at him, raising his arm to deflect a spray of stones hurled at him by Sergan. "You can come with me!"

Obriem lunged, striking out with his shield. Markus knocked it aside and brought his sword up under it.

His blade caught on something and was nearly wrenched out of his grip. He jerked back on it, hard, fanning blood across the cavern.

Startled, Markus sprang backward just as Obriem fell to one knee, dropping his shield and bracing himself upright with his sword. For a moment, Markus just stood there, trying to figure out what Obriem was holding with his other hand.

Then his eyes went wide, and he gasped, realizing that Obriem was clutching his neck in an attempt to stem the gush of blood that spilled from a deep slice in his flesh.

Markus stiffened, frozen by shock. Obriem uttered a gurgling wheeze then slumped forward, curling into a ball and making raspy, frothing sounds.

Markus glanced up to find Sergan glaring at him with cold contempt in his eyes. He raised his white-gloved hand and clenched his fist.

Markus scooped up Obriem's shield, expecting another shiny lance of rock to dislodge itself from the ceiling and come flying toward him. When it didn't happen, he turned to look at Sergan.

He didn't see the stone that slammed into the back of his head with such force that it knocked his helmet off.

Sergan drew his dagger and approached Markus warily, unsure if he was dead or unconscious. The large rock had hit him in the head with enough force to cave the side of his helm in and send it flying across the cave, but he wanted to make sure. He never left an enemy behind.

He stopped and knelt beside Markus's prone body, intending to roll him over and slice his throat.

"Stop," rang a commanding voice.

Sergan rose, turning slowly back around.

A familiar figure emerged from the shadows, and the sight of him filled Sergan with a heady mixture of fear and relief.

"Aram Raythe," he breathed, shaking his head.

An inferno of rage scorched Aram's insides as Sergan turned his way. He wasn't sure if Markus was dead or alive, but in order to have any chance of helping him, he would have to get past the sorcerer.

Seeing him coming, Sergan sheathed his dagger and drew a vial of essence from the strap that crossed his chest. Popping the cork stopper, he tilted his head back and downed the liquid in one gulp. He backed away slowly as Aram advanced, keeping space between them, maintaining a frozen smile on his face.

"I was hoping you'd come." Sergan's eyes shone with the light of stolen essence, his many-colored aura rippling around him like a billowing cloak. "I take it you've learned how to bind?"

Aram didn't respond. Instead, he raised his arms and grasped a handful of ethereal tendrils and started knotting, just as he'd done with rope as a boy back in his cave. His fingers danced over the strands, shaping them quickly into a spear of blue energy just as sharp and deadly as his wrath. He hurled it with all his might at Sergan.

The sorcerer knocked it aside with a casual wave.

"That's a start," Sergan said, still slowly backing away. Somehow, he didn't trip over the uneven surface of the cave, as though his awareness was enhanced by the magic within him. "What else can you do?"

Aram's fingers flew over knots of air. He formed a noose of crackling energy and slipped it around Sergan's neck, yanking it tight. But the sorcerer simply cut it away with a slicing motion of his hand, dispelling it with a flare of light. He rubbed his neck with his fingers, stepping sideways.

"So, you can bind in the defense of someone else," Sergan said. "But can you use magic to save your own skin?"

He made a throwing gesture, and a ball of light shot from his hand.

Aram reached out with his mind, ready to weave a shield to block it. But the colorful strands of aether slipped through his fingers like water.

He dodged sideways.

The sizzling ball of energy whizzed by, nearly hitting him in the head.

"I suppose not," muttered Sergan. He stopped walking. Bending, he picked up Obriem's fallen sword. "Now we know why Auld Champions needed Wardens. I never knew they were so helpless without them." He gestured with the sword, pointing it at the ground. "Kneel."

When Aram made no move to comply, Sergan said, "Kneel and surrender, and I'll do what I can to save your friend."

A cold feeling came over Aram, and he was suddenly back in Anai, standing in the alley with the young Exilar threatening his mother's life. This was the same situation. Only, this time, it was Markus's life that was being threatened. Now he understood why the Overseers had chosen that test, and why he had almost failed it.

His love of others was his greatest weakness.

Yet knowing that didn't help.

Fear is your enemy. Don't surrender to it.

His father's words.

He couldn't surrender. Not because of his fear of the cellars, but because he couldn't yield to the enemy and give them that kind of advantage. He wouldn't give the Exilari another drop of his essence. Just as he had with the sorcerer in the village, Aram shook his head.

"No."

Sergan's eyebrows flew up in surprise. "Really? You've actually got the balls to defy me?"

Instead of answering, Aram swept his arms up, capturing every strand of aether he could hold, and started weaving for Markus's sake. This time, he didn't move his fingers, for he didn't have enough of them for all the strands he was working simultaneously. This time, he wove solely with his mind. Colors and patterns swirled dizzily around him, flitting by faster than the speed of thought. Tendrils of aether knit together in structures of increasing complexity, spilling out before him. He tied off the last threads of his creation with a defiant growl then hurled the whole glowing mass at Sergan.

A flash of light brighter than the sun exploded in the cavern. Sergan was lifted off the ground and went flying backward, crashing high up into the wall behind him. But instead of falling, his body clung there as if nailed in place. Cold horror froze his face, and the color drained from his cheeks.

Slowly, his body peeled from the wall and slid to the ground, leaving a streak of blood behind. Aram saw the spikes his back had been driven into. There were two of them, as long as his hand, unless there were others that had broken off inside him. The sorcerer sat leaning back against the wall, legs splayed, gazing slack-jawed at Aram with a look of terrified disbelief. Aram glared back at him with glowing eyes that blazed with power and hatred.

Sergan growled, thrusting out his hands.

Aram leapt sideways, but not in time to avoid the concussion of air that clapped together where he'd just been standing. His head thundered as if struck by a hammer wielded by the gods.

Motes of light danced across his vision, and he slumped to the ground. For a moment, darkness encased him. Then the world came swimming back into focus.

Aram lifted his head and spat a mouthful of blood. He opened his eyes.

Sergan was gone.

He looked to where Markus lay unconscious or dead on the floor of the cave. Grimacing in pain, he pushed himself off the ground. He wobbled for a second then staggered toward his friend, heart pounding with fear.

When he reached Markus, Aram rolled him over gently. He was still alive, though blood ran freely from a wound in his scalp, drenching his

face. Aram threw his head back in despair, for he didn't know what to do. Markus was bleeding heavily. His helmet lay across the floor from them and, looking at the size of the dent in it, his skull could easily be cracked. Aram tried to summon magic to heal him, but he didn't know how. And when he tried to twist the strands into something that could stop the bleeding, they simply melted in his hand.

He wanted to scream. Markus was Impervious.

No amount of magic could heal him.

Aram started tearing at his clothes, wadding torn strips of cloth and pressing them against the wound.

The cloth became saturated almost instantly.

He didn't know what to do. There had been a man in his village who had died of a head injury, when the halyard of a ship cracked his skull. He'd lived three days after the accident, but he'd never woken up.

Markus had to wake up.

He *had* to.

Glancing behind him, Aram considered the glowing waters of the Wellspring.

There was great power in Wellsprings, Harak had told him. Great power of healing. And it wasn't active magic. It was *passive* magic. Not the magic of the aether, but the magic of the earth itself.

Perhaps it was a kind of magic Markus was not immune to.

Heart thundering, Aram gathered his best friend in his arms and dragged him backwards, being careful not to jostle Markus's head. The action made his shoulder throb fiercely, and he figured he must have hit it when he fell. His body felt terribly weak for some reason, but he managed to lift Markus over the worst of the uneven ground and wade with him out into the shallow waters of the glowing Wellspring.

There, he knelt with Markus cradled in his arms, holding his head above the water's surface. Tendrils of blood rose around them, snaking through the water, far more blood than he ever would have expected. Cupping his hand, Aram washed the wound in Markus's scalp with the water of the Wellspring. He drizzled some into his mouth, making Markus choke and sputter.

A raw ache of desperation gripped Aram's heart as the water surrounding them darkened. Still, Markus didn't wake up. Desperate, Aram drenched the torn cloth and pressed it against the injury. His shoulder throbbed fiercely, and he wanted to rub it, but he didn't want to jostle Markus. After several minutes, he removed the cloth and checked the wound beneath it.

Aram gasped.

The bleeding had stopped.

He gave a long sigh of relief. Markus still wasn't out of danger, but it was something. Cradling his friend's limp body in his arms, Aram determined to remain with him in the pool until Markus either awakened or succumbed to his injuries.

Hours went by.

Marcus remained unconscious, his breathing regular, as though he were deep asleep. Aram thought that some of the color might have returned to his face. He propped himself up against a boulder, resting his head against the uncompromising rock.

His temples throbbed from the explosion of magic Sergan had tossed at him, making him feel weak and dizzy. He started shivering, though he didn't understand why. The water around him was warm, far warmer than the cave.

Aram caught himself nodding off and had to jerk himself awake. Then he heard it: the sound of voices echoing through the cavern. Fear gripped him, and he hugged Marcus protectively. Those voices could be friends, but it was more likely Sergan returning to claim them both. Not knowing what else to do, he pulled back behind the boulder.

The voices grew closer, echoing off the cavern walls. Aram squeezed his eyes shut and listened, straining to recognize them. But the sounds rang hollowly off the walls, and he couldn't tell who was speaking. He pressed his back up against the boulder as hard as he could.

The footsteps entered the room.

Aram chanced a glance around the rock and just about sobbed in relief when he saw that it was Vandra, accompanied by some of the riders from the fighting Wing. With a gulp of joy, Aram moved out from behind the rock and surged toward her through the water.

"By the wind!" exclaimed Vandra.

She plunged into the water and, together, they carried Markus to the shore, where they laid him out on the rocky floor of the cavern. Vandra bent to examine him, and Aram knelt at her side.

"Is he going to be all right?" he croaked.

Vandra turned her attention from Markus's scalp to examine the rest of him, lifting his eyelids and pressing an ear against his chest to listen to his breathing. Looking at Aram, she smiled in reassurance.

"I think he's going to be all right." Her smile froze. "You're bleeding."

Aram looked down and saw she was right. His left shoulder was stained dark with blood.

"I'm fine," he muttered.

Then the world went dark, and he collapsed into Vandra's arms.

Aram awoke to the familiar scent of cloves and roasting meat. He was staring up at the ceiling of a cave, only, this cave was tall and smooth, not embellished with stalactites. He was warm, encased in a cocoon of blankets, his head cradled by a feather pillow. Turning over, he closed his eyes and stretched, wondering why he felt as though he had been sleeping for a week. When he opened his eyes, he was startled to find himself looking at Esmir, who was relaxing in a chair that had been pulled up beside his sleeping pallet. At the sight of the old Warden, everything that had happened since his return from the Portal Stones came back.

"Markus—"

"Recovering." Esmir nodded past Aram, and he turned to take a look.

There, on the other side of the small room, lay Markus, by all appearances sleeping peacefully. His head was wrapped in bandages, but otherwise, he looked healthy. At the sight of him, Aram let out a great, long sigh, feeling almost dizzy with relief.

"I thought he didn't have a chance," Aram breathed.

Esmir lifted his bushy gray eyebrows. "He's lucky to have a friend that acted quickly. How did you know the water would work on him?"

"I didn't. I just hoped."

There was a crashing noise as the eyrie's door burst open.

"Are they awake?" came a loud voice.

Aram turned at the sound of rushing feet to find Jeran, Kye, and

Corley running toward them.

Esmir surged halfway out of his chair, holding his hands up, a ferocious look on his face. "Would you louts be quiet? Markus needs his rest!"

The young men halted with grimaces of apology, tiptoeing the last few steps to flop down at Aram's side.

"I can't believe you saved the Anchor all by yourself!" Jeran exclaimed in a whisper.

"Hell, he saved the entire Wing!" gushed Kye.

"Are you feeling all right? You had us worried!"

Aram wanted to cover his ears from the assault of questions.

"Why are you worried about me?" he asked. "It's Markus that's hurt!"

He tried to sit up, but a sudden, shooting pain made him think better of it.

"Are you joking? You have a gaping hole in your shoulder!"

Aram brought a hand up and discovered that his shoulder was heavily bandaged. He glanced at Esmir in alarm, and the old Warden nodded.

"I don't understand…how could I be hurt and not know it?"

Come to think of it, his shoulder *had* ached something fierce. And he didn't remember leaving the cavern. The last thing he remembered was Vandra telling him that Markus was going to be all right.

"Did I pass out?"

"You could say that." Esmir smiled. "You'd lost a lot of blood. But the Wellspring sped the healing remarkably. What affected you more was the amount of magic you used. That much magic doesn't come without a price."

"You've been out for three days!" exclaimed Kye. "We kept coming to check on you, but he kept kicking us out."

Esmir snorted. "Because you have no idea how to be quiet! Now. All of you! Aram needs to recuperate, and he doesn't need you loudmouths hounding him!"

Chastised, the three youths said their goodbyes and departed. Esmir rose from his chair and went to the fire pit, returning with a bowl.

"See if you can sit up and eat," he said, groaning as he lowered himself to the floor at Aram's side.

With Esmir's help, Aram was able to eat nearly the entire bowl of soup, but by the end of it, he started to tire, so Esmir left him to his rest.

As Aram slept, he had the strangest dream. In it, he was being carried by the void dragon. Only, this time, he didn't ride clutched in the creature's talons, but rather on its milky-white back. The void dragon tucked its wings and veered downward into a steep dive, angling straight into the great fissure in the earth at the bottom of the gorge. Instead of pulling up, the dragon continued on down into the yawning crack, maintaining its speed as darkness closed in around them. For several seconds, they flew straight down, deep into the ground, Aram clinging as hard as he could to the dragon's back as blasting-hot wind sped past them.

Far below, a deep red glow appeared, winding like a thin river through the darkness. It was rushing up to meet them, the walls of the fissure closing in, and still the dragon continued its descent, picking up speed.

Suddenly, the dragon lost control and started tumbling.

Aram gasped as he startled awake.

He was panting, and an aching anxiety squeezed his heart. The void dragon had saved his life, and in turn, had given its own. It had fallen into that great crack in the earth, into that searing darkness.

But why?

Why had it saved him? Why had it not saved itself?

Aram lay awake long into the night, pondering these questions, until exhaustion won out and sleep claimed him.

He awoke to daylight.

Opening his eyes, Aram sat up anxiously to see if Markus was awake and found Vandra there, kneeling beside Markus. The Wingmaster was changing his bandages. The whole while she worked, Markus remained sleeping.

Vandra finished tying off the bandages and started gathering up the old ones but, seeing Aram awake, she turned toward him. A quiet smile passed her lips, and Aram thought he'd never seen such a look of warmth on Vandra's face.

"I owe you thanks," she said. "We all do."

Aram ducked his head self-consciously. "No. It's Calise you need to thank. Without her, I don't think I would've made it out of the Henge."

Vandra shook her head. "You must learn to take credit when credit's due. Without you and Markus, we would have lost the Anchor and most of the Wing."

Aram's cheeks heated, for he didn't deserve the compliment. He'd just done the only thing he *could* do—there'd been no other choice.

"Markus killed Obriem and stood up to Sergan," he said softly. "I didn't do much."

Vandra cocked her head slightly. "How about this. Why don't you tell me what happened, and let me be the judge of who saved what."

Aram smiled shyly. As best he could, he described what happened, telling Vandra about how Markus had killed Obriem, and how he'd taken on Sergan too—a fully-fledged sorcerer. He didn't intentionally try to minimize his own involvement, but he didn't really try to dwell on it, either. But Vandra kept pumping him with questions, until the full story finally came out.

When it did, she shook her head slowly, her eyes going distant. "That is…remarkable. I wouldn't have thought anyone but a Champion could defeat an Exilari sorcerer."

"He got away," Aram said, "so I really didn't defeat him."

"It still counts as a defeat." Vandra smiled and stood up. "In a couple of weeks, the rest of the apprentices are going to be inducted into the fighting Wing. So will you and Markus. I'll be proud to serve with you."

Aram frowned. "But I can't bond a dragon, so how can I be a member of the Wing?"

"It doesn't matter," Vandra assured him. "You still have valuable skills that are assets to the Wing, and the fact that you don't have a dragon of your own hasn't slowed you down yet."

She walked across the room to where Esmir sat at his table, a ceramic cup cradled in his hands.

"I need you to get Aram ready for the Trials," Vandra told him. "He's proven he's capable, and we don't have any more time to delay. You've got one month."

"The hell you say!" Esmir barked, sitting bolt upright and slamming down his cup. "He's nowhere near ready—"

"Then what's it going to take to *get* him ready?"

"Time!" Esmir scooted his chair out with a nerve-grating screech and rose, towering head and shoulders over Vandra. "I need time—*he* needs time! You say he's capable, but I say we almost lost him! There are *four tests* he'll have to survive to pass the Trials, and each is exponentially harder than the one before it."

Aram didn't understand why Esmir was arguing with Vandra. If they needed him, then they needed him, and it was as simple as that. Gathering his blankets about him, he rose unsteadily to his feet, walking around the fire to stand beside Vandra.

"What changed?" Aram asked. "Why the rush?"

Esmir glared at Vandra, his eyes narrowing in burning accusation.

"There was a sorceress with their army," Vandra said. "She was the one who called down the lightning upon us. Esmir thinks she's a Champion. An enemy Champion."

Shocked, Aram glanced at Esmir. "How's that possible? Would the Overseers allow someone like that to become a Champion?"

The old man brought a hand up to roughly scratch his whiskered cheek. His skin and hair looked oily, as though he hadn't bathed in weeks. Come to think of it, Aram couldn't remember Esmir ever bathing at all.

Vandra crossed her arms. "We need a Champion to fight a Champion. And if we keep using Aram constrained the way he is, we're going to get him killed."

"And if you force him into the Trials before he's ready, you'll accomplish the same damn thing!"

"I'll do it," Aram said.

"And if he—" Esmir started.

"I'll do it," Aram repeated more firmly, meeting and holding Esmir's gaze. "Wingmaster Vandra's right. Sergan almost killed me because I couldn't defend myself. And if I can't defend myself, I'm no good to anyone."

Vandra caught Esmir's arm. "They're already regrouping. We're fighting the Archons of two worlds, and we can't fight them alone."

"Come on, now," came a weak voice from behind them. "Can't you argue somewhere else?"

Aram whirled at the sound of Markus's voice. With a yelp of joy, he sprang to his friend's side. Markus still looked pale and haggard, but his eyes were full of life and light. Aram threw his head back and laughed. For a moment, the two friends just sat together without speaking, for what passed between them didn't need words. Vandra came and knelt beside them, draping a hand over her knee.

"How do you feel?" she asked.

"Like a dragon bit me." Markus smiled his usual, lopsided grin.

Vandra chuckled. "I suspect a dragon would have caused less damage. Fortunately, you have a thick head and a quick-thinking friend." Reaching out, she mussed Aram's hair.

She stood and said to Esmir, "I'll give you a month. No longer."

"My birthday is in a month," Aram muttered, wondering if that was coincidence or portent.

"Then we'll set the date of your Trials the day before," said Vandra, "that way you can celebrate your birthday as a Champion."

Esmir didn't say anything, but the glower on his face wasn't difficult to interpret. After Vandra was gone, he walked over to his table and splashed some whiskey into his cup, grumbling under his breath.

"What was that all about?" Markus mumbled, closing his eyes.

Aram leaned over and pulled his friend's covers up but didn't bother to answer. Markus was already asleep.

Esmir had Aram up in the Henge the very next day, despite the fact that he was still recovering. Over the next several days, he worked him harder than ever before, making him spend more and more time inside the first portal, until he was entering the Shadow Realm several times a day. The tests the Overseers gave him seemed to be increasing in difficulty every time he went in. Sometimes, the tests were physical, while at other times, they required a magical response. His shoulder didn't really bother him much anymore, which helped, and Aram found that the mental tests were often the hardest to endure.

It was another few days before Markus was up and moving around, and even then, Calise insisted his head wasn't ready to go back to training. He still got headaches often and felt dizzy sometimes when he stood up. He seemed to be improving every day, though, and his spirits were good. It helped that some of the apprentices came by to spend time with them in the evenings, mostly Jeran and Kye, though sometimes Corley and Eugan came with them. Iver even made an appearance, though he was quiet and didn't say much.

Esmir decided that they should live with him until after Aram's Trials, for he needed every moment he could get to work with him, so they didn't return to the dormitory. Markus didn't object, and Aram knew his friend was worried sick about him. Markus had been very vocal about his concerns over moving up the Trials—until Vandra reminded him that Aram was incapable of defending himself with his magic locked. After that, he'd stayed quiet, though his worry still showed whenever the subject came up.

After supper one evening, their friends spilled into the eyrie bubbling with excitement. It took over a minute before both Markus and Aram understood the source of their delight, for they were all too giddy to stop talking over one another.

"Dragons!" Kye exclaimed. "We're going to get dragons!"

"Dragons?" Markus asked.

"The *eggs*," said Corley, coming over to plop down at his side. "The eggs are ready to hatch! Vandra said it could be any time!"

"There's enough for all of you," Aram said, excited for them, even though he knew he wouldn't be getting a dragon of his own.

The smiles disappeared from the apprentices' faces when they remembered that Aram was destined to stay dragonless.

"I'm sorry, Aram," said Corley. "I'm really, really sorry. I forgot!"

"You don't have to be sorry," Aram told him. "I'm glad for you. I really am. If I ever need a dragon, I can always just borrow one. They don't seem to mind giving me a ride."

Even though Aram insisted that it didn't bother him, the joyous mood had been broken. The apprentices left a few minutes later, congratulating each other, mired in a guessing match over which of them would end up with which egg, all agreeing that Corley would probably end up with the runt.

When they were gone, Esmir pulled a chair over and sat next to them, folding his hands on his lap. Aram glanced at Markus, who stared back, for it was easy to tell that something was wrong by the look on Esmir's face.

"What is it?" Aram asked.

"Markus won't be bonding one of the hatchlings," Esmir said, a statement which shocked Aram.

"Why not?" he gasped, at the same time as Markus shrugged and whispered, "That's all right."

Esmir smiled slightly. "You won't be bonding a hatchling because you're already spoken for, you see."

When both Aram and Markus just stared at him blankly, the old Warden explained, "We wanted to wait a bit before telling you, to make sure he didn't change his mind. This kind of thing doesn't happen very often, you see. Not in the last hundred years, that I can remember."

Markus and Aram exchanged confused glances.

"What are you talking about?" Markus asked. "*Who* are you talking about?"

"After we found you in the cavern, Siroth was so distraught that he decided to linger in this world until he knew you were out of danger. And then..." Esmir shrugged. "I think his concern for you overrode his natural instinct to accompany Faril to her grave. He let us bury her, instead, and he remains with us." For a few seconds, Markus just stared at him as though he wasn't sure what Esmir was trying to say.

"You mean…"

"Siroth has become quite fond of you," Esmir confirmed.

Markus's eyes grew wide, his jaw slackening. "But I thought…I thought that wasn't possible."

"It's possible, just very rare. Very rare indeed."

Aram asked, "Can humans survive the death of a dragon?"

Esmir shook his head sadly. "No. No, we can't. We are not so resilient as dragonkind."

A startling thought struck Aram, and he frowned. "Esmir, how is it *you're* still alive? Didn't your dragon die?"

The smile departed from Esmir's face, and he bowed his head. He took a moment before answering. "When Daymar was captured, our dragons were caught in the space between the worlds." He drew in a deep, troubled breath. "Faranth…she isn't dead. She's a void dragon now, as is Daymar's dragon, Agaroth. Or, at least, he was."

"Was?" Aram asked. "What happened to Agaroth?"

The frown on Esmir's face intensified, growing as deep and dark as the chasm below.

"Agaroth was the void dragon who brought you here," he said at last. "The one who fell into the abyss."

69

Sergan took one last glance around his tent, making sure he had everything he needed, for he hoped he would never be coming back. He spied a bone-handled knife that had belonged to Obriem and decided to take it, since it was finer than his own. He winced in pain as he stooped to collect it, his injured back shooting hot daggers throughout his torso. It had been only a week since he'd been slammed into a wall full of short but painful spikes, and some had punctured deeper than others. Fortunately, Lazair's healers had proven skilled, more so than any he had ever met.

He picked up his pack, carrying it at his side instead of throwing it over his shoulder. Outside, the morning sun hadn't yet crested the horizon, and the early morning shadows clung to the ground. Even the birds hadn't stirred awake yet, and there was a lingering stillness broken only by the crackle of the campfires. He stood for a moment looking out across the gray dawn, thinking there was no way in hell he was going to miss this place.

"Where are you going?"

Sergan turned to regard Lazair, who was sitting at the fire in front of his tent. Her pale hair was bound in a long, thick braid, and she wore lamellar armor that consisted of lacquered black scales. Her features were so pale and emaciated that he still couldn't decide whether she was ugly or gorgeous. He supposed it made no difference. She was dangerous, and that's what was important.

"I'm heading out early," he said. "It's a long ride back to the rupture."

She rose, dusting off her armor's skirt, and walked around the campfire toward him. "Why are you leaving?"

He couldn't believe she'd have to ask such a question, for he thought the answer obvious. If it hadn't been for his wounds, he would have left a week ago. "Because we *lost*. There's no point of continuing."

Lazair waved her hand dismissively. "A minor setback."

"That was more than a minor setback for me. In the past few weeks, I've gone through two Shields and four flasks of essence, not to mention coming damn close to getting killed by an untrained adolescent."

"I think we both know that Aramon Raythe is far more than just an 'untrained adolescent.'"

"I agree." He sneered. "So good luck with him."

Lazair's gaze turned skyward as the shadow of a dragon passed over them. He had no idea if it was one of Lazair's tame dragons or one of their enemy's and, frankly, didn't care. Dragons and adolescents were no longer his problem.

She caught his arm, preemptively stopping him from walking away. "My master wants to make him a priority."

Reaching up, Sergan calmly extracted her hand. "Aram should have already *been* a priority. If he's this dangerous now, what do you think he's going to be like if he becomes a Champion?"

Sergan was genuinely frightened of the thought, and he didn't scare easily. In the cavern of the Wellspring, he had gravely underestimated the boy. He shouldn't have toyed with him, and he wanted to kick himself for it. Aram couldn't even defend himself—and yet he'd still almost killed him. It was so odd that a person's magic could be locked in such a way. He hadn't known that before, that there were rules to Auld magic. If he had, the boy would have never gone to the Extractors.

"He won't pass the Trials to become a Champion," Lazair promised.

"And why is that?" Sergan lifted an eyebrow, feigning interest, even though he'd already grown bored with the conversation.

"The Trials are administered by a race of creatures who call themselves the Unan," she explained. "Gifted people who fully enter their realm return with their Gift unlocked—if they return at all. In my time, the Unan were called the Overseers and they were thought to be gate-keepers of magic. We thought they were some type of higher race whose job it was to make certain Auld magic would not be used for evil. But we were wrong. Like we were about so many things."

"Indeed," he mumbled.

Bored, Sergan looked out across the encampment. The soldiers were already up and about their daily routines, stoking the cook fires, gather-ing water, and collapsing the tents for the day's march. The air was filled with the scent of wood smoke and cooking meat, odors that made his mouth water.

Lazair guided him to the fire, where one of her soldiers was tend-ing an iron skillet. Strips of meat that resembled pork belly, but likely weren't, sizzled in the pan. Lazair crouched next to the fire, patting the ground next to her. Sergan declined, not wanting to mar the perfection of his blue mantle.

"So, why do they do it?" he asked. "What do these Overseers gain by administering the Trials?"

Lazair plucked a strip of meat from the pan, holding it in front of her gingerly, so as not to burn her fingers. Blowing on it, she slipped it into her mouth, making him wait as she slowly chewed. "It turns out that the candidates who end up 'passing' their Trials are those who have actually *failed* them, in the minds of the Overseers. They're looking for Gifted humans with little mental fortitude, you see. Basically, people that can be easily dominated and enslaved. These, they take to become their thralls—which explains why so many of the candidates who enter their portals never come back out again."

Sergan plucked his own strip of meat from the pan, waggling it in the air to cool it before biting off a piece. "That *is* interesting. What about the people who come back insane?"

"People who are too strong of will are perceived to be a threat," Lazair said glibly. "They are either killed or their mind is broken."

Sergan pondered that, reflecting on what he'd learned of Aram Raythe from the short time he'd spent as his mentor. The boy had been very shy and very awkward, and he walked just a little out of step with the rest of the world. He was a congenial boy, though, who had tried hard to please. In the little time he'd known him, Sergan had almost grown fond of him.

"Aram is very biddable," he said at last. "If I had gold to put on it, I'd wager he's exactly the type of person these creatures are interested in taking."

"Fortunately, my master has an arrangement with the Unan. They're interested in more than just humans, you see. They actually prefer Elesium to men. So we've been trading them—for every human they return to us alive with their Gift unlocked, we offer them an Elesium foal." She smiled broadly. "I'm certain they would be happy to accept a colt or two in payment for one boy."

Her smile was infectious. Sergan found himself grinning too. Perhaps he'd remain, after all. It seemed things were just about to get interesting.

"I want you to stay," Lazair said. "You may name the price for your services. As long as it's not too extravagant, I'm certain my master will accommodate it."

Sergan would have to think about that long and hard, because the reward had better be worth it. "So, what's our next objective?"

"I received word today. Your Emperor has promised us ten more of your Exilari. My master has grown impatient with our lack of progress. We are to direct our efforts at the keystone Anchor, what's known as the Heart of the Mother. The Veil has already been destabilized, so if the Heart of the Mother falls, then the rest should fall with it."

"Are you sure you want me here?" Aram asked.

Markus looked up in surprise. "Why wouldn't I? You're the closest thing I have to family. Of course I want you here!"

Aram felt profoundly moved by his best friend's words. In truth, Markus was the closest thing he'd ever come to having a brother. He felt deeply honored that Markus would want him to be present at such an intimate occasion as the bonding of dragon to rider, the twining of two souls until the end of time. He was not jealous of Markus, even though he knew he would never bond a dragon of his own. He felt truly glad for him and especially glad for Siroth, who had found, in Markus, a reason to live.

Vandra appeared in the doorway, dressed in a tunic that wasn't quite ceremonial, yet definitely an improvement over the war-beaten leathers that were her usual apparel. Seeing her, Markus's eyes flicked to Aram.

Aram squeezed his arm in reassurance. "You'll do fine."

Markus smiled with all the nervous anticipation of a bridegroom.

"Are you ready?" Vandra asked.

When both young men rose and moved toward her, Vandra raised her eyebrows in surprise. But Markus didn't say anything, so Vandra walked past them and pulled back the wicker screen that guarded Esmir's quarters, letting in the sunlight and a cool afternoon breeze. Aram and Markus followed her through the eyrie and out onto the terrace.

There, they waited, the wind teasing their clothes, eyes drawn to the sky. Vandra lingered back against the wall alongside Esmir, while Aram took his place at his best friend's side, feeling nervous enough for the both of them. For his part, Markus looked remarkably at ease, the only outward sign of tension the occasional twitch of his cheek. And even though the wind whipped his dark hair about his face, he looked oddly dignified.

They stood there for a few minutes, just long enough for the apprehension that gripped Aram's stomach to loosen somewhat.

A long shadow fell over them, eclipsing the sun.

Aram took a step back, craning his neck and shielding his eyes as a large black dragon descended upon them, alighting on the terrace with predatorial grace. For a moment, Siroth stood frozen in the action of landing, wings spread and horned head tilted at an angle, peering down at them with molten gold eyes. He settled slowly into a crouch, as though wary or uncertain of this place. Then his eyes came to rest on Markus and their gazes locked, his sleek obsidian body tensing as though to spring.

Startled, Aram had to restrain himself from stepping protectively in front of his friend, for he had never seen a dragon look so fearsome.

Markus stood his ground, though his breath came in sharp gasps. He glanced at Aram as though seeking reassurance. Aram set a hand on his friend's back.

"Go to him."

Markus swallowed hard, then walked forward in a measured pace, looking very much like an unkempt groom arriving before his ferocious bride. He approached the dragon cautiously, and then he paused, looking uncertain about what to do next.

It was Siroth who made the next move.

With a low rumble, the black dragon lowered his head. Hesitantly, Markus reached up and laid a hand upon Siroth's scaled brow, and their eyes met. For long moments, the two simply stood in regard of one another, two warriors paying respectful homage in a gesture that was strangely noble.

Then something changed.

Markus sucked in a sharp breath, his eyes widening for just an instant before closing completely. His body wavered, and Aram almost rushed forward to steady him.

But it was not Aram that Markus needed in this moment of vulnerability, for that honor was meant for another. Siroth curled his neck around Markus and let him sag against him, catching him against his muscular chest as Markus clung to the soft spines that ran the length of his dragon's body. Siroth gave a low rumble, and the two simply stood there, locked in a mutual embrace, as something significant passed between them. When at last Markus recovered somewhat, he glanced back over his shoulder with tears in his eyes, flashing Aram a joyous smile.

Aram smiled back, for he was glad for his friend. Siroth was a valiant and fearsome soul, and he was everything that Markus deserved. When Markus climbed onto his dragon's back for their first flight as a bound pair, Aram watched in awe as Siroth launched from the terrace with a wind-gusting downstroke of wings. The sight of them gliding over the canyon was exhilarating, and yet, at the same time, it made his heart ache. For even though he was happy for his best friend, Aram was also very aware that *he* would never know a love so profound.

When he turned away from the terrace, he found Vandra and Esmir looking at him, and at first, he felt ashamed, for they had surely seen the sadness on his face. He forced a smile as best he could, deciding to focus on Markus's happiness instead of his own self-pity.

"I'm sorry," said Vandra, and the compassion in her eyes told Aram that she truly understood.

Esmir gave him a look of sympathy, for, more than anyone else, the old Warden knew what it was like to be dragonless.

"I'm happy for them," Aram said, his gaze following Markus and Siroth as they soared across the sky.

"I know you are," said Vandra, placing a hand on his shoulder.

Aram spent the remainder of the morning at the Henge with Esmir, drilling sword forms over and over until sweat drenched his clothes and his arms hung limp with exhaustion. When the sun reached its zenith, Esmir threw him a water skin and a damp cloth to wrap around his head and called him into the shade of one of the monoliths for a rest. Aram sat down heavily, his back against the stone, breathing hard and gazing down at the dulled blade in his hands.

"What about my own sword?" he asked, the thought suddenly occurring to him. "And my armor? Are they going to be ready any time soon?"

"Your armor will be ready in the next couple of days, I'm told," Esmir assured him, then took a swig from his water flask. Stoppering it, he set the flask back down in the dirt. "Your sword is going to be the problem. I asked Onsel if he could speed the process up, and he assured me that he was already doing everything in his power. Unfortunately, it has to pass through the hands of several different craft masters. Right now, it's with the polisher, and then it will go to the woman will put the final edge on the blade. I'm told those two steps cannot be rushed."

Aram nodded. More than anything, he did not want Onsel to sacrifice quality. If he passed his Trials, his life would depend on that sword. It was good news about his armor, though. He was eager to see it and even more eager to wear it.

"All right," Esmir said, gesturing with his cane toward the first portal. "Let's see what kind of tests the Overseers have for you today."

Aram sighed heavily, for the last two times he'd entered the portal, his resolve had been sorely tested. He was not looking forward to finding out what kind of assaults they would throw at him today. Reluctantly, he laid down his sword and bent to remove his clothes.

"What will happen if I don't survive the Trials?" he asked quietly. "What will you do?"

Esmir opened his mouth but then closed it again, his eyebrows drawing together. "I don't know."

Aram knew it was an honest answer, and it made him a little sad. Tossing his clothes on the ground, he walked toward the portal and, drawing a deep breath, stepped through.

Looking down at himself, Aram saw that he was dressed in dragon-scale armor, though it was different from the mail he had seen in Master Krommer's shop. This cuirass had scales lacquered with black enamel that glowed orange in the light of flames. The flames themselves were cast by torches hung from sconces all around the dark, circular room he found himself within. Aram turned slowly in place, raising the sword in his hands.

It wasn't the star-steel blade that was being crafted for him, but a similar sword of far less quality. For a moment, Aram looked around in confusion, trying to understand the nature of this test. The timing of the sword and armor appearing after his conversation with Esmir was not lost on him. He thought perhaps this exercise was a direct result of it.

The floor shivered beneath his feet.

He sprang away as the shadows rushed from the walls and converged on the spot he had just been standing. There, they solidified into the form of a man. It was no ordinary man, but one that looked like a blackened corpse covered in armor that glowed red as though slightly molten. It held a round shield in one hand and a short sword in the other. The corpse stank of death and rot, wheezing breath through gaping rents in its chest.

In the past several days, Aram had been presented with a menagerie of frightening adversaries. For some reason, this one seemed worse than most. For one thing, he was already at a disadvantage, for this opponent bore a shield, while all he had was a fragile, mundane sword.

The corpse—or whatever it was—didn't hesitate, but conjured a lance of magic that Aram wasn't expecting because he'd been so focused on the weapons. It slammed into his chest, hurling him backward. He hit the ground and lay there dazed, his body numb from the shock, the air driven from his lungs.

As he struggled to regain his feet, the corpse's head elongated and shot toward him like a striking snake. He rolled away just in time to see the head reshape itself into a mercurial sword that cleaved the earth where he'd just been lying.

Somehow, he ended up on his feet in a fighting stance.

The creature changed back into its human form and threw itself at him, striking out with its sword. Aram brought his own sword up to block then swung it around, severing his opponent's arm. Its weapon went flying, and the creature recoiled with a snarl.

There was a sick, oozing sound, and the corpse somehow cleaved in half, both halves leaping in opposite directions. Suddenly, he was fighting two corpses instead of one. Aram swung low and carved a slice out of the leg of one then kicked out at the other, knocking it backward.

The first creature went down with a snarl, while the second came back at him. This one had two swords, which it jabbed at him in a scissoring motion. He dodged back out of reach, bringing his blade around just in time to deflect a strike coming at him from a third adversary that had appeared from out of nowhere.

With a growl, Aram spun sideways to avoid one sword, only to find himself confronted by another. This, he smacked aside with the flat of his blade, continuing the motion to drive the pommel of his hilt into the eye socket of the corpse.

Scalding ichor spattered his face. He wiped it out of his eyes just in time to see the edge of the shield that smacked him in the head.

Aram went down and rolled away as a blade pierced the ground where his chest had just been. Spitting blood, he pushed himself upright, but the moment he regained his feet, the first creature swept his legs out from under him. He could feel his knee give out, and he fell to the ground with a pained cry.

When he glanced up, three living corpses loomed over him, and he feared he was beaten. The three fell upon him at once, stabbing with their swords.

With a sweep of his hand, Aram wove strands of air into a shield that turned the blades aside. He wrenched himself to his feet, braiding another handful of aether into a burning whip, which he lashed out with at one of the demons. At the same time, he arced his blade toward another. His sword arm jarred as his weapon connected with bone and sinew, cleaving one of the three bodies entirely in half.

He cracked the flaming whip at the creature on his left, sending it shrieking and chattering to the other side of the room. Then he swept his sword around, cutting a deep slice into the torso of another. Black gore spilled from the wound, and ropes of steaming entrails squirmed to the ground. The thing collapsed, crumpling as though squeezed by an enormous fist.

Which left only one last adversary. Favoring his leg, Aram turned toward it and drew his sword back, preparing to strike.

"Aram!"

He whirled at the sound of his mother's voice.

Another corpse had appeared, standing behind his mother, holding her firmly by the hair. Dark bruises and open wounds covered her body, and she was sobbing uncontrollably. Blood drenched her clothes and streaked her face.

Aram froze. He didn't dare strike out at the corpse with his mother in the way, and the other creature was advancing. He had no idea whether or not she was real, but he couldn't risk it. The wounds that he took in the Shadow Realm followed him outside, so he had to assume that whatever happened in here was more than just illusion.

He dropped his sword and raised his hands.

"Please!" his mother shrieked. "Stop coming here!"

"Why?" Aram asked, watching the other corpse warily out of the corner of his eye.

"They'll kill you!" she wailed. "Go away! *Go away and never come back!*"

Aram gritted his teeth, his resolve slipping. He couldn't kill the creature behind his mother without cutting her down. But now he wasn't so sure that this woman was truly his mother. His real mother would never ask him to run away from duty.

Suddenly, he understood the nature of the test.

His hands started shaking when they realized what he was about to do. He adjusted his grip on his sword then drew the blade back over his shoulder, whispering, "Forgive me."

And then he struck.

Not at the creature, but at his mother. His sword met her neck, severing it with little resistance. Aram screamed as he saw her head come away, her body toppling to the ground.

"Aram!"

He moaned at the feeling of someone striking his face over and over. "Aram! Wake up!"

He opened his eyes with a cry, scrambling for his sword.

But it wasn't there. He was lying flat on his back in front of the Portal Stone, staring up into Esmir's whiskered face, which was grave with apprehension. His breath came in gasps and his heart pounded furiously against the walls of his rib cage. He sat bolt upright and bent forward, hugging himself.

"Is it real?" Aram demanded. "Did I kill her?"

Esmir sank down to his haunches with a troubled look. Aram grasped him by the fabric of his sleeves, shaking him.

"Is it real? Tell me, Esmir!" Tears drained like lifeblood down his face. "Tell me I didn't kill her!"

The old Warden shook his head, his mouth open, his eyes wide and moist. "I don't know."

Aram let out a strangled sob, all of the strength draining from him. "You *don't know?* How don't you know?"

Esmir glanced down, and he seemed to be trying to compose himself as Aram clung onto him, his hands shaking.

"I don't know," Esmir repeated. "Some believe it's real. Some don't. What do you believe? Do you think it was real?"

Aram thought of how his mother had begged him to surrender. He couldn't dismiss the possibility entirely but, deep down, he did not believe his real mother would have done that. She had always been overprotective. But she had raised him with the right values, and running from duty was not one of them.

"No..." he whispered finally. "I don't think it was her. I hope it wasn't her..." Tightening his jaw, he looked up at Esmir and wiped his eyes.

The old man heaved a sigh and nodded, looking frail and exhausted. "We're done here today."

Over the next few days Aram had trouble sleeping, for his dreams were haunted by nightmares. Many of them were a painful rehashing of his experience in the Shadow Realm. In them, he found himself pleading with his mother for forgiveness before killing her over and over. Sometimes, it was *her* apologizing to *him,* and those nightmares were somehow worse. In other dreams, it wasn't his mother he pleaded with—it was the void dragon. And in those dreams, the dragon answered his pleas of forgiveness with projected feelings of understanding and compassion.

When he awoke each morning with a gasp, it wasn't his mother's image that lingered in his mind. It was a dragon's golden eyes, noble and compassionate, and yet full of weariness and pain. And every day, Aram awoke with a growing certainty that, unlike the visions of his mother, his dragon-dreams were true.

By the end of the week, he was convinced that somewhere, deep down in the darkest reaches of the abyss, Daymar Torian's dragon was somehow still alive.

And it needed him desperately.

Esmir adjusted his tunic nervously, running his hands over the fabric to smooth out the age-old wrinkles. He turned his attention to his hair and gave it a good finger-combing then berated himself for not spending more time on his appearance before reporting to the Council chamber.

But it didn't matter, for the door was already opening.

Leaning heavily on his cane, he limped into the room in a lurching stride. Many of the faces before him held irritated expressions, while others frowned in outright disdain. He glared right back at them. Once, he had welcomed their scorn, considering it a fitting punishment. But now all their resentment did was get in the way, and he didn't have time for it.

Luvana greeted him with a smile that was patient, but far from warm. He walked around the fire to take his rightful position at her side, a place he hadn't occupied in centuries, then glanced around at the dozens of disapproving faces, returning their glares in kind.

"Why, Esmir, so good to see you."

Esmir fought the contempt off his face, beating it down beneath his skin. "I came to beg a boon."

Luvana's eyebrows arched upward. "A boon? Truly?"

"Yes, Luvana. A boon." His eyes scanned the people seated around them. "I need time. *Aram* needs time. I need at least six months—"

"Six *months?*" Luvana's gaze flicked from Esmir to Vandra. "I thought you said the boy was ready now?"

Vandra started to reply, but Esmir spoke over her. "When Aram first came to us, you told me not to make the same mistake with him as I did with Daymar. I was rash and imprudent, and I led Daymar to his grave. But now you're asking me to do exactly that with Aram! This boy has an incredible Gift. But he is still just a boy."

"He is not a boy." Vandra rose from her seat on the floor, addressing Luvana with a stern face. "Aram is a young man. A young man who saved us when we otherwise could not be saved. He proved his fortitude—"

"*Bah!*" The word sent a spray of spittle from Esmir's lips. "He proved his *heart,* not his fortitude!" He glared back at Luvana. "Do you want him to end up like his father?"

For the first time since he'd entered the room, he saw Luvana's confidence slip.

She said carefully, "Darand Raythe wasn't a True Savant."

"No." Esmir lifted his chin. "But that's not why he failed."

He swept his gaze around the gathering and saw that all side-conversation had ceased. All eyes were upon him, and he felt assured that he finally had their attention. Every one of them had known Darand Raythe, and they would take his warning to heart.

"I beg you," he said to Luvana. "Don't condemn Aram to the fate of his father."

"Kathrax's army is advancing into the Winmarch," Vandra said. She stood and walked into the center of the ring. Standing beside the hearth, she let her gaze pass over each of the members of the Council. "We must assume their objective is the Heart of the Mother. Our scouts have reported that they've summoned more Exilari. Rumor is that Kathrax himself is on his way to lead them."

Esmir closed his eyes, tasting defeat, for that last piece of information had pounded the final nail into his argument's coffin. He sagged, bowing his head.

"Do you understand now?" asked Vandra, crouching at his side and setting a hand on his arm.

Esmir gave a defeated sigh. "That's a lot of weight to be carried on the shoulders of one young man."

"Two young men," Vandra corrected him.

A ram tossed Markus a towel then took one for himself. The bath had felt good. His muscles were tired and aching from the day's exercises, and the hot water was soothing. It had been days since he had last felt really clean, and he regretted having to put on the same dirty clothes he had taken off before he got in. He was down to one pair of trousers and a single, sleeveless vest. With the increased training regimen and all the food Esmir had been stuffing down his throat, he had grown out of every other outfit he owned. He needed to pay a visit to the tailor down in Hearth Home.

"Are you really going to wear that?" Markus asked, eyeing his ill-fitting, rumpled clothing.

Aram chuckled softly, fingering the frayed hem of his vest. "I suppose I should have found something else."

Markus threw his wet towel into the corner, where there was a pile of other towels. "You think so?"

Aram grinned. He wasn't looking forward to standing before a gathering of the entire Wing dressed in threadbare clothes, but he really didn't have a choice. It was his own fault for not telling Esmir.

They left the bath and returned to the eyrie, finding it empty.

As soon as they entered, Markus asked, "What's this?" and started across the room to where two new chests had been pushed up against the far wall. "Do you think they're meant for us?"

"I don't know," Aram said, staring thoughtfully at the polished wooden chests. "Don't open them, just in case they're not."

Markus stopped in front of the closest chest and stood contemplating it. "Well, there's two of them and two of us. Putting that together with the fact that tonight's our induction, I'd figure there's a good chance—"

"A good chance of what, Master Galliar?"

Aram flinched at the sound of Esmir's voice, and Markus froze. The old Warden limped into the room, hobbling on his cane. He cast an accusatory glance first at Aram then at Markus, lifting a bushy eyebrow.

"Nothing, Warden," Markus said, then looked over his shoulder at Aram and grinned. "Oh, hell. We're wondering what's in the chests."

"Well, then." Esmir gestured toward the chests with his cane. "Why don't you find out?"

When they both scrambled forward at once, he raised his voice and added, "The one on the right is for Markus. The one on the left is Aram's."

Aram stopped beside Markus, figuring they should take turns opening the chests. He watched over his friend's shoulder as Markus opened the heavy oak lid, exposing a large bundle wrapped in cloth. Markus folded back the white linen, revealing a gleaming cuirass made of black-enameled scales. His breath caught, and his eyes went as wide as platters.

"By the gods," Markus whispered, holding the dragon-scale cuirass up with a look of wonder. "I don't know what to say."

"'Thank you' would be nice." The old man chuckled.

"Thank you," Markus whispered, and Aram didn't think he'd ever heard words sound more sincere.

"There's more," Esmir prompted.

Turning back to the oaken chest, Markus withdrew a dragon-scale skirt made of two pieces, split for riding, that could be strapped to the cuirass. There was a pair of enameled spaulders and lacquered braces that were long enough to cover his elbows. Packed beneath all that was a padded wool gambeson and a pair of rigid leather boots. Last was a cylindrical helm with a wide nasal and cheek-guards, fitted with a short curtain of mail to protect the neck.

"For your induction, it is tradition that you come armed and armored to the occasion," Esmir explained. "Go ahead, Aram. I'm curious to see how yours fits, considering the fact that you've just about tripled in size."

Aram felt a moment of panic, for Esmir was right. He'd filled out an awful lot since Master Krommer had first taken his measurements. He moved to his own chest and folded back the cloth wrappings within, revealing a similar set of scaled armor that differed by only minor embellishments. It was lighter than it looked and lined with soft material to prevent chafing. His helm was also different from Markus's, in that it was more rounded with a narrower nose-guard.

"Thank you," he said to Esmir, staring down at the black cuirass, admiring it for the work of art that it was. "This is...too much. Far too much."

"Nonsense." The old man limped over to stand behind him. "I didn't spend all these days training you just to have you struck down by the first lout with a lucky swing. Now, turn around, let's get this on you and pray like hell it fits."

With both Esmir's and Markus's help, Aram donned his new suit of armor. There were so many straps and buckles that hooked one piece onto the other, he doubted he could have strapped it on by himself. When it was all assembled on his body, he stood with his hands out as Esmir walked slowly around him, tugging at the cuirass and slipping his fingers into the gaps to make sure there was enough clearance for him to move without restriction. At last satisfied, the Warden blew out a heavy sigh.

"I told Master Krommer to anticipate you putting on a little meat, but I never imagined you'd sprout this much muscle." He gave a slight chuckle. "Fortunately, he must have been more optimistic than I was."

They helped Markus into his armor, tightening the various buckles and straps.

"He'll still need to make final adjustments," said Esmir. "But this will do for now." He stood back with a satisfied nod. "You two almost look presentable."

Aram and Markus exchanged smiles, taking in the sight of each other in the armor of a Champion and his Warden. The sight of Markus looking so fierce and daunting in the black lacquered scale made Aram shiver, and he wondered if he looked even half as formidable in his own gear. By the look of surprised wonder in Markus's eyes, he imagined he did.

"Gentlemen."

Aram turned to find Esmir holding a long, thin bundle wrapped in scarlet silk. A tingling sensation crept up the back of Aram's neck, for he thought he already knew what it was. Esmir handed the silken bundle to Markus, who received it in both hands. He parted the folds of the wrapping to reveal a magnificent two-handed longsword with a thin crossguard and a scalloped pommel.

He held the sword up before him, his face slack with an expression of awe. The hilt had a leather grip that was bound by wire and painstakingly worked. The blade itself was contained in a leather scabbard with brass fittings. When Markus drew the weapon, Aram stood quietly admiring it. The sword had an elegant blade that shimmered like satin, wider at the hilt and tapering toward the point. It was an exquisite piece of craftsmanship.

Sheathing his sword, Markus swept Esmir into a tight hug. The old man griped and grumbled until Markus released him, but there was a light in his eyes that made Aram think he appreciated the gesture.

"Put it on!" Aram urged.

Esmir left the room as Markus strapped the sword belt around his waist. The old man returned a few moments later with another parcel in his arms. Just as he had with Markus, Esmir handed Aram his sword with both hands. For a long moment, Aram just stood there, staring down at the layers of silk wrappings, hesitant to look beneath them. It took a nod from Esmir to get his hands moving, parting the folds of silk to reveal the sword underneath.

When he saw his star-steel blade for the first time, it took Aram's breath away. The scabbard alone was a work of art, lacquered with a gradient that started out deepest red, fading to black, and embellished with a sinuous dragon painted in gold leaf. With solemn reverence, he gripped the bone hilt and drew the blade from its scabbard, holding it up to catch the light. His hand was trembling, and his vision clouded as he gazed upon the sleek curve of the blade he had helped forge. The steel glinted in the light, all the thousands of glittering layers seeming to swirl like the surface of the Wellspring. It was the most beautiful thing he had ever beheld, and it felt graceful and perfect in his hand.

Replacing the sword in its sheath, he, too, took Esmir in his arms, hugging the old Warden as tightly as he could.

"That's enough!" Esmir barked. "You have your armor and your swords. There's no damn need to make a fuss about it!"

Aram let him go then turned to Markus, moved beyond the capacity for words. Markus nodded in understanding, for his eyes, too, glimmered with emotion.

"Do our swords have names?" Aram asked.

"Your sword's name is *Hope*," Esmir informed him. He turned to Markus. "Yours is *Faith.*"

Aram gazed upon his sword without speaking, stricken by wonder. *Hope* and *Faith*. He couldn't imagine names more fitting and symbolic.

"Now, let's go!" Clapping his hands, Esmir shooed them toward the door. "If you stand there making moon-faces at each other any longer, you're going to miss your own damn induction."

Markus barked a laugh but waited for Aram to buckle on his sword belt before moving toward the door. Side-by-side, the two friends left the eyrie, Esmir hobbling in their wake. They took the stairs to the Southern Eyrie, and when they entered the enormous cavern, they found themselves emerging from the stairwell behind a crowd of people who had gathered before Vandra in the center of the great cavern.

The rest of the apprentices were already there ahead of them, standing off to one side, and Aram and Markus went to join them. The girls who had trained with them stood in one line, the boys in another. All of the other young men were giddy with excitement, for they had bound their hatchlings just that morning. They welcomed Aram and Markus with bright smiles and congratulatory slaps on the back, for they would all be inducted together during the ceremony. They had all worked many years for the right to stand here today—even Markus, if the years he had spent training with the Exilari were taken into account.

But that left Aram feeling like he didn't fit in. He had spent far less time working toward this goal than any of his peers. He greeted their smiles with self-conscious nods, hoping that they didn't feel resentful of him. He couldn't shake the feeling that he was undeserving of such an honor.

But as it turned out, he didn't have time to think much before the crowd parted and Vandra motioned them forward. The apprentices exchanged nervous glances, then made their way through the crowd, Iver and Eugan in the front, Markus and Aram bringing up the rear. When they reached the center of the circle, they arranged themselves in a line behind Vandra, joining the young women who would be inducted with them. They stood shifting and scratching nervously as they stared out at a crowd composed of over a hundred windriders and several dragons standing in the rear, observing the proceedings with aloof interest. Vandra waited until the buzz of the crowd settled and quiet descended upon the gathering. Then she spread her hands, indicating the apprentices lined up behind her.

"These young men and women have each earned a place among you," she announced. "Today, we gather to accept their pledges as they cleave themselves to us, welcoming them into our family, our arms, and our hearts." She turned to regard the young men and women behind her. "Do each of you swear to uphold our laws, our values, and each other?"

"I do," Aram said at the same time as the others.

"And, should you be called upon, will you come to the defense of all that we honor and hold dear, to fight with courage and without surrender, unto the very last of your breath?"

"I do," Aram whispered, feeling the weight of those words settle upon him.

Vandra spread her arms, smiling graciously. "Then welcome home, windriders!"

The chamber erupted in applause and shouts. Aram flushed, embarrassed, but forced himself to stand with his head held high and his back straight. His gaze fell on a black dragon in the back, and he recognized Siroth, who stood gazing upon Markus with a look of burning pride in his fierce golden eyes.

When at last the crowd quieted, Vandra announced, "Ladies and gentlemen, I present to you the new women of the fighting wing." As she listed the names of the young women, Aram stared at them in curiosity, for they were his new sisters. Though he had never trained with the older girls, many of his friends had, and he saw Corley and Iver smiling and winking at a couple of them as Vandra recited their names.

The Wingmaster continued, "And may I also present to you Kye Rennon, Iver Soren, Corley Eban, Jeran Hanmere, Eugan Remes, Markus Galliar, and Aramon Raythe."

More applause erupted, growing in crescendo as Vandra spoke, until she announced Aram's full name.

And then the applause faltered.

The clapping slowed and then finally dwindled, while some of the men and women exchanged looks of confusion.

Aram felt his cheeks heat and his brow prickle. Why had they stopped clapping? Did they know, as he did, that he didn't belong? That he hadn't worked as hard or as long as his peers, that he didn't deserve their applause? Swallowing heavily, he dropped his gaze to the ground, trying not to let the mortification he felt show on his face.

A ram barely noticed as the crowd turned and departed, filing out the door toward the hall where the Wing took their meals together. He stood blinking in confusion as his friends laughed and congratulated each other and Vandra came to shake each of their hands. When Vandra took his own hand, Aram thought her grip seemed weaker than it should, though he wasn't sure.

"Let's go change and get some food!" erupted Markus, urging him forward with a hand on his back.

Aram nodded, the smell of the banquet making his mouth water. He followed Markus back to Esmir's eyrie, where they exchanged their armor for tunics, then hurried back down to the dining hall, which was filled with cloth-covered tables arranged in long rows, with a wide space at the front where people could gather. There were tapestries on the whitewashed walls that depicted battle scenes, dragons and their riders engaged in glorious combat. The room was well-lit by foul-scented candles impaled on tall iron candlesticks. Vandra and her officers sat on a dais at the upper end of the hall, goblets and heaping plates arranged before them.

Aram sat next to Markus at the end of one of the tables, his stomach rumbling, anxious for the cupbearers to serve the wine and for the food to be brought out. As he waited, his mind worried on the problem of the applause dying at the mention of his name. He almost asked Markus what he thought was the cause, but then he decided against it. His friend would probably just tell him what he always told him whenever Aram confided his insecurities—that it was all in his mind.

But, this time, Aram didn't think it was.

When the food was brought out, each person shared a dish with the person next to them, one breaking the bread and cutting the meat for the other. The wine was soured and smacked of pitch from the barrel, and the pheasant that was brought out was so overcooked that it was nearly unrecognizable. Still, it was one of the best meals Aram had ever seen. The sweets were made with real sugar, and the spoons, cups, and salt dishes were all polished silver.

When he reached for the knife to carve the pheasant, Markus plucked it out of his hand with an amused smile, saying, "I'm going to be your Warden, remember? I'm the one who's supposed to be breaking your bread!"

Aram was startled, for he really hadn't thought about it like that. He had never imagined being put in a position to be served by another—especially not by his best friend. He hesitated, staring down at Markus's hands as he carved the pheasant, a cold feeling creeping over him. He didn't like it. He didn't want to be treated differently by him. Uncomfortable, he muttered his thanks, avoiding Markus's eyes.

As he ate, he watched the servants swarming the hall, carrying basins and ewers.

He also noticed a few of the men and women around them watching him curiously as he ate. At first, he ignored the stares, thinking it was all just him. But they persisted, until there came a point that he wondered if he wasn't doing something wrong. But Markus was tearing into his pheasant like a wolf ravaging a kill, and he wasn't getting any stares—which made Aram feel even more uncomfortable.

After the last course was served, Vandra stood and led the toast. Then, from a gallery above the dining hall, a group of minstrels started playing. Cheers went up, and people rose from their seats and rushed to the front of the hall, where there was a space cleared for dancing.

Aram watched them with unabashed curiosity. People from his village danced all the time at celebrations, but this dancing was altogether different than any he had ever seen before. Instead of everyone standing in a ring and holding hands, couples danced together in each other's arms.

His attention went to Markus, who had picked up a conversation with Kye.

"I'm still dying to know who got which egg," Markus was saying.

"I got the little green one and Corley got—"

Corley rose half out of his seat. "Wait! Let me tell it!" Leaning over the table, he spoke quickly over Kye, "So Eugan's egg hatched first and out popped the ugliest little—"

"Shut up, Corley!" Eugan cried from across the table. "There's nothing wrong with Nanneth!"

"Anyway," Corley said with an eyeroll, "out popped this little dragon still covered in membrane, and you've never seen a slimier—"

"I said shut the hell up!" Eugan slapped his hand on the table, jolting the servingware. "It's not like yours is any prettier!"

Aram looked away and caught the glances of two more men who seemed to be staring at him. Suddenly uncomfortable, he set his napkin down and leaned over, muttering to Markus, "I'm going to go find some better wine."

He took his cup and rose, wanting to get away from the stares more than anything. He glanced around, looking for a quiet place he could retreat to. His eyes fell on Calise, who sat across the room at a table of young women. Her hair was done up, which gave her a very different look than what he was used to, and he couldn't help but stare.

She glanced up from her conversation and, for a moment, their eyes met, and she smiled. Embarrassed, Aram jerked his gaze away and hastened toward one of the screens on the wall that the servants kept disappearing behind. Ducking behind the screen, he found himself in a buttery full of jugs and bottles. A startled servant holding an ewer frowned at him. He realized he probably wasn't supposed to be there and ducked back out again.

Turning, he practically ran into Markus, who took his arm with a grin.

"I saw that," he said.

"Saw what?"

"Saw her smiling at you right before you turned and ran." Markus's wide grin made Aram's face flush.

"I wasn't running."

"Yes, you were." Markus glanced back over his shoulder in the direction of Calise. "Why don't you ask her to dance?"

Aram's jaw dropped. He said in a frantic whisper, "No! I couldn't!"

"Why not?"

"Why don't *you* go ask someone?" he asked, parrying the question. "I'm going to sit down. My feet hurt from all the running I did today."

But Markus shot his hand out and caught him before Aram could move. "Oh, no, you don't! I'm not letting you off that easy. Why can't you ask her?"

Aram squirmed, floundering. "I'm just not the kind of person girls like."

"Why do you say that?"

"I don't know how to talk to girls."

Aram thought of pretty Mora Haseleu and the lanyard he had knotted for her all those years ago. Mora had been the only girl in his village who had ever said more than two words to him. The rest had either ignored him completely or scrunched their noses whenever he came near.

"You know how to talk to girls," Markus insisted. "You talk to Calise all the time!"

"That's different."

"How's it different? We're talking about the same person!"

Aram licked his lips, having to think hard about it. "Talking to her like a friend is one thing. Asking her to dance—it's not the same!"

The music had changed to a slow ballad. Not wanting to look at Markus, Aram let his gaze drift upward toward the gallery where the minstrels were playing.

Markus took him by the shoulders, forcing Aram to focus on him. "Look. There's nothing wrong with you—there never has been! And if anybody thinks there is, then there's something wrong with *them*. You're different from the rest of us, but that's your strength, don't you get it? I can't do what you do, and neither can anyone else in this room. Not even close. The only one here who looks at you and doesn't see someone extraordinary is *you*. Now stop standing here acting like a toad and go ask the girl to dance!"

"Ask *which* girl to dance?"

Aram closed his eyes.

Calise was behind him.

Her voice struck a mortal wound to his courage, and he groaned as all the blood poured from his head and pooled in his gut. His vision swam, and the world tilted dangerously. He opened his eyes to find Markus's face red and twisted from the strain of containing a fit of laughter.

Calise took hold of Aram's arm. "Who do you want to dance with? Maybe I can introduce you."

Aram threw a hard glare at Markus, then turned slowly to face his worst fear.

As he looked at Calise, all he could think of was Mora Haseleu and the humiliation he had suffered when Jory had caught him speaking with her. He'd been a bundle of nerves then, but that was nothing compared to now, and he didn't think he could stand being humiliated like that again.

Markus cleared his throat conspicuously. He patted Aram's arm then walked away, leaving him alone with a beautiful girl who surely wanted nothing to do with him.

Calise looked at him sideways and raised her eyebrows.

He was done for.

Drawing a deep breath, Aram decided then that if he ever had to mount the gallows, he would do so with a smile on his face and a spring in his step—for surely that would take far less courage than this.

"Who do you want to dance with?" Calise asked again.

There was nothing else to do, so he gave her a slight, defeated grin. "You."

To his amazement, the word came out right.

Calise blinked, a shocked look flitting across her face. "Really?"

That wasn't the reaction he'd hoped for, and he couldn't tell if her surprise was the good kind or the bad kind. But he was already committed, so he had no choice but to follow through.

He extended his hand, willing it not to tremble. "Will you dance with me?"

This time, she flashed him a smile that was genuine, even gracious, and accepted his hand. "Of course."

Hearing those glorious words made his knees nearly buckle. Dizzy, Aram led her by the hand toward the front of the room, passing rows of tables and staring eyes. He floated the whole way on a sea of bliss, though the hall around him listed like it was ready to capsize. When they arrived on the dance floor, Calise turned to face him, smiling into his eyes as he stood panicked, not knowing what to do next.

"Put your hand on my back," she whispered.

Giddy with terrified euphoria, he did as she asked, and she leaned into him, taking his other hand. The song faded from his hearing, and the entire world was reduced to the feel of her touch and the smile in her eyes.

He let her lead, following as best as he could, struggling to keep his feet moving to the tempo of the music instead of the race of his heartbeat. He stumbled once, which made her smile and laugh. For the rest of the song, all he could do was grin and blush, and by the time the music ended, he was breathless.

Seeing his condition, she giggled and asked, "Want to step out for a rest?"

He didn't remember saying yes, but suddenly she was leading him away, weaving through clumps of people toward the door to the hall. Aram shot a panicked glance at Markus, who grinned back and waved at him smugly. He followed Calise through the eyrie to its cavernous entrance and out onto the wide terrace that was usually brimming with dragons. Now it was empty, for all the dragons and their riders had gathered inside.

Still holding his hand, Calise led him almost to the edge of the cliff, where she stopped and turned away from him, looking out across the dark gorge. A slight breeze tossed the loose strands of her hair that fringed her face. She gave him a quiet smile, then inclined her head toward the looming canyon walls that soared around them taller than the sky.

"It's beautiful, isn't it?"

Yes. She was.

Calise frowned. "Is something wrong?"

Aram looked away. He didn't know how to tell her what he felt. He tried to swallow, but his throat was too dry.

"There's something I've been wanting to tell you," he finally admitted, smiling shyly.

She raised her eyebrows. "So, what's been stopping you?"

Fear was stopping him—that singular emotion he was supposed to be conquering at all cost. But one look in her eyes made him quiver with trepidation, and every ridicule he'd suffered as a child came rushing back to conquer him.

Dropping his gaze, Aram licked his lips. "I guess I'm afraid you'll laugh at me."

"Why would I laugh at you?"

"Girls always used to laugh at me."

She made a disbelieving face. "Did you ever try laughing at them?"

He stared at her, speechless, for her statement was absurd. His mind had to grapple with it for a moment before he finally realized she was joking. And it was a really funny joke, now that he thought about it.

He grinned. "No. I never laughed at them."

"Maybe you should have." Her face grew serious. "So, what is it you want to tell me? I promise I won't laugh."

He hoped with every bit of his heart she didn't. Closing his eyes, he took a deep, deep breath. "I want to tell you that…that…" He swallowed. "I really like your freckles."

Aram opened his eyes. For long moments, he stood holding her hand and quivering in fear, waiting for his hopes to be dashed.

"Thank you," Calise said simply.

She wasn't smiling anymore. He didn't understand the look on her face. He started to draw back, thinking that maybe he'd made a mistake, but she tightened her grip on him, pulling him nearer.

"What do you like about my freckles?" she asked.

"I..." Nerves made his voice tremble worse than his hands. "I like them because they're not symmetrical. I mean...I like things symmetrical, but just not you." He cringed, squeezing his eyes closed. "What I'm trying to say is, I like it that you're not symmetrical. You're unpredictable—just look at your clothes!"

Calise glanced down at herself, a look of confusion on her face. She was wearing an unbleached linen skirt with a leather riding shirt. He loved the way her clothes were always mismatched, as though she purposefully mixed the pieces of different outfits for a variety.

"Every time I think I know you, I find out I don't," he admitted. "And that's what makes you beautiful. Your freckles just show on the outside what you're like on the inside. That's why I like them," he finished lamely, glancing down.

Calise stood for a long moment without saying anything. Then she raised her hand to his face and, leaning forward, pressed her lips gently against his. Aram's stomach plunged, and his blood burned in his veins. He wrapped his arms around her and returned the kiss softly. When they parted, he stood in a trembling daze, his breath coming in soft gasps.

Gathering him close, she kissed him again then simply laid her head on his shoulder. He stood with his arms around her, his cheek pressed against her hair, rocking her softly and staring out across the shadows of the canyon. He held her that way as the breeze moved past them and the mist drew close overhead. Long moments passed timelessly, and yet they still weren't long enough.

"Let's go dance some more," she whispered.

Holding her hand, Aram led her back off the terrace and into the warmth of the eyrie. As they crossed the wide-open space in the center of the cavern, he could see the forms of the dragons resting in their alcoves, and he got the strongest impression that they approved.

He walked with her back to the dining hall, pulled by the soft strains of music and the promise of another dance. He moved in a blissful daze, weaving through the press of bodies, feeling her soft fingers stroking his.

Walking around one of the tables, he felt a tap on his shoulder and halted, looking back.

A tall, middle-aged man had risen behind him and stood offering him his hand. Aram accepted the handshake automatically, frowning in confusion. He had never seen this man before, although he wore the armor of the fighting Wing. His hair was thin and starting to gray, and there was a long scar slanting across his face.

"Corin Bandor," the man introduced himself, his grip firm. "I wanted to congratulate you. I'm sorry, but I never knew your family name before it was announced tonight. Are you any relation to Darand Raythe?"

Aram stiffened, his hand slipping from the man's grasp. His gaze fixed on Bandor's face, his confusion rampant.

He said warily, "Darand Raythe was my father."

The man gave him a warm but sympathetic smile. "I'm sorry. I didn't know, or I would have introduced myself sooner. Your father was my friend, the finest man I ever knew. You have my sincere condolences."

Aram's breath caught, his chest tightening. "You knew my father?"

The man nodded with a frown of confusion. "Of course. Everyone did."

Dazed, Aram's gaze drifted away from Bandor, coming to rest on Eraine Vandra, who stood behind them looking on, her face slack with dismay. When their eyes met, Aram's throat constricted with emotion.

Vandra ducked her head, her eyes filled with regret.

73

Aram sat on his straw pallet in Esmir's quarters, knees drawn up to his chest, a bit of twine in his hand that he was knotting and unknotting with rapid, brisk motions. He'd cast aside his rough wool blanket, even though Esmir insisted he sleep with it every night. To Aram, the wool felt painful against his skin, but he usually forced himself to endure it. Tonight, he just didn't want to deal with it, so he shivered instead. It was hard to tell if the shivering was more from the cold or from the emotions chilling his insides. He had always heard that anger burned hot in a person's blood, but the anger he felt was more like ice.

He heard a low growl coming from the other side of the chamber. Ever since Markus had taken Siroth into the eyrie, he had moved his pallet to the other alcove and slept next to his dragon. They were there now, settling in for sleep. Markus had graciously left him alone with his thoughts and his resentments. Aram appreciated that, knowing he wouldn't make for good company. Even Esmir had made himself scarce, which was a good thing. Aram didn't want to speak with him yet.

The door to the hallway opened. Aram looked up to see Vandra entering the dim cave—the last person in the world he wanted to see. He could tell by the look on her face that she regretted her part in keeping knowledge of his father's death from him, and yet Aram knew he wouldn't be able to forgive her easily. His father's disappearance had haunted him all his life and had been the source of much of his self-doubt. Knowing anything about his father—*anything*—could have made a world of difference. But the people who had the power to set his mind at ease had made a decision not to.

That hurt. It hurt terribly.

He looked up at Vandra with an accusing glare. Silently, she moved into the room and sat down on the floor next to him. For a moment, she just sat there, hunched over and staring downward at the ground, her dark hair dripping into her face in greasy ropes. Aram didn't try to keep his resentment off his face, instead letting it burn in his eyes, hoping it scorched her. He had placed his trust in this woman, and what he felt was the pain of betrayal.

"Why didn't you tell me?" he asked at length.

With a heavy sigh, Vandra looked up at him. "When you first came to us, we were all very worried about you. You'd already endured more suffering than most people will know in a lifetime. We wanted to give you time to mend. And then, after that..." She shrugged. "We wanted to give you the best chance we could to pass the Trials. We feared that hearing your father's story might strike a blow to your confidence. We didn't want it to be a fatal blow."

A lot of what she said made sense, but it fell far short of justifying their actions. He said in a low growl, *"I needed to know."*

Vandra nodded, then sat for a time in silence. At length, she whispered, "How much do you know about your father?"

"Not much. I guess he never spoke about his past. My mother thought he may have been some kind of soldier, but he never would admit it. He was always going into town for business. And then, one day, he just didn't come back. They did a search, but they never found his body. Everyone thought he'd run away and left us."

"No. He didn't run away." Vandra blew out a long sigh, tossing her hair back from her face. She rose, pushing herself to her feet. "Let me just pour something to drink."

She stood and walked to the table where Esmir his supply of liquor. Vandra picked up the first jug and took a sniff, crinkling her nose before sealing it again. She reached for the orange-glazed jug next to it. From it, Vandra poured two cups, handing one to Aram before settling back down in front of him.

"Your father was born here. In Skyhome," she said. "He was Wingmaster of the Southern Eyrie long before me. He had this magnificent dragon named Maranth, the biggest dragon I've ever seen. Darand was different, just like you. He wasn't a Savant, but he was very Gifted, more so than any of us since Torian."

She took a sip of her liquor, making a face. "At the time, Kathrax was just starting to assert his power again after hundreds of years of quiet. He'd somehow managed to tame therlings and void walkers to flesh out his ranks. We were at an extreme disadvantage; we didn't have a Champion that could oppose an Archon, and we didn't have much of a chance without one. Your father was the closest thing we had to a True Savant. He could see the strands in detail and was a natural at manipulating them. He wasn't like you, though—he couldn't see them in color. And, just like all Auld mages, he could only use his Gift in the defense of others."

Aram sat staring into his cup as he listened, unable to bring himself to taste it, and unable to bring himself to look at Vandra. As she spoke, emotion curled around Aram's throat like a strangling snake, slowly constricting.

"We needed a Champion," Vandra continued, "and Darand was agreeable. So the Council decided that he should be trained."

"But why would they let him train, if he wasn't a Savant?" Aram's voice seethed with resentment and grief.

"True Savants have always been exceedingly rare, and not every Champion was one. Your father was very Gifted, which should have been enough. Luvana was assigned to be his mentor—"

"Luvana?" Aram interrupted. "Why not Esmir?"

"Esmir fell out of the Council's good graces a long time ago. It was thought that Luvana could do a better job. But they were wrong." Vandra spread her hands. "She did her best. Darand was as prepared as she could make him. He was already the best warrior I ever knew, and he always gave everything of himself. But there was one thing he needed that Luvana couldn't give him: a mentor who truly understood and appreciated the particular needs of a Gifted mind."

"He needed Esmir," Aram guessed softly.

Vandra nodded. "He did. Esmir spent centuries with Torian. He knows more than anyone what it means to be truly Gifted, but no one thought about that. So, when it came time for your father's Trials, he was lacking in some important ways."

"So he failed," Aram summarized, his voice ragged.

"Yes." Vandra took a gulp of her drink. "He failed. And it broke him."

Aram squeezed his eyes shut, the resentment within him gathering like a great, darkening storm. Luvana and the Council had abused his father badly. And then they'd kept their silence about it, a crime nearly as bad.

Vandra heaved a sigh. "Darand returned to us from the Portal Stones, but he wasn't the same man. He barely spoke and never left his room. Even his dragon could not console him. Then, one night, Luvana caught him in the act of throwing himself off the cliff. She wasn't in time to stop him, so she did the only thing she could think of: she wove a rupture beneath him, and he fell through it. It was the last we saw of him for a very long time."

Aram lifted his cup to his lips, taking a heavy drink. He grimaced from the bite of the liquor. It wasn't wine, but something far more powerful, and he was grateful for it.

Vandra glanced at him through snarls of hair. "About twelve years ago, your father returned to us. He wouldn't speak of where he'd been, but he was renewed, mended. Somewhere along the way, he'd found a new reason to live." Vandra gave a sad smile. "Looking back on it, my guess is that reason was you."

Aram ducked his head. Hearing Vandra say that made him feel worse instead of better. If he had truly meant so much to his father, then why hadn't he stayed?

Vandra said, "Things had gotten bad here during the time Darand was gone. Kathrax had invaded the Greenwood and our forces were losing."

She paused and sipped her drink. "I guess word of our losses had reached the other side of the Veil. Darand said that a bard had come to the village where he'd been living and shared the news. He came back to see for himself how bad it was.

"As you can imagine, we were all very shocked to see him not just alive, but *sane*. Luvana begged him to lead the Wing just one last time. He disappeared again, and we thought he'd fled. But then Darand returned and took up his star-steel blade. He mounted Maranth and led the offensive to take back the Greenwood."

Vandra looked at him with eyes moist and intense with remorse. "I've never been prouder to fly with a man. Darand Raythe wasn't a Champion, but he was *our* champion. He left behind the life that had made him whole again and returned to lead our Wing."

She bowed her head, taking a deep, shuddering breath. "Kathrax himself joined the battle. I'm guessing he recognized your father's power and perceived him as enough of a threat to challenge him personally. Darand couldn't defend himself, not with his Gift still locked. Against an Archon, he never stood a chance."

She drained the last of her drink, tilting her head back. "But what he did accomplish was distract the enemy long enough for the rest of us to retreat and reestablish our line. We lost the Greenwood, but without Darand, we would have lost the entire Wing. And we halted their advance." She looked at Aram with blazing eyes. "Your father was, in every sense, a champion. Never doubt that."

Aram stared at the floor, mired in grief and anger and a dozen other tangled emotions that his mind couldn't separate. His cup trembled in his hand, and it was all he could do to hold back the tears that wanted to come. It was a long time before he trusted his voice enough to speak.

"Thank you for telling me."

Vandra rose and set her empty cup back on the table. "I should have told you sooner. I regret that now. I know it's a lot for you. We'll push your Trials back—"

"No." Aram's opal eyes narrowed, burning with anger. "This doesn't change anything."

For a moment, Vandra looked like she wanted to protest. She stared hard into Aram's face as though searching for something. At last, she nodded.

"Were you his friend?" Aram asked.

"Yes."

Hearing that, his resentment lessened ever so slightly. "What was he like?"

Vandra gave him a small, reassuring smile. "He was a very brave man. A very *kind* man." Her gaze drifted to the side. "And a very wise one."

Aram nodded, his gaze faltering. "Thank you."

Vandra turned and left. When the door closed behind her, Aram sat for a while in silence, finishing the rest of his drink as the coals in the hearth slowly faded to gray. He thought on Vandra's words with a heavy sadness in his heart, but also with relief. For the first time in his life, he knew—really *knew*—that his father hadn't abandoned his mother because of him.

He was still awake when Esmir returned. When the old man's eyes fell on him sitting in the shadows, he frowned deeply. He, too, had kept his silence, and Aram begrudged him that. Esmir hesitated, looking as though he wanted to say something, but he didn't. Aram peered up at him, wanting to ask a hundred questions. But in the end, there was really only one that mattered.

"Do you think I'm ready?" he asked.

"Maybe."

Aram appreciated Esmir's honesty. Without responding, he stood and picked up his pallet. He carried it to the partition that enclosed the alcove where Siroth and Markus now made their home. The two were sleeping when he entered, though when he spread his pallet out next to them, Siroth opened a great golden eye and gave a low rumble of understanding.

Aram lay down and closed his eyes, listening to the sounds of Markus's snoring and warmed by the heat of Siroth's inner furnace. Still, it was a long time before he could sleep. His thoughts were of his father, but also of the abyss at the bottom of the gorge.

Somewhere down there was the void dragon, and Aram's soul yearned for him.

If it hadn't been for Siroth's comforting presence, Aram doubted he would have slept at all.

When he woke, he felt a little better. What Vandra had said about his father had given him a reason to be cautiously optimistic. While the consequences of failure now seemed much more personal, Aram also recognized that he had two great advantages over his father: he could see the world in color and, also, he had Esmir. He wasn't sure which gave him the greater edge, but both gave him hope.

Aram rose, drawn by the sound and smell of meat sizzling over a fire. He was alone in Markus's alcove. Siroth had gone out to sun on the terrace, and Markus's pallet was empty. He rolled over and stretched, his head aching from lack of sleep.

It was the day of the Trials, the day he had been dreading for over a year. It might be the last day of his sanity or even the last day of his life. Both were real possibilities. But what *was* certain was that this was the last day of his childhood, and that scared him more than anything.

Rising, he slid back the partition and found Esmir attending an iron skillet. Markus knelt next to him, stirring something in a wooden bowl. More bowls and plates were arrayed around them, and for a moment, Aram wondered if they were making a feast.

He moved toward them blearily, rubbing the sleep from his eyes, and stood appraising the spread of food laid out before him, his mouth already watering. There was pork belly and eggs, aged cheese and fresh-baked bread, along with a bowl of fruit that looked ripe.

"You made my favorite breakfast," he said, kneeling on the rug next to Markus.

"You need all the strength you can get." Esmir bent forward to flip a sausage in the pan, but it got away from him and fell into the fire. He looked like he wanted to grumble, but he didn't. Instead, he smiled, which was completely out of character.

Aram frowned, suspicious. Esmir was too cantankerous to let something like losing a sausage go unremarked. He must be a lot more nervous than he looked. Aram accepted a plate from Markus and nodded his thanks.

The breakfast was everything he could have hoped for; it was the conversation that was lacking. The few words that were exchanged between the three of them were awkwardly positive and punctuated by long gaps of silence. By the time the meal was finished, Aram was ready for it to end. Both Esmir and Markus had done their best to set him at ease, and he appreciated their efforts, but for some reason, their forced positivity made him feel worse.

He stood and started toward where his clothes hung from a peg, but Esmir caught his arm. "You will need something different today."

He stood and handed Aram a folded outfit. It was a plain gray cloak with a matching tunic, and Aram recognized it immediately. It was the same outfit the Overseers had clothed him in the first time he had entered the Shadow Realm, the only thing they had ever given him that he'd been allowed to keep. The garments were torn and blackened, and in some places stained brown with his own blood. Aram glanced a question at Esmir, wondering why the old man had saved them.

"It's tradition," Esmir said. "You are to wear this when you go in. If you pass the Trials, then you will emerge with this clothing remade. Just as you will be."

Aram donned the scorched outfit with an intense feeling of foreboding. There was something about wearing the ruined garments that made him feel like he was already defeated. He shivered, hoping that feeling was not a premonition of what was to come. But he managed a weak smile, turning to Markus and spreading his arms.

"How do I look?"

Markus made a valiant attempt to grin in return. "Absolutely dashing."

"All right, you two lovebirds," Esmir grumbled. "You can fawn over each other later. People are waiting!"

Aram winced. "People?"

"You didn't think this was going to be a private affair, did you?"

Aram hadn't given it a thought, for he had always entered the portal alone—and naked. The thought of others watching him strip...

"Oh, no—I can't—"

This time, Esmir laughed. "Don't worry. You get to keep those on. After all, they did give them to you."

That was true. Aram breathed a heavy sigh of relief. "All right, then. I'm ready."

As they walked toward the door, Siroth let out a soft growl that Aram couldn't interpret, for the images it provoked were conflicting. He glanced at Markus, wondering if his friend had a better idea of what the dragon was trying to tell him.

"He has hope for you, but he also fears for you," Markus said, his eyes sad and distant.

Aram appreciated the dragon's sentiment, for it was honest, and it echoed his own feelings. They left the eyrie and started down the hallway, Aram walking with Markus and Esmir at his sides. He held Esmir's arm and helped him mount the steps, concerned that the old man seemed frailer than he ever had before.

When they arrived at the top of the bluffs, Aram halted, staring across the Henge in shock.

Everyone in the world who mattered to him was standing at the top of the stairs, forming a path consisting of two lines of people between the stairs and the stones of the first portal.

He hadn't expected that.

Aram lingered a moment, overwhelmed by emotion, taking in the familiar faces arrayed before him. There were his friends from his dorm:

Corley, Eugan, Jeran, Kye...only Iver was missing. There were also the novices he had trained with for a short while, all staring at him with solemn faces. Many of the windriders were there as well, all dressed in the armor of the fighting Wing. Aram didn't understand why they were there, then realized that many of these men and women probably had been friends of his father. At the end of the line, nearest the first portal, stood Vandra and Luvana, Vandra in her typical leathers, Luvana in long, silken robes.

Licking his lips, Aram started forward, nodding his gratitude at the people who had come to support him. As he moved past Eugan, the young man caught his arm.

"Iver couldn't be here," Eugan said. "He couldn't... But he wanted me to wish you luck."

Aram smiled his understanding. "Tell Iver I said thanks."

When he at last arrived before Vandra and Luvana, he shook Vandra's hand then caught Luvana's gaze and held it defiantly. He wanted her to see the anger in his face, and he glared at her until she looked away.

As he paused in front of the stone archway, the witnesses spread out, positioning themselves among the outer ring of stones. Only Markus and Esmir remained with him in the center of the Henge.

"Good luck," Markus said, holding out his hand. But when Aram went to take it, Markus hugged him instead, whispering, "You'll do fine."

Aram pulled back but held onto his shoulder. "I wish I could have you in there with me."

Markus smiled. "I'll be here when you come out."

Esmir stepped in front of him. "Each portal you return from will unlock the next, but it will only remain unlocked for a short while. You won't be able to stop and rest going from one to the next."

Aram nodded. When Esmir stepped aside without saying goodbye, he almost felt grateful. He started toward the portal but then paused when he heard someone say his name.

Turning, he saw Calise hurrying toward them across the sand. Seeing her brought a smile to his face, and he walked to meet her halfway. He stopped in front of her and took her hands. A silent moment passed between them in which everything that needed to be spoken was said.

Suddenly remembering the woven necklace he wore, Aram reached up and touched it. He'd almost worn it in there again, and only the sight of Calise had made him think about it at all. A shiver passed over him, and with a wash of intense relief, he removed it and pressed the heart knot into her hand.

"Would you hold onto this for me?" he asked.

Staring down at the necklace, Calise nodded, her eyes growing moist.

"Thank you," he whispered. Then with a last, apologetic smile, he turned and made his way toward the portal.

The world obscured and faded to murk.

Aram still stood within the ring of standing stones, though now the Henge was empty of other people and suffused with a dim, surreal twilight. A putrid glow emanated from every direction at once, and the craggy faces of the monoliths glowed of their own accord with an odd, vacillating light that made them writhe like tormented things.

Glancing down, Aram saw that he was no longer clothed in the ruined tunic and cloak. Instead, the Overseers had seen fit to supply him with his own dragon-scale armor and his star-steel blade. The elegant sword hung suspended in its lacquered scabbard from his belt, along with a matching dagger he had never seen before.

Curious, Aram drew the sword and was surprised to see that the blade glowed with an ethereal blue light that rippled like ribbons of blue flame. At first, he didn't understand what that flame was or what it meant, and it took a while for its implications to sink in.

For this Trial, his Gift had been unlocked, and his blade burned with the fierce power of the magic within him. The Overseers had supplied him with the best of everything he could possibly need: his own weapon, his own armor, even his own magic. Apparently, they thought he would be needing it all.

It was a harrowing thought.

Glancing around, Aram paced warily toward the center of the circle. There was something about the muted light that reminded him of the first time he had entered the Shadow Realm, when the Overseer had attacked him and set him on fire. That time, the Henge had been filled with the same nondirectional light that came from everywhere and cast no shadow.

But this time, the Overseers were nowhere to be seen. The stillness stretched, and the longer it did, the more anxious he became. It was the anticipation that was disarming, for he couldn't help but wonder what kind of foe would require all of his weapons and the sum of his magic to defeat.

When the attack finally came, it was without warning.

A humanoid shadow appeared in front of him, wielding two thin swords: one longer, the other shorter. It did not pause a second before attacking, coming at him with both swords at once. Aram parried the longsword and dodged the shorter blade, twisting back. But the shadow-creature didn't give him a chance to recover. It came at him like a thousand knives tumbling toward him all at once. This time, he didn't try to block, but retreated across the circle of the Henge, backing away as fast as he could.

His shadowy opponent was too skilled. Even if it had possessed only one blade, he would have been hard-pressed to defend himself. With two blades, this foe was unstoppable. Aram realized why the Overseers had unlocked his Gift for this test. Martial skill alone wouldn't be enough to defeat this adversary.

He reached out with his mind, seeking the colorful strands of aether that made up even this shadowy world. They were all there, strung out before him like the fibers of a loom, waiting for his mind to start weaving. He grasped a handful of strands and started binding, spinning them instantly into a net that he threw over his adversary, hoping to at least slow it down.

But his opponent merely cut the net to shreds with its sharp blades and set upon him with renewed determination.

Backing away, Aram reached for the dagger at his waist, drawing it just in time to block the long sword even as the shorter blade sliced at his throat. He danced backward, yielding more ground, using both dagger and sword together at once.

Attacking with the sword and defending with the dagger, he unleashed a crisp sequence of attacks that his foe evaded effortlessly. The dagger was no match for the short sword, just as he was no match for his inhuman opponent.

In the end, he wasn't going to win.

Desperate, Aram reached again for the colors of the world and started weaving an elaborate braid. He tied it off then lashed out with it like a whip. The air between them erupted in an explosion of light and roiling flame.

His adversary merely absorbed the flames, sucking them right out of the air. Then it pressed forward with its twirling blades, and it was all Aram could do to move fast enough to dodge and deflect the attacks.

He couldn't evade them all. He felt the bite of the short sword slice through his armor and score a deep cut in his side.

Aram didn't have time to react to the injury. The blades coming at him were relentless, and he couldn't keep up with them. He realized there was no way he could win this fight. He hadn't once even grazed his opponent, and now he doubted that he even could, for how does one cut a shadow? The Overseers had given him every weapon in his arsenal to defeat this foe, and yet none of them worked.

Which meant weapons weren't the answer.

Retreating, Aram considered the sickening twilight around him that came from everywhere at once. All it took was one glance at his opponent to make him understand that it was the light he fought in this place, not the shadow. It was the magical energy of this plane that was his true enemy.

Reaching out with his mind, he grasped at the strands of aether that made up this world and started ripping them apart. There was a terrible shriek that echoed from every direction as his enemy reacted to his attack.

The shadow-man started forward to press its assault, but then it wavered, its twin blades faltering. Aram didn't hesitate, but ripped and tore the energy right out of the world. Gradually, the light around him faded like the horizon after sunset, until a starless midnight fell upon them.

With a ghostly moan, his shadowy opponent disappeared, swallowed by the darkness. Aram dropped his sword and clutched his side, which stabbed him with fire. He stood for a moment panting, glancing around at the lightless world he had created.

Then the ground beneath him heaved, and he was wrenched somewhere else.

Aram staggered out of the portal, his side pulsing with heat. His sword and armor were gone, but somehow he retained the dagger. The cut his opponent had given him slicked his hand with syrupy blood.

He glanced up as Markus and Esmir rushed toward him. Markus caught hold of him, and Esmir bent to press wadded bandages against his wound.

"I'm fine," Aram said, gritting his teeth. "It's not that deep."

"The hell it is," snapped Markus. He glanced worriedly at Esmir. "Do we have time to bind it?"

Retracting the blood-saturated cloth, Esmir shook his head. "He's got to go."

"Wait—"

Ignoring Markus, Aram sprinted across the Henge toward the second portal and dove through the opening.

He stood on a hill above a battlefield.

The rage of battle and the screams of men clawed toward him through the air. Below, the soldiers of three armies were engaged in melee, while hundreds of unarmed civilians looked on in terror, their fates to be determined by the outcome of the fight.

Looking down at himself, Aram saw that he was robed in a golden tabard and mantle. In his hand was a recurve bow that gleamed with the silver aura of an untainted soul. He didn't know how he knew that, only that he did. Below, the army of Nimarae was being swallowed by the combined forces of Sor and Demalkia. The knowledge came to him with a wash of dizziness, and he wavered for a moment, bringing a hand up to steady himself. He had no idea why he was here or what he was supposed to be doing. All he knew was that something inside him was unlocking, opening wide like a vault, and information he had never known was being revealed to him...though it felt more like he was remembering something long forgotten.

He started to turn but winced as the motion brought a sharp stab of pain. Looking down, he saw blood spreading across his golden tabard from a deep injury he barely remembered receiving. Aram cursed. He had no time to have the wound tended. People he loved were dying.

Down below on the field, the battle he was commanding had taken a turn for the worse. The ranks of defenders were collapsing, an entire wing of his army caught in a pincer between two larger forces. Even more heartbreaking was the plight of the civilians they fought to protect: refugees from the fallen city of Tel Aru who had traveled a dozen days to reach the fortress of Eld Atai, only to die in sight of it.

He didn't have the resources to protect both the civilians and the fortress.

Now he found himself in the dreadful position of having to decide which to sacrifice.

Walking to the very edge of the cliff, he looked out upon the flagging battle below. He could smell the blood from where he stood; the field was flooded with it. Dark clouds of birds circled the skies, landing in droves on the piles of bodies still moving with wounded. Horns sounded and dark smoke clotted the air, and still the killing continued.

An explosion near the refugees threw up a large cloud of dust, raining bodies and debris across the field. Screams erupted from the column of civilians and part of the Nimaraean line collapsed in disorganized chaos. There was another explosion, followed by another. His gaze scoured the battlefield, trying to determine the source of the attacks.

And then he saw it: across the field, one of the Disavowed sat upon a white horse, encased by soldiers of his personal guard. The Archon flung his hands out, and yet another explosion tore deep into the Nimaraean ranks, hurling soldiers into the air and rending flesh.

Aram clenched his jaw and tried to concentrate, but the pain in his side throbbed worse with every heartbeat. His tabard was wet with blood.

Sweat rained from his brow as frustration got the better of him. He would have to make a decision. The civilians down there were his own people, but the fortress was a strategic position they couldn't afford to yield.

"Father Ahn, forgive me," he muttered then turned to his general. "Order a retreat. Fall back to the fortress."

"But, Lord! The civilians!"

"The fortress has to be our priority." He squeezed his eyes closed, feeling the weight of the decision crush his heart.

"Lord! Please!"

"You've heard my command," he snapped, knowing that he had condemned the civilians to death...along with his own soul. He stood bleeding as the order was relayed to the drummers who thundered the death-knell of the people of Tel Aru across the battlefield.

The hill beneath him jolted.

He staggered and almost lost his footing. The ground lurched again, knocking him off his feet.

Aram spilled out of the portal, collapsing to his hands and knees in the sand. He quickly pushed himself up but staggered, weak and disoriented and drunk on self-loathing.

What had just happened? Had that been real? Had his word just condemned hundreds of people to death?

Seeing Markus rushing toward him, he raised his hands to fend him off. Both of his hands were now slick with blood, his clothing saturated with it. He had no idea what had just happened in the portal, and he didn't have time to come to terms with it. He was already weak from blood loss, and he still had two tests left to go.

Backing away from Markus, he turned and jogged toward the third set of Portal Stones.

Aram squatted in the darkness. Casting his hands out, he felt cold walls around him, close on either side. The feel of them brought a shiver of fear rushing up his spine toward his neck. Hands groping, he pushed himself upright.

He heard the sound of a latch, and a door opened.

A wash of torchlight spread over him, illuminating the close space he was in. When he recognized where he was, cold panic nearly ripped his mind from him.

He was back in the essence cellars.

A scream tore from his throat as a human-shaped silhouette reached in and grabbed his arm, jerking him forward. He struggled and fought, but his body was weak with emaciation and blood loss, and there was little he could do. His fists beat pathetically against an iron cuirass, succeeding only in producing a dull clanking noise. Desperate, he reached out for the strands of aether—

But he couldn't touch the aether, not to save his own life. There was nothing he could do but flail and scream as he was lifted and carried to the extraction chamber. As they buckled the leather straps about his arms, legs, and torso, he sobbed in anticipation of the agony.

Oh, gods, please…let this not be real.

Let this be a hallucination…

In the end, it didn't matter.

The pain came immediately. He arched his back, jerking against his bonds and screaming until his throat burned raw. The pain intensified, relentless and merciless. His fingernails bit the palms of his hands and his toes curled, but still the pain clenched him and wouldn't let him go. His skin burned and cracked and the fat beneath it sizzled. Acid melted his insides to jelly, and dull spikes drove all the way to the center of his brain. He begged the gods for the pain to stop, for his heart to stop, for his mind to shatter.

Anything, he didn't care.

Anything to take away the agony.

At last, hours later, the pain subsided.

Hands were upon him, tightening the buckles of his restraints.

"Welcome home," said a voice he recognized. It was one of the Extractors, an older man who had been present at almost every one of his sessions and seemed to take great pleasure in watching him scream.

"*Please…*" he wheezed, his voice raw from screaming. "No more…*No more! I can't stand it…*" His voice collapsed into choking sobs.

CONCEDE.

The words rocked his mind with all the fury and thunder of an avalanche.

Oh, gods, that was them. That was the Overseers, giving him a choice. Giving him a chance. All he had to do was concede and the pain would stop. It would all go away. He would either die or go insane, but either would be better than this. So much better.

The Extractor raised a glowing-hot poker, leveling it at Aram's right eye.

"*I…*" His throat clenched.

He let out a strangled sob.

"No," he croaked. "I won't concede. I won't… oh, dear gods…"

He screamed as the poker drove toward his face.

Aram opened his eyes, shocked that he still *had* eyes.

He lay on his belly in front of the third portal. Tears drenched his face and dark blood coated his skin. He was shaking so hard, he could barely get his hands under him to turn himself over.

He heard footsteps running toward him.

People surrounded him, helping him upright.

He looked up, startled, into Markus's face, and shook his head wordlessly.

"That's enough," Markus gasped, catching him up in a strangling embrace. "You gave it your all, but you don't have any more to give. You did your best."

"No," Aram wheezed, shuddering. "I'm not done."

Markus drew back, clutching him by the shoulders. He glanced behind him. "Esmir, help me get him up."

"No." Aram pushed himself to his feet and took a staggering step backward.

Fear on his face, Markus reached for him, but Aram shook his head.

"I have to do this. I have to."

Markus stood unmoving, his face contorted with grief. At length, he issued a slight nod, and Aram knew he understood. Then he turned away and, with the leaden steps of a condemned man, walked toward the fourth portal.

He stood on a cliff above a vast expanse of forest.

At first, he thought it was the Eldenwood, but then he realized that it couldn't be. This woodland was still alive and vibrant, and he could feel the health of the land below him. A calm layer of mist clung to the air above the forest, spreading over the trees like a soothing blanket. Rolling mountains were painted in pastel against the horizon, the sight of them almost lost to the haze of distance.

Somewhere down in that forest was a Wellspring. Aram could sense it, even from far away. The entire forest was suffused with the Wellspring's essence. Or perhaps the entire forest was itself the Wellspring.

He saw that he was clothed once again in the charred and tattered robes the Overseers had given him. Only a common, dulled practice blade hung at his side. It was as Esmir had warned him: in this last portal, everything he needed would be taken from him.

Including his lifeblood. He was exhausted and trembling, his body cold, his pulse weak and racing. If he didn't pass this final test quickly, he wouldn't be leaving the portal.

A murderous growl made him turn.

Behind him crouched a magnificent black dragon, bigger even than Siroth, with fearsome horns and fangs the length of daggers. Its wings were mantled, and the air in front of the dragon roiled with the heat of its breath. The ground around it shimmered, as though the dragon stood in the midst of a mirage. It was either injured or defending something—or both; he couldn't tell. Its attention was not on him.

Aram followed its gaze.

He stood beside a narrow cleft in the earth. The rock around it was charred and battle-scarred. Red magma bled from the fissure, as though it were a wound sliced into the hide Hyatt of the world, from which hot giant's blood gushed. Aram could feel the heat of it on his face, the kind of heat that radiated from Onsel's forge. The wound in the earth looked recent, the product of whatever events were taking place around him.

He was in a precarious situation, caught between the dragon's scorching breath and the smoldering scar in the ground.

He heard a groan.

The dragon had shifted enough for Aram to see what it was guarding. A man lay in the shadow of its wings, by all appearances gravely injured. He wore a dark cuirass of dragon-scale armor, and at his side was a blade that glowed dimly blue. A star-steel blade, just like his own.

Aram stood there for a minute, taking in the scene through the fog of blood loss, letting it slowly penetrate. A black dragon. A wide forest, and an injured man who was almost a Champion.

"Da..." he whispered.

The dragon must be Maranth. Heart thrumming, Aram took a step toward it, but was halted by a threatening growl. In Maranth's eyes was none of the intelligence and wisdom he was used to seeing in a dragon's golden gaze. Instead, there was only a feral anger and anguish that recognized no difference between ally or foe. If he tried to approach, he had no doubt the dragon would slay him.

FOOL.

The voice in his head was so thunderous and echoing, that at first, he thought it was the dragon somehow shouting in his mind. His second thought was that it was the voice of the Overseers. His gaze jerked skyward, for part of him expected to see them standing in the sky, staring down at him like callous gods. But the sky was devoid of anything, save clouds. His attention was drawn once again to the steaming crack in the earth.

That's when he saw his opponent.

At first, Aram couldn't tell whether he was looking at monster or man. This new adversary was larger than any human he had ever seen, swathed in obsidian armor and armed with a sword enveloped by dark flames. It wore a visorless helm to which long, spiraling horns had been anchored. From its shoulders hung a fur-lined cloak of purple silk that billowed in the air despite a complete lack of wind.

Woven around his opponent's body was a thin, eel-like creature the color of lard. It hovered in the air as though ignored by gravity. A therling, Aram realized, for it looked just like the monster that had attacked him when he'd opened the rupture in the longhouse. It was a creature birthed in the void itself, not a product of his own world, and he had no doubt that its presence here was an abomination. Somehow, his adversary was able to control it.

Which could mean only one thing: the enemy who challenged him was an Archon. He assumed it was Kathrax, who had struck Maranth from the sky and slain his father.

WHO ARE YOU?

The voice resounded again in his head, agonizingly loud, reverberating through his skull.

Aram brought his hands up, covering his ears—a futile reaction that couldn't hope to keep the creature out of his mind.

He considered the Archon across from him with a growing sense of defeat. He was not a Champion, so he did not have the ability to fight it. And yet he could not become a Champion unless he did.

Aghast, Aram realized the brutal nature of this final test: the Overseers had placed him in a no-win situation, with his father's life in the balance. And he had no idea if this was real or simply a vision. Had they somehow transported him back twelve years in the past, to the day his father fell? Could he somehow change the course of events?

It didn't matter.

He could not defeat an Archon by himself.

And yet he didn't have a choice. Not if he was to save his father.

"I'm Aram Raythe," he shouted across the fissure, "son of Darand Raythe! And I'm here to slay you!"

Distorted by heat waves, the helmed figure regarded him darkly. There came no answer to his challenge, and yet, somehow, Aram could feel the utter disdain this enemy held for him. He was beneath the Archon's contempt, not even an inconvenience. Much more threatening was the beast that crouched behind him.

A shiver of doubt trembled Aram's spine. He could not let Maranth be defeated, for if the dragon didn't survive, then his father couldn't either. Perhaps that was his business here: not to challenge Kathrax himself, but to give his father's dragon a fighting chance.

He turned to Maranth and extended his blood-slicked hand, a silent offer and pledge he hoped the dragon would understand. In response, Maranth let out an infuriated roar, for he did not know him. He could feel the dragon's distrust and fear. Aram noticed for the first time that Maranth was gravely injured. A deep wound was carved across the center of his breast, leaking dark brown gore upon the ground.

"Fight with me," Aram proposed, taking an unsteady step toward the dragon. "I can't defeat him, and neither can you. But perhaps, together, we have a chance."

YOU DO NOT.

The world trembled from the aftershocks of that voice.

Aram stood with his hand outstretched, silently begging the dragon to heed him. "He'll kill you both—I know this for a fact. Fight with me!"

Maranth gave an almost imperceptible nod. He lowered his great head and gave Darand Raythe a tender nudge, then took a step toward his rider's son with blazing defiance in his eyes.

An accord had been reached.

Without hesitation, the dragon sprang from the ground and swept toward him, touching down only long enough for Aram to haul his injured body over its back. Then Maranth vaulted into the sky, spewing torrents of flame upon the Archon.

But Kathrax merely raised his hand, extinguishing the dragon's flames.

Maranth growled his rage, wheeling on wing to come around for another pass.

This time, Kathrax was ready. He drew his awful sword back and carved it around in a mighty arc, just as a reaper swings a scythe.

A ball of dark flame blazed toward them. With a furious cry, Maranth keeled to avoid it, and the terrible magic sped past them, narrowly missing.

In response, Maranth dove toward the earth. Before the dragon could touch the ground, Aram leapt from its back, weaving magic to soften his fall. Even so, he hit the ground hard, dropping into a crouch only feet away from the Archon as his side exploded in agony.

Grimacing in pain, he pushed himself to his feet and stood wobbling like a drunken man.

Kathrax ignored him, distracted by Maranth. Knowing that this might be his only opportunity, Aram raised his sword and plunged toward his opponent, throwing himself at the Archon with the last of his strength.

His dull blade scored the dark armor but failed to penetrate. With a roar of fury, Kathrax swept his arm around, and a tidal wave of magic picked Aram up from the ground and hurled him backward.

The Archon drew his sword back over his shoulder then hurled it into the sky. The Baelsword tumbled through the air and slammed into Maranth as he passed by overhead. Aram watched in horror as the dragon let out a mortal cry and fell from the sky, spewing blood and fire from a rent in its gut. It crashed into the crest of a ridge, hurling dust and debris high in the air. And then it tumbled, rolling in a flailing mass, to slide into the steaming fissure.

Aram opened his mouth to scream, but another voice took up the scream for him, shrieking a soul's weight of agony across the landscape. Aram whirled to see his father on his knees, shoulders heaving with tormented sobs. Though he stood across the fissure, Aram took a step toward him, but his motion was halted by a sword of blazing darkness that raised to block him.

Aram glared his wrath at Kathrax, his vision swimming with defiant tears.

"Leave him alone, you bastard!" he shouted.

But then the last of his strength left him, and he collapsed.

Aram lay on the ground, panting, his vision going dim. Kathrax advanced toward him like an evil apparition, swathed in an aura of dark flames.

YOUR SOUL FOR HIS.

"What?" Aram whispered, clutching his side as the last of his life bled out of him.

Kathrax halted over him. Slowly, he raised his sword.

CHOOSE.

Understanding drove a jagged lance straight through Aram's heart. The sword of flaming shadow was a Baelsword, and it hungered for his soul.

At last, he fully understood the tragedy that had befallen his father. Darand Raythe had lost more than his life that day in the Greenwood.

He had lost his soul.

And he would again, unless Aram chose to save him.

His life for his father's life.

His soul for his father's soul.

This was the test.

He heard a cry behind him and turned to watch the man he loved more than anything in the world pull himself to his feet.

For a moment, his father's eyes met his own, and their gazes locked. Aram had no idea whether his da recognized him, but he hoped that he didn't.

His body shivered uncontrollably, and tears filled his eyes, for he knew that sacrificing himself for his father was not the purpose he was born for.

Using hatred to fuel what little strength he had left, Aram wiped his tears and glared his defiance into the shadows of that dark helm.

"Take him."

The hoarse words clawed their way out of his throat, more painful than any torture he had ever endured.

The Archon stood without moving, as though it hadn't heard him.

Then, ever so slightly, it inclined its head in acknowledgment.

Aram screamed.

The world jolted and wrenched away.

He awoke, naked and in chains.

Gasping, he found that he had been staked out, limbs splayed, upon a circular slab of stone under the vault of a clouded sky. His breath came in weak, panting gasps, and his vision was dark from blood loss. Aram knew for a fact that he was dying, and he struggled to care.

Around him in a ring loomed the horrible creatures that had designed this fate for him. The Overseers, all doing nothing but observing him die. As he felt the last of his blood trickle out of him, Aram shook his head in confusion.

"Why...?" He gasped weakly. "I did everything right."

A pinpoint of light moved toward him, and he turned his head, struggling to see through his dimming vision. It was another of those horrid creatures, leading a gleaming Elesium colt. The sight of the foal confused him more, making his mind return to the scene of the terrible slaughter he had witnessed.

They had taken the colt.

"Betrayers..." he whispered.

Let him die.

A waste. We can make use of him.

His soul is too powerful.

He will be broken.

But the agreement...

They will not know.

No. He could not be controlled.

Let him die.

Let him die.

Yes. Let him die.

Aram's vision faded until only the silver light of the colt's aura remained in his darkening world. The colt's eyes met his, and in that brief moment, something passed between them, the acknowledgement of defeat. But it was more than that. He could feel the colt's great heart harden with resolve, and a sharp dagger of understanding lanced through him.

No! his mind screamed, too late.

The Elesium reared, throwing back its captors, striking out at the nearest with its forelegs.

The Overseer put its hand out. Dark fire gushed from its palm, enveloping the young horse in black flames.

"NO!" Aram screamed, and lashed out with all his wrath and the full force of his mind.

The world exploded in fire, the air filled with the ghastly howls of dying creatures that flailed around him in the heat of the inferno. The flames savaged the circle all around him, everywhere but where he lay.

Through the flames streaked a blazing light, and suddenly the glowing Elesium colt was rearing over him, its silver aura glowing brighter than the sun, haloed by flames. It was a powerful and arresting sight, agonizing to behold. The colt came down on top of him then reared again, its hoofs striking off the manacles that bound his arms and legs.

Then it wheeled and fled back into the raging fire.

"NO!!!" Aram screamed.

But it was too late.

The colt was gone, consumed by the flames.

Markus shivered as he stared at the fourth portal, his throat clenched with suppressed emotion. Every passing second tightened the grip of dread that strangled his heart, until the agony of waiting grew unbearable. He had known, watching Aram stagger beneath that last arch of rocks, that his friend wouldn't be coming back out. He had known it in his heart, and yet he had refused to give up hope.

But it had been too long. Far too long. When the tears came, he realized that the Trial had reached its inevitable conclusion. He could stand there all day, staring at an empty doorway, but that wasn't going to change anything.

Aram wasn't coming back.

A terrible silence clenched the Henge in a trembling fist. All around the ring of stones, men and women stood with their heads bowed and hands clasped, faces somber in grief. No one spoke, for words would be inadequate, not to mention inappropriate, at such a time. So they stood in silence, each of them marking the end of a life in their own quiet way.

Markus looked to Esmir, and something passed between them that was profoundly intimate. For, in that moment, they had ceased to be mentor and student, and stood before each other as two fellow Wardens united in the solidarity of grief, mourning the loss of the loved ones they had been entrusted to protect.

The moment was broken when he heard the sounds of footsteps moving away. The others were leaving, for the time for hope had come and gone. He heard the sound of quiet weeping and looked to see Calise standing against a pillar of stone, clutching Aram's knotted necklace.

That was it, then.

It was done.

Markus bowed his head and stood in silence for a time, until he felt the touch of a hand rest on his shoulder. Looking up, he saw that Wingmaster Vandra had come up next to him, her face long and haggard.

"I'm sorry," she said, her voice ragged.

But then her breath hitched, and her eyes widened.

Markus turned, following the direction of Vandra's gaze, just in time to see a flash of light accompanied by a falling body.

He was running before the body hit the ground.

He skidded to a halt next to where Aram lay, face down in the dirt. Esmir and Vandra rushed to his side, and together they rolled him onto his back. Vandra tore at his clothing, exposing the long gash that had opened his side. Esmir started ripping at his own clothes, shredding his shirt into strips of cloth that he pressed against Aram's side in an attempt to stop the bleeding. Dark brown blood pooled on the ground, soaking into the sand.

Vaguely, Markus was aware of the people rushing to cluster around them. Someone handed Esmir a bottle of Wellspring water. He took it and poured most of it over the wound. Then he handed the container to Markus, who lifted Aram's head into his lap and tried to dribble some of the life-saving water down his throat. Aram coughed and sputtered, water leaking from his mouth, and Markus wasn't sure if any made it down.

"This isn't working," growled Esmir, panic in his voice. He pressed the bloody rags into Markus's hands. "Keep pressure on it!" With that, he rose and moved quickly away through the crowd.

Suddenly, Calise was there. She moved the blood-soaked rags aside and pressed her bare hands over the wound, squeezing her eyes closed. A fierce light appeared around her, streaming outward in golden rays. The light poured down her arms, running over Aram's body like liquid, melting into him.

"Gods, help him," someone gasped.

Looking up, Markus saw that they were surrounded by a crowd of people, all looking on in fear and awe, faces lit by the golden light streaming from Calise. Markus looked on with held breath, knuckling his mouth. Calise seemed entrenched in a desperate struggle, her jaw clenched, her face pinched in effort. Glistening sweat broke out across her skin.

Suddenly, Calise threw her head back and cried out. Then she toppled over, unconscious. Vandra caught her as she collapsed and laid her down on the sand at Aram's side.

Markus scrambled forward and gasped in relief when he saw that Aram's bleeding had slowed substantially. The wound looked well on its way toward closing. By the time Esmir returned with a bag full of medical supplies, the bleeding had stopped entirely.

Vandra retrieved a needle and held it between her teeth as she threaded it with catgut. Crouching over Aram, she started stitching the wound while Markus looked on. Her work wasn't neat, but it did the job. Within a few minutes, she had him sewn up and bandaged. She turned Aram over, checking him thoroughly for other injuries. Other than bruises and abrasions, he seemed to be whole, at least in body.

"Do you think his mind's broken?" Markus asked Esmir.

"No." The old man shook his head firmly. "They didn't break him."

"How do you know?"

"His clothing's black." Esmir grasped a handful of Aram's cloak, holding the fabric up.

It took Markus a moment to understand the significance of the color, to remember the cloak had been gray and tattered when Aram had entered the portal. Now it was black and looked almost new.

"But all is not right," Esmir continued, his face haggard. "He should have never been returned in such a condition. They should have healed him." He looked down at Aram's ghost-pale face, shaking his head slowly. "I don't know what happened to our friend, but the Overseers were certainly not on his side."

"So, something went wrong?" Markus asked, a deep-seated fear returning.

"It did. I just don't know how or what it means."

They loaded Aram and Calise onto stretchers and carried them down the stairs past scores of anxious onlookers. Vandra took Calise down to the infirmary while Esmir and Markus carried Aram to their eyrie. There, instead of placing him on his pallet, they tucked Aram into Esmir's bed, smothered in blankets.

Markus stayed up late into the night drizzling Wellspring water little by little down Aram's throat and monitoring his condition. Esmir, meanwhile, slept on the floor, his sleep aided by copious amounts of honeywine provided by well-wishers.

When the morning arrived, Markus was glad to see that his friend looked much stronger. Aram's face was less pale, and the deep shadows had retreated from beneath his eyes. Markus was convinced that his improvement was entirely due to Calise's intervention, for he had never seen anyone bleed as much as Aram had and survive the night.

In the early afternoon, Esmir answered a knock at the door and admitted Calise. She came in tentatively, glancing around as though uncertain she should be there. Markus pulled another chair over beside the bed for her to sit on. But instead of sitting, she simply stood at Aram's bedside, her hand worrying the knotted necklace she wore around her neck.

"Is he better?" she asked, her voice fraught with worry.

"Yes." Markus straightened Aram's covers that had fallen down over his chest

Reaching down, Calise brushed a lock of his hair back from his face, her hand lingering on his cheek. "Will he be the same?"

"No," Esmir said from where he sat at the table. "Definitely not." He sat in silence for a long moment, his gaze lingering on Aram's face with a sad and distant expression.

"He is no longer a boy, or even a man." Esmir sighed. "He is a Champion, now, and that's an altogether different thing."

Aram awoke to the familiar light of Esmir's eyrie. He was covered with blankets that were soft and snug, not the scratchy wool of his own blanket. They were not as warm, though, and his body shivered beneath them. There was a pillow under his head, a comfort he had only felt a few times before in his life, and his body sank languidly into a mattress of goose down.

"Welcome back."

He turned toward the sound of the voice, Markus's face coming into bleary focus. His friend was sitting next to him in a chair, smiling the same crooked smile that always made Aram smile back. He was so happy to see him, he wanted to cry. He had resigned himself to the fact that he was dying and was actually shocked that he was still alive.

"How do you feel?" asked Esmir, coming to stand behind Markus.

Aram closed his eyes, probing within himself. The wound in his side seemed on the mend, so much so that it actually itched more than it stung. He was still weak from blood loss, though, and that would take time. But there was something more than that, he sensed. A strange queasiness that had nothing to do with his injuries. The air seemed to squirm a bit around him, all of its beautiful colors much more saturated than usual.

"I feel different." He squinted, trying to keep the colors from twisting. He was still shivering, and he pulled the blankets closer. "It's cold."

Markus stood immediately. "I'll throw some more logs on the fire."

When he moved away, Esmir took his place in the chair and bent over him, examining him up and down with a critical eye. He checked Aram's pulse, then peeled the blankets back to take a look at his bandages.

"How long was I out?" Aram asked.

"Not long. Only a couple of days."

A couple of days sounded long to him. He turned his head and watched Markus feed the fire with fresh wood. The logs didn't catch as quickly as he wanted them to, so he twisted the colors around them, infusing them with energy.

Markus sprang back as the fire flared up, sending sparks shooting into the air. He cast a startled glance at Aram before his eyes slipped to

Esmir, his mouth open in shock. Aram stared at the fire in mute aston-ishment. He hadn't meant to do that—or at least, he hadn't expected that to happen. He had never done something with magic as mundane as lighting a fire in a hearth, and the mere act made him shiver harder than the cold.

"Tell us what went wrong," Esmir said softly. He wasn't referring to the fire, Aram could tell.

He didn't want to think about his experience in the portals, especially the part about his da. If he never thought about that again, it would be too soon. But his chest tightened, and his skin prickled. There *was* something he had to think about, for it scared him, and he didn't know what it meant.

Staring up into Esmir's face, he whispered, "I killed them."

The old man frowned, his thick eyebrows pinching together. "Killed whom?"

"The Overseers."

"What?" Esmir's face screwed into a disbelieving grimace. He started shaking his head, as if ready to tell Aram he was wrong.

"They betrayed me," Aram said quickly. "They had made a bargain with someone...or something. They were supposed to kill me..." He strained to think back on it. The whole memory was hazy and already fading from his mind. "They were arguing. Some of them wanted to keep me... Others said I was too powerful, that I couldn't be controlled. In the end, they decided to kill me. So I killed them. They had stolen an Elesium colt...it saved my life...it died for me..."

Esmir's gaze slipped far away, his face slack and paling. At length, he scrubbed a hand through his hair and heaved himself out of the chair. "The Council has to know of this." He walked across the room to gather his overcoat.

"I need to speak to Luvana," Aram said. "Can you tell her to come?"

Esmir paused in the process of tying his coat. "Are you certain you're strong enough?"

"Yes." His body craved more sleep, but this was far more important.

Removing his coat, Esmir gestured to Markus. "You go get her. Let her take *your* head off."

Markus nodded and headed for the door. Aram watched him leave, then let his gaze drift to the ceiling as he struggled to stay awake. Apparently, his struggles didn't work, for the next thing he knew, he awoke to Luvana's hand touching his and found her sitting at his bedside. There was deep concern in her eyes, and he realized that her concern was for *him*, and not just the situation, which surprised him. He had never liked Luvana, and didn't think she liked him. She had withheld the information about his father, and he wondered what else she was holding back.

"The Archons are harvesting souls," Aram said. "Why?"

A look of shock passed briefly over her face, and she hesitated before responding, "They devour the essence of the wondrous, to become greater than what they are. To ignite the spark of the divine, so to speak. Kathrax and his brothers desire to ascend to the throne of their mother, the goddess Senestra. To that end, they have been drinking the souls of the Gifted for centuries, feeding their undying thirst for essence and blood."

Aram glared up at her, wanting her to know in no uncertain terms what he felt about her. "Did you know Kathrax took my father's soul?"

A blink, followed by a long pause.

"Yes."

He appreciated the truth, though he would never forgive her. "You should have told me."

"I don't agree," she said glibly, "and I'm sorry you found out. There is nothing you can do with the knowledge. It will only bring you pain."

She didn't have the right to protect his feelings. They were *his* feelings, not hers. And the information he had learned was very pertinent to their current situation.

"There *is* something I can do about it." Aram had a hard time keeping his voice steady. There was a fire within him that he had never felt before, the fire of righteous anger, and Luvana deserved to feel the heat of it. "I can slay Kathrax and release the souls he has consumed."

She gazed down at him, undaunted by his ire. "Kathrax has grown substantially since the start of this campaign. He has gorged on essence to the point that he is on the verge of ascendance. Powerful as you might be, you cannot slay a god."

"Perhaps," Aram allowed. "But I still have to try, don't I?"

"We'll discuss it later." She smiled kindly. "For now, you need to rest and regain your strength." She rose from the chair but paused before leaving. "There will be a Council meeting in a few days. We'll talk more then, if you're up to it."

Aram was surprised by that. "You want me to attend a Council meeting?"

Luvana raised her eyebrows. "Of course. You are an important part of the Council now."

Aram stared after her as she left, processing that information. Before his Trials, no one had taken him very seriously. He was young and inexperienced, and he had never held any type of leadership role, even among the apprentices. He didn't know what he had to offer the Council, but he was thankful they wanted to include him.

When Markus slid into the empty chair, Aram smiled up at him. "Did you hear that? I'm an important member of the Council."

Markus chuckled. "I heard. That's great! Odd, but great."

"So is Markus," said Esmir. "After all, he's your Warden. Well, he will be, after he pledges himself to you."

"Oh," said Markus, looking surprised, for Esmir hadn't ever mentioned anything about that. "I didn't know I had to pledge something. When am I supposed to do that?"

Esmir shrugged. "Now's as good a time as any."

Markus stared up at him, looking lost. "What do I say?"

"Just pledge your life to his."

Aram and Markus exchanged glances. "That sounds a lot like marriage."

Esmir chortled. "It's more like parenting. You'll spend the rest of your life trying to keep him out of harm's way."

At that, even Aram had to laugh. It was hardly a role change.

"All right," Markus said. He looked around uncertainly, at last pushing his chair out. Awkwardly, he lowered himself to one knee, as though pledging fealty to a feudal lord. While Aram stared down at him in dismay, he stated, "Aramon Raythe, from this moment forth, I pledge my life to yours. I will be the Shield that guards you from your enemies... Also, I will..." His face squirmed, for he had apparently run out of words.

Esmir prompted, "You'd better add that you'll try to save him from himself."

Markus grinned at Aram. "And I will do my best to save you from yourself."

Aram laughed, for he didn't envy Markus that task. He said sincerely, "Thank you very much. You've no idea how much this means to me. I'll do my best not to let you down."

Esmir clapped his hands. "Now. Let's get some stew into him before he fades to nothing again."

Aram let Markus spoon him some of Esmir's flavorless stew. After that, he slept. When he awoke again it was evening.

Aram sat up in bed, weak and shaky and momentarily disoriented. He looked around the cavern, at the shadows of the firelight contorting the walls. His gaze at last settled on Markus, who was seated against the wall with his sword across his lap. He appeared to be just staring at it, as though he didn't believe it possible that he could own such a weapon. Esmir was in his usual chair at the table, by all appearances already in his cups. Aram smiled, for the sight gave him a comforting sense of normalcy.

Until the door burst open and a flock of boisterous young men swooped in.

When Aram saw his friends spilling toward him, his throat tightened with emotion. For too many years he had been friendless, so the sight of five people who actually cared enough to come visit him in his sickbed was overwhelming. When they arrived at his side, he couldn't speak, but could only stare up at them gratefully.

Kye broke out in a jubilant smile. "You're alive! I can't believe it!"

Aram returned the smile faintly. "Yeah. I guess I looked pretty bad."

"You still look like something a cat hacked up." Corley grinned.

"It doesn't hurt as much as it looks."

The boys traded glances of disbelief. Corley turned and coughed "Bullshit!" into his hand. The others burst out laughing, clapping Aram on the shoulder and congratulating him as Markus came over and joined in the banter. They stayed there for a while, just talking, as though they were back in the dormitory, and for a time, Aram could almost believe that things between them hadn't changed. But then Eugan's face grew serious, and he lifted his hands.

"Is it just me, or do the rest of you feel that?"

Aram looked at him in confusion as the others quieted, turning to Eugan with troubled expressions.

"What are you talking about?" asked Corley, but Eugan waved him silent.

He turned to look at Aram, his hands raised over him as if feeling the heat coming off of a fire. Aram glanced down at himself, wondering if something was wrong or if he was bleeding again.

The other boys stared at Eugan with frowns of confusion. But then Kye's eyes widened, and his gaze snapped to Aram.

"I do! I feel it!" he gasped.

"I feel it too," said Jeran, looking at Aram, his face suddenly very serious.

"What?" Aram asked, looking from face to face, concerned and confused.

"It's you," Eugan said in a wary tone. "It's like I can feel the power coming off you."

Aram lowered his gaze, self-conscious, wondering exactly what it was they were sensing, for he couldn't feel it. Markus hadn't said anything. But then again, Markus didn't feel magic. Esmir hadn't said anything either, but maybe the old man had just expected the change and didn't think anything of it.

"I'm sorry," he said, feeling suddenly embarrassed. For the first time, he became aware of the gulf that had widened between him and his friends, and he was suddenly nervous about it.

Iver came forward to stand beside Eugan. "How did you do it?" he asked, his voice quiet and full of awe. "You just kept going back in there." He shook his head. "I couldn't have done it."

Aram shrugged. "I just knew I had to." It wasn't like he'd done anything brave or courageous. He'd just done what he had to.

In the end, Esmir came to his rescue, clapping his hands loudly. "All right, you louts, that's enough! Let the young man get some rest!"

His friends left the room with a chorus of well-wishes. Aram gazed after them long after they were gone, grateful to have such friends. He also felt a little sad, for there was one friend he wanted desperately to see, who hadn't visited him yet, and her absence troubled him more than the wound in his side.

PART IV

CHAMPION

A ram slept all day and night and into the next afternoon. When he awoke, he felt much better. Rested. He reached under the blankets and groped at his bandages and was surprised when the only tenderness he felt was the tugging of his stitches. Whatever ointments Esmir had chosen to treat his injury seemed to be working miracles.

Seeing him awake, Markus slid into a chair next to his bed, leaning forward with his hands clasped. "Hey there, knot-head! How're you feeling?"

"A lot better," Aram said. Shockingly so. He was much less weak, as though Esmir's lackluster stew had increased the amount of blood in his veins.

With Markus's help, he sat up and swung his legs over the side of the bed. The world went dark for a few seconds before his vision faded back again. Reaching up, he caught his head in his hands.

"Here. You need to drink something."

Markus handed him a jug of Wellspring water, which Aram guzzled, not sure whether he got more down his throat or down the front of him. When he was done, he handed the jug back and asked, "How long before the Council meeting?"

Hearing the question, Esmir rose from the table and moved to stand behind Markus, gazing down at Aram with a skeptical expression. "It's too soon. You shouldn't be getting out of bed yet."

Aram shrugged dismissively. "I'm feeling a lot better. I'll be fine."

Esmir harrumphed and turned away, a sound that usually made Aram and Markus exchange grins. Only, this time, Markus looked in complete agreement with Esmir.

"I *will*," Aram insisted.

He spent the remainder of the day recuperating, letting Markus and Esmir stuff food and honeywine down him until he was uncomfortably full. All throughout the day, his gaze kept drifting toward the door, for he was sorely hoping Calise would stop by to see him. When evening came, and she still hadn't paid him a visit, he felt more than a little disappointed.

After Markus crammed a supper of lentils down his throat, Aram figured he should probably start getting ready. He wasn't going to let the first Council meeting he had ever been invited to participate in pass him by.

"Here, let me help you up." Markus came forward and passed an arm around Aram's back, helping him to his feet.

Aram wavered for a minute, his vision dimming again before coming back. It took him a moment before he felt certain he could stand unsupported. He gave Markus a weak smile. "Some fine Champion, aren't I?"

"Give yourself a break," said Markus. "You've been through hell and back."

"It wasn't hell." Aram frowned, trying to remember the features of the Overseers' domain. "At least, not hell the way I'd imagine it."

Markus chuckled. "I meant *figurative* hell."

"Oh. Sorry."

Esmir came over with a stack of clothes that he sat upon the bed. "Here. Put this on."

Aram picked up the first garment, a black knee-length tunic with a large dragon embroidered on the chest in gold thread. He stared at the dragon emblem for a moment, realizing it was made from an elaborate pattern of interlaced knots. Beneath it was a folded pair of trousers and a black mantle and tabard trimmed in golden embroidery. All four garments were made of exceptionally fine fabric, softer than anything he had ever touched, soft enough to make his skin yearned for them.

"What are these?" he asked.

"This is the uniform of a Champion," said Esmir. He brought over another pile of garments and handed them to Markus. "And his Warden."

Aram frowned at the embroidered tunic, which looked more suited for a nobleman. "I don't know, Esmir..."

Esmir looked offended. "They were good enough for Daymar and every Champion who came before him."

Feeling sheepish, Aram muttered, "I spoke before I thought. Thank you, Esmir."

The old man nodded curtly, stepping back. "You can toss away your old clothes. By tradition, this uniform is what you are to wear, every day of your life, so that you can be recognized for what you are."

Aram looked upon the new garments with a feeling of dismay. He would have to look like this all the time? What if he had to go clean out a stable or dig a hole somewhere? He'd look rather silly. But then, he supposed it was unlikely that he'd be cleaning out too many stables, which was a thought that made him a little sad.

Aram sat on the bed and let Markus change his bandage and help him into his new clothes. Then he stood staring down at himself as Markus dressed, still not sure what to think of himself.

"Ready?" Markus asked.

Aram turned to Markus and stiffened, his face going slack, for he hardly recognized his friend. Markus's uniform was similar to his own, only his tabard and tunic were gray. With his sword at his side, the black mantle wrapped around him, he looked like nobility.

Markus stared at him sideways. "It's pretty unbelievable that you're the same boy I plucked out of the mud all those years ago."

Aram chuckled, supposing they had both come a long way since that morning in Anai.

When Markus came forward to take his arm, Aram shook his head. "I can walk on my own." He took a step forward but then paused, wavering as the floor rocked beneath him. He looked up at Markus sheepishly. "Actually...I can't."

With Markus on one side and Esmir on the other, Aram managed to walk out into the hallway and take the stairs down to the level of the Council chamber. There, they exited into a bustling corridor that served as a main artery between Hearth Home and the eyries it supported. Seeing people staring at him, Aram became nervous, wishing intensely that he wasn't wearing the new uniform, which made him stick out. He pulled his arm out of Esmir's grasp and squared his shoulders, making his best attempt not to appear as weak and anxious as he felt.

As they walked through the corridors, people paused to let them by, moving to the side of the walkway and bowing their heads. At first, Aram thought they were just being kind, clearing a path for someone obviously infirm. But the further he walked, the more it became apparent that people were stepping aside, not out of courtesy, but out of respect.

He glanced sharply at Esmir and asked under his breath, "Why are they doing that?"

The old man muttered back, "Because you're a Champion."

Aram felt his face pale. "I don't want them to do that."

"It doesn't matter what you want."

Aram didn't like that answer, just like he didn't like the clothes he was wearing. He opened his mouth to protest but then thought better of it, for Esmir was right. People were going to do what they were going to do, and he had no control over it. He continued in silence down the corridor, nodding at the people who stepped aside in deference. Even people he knew lowered their eyes, which made him feel even more uncomfortable, like an outsider in his own world.

By the time they reached the Council chamber, he felt drained and dizzy. Nevertheless, when Esmir opened the door to admit them, he let go of Markus and walked into the chamber without support.

As he entered, the people gathered in the room turned toward him. Most bore white hair and wrinkles, and many were hundreds of years old. Some, like Luvana, were over a thousand. And yet, at the sight of him, all twelve members of the Council rose to their feet.

Luvana raised her hand, beckoning him forward. "Champion Raythe. Welcome. Your place is here."

She gestured at the woven rug laid out beside her. Stiffly, Aram made his way around the firepit. He was grateful to have a seat, for he was exhausted, and he didn't think he could stand any longer without assistance. Markus lowered himself down at Aram's side, removing his longsword and laying it behind him.

Aram could feel the stares of the Council members upon him, though he tried to avoid eye contact. Even Vandra was regarding him with a kind of wary respect. Aram sat cross-legged on the rug and stared into the hearth's dancing flames, struggling to keep his eyes open.

"Let us begin," Luvana said as the others took their seats. "Our first order of business is welcoming our new Champion and his Warden to this Council. It has been four hundred years since the places beside me were last occupied. I'd say it's high time."

There were nods of acknowledgement from all around the fire. Aram had expected many of the Council members to bear him some level of resentment, for not only was he far younger than any other person in the room, but many of those gathered had opposed his training. He was surprised to see that there was no ill will in the looks he was receiving, which ranged from solemn respect to awe and curiosity. It was all so surreal, he almost wondered if he was still sleeping.

"Thank you," Aram said to Luvana, feeling some of his own resentment ease.

For the first time, he was starting to realize what it truly meant to be a Champion, and the more he thought about it, the more daunting the role seemed. The members of the Council, even Vandra, seemed to be deferring to him, and Aram found their behavior deeply unsettling.

Luvana said, "Wingmaster Vandra. You have a report for us?"

"I do." Vandra stood and stepped back from her place by the fire pit, positioning herself so that every member of the Council could view her easily. "The armies of Kathrax are advancing toward the Winmarch and are now a week out from Eld Anoth. They have expanded their ranks considerably since we met them in Altier, supplementing them with tamed therlings from Araghar. Also, they've acquired dragons."

Her words provoked a flurry of questions and whispered conversation, although Aram was not surprised, for when Vandra had taken him to the place where the Elesium had been slaughtered, he had seen visions of enemies mounted on dragons.

"They were once ours," said Vandra, "struck down in battle. Somehow, Kathrax or his sorcerers found a way to corrupt them."

"How can that be?" asked a craggy man with a hawk-like nose, his hair streaked with silver. "Dragons are soul-bound to their riders!"

Aram said quietly, "He has a Baelsword."

Every person in the room turned to look at him.

"What was that?" Vandra asked.

"Kathrax has a Baelsword," Aram repeated, remembering the sword that brought down his father's dragon. "He claims the souls of his enemies…" he glanced down, "and he severs the bonds that connect them."

The Council members stared at him with expressions of disbelief and horror.

"How do you know this?" asked Luvana, her voice tight.

"I saw it. During my Trials…I experienced things."

"And do you trust these experiences?"

"I do." His knowledge of the details of his father's death spoke to the truth of the visions. He glanced over the faces in the room and saw that there was no trace of doubt in the eyes that regarded him. Just yesterday, his claim would have been questioned and probably dismissed. Not today.

Face pale, Luvana addressed the Council, "They are marching toward the Heart of the Mother. We can't let them enter the Winmarch."

Vandra bowed her head solemnly. "I'll send riders to reinforce the fortress of Eld Anoth."

Luvana turned to Aram. "Do you have any advice for how we might defeat this enemy, Champion Raythe?"

Aram was taken aback that she would ask his opinion. Out of every person in the room, he had the least experience with such matters. He thought back to his Trial in the second portal, where he had been in command of an unknown army and had ordered the sacrifice of a large group of refugees. He had no idea if that vision had been real or not, whether it had been his own skin he was wearing, or someone else's. At the time, he had known things he couldn't have possibly known, and he assumed that knowledge had been planted in his head by the Overseers. Nevertheless, he still retained some of that knowledge. Perhaps it had been left there for a reason.

Looking at Luvana, he said, "Our forces are inferior, and they control the skies, so that eliminates the advantage of our dragons." He paused in thought, staring deeply into the flames of the hearth. "Kathrax has dragons and Exilari and a Champion of his own—as well as an army of creatures from the void. We cannot rely on the strength of Skyhome to win this war. We need numbers. We need bodies. Send riders to the corners of the world. Call on the Dedicants."

Looking up, he saw the dismay on many of the faces looking at him. In truth, he didn't know where any of those words had come from—they had flowed from his mouth of their own accord. He was about to apologize for overstepping his place, but he was suddenly hit with a terrible feeling of weakness. His vision darkened, and he caught hold of Markus, struggling not to pass out.

"What is it?" Luvana set a hand on his back, her expression concerned.

Aram scarcely noticed her, for while his eyes were still staring into the fire, his mind had gone to another place. An image of the void dragon filled his mind.

He could feel it. It was alive, though barely. It was reaching out to him with the last of its strength. It had waited as long as it could, but it could wait no longer, for it needed him desperately.

And he needed it.

Dizzy, Aram brought a hand up to mop his brow, which was suddenly cold and drenched in sweat.

"Aram?" Markus asked.

"Excuse me, please," Aram whispered.

He rose unsteadily amidst a chorus of whispers. Markus rose with him, taking his arm, his face darkened by concern. Aram leaned on him heavily as he exited the chamber, every stare following his progress with looks of stunned shock.

Sergan leaned against a picket, sweat dampening his skin and saturating his clothes. He despised this Southern heat. The only time of day that was livable was the first hour after sunset. By noon, it was unbearable. And it didn't let up but continued relentlessly after sunset. Nights were the worst, for he'd lay awake sweating in his tent, unable to sleep, denied even the simple comfort of a breeze. One night, he'd actually dragged his bedroll outside and quickly learned why tents here were a necessity. The mosquitoes were rampant, along with other, larger bugs that were drawn to the light of the campfires.

Untying his white scarf, he used it to dab at the perspiration on his brow then returned his attention to the makeshift arena some of the soldiers had improvised. It turned out that the tribes of the North had a rather tenuous alliance. It was only due to the officers' harsh imposition of order that they were able to fight a common enemy instead of one another.

When they weren't on the battlefield, their thirst for the blood of their rivals was appeased by permitting gladiatorial fights whenever time permitted. It turned out to be a brutal pastime that Sergan found himself enjoying. During the afternoons and evenings after the days' march, he had watched—and even bet on—hours' worth of bloodshed.

The arena they had constructed today was a simple corral about a hundred paces wide. The ground within had been trampled and darkened by the blood of the defeated. Dozens of bouts were usually fought every evening, and sometimes there were deaths. Even the weakest Northern warriors were capable of skull-crushing blows and tearing limbs from sockets.

The last fight of the evening turned out to be more of a coming-of-age rite than a grudge feud. The challenger, a young man of the Raven Clan whose skin bore only the first of the many sets of tattoos he would gather throughout his adulthood, had selected a much older opponent, a leather-faced old warrior of the Wolf Clan. Sergan figured that was a mistake; even his untrained eye could see that the old warrior's age belied the threat he posed. The Wolf Clan warrior walked with a confident stride toward the arena and ducked through the posts like a man half his age. He reminded Sergan of a gnarled but solid oak, and he looked like he still had a few good years of trouncing challengers left in him.

Seeing his young opponent climb into the arena, the oaken-faced warrior hawked a glob of spittle onto the sandy ground. He was clad in a leather jerkin and greaves, and he bore a broadsword and a small round shield. He rolled his shoulders and rapped his sword against his shield, circling his foe slowly.

The younger man wore a similar outfit, though his jerkin was ornamented around the neck with raven feathers, and he carried a curved blade. He didn't seem troubled by the older warrior's display of aggression, for he came strutting and swaggering into the center of the arena, casting a sneering sidelong grin at the crowd.

The gathered mob was already baying for blood. The arena master wasted no time bringing his hand down in a chopping motion, starting the fight.

The younger man darted forward, closing the distance between him and his opponent rapidly, leaping the last five paces to thrust his sword toward his opponent's heart. The blade *thunked* off the metal boss of his foe's shield, and the old warrior's sword came in under his guard, angling for his gut. The younger man snarled, and the crowd roared. Sergan couldn't tell if the slice had landed, but by the audience's reaction, he would guess some amount of blood had been spilled.

The young man staggered back, raising his shield to deflect a barrage of blows as the old warrior glided effortlessly from one form to the next. He brought his sword down hard, punching through the younger man's shield, raining splinters and shards of wood upon the sand of the arena.

The younger man leapt away with terror in his eyes, for he had to know with certainty that he was done for. And his fear was proven justified not five seconds later, when the sword of his opponent drove through his collarbone and down into his rib cage. The younger man's sword slipped from his grip, and he fell. He lay prone, one foot drumming the dirt, his lifeblood feeding the sand and the audience's bloodlust.

Another victory for the Wolf Clan.

Sergan nodded respectfully at the old warrior as he exited the arena then turned away with a smirk on his lips. Almost, he regretted not placing a wager on the match. Wiping his brow, he turned away from the sight of the boy's body being dragged away through the dirt. The men of the Raven Clan erupted in fury, while the Wolf Clan shook their spears and howled like their namesakes.

Sergan turned away and started back toward his tent, having had enough of dust and swelter for the evening. As he walked, a shadow passed over him, blocking out the moonlight for just an instant. He glanced into the sky and saw a black serpentine body attached to a pair of bat-like wings. One of Lazair's tame dragons came slithering gracefully out of the sky to alight on the ground in the center of the encampment. This one had come from the North, from the direction of Araghar. Curious, Sergan made toward it, wondering what kind of dispatches the rider brought.

He reached the dragon just as Lazair did. The pale woman shot him a smile that was both welcoming and poisonous at the same time. She had a unique way about her. If she'd been just another woman on the street, he would probably find her irresistible. As it was, he thanked the gods every day that he wasn't tempted to risk such a dangerous liaison.

The emissary from the North handed her a wooden scroll case. Lazair opened the end of the tube and shook out the scroll within, unrolling it and holding it vertically as her eyes scanned the leather. Sergan stood behind her, looking on over her shoulder, and was instantly fascinated by the script, which flowed in a single column of elaborate logograms down the page. The leather they were written on was like nothing he had ever seen before, thin and almost translucent, more reminiscent of lambskin than cowhide.

"Is that *human* skin?" he asked, genuinely intrigued.

Lazair nodded absently as her eyes scanned the page, at last rolling the scroll back up and returning it to its case. She turned to Sergan with a severity in her eyes that he'd never seen before and yet looked thoroughly at home on her face.

"Bad news?" he asked.

"The boy passed the Trials and has become a Champion," she informed him. "My master wants him taken alive."

A shiver of excitement passed over Sergan. In a way, he felt vindicated, for his early suspicions of the boy's talent had been confirmed. Yet it was also grave news, for it complicated matters terribly.

"How did he pass?" Sergan asked. "I thought you had a bargain with the Overseers."

"The boy killed them," Lazair stated flatly.

Sergan's eyebrows flew up. "That's possible?"

"I wouldn't have thought so." As the dragon launched back into the sky, Lazair turned and walked away. Sergan had to hurry to catch up with her.

"I want him, Lazair," he said. "You asked me to name the price for my services. This is it."

"No. He's ours. Pick something else." The tone of her voice brooked no argument, and neither did the hardness in her eyes.

"I'm the one who found him to begin with. He was my apprentice—"

She stopped to regard him with cold ire. "And what would you do with him, Exilar? Stick him back in your essence cellars? You tried that once before, remember? How did that work out for you?"

But that wasn't Sergan's plan for the boy. Rather, he wanted to consume every drop of Aram's essence himself. A yearlong magical orgy. Drink him dry and then wallow in his power. Not only would such an experience prove more euphoric than any drug, he was certain that much essence would sustain him the rest of his life. He could operate independently of his Order. He would have no trouble making a place for himself at the Imperial Court, the place his own father had denied him when he'd disinherited him all those years ago.

"You told me to name my price," he reminded her. "This is what I want, Lazair. I want Aram."

The woman crossed her arms and stared at him rigidly. "My master has plans for him. He will not negotiate."

Sergan wanted to grind his teeth. Lazair carried her master's Baelsword at her side, and she was not a person Sergan wanted to argue with.

He sighed heavily. "Then give me Markus." When she opened her mouth to protest, he cut her off quickly. "You've got to give me *something.*" Markus was a True Impervious, one of the rarest people in the world. Perhaps, with the right leverage to control and motivate him, Markus might be of some use to him.

She stared at him hard a moment longer, at last nodding. "You may have Markus."

Sergan sighed. "Fair enough. Out of curiosity, why does your master want Aram?"

A breeze stirred her hair. She smiled slightly. "Kathrax desires to drink his soul and devour his flesh."

A ram sat on the terrace of Esmir's eyrie, the spray of the waterfall misting his face as he stared out across the canyon toward the cliffs on the other side. The fissure that cracked the earth was called an abyss for a reason. It hadn't been made by the action of a river, but by the Sundering, a great crack that had almost physically split the world in two, or so it was said. He didn't know what was down there, for he had heard conflicting tales and had no idea which ones were true. Some said the fissure descended all the way into Senestra's lair, and that it was the brimstone of that world that flavored the breath of the abyss so powerfully with the smell of rot. Others said it led to a great volcano way down deep within the earth, and a lake of lava was down there. Others had different explanations. Some thought it led to the void, while others thought it led to the World Above. Aram had no idea which to believe. All he knew was that he had to find out.

He heard footsteps behind him and turned just as Markus sat down at his side, staring at him hard with a look of grave concern.

"Are you feeling better?" he asked. "Everyone is worried."

Aram shrugged his shoulders, not taking his eyes off the chasm. "Better. But useless. Without a dragon, I can't defend anyone."

Only a dragon would give him the advantage he needed to do any good. And not just any dragon. He needed one of the Great Ones, a dragon powerful enough to share his mind.

His eyes slipped to the abyss.

"Are you just going to give up?" Markus asked. "Or figure out another way to fight?"

At first, Aram wondered if Markus was trying to appeal to his sense of duty, but then he saw the sincere concern in his friend's eyes.

"No. I won't give up." He nodded down at the crevasse below them. "The void dragon is down there somewhere. It's my fault it's there."

A silent moment fell between them as Markus's gaze followed his stare. "It's not your fault."

"It is," Aram whispered. "I'm sorry, Markus. I'd like to be alone."

Markus stared at him for a long, searching moment, at last rising reluctantly. "I'll be in the Southern Eyrie. Come get me if you need anything."

Aram listened to his footsteps moving away, to the sound of the eyrie door opening and then closing. Only when he was sure he was alone did he rise and wander over to where Siroth was resting on the far side of the terrace. As he approached, the black dragon raised his head and peered at him with golden eyes that expressed the same concern his rider had. Aram reached up and placed a hand on the dragon's face, caressing his cool scales.

"I need you to do me a favor," he said. "I need you to call Zandril here."

He felt rather than heard the dragon's question in his mind.

"I...can't tell you. I just need you to trust me."

Siroth glared at him a long moment, emitting a low, stomach-rumbling growl. At last, he inclined his head and stepped aside.

Lowering his hands, Aram let out a grateful sigh. "Thank you."

As he waited for Siroth to relay his request to Zandril, Aram wandered over to the edge of the terrace, the dragon watching him with wary golden eyes. There, he stood and looked down into the abyss. The walls of the fissure plunged downward until they were lost in shadow and steam. When he had first come to Skyhome, he had mistakenly thought there was a river down there, somewhere way down deep. He didn't believe that anymore. The images that came to him in his nightmares were steeped in darkness and overwhelming heat.

Whatever was down there, he feared it greatly.

He closed his eyes and tried to reach out with his mind to the dragon who had touched him in his dreams. But there was nothing there. Perhaps it was sleeping or had died in the night, or perhaps it had never been there to begin with, and the Trials had driven him insane without him realizing it. The last thought made him shiver, for he knew that was a real possibility.

The sound of rushing air prompted him to step back from the cliff's edge just as a golden dragon swooped in for a landing. Zandril alighted perfectly on the edge of the terrace, gracefully folding her wings. She froze and simply stared at Aram for a long moment, at last lowering her head in a kind of reverence. Not knowing how to respond, Aram bowed to her, and if a dragon could ever appear shy, Zandril somehow managed it.

Walking toward her, Aram stopped at her side and ran his hand over the cool scales of her sleek neck. Closing his eyes, he opened himself to her, trying to convey what he wanted, along with the urgency of his need. Understanding his intent, Zandril flinched back with a hiss, the ridges of her spine springing erect. It took minutes of coaxing before she at last yielded and nodded her acquiescence, albeit grudgingly.

That was all Aram could hope for. She lowered herself for him to climb onto her back.

"Thank you," he told her as he buckled himself into the straps of her harness. "All I'm expecting is for you to take me as low as you can. I'll find my own way from there."

A vibration quivered her skin, a feeling somewhat like a cat's purr, though he knew it had nothing to do with contentment. It was Zandril's way of politely disagreeing with him.

"If I don't think I can do it, I won't," he assured her. "Please trust me."

Her quivering ceased. She spread her wings and leapt off the edge, gliding gracefully over the chasm. As they flew, Aram surveyed the crack beneath them, looking for a good place to begin their descent. The fissure wound for miles through the mountains, jagged as a saw blade.

In some places, he could see farther down into the rent than others, but even then, the view was lost eventually to shadow. In other places, steam rose in convoluted clouds that collected in the air above the fissure. After minutes, he located a place where the crack was wide enough that Zandril would have plenty of wing-room to maneuver for a good distance. He pointed it out to her as they passed over, and with only a slight hesitation, she wheeled in the air then dove toward it, plunging almost straight down the walls of the canyon. His stomach dropped, and he squinted his eyes against the cold air rushing past his face.

As they sped downward past the lower eyries, Aram saw a good number of people lining the ledges, and he was certain that many noticed their descent. He sent a panicked thought toward Zandril, urging her to hurry, in case anyone realized what they were about and decided to give chase.

At Aram's prompting, Zandril tucked her wings in closer, speeding their descent. The shadows around them thickened quickly to darkness. When it became impossible to see, Aram wove a light ahead of them. The air was becoming thicker and hotter, reeking of brimstone, and deep down below, a red glow appeared in the distance.

Scorching wind and shadows flew by, and yet Zandril plunged ever lower down into the darkest reaches the chasm. Sweat streamed from Aram's brow as the heat condensed around them. In his mind, he could feel Zandril's determination and her discomfort. She couldn't take much more of the heat. Neither could he. The dark red glow of some type of hell seemed still so far below.

The shadows around them darkened, the close walls of the rift speeding by. Searing heat gusted past them, scorching his skin. Zandril couldn't go any further, Aram realized. He couldn't ask her to. If something happened to her, Calise would also perish, and that wasn't something he could endure.

"Stop," Aram croaked, his throat too dry and aching to form proper words. Zandril heeded, splaying her wings and arresting their descent. As they hovered in the air, he could feel the relief pouring out of her. Reaching down, Aram caressed her back.

"That's far enough. You go back."

A questioning thought probed his mind, edged with concern.

"No, I'm not coming."

His dragon was down there, so close. He could feel him, though weakly. Somehow, Agaroth had fallen down into the bowels of the chasm and had managed to remain alive all this time. If a dragon could survive the extremes down there, so could he. At least for a little while.

He felt Zandril's alarm when she realized what he was intending to do.

"He had faith in me," Aram explained in a wheeze. "I have to have faith in him."

With that, he unbuckled himself from the riding harness and let go.

Markus angled across the eyrie toward the soaking pond. The pond contained fresh water brought up from the springs beneath Skyhome by pipes that lifted water up the cliffs using helical shafts that twisted like cork screws. The pipes provided water for not just the eyrie's dragons, but also for its human inhabitants and all the industry of Hearth Home. The soaking pond was a popular place, for it was also a gathering area where the men and women of the eyrie met to socialize while their dragons bathed.

Jeran and Iver were there with their hatchlings. Jeran's was a small gray dragon named Gananth. Of all the hatchlings, Gananth was the smallest and friendliest, and, just like its rider, the little dragon was inquisitive and intelligent. Iver's hatchling was much bigger, a beautiful dark blue male named Tandriel. Even though he was still young, Tandriel carried himself with an air of dignified nobility and had a way of looking down his angular nose at any human except his rider.

Seeing Markus approach, Jeran raised his hand in greeting and elbowed Iver. "Look what the wind blew in!"

Markus grinned, coming up to stand in front of them. Iver was shirtless and stood mopping water off his muscular body with his tunic. Seeing Markus, he tossed his wet hair back with a shake of his head, spraying water everywhere. Apparently, he'd been bathing in the soaking pool alongside his dragon, a common practice.

"I can't believe how they've grown," Markus said, shocked at the size of the two young dragons. "If they keep this up, they'll be as big as Siroth in another month or two."

Gananth's spines raised eagerly at the compliment, but Tandriel somehow managed to look offended. That didn't bother Markus, because he knew that Tandriel took offense to everything, so it wasn't personal. He hoped the dragon grew out of it. Moodiness was hard enough to take in a human, much less a dragon, although it wouldn't surprise him if Iver's dragon turned out to be just as insufferable as he was.

Iver scrubbed his shirt through his hair, toweling it dry. "So, what brings you down here among the rest of us commoners? Got tired of Wardening already?"

Markus shrugged. "There's not much to Warden right now. I figured I'd come down here and annoy you."

"Lucky us!" Iver laughed and pulled his shirt on over his head, heedless that it stunk like wet dragon. He motioned at Markus. "I guess a Warden's clothing allowance is a lot better than a windrider's. I mean, look at this!" Reaching out, he plucked at Markus's tabard before he could react. "I bet Esmir makes you wear that so you can walk around next to Aram and make him look important."

Even Markus found himself laughing, because it wasn't far off from the way he felt about the uniform. Looking down at himself, he really did feel like a spectacle.

"Hey, now—"

An outburst of shouting toward the cave mouth cut him off midsentence. He glanced back over his shoulder to see people running toward the terrace. Drawn by the commotion, more people poured out of their alcoves, gathering at the entrance to the eyrie.

"What's going on?" Markus asked.

"I don't know." Iver started forward with a look of intense concern.

Jeran hurried after him, and Markus moved to follow, but he halted when he saw Calise dashing toward them. The sight of her face made him draw up short. Her mouth was contorted in a grimace, and her cheeks glistened with tears. Rushing toward her, he caught her by the shoulders.

"What is it?"

"He took Zandril!" she gasped, panic sharpening her voice. "Why would he take Zandril?"

"Who?" Markus asked. "Who took Zandril?"

"Aram!" Calise sobbed, covering her mouth with her hands. "He flew her down into the abyss!"

Markus's heart stopped. *"What?* Tell her to turn around! Tell her to come back!"

"I tried!" Calise cried. "She closed herself to me! I can't feel her anymore! Please—you have to stop him! He's going to kill them both!"

Someone shouted his name, and Markus turned to see Vandra running toward them.

"What is he doing?" she demanded.

"I don't know!" Markus knuckled his hair. "He was upset after the Council meeting. He said there wasn't anything he could do without a dragon." His eyes went wide, a terrible thought occurring to him. "The void dragon," he gasped. "The one who brought him here. He said it's down there somewhere…" His breath hitched. "Oh, gods…"

"Damn the wind!" Vandra snarled.

Markus sprinted for the hallway, taking the stairs up to Esmir's eyrie. Flinging open the door, he confirmed that the chamber was empty, save for Siroth. He ran to his dragon, climbing onto his back. "Why didn't you tell me?"

All he got in answer was a burst of scattered images that he didn't have time to try to understand. He had never heard of a dragon keeping secrets from its rider. His anger flared, though it was overshadowed by panic.

Below them, dragons spilled from the mouths of the eyries, plunging into the gap of the chasm. Markus willed Siroth to follow them, but as soon as Siroth prepared to dive into the crevice, he saw the other dragons who had gone ahead reemerging, returning from the depths to land on an outcrop. Why had they abandoned their pursuit?

He directed Siroth past them, and together, they swept into the fissure.

The moment they entered, Markus saw that the walls were much closer than they looked from above. There was no room to maneuver or ease their descent, so Siroth plunged straight into the dark crack. The air coming up at them was searing hot, and dense shadows encased them quickly. It took only seconds of darkness to convince Markus that it was too dangerous to go deeper. Maybe Aram had protected Zandril with magic, but Markus had no way of protecting Siroth.

With a cry of frustration, he ordered his dragon to turn around. Feeling utterly defeated, he let Siroth carry him back up the cliff, landing on the large terrace of the Southern Eyrie. He didn't want to be alone, and he didn't want Calise to be alone either.

Sliding from Siroth's back, Markus raised a fist, clenching it in frustration. Incensed, he punched out at the air, raging at his dragon:

"Why?"

But he already knew the answer.

The void dragon is down there somewhere. It's my fault it's there. That's what Aram had told him, what he believed.

Markus closed his eyes and bowed his head, fearing those words might have been Aram's last.

Scorching wind clawed at Aram's face, rushing past him as he tumbled through the darkness. Below, a terrible red glow awaited him, but now he wondered if he would live to reach it. His skin felt like it was on fire, broiling in the heat upwelling from below, and every breath he took into his lungs seared his throat. As he fell, he groped at the threads of aether around him, failing to catch more than a couple. Those broke quickly, too frail to arrest his hurling descent.

Frantic, he managed to catch hold of a handful of strands. These he wove quickly, tying them into a sheet of aethereal fabric which spread above him and slowed his fall somewhat. Grasping more threads, he formed them into a net of fibers that he wove around himself like a cocoon. The heat around him cooled faster the harder he worked, for the knots he cast were of the kind that sucked heat from the air and locked it away. The shield took precious, painful moments to weave, but at last, he was able to breathe easily. The bonds he had woven would keep the heat at bay, at least for a while. More of a problem was slowing his fall.

The close walls of the fissure grew further apart and then opened up around him. Though he couldn't see much of anything, he got the impression that he was falling through an immense chamber as tall and wide as a mountain. At the bottom of that chamber was a river of lava, and it was from there that the heat and foul breath of the abyss emanated. It was as wide as the chamber, thick and glowing an incandescent red, its surface fractured by bright streaks of gold that looked like veins.

In places, fire erupted from the surface of the magma, breathing sulfurous smoke that rolled upward in dark plumes. It churned sluggishly, like a pot boiling in slow motion. Having witnessed the color of the steel ingots in Onsel's forge, Aram had some idea of how hot that molten river had to be.

Hot enough to kill him instantly.

Desperate, he wove a rope of aether and tossed it toward the wall of the chamber, but it fell well short of the rock. Working as quickly as he could, he wove another net, this time below him, reinforcing it with knots that he felt sure wouldn't slip. He tied it off and cast it down just in time. The force of his body colliding with the net stretched the fibers so far, they nearly broke the surface of the lava. But the net rebounded quickly, flinging him upward toward the side of the cavern.

Aram wove a lasso, which he flung over an outcropping of rock. The fibers snapped taut but held. He clung desperately to the tendrils of aether, dangling over the surface of the wide river, swaying in a broad, pendulous arc. The half-healed wound in his side shot pain all the way to his spine, and it felt like it would split him all the way in half.

He clinched his jaw, his hands shaking from the strain of holding the tether. It took all of his concentration, and the protective net around his body started to unravel. The heat of the air was once again scorching his skin, threatening to overwhelm him quickly. He had to do something fast.

Desperate, he wove a splice into the tether of glittering aether, lengthening it, and lowered himself almost all the way to the bottom of the cavern. There, he managed to cast a line out at the rock wall, which caught and held.

Aram drew the line taut and kept pulling, hauling himself over the river of lava. He could feel his skin searing in the heat of the flames that leapt off the magma. When at last he had maneuvered his body over the shore, he let go and fell to the scorching ground, unable to hold onto the rope another second. The drop was longer than it looked, and even though he used magic to soften his fall, the impact still jarred him off his feet and nearly knocked him unconscious.

Groaning, Aram opened his eyes and saw that he was lying on the black rock of the shore. His skin felt like it was on fire, his body wet with sweat, and every breath he drew hurt his throat. The only reason he was still alive at all was because of the absorbent shield he had woven around himself, though it had grown thin and frail, riddled with holes.

The close walls of the abyss loomed above him thousands of feet, their features obscured by shadow. Beside him, the river of lava moved sluggishly, suffusing the air with a sulfurous miasma, flames erupting from its surface.

Holding his side, Aram pushed himself to his feet. He had no idea where to go. All he knew was that he couldn't stay there, for to do so would mean his death. The chamber was too hot, and he couldn't keep the cooling net around him indefinitely. Eventually, he would run out of the essence to maintain it.

His head throbbed. He took a step with legs that felt made of jelly and, for a moment, he thought he would pass out. Shooting his arms out, he caught his balance and, eventually, the ground stabilized beneath him.

Squinting, he looked out across the dim bottom of the gorge, the surrounding air rippling with heat waves. There was nothing around him but molten rock and shadows. The lava ran its course, just like a river of water, and he couldn't see what lay beyond a bend in the canyon wall ahead. He had no way of knowing which direction to go—upstream or down.

He closed his eyes and reached out with his mind, seeking the creature he had encountered in his dreams. But the only thing his mind met was an overwhelming stillness, and he began to doubt that the void dragon was alive at all. Growing desperate, Aram glanced up and down the length of the river, trying to decide which way to go. The dragon had slipped down into the abyss from the terrace of Esmir's eyrie, so he felt it had to be somewhere close by.

There was only one thing to do. He would have to make a guess and put his trust in fate.

Resolute, he made his way over uneven, black rock toward the first bend in the gorge, following the slow-moving river downstream. The air was sulfurous and scorching, and no matter how tightly he wound the cooling web about him, he couldn't keep the sweltering heat at bay. His clothes were so wet they stuck to his skin, and his hair was dripping with sweat, as though he were a castaway disgorged by the ocean. He was nauseous and dizzy, but he willed his feet to keep going, following the bend in the gorge.

The river of magma hissed and grumbled, belching plumes of fire. The path he followed narrowed, forcing him to be particularly careful of his footing, with lava on one side and the cavern wall on the other. The walls closed over him until he was stooping, picking his way through a dark tunnel lit only by the hellish glow of the molten rock. Within that tunnel, the temperature became unbearable. His gait became a stumbling shamble, and his vision grew dim. He tried to strengthen the shield around him, but it was saturated, unable to take much more heat.

Just when he felt sure he was near his end, the tunnel opened into a wide cavern that was mercifully cooler. Gasping, Aram leaned forward with his hands on his knees, swaying from heat exhaustion. His vision swam in darkness for a few seconds, then faded slowly back. When he felt a little steadier, he drew himself upright.

And froze.

Across the chamber, his eyes fell upon the object of his search.

The void dragon lay just ahead, curled on the shoreline beside the glowing river of magma. One glance confirmed his fear: the dragon was dead, its body petrified, just like the stone dragon he had seen in the upper eyrie.

The sight of the dead dragon broke Aram's spirit. All his effort, all the training, all the sacrifices his friends had made for him, had been for nothing. He had wasted his life on a whim.

A crushing mountain of despair drove him to his knees.

It was unbearable. He threw his head back and screamed in fury and self-hatred. He knelt there, staring straight up into the shadows of the chasm overhead, longing for just one last glimpse of the sky. But he couldn't see it, not even a thin crack of daylight. He was too far down. Too deep. There would be no rescue, for no one above could ever reach him.

The overwhelming grief he felt had nothing to do with his own impending death. Instead, he grieved for the friends he would leave behind. That, and the loss of the dragon that should have been his. He looked again at the sad form of the void dragon, its body hardened to granite, the sight filling him with excruciating sorrow.

If he was to die, then he wanted to die alongside his dragon.

With the last of his strength, Aram crawled on his hands and knees along the shore of the molten river, coughing and choking. The caustic air clawed tears from his eyes and corroded his airways. He crawled with his eyes squeezed shut until his hands felt the smooth surface of granite stone. Then he collapsed on the searing ground at his dragon's side.

With the last of his waning strength, Aram kissed his fingers and laid a hand on the void dragon's petrified hide.

Beneath his hand, the stone rippled.

Aram heaved a sob. Though nearly stone, there was enough left of his dragon to respond to his touch. He wept openly at the unfairness of it.

"Forgive me," he whispered.

He tried to take comfort in the fact that at least they would die together. But even that thought did not quell the raging guilt within him. If he had just passed his Trials sooner, he could have saved them both.

But now it was too late.

Unless...

Aram stiffened, his eyes going wide. The void dragon had slipped into the abyss because he had been drained of essence. Aram was full of essence, brimming with it. And none of that essence would do him any good after he was dead.

He had nothing to lose by giving it all away.

Placing both hands on the creature's stony body, he opened himself to the dragon, just as he had that day in the forest, all those years ago, and gave it what it needed.

The pain was excruciating, but he didn't scream. It was a kind of agony he was used to, the pain of extraction he had endured every day in the essence cellars. Then, the extraction had been forced upon him, but now he gave it freely, which somehow made a difference. So, instead of screaming, he merely closed his eyes and surrendered to the pain.

As he slipped away, Aram smiled faintly, for he could feel the stone beneath his hands start to soften.

For heartbeats, Markus stood next to Siroth on the terrace, peering down into the gaping abyss. His gaze roved over the long fissure, searching for any sign of movement from below. But there was nothing. All the dragons that had gone down after Aram had returned. He was about to turn away when a flash of movement caught his attention.

Far below, a small golden dragon emerged from the crack in the earth. Markus's head filled with a dizzying relief that quickly died.

Zandril was riderless.

Oh, gods, no….

His gaze followed the small dragon as she rose from the chasm, pumping her wings furiously to gain height. He watched through blurry vision as she flew directly toward them and landed on the terrace next to Siroth, who bent his head and touched his nose to hers. Feeling weak and disoriented, Markus just stood there, staring off into the distance, his body numb.

Calise rushed to Zandril's side, throwing her arms around her dragon's neck, her shoulders heaving with sobs. Everyone on the terrace gathered around them, men and women of the fighting Wing, faces pale and grave. They stood with heads bowed, gazes lowered, looking far more shocked than grieved.

Markus couldn't do anything but stare at Zandril, stunned. He stood locked in a mixture of confusion and despair so powerful that he couldn't even summon tears. Looking across the eyrie, he saw that Vandra's face had gone red, not in grief, but in fury. Markus understood. Aram had died a selfish death. Through rash stupidity, he had taken from these people what they needed most: their Champion.

On legs that were made of clay, he walked over to Calise and drew her into a hug. She cried against him for minutes before looking up, staring plaintively into his eyes. "He let go. He didn't fall. *He let go.*"

Finally the tears came, for at last, Markus understood.

Aram had taken his own life on purpose.

He saw Vandra's eyes on him, full of anger and dismay, but they also held sympathy. Markus turned away and strode heavily for the stairs as a tidal wave of despair broke over him. Vision blurred, he jogged up the steps to Esmir's eyrie and shoved the door open violently. Startled, Esmir shot out of his seat, face shocked and questioning. Markus closed the door more softly than he'd opened it.

"Aram's gone," he said, his voice rough with emotion.

Esmir stared at him sideways a long moment. "Gone?"

Markus nodded. "He killed himself. Jumped into the gorge."

The old man's gaze slowly lowered. For a moment, he stood teetering as though drunk. Then his knees gave out, and he slumped back into his chair like a marionette whose strings had been cut.

Markus crossed the room in a daze and slipped through the partition, leaving Esmir to his grief. His own feelings were strangling him hard enough; he could barely breathe. He strode out onto the terrace and walked to the edge. There, he fell to his knees and wept.

He stayed there on the terrace the remainder of the day and well into the night, staring out across the gaping silence of the chasm. Siroth landed and settled next to him, and he was grateful for his dragon's presence, for Siroth's steadying personality helped keep the despair at bay. Sometime after sunset, Esmir joined them, hobbling out and sitting down at his side. For hours, the two of them just sat there in silence, two failed Wardens bereft of the Champions whose lives they had pledged to protect.

"What happened?" Markus asked at last. "Did he just break?"

Esmir bowed his head, shaking it sadly. "More likely, he was already broken. Perhaps we were too quick to assume Aram passed his Trials."

To Markus, that made sense. It was comforting, in a way, for it meant that it wasn't Aram's fault. Thinking of it that way cooled his anger, and let grief take its place. But guilt came along with grief like an inevitable companion. He couldn't shake the cruel feeling that it wasn't Aram who had failed…but rather it was *he* who had failed Aram.

"I didn't keep my oath," he murmured. "I didn't save him from himself."

Reaching up, Esmir patted Markus's shoulder in a gesture of sympathy. Then he pushed himself up and limped back into his eyrie.

Markus awoke to the brilliant light of morning warming the rock beneath them. Siroth lay stretched out at his side, the dragon's long neck curled around him protectively. Markus sat up and rubbed the sleep from his eyes. His back ached from spending the night on the hard stone, and his eyes felt grainy, like he'd scrubbed sand into them. He supposed he wasn't going to get any more sleep, though he needed it. He rose reluctantly with a murmured word of thanks to Siroth for his company. Then he paused, not sure what he should be doing. For a moment, he just stood stunned, his gaze wandering the empty air in front of him.

For the first time in his life, he had awakened without a sense of purpose.

When he entered the eyrie, he noticed that Esmir was gone, though the old man had left a pot of something simmering over the fire. Markus wrapped his hand in a towel and took the kettle off the flames, setting it down on the floor. He ladled himself a bowl of watery porridge, but only managed to get down a third of it before his stomach rebelled. Pouring the remainder back into the kettle, he decided to dress and go downstairs, hoping that Vandra could put him to work—anything to get his mind off Aram.

But when he reached for his clothes, his hand stopped short of grasping them.

They were the clothes of a Warden. The sight of the garments made him sad, but also disgusted. Tossing the uniform aside, he found some of his old garments and pulled them on.

The sound of rushing wings made him flinch.

Markus whirled toward the mouth of the cavern just as a violent gust of wind blew in from the outside, fanning his hair and crackling his tunic, billowing Siroth's wings. He raced toward the cave mouth just in time to see an enormous red dragon sweep across the sky, occluding the sun. Its great wings were easily twice the span of Siroth's, black on the leading edges, transitioning to crimson. The dragon banked sharply and, with graceful precision, alighted on the terrace.

Aram's body slipped limply from its back.

With a gasp, Markus sprinted forward, his mind spinning with a heart-stopping combination of joy and disbelief, for not only was Aram alive, but he had achieved the impossible—he had returned a Greater Dragon to the world.

But the red dragon reacted violently to his motion, mantling its wings protectively over Aram and baring teeth as big and sharp as swords. An intense and irrational hatred filled its eyes. It opened its mouth wider until he could see down its gullet, to the heated core within. For one, terrifying second, he thought the monster was going to sear him with dragonfire.

"No!" a commanding voice rang through the eyrie.

The enormous dragon flinched, closing its mouth with a snap. Its viper-like head pivoted, and it issued a sharp hiss. Markus turned to find Esmir standing frozen in the eyrie's entrance, staring at the massive dragon in open-mouthed shock. For several long moments, he stood rigid and didn't move, and neither did the dragon. Their gazes locked, each held fast by the other, and Markus got the strong sense that he stood between two old enemies reunited in hatred.

"Agaroth," Esmir whispered. Then he slumped, crumpling in on himself, and wept openly into his hands as the dragon glared at him hatefully.

Sensing a break in the tension, Markus inched forward, hands raised, hoping the dragon would allow his approach. Aram lay unconscious beneath it, the skin of his face raw and blistered. Sensing his motion, the great head recoiled like a snake preparing to strike.

"We're his friends," Markus said, taking a mincing step closer, his hands still raised. "He needs help. Please, let us take care of him."

In response, the dragon gave a threatening growl produced low in its throat.

Markus pointed at Aram. "I'm his Warden. He needs help."

The dragon's gaze slipped from Markus to Esmir, its eyes filled with rancorous distrust. It was only then that Markus made the connection.

He drew in a gasp. "Agaroth…" he whispered. Turning to Esmir, he asked, "Is this Torian's dragon?"

"Yes." Esmir wiped his eyes on his shirtsleeve. "And he blames me for Daymar's death, as he rightfully should."

Markus looked back and forth between the old, broken man and the vengeful dragon, at last understanding the dynamic that crackled like lightning between them.

"Don't blame him!" he said to the dragon. "It wasn't his fault. If it wasn't for Esmir, Aram would be dead too!"

Agaroth glared at him with eyes that seemed to burn right through him. To Markus, it felt like he was locked in a battle of wills with a demon. After what seemed like eternity, the dragon let down its guard somewhat, just enough for Markus to reach out to it with his mind with an offer of truce.

Warily, he opened himself to the dragon and showed it a quick succession of mental images that tumbled out of him like a gush of water. Most were memories of the experiences he had shared with Aram, starting with the day he had saved his friend from a beating all those years ago. The dragon got to see Aram through Markus's eyes, and at last gained some measure of understanding. Slowly, the expression of hatred eased on its harsh, reptilian face. Agaroth's wings relaxed, and the dragon took a step back.

Markus hastened forward, dropping to Aram's side. The skin of his face was raw, as though scorched by steam. His clothing was singed, and he stunk of brimstone. Esmir dropped down next to him, laying a hand on Aram's brow.

"He needs essence," Esmir said, his voice trembling. "Fetch me the Wellspring water!"

Markus rose immediately and ran to retrieve the crystalline decanter Esmir always kept on his table. Returning with the water, he lifted Aram and drizzled the water down his throat while Esmir went to fetch a healer.

The water made an immediate impact on Aram's coloring. The warmth of his brown blood returned to his cheeks, and his breathing slowed and stabilized. Above them, Agaroth uttered an approving rumble and backed away, looking much more at ease.

Little by little, Markus got half the container of water into Aram before the healer arrived, an older woman who came stumbling into the eyrie and nearly collapsed at the sight of a Greater Dragon looming above her patient. Together, they got Aram settled into bed, his scalded skin glistening with salve.

Markus returned to the terrace, where Siroth and Agaroth seemed to be getting acquainted. Agaroth was easily double Siroth's size, and yet seemed to accept him as an equal. For his part, Siroth regarded the red dragon with a mixture of excitement and reverence, displaying no sign of being territorial about sharing his eyrie.

Esmir yielded his alcove to Agaroth, the space he had once shared with Daymar Torian. Together, he and Markus moved Aram's pallet to the center of the floor and laid him down upon it. Agaroth curled his great, sinuous body around Aram and shared the warmth of his inner fire with him, fiercely protective of the powerful young man who had not only saved his life but had also redeemed his spirit from the void.

When Aram awoke, there was a chill to the air, a welcome relief from the brutal heat of the abyss. His body ached with scalding pain that felt like someone had dunked him in a pot of boiling water, and when he lifted his arm, he saw that his skin was red and blistered. His throat was raw, and every breath he drew made his lungs burn. With a groan, he rolled over and opened his eyes.

And flinched with a gasp.

A great golden eye was watching him.

Aram sat bolt upright, scrambling backward. An enormous dragon loomed over him, peering down at him with a look of wary curiosity. Aram's thoughts clotted like spilled blood, his mind struggling to understand the miracle of the creature standing before him. It was the void dragon, though it was no longer milky-white, but the deepest shade of crimson, darkening to black at the extremities. It was one of the Greaters, easily twice the size of even Vandra's Ragath, with twin spiraling horns swept back from its viper-shaped head. The dragon's scarred wings were mostly black, and though they were folded, Aram could imagine its magnificent wingspan.

Somehow, the void dragon had saved his life again, and returned him to Esmir's eyrie. Mouth open in wonder, Aram rose unsteadily to his feet and stared upward into the dragon's fearsome gaze.

"His name is Agaroth the Red."

Aram turned at the sound of Esmir's voice, finding the old man standing in the entrance to the alcove. The dragon reacted as well, its black spines going rigid, its golden eyes narrowing in anger. Aram could feel the hatred radiating off the dragon like waves of heat, and at first, he was scared it might attack. But Agaroth stood firm, glaring at Esmir, teeth bared, nostrils distended.

"He hates you," Aram whispered.

"He blames me for Daymar," said Esmir.

The old Warden moved around them, giving the dragon a wide berth. He went to the table where he always sat and started stuffing items into a burlap sack. Then, without speaking again, he left. Aram glanced around for Markus, but both he and Siroth were gone. He was alone with Agaroth, and he could not tell from the dragon's expression whether he saw him as friend or foe.

For the first time, it occurred to him that maybe Agaroth wouldn't want anything to do with him. Daymar Torian had been dead for hundreds of years, but that did not mean Agaroth's heart wasn't just as broken as the day he'd lost him. Siroth was the only dragon Aram had ever heard of that had survived the death of its rider. The more he thought about it, the more he realized that he should have never assumed that Agaroth wanted to live. Perhaps he had been content to die down there in the molten bottom of the abyss. Aram sighed heavily, dropping his gaze, suddenly feeling guilty and unsure.

The sound of a low, rumbling growl made him look back up. Agaroth was considering him with a complex expression, as though the dragon didn't know quite what to make of him. Aram wondered what Agaroth saw when he looked at him—did he see a weakling boy or a young man full of hope? A Friend? An enemy? It could be any one of those or none; he simply couldn't tell.

A questioning rumble trembled the chamber, and the great horned head lowered toward him. Resisting the impulse to retreat against the wall of the alcove, Aram moved forward instead. Hesitantly, he reached out to touch the dragon's head, meeting him halfway. As his fingers brushed the scales of Agaroth's face, something inside him shifted.

Aram reeled as the entire cavern lurched, all of his senses suddenly

upended. It was as though he had been thrust outside his own body, looking down from a height at someone he did not recognize: a man who blazed with ferocious power, and yet somehow projected a sense of innocence that seemed completely at odds with his strength. Aram winced, for it suddenly occurred to him that he was looking down at himself through the dragon's eyes.

Was it possible? Was that truly what he looked like?

Yes.

It wasn't a word, but rather a conviction, and it rolled through his mind with the force of an avalanche. Aram raised his gaze and stared up into the dragon's mighty face, shocked and profoundly humbled by the revelation. Agaroth seemed to nod slightly, as though in confirmation, and then closed his golden eyes.

Aram felt the dragon's mind press upon his own. Every emotion he was capable of feeling stirred awake all at once, an overwhelming gush that sent him reeling as his sense of self was yanked away, replaced by a feeling of plurality. He felt the dragon's soul twine about his own, and a bliss like no other filled him completely. He could feel Agaroth's great sense of relief as the ache of loneliness lifted from him, the terrible despair he had endured ever since the loss of Daymar Torian.

A vision flitted across Aram's mind: that of a young man with warm brown skin and a carefree smile that belied the strength of the power that shone within him. He stood at the side of another young man who was tall and physically strong, with an air of noble confidence that was arresting. It took Aram a few moments to understand what was being shown him. This was Agaroth's memory of Daymar and Esmir, two partners in life and battle, who had loved each other fiercely.

"I'm so sorry," Aram whispered, his voice shaking with emotion. "I'll never be like him. But you have my word, I'll try my best."

The dragon gave a disapproving growl that needed no translation. Agaroth had no tolerance for self-doubt, a weakness he deemed debilitating.

Aram swallowed, finding himself confronted by one of the most daunting quandaries he had ever faced. All his life, he had known with certainty that there was something wrong with him, something that drove other people away. This concept of worthlessness was the foundation upon which his identity was built. The idea of thinking different in any way rubbed against his every grain. He wasn't sure he could do it, even for a dragon as mighty and terrifying as the one glaring down at him.

But, for that dragon's sake, he had to try. So he licked his lips, at last nodding.

He let his gaze roam over his soul-bound companion, slow degrees of awe creeping over him. Agaroth was part of him now, their thoughts and feelings intertwined, and Aram knew that he could no sooner exist without him than he could exist without his heart. For this was what it meant to be dragon-bound. Before, he was but a thin fracture of a soul, and now he was complete.

He stood for a time in the shadow of that powerful gaze, feeling terribly self-conscious, letting Agaroth explore the deepest recesses of his mind and personality. At first, he was afraid that the dragon would take his measure and find him lacking, but that fear was quickly assuaged, as Agaroth would have none of such nonsense. Once again, the mental image appeared in Aram's mind of a young man blazing with power, and this was paired with the dragon's memory of Daymar. Aram looked between the two young men and realized how similar they were in appearance, though in strength, *he* blazed even brighter—he was far more powerful than Daymar.

It was a chilling revelation.

"I hope I'm not interrupting."

Aram turned to find that Markus had entered the eyrie and was cautiously approaching them. Agaroth did not seem to mind his appearance; in fact, he issued a grunt that sounded like a greeting. Aram felt the dragon's reactions as though they were his own and sensed Agaroth's regard for Markus as something along the lines of respect for a colleague.

Markus paused before Agaroth and gave a slight bow, a gesture that seemed to please the great dragon, for his spines lifted slightly and he gave a faint rumble. Markus then turned to Aram and lifted his chin slightly.

"Hey."

There was no emotion in his voice, which gave Aram pause.

"Hey," he echoed.

Searching Markus's face, Aram thought that his friend was angry with him. Though it hurt, he couldn't blame him. He had acted in a way no friend should ever behave.

"You're looking better," Markus said with a guarded expression.

"I feel better." Aram's chest tightened as it sank in how terrible of a friend he had been to Markus. At the time, he hadn't thought about it, or at least not thought it through. A cold fear came over him when he realized how different Markus was acting. Had he gone so far as to damage their relationship?

He thought maybe he had.

Markus nodded once then turned to leave. But before he got to the door, he hesitated and turned back. "You took a hell of a risk without warning me."

Shame reddened Aram's cheeks. He bowed his head. "You have every right to be angry with me."

"Yesterday, I was madder at you than I've ever been at anyone except Sergan."

Aram sucked in his lips, at last nodding. Markus's words hurt, even though they were deserved. The more Aram thought about it, the angrier he was at himself.

"I hope you can forgive me," he whispered.

"I will," Markus said, though something about his tone suggested that his forgiveness would not be immediate. "I'm just going to ask that the next time you want to risk your life on something, you at least talk to me about it first. I'm supposed to be your Warden. I can't do my job if you keep secrets from me."

Aram nodded. "If I'd told you, would you have let me go?"

For a moment, Markus seemed to ponder the question. "Yes," he said at last. "I wouldn't have agreed with it, but I wouldn't have stopped you. You see, I trusted you."

Aram didn't miss Markus's intentional use of 'trust' in the past tense. Never before in his life had he felt such depths of shame. He had done things wrong before. Many things. But never had he done anything deliberately hurtful to someone he cared about.

"You have my word," Aram said. "I'll never keep anything from you again."

Markus contemplated him in silence before finally nodding.

When he was gone, Aram dressed then crossed the main chamber to the hearth, finding the embers gray and cold. Looking around, he saw that many of Esmir's possessions had been removed from the alcove, and he feared that the old man had moved out. His gaze wandered to Agaroth, and he thought he knew the reason why. Nevertheless, it wasn't right. This had been Esmir's home for hundreds of years. If only one of them could live here comfortably, then it should be him.

Aram spent the next few minutes gathering up his possessions into a sack as Agaroth watched him with patient curiosity. Glancing at Markus's belongings made him feel sad; he didn't suppose Markus would want to move with him. The only thing big he had was the chest that Esmir had given him, where he kept his armor. Aram left it there, figuring he would come back for it later.

"I'm going to let you pick out a new eyrie for us," he told Agaroth. "Whichever one you like."

He felt a question form in the dragon's mind, and he shook his head. "No. Just us, for now." He frowned, his eyes going toward the terrace, to where Siroth lay basking in the sun. A deep sadness came over him when he thought about how many people he had hurt. Markus, Esmir, Calise, even the dragons... He doubted any of them would want him around for a while.

Gathering his sack of belongings, he fetched up his sword and moved toward the dragon. Agaroth wasn't wearing a riding harness, and Aram had no idea where he would get one that would fit him, anyway. He was also presented with the problem of how to mount such a large creature. Even lying flat on his belly, Agaroth was taller than a horse.

The red dragon snorted, dismissing his concern. He stalked toward the mouth of the eyrie, where he pressed his head against Siroth's in greeting. Then, moving into the bright sunlight, he spread his mighty wings.

Aram followed him out onto the terrace, overwhelmed by his dragon's sheer size and majesty. In the sunlight, Agaroth looked both magnificent and ferocious, easily the most lethal-looking creature Aram had ever seen. He stalked with a predator's grace, and his wingspan was enormous, extending well beyond the edges of the terrace. His deep red scales reminded Aram of the warning coloration he had seen on many snakes.

The dragon lowered himself to the stone, raking back his wings and raising a leg for Aram to mount. Pulling himself up by the dragon's soft spines, he took a seat high on Agaroth's back above his shoulder blades. He dearly missed having a riding harness, and for a moment, he almost lost his nerve.

Before Aram could protest, Agaroth kicked off from the stone. Startled, he scrambled to hold on. For a moment, the dragon hovered over the terrace, and Aram could feel the great muscles of his shoulders rolling beneath him. His pulse thundered and his breath came in gasps as he clung to the dragon's back with all the strength in his legs.

Agaroth tucked in his wings and plunged down the mountainside.

Aram felt himself lift, and he only kept his seat by gripping the dragon's body with his legs. He clung to the black spines of Agaroth's neck as the dragon pulled out of the dive, soaring away from the cliffs and out over the gaping abyss. Cold wind gusted against Aram's face, making him squint. The dragon's great wings stretched straight out to either side, parting the air like blades. They glided over the canyon, rocking first one way and then the other, as Agaroth adjusted the direction of their flight. Aram could feel the dragon's own exhilaration, his vast relief at being made whole again after so many centuries of lonliness and despair.

Behind them, the structures of Skyhome grew small and distant. On a bluff above them was the Henge and its ring of standing stones. The cliffs below were studded with terraces and pockmarked with caves, entrances to the abandoned eyries on the Heights where the Great Ones had once dwelled. Agaroth banked, turning back, his shadow skimming the rooftops of Hearth Home below.

Aram could see people on the streets pointing upward, shielding their eyes against the glare of the sun. It had been four hundred years since the last Greater Dragon had graced the skies above the eyries, and the sight of Agaroth drew people from their homes and businesses. Children ran in packs through the streets, following the path of their flight. Dragons on the terraces scattered, abandoning their perches in screeching droves and flocking from the cliffsides as a Great One swept by.

Agaroth banked, gaining elevation, skimming the tops of the bluffs and passing over the monoliths of the Henge. The dragon's body rolled slightly, veering toward the wide terrace of an eyrie at the very top of the cliff, even above the level where they had found the dragon cairn. With exquisite grace, Agaroth backstroked to a landing on the wide terrace and there folded his great, black-tipped wings, claiming the eyrie as his own.

Panting with exhilaration, Aram slid from his dragon's back and ran to the edge of the terrace. There, he stood looking down at the streets of Hearth Home, where hundreds of people had gathered, all looking upward, cheering the return of a Great One to the Heights.

83

Aram walked to the entrance of the abandoned eyrie and gazed around at their new home. The cavern was dark and full of centuries of dirt and dust, and it stunk of mold and either bird or bat guano. Pieces of rock had crumbled from the ceiling, adding to the debris on the floor. There were a few pieces of furniture in various stages of decay, all covered in a thick layer of fine gray dust: a long trestle table with a bench, the remains of an ancient cupboard or wardrobe, and the frame of a massive four-poster bed, black with wood rot. There were also various items scattered everywhere: tin cups and broken ceramic vessels, a large iron kettle and candle holders, among various odds and ends.

As he walked slowly forward, his feet crunched on brittle twigs and ancient leaves. The eyrie was going to take a lot of work to restore it to a livable space, and Aram figured he'd better start working. He labored the rest of the morning clearing a dragon-sized area, loading piles of debris into pails and throwing them over the edge of the terrace as Agaroth looked on. There was a second chamber adjoining the first with the remains of a smaller bed, the ceiling lower, yet still tall enough for a good-sized dragon. There was a fresh supply of water; the ancient pipes that had once filled the eyrie's soaking-pool still functioned, though they had been plugged with debris. Once he had cleared the pipes, fresh water once again trickled down the wall into the pool in a thin cascade. It took some time before the water ran clear, and it would take days to fill the entire pool, but at least they had a water supply.

When the time for supper came along, hunger finally pried him from his work. Aram had no wish to go down and dine with the fighting Wing. After his conversation with Markus, he was too ashamed. So, instead, he took the stairs down to Hearth Home, intending to acquire pantry supplies to stock his new home.

Walking through the streets, he got plenty of looks. People moved out of his way, bowing their heads in deference. Aram walked with his gaze lowered, trying his best to be inconspicuous, though it didn't work, for people noticed him anyway. He wished he had changed into his old clothes, even though Esmir said he shouldn't wear them anymore. Deep down, he longed for the anonymity he had enjoyed before passing his Trials. He didn't like the looks in the eyes of the people who recognized him as he passed, looks of trust and faith he hadn't earned.

He requisitioned wood and supplies at the market, more than he could carry, and arranged for the rest to be delivered. The merchants bowed and thanked him profusely, making Aram feel terribly uncomfortable. Turning away from the last stall, he scrubbed his hands over his face, which was coated with a grimy layer of dust. Only then did he looked down at himself and realize how rumpled and filthy his new uniform was.

He hurried back to the eyrie with his bags of supplies, which included two chickens that weren't happy about being shoved into a sack. Back home, he set the chickens loose with a spread of greens and grain to forage on. He ate as quickly as he could then busied himself with more work, hoping that staying distracted would keep away the feelings of guilt and shame.

By the time sunset cast its shadows over the canyon, he had most of the floor cleared down to the ancient stone, and a good-sized fire was blazing in the hearth for the first time in centuries. He fed the fire with more logs then sat beside it in silent contemplation, feeling more alone than he had in years. When it was time to go to sleep, he realized he'd left his pallet in Esmir's eyrie, so he simply curled up at his dragon's side, taking comfort in Agaroth's soothing warmth.

Over the next couple days, Aram finished cleaning out the eyrie and restocking it with provisions, all the while avoiding as many people as he could. He found some treasures buried within the rotten wardrobe and discovered an iron-shod chest that had been hidden beneath some type of abandoned nest in the corner. One of the things that had been left behind by the eyrie's previous inhabitants was a riding harness made of ancient leather that was hardened and cracked. This, he gave to one of the leather workers down in Hearth Home and asked her to replicate it so he could have a harness that would fit Agaroth.

Deep in a corner, he also found a chest of ancient dragon scale armor that was curiously similar to his own. He'd been suspecting the eyrie might have belonged to a Champion at one time and finding that armor validated his guess. He found other trinkets, all ancient, and there were a few that he couldn't even guess the purpose of. These he set aside on a ledge, a small collection of treasures he couldn't bring himself to discard.

On the third morning, a knock at the door broke him from his work. Aram opened the door hesitantly, hoping and yet fearing that it was Markus. To his surprise, he found Calise standing in the hallway. He hadn't seen her since the morning of his Trials, and just the sight of her robbed him of his last scraps of dignity and courage.

Immediately, his hand went to his tunic, which was just as dirty as it had been three days before—he hadn't taken it off. Embarrassed, he opened the door wider and stepped back, unable to find words to greet her. He couldn't tell by the look on her face whether or not she hated him.

She entered the room and froze the moment her gaze fell upon Agaroth, a look of startled awe upon her face. She stood staring at the blazing red dragon for several seconds, blinking slowly. Looking away from Agaroth, she turned and glanced around at the stark emptiness of the eyrie, her gaze at last coming to rest upon Aram with an expression just as bleak as the walls surrounding them. Unable to look at her, Aram stared instead at the floor between her feet, shifting awkwardly. He was too ashamed to say anything. He had almost killed her dragon, and he could tell by the set of her face that she hadn't forgiven him for it.

"You broke my heart," she said at last.

Her words shocked him, and he felt his stomach plunge. "How?"

She shook her head slowly, face heating to red, her eyes glistening with moisture. "Because you almost took away from me the two people I care about most."

As Aram stood gaping at her in dismay, she took his hand and placed something in his palm, squeezing his fingers closed around it. Looking down, he saw that she had given him back the heart knot necklace he had entrusted to her before his Trials. It was all wadded up into a little ball of twine, a sad-looking thing that made his chest ache.

He waited for her to say more, but instead, she simply turned and made her way back toward the door.

"Calise," he called after her. When she stopped and glanced back at him, he whispered softly, "I'm sorry."

Her lips compressed into a thin line, her eyes filling with sadness. "I know."

When she'd left, he tossed the twine necklace into the corner of the cave and went to sit on the terrace with Agaroth. The dragon seemed to sense his mood, his golden eyes conveying a look of understanding. He settled down at Aram's side, looking out over the broad expanse of the canyon with its painted walls. Aram stayed there for a long time, his knees drawn up against his chest, the cool morning breeze playing with his matted hair. It was only when Agaroth left to hunt that he finally rose and dusted off his trousers, looking helplessly around the eyrie.

There was nothing left to clean, nothing left to do. He had spent half the week avoiding both people and responsibility, and now he had no excuse not to get back to them. And yet, he couldn't bring himself to leave the Heights. He walked to the soaking pool and knelt beside it, cupping his hands and filling them with water, which he splashed over his face. Rising, he paced back toward the corner where he'd stacked some empty crates, thinking that maybe he could make some nesting boxes for the chickens.

"Are you just going to hide up here the rest of your life?"

Startled, Aram turned to find Markus standing behind him. His old friend was still wearing his gray tunic, his black hair tied back from his face. He looked confident and knightly, the embodiment of everything a Warden should be. Aram couldn't help glancing down at himself out of embarrassment and shame.

He drew in a deep sigh. "I'm not hiding. I just figured it wasn't fair to make Esmir move out of his own eyrie."

Markus pressed his lips together. "Look. I forgive you," he said at last. "I was mad but…now, I'm just happy you're alive."

Staring at the floor, Aram whispered, "Thanks."

Markus took a step forward, concern in his eyes. "When's the last time you had a bath?"

Aram shrugged.

A long silence stretched between them as Markus simply regarded him. At length, he said, "Well, you can't just hide away up here and rot. Why don't you come down and dine with the Wing tonight? You've been missed."

"Thanks. I will," Aram whispered, though just the thought filled him with apprehension, for he feared the other riders would look upon him with resentment.

Markus nodded. "Take a bath," he ordered, starting for the door. "Don't forget to shave."

Aram ran a hand over his face, realizing that his cheeks were covered in a growth of scraggly whiskers.

"Markus…" He said, his stomach clenching. "Are you still my friend?"

Markus looked at him with a sad smile. "I stopped considering you a friend a long time ago. I consider you my brother."

The relief that washed over Aram made him waver. His eyes burned so hard he squeezed them closed. He stood silent for a moment, gathering his emotions, until Markus came over and gave him a tight hug. Aram hugged him back as hard as he could, not wanting to let him go.

"You really picked the nicest eyrie in the place," Markus said, squeezing his shoulder and looking around.

Aram wiped his eyes. "I didn't pick it. Agaroth did. It's kind of big for just the two of us, though. If you want, you and Siroth can have the alcove over there." He nodded toward the adjacent chamber, where the second bed had been.

"I'd like that. And I'd bet Esmir will appreciate having his eyrie to himself." Markus wrinkled his nose. "You smell like wet dragon. Go take a bath. I'll get my things."

When he'd left, Aram went down to the baths and soaked for a good, long time, scrubbing the filth off his skin with harsh lye soap. When he returned to the eyrie, Agaroth looked at him with an expression of surprise, to which Aram could only smile.

"Was I that bad?"

Amused, he put on the second set of clothes Esmir had ordered for him. He was just finishing shaving when a gush of wind blew in through the opening of the cave mouth, alerting him to Siroth's arrival. Wiping his face dry on a rag, Aram hastened toward the terrace, arriving in time to see the two dragons greeting each other.

Markus slid from Siroth's back, holding a bundle of cut wood held together by a cord and carried by a branch handle. He walked with the wood out to the end of the terrace, to the ancient brazier that was there, and started feeding the wood into it.

"What's that for?" Aram asked.

"A housewarming present from Esmir."

It took Aram a moment to remember that every eyrie occupied by a Greater Dragon had once had its own beacon fire. The brazier on this terrace hadn't been lit for hundreds of years. Markus fed it one last log and, of its own accord, the kindling burst into flames that crackled, throwing sparks into the air, signaling to the world that a Great One looked down upon them, guarding them from the Heights.

They spent the remainder of the morning making a space for Markus and Siroth in the abandoned second alcove. Aram had to chase the chickens out, for that's where they had gone to roost, terrified of dragon-scent. By noon, they had Markus pretty much settled in, and they took lunch on the terrace beside their dragons, their backs pressed up against the cliff behind them.

"Do you ever regret coming to my rescue, that day back in the village?" Aram asked. "I mean, if you hadn't, you'd still be living in Anai right now. You'd probably be married."

"No." Markus tore off a last bite from the chicken leg he was holding then tossed the bone over the edge. "Not once have I regretted it. I didn't rescue you. You rescued me from a life of being my father's whipping boy."

Eyes distant, Aram said softly, "If it wasn't for me, Master Ebra would still be alive, and you could have been his apprentice. Who knows? You could be a master bard right now."

Markus shook his head. "If it wasn't for you, Master Ebra wouldn't have taken me for his apprentice in the first place."

Aram supposed that was true. A heavy silence settled between them, and for a while, neither friend spoke a word. Aram sat gazing absently down at his hand. Streaks of colored light appeared around his arm that reminded him of the auras he saw around most people—pretty much everyone but Markus and Esmir. Only, the colors he produced were intentional. In the last couple of days, he had taken to the habit of knotting strands of aether out of anxiety and boredom, the way he'd used to do with bits of string, finding the exercise comforting.

"What's it like?" Markus asked.

Realizing what he was doing, Aram let the strands of aether go. "It's…intimidating. Every time I look at it, it makes me think about all the responsibility that comes with it." He brought the light back again, holding it in his hand like a ball of soft, radiant yarn.

Markus raised his eyebrows, grimly considering the globe of light Aram held in his palm. "I bet it does."

"The truth is, it's terrifying," Aram admitted. "I just…I wish I wasn't the only one. I wish there were others like me. What if I fail? What if I die? What happens then?"

"I feel the same way," said Markus, his eyes sad and serious. "I'm charged with protecting the only Champion the world has left. What if *I* fail? What if I let something happen to you? Then not only have I lost my best friend, but who will stand against Kathrax?" He sighed, draping a hand over his knees.

Aram didn't have an answer to that. He let the ball of energy fade, his gaze returning to the distant cliffs.

That evening, at Markus's encouragement, Aram accompanied him down to the dining hall for supper. He would've much rather stayed in the eyrie, but Markus was right. He had to emerge sometime. Still, it took all of his courage to enter the hall after such a long period of absence. He saw an open space at one of the tables in the back and made toward it quietly, hoping no one would notice him. But he and Markus hadn't gone more than a few steps before they were noticed and, to Aram's shock, every person in the room stopped what they were doing and rose to their feet, applauding and cheering.

Aram froze, wanting to turn and run from the room, but Markus caught the back of his tunic, denying him any hope of retreat. Ducking his head, he started toward the back table, but the sight of Vandra shaking her head made him stop. The Wingmaster sat on the dais at the front of the room, accompanied by some of the senior members of the Wing. There were two empty chairs next to her, and she motioned Aram toward one of them.

He groaned out loud.

Averting his eyes from the scores of people that stood in respect, Aram made his way to the front of the room past rows of trestle tables, at last taking his place beside Vandra. The applause had stopped, but for some reason, the people were still standing. Aram looked to Markus for direction, but his friend only shrugged, looking as lost as Aram felt.

Leaning toward him, Vandra said quietly, "They're waiting for you."

Awkwardly, Aram took his seat, the rest of the room following suit. A cupbearer arrived behind him and poured him a cup of wine, which Aram picked up immediately as a pretext to be seen as occupied. He sipped his wine and stared down at the table as conversation picked up around him, droning in his ears. In his lap, he fingered the heart knot necklace that he'd rescued from the floor, replaying the painful conversation with Calise in his mind. It wasn't until Markus nudged him that he looked up, jarred from his thoughts.

"Did you hear that?" Markus asked.

Aram shook his head. He looked at Vandra, who was staring at him expectantly.

"I said, I'm glad you came." Vandra's expression was irritated, probably from having to repeat herself. "You saved me from having to go get you."

"Why is that?" Aram asked.

"There's been a problem. Our scouts in the Winmarch failed to report back this morning."

Aram frowned. "How many scouts?"

"All of them."

The silver-blue of moonlight reflected off the Winmarch, transforming the grassland into an expansive, rolling sea. Mandrel looked out across the swells of glowing grass with a growing unease, for there was something about the evening that didn't sit right with him. The horses had been restless, stomping their feet and tossing their heads, giving soft nickers of apprehension. There didn't seem to be any reason for their behavior. There were no predators about, and no storms hung over the horizon. Just a tight, lingering tension in the air that Mandrel couldn't place.

He stood at the edge of the village, Elder Hammon at his side. The expression on Hammon's face was long and grim, the copper rings of his thin gray braids tinkling softly. He stood with his hands on his hips, regarding the shadows beyond the village with a persistent frown.

"Something comes," he said, and Mandrel agreed, though he didn't know what.

His gaze followed the direction of Hammon's stare, and his stomach tightened. To the north, there was a patch of sky that seemed darker than the rest, as though clouds had blotted out the light of the stars in that place. But there were no clouds in the sky; it was a clear night, and all the other myriad stars glimmered like gems strewn across the velvet darkness. Except for that one, dark swath of sky, low on the horizon.

"Something comes," he agreed. Mandrel glanced back over his shoulder at the center of the village, where his people had gathered around the evening bonfire. Their songs and laughter drifted toward him, sounds of normalcy and blissful ignorance. Every person he cared about was seated around that fire, a thought that made him shiver.

"Send the women and children away," he told Hammon. "Have them flee but do not ask where they are going, just in case. Warn the stallion of what comes." With that, he drew the sword he always wore at his side, a weapon he trained with unceasingly and yet had never wielded in war.

"At once, Dedicant." Hammon bowed curtly and left, striding back toward the sod huts of the village.

Mandrel kept his attention fixed on the north, on the dark expanse of shadow that seemed to be growing larger by the second. Behind him, the cheerful sounds of evening were replaced by cries of dismay, shouts and clamor destroying the peace of the night. The village collapsed quickly into disorder as men scrambled to collect their weapons and women rushed to collect their children. Within moments, Mandrel was joined by a line of shirtless men who stood with swords and bows, sheaths of arrows dripping from their bodies and clustered about them on the ground.

"What is it?" asked Namud, a tall and muscular man who was considered the strongest warrior of the village. His eyes scanned the horizon, at last narrowing when he spotted the nothingness that approached.

"The horse-killers come," Mandrel informed them all. Never had he seen them, but he knew their wickedness. They came from the north on black wings.

"The Disavowed," said Hammon, and Mandrel nodded.

The sounds of hoofbeats rose and then grew distant behind him, bearing his loved ones away to safety. His heart and prayers went with them, though their lives were not important. It was the Elesium that must be saved at all cost, the Great Horses of the plains, purest spirits born of the blood of the Mother.

As the sounds of hoofbeats faded, stillness enshrouded the village, chilling the hearts of the men who had stayed behind. They were warriors, one and all, born and bred to defend the Great Horses of the plains. It was that sacred duty that burned hot in their blood and gave them the courage to stand against the evil that rode the shadows toward them.

"Go," Mandrel ordered Hammon. "Ride to the dragonmen and bring them word of our fate."

For a moment, the old warrior made no move, but stood considering him with a look of profound respect and weary sadness. Then he nodded, touching his hand to his brow. "May your spirit ride the winds home."

Mandrel touched his own hand to his brow, though he did not reply, for he knew that his spirit would never find the Greenest Pastures. He watched Hammon sheath his sword and walk away, wading out into the grass of the plains, where he would summon a stallion to bear him away. After he was gone, Mandrel stood in silence with the rest, waiting for hell to descend.

He did not wait long.

The stars overhead disappeared one by one as though gobbled up by shadows that expanded to consume the sky. The evening chilled and darkened, the grass losing its silver glow as night advanced upon them. The wind stilled, as though the earth itself had paused, holding its breath in anticipation.

They crossed the grasslands like a swarm of locusts, dark forms that moved like insects, advancing at impossible speed, teeming over the prairie like spiders erupting from an egg sac. A terrible screech echoed across the sky and a winged form glided by overhead, a black dragon of the enemy. Upon its back sat a human rider garbed in dark armor, wearing an iron helm with two horns swept backward like a goat's.

There were hundreds of them, perhaps thousands. They chattered as they advanced, mandibles clicking in an insectoid tongue that sounded like an army of cicadas. All up and down the line of men, he heard the sounds of struggle followed by the guttural moans of death. When the first creature came at him, Mandrel found himself confronted by a demon armored in a black enameled carapace that was segmented at the joints, its forelimbs ending in sharp spikes. Though humanoid, it wasn't human, but had the jaws and long, slanted eyes of a mantis.

Summoning every drop of fortitude that he could muster, Mandrel swung his sword, driving it hard into the creature's shoulder, in the gap between plates of armor. The thing screeched, black ichor splattering his face. He screamed as the caustic fluid ate away at his skin, dissolving his flesh with a hissing noise.

The screams of the dying assaulted his ears, and it was all he could do to kick the insect -like creature off his sword. He barely raised his weapon in time as the next one descended upon him. He swung his sword widely with all of his might behind it, cleaving the creature's head off. Caustic ichor sprayed, saturating his face. Something *cracked* against his head.

Then, there was darkness.

An enormous dragon landed amongst the burning huts of the village, folding its elongated, batlike wings, scanning the battlefield with eyes blackened by shadow. Centuries before, it had been one of the Great Ones, a true master of the skies. But no longer. Now, it was something else, something tainted, and its blood ran dark and cold with hate.

Lazair slipped from her mount and paused, stroking the dragon's long, sinuous neck as she surveyed the carnage of the village through the T-shaped opening of her helm. All around, smears of gore that had once been men slicked the trampled grass of the prairie, a sight that gave her a sense of satisfaction. The horse-thralls had resisted long enough. It was long past time they were put to the sword. But the humans were not the reason they were here. She had come for those they warded, and now there was no one left to stop them. She could almost taste the blood of Elysium on her tongue, and the thought made her salivate.

A tingling sensation came over her, and she sensed a presence she hadn't felt in a very long time. Turning slowly, she stared out through the shadows of her helm, her gaze fixing on a lone stallion that waded toward them through the long grass of the prairie. The stallion was the color of burnished gold, its mane and tail like spun glass. It stopped and considered her with dark eyes that held no fear of death or pain. Lazair nodded acknowledgment of her opponent.

The ranks of therlings parted to admit the lone stallion into their midst, and Lazair slipped her Baelsword from its sheath. It was the same sword that, ages ago, had slain Raginor, Lord of Eyries, and today would reap the soul of this far less worthy opponent.

The Elesium's silver aura swelled to brilliance, as though it sucked every drop of starlight from the sky and reflected it back. Lazair raised her Baelsword, allowing it to drink of the stallion's essence.

Still paces away, the Elesium paused. His ears laid back flat against his head, his teeth bared. One golden hoof stamped at the soil of the prairie. His distended nostrils blew warm mist into the cold night air, and his noble eyes blazed with wrath and fury. He was the embodiment of grace and all that was wholesome, and her sword hungered for his spirit.

Trumpeting a challenge, the stallion tossed back his head and reared to his full height, pawing at the air. Coming down, he hurled himself at his enemy.

Arrogant and ruthless, Lazair drew back her sword and waited to receive her charging foe. But before the stallion came within range, a brilliant light shot out from him, slamming into Lazair and hurling her backward. She landed hard on her back, and before she could regain her feet, the stallion reared and came down on her with its forelegs. Its hooves slammed into the black armor of her cuirass like a meteor crashing to earth. But the fortified armor held, only denting. When the stallion rose again, Lazair brought her sword up, blade angled at his chest.

Another blast of solidified light hurled her body across the ground. She rolled, nearly losing her grip on the sword, but somehow, she hung onto it. The stallion came forward, lowering his head to charge, but this time, Lazair was prepared for it. When the force of the stallion's great spirit slammed into her, she brought the Baelsword up to parry.

The Elesium screamed in pain and outrage, wheeling away. Lazair lunged after it, determined to exploit the opportunity before her opponent could recover. In one impossible stride, she closed the distance between herself and the stallion and lashed out with her blade, slicing a deep wound across the stallion's hide.

The Elesium reared, battering Lazair with his forelegs while lashing out with his fortified spirit. The power that slammed into her would have been devastating, but she brought her blade up in time, absorbing the force of the stallion's fury before swiping out in a counterattack.

The Baelsword cleaved a gash deep into his flesh, opening his neck from jaw to shoulder. Hallowed blood showered the ground, raining like teardrops upon the plain. Releasing a sigh, the stallion staggered then slumped to his knees, head bowing to the ground, the radiant glow of his spirit fading as his lifeblood drenched the grass.

Lazair knelt and scooped up a handful of hot blood fresh from the vein, bringing it to her lips. She slurped it down ravenously, licking her fingers clean as a shivering thrill electrified her body, making her gasp. She stood and raised her sword to administer the coup de grâce, but the sound of weeping made her pause. She turned toward the noise, lowering her blade.

Kneeling on the ground, hands bound behind his back, one of the pathetic horse-thralls wept openly, a man with long gray hair and a scar upon his face. Lazair turned from the dying stallion and walked toward the old man, her heavy iron boots crunching on the charred bones of his fallen kinsmen. Pausing over him, she gazed down upon the old warrior for a long moment, taking pleasure in his grief.

But it was another's grief she was more interested in.

Kneeling beside the horse-thrall, Lazair made sure the dying stallion was watching as she softened the flesh and bone of the old man's chest and forced her hand through his rib cage. He threw his head back in a tortured scream, the tendons of his neck pulling taut in agony. One by one, Lazair grabbed hold of the man's ribs and pried them out of his flesh, tossing them on the ground as the dying Elesium looked on.

With a satisfied smile, she glanced to the south, where she felt the presence of another opponent, this one far greater, and a quivering anticipation passed through her.

"What do you need from me?" Aram asked Vandra as a servant in a floor-length robe set a plate of roasted coney between him and Markus.

"Nothing for now," Vandra said, nodding her thanks at the servant, who set another plate between Vandra and the woman seated next to her, Imal Padra, one of the newest members of the fighting Wing. Like himself, Imal seemed too young to have already earned the privilege of sitting at the head table. He'd seen her around the eyrie, but he didn't know much about her. She was around Markus's age, with long brown hair and skin darker than most of the Auld, so much so that he couldn't help wondering if one of her parents were human. She cast a shy glance at Markus who, predictably, didn't notice.

"We'll see if we hear anything by tomorrow," Vandra said around a mouthful of meat. "If not, maybe you and Markus can fly to Winhome and make sure everything is all right."

Aram broke a leg off the coney then leaned back in his seat to clear a visual path between Markus and Imal. His gaze scanned the rows of tables that filled the room, looking for Calise, but he didn't see her. A heavy weight settled deep in his chest, making it hard to swallow. He set the leg down and lifted his wine.

From the corner of his eye, he caught Imal chancing another glance at Markus. At that point, there was only one thing a good friend could do: he prodded Markus's foot with his own, nodding his head at Imal ever so slightly. At first, Markus frowned in incomprehension, but then his eyebrows flew up. After that, Aram had a hard time staying out of the way as his Warden squirmed forward and backward in his seat to get a better view of the pretty young windrider.

By the time supper was over, Aram still hadn't caught even a glimpse of Calise. He was still looking for her as everyone in the hall rose to leave.

Before he and Markus could exit the room, they were accosted by their friends, who were all dressed in riding leathers and bubbling with exuberance. Aram smiled broadly, happy to see that at least *they* weren't mad at him.

Corley spoke first, "Eugan was wondering if—"

"It wasn't just me!"

Corley scowled with an irritated glance at Eugan. "*We* were wondering if we could meet your dragon."

"Is it true he was Daymar Torian's?" Kye asked.

"Why don't you come on up?" Aram smiled, glad that at least some things were returning to normal. He glanced at Markus, but Markus wasn't paying attention. Instead, he was staring across the room to where Imal lingered against the wall, talking to one of her friends.

Markus muttered, "I'll be up in a moment," then walked away, making a beeline across the room toward Imal, who was conspicuously acting like she didn't notice his approach. Seeing his trajectory, Corley prodded Iver with his elbow then nodded at Markus. Iver winced, rubbing his side were Corley's elbow had jabbed into his ribs.

Aram led them up to the level of the new eyrie, hoping that Agaroth wouldn't mind being gawked at. As it turned out, the great dragon seemed to enjoy the attention, spreading his massive wings in display and even letting them touch him. Aram got the feeling that indulging human curiosity was nothing new to Agaroth, and indeed, the dragon flashed him images of he and Daymar surrounded by crowds of eager people.

"I just...I can't believe it," muttered Eugan, staring up at Agaroth with wide, incredulous eyes. Turning to Aram, he said, "When I first met you, I felt sure that Vandra was committing cold-blooded murder making you face the Trials. I really didn't think you stood a chance."

Smiling, Aram admitted, "I didn't think I had much of a chance either."

Eugan looked at him as though really seeing him for the first time. "How did you do it?"

Aram had never thought about it. In his mind, he had just done what people had told him to do, whether it be Esmir or Vandra or Master Henrik. Then he remembered something Esmir had told him a long time ago: *you'll do it because it would be unthinkable for you not to*, a phrase which pretty much summarized it.

He shrugged. "I didn't have a choice. So I just did."

Jeran came to stand next to Eugan, giving Aram a look he couldn't interpret. Softly, he asked, "How powerful are you?"

Aram answered honestly, "I don't know."

"How don't you know?"

"I've never really been tested, outside of the Henge."

"Well, don't you think you should find out?" asked Kye. "Before there's a battle?"

"I suppose I should," Aram said thoughtfully. "I just don't really know how."

Corley shot Iver a wry grin. "Maybe you can fix Iver's broken heart. Ever since Maddy Paden broke up with him—"

"*I* broke up with *her!*" Iver exclaimed, face red as a beet.

"At least fix his nose so he's not so ugly," said Kye.

Everyone erupted with laughter, except for Iver, who stood fuming, staring off to the side with his hands on his hips. Jeran tried to pat his back, but Iver just batted him away. Aram led them off the terrace, figuring the two dragons needed some peace. Settling his friends around the fire, he went and fetched a jug of whiskey.

Iver took a swig from the jug then passed it to Eugan. Wiping his mouth, he asked Aram, "So, what's going on between you and Calise?"

Aram shook his head sadly. He'd been hoping to see Calise in the dining hall and wondered if she was avoiding him on purpose. He hoped not. He didn't want to think that he made her feel so uncomfortable she couldn't eat with her friends.

"I shouldn't have taken Zandril," he muttered.

"No," Iver agreed. "You fucked up."

Nods and murmurs of consensus echoed from around the fire.

"I fucked up," Aram agreed, accepting the jug of whiskey from Jeran. He took a healthy gulp, wincing as it went down. It was strong and tasted terrible, and it burned his throat. He smacked his lips with a grimace, passing it along.

The door opened, and Markus entered, a wide grin on his face. He came directly over to the fire and flopped down next to Aram. Accepting the jug of whiskey, he knocked back a healthy swallow.

"How did it go?" Eugan asked.

Markus glanced down with a sheepish grin.

"Oh, come on," Kye prodded. "You couldn't have done worse than Aram!"

Aram smiled, for it was true. Jeran thrust the jug back at him, hitting him in the chest with it. Taking a drink, Aram handed it to Markus. "So, did you do better than I did?"

"I did. Sorry." Accepting the jug, Markus upended it and drained the last of its contents.

"That's great," Aram said. "She's really pretty."

"Yeah, she is." Markus had a distant and dreamy smile on his face.

The sound of the door opening made Aram turn. One of the younger men from the Wing strode in, an apprehensive look on his face. His eyes wandered over the group of friends, at last coming to fix on Aram.

"Vandra needs you," he said, walking swiftly forward. "In the Council chamber."

Concerned, Aram rose to his feet. "What is it?"

"There's been an attack on Winhome."

Aram paused just long enough to gather up his sword as his friends jumped to their feet, erupting with questions. He didn't wait but sprinted out of the room with Markus on his heels. They rushed down long flights of stairs to the level of the Council chamber, then dodged through the halls as people scrambled to move out of their way.

Entering the chamber, Aram found a meeting already in session. He picked his way around the circle and took his place beside Luvana. Conversation stopped as he entered, all eyes going toward him and Markus. Aram took a seat as quickly as he could, muttering an apology for being late.

Luvana sat in her usual spot, her head covered by her blue headscarf. Before her sat a wiry man with braided gray hair, a wool blanket thrown over him as though he were ill or infirm. To Aram, he looked familiar, but it took him a moment to remember that he had seen this man before, when he had visited Winhome with Vandra. Then, Aram had gotten the impression he was one of the leaders of the village.

Luvana raised her hand, indicating Aram and Markus. "Elder Hammon, this is Champion Aram Raythe and his Warden, Markus Galliar."

The old man grimaced. "I know who he is." He pointed an accusatory finger at Aram. "You promised you would help."

Aram went cold, for he knew what the man was talking about. He had promised Mandrel that, after his Trials, he would find the people who had slaughtered the Elesium. But with all that had gone on, he hadn't had the chance.

"I'm sorry," he said, forcing himself to look the man in the eyes, even though it was almost painful to do so. "I hadn't forgotten, but—"

Elder Hammon bared his teeth. "Dedicant Mandrel is dead, along with all of the men of Winhome."

Exclamations of fury erupted all around the council fire, and Vandra raised her hand in an effort to instill calm. She turned to Elder Hammon. "Champion Raythe only passed his Trials last week, and he did so far sooner than anyone thought he could. He is not to blame."

The expression on Hammon's face did not change. He sat glaring at Aram as though he held him personally responsible for the tragedy that had befallen Winhome.

"Please, Elder Hammon," Luvana said. "We want only to help you. But first, we need to understand exactly what transpired."

The old man at last broke his stare away from Aram and turned to address the Council. "A raiding party from Araghar descended upon us. The women and children escaped with the Elesium, but our men stayed behind to ward their flight. Dedicant Mandrel sent me to you, to bear word." His gaze swept around the room, traveling from person to person. "I went back. I shouldn't have, but I did. They were all dead. Every one of them, slaughtered, along with an Elesium stallion. Dedicant Mandrel…" He bowed his head.

Aram felt a great sadness, for he had thought highly of Mandrel, and he couldn't help but blame himself.

"What of those who fled?" asked Vandra.

"I do not know. I came straight here."

Which meant that his people could still be in terrible danger—or dead already. Aram couldn't bear it. He couldn't have more deaths on his conscience, especially not women and children and Elesium.

"What of the armies that were gathering? Are they anywhere nearby?"

"They're close," Vandra informed him.

Aram turned to Luvana. "I'll fly to Winhome. I'll read the strands there then go find the refugees and make sure they're safe."

"No," said Vandra immediately.

Aram started to protest, but Vandra cut him off. "The main body of Kathrax's army is nearing the fortress of Eld Anoth, which guards the entrance to the Winmarch. We need you here."

One of the older men raised his head, a look of defiant pride smoldering in his eyes like banked embers. "Eld Anoth is the most defensible fortress in the world. Not once in history has it fallen."

Elder Hammon's stare fixed on him, his eyes narrowing. "Do not take them lightly. You have not seen what I have seen."

Looking at Luvana, Aram argued, "I can make it to Winhome and back in a few hours." He would have more than enough time, especially if he left immediately.

"We need you here," Vandra insisted. "Only you and Markus can fly over their army, and we need reconnaissance. We must stop them at Eld Anoth, before they reach the Heart of the Mother."

Aram clenched his fists in frustration, for every fiber of his being was opposed to that idea. Something inside him was pulling him toward Winhome, and he knew it was the kind of feeling that he couldn't ignore. Looking at Elder Hammon, Aram held the man's gaze firmly. "Markus and Siroth can surveil Kathrax's army without me. I *need* to go to Winhome."

Markus sat bolt upright. "I go where you go—"

Aram refused to be deterred. He turned back to Luvana. "We need to know why this happened, what their objective is. I'll just go read the strands and then return. That's all."

Luvana at last sighed. "You may go. But return immediately. Do not engage them."

Markus didn't look very happy about it, but he relented with a scowl. Elder Hammon inclined his head, a gesture Aram appreciated more than the man would ever know. With that, the meeting was adjourned, and people started filing out. Before Aram could follow, Vandra caught both him and Markus by the arm, pulling them aside.

She raised a finger at Aram. "The moment you find something, come right back. Don't do anything rash." She turned to Markus. "Candon Laiel is right—Eld Anoth *is* the most impregnable fortress in the world. I need to find out why Kathrax thinks his army can take it. Until we know that, we know nothing." With that, she clapped both their shoulders and strode out of the room.

Markus turned a resentful glare on Aram. "If you see one damn thing—"

Aram raised his hands. "I know. I'm just going there to read the strands. And I won't be alone—I've got Agaroth."

Markus ground his teeth, but he didn't say anything more. Aram followed him toward the door but paused, turning back. He crossed the room to Elder Hammon and bowed his head deeply.

"I'm truly sorry about Dedicant Mandrel," he said. "I promise I'll do everything I can."

The old man gazed at him harshly for a long, silent moment before saying, "I will hold you to that promise, Champion Raythe."

Aram stood looking at him a second longer, then bowed formally.

Dedicant Mother Althea stumbled over a hollow in the ground and would have fallen, had it not been for Nadira, her teenage acolyte who walked at her side, holding her arm. The night was dangerously dark, and the shadows that dappled the ground were even darker. After their wild flight across the prairie, the people of Winhome were exhausted, and Althea was no exception. She had lived for hundreds of years on the plains, yet her body was no longer young and agile. She felt every jarring stride in her joints and knew she did not have many leagues left in her.

She walked at the head of a column of women and children, refugees from the terror that had befallen their home. Every time Althea glanced behind, the shadow that obscured the northern horizon seemed ever more oppressive. As the night wore on, that shadow deepened, and she knew with growing desperation that they would not reach safety in time.

The people who walked behind her were strong both in body and spirit. They were people of the plains, servants of the Great Horses, and they had known their share of hardship. But nothing like this. Every one of these children had lost a father this night. Babes cried from their swaddling and toddlers wailed in trauma and fear. The older children and women did not weep, however, for they understood that their lives were inconsequential. It was the lives of the Elesium they warded that must be preserved at all cost.

Nearly fifty of the Great Horses had fled with them from Winhome.

They walked beside the column, their glowing spirits shining like beacons in the night. Althea had hoped they would flee to the fortress of Eld Anoth. But the Elesium were proud, and they disdained the walls of men. They were fleeing toward what they knew, and she couldn't blame them for it, for that was their instinct.

Althea stumbled, her ankle turning. She stifled a gulp of pain and nodded at the girl next to her, assuring her acolyte that she would be all right. But when she continued forward, she could not hide the limp that plagued her stride. Sweat beaded on her brow, and she bit her lip in determination. But all the determination in the world would not help her if her body failed.

Glancing behind, she took note of the shadows and felt her heart quail, for they appeared much closer than they had just minutes before. She trembled, for she knew it was no mere shadow that plagued their trail, but an army of creatures shunned from the world, unnatural and despicable, against whom they had little protection.

"Mother Althea," Nadira said, her voice barely audible. "Do you need to rest?"

"No." The Dedicant Mother shook her head. "There is no time to rest."

The girl glanced behind them, her eyes widening. "We will not make it."

Althea feared she was right, though her heart still clung to hope. She patted the girl's hand on her arm. Her eyes went to the sky, searching there for signs of movement. She saw nothing. For now, the sky was clear of dragons. But one by one, the stars overhead were winking out, and her hopes were fading with them.

With a deep sigh, Althea stopped and turned back.

The people of Winhome stopped with her.

She let her gaze rove over them: mothers and daughters, small boys with thumbs in their mouths, babes carried in arm or by sling. All stood before her with bleak and haunted faces, eyes drawn to the shadows behind. Flanking them were the golden Elesium who had fled with them, arrayed in a large crescent that stretched out before and behind their column like the wings of a butterfly.

Raising her voice, Althea informed them, "We can go no further."

The people exchanged fearful glances but said nothing. They trusted her, even in this. Never before had she felt so grateful to have been chosen as Dedicant Mother of these people. Most knew her words foretold their death, and yet none spoke in protest. They trusted her to make the right decisions, and they knew that, ultimately, it was the lives of the Elesium that mattered. Not theirs. They knew that she would help them if she could.

She could not.

Walking forward, Althea made her way toward the nearest stallion and laid her hands upon his velvet coat. The stallion uttered a soft whinny, breathing warm breath into her face.

"We have served you as well as we can," she told him, "but now our presence only slows your flight. Go with our love, and may the speed of the wind carry you."

Removing her hand, she bowed her head.

The stallion snorted, stamping his feet. Then he reared halfway, neighing his acknowledgment of the respect she had paid him and his kind.

But instead of turning to leave, he walked past her and stopped beside a woman holding a small boy. Stretching out his head, he nuzzled the child.

The woman's face slackened, and her eyes widened in awe. Moving around to his side, she lifted the boy and set him upon the back of the Elesium stallion. Althea brought a hand to her face in shock, for never in her life had she known an Elesium to bear a rider. The boy sat astride the magnificent stallion without fear in his eyes, small fists clenching the silver mane. All around the column, the Great Horses came forward, offering to accept the burden of a rider upon their backs. There were not enough horses to carry them all, though.

Some would have to remain.

Althea knew better than to protest when a stallion came forward and offered to carry her, and she allowed her young acolyte to help her onto the Elesium's tall back.

Nadira wasn't so lucky. No horse came to bear her away. Instead, she moved to stand with the women and older children who would not be saved, who were doomed to remain behind. Althea felt her eyes moisten with tears, for she loved each of them dearly. They were her kin, her daughters and sons, and it was unbearable that she would be borne away, leaving those she loved to perish. As the stallion started forward, her eyes were drawn to the shadow behind them, and she knew she did not have time to grieve.

Markus leaned forward over Siroth's neck, squinting against the wind as his eyes scanned the ground far below. The speed of their flight tore the breath from his lungs and filled him with an exhilarating rush. It didn't matter how many flights he took on Siroth's back, every flight was just as exciting as the first. He felt born to the sky, far more comfortable on his dragon's back than on a horse. In the sky he felt truly alive, truly awake, in harmony with the dragon beneath him and in awe of the world below.

They soared over a landscape drenched in moonlight. Ahead, the plains spilled like a silver tide in all directions, while below them, snow on the high mountain peaks glowed a luminous white. Siroth's wingtips parted the clouds as he glided gracefully down the flanks of the mountains, the land tumbling away beneath them. At the base of the foothills was their destination: Eld Anoth, the ancient fortress that guarded the entrance to the Winmarch, its many towers and high walls forming a roughly circular perimeter that ambled over the irregular landscape.

His eyes were drawn to a darkness on the ground, and he willed Siroth toward it. The dragon complied, banking gracefully, giving Markus an unobstructed view of what looked like a wide, black lake ahead of them.

As they grew closer, he realized that the darkness below wasn't a lake at all, but the encampment of an army. A vast army, numbering in the tens of thousands, their campfires dotting the plain. In the distance, he could make out the silhouettes of four dragons circling like vultures over the encampment. He urged Siroth lower, wanting a better look at the enemy. The dragon dipped toward the ground, taking him low enough to see individual tents and soldiers arrayed there.

What Markus saw shocked him.

Behind the encampment of humans was an army of void walkers. He could recognize their pale and emaciated bodies from the air. They were mixed in with therlings and dark insect-like creatures with segmented bodies that sheltered together like a tremendous swarm.

Light flashed, and a peal of thunder jarred the sky. It was as though the air itself had been jerked out from beneath them. They lost altitude quickly, but then Siroth recovered, flapping to gain height. Markus's bones felt frozen, and he knew for a fact that he had repulsed an enormous lance of magic. If it had been any other rider on Siroth's back, they wouldn't have survived the attack.

Another bolt of lightning stabbed at them like a spear, the clap of thunder that followed shuddering the air.

"Turn back!" Markus cried, and gripped the spines of Siroth's neck as the dragon rolled sideways, pivoting in the air. Pumping his wings, Siroth surged back toward the foothills, Markus glancing frantically behind.

As they gained the slopes of the mountains, Markus urged Siroth faster with a gnawing anxiety, for he knew how dire the news was that he carried. Somehow, Kathrax had tripled the size of his army. And they would be arriving at the walls of Eld Anoth a day sooner than expected.

Siroth soared faster than the wind, cutting like a dagger through the night sky. He gained the summits of the mountains then flew out over the gorge, navigating its twists and turns with expert precision, at last gliding to a stop upon the wide terrace of the Southern Eyrie.

There, Markus slid from his back and sprinted into the cavern, looking for Vandra. He found her in her alcove, sleeping on the ground alongside her dragon. Markus crouched over her, panting and trembling, and shook her awake.

"They're there already!" he blurted as Vandra sprang upright. "They'll arrive at the fortress tomorrow morning! And there's a lot more of them—I saw therlings and void walkers. And dragons! They called lightning—"

Vandra threw her hand up, cutting him off. She pulled on her leathers and grabbed her sword off the floor. Marcus followed her as she ran out into the cavern, shouting orders and obscenities at the top of her lungs. Windriders rushed from their alcoves, quickly surrounding her.

"Send a messenger to the commander of the Altierian army," she ordered one of her captains. "Tell him if he can't get reinforcements there by the afternoon, then there's not going to *be* a fortress. Hell, send riders to every nation! Find out where the forces are that they promised us months ago!" She glanced toward the mouth of the cavern, her expression pale and grim. "We need Aram."

"I'll go get him," Markus said, but Vandra shot out her hand, stopping him.

"We can't wait. I need you to fly me down to the fortress."

Markus sighed, casting a dispirited glance back at the cave mouth, wondering what could be keeping Aram.

87

Althea rode bowed forward, clinging to the neck of the Elesium stallion that bore her, galloping, across the plains. Her bones were old and her muscles weak, and it had been years since she had last ridden more than a few leagues. But the stallion's gait was preternaturally smooth, and though his speed rivaled the wind, his hoofbeats did not jar her.

Behind them, the shadow that had pursued them throughout the night was taking on definition. When Althea glanced behind, she saw that the darkness was an infestation of thousands of insectoid bodies, the kind born of the void, their numbers supplemented with eel-like creatures with long, triangular jaws lined with sharp rows of teeth. They came clacking and skittering along behind them at great speed, their segmented legs blurs of motion.

"Faster," she breathed into the Elesium's mane. Beneath her, she could feel the great stallion's muscles gather for a fresh surge of speed. Neck outstretched, tail swept back behind them, he raced in the direction of the foothills, the mountains looming over them like jagged sentinels. Althea squeezed her knees into the horse's sides and clung desperately to the stallion's back, his mane whipping her cheeks.

With a powerful surge of muscle, the stallion cut across the prairie and began its ascent into the foothills. There, they rounded a ridge of green, rock-encrusted hills and entered a narrow ravine, its walls formed of craggy layers riddled with cracks and seams. The sound of their stampede clattered off the walls of the ravine, echoing sharply.

There, the stallion slowed his gait, drawing back from a gallop to a canter and then to a trot as they rounded a steep bend. Realizing where they were, Althea sucked in a gasp. The Great Horses had borne them to Ayar Elysse, the sacred valley of the Elesium.

Her eyes widened, and she sat upright, her heart beating furiously as she looked upon this hallowed place. Before her stretched a wide lake whose glassy waters were clear and glowing with the light of a Wellspring. Its shore was lined with edylberry trees, whose pink blossoms shimmered on their weeping branches. The lights of fireflies zipped through the shadows, weaving a dance of light over the shimmering lake, and the fragrance of spring filled her nostrils with the scent of rebirth and renewal.

Tears gathered in her eyes as she realized the danger they had brought to this place.

What had they done? All around her, the fleeing Elesium halted and collected before the lake, snorting and neighing, tossing their heads in apprehension as the refugees slid from their backs. Althea followed them to the ground, leaning heavily against the stallion's lathered side as she fought back a dizziness that threatened to overwhelm her. Taking in the awe and the majesty of the surrounding valley, a terrible fear trembled her bones.

They could not stay here. They could not bring death to this place.

"Go back!" she shrieked, staggering toward the mouth of the ravine. "We must leave! Quickly!"

The stallion surged forward, inserting his body between her and the valley's exit. He turned his head and regarded her with a proud fire in his eyes, reminding her firmly that it was *she* who served *them*, and her life was not hers to give. Broken, Althea fell to her knees, weeping into her hands. *Why?* Why had the Elesium spared them, their thralls and servants, at the expense of their sacred birthplace?

The stallion reared on its hind legs and pawed at the air above her. Althea raised her hand reflexively to ward her head. But instead of coming down on top of her, the stallion whirled and charged toward the lake, tail carried high, neck proudly arched. He stopped at the shore of the Wellspring and lifted his gaze.

In that moment, a profound darkness eclipsed the sky, and the refugees moaned and huddled together. A harsh wind rose, whipping the manes and tails of the horses. A gusting *whoosh* of beating wings echoed off the valley walls, and from out of the sky, an enormous red dragon appeared and landed before them.

Althea went rigid in terrified wonder, for it had been centuries since her eyes had last looked upon a Greater Dragon. Dizzy with disbelief, she staggered to her feet and lurched forward, her hands raised in front of her like a blind woman groping for sight. All around the meadow, Elesium tossed their heads and whinnied, bucking and rearing in excitement, while the women and children stared fearfully at this monarch of the skies who had descended into their midst.

The great creature spread its massive wings and raised its head, emitting a mighty roar. A helmed man armored in black slid from the dragon's back and strode toward them. Althea gaped into the shadows of the man's helm, desperately searching to make out the features of his face. But it was only when he stood before her and removed the helmet from his head that her eyes widened in recognition.

"I remember you," she whispered in a haggard voice. "You were the boy who sees in color."

Lifting her trembling hands, she closed her eyes and touched his face. What she felt made her insides tremble. This was no boy who stood before her. She could feel the power within him burning with the might of a thousand angry suns. No longer were his body and spirit as she remembered it, young and frail, but he contained a force of presence that eclipsed even the silver radiance of the Elesium. Althea gasped, flinching back.

"You have grown," she whispered.

The young man blinked his burning eyes, and uncertainty darkened his face. His gaze left hers and scanned the surrounding valley, lingering on the Elesium arrayed before them.

"What is this place?" he asked.

Althea drew herself up as much as she could and stood before this formidable man with all the strength of spirit her old body could muster. "This place is Ayar Elysse, the Loins of the Mother. It is Her sacred womb, the birthplace and bastion of the Elesium. Our enemies have come to defile it. To defile *them.*" She glanced toward the Great Horses who stood ringing them, looking on.

The young man nodded slightly, taking in the surrounding valley with an intense and distant stare. His hand rested on the hilt of the star-steel blade he wore at his side. Behind him, the last Greater Dragon in the world regarded them all with ferocious eyes.

"I am Althea, Dedicant Mother of Winhome. What is your name?" she asked.

"Aramon Raythe."

Althea closed her eyes, absorbing the name of this tremendous soul who felt so comfortingly familiar, as though she had known him all her life. She drew in a deep, lingering breath, and held it in her chest for heartbeats. Then she turned to face the contingent of radiant spirits that surrounded them.

Opening her eyes, Althea raised her hands and voice and cried, "Mighty Elesium! A son of Raginor has returned to this world! Let not your heads be lowered nor your hearts despair, but come forth and greet Aramon Raythe, who has arrived to Champion our cause!"

At that, each of the Great Horses neighed loudly, then bowed in deference to the only mortal worthy of their homage. The young man stiffened, his face paling, as though appalled by their behavior. Raising her hand, Althea took his arm.

"Be not ashamed, for it is a great honor they pay you."

The young Champion nodded. "Tell them thank you."

Althea smiled. "There is no need to thank."

The radiance of the Elesium swelled, and their ranks parted. When she saw who approached, her heart stilled. "Look," she whispered in incredulous awe. "He comes!"

The ring of Elesium cleaved to admit one of their number, a stallion of purest white that gleamed with an argent light. He strode toward them at a stately pace, the grace of his stride matched only by the pride and majesty in his face.

"Madiveron," she whispered, "Steed of Raginor, Father of Horses."

The fierce young Champion sucked in a gasp as Madiveron drew up before him, the stallion's gaze regarding him piercingly. Hesitant, Aramon Raythe rested his palm against Madiveron's mighty brow and closed his eyes. A shiver passed over him.

"He wants me to ride him," he said in a tone both solemn and shaken.

"Then you must do as he wills, Champion Raythe," Althea said, moving back.

Aram ran his hand over the stallion's gleaming neck, dazed and over-awed. The coat beneath his fingers didn't feel like horsehair, for it was as soft as velvet, and the Elesium's long mane had the appearance and texture of spun glass. The muscles rippled beneath his touch, and the stallion nickered at him softly.

Overwhelmed, he glanced back at Agaroth, and saw that his drag-on's attention was fixed on the mouth of the ravine, his golden eyes nar-rowed dangerously. Aram felt through Agaroth's senses the presence of something nearby. Something evil. He took hold of Madiveron's mane, and the stallion started forward, striding toward the mouth of the ravine without any prompting. Behind him, Agaroth bared his teeth and emit-ted a low growl.

As they headed toward the gap between ridges, the host of Elesium fell in behind them, their combined radiance illuminating their pas-sage. The rocks closed in around them, and the air seemed to stiffen with tension. The ravine was narrow and winding, but it wasn't long. Eventually, it opened onto a wide escarpment that flowed downhill onto the plains below. The night deepened as the rock walls opened up, and Aram squinted into the shadows that confronted them.

The stallion halted.

Spread out across the plain were thousands of creatures, none of them human. Most had the look of bulbous arachnids with thin, hairy legs that ended in a pair of dagger-like talons. They rocked as their legs seem to dance beneath them, the joints of their dark, chitinous bodies making clacking sounds that buzzed like the roar made by a swarm of bees. Within the ranks of the spider-things were pale, eel-like creatures that Aram recognized, for it was the teeth of such a monster that had savaged his leg when he was a boy. There were other such creatures, too, pale things with rent flesh, that once might have been natural before they had been warped into something profane.

One and all, these were monsters of the void. The spider- and eel -like therlings had originated there. But the others—the pale and tormented things—were void walkers and had once been creatures of this world.

He thought of Agaroth. His dragon had been like them. Perhaps, like Agaroth, these distorted creatures could also be saved from their obscene existence. He couldn't imagine how much essence it would take to return to them the life or death that had been denied them for so long. Far more than he had within him, certainly. But before pity got the best of him, Aram reminded himself that no matter what these creatures had once been in life, they were now the enemy, and he could see the hunger in their eyes as they looked upon him. One and all, they wanted to feed. On him. On the Elesium. To drink their lifeforce.

He shivered.

A shrill cry knifed through the air, echoing down from the sky. Aram glanced up just as a black dragon swooped down and landed in the space between the army of therlings and the line of Elesium that had formed to either side of Madiveron. A helmed figure in dark armor slid from the dragon's back and stalked toward him with long, arrogant strides. A resounding roar trembled the air, and Aram glanced back to see that Agaroth had settled upon the high cliffs above them and stood crouched forward with wings swept back, as though ready to pounce upon this new foe.

Madiveron snorted and pawed at the ground, laying his ears back at the approaching figure. Aram caressed his neck and dismounted. As he did, he felt a stab of apprehension from Agaroth. His dragon did not trust this foe. Neither did Aram. He walked toward the figure at a measured pace, hand on his sword, nerves stretched thin. He did not halt until he stood before the stranger. Reaching up, he undid the buckle of his chinstrap and pulled his helm off his head.

His opponent followed suit, removing off a barbute helmet and releasing a waterfall of silvery hair that rivaled Madiveron's lustrous mane. Aram's breath caught as he realized he was confronted by a pale, striking woman, taller than himself and delicate of build, her eyes full of intelligence and yet steeped in shadow. Looking upon his face, she smiled a confident and gloating grin. Her aura blazed with purple brilliance, a color that screamed corruption and wrongness.

"The boy-Champion has come to stand against us this day," the woman said, her eyes glinting, a sneering smile on her lips. "How fortunate. My master desires your soul as much as he craves the flesh of those you ward. Today, he will feast on both."

She patted the weapon at her side, and for the first time, Aram recognized the sword for what it was: a Baelsword, like the one Kathrax had wielded in his vision. This sword was different; its hilt was carved of dark bone into the distorted likeness of a panther. The sword had an aura of its own, and it gleamed black like the breath of night, coruscating over the length of the scabbard.

Aram's eyes burned with anger. "Tell your master his armies will find only defeat in the Winmarch."

The woman sneered, tossing her hair. "The defeat will be yours, child. You have surrounded yourself with the vanquished. I see behind you the coward Steed of Raginor, who fled the field when his master was slain. And the dragon who failed Daymar Torian and didn't have the decency to die. Where is your Shield, Champion? Was he vanquished too? Who will protect you from the thirst of my blade?"

Aram ground his teeth at the sting of her insults. He was used to taunts, for he had known them all his life. What he could not suffer were affronts to his friends and allies.

Fear is your enemy, his father's voice echoed in his mind. *Don't surrender to it.*

"I don't fear you," he growled, and donned his helm.

"You should, boy."

Ignoring her, Aram started back across the ground to where Madiveron waited with the glowing line of Elesium.

He had gone only a few steps when he heard the unmistakable metallic rasp of a blade being drawn. Aram bared his own sword and whirled, barely avoiding a blow that almost severed his hand from his wrist. His sword glowed with the blue light of the power within him, and it met the woman's Baelsword with a sound impact that jarred through his body, rattling every bone and nerve.

He staggered, feeling an instant of panic. This was no woman he fought, but something far more insidious. Magic suffused her, lending her an inhuman strength that no mere mortal could oppose. The blade of the Baelsword in her hands was like a black wound in the world, sucking light and life from the air around it.

A thunderous roar exploded around him as the two sides engaged in battle. The Elesium fought with the might of their hooves and souls, and he could feel their presence bolstering him, lending him their strength.

Aram struck out with a downward slice, infusing his weapon with aethereal strength. But his opponent was just as fast and just as powerful, and the Baelsword deflected the strike and continued upward, seeking his neck. Aram was quick enough to turn her blade aside, but the pommel of her hilt struck him in the head, a blow that would have incapacitated him had he not diverted magic from his sword to his helm at the moment the strike impacted.

Still, the blow was enough to ring his head, and his next reaction was delayed.

The woman struck out with an armored boot, kicking him forcefully in the thigh, at the same time pressing forward with a lightning-quick barrage of cuts. Aram staggered backward, blade raised defensively to absorb the blows. It took every drop of magic his mind could weave to hold back the torrent of dark steel raining down upon him.

This woman had to be their Champion—there was no other explanation for the strength and proficiency of her attacks. With the Baelsword lending her its might, she was far more powerful and competent than he was. Had Markus been there with him, Aram thought he might have stood a chance. But now, he feared he did not. Little by little, she was overpowering him, wearing him down. It was just a matter of time before he reacted too slowly or made a fatal mistake.

A black mote of darkness the size of a fist shot out of the woman's hand, taking him in the face. Aram cried out as he felt the heat of it burn his skin. Reflexively, he disengaged and staggered away, bringing a hand up to his face. She charged him, closing the distance in a heartbeat, her obscene blade thrusting for his chest.

Aram managed to turn her sword aside, but he lost his footing. His ankle turned, and he fell to the ground. She was on top of him in an instant, her demon-blade pressed against his neck. Aram stared up into her face, aghast, realizing he had lost the fight.

The woman went flying backward, hurled off of him with a scream.

Aram scrambled to stand, gaping at Agaroth, who lunged past him. But just as the dragon's mouth was ready to close around her, the woman brought the Baelsword up, its blade raking across the scales of Agaroth's neck. The dragon hissed in pain, recoiling, blood pulsing from the wound.

Enraged, Aram thrust his hand out, gathering fibers of aether and bending them to his will, forming them into a massive fireball that shot toward her.

The tangle of aether exploded, engulfing his opponent in a wreath of flames. The pale woman screamed and dropped to the ground, rolling and weaving darkness to extinguish the blaze. The fire hissed out of existence, but the damage had been done. Her beautiful white hair had been burned to black char that clung to her heat-ravaged face.

Aram heard a whistling scream and turned in time to see an Elesium go down, its belly torn open by a dagger-length claw. He cried out in horror, but it was too late to do anything. Its scorpion-like attacker whirled toward him, stinger raised and oriented at him.

Agaroth pounced, catching the creature up in his jaws, his teeth crunching on the hard carapace. Black ichor sprayed from the creature's abdomen as the dragon shook it back and forth the way a wolf snaps the neck of a hare.

Aram whirled back around, but the woman was gone. He turned slowly, glancing every which direction, but didn't see her. Suddenly, her dark blade came from out of nowhere, slicing through his armor and opening the top of his arm.

Aram hissed in pain, going cold as the bite of the Baelsword took more than blood out of him. Even the mere split-second of contact had been enough to sap a good deal of his strength, and his next motions were sluggish. Before he could bring his blade up, the Baelsword was already coming back again.

He dodged sideways, though not quickly enough. The motion of the Baelsword had been a feint, and the woman's gauntleted fist hammered his jaw with the might of a sledgehammer. Aram staggered, dazed, and reflexively wove a net of energy in the air between himself and his foe.

The net saved his life.

It caught the Baelsword as it was coming around for him. Reaching out, Aram knocked the sword from the woman's hand. Before she could react, he lashed out at her with a solid gust of air that slammed into her, flinging her to the ground.

Without hesitation, Aram rotated his blade to high guard then brought it down with the full strength of his magic behind it.

The woman screamed and threw her hand up, but his sword cleaved through her arm and continued downward, colliding with her breastplate, which was made of fortified steel, designed to withstand such a frontal attack.

It split anyway.

With a terrible crunching sound, Aram's star-steel blade ripped right through her cuirass and buried itself deep in the woman's chest, slicing right through her breastbone.

Wrenching his blade out of her, Aram stepped back just as something slammed into him with horrendous force. He was lifted off his feet and hurled backward. He landed hard against the ground, the wind knocked out of him. Before he could recover, a heavy foot kicked his helmet, ringing his head like a bell. He tried to roll away, but another kick took him in the ribs and, suddenly, he was being trampled.

There was a ferocious roar, then bodies started flying off him. Agaroth's head snaked down, his teeth closing around Aram's body and yanking him off the ground.

The dragon dropped him at his side, and Aram scrambled to get his feet under him. He grabbed hold of Agaroth's harness, taking a moment to recover his balance and get his bearings. Seeing a wall of insect-creatures pouring toward them, he shouted a warning to the Elesium.

As soon as the Great Horses retreated, Agaroth opened his mouth and disgorged a great gush of flames that saturated the battlefield. Creatures shrieked and screamed as they burned, writhing in the inferno. The dragon stalked forward, dousing the enemy ranks in a wash of roiling dragonfire. Everywhere Aram looked, therlings succumbed to the heat, their meat cooking inside their shells. Only the Elesium were unaffected, withdrawn beyond the radius of the flames.

Emboldened, the Great Horses pressed forward, spilling blinding radiance as they waded into the inferno, which didn't seem to affect them. Spinning a cooling web of aether around him, Aram raised his sword and walked ahead of them.

They passed through the wall of flames and emerged unharmed on the other side. There, the insect-things were regrouping, collecting into a mass like a ball of fire ants. Aram swept his sword back over his shoulder and swung it like a club, using the star-steel as a conduit to unleash the full force of his magic.

A blinding flare of energy shot out from the sword that impacted with horrendous force into the enemy ranks, ripping limbs from torsos and shredding meat, spraying ichor across the field. Aram swung again, slicing through a line of therlings, their bodies yielding like stalks of grain before the farmer's scythe. Agaroth paced at Aram's side, gushing white fire, while Aram swept his sword in deadly arcs of magic, mowing down the enemy before they could escape.

But eventually exhaustion overcame him.

Aram halted, panting, and stood looking around, blinking and disoriented. When he realized that all of their enemies were dead, he staggered, the strength leaving him. The amount of magic he had woven on the battlefield by far exceeded anything he had ever imagined he was capable of, but it had taken its toll. His knees buckled, and he slumped to the ground, landing in a heap of gore.

Markus stood at Siroth's side, one hand on his dragon's smooth and muscular neck, waiting for Vandra to return. The Wingmaster had gone to inform Luvana and the other members of the Council of the threat to the fortress. If Eld Anoth fell, then there was nothing that could keep Kathrax's main host from advancing into the Winmarch.

Vandra had been gone a long time. Markus had been expecting her back before now. His gaze kept darting to the mouth of the eyrie, hoping for Aram. He was starting to get nervous. Aram had been gone all night, and Winhome wasn't that far away on dragonback. But every time he looked out onto the terrace, it was always empty.

Vandra returned, jogging across the eyrie toward him, carrying an enormous sword.

Seeing the sword, Markus guessed her intent. "Do you think Siroth can fly us both?"

"Siroth's a big dragon," Vandra responded. "He can handle two people on his back." Reaching Siroth's side, she gave him a friendly pat. "We'll fly down there and help organize their defenses. Hopefully, Aram will show up before anything happens. If not, I'm going to need you to help counter their sorcerers."

Markus's stomach tightened, for he knew that meant he might be facing Sergan again. All it would take was for the sorcerer to toss a boulder at him, and he would be just as dead as any other man. All he was good for was blocking magical attacks—he wasn't supposed to be a mage-assassin.

Through words and images in his mind, Markus communicated their mission and the importance of it to Siroth. If dragons could frown, then Siroth would be glowering. An image of Markus alone surrounded by thousands of insect-like creatures crossed his mind like an accusation.

"Don't worry." Markus smiled fondly. "I don't intend to die today. And you're not allowed to either." He glanced worriedly at Vandra. "Are you certain he can carry us both?"

The question earned him a rumble of reproach from his dragon, making Vandra cock an eyebrow at him.

"There's your answer."

Markus smiled nervously. "I guess it is." He mounted and waited for Vandra to climb up behind him. As soon as they were secure, the dragon leapt from the terrace, spreading his wings to soar over the gorge.

Markus resisted the impulse to take one last look back, hoping for a sight of Aram. He had to stop worrying and focus his thoughts on the mission at hand. As Siroth banked toward the mouth of the gorge, Markus leaned forward, gripping his dragon's spines with his hands. Siroth didn't seem strained by the weight of two riders as he glided down through the winding canyons, tall sandstone bluffs rising around them on every side. Dipping and weaving, he flew through the eye of a natural rock arch then banked swiftly as the canyon veered ahead of them.

They flew for long miles over the mountaintops, until the plains came into view and they looked upon the encampment of the enemy below. They were approaching the fortress of Eld Anoth, which sat upon a tall bluff above the plains. It had an enormous curtainwall that enclosed concentric rings of battlements complete with bastions and towers. Inside the curtainwall, there was a long reservoir of water that extended all along the wall at the top of the cliffs, flooding a portion of the fortress's interior. It was an intriguing feature, like a moat, though on the wrong side of the wall. On the other side of the reservoir were towers, some of them as tall as ten stories. One tower in particular rose above all the rest, slender, with a weathered copper dome.

Siroth circled low over the fortress, picking out the best place to land. At last, he descended onto the top of one of the fortified towers above the main gate. Markus climbed from his back and stood leaning against him for a moment until the world stopped rocking beneath his feet.

"I'm fine," he mumbled at the dragon's unspoken question. The flight had been a bit rockier than most, perhaps from Vandra's added weight.

He heard the sound of rushing feet, and a group of soldiers spilled onto the roof of the tower and stopped in front of them, raising their hands to their hearts in a gesture that Markus returned awkwardly. They were not Auld, but men with exceptionally dark skin reminiscent of the people of Odessia in the World Above. They wore quilted armor of bright colors and were armed with swords and quivers of throwing javelins. They stood in silence, gazing down upon the army below with grim faces that bore no trace of fear.

Vandra walked forward, halting in front of a man that Markus took to be an officer despite any outward sign of his rank.

"You came," the man breathed, though the look in his eyes was any-thing but relieved. "Where are the others?"

Vandra shook her head grimly. "There will be no others. None could get through because of their sorcery."

This, the soldier accepted with a resigned bow of his head, the way a man found guilty of murder might accept word of his conviction. After a moment, he looked up at Vandra and asked pointedly, "Then you came to die with us?"

"Not if we can help it." Vandra jerked her head toward Markus. "This is Warden Galliar. He is Impervious to magic, and by his virtue, so is his dragon. They cannot be brought down by sorcery."

The officer's gaze slipped from Markus to Siroth, the lines of his brow furrowing. "One dragon will not be enough. They have four."

Markus looked out through the slots in the parapet at the army be-low. The officer was right. They would not be enough. He closed his eyes and silently prayed for Aram to hurry.

89

Markus stood with Vandra at his side, gazing out between the tower's crenelations at the foothills below the fortress. The army of Kathrax was very visible in the morning light. The enemy had broken camp and were advancing up the slope that rose out of the plain, ascending the hill crowned by the walls of the fortress. From the ground, their numbers looked much more intimidating than they had from the air. The vanguard of the army was a hodgepodge collection of misshapen creatures that looked more at odds with each other than they did with their adversaries. Markus couldn't help comparing them to the well-disciplined legions of the Abadian Empire, professional soldiers who fought and died for a living. The army arrayed on the slopes below them was something different entirely. There was no order to them, no banners or heralds, and they shared nothing by way of identity—not even uniforms—and he wondered what could possibly be holding together such unlikely allies.

The insect-like creatures advanced at a faster rate than did the rest of the army, their spindly legs moving quickly at awkward angles, giving them a rigid, jolting stride. After them came a diverse group of void walkers: pale, misshapen creatures that resembled sick parodies of nature. There were hairless deer and foxes, wolves and antelope, hawks and eagles soaring on tattered wings. Behind them came what looked like an army of albino humans. Many appeared wounded, their stride faltering, while some leaned on others for support. Between them swarmed eel-like therlings: white, sinuous ribbons that rippled as they floated above the ground, mouths lined with jagged teeth.

"Where did they all come from?" Markus asked, for when they had met this army before, it looked nothing like it did now. "How can therlings survive so long outside the void?"

Beside him, Vandra stood with an arm draped casually over the dressed masonry of a merlon. She leaned forward and spat a glob of spittle over the parapets. "Kathrax has been draining all the Wellsprings he's taken. Now we know why: he's been building an army of void creatures."

"But that makes no sense." Markus's eyes studied the advancing figures below, wondering who and what those people and animals may have once been. Most of them had been lost from the world during the Sundering, he was sure. But why would they ally with Kathrax? And if they were being fed essence, then why did they look so hideous? The only explanation he could think of was that they were only being fed just enough to keep them alive this side of the void, but not enough to truly make them whole. These creatures were most likely slaves to those who fed them, forever hungering for more essence than their captors were willing to give.

Markus stared down at the enemy forces in dismay, realizing that there would be no end to them. For every creature their own soldiers cut down, Kathrax's sorcerers could simply bring more through the Veil. There would be only one way to truly defeat them: to kill the sorcerers who were creating and maintaining the ruptures.

Markus's throat felt as dry as desert sand. He didn't stand a chance against a sorcerer without Aram. Alone, there wasn't much he could do. Perhaps if he caught one by surprise, he could drive his sword through them before they realized he was Impervious.

Turning away from the parapets, he drew in a long, regretful breath.

"Dragonfire's still our best strategy." Vandra sounded grimmer than she had when they'd first arrived. "We have to find a way to reduce their numbers before they overrun the walls. Look at those things." She gestured at the insect-creatures. "They don't look like they'd have any problem scaling a wall. When the battle starts, send Siroth up to attack from the air. You stay with me."

"He's going to need me—"

Vandra shook her head. "He'll be protected by the bond. What's part of you has become part of him."

Markus didn't argue, because it made sense. There was not a part of him that wasn't intertwined with Siroth, as though they were two aspects of the same soul.

"What would you have me do?" he asked.

Vandra appeared thoughtful. "They don't have siege weapons. They must plan to use their sorcerers to break the walls. Stay by me. We'll defend the gate. Just remember—you're not here to be a soldier. You're here to counter magic. That's it. So stay out of the fight."

Markus turned and scanned the fortress behind them, his gaze roving over an uneven landscape of concentric walls interrupted by thin towers made of limestone masonry. A warm breeze ruffled his hair that smelled of cook fires and nervous sweat. He hadn't expected Eld Anoth to be as big as it was. The fortress was the size of a small city, and it must have been even larger at one time, for the buildings no longer filled the walls that ringed it. Within, there were dozens of pools and reservoirs flanked by trees and gardens, and the foothills outside the walls were cultivated with olive orchards.

A shadow passed over him, drawing Markus's attention upward. A small dragon flew by overhead with a rider on its back. Siroth gave a low and menacing growl, the spines on his back raising. Markus could feel his dragon's loathing for this corrupted creature that had once been its kin. Siroth didn't understand how any dragon could turn against men and was both confused and repulsed by it.

As he stood looking up at the dragon flying over, a terrible cold gripped Markus, making his insides shiver. He gritted his teeth and clutched a stone merlon for stability, feeling as though a bucket of ice water had been thrown over him. Beneath his feet, the wall shuddered. The battlements heaved with a terrible groan, raining pebbles and mortar down their faces.

Magic.

The dragon's rider was a sorcerer and had attacked the wall on which they stood. Marcus had unwittingly repulsed the brunt of the attack, which was probably the only reason why the wall was still standing. All around him, the defenders were scrambling and looking to the sky, shading their eyes against the glare of the morning sun. Two more dragons rose from behind the advancing army, pumping their wings to gain altitude.

"Let me take Siroth up," Markus said. "We can go after them—"

"No." Vandra shook her head. "I need you here. When the fighting starts, send Siroth up alone."

Markus glanced nervously at the sky. Where was Aram? He clenched his hands into fists. Aram should have been there already, unless something had gone terribly wrong.

Below, smoke rose from the orchards. The ranks of the enemy had reached them, and they were setting the trees ablaze. The insect-things spilled through the orchards first, pouring impossibly fast over the ground like waves breaking upon a beach. They moved with a blurring roar that sounded like thousands of blades pressed against grinding wheels. They reached the bottom of the cliffs that supported the fortress's walls and then continued straight up the cliff face.

Immediately, the defenders began raining rocks and hot sand down through murder holes, which seemed to have little effect. For every bulbous body knocked off the rock face, three more scampered upward to take its place. The buzzing roar grew louder, became deafening. Markus had to resist the impulse to cover his ears. He raced to the edge of the parapet and looked down, trying to see the therlings advancing on his own position, but the wall hung too far out from the cliff, and he couldn't see what was straight below them.

The parapet beneath his feet heaved.

The tower across the gate from them erupted in an explosion of fire, spilling rocks to the courtyard below. Screams cut through the sounds of mayhem as men burned, falling to the ground in balls of fire. The day around them flared brilliant white for only an instant, then the wall was jarred by a deafening thunderclap.

A barrage of lightning strobed the air around them, stabbing down like needling lances at the square behind the gate. Soldiers screamed and fell to the ground, writhing in smoldering anguish as electricity clawed over their bodies.

A horrendous cold gripped Markus, making him stagger. Clutching himself, he glanced up just in time to see one of the enemy dragons gliding by overhead. Feeling every hair on his body rise, Markus saw that all the soldiers along the wall were staring at him with expressions of awe. They all realized that he was the reason why they hadn't met the same fate as their counterparts in the courtyard.

Vandra turned and shouted, "Abandon the Ward! Go! Get the hell out of here!" Then she turned to Siroth and pointed up at the sorcerer's dragon slithering across the sky. *"Kill that damn thing!"*

Siroth immediately spread his wings and vaulted into the air, gaining altitude quickly to avoid the arrows of the enemy. Markus watched Siroth bank toward his foe, his throat clenching in anxiety. Siroth was just as fierce a warrior as any, but he hated not being there to fight at his side.

"Let's go!" Vandra's voice broke Markus's attention from his dragon.

She started toward the tower steps, her dark hair fluttering behind her in the wind. Raising his sword, Markus followed her toward the steps to the courtyard. There, they stumbled over debris and smoldering corpses toward the gate, which was cracking and shuddering under whatever force was being applied to it. It couldn't be a battering ram, so Markus guessed that there was probably a sorcerer on the other side, attacking the gate with magic. The defenders had propped wooden beams at angles against the gate to reinforce it, but even those were starting to give. Dozens of men lent their own body weights to the effort, pushing with all their might against the thundering gate with their backs to it.

Up in the sky, Siroth roared a challenge to his foe. Markus glanced up just in time to see him swoop toward the enemy dragon. The two collided in the air and tumbled in a fiery mass through the sky before breaking apart. Before the smaller dragon could flee, Siroth vaulted after it. He caught hold of it by the neck and tore into it with teeth and talons.

"Markus!"

The gate exploded. He was picked up and slammed to the ground, shards of wood spearing the courtyard all around him and ricocheting off his armor. An enormous cry went up, and then a horde of black-armored creatures came spilling in through the gap left by the gate.

Markus barely had time to get his sword up before he was being assaulted by spear-tipped legs that stabbed at him like lances, and his only defense was to swing his sword as widely as he could, clearing a space around him while trying to fall back. Their position was quickly overrun, the soldiers in the courtyard dropping dead, skewered by stingers and spike-like claws, their faces chewed by jagged mandibles. Reinforcements rushed forward from the ward behind them, flooding through sally ports.

The tide of the battle changed as the defenders gained ground, driving the creatures back. Markus found himself falling into a rhythm of slashing and dodging, driving chitinous bodies back out of his way. His blade severed legs and antennae, splitting heads and blinding compound eyes. Vandra fought at his side, swinging her sword with all the strength of a burly man twice her height.

For the first time, Markus understood the nature of Vandra's Talent. Not only did her sword move with the power of Auld magic, but her mere presence seemed to lend courage and resolve to the men and women who fought around her. Black ichor coated her face like tar, mixing with blood from a wound in her scalp. Her eyes blazed with battle-rage. No foe could stand before her.

A lightning strike lit the world around them, dropping a score of defenders where they stood. Many more scattered, running for cover as panic claimed them. Markus glanced around, frantically seeking the sorcerer summoning those deadly spears of magic.

Through a squirming mass of bodies, his gaze fell on two people wearing blue mantles, walking unmolested through the battle: an Exilari sorcerer and their Shield.

Clamping his jaw tight, Markus started toward them, cutting his way through a clot of insects. He was almost within striking distance when the Shield must have sensed him, for he whirled toward Markus, sweeping his weapon back.

Markus halted, frozen mid-stride.

It was Poda.

His old friend stared at him as though looking at an apparition, mouth open and eyes wide. At the same time, the woman at his side turned, and when their eyes met, Markus found himself gaping into Peshka's glowing blue gaze.

Markus stayed his blade, for he had only known Poda as a kind and gentle friend. He couldn't bring himself to strike.

So Poda struck first.

Markus threw himself backward, but not quickly enough. Poda's sword impacted with his shoulder, not hard enough to penetrate his armor, but hard enough to *hurt*. Markus almost lost his grip on his sword. His chest froze with ice as he repulsed a magical attack from Peshka, and Poda's blade was coming back around for another swing.

Markus dropped to the ground and struck out with a kick, taking Poda in the knee, at the same time reaching for his dagger.

Poda fell, landing on top of him and trapping Markus's dagger against his chest with his weight. Markus struggled, grappling with Poda for control of his sword. Poda brought a fist back and clubbed Markus in the face through the opening of his helm.

Markus rolled, pinning Poda's arm against the ground as he struggled to get the dagger out from between them. Suddenly Peshka was there, kicking him in the head, her heavy boot clanging against the thick iron of his helm.

He shifted just enough to free the hand holding the dagger. Wrenching upright, he thrust it through a gap in Poda's armor beneath his arm, plunging it down through his chest and into his heart.

Poda's back went stiff, his eyes widening, his sword arm slowly wilting like a droughted stem. And then he slumped backward as Peshka scrambled away from him with a soul-wrenching cry. Scooping his sword up, Markus rose and lunged at her, burying his blade in her chest and silencing her scream.

She slid backward off his blade, collapsing like a ragdoll to lie on the ground, groping at the rent in her chest.

Markus staggered, his stomach heaving as the horror of what he'd just done slammed into him. He brought a hand up to his mouth, choking, unable to break his eyes away from the pathetic sight of Peshka gulping for air like a fish caught in a net.

He heard his name.

Whirling, he glanced back over his shoulder. Across the courtyard from him, Vandra stood with her hands clutching her neck, her face turning a deep shade of red. Markus sprinted toward her, but before he could cross half the distance, she collapsed, and Markus saw the man standing behind her.

Sergan Parsigal.

"No!" Markus cried, sprinting forward and drawing his sword back over his shoulder.

A smile grew on Sergan's face as his eyes met Markus's. Raising his hand, the sorcerer clinched it into a fist. On the ground, Vandra thrashed and moaned.

All Markus could think about was sinking his sword hilt-deep into the sorcerer's chest. Just as he leapt over Vandra to run Sergan through, something thundered into him, bowling him to the ground. A heavy weight slammed into the side of his helmet, then the entire world bucked and went dark. It took a moment for the light to fade back again, and when it did, he found himself lying on his back, staring up into Sergan's face. The sorcerer was standing over him, smiling down, eyes blazing with the terrible light of sorcery.

Someone grabbed him, hauling Markus upright. Another man moved in to help restrain him. Markus fought, but there were too many of them. They pulled him back away from where Sergan was standing, watching Vandra struggling to breathe.

Just then, a raging gust of wind swept over them, accompanied by a ferocious roar. Markus looked up in time to see Siroth falling upon them from the sky in a gush of flames. The people holding Markus screamed and scattered as the dragon landed in their midst, lashing out with his tail and spewing fire all around the courtyard.

The flames stopped just shy of Sergan, for Siroth saw Vandra lying at his feet. With a roar of frustration, Siroth leapt into the air, snatching Markus up with his talons.

"No!" Markus cried as the ground fell away beneath him. "Take me back!"

He couldn't leave Vandra there to die.

But Siroth ignored him, his powerful wings straining to gain height as they soared away from the overrun fortress.

Siroth carried Markus to a ridge high above the fortress, where he set him down. Markus dropped to his knees, dazed with shock, and gazed upon the smoke wafting up from the walls below. Vandra was down there still, with Sergan. She might still be alive. There had to be some way to get back to her—

Siroth's head snaked toward him, and the dragon let out a threatening growl. Images of himself lying dead next to Vandra came to Markus's mind, but he shook them roughly out of his head.

"I can't just leave her!" he shouted.

But the dragon would have none of it. With a jerk of his head, Siroth ordered him onto his back. Markus's shoulders slumped as despair took hold, wringing the strength out of him. Vandra was one of the best people he knew. She had stood up for himself and Aram, even when it seemed the whole world stood against them. Never had she lost faith in them.

She didn't deserve this. Not this.

He knelt there for a long time, watching smoke pour from the fortress's towers in a great, dark plume. At length, he pushed himself to his feet and walked back to Siroth. With heart-numbing regret, he climbed onto his dragon's back.

Siroth walked forward and stepped off the ledge of the cliff, falling for a heartbeat before stretching his wings and catching the air beneath them. They banked sharply over the fortress then gained height, following the ridgelines to where the deep furrow of the gorge opened out of the surrounding bluffs. The whole flight home, Markus fought back tears of sorrow, feeling strangled by grief and self-contempt.

Eraine Vandra knelt on the ground at the sorcerer's feet, hogtied, a rope running from her ankles to her wrists. She had stopped struggling against the bonds. They were tied too securely, and all she'd succeeded in doing was abrading her wrists. The sorcerer still maintained the invisible stranglehold around her neck, forcing her to fight for every breath. The struggle for air filled her with a desperate panic that she couldn't shake, which was worse than the physical pain she felt from the wounds she had taken during the fight.

The sorcerer reached down and patted her head as though she were an animal. "I'm sorry about this," he said in a conversational tone. "I'm almost out of essence, you see. There's a pathetic amount in you, but it may be enough to fill a vial or two. Unfortunately, the procedure's not comfortable, and since I'm not an Extractor, I'm going to have to do some real damage to your body to achieve the levels of pain that are needed." To a leather-clad man standing next to him, he said, "Take her over there. Strap her down."

The man bowed and moved quickly to comply, dropping down behind Vandra and drawing a large knife. He sawed quickly through the ropes that bound her ankles then jerked her upright. More men came forward, taking her roughly by the arms and forcing her toward an enormous block of stone that had fallen from the tower above them. They lifted her onto the stone slab and tied her down with leather straps.

When Vandra saw the man walking toward her with a sledgehammer, a heavy-handed fear choked her, and she clenched her jaw in expectation of the pain. The one thought that gave her comfort was of a boy she knew who had survived four years of such torture. If Aram could endure it, then so could she.

"We'll start with your feet and hands," said the sorcerer. "Then we'll work our way up."

Markus was barely aware of the cliffs moving by them in a blur. He had no idea they were close to Skyhome until Siroth slowed his flight and descended onto the large terrace of the Southern Eyrie. Seeing them land, people rushed toward them with looks of concern. The entire Wing knew he had left with Vandra. They also knew he hadn't returned with her.

Climbing down from Siroth's back, Markus leaned heavily against his dragon's side, gripping the riding harness for support. He couldn't bring himself to look up, to meet their eyes, to admit the magnitude of his failure. The crowd parted to admit a tall man with wind-whipped hair and a face like sunbaked leather. Markus recognized him as Ansul Stroud, the Wingmaster of the Lower Eyrie.

"Where's Vandra?" Stroud demanded. "Ragath's beside himself!"

Markus grimly shook his head, unable to speak. There were cries of dismay and denial from the people surrounding him, but then it grew quiet as the loss sank in. Stroud stood glaring at Markus in shocked dismay, looking frozen between sentences. He clenched and unclenched his fists, the muscles of his jaw bunching in anger. Grief and guilt-stricken, Markus wanted nothing more than to flee the eyrie. He turned and put a foot into Siroth's harness, but a hand on his arm stopped him from climbing up.

He turned to see Calise standing next to him, her face pale and damp with tears. She asked, "Is Aram with you?"

Grimacing, Markus shook his head. "He never came."

Visibly upset, she turned and made her way back into the crowd. Markus watched her go, a heavy weight of despair bearing down on him.

"The fortress is lost?" asked Stroud.

Markus nodded.

"What happened? Where is Raythe?"

Markus slumped back against Siroth's side, leaning heavily on his dragon's strength as he recounted the story of Eld Anoth's fall to all who stood around them. When he came to the part where Siroth pulled him away from Vandra and the battle, his voice broke, and he couldn't continue, for the weight of guilt compressed his chest so hard, he couldn't speak.

"There's nothing you could have done." Stroud squeezed Markus's arm consolingly, though the gesture did little to help. "Your dragon did the right thing. Sometimes they know better than us what is best." He stood quietly for a moment, gaze downturned, then, at last, turned to address the people gathered around them. "It doesn't end here. It's only beginning. They'll be marching on to Eranor. We must prepare."

Sergan knelt next to the woman who lay moaning on the stone slab. In his hand, he held a cobalt-glazed distillation flask. His eyes were closed in concentration, sweat beading on his forehead. He wasn't an Extractor; he had little Talent for it. The woman whose essence he harvested was on the verge of passing out, which made the extraction easier, the way applying grease to an axle allows the wheel to turn freely, though he couldn't let her slip entirely out of consciousness. There wasn't a lot of essence in her to begin with, and the process was taking time, along with all of the concentration Sergan could muster. In the end, he could barely wring more than a few a vials out of her.

When the flow of essence from her slowed to a trickle, he removed his hand and stood, for a moment feeling dizzy. He raised the flask to his nose and inhaled deeply.

"*Phaw,*" he spat, corking the flask. He had never known such a hard, unbreakable woman, and he feared her essence would taste like acid going down.

Grimacing in annoyance, he patted his victim's shoulder and nodded at the men of the Lizard Clan who had gathered to look on. "Carry her to my tent. Make her comfortable." He grimaced, too weary to appreciate his own irony.

"Your pardon, Exilar," said a voice behind him.

Turning, Sergan quirked an eyebrow at the pale and sickly-looking man who had come up behind him. The void-man bowed low, spreading his hands in the tradition of ancient Nimare. The man had white hair that flowed to his waist and wore a long, uncut piece of cloth stitched up the side and pinned at the shoulder. His features were skeletal, his skin paper-thin, with the texture of parchment. Tiny veins could be seen squiggling beneath it, dark with inky blood. The man's eyes glowed with the cold, empty blue of the void.

"I bear word for your ears alone," the Nimarean man said in an accent so thick that Sergan could hardly understand him.

He sighed heavily, glancing down in irritation at his moaning victim. "Fine."

He allowed the void-man to lead him away from the group of soldiers toward one of the very few walls of the courtyard that had somehow remained intact. Sergan stared at the wall warily, not trusting it to remain standing. He was almost ready to suggest they find another location when the man halted and caught his arm.

"Our Lady Lazair has fallen in battle," the Nimarean said in a lowered voice.

Sergan blinked, convinced he hadn't heard the man right. For seconds, all he could do was stare at the void-man in shock. *"What?"*

"I said—"

"Yes, I heard you!" the sorcerer snapped. "How the hell did that happen?"

The pallid man spread his hands again, a pithy gesture of apology or deference. "Exilar, the Lady Lazair was slain by their Champion."

"Aram Raythe killed *Lazair?"*

He had a hard time believing that. Hell, he *didn't* believe that. The void-man had to be wrong. Perhaps the boy had been there, but to kill Lazair all by himself... A tingle went down Sergan's spine, and he felt his skin pale to the shade of the Nimarean's. He remembered the brilliance of the boy's radiance, how rich his potential had been, even when his body had been weak and near death.

Apparently, Aram had grown into that potential. Perhaps he truly was a Champion.

Sergan shivered, for the very thought terrified him. If Aram could dispatch someone of Lazair's talent, what could he do to a mundane sorcerer?

"My Lord," the Nimarean said, and motioned to someone behind him.

"What now?" Sergan asked, for it had been Lazair who led this bizarre coalition. "Who's in charge?"

The Nimarean man inclined his head. "Exilar, we have received word that the Divine One himself is on his way to personally lead the assault. He is expected imminently."

Sergan felt the rest of the blood drain from his flesh. "Kathrax. Himself. Coming here?"

The Nimarean winced, his face pinching into a grimace. Sergan wondered if the reaction was in response to his speaking the Archon's name.

"Yes, Exilar." More bowing and hand-spreading. "The Divine One himself is on his way. But until he arrives, it would seem you are in charge."

A man came forward bearing a bundle wrapped in black cloth, bowing before presenting the parcel to Sergan. Sergan accepted it with a frown and was shocked when his hands grew cold the moment the fabric touched his fingers.

Pulling back the black silken cloth, Sergan's breath caught at the sight of the Baelsword's bone hilt.

It was nightfall, and Aram still hadn't returned.

Markus sat beside the hearth in Esmir's eyrie, staring down at the bowl of cinnamon-flavored *namas* the old man had prepared for him. When he had first arrived in this world, the flavor of *namas* had seemed a betrayal to everything that supper was supposed to be. In the Vardlands, cinnamon was a spice used only in pastries. Never before coming to Skyhome had he tasted a main dish seasoned with it. But the peculiar flavors of the food here had grown on him, and he usually looked forward to *namas*, even when it was Esmir cooking it.

Not today, though. He wasn't hungry. Markus set the bowl down and stared into the fire.

"You're not going to eat?" asked Esmir.

"No." Markus offered him the bowl. "Thank you, but I can't."

Esmir grunted but didn't take the bowl. Markus set it down in front of him and stared at the contents, watching steam curl from the broth. The smell of cinnamon reminded him of happier times. His eyes kept going to the mouth of the eyrie, hoping for a glimpse of Agaroth's red body. Esmir's eyrie was on the level below their own, and it would be impossible for a dragon as big as Agaroth to return home without being seen. But there was still no sign of the crimson dragon, and Markus was ill with worry.

"He should be back now," he grumbled.

"He should." Esmir leaned forward to stir the *namas* in its pot. "But that doesn't mean something went wrong. Aram is not incapable, you know. His task could have proven much bigger than we thought."

Markus's fingers tapped out an anxious pattern on the floor at his side, and he did nothing to still them. "I want to go look for him."

Esmir shook his head. "The Winmarch is a very big place. You could search for days and never find him. And we need you here, not out looking for one blade of grass in a literal prairie. What if something else happens while you're gone?"

"Some people are blaming him," Markus said, staring blearily into the fire.

Esmir plopped the ladle into the kettle and leaned forward, casting Markus a sidelong glare. "Don't let them get away with that. It wasn't Aram's fault, and they need to be made aware of that. That's one of the burdens Champions have to live with. People expect them to be everywhere at once, and when they can't be, they take the blame. It can be a heavy weight for the soul."

Markus hung his head, for Esmir was right. When Aram returned to find that Vandra had been left behind, he would blame himself. He would have a hard enough time without having to deal with the accusations of others.

"He's going to need you," Esmir said, poking at the coals of the fire with a stick.

Markus nodded. Sighing heavily, he pushed himself to his feet and walked stiffly out onto the terrace to where Siroth lay stretched out across the rocks. Hearing him approach, the dragon opened an eyelid and peered up at him. He felt Siroth's question in his mind, and he shook his head in answer.

"No," he said, kneeling to scratch a place on Siroth's neck that was always itchy. "Nobody's heard anything yet."

The dragon let out a long sigh, echoing Markus's own.

"He'll come," he said at last, staring out into the night.

Aram awoke to find himself lying in a bed of straw, a cloudless night stretched above him in all its star-filled glory. He started to sit up but cried out as a shooting pain stabbed into his side. He rubbed his ribs, wondering whether they were just bruised or cracked. Other parts of him ached, too, but his side was the worst. With a groan, he managed to push himself upright.

He was in the slender valley of the Wellspring, surrounded by dozens of edylberry trees whose weeping boughs glittered silver in the moonlight. Dozens of fireflies danced above the lake, the lights of their bellies flickering in the darkness. From somewhere far away, he heard the mournful cry of an owl. Other than that, and the crackle of a small campfire, the evening was silent and still. Agaroth lay on the far side of the fire, surrounded by Elesium who stood with necks downstretched, grazing in the moonlit grass.

"You're awake," said a voice.

Althea stepped around the campfire and knelt at his side. She still looked haggard, though much better than she had. She took him by the shoulders and ran her gaze over him critically.

"Your wounds are mending quickly," she said. "How does your side feel?"

Aram groped at his ribs. "It hurts."

The smile that flitted across Althea's lips was as brief as the fireflies' flickering lights. "I'm sure it does. You took quite a blow."

"I don't remember," Aram said with a frown. He brought his hand up to feel the skin of his face and was shocked to find that it was peeling. "How..."

"I'm skilled with healing, especially burns. Not so much with deeper injuries. That was Mandrel's Talent."

Althea must be very skilled, for Aram remembered the excruciating pain of Lazair's magic scorching his face. He trailed his fingers over his cheeks, unable to believe that he could recover from such an injury without lifelong scars.

"Thank you," he breathed.

With a groan, he pushed himself to his feet. It felt like every inch of his body was covered in bruises and scrapes. As he walked stiffly toward the campfire, Althea's people noticed him and stood. One and all, they inclined their heads toward him.

Aram raised his hand. "Please. Don't."

"We reserve the right to feel grateful," Althea said, coming to stand at his side. "Without your intervention, the Elesium would be slaughtered, and this sacred place would be defiled."

Feeling uncomfortable in more ways than one, Aram averted his eyes, unable to look at them. "Thank you," he whispered again, staring at the ground.

The old woman kissed his cheek.

Agaroth raised his head and regarded Aram with a trace of irritation in his eyes, for humility was something the dragon did not understand or condone. But it wasn't humility that Aram felt; he simply didn't understand the magnitude of what he had done.

But the people around him did.

Morning arrived, bearing with it a spectacular golden light that angled down upon the valley of the lake, making the silver waters sparkle and the coats of the Elesium glow iridescently. Aram climbed gingerly from his bed of straw and walked toward a nearby hill, upon which Agaroth had made his perch. As he made his way through the camp, the people smiled and brought their hands to their brows. He gestured back, happy that, for the most part, Althea's people seemed healthy and well. The water of the lake had worked its wonders upon them, and those who had survived the flight from Winhome would recover.

When he reached his dragon, Agaroth tilted his head, considering Aram with concern in his golden eyes.

"I'm fine," Aram assured him, bringing a hand up to feel his injured ribs. "How are you holding up?"

He reached to examine a wound on the dragon's shoulder that had parted the scales. Agaroth flinched but then suffered his touch. The wound was not deep and had already closed. Apparently, the waters of the lake worked its wonders on dragons as well as men.

"Do you think you can fly with that?"

In answer, Agaroth rose and stretched his wings as though eager to be away. Aram smiled, patting his neck. "All right. Just let me say goodbye, then we'll be off."

He made his way back to where the others were gathered. He rounded up his star-steel blade, and Althea helped him into his armor, an excruciating labor he could have never accomplished on his own. After he thanked Althea for her care, people and Elesium alike came forward to see him off, standing in a circle around Agaroth as Aram climbed stiffly onto his dragon's back.

Agaroth kicked off from the ground and vaulted into the sky, banking sharply over the valley before gliding out over the plain where the battle had taken place, now smoldering with cremated remains. Through the link he shared with Agaroth, Aram could feel the wound on the dragon's shoulder. It ached with each stroke of his wings, yet no more so than his own injuries. The waters of the lake were indeed potent, and he was more than grateful for the care shown them by Althea and her people.

It took them the rest of the morning to make it back through the ridges and canyons of the Kemeri Mountains to the gorge. As they flew over the streets of Hearth Home, people looked up and pointed at the great crimson dragon that was, to them, still an anomaly, a creature from a lost past, a greater time, a symbol of hope.

Reaching their eyrie, Agaroth turned lithely in the air and touched down upon the terrace. Siroth came forward immediately to greet them, appearing unsettled.

"Aram!"

He turned to see Markus rushing toward them, his face haggard and his eyes rimmed with red. Instantly alarmed, Aram felt a chill seep into his body, knowing in his bones that something had gone terribly wrong.

"What is it?"

When Markus reached him, he took Aram's bruised and peeling face in his hands, turning his head from side to side. "That isn't sunburn. What happened?"

"There was a battle." Aram said absently, wincing away. "What's wrong? Something's wrong, I can tell."

Markus's face darkened in anger and dismay. "You fought a battle without me?"

"I didn't have a choice," Aram said. "They sent a raiding party after the Elesium. I'm not—"

"What about the rest of you?" Markus stepped back, his gaze scouring Aram for signs of injury.

"I'm fine," Aram assured him. "Just bruises and scrapes."

Planting his hands on his hips, Markus turned and paced away, raking a hand through his hair. "There was a battle here too."

"What happened?"

Aram listened in trepidation as Markus described the battle for the fortress and Vandra's capture in great detail. When he was done, Aram stood staring past him, numb with grief and aching with guilt that he hadn't been there.

"But she's alive?" Aram whispered.

Markus nodded heavily. "Ragath's still with us. But he knows he can't fly down there and risk himself, so he's practically insane." He bowed his head. "The fortress was overrun. I couldn't save her."

"It wasn't your fault," Aram said. "If anything, it's mine, for not being here." He picked up a twig off a tall stack of kindling and held it in his hand, squeezing it. "And it was Sergan? Are you sure?"

"I saw him." Markus's voice shook in grief and anger.

The twig snapped in Aram's hand. He looked down at it in surprise. Opening his hand, he let the pieces drop to the floor. He hated Sergan more than any other person he had ever known.

"I'll kill him," Aram vowed. Standing, he started toward the terrace.

"Where are you going?" Markus called after him.

"I'm not going to just leave her there," said Aram. "I'm going to get her back."

Markus rose. "The hell you are! The only place you're going is the infirmary."

"I told you, I'm fine."

Striding forward, Markus caught his arm. "Why don't we let the healers decide that."

From the terrace, Agaroth gave a growl of agreement. Aram sighed. Reluctantly, he let Markus lead him back across the eyrie to the door, trying hard not to limp.

He followed his friend down the hallway, letting his gaze trail over the intricate knotwork carved into the walls as they walked. He recognized many of the types of knots portrayed in the stone, even though they were ornamental. Ever since he'd started his training, he'd begun thinking of knots more in terms of magic than in terms of cordage. And now, for the first time, it occurred to him that perhaps the walls of Skyhome might be more than just ornamental.

For just a moment, he felt a tingling of excitement. But as he studied the walls harder, his excitement faded, for though he could make out the individual knots, he didn't understand the larger picture. Disappointed, Aram let his attention drift away from the walls. Only then did he realize that Markus had been speaking to him the entire time they'd been walking.

"Their army's continuing on," Markus was saying. "It's headed for the Hills of Eranor. Somehow, we have to figure out a way to get our dragons down there past their sorcerers."

Eranor. The keystone anchor was there, the Heart of the Mother. If Kathrax destroyed that Anchor, then the two worlds would come crashing back together and there would be nothing he could do to stop it.

"I killed their Champion," he said with a shiver. "Maybe that will slow them down. It's one less sorcerer, at least."

Markus glanced at him in shock. *"You killed their Champion?"* He shook his head roughly. "I should have been there."

His regret sounded just as plaintive as Aram's own. Neither of them said another word all the way down to the lower level, where the infirmary was located. When Markus escorted him through the door, Aram halted abruptly.

Calise was there, talking to one of the other healers. She glanced up and noticed him standing in the doorway.

Aram flinched, having to stop himself from turning around and walking back out again. As though sensing his reaction, Markus took hold of his arm, denying him any possible hope of escape. Aram's heart flailed in panic, for he had no idea how to act in such an uncomfortable situation. Sweat broke out on his brow, and he felt his courage waver more than it had on the battlefield. When Calise turned and walked toward them, he averted his eyes from her.

"What's wrong with him?" she asked Markus. Even though her voice was full of concern, Aram didn't miss the detail that Calise was addressing Markus instead of him.

Markus answered, "He claims he's just bruised up, but I figured I'd let you check him out, just in case."

Aram glanced back at him in panic as Calise led him away to a corner. There, he stood staring intensely at a dark stain on the wall as Calise looked him over.

"You're going to need to remove that," she said, nodding at his armor.

Aram winced at the mere idea. He couldn't bring himself to move his arms, much less unfasten all the straps that held his armor in place. So Calise took over, unbuckling the straps and setting the various pieces on the floor while Aram stood gritting his teeth, trying hard not to groan. When he at last stood shirtless and ashamed before her, she looked him over critically, only patience and professionalism in her expression.

That hurt more than his wounds.

She bent to examine the deep purple bruising on his side, a large mark in the shape of a crescent moon that wrapped all the way from his chest around to his back.

"Take a deep breath," she ordered.

Aram tried to comply but stopped when a sharp pain speared him all the way to his spine.

"Broken," Calise confirmed, frowning heavily. "What happened?"

"I was hit with something," Aram mumbled, staring at the wall behind her. "Magic, I think. I don't really know…"

She scowled as though irritated by the answer but motioned to a pallet that lay on the floor behind her. "Sit. This is going to make you woozy."

Aram obeyed, looking up at Markus helplessly. Markus gave him a beleaguered smile, but one glance from Calise washed the expression off his face.

She sat next to him and placed both of her hands over the injury. "When I count to three, hold still and don't breathe."

Aram nodded, biting his lip, finding her touch almost painful. Not because it hurt his ribs, but because it felt so heartbreakingly good.

"One... Two... Three."

Aram held his breath. A burning warmth bloomed in his side, and he resisted the impulse to suck in a gasp of air. He clenched his hands instead, squeezing his eyes shut hard. The warmth spread down his side and toward his back like a wash of scalding water.

Calise sat back, bringing her hands up to her temples as though warding off a terrible headache. Aram wavered, feeling just as dizzy as she'd promised. The light in the room dimmed, and he thrust out his hands to stop himself from falling over. Eventually, the world stabilized and the sound of his pulse in his ears faded.

Calise said to Markus, "Make sure he rests for a couple days."

"Like that's going to happen," Markus grumbled as he helped Aram up, then bent to collect his armor off the floor.

Aram protested, "Vandra doesn't have a couple of days—"

"And if you do something stupid, neither will you," snapped Calise.

Deflated, Aram said nothing as Markus thanked her and led him away, hurrying him down the hallway in the direction of the stairs. He still felt terribly dizzy, and the floor rocked beneath his feet, so he was grateful for Markus's steadying grip on his arm.

"If we leave now, maybe we can—"

"Don't even think about it," Markus growled. "There's nothing you can do, anyway. I can't protect you from an entire army."

Aram's body wilted as the futility of the situation finally seeped in. Vandra was truly gone. Even though she was still alive, there was absolutely nothing he could do to help her. Aram threw his head back, squeezing his hands into fists. What good was magic if he couldn't even save a friend?

"Come on," Markus said. "Let's get you back."

They walked in silence the rest of the way back to their eyrie. Once there, Aram forced down some soup then wandered to his bed. Whatever Calise had done had made the bruise on his side fade to a dull yellow-green but had also sapped his strength. He lay down on the straw-stuffed mattress and drew his scratchy wool blanket up around himself. The last thing he thought of as he drifted off to sleep was the way Calise's soft hands had felt against his skin.

When Aram woke again, it was evening, and the smell of roasting meat filled the eyrie, making his mouth water. When he sat up, his ribs didn't stab him. He moved to the fire, nodding at Markus, and poured himself a cup of wine.

"Doing better?" Markus asked.

Aram nodded, not feeling like talking. He sat gazing into the flames while Markus turned the leg of lamb he was roasting on a spit. The logs in the fire cracked, raining a shower of embers his way. Aram absently brushed them back toward the fire, struggling to clear the drowsiness from his head.

Markus made small talk over supper, conspicuously avoiding the subject of Vandra. An uncomfortable heaviness hung over the room, weighing down on both of them and making conversation difficult. Even the dragons seemed to sense it and fled the tension by leaving to hunt.

After supper, Aram cleaned their plates. He was about to go down to check on Esmir, but a knock at the door changed his plans. He glanced at Markus, who walked to the door and opened it.

It was Calise.

Markus glanced back at Aram then opened the door wider. Calise smiled a greeting at him as she entered, her gaze flitting hesitantly toward Aram. Aram could only stare back at her, his jaw slack, terrified and achingly hopeful all at the same time.

Markus muttered, "I'll be downstairs."

Aram barely noticed him leaving. Suddenly the door shut, and he was alone with Calise. She stood with her arms crossed in front of her, though he didn't think she was angry—the look on her face didn't match her body posture, which confused him. In truth, he didn't know what to make of her. When she gave a tentative smile, that set him at ease a bit, though his heart still ached with regret.

"You look better," she said, coming toward him.

"Whatever you did helped a lot." He reached down to touch his side, which barely hurt at all anymore. "I wished I could do magic like that."

Calise's magic was beautiful, and it came from an even more beautiful place within. It wasn't like his. She was limited in what she could do with it, but in some ways, it was even more powerful than his own.

She stopped in front of him and looked steadily into his eyes. "I came to say that I forgive you for taking Zandril."

The gratitude he felt nearly took his breath away. "You don't have to forgive me."

"I know. But I'm going to anyway, because I feel like it." Her gaze wandered to the hearth. "Can I sit down?"

"Please." Aram moved rapidly to grab a cushion for her, setting it down beside his own. As she took a seat and adjusted her skirt over her legs, he went to fetch a sack of honeywine from the decrepit cabinet that served as the larder. He poured her a cup, which she accepted with a grateful smile and a murmur of thanks.

He lowered himself onto his cushion, sitting with his legs stretched out. Nervous, he longed for a piece of string or just something to fidget with in his hands, but she might notice, and that would be embarrassing. Instead, he settled for twitching his toes.

She took a sip of her wine, cradling her cup in her hands. Softly, she said, "When I was young, Lowland Fever took my parents."

Feeling terrible for her, Aram whispered, "I'm sorry."

"Don't be sorry," she said, taking another sip of wine. "They weren't nice people. Anyway, I grew up raising my younger sister, just her and me. We did everything together. We were best friends. All we had was each other, but I think we were better for it. She was the most lovely, gentle person. I loved her more than anything in the whole world."

He gazed at her as she talked, for he found her beautiful and baffling. She had her hair up in a sloppy bun atop her head, but wispy strands had escaped, fringing her face. She spoke quickly, as though nervous, and never looked at him. But when she raised her cup to her lips, she did so with meticulous grace.

"One day my sister just disappeared," Calise continued. "She knew I liked truffles, and she wanted to surprise me with some. So she took our sow out rooting for them in the forest behind our hut. She didn't tell me what she was doing or where she was going. Anyway, a storm came through that no one expected, and she was caught out in it. The sow came home. Nedira didn't. I told myself she'd just gotten lost in the storm, and I looked for her for days. Eventually, I gave up. All I could do was wait and hope for her to make her way back. Every day I'd wake up thinking this was going to be the day Nedira found her way home. But it never was. Years later, a couple of trappers found her bones. She'd fallen down a ravine in the storm and gotten carried away by a flood. All because I liked truffles."

She smiled, but it wasn't a happy smile. It was a sad, sad smile that made Aram wish he could do something to take it away.

"I'm very sorry," he said.

"You don't have to be sorry. It wasn't your fault." All traces of sadness were suddenly gone from her face, as though washed away.

She was right; it wasn't his fault, but he didn't know what else to say. So he lowered his eyes and gazed into the fire and said nothing. They sat in silence for a time, watching the flames dance over the graying logs. The silence grew uncomfortable, so much so that Aram started feeling a mild kind of panic. He feared he was supposed to be saying something, and he found himself groping for a subject to talk about. Nothing came to mind, and the more desperate he got, the less he could think.

Calise said, "When Zandril came back without you, I felt like I was right back there again, waiting for Nedira to come home."

"I'm sorry," he said before he could stop himself. He clamped his mouth shut, knowing he'd screwed up.

"Good." She looked at him directly, her eyes digging into him. "You *should* be sorry about that, because that *was* your fault."

He hung his head. "I know."

Aram wished he could tell her he regretted taking Zandril, but that would be a lie. He had needed Agaroth, and Agaroth had needed him. Because of that, he couldn't regret what he'd done. But he did feel terrible about it.

"Look at me," she ordered.

He raised his eyes and looked at her, even though it was painful to do so.

"I didn't want to fall in love with you, because of what you are," she told him softly.

It hurt to hear that. He looked away quickly, trying to hide the pain he felt, which had to show in his eyes. "It's all right." He shrugged. "Girls don't fall in love with people like me."

She set her cup down at her side. "There's nothing wrong with you," she insisted firmly. "It's what's wrong with me. I didn't want to fall in love with a Champion. I didn't want to spend the rest of my life worrying about whether or not you'd be coming home."

He understood completely, though it still hurt. He couldn't blame her, not after what she'd told him about her sister. Suddenly, he felt bad for ever wanting to kiss her. More than anything, he wanted to give Calise what she needed. And what she needed wasn't him.

"I never want to hurt you," he said, his voice gruff. "I won't bother you again."

He started to push himself up, but her hand caught his arm. He sat back down, looking at her in confusion.

"It's too late for that," she said.

He sighed dismally. "I know. I already hurt you."

"No. I mean I already love you."

He sat frozen for a moment, just staring at her. How was that possible, after everything she had just said to him? He was exactly what she didn't want, exactly what she didn't need.

She took his hand. He stared down at her fingers clasped around his, feeling suddenly frightened, though he didn't know why. Part of him was shouting that this couldn't be happening, that it was all his imagination. She couldn't be sitting here holding his hand, telling him she loved him. It was impossible. Things like this didn't happen to people like him.

"Can I kiss you?" she asked.

The question filled him with a terrified euphoria. It overwhelmed him, so much so that all he could do was stare at her in shock.

She brought a hand up and touched his face.

"Relax," she whispered, drawing close, so close he could feel her warm breath feathering his cheek, smelling sweetly of honeywine and herbs.

He felt her lips touch his, and his entire world was reduced to the feel of that kiss. He moved his own lips awkwardly, struggling to remember how he'd kissed her before, that time when they'd danced. It seemed like a lifetime ago. Her hand slid behind his back, and she kissed him deeper, and all thoughts and worries fled his mind. Just when he was about to put his arms around her, she pulled back just enough to look at him with a smile.

"I thought you said you didn't know how to kiss."

"You taught me," he whispered.

Then she was kissing him again. Something came over him then, and every thought and worry fled his mind, for he no longer felt clumsy and lost but profoundly thankful to be found. They stayed up late into the night, holding each other and talking. It felt so good to laugh with her. When morning came, and she rose to leave, Aram caught her by the hand.

"I love you," he said, gazing into her eyes.

"I love you too."

She smiled at him, and it was the most beautiful smile. His heart burned with gratitude.

92

Markus returned in the morning, just as Aram was headed out. "Where are you going?" he asked.

"I figured I'd go down to the kitchens and get something to eat," Aram answered. He set out down the corridor with a smile and made his way down to Hearth Home. It was still dark out, and when he exited the stairwell, the smell of baking bread permeated the air. There were only a few people out in the streets, and yet the roosters were already crowing, and the mockingbirds were at it, making a racket in the treetops overhead.

He gathered a couple of fresh-baked loaves from Rienne, one of the Master Baker's apprentices who had always been nice to him. He swaddled the loaves in a cloth and held them against his chest, determined to keep them oven-warm all the way up the long flights of stairs. He hurried as quickly as he could, but when he opened the door to his quarters, he didn't find what he was expecting.

Markus stood by the hearth speaking with two other people. All three turned toward him as Aram entered, and he recognized Ansul Stroud and Ethora Lorine, Wingmasters of the Lower and Eastern eyries.

Looking from one person to the other, Aram asked, "What's going on?"

Ansul Stroud nodded at him in greeting. "The last of the Dedicants and their apprentices have arrived. Luvana is convening the Council."

"Right now?" Aram asked with a glance at Markus.

"Right now."

Disappointed, Aram set the bread down on the table. "I guess we'll eat this later."

On second thought, he broke off a piece for himself, tossing another to Markus. They donned their mantles and followed Stroud and Lorine down the stairs.

When they reach the Council chamber, Aram was surprised to find it packed with people, many of whom he'd never seen before. And no one was sitting; rather, they'd gathered in several different nodes of conversation. When Aram and Markus entered, people turned to look at them with a mixture of expressions. Aram nodded greetings as he made his way through the crowd to where Luvana was standing, cradling a drink and speaking with an ancient-looking woman who wore the headscarf of a Dedicant Mother, though this woman's scarf was green, like the leaves of a forest.

"Aram," Luvana said, motioning him over. When he reached her, she set her hand on his back and introduced him to the woman she was speaking with. "I would like you to meet Carlova, Dedicant Mother of Lorinfel."

Aram gave a short bow, bringing a hand to his brow. "Very pleased to meet you, Dedicant Mother."

Reaching out, the woman clasped his hand with her own cold and bony fingers. "The wind brought you, Champion Raythe."

Luvana said, "Dedicant Carlova will be coming with us to the Hills of Eranor. She is very skilled at hardening the strands."

Aram looked at Carlova in curiosity. "Forgive me, but I'm not sure what that means."

"Watch," the old woman said, and Aram saw the strands of aether between them snap tight, as though under tension. As they stretched, they began to glow, the light physically wrung from them. Reaching out, Aram groped at the air between them and found it solid, like touching a brick wall. It was a useful technique, one he'd have to remember.

He looked at the Dedicant Mother and smiled. "That could be helpful."

"I can only do it over a short distance." The old woman gave him a bleak smile, releasing the tendrils and letting their light fade. "But perhaps it'll come in handy."

"I'm sure it will." Aram was about to say something further, but the sound of his name turned his attention away.

Glancing behind him, Aram saw Ansul Stroud motioning him over. Markus stood at his side, conversing with a woman next to them. The Wingmasters and their captains had gathered around a table with a map rolled out on it, weighted down on one end with two cups and on the other with a small knife and a stone from the hearth. Someone had set an arrowhead just off-center on the map, and there were a bunch of dark pebbles scattered across the parchment, forming a trail, while another path of lighter pebbles approached from the opposite direction. Aram gazed down at the map, recognizing the rolling curves that formed the Kemeri Mountains and the jagged line of the gorge. The arrowhead, then, must be the Hills of Eranor, and the dark pebbles must be Kathrax's army. It didn't look like they'd made it very far from Eld Anoth.

"How recent is this information?" he asked.

"Yesterday evening," answered Stroud.

"That doesn't make sense." Aram frowned. "They could have been most of the way to the hills by now."

He studied the map harder, feeling like there was something he was missing. The Army of Araghar was barely a half day's march from the fortress they had conquered. Which didn't make any sense, for why would they linger?

"They're waiting for something," he muttered.

"Waiting for what?" asked Stroud.

Aram set two fingers on the map, at the head of the swath of pebbles. In two days' time, they should be most of the way to Eranor. "Do you have scouts to the west?"

Stroud answered, "The West has gone silent."

Aram noticed that many of the people in the chamber had halted their conversation and were looking at him. He felt suddenly hesitant, almost regretting that he had mentioned anything. His gaze slid from the grouping of lighter-colored pebbles to the arrowhead.

"What are you thinking?"

Aram looked up, not realizing that Luvana had come up beside him.

"By waiting, they're letting us arrive first," he said. "By the time they get to Eranor, our forces will be pretty well entrenched. So, what's so important that is keeping them there?"

His question went unanswered. He looked up and glanced around the circle of people gathered around the table, all staring down at the map with faces equally long. None of them had an answer, he could tell.

"Whatever they're waiting for, it must be worth it." Aram sighed heavily. "I wish Vandra were here." She would know what to do. Markus caught his gaze, his face tightening.

Aram was quiet after that, letting the more experienced minds hash out strategy, for he felt far out of his element. Almost unconsciously, he withdrew to the side of the room, working his way toward the corner, where he felt more comfortable. There, he leaned up against the wall, his mind gnawing on the problem of what could possibly be important enough that would cause the enemy to give up a strategic advantage.

"You look like you're feeling disregarded."

Aram looked up into the face of Elder Sabrien, one of the oldest members of the Council. He was a frail man with youthful eyes that held a sparkle of mischief in them.

"Not disregarded." Aram conjured a faint smile. "More like out of my depth."

Sabrien nodded back toward the table where the Wingmasters had gathered with their captains. "They find you intimidating."

"Intimidating?" Aram wondered if the man were joking. "I'm barely more than a recruit. I have very little experience in any of this."

The old man raised his thinning white eyebrows. "Perhaps not, but you have something better. We'll call it 'informed intuition.'"

Aram frowned. "What do you mean?"

Elder Sabrien spread his hands. "You're a True Savant. Consciously or not, your mind is always reading the strands. You have insight that others lack. To you, it might feel like a gut feeling, but for the Gifted, that kind of feeling is far more than just a hunch." He inclined his head toward the others. "They know this. They're just having a hard time reconciling your youth with your capabilities."

Aram glanced to Stroud and the other Wingmasters. "I don't feel very capable."

"You don't give yourself enough credit." The old man patted Aram's arm then walked away, inserting himself into a conversation Luvana was having with some of the other Dedicants. Aram wondered if Sabrien was a Dedicant himself. He seemed to know a lot about the Gifted, and Aram wondered how he had come by the knowledge. By the looks of him, Aram guessed that Sabrien had to be well over a thousand years old. He looked even older than Esmir, who was old for even an Auld's generous span of years.

Aram wandered back over to the table and listened while the Wingmasters finalized their plans. Apparently, it had been decided to risk the dragons and fly the Wings to Eranor. Stroud's argument was that, like a flock of birds, they would be protected by sheer numbers.

"They can't bring us all down," he argued.

"No," said Aram, gazing at the map. "But they can kill a lot of us." To him, even one dragon lost to lightning was too many. He bit his lip, thinking hard. "If you insist on taking the dragons, you should wait till nightfall. Their sorcerers have to be able to see us to strike. If we're lucky, there'll be cloud cover."

Luvana nodded her approval even as Stroud looked like he was about to differ. But he kept his silence, gazing at Aram for long seconds. At last, something in his face softened, and he gave a terse nod.

The Council broke up shortly after that, the Wingmasters and their captains striding with purpose out of the chamber, determined to take advantage of the enemy's hesitance. Markus left with one of Stroud's captains, mired in some conversation. He was a lot more outgoing than Aram was, fitting seamlessly into any social situation he found himself in.

Aram was undecided about whether to return to his quarters or to try to find Calise. He had no idea what the proper thing to do was, after what had passed between them. Did she want time to herself? He didn't want to come off as smothering. But he also didn't want her to think he was avoiding her.

If she had been a woman of his village, he would have been planning a marriage proposal. But the traditions of the Auld were different than those of his own people, and here marriage was a rare thing, perhaps because of their longevity. He wondered what it would be like to be married to the same person for centuries. If it were Calise, he thought those centuries would be happy ones.

As he walked, Aram let his gaze trail along the elaborate wall carvings. On this level, the patterns had a repetition to them that were absent on other floors. He stopped and studied the intricate design, made of one strand woven about itself with hundreds of different crossings. In his mind, he envisioned what form the knot would take if someone were to tug those crossings tight. He imagined it would look like a turban knot, or perhaps a knob knot.

He was still pondering the carvings when he heard footsteps and turned to find Elder Sabrien approaching him. Seeing Aram's interest in the wall, the old man beamed.

"Do you know how to read Elaric?" Sabrien asked.

"No. What's Elaric?"

The old man gestured at the wall. "The Kingdom of Elara existed during the Age of Chaos, after the Sundering. The language of Elara was not written in letters but rather as a system of knots tied in cord or, sometimes, graven in stone."

Aram sucked in a breath, for he had wondered if the walls of Skyhome had something to do with magic. His interest intensified, for the parallel between a knotwork writing system and the actual binding of aether was too uncanny to be coincidence. He raised his hand and ran his fingers across the textured stone.

"What does it say?"

"It's a ballad."

Aram was amazed. He glanced up and down the length of the hall, wondering how long a ballad it could contain. Imagining that each individual component of the knot formed a word, it was entirely possible that each section of the corridor between doorways could contain an entire stanza. He thought immediately of Master Ebra, of how excited the bard would have been to have seen such a masterpiece.

"It's called the *Eyana Eman*," the old man said.

At that name, the entire world shifted under Aram's feet.

"What?" he whispered.

That had been the ballad Master Ebra had recited in the longhouse, the night Aram had created the rupture. It was uncanny, and he doubted it was coincidence. Why had the bard chosen that particular ballad to play? How had he known of it? He thought back to Master Ebra's brilliant red aura, a color he had never seen before on a man. And had never since.

"The *Eyana Eman* was originally woven into a tapestry composed of forty-six panels that were later translated into forty-six tablets," Sabrien informed him, running his fingers over the stone. "The walls of each floor of Skyhome each contain one tablet."

"Where's the Ballad of Raginor?" Aram asked, his voice breathless.

Sabrien's brow furrowed. "On the fourteenth floor. You know the *Eyana Eman?*"

"Just the part about Erok and Raginor." Aram glanced down the hallway. An excited tingling caressed his skin like the light touch of a feather, and beads of perspiration broke out across his brow. He had only heard it once, but he recalled the Ballad of Raginor word for word.

"That's how I came here," he whispered. "The ballad..."

It had been the words of the ballad that had moved him to create the rupture in Anai. Somehow, his mind had taken the scant references in the lyrics and reasoned that the Veil had something to do with his father's disappearance. It had been quite a leap to come to that conclusion, and yet, all along, he'd been right. Perhaps it was the same kind of 'informed intuition' Sabrien had told him about. Regardless, the *Eyana Eman* was important, not just to him, but important enough to be carved across all the floors of Skyhome.

"I've got to go," he whispered then turned to hurry down the corridor, the refrains of the Ballad of Raginor echoing in his mind. By the time he reached the stairs, Aram was running.

93

Aram spent the remainder of the morning wrestling with the words of the ballad the bard had sung that night in the longhouse so long ago. The lyrics detailed the mythical events that had led up to the Sundering of the World. It spoke of a battle between Ahn, the Father of All, and his immortal lover Senestra, who had brought the Archons into the world to serve Ahn's children, the Auld. But the Archons had turned against the Auld. The ballad labeled them 'the Disavowed,' for they had broken their oaths. Aram was convinced that Ahn's champion Raginor had been a true Champion in every sense, and that his lover Erok had been his Warden. Raginor had been slain in the ensuing battle between the gods, and his death had provoked Erok to bring about the Sundering, separating the world of magic from the world of Men.

Aram knew that, somehow, the *Eyana Eman* was critical to their current situation, though he didn't know how he knew it. Just as when he had first heard Master Ebra recite the ballad in Anai's longhouse, Aram's intuition was screaming at him, and he couldn't ignore it.

All day he walked the halls of Skyhome, studying the flowing, interlaced knotwork, wishing he could read it like a script. He was convinced that he could, given time to study it—which he didn't have. So, instead, he appeased his mind by walking the halls with a ball of twine in his hand, transcribing the language of stone into a language he understood better than any other: the language of cord. By the time he arrived at the lowest level, he had amassed a collection of small, braided panels, each

747

composed of hundreds of knots. These, he carried back to the eyrie and laid them out across the terrace in the sunlight, where he compiled them into one, large tapestry.

When the entire ballad was assembled, Aram hung it on the wall and then stood back, running his gaze over the woven text. He stood there for perhaps an hour, until he had the entire structure of the ballad memorized. Yet, the more he stared at it, the more disappointed he grew. He had been hoping that, compiled, the complete ballad would offer him some important insight or piece of knowledge.

But it didn't. In the end, the *Eyana Eman* was just a beautiful tapestry, and a beautiful story woven in a language that no amount of staring at would help him understand. Sighing, Aram turned away from his creation, disappointed that he had wasted precious hours for nothing.

He ate then went down to the infirmary, looking for Calise. When he didn't find her there, he took the stairs to the Southern Eyrie, where the fighting Wing was preparing to depart for battle. He looked around the eyrie with an intense feeling of dread, fearing the risks of such a flight. Once again, his intuition was shrieking at him.

Distraught, he found Calise in the alcove she shared with Zandril, fixing bags of supplies to her dragon's riding harness. When she saw him, Calise broke into a smile that quickly capsized to a frown.

"What's wrong?" she asked.

"You're coming with us?"

Tightening the strap she was working on, Calise straightened, rubbing the redness out of her hands. "Of course. I'm a healer. If there's going to be a battle, that's where I belong."

Aram squeezed his lips together, despising that answer. He glanced nervously at Zandril, silently pleading with the dragon to talk some sense into her rider. But Zandril just answered with a purring rumble, chastising him for his interference. Aram scrubbed a hand roughly through his hair.

"They have sorcerers," he said. "You can't take Zandril down there."

"*You're* going down there."

"Yes, well I'm—"

"Going to be in far more danger than I am." Calise planted her hands on her hips.

There was a growing irritation in her eyes, and Aram knew his concern was making her upset. He didn't want to make her mad, but he also didn't want her to go. He glanced up at the ceiling, searching for a way he could convince her to stay.

In the end, he decided she was right. If there was going to be a battle, then that's where they both belonged. He couldn't ask her to stay behind and wait for him to return, because he knew that was her greatest fear, and he couldn't do that to her.

His shoulders sagged in defeat. "Just promise me you'll stay out of the battle."

"Will *you?*"

Calise chortled a laugh, turning her back on him and moving to the other side of the alcove to grab her gear. She was wearing her riding leathers, the only outfit she owned that actually matched. Because of that, they didn't look right on her.

She shouldered a large pack and, straightening, walked toward him with annoyance in her eyes. "Don't worry about me. Worry about *you.*"

Aram licked his lips. "All right." Backing out of her alcove, he stabbed a glance at Zandril. "Fly above the clouds."

"Aram!"

He raised his hands. As he left, he shot a glare back at Zandril and pointed upward, shaking his finger. Then he turned and strode across the floor the eyrie, hurrying away. In the back of his mind, he felt somewhat comforted, for he knew the golden dragon would take heed.

By the time he returned to their eyrie, Markus was already there and geared up.

"Where have you been?" his Warden demanded, rushing forward. "People have been looking for you!"

"I had something I had to do."

Aram cast a frustrated glance at the new tapestry on the wall, wondering if Markus had noticed it. He had wasted most of the day chasing a fancy. Even Agaroth was glowering at him, staring at him with accusing golden eyes.

"Well, hurry and get your gear on," Markus said. "Bring it here. I'll help you into it."

Aram went and gathered the various components of his armor then stood still as Markus tightened all the buckles and straps that held it together.

"They want us to fly ahead of the Wings," Markus informed him, cinching the final strap. "That way, if we run into a sorcerer, they'll strike us first, and hopefully the rest will have a chance to scatter."

"Hopefully?" Aram scowled in disdain. Scooping his sword up, he headed toward the terrace. "What then?"

Markus shrugged. "I don't know."

That was the problem. Aram didn't know either. If there was a sorcerer anywhere between Skyhome and the Hills of Eranor, scattering the Wings wouldn't do much to deter them, since all a sorcerer needed was line of sight.

He climbed onto Agaroth's back, mulling over the problem. As the great dragon walked to the edge of the terrace and gathered its muscles, Aram took one last glance back at the tapestry he had braided.

Agaroth leapt from the terrace, unfurling his wings and catching the air. All throughout the length of the canyon, dragons rose from their terraces, taking flight like great flocks of birds. Aram stared at the breathtaking sight, having never seen the combined might of all the eyries together at once. There were hundreds of dragons of every color, many more than he would have ever believed.

Agaroth pumped his mighty wings, gaining speed to fly ahead of the rest, then soared low over the abyss, banking slightly as he followed the meandering path of the gorge. So great was his wingspan that it practically stretched the width of the canyon in some places. Markus and Siroth flew at his side, the others spread out behind them in a great wedge that filled the sky.

They followed the ridges of the mountains north and then turned west, chasing the sunset. The shadows lengthened as they flew over the high passes of the Kemeri Mountains, and by the time they reach the foothills of the plains, the sky had darkened, the sunset only a blood-colored streak on the horizon. As they leveled off over the grasslands, Aram glanced back, taking in the sight of the rising moon whose light would work against them.

He frowned, for the moonlight reflected off the wings of their dragons, making them very visible to anyone who might be in the air. Fortunately, he knew what to do about it. Reaching out with his mind, Aram wove a blanket of shadow that he cast above them, blocking the moon's light. From the ground, the passage of the Wings would look like nothing more than a large patch of solid night unadorned by stars.

Below on the plains, he saw no signs of campfires. With luck, Kathrax's armies were still a day behind, which would give them a chance to get ahead and dig in. All he saw between their position and the hills to the north-west was a vast tract of prairie unmarred by the presence of man.

A streak of light strobed the sky, followed by a crackle of thunder.

It hit the shadow-net first, tearing through the gossamer filaments. Before Aram could bind another, the lightning struck again. Behind them, a dragon let out a shriek as its wingmate dropped like a stone from the sky.

"Bank!" Aram cried, and Agaroth obeyed, turning on wing to fly back in the direction they'd come. But even as Aram scrambled to thicken his web of shadow, he knew it was useless, for he had to cast it too thin to be any real kind of barrier.

In front of him, a dragon exploded.

"NO!" he cried.

There had been no lightning. No thunder. Just blood, shock, and gore.

Aram's stomach heaved, and he clamped his hand over his mouth to keep from vomiting.

This wasn't working. He had to do something. The next dragon to fall might be Zandril. He brought Agaroth around, flying parallel to the Wings, his eyes searching the sky and ground for the source of the attacks. But the enemy sorcerers could be hidden anywhere, and he saw no sign of them.

Aram growled in frustration.

How had Raginor done it? How had he kept his dragons in the sky against the forces of the Archons? His mind groped through the panels of knotted cords he had tied and hung on his wall, desperate for an answer.

The strains of the ballad kept running through his mind. Suddenly, his eyes went wide, and he quoted a verse: "'And he led the host in glorious raiment...'"

Glorious raiment...

That was the solution. All along, he'd been wrong. It wasn't shadow they should be hiding behind, and he needn't waste his energy covering up an enormous swath of sky.

"Fly back!" he gasped, and Agaroth wheeled again in the air, nearly dislodging him from his seat.

As they neared the vanguard of the Wing, Aram lifted his hands and started weaving. A golden light bloomed around Ansul Stroud's dragon, brilliant and glimmering, a shroud of light that would reflect any energy thrown its way. As he flew down the length of their formation, one by one, dragons flickered ablaze with streaming rays of golden light.

Lightning struck, streaking up from the ground.

And yet, it accomplished nothing. The gleaming armor of the dragon it struck merely flared for a moment.

Exuberant, Aram turned Agaroth back toward the front of the Wing. They were halfway across the grassland by now, and it would be almost time to descend toward the rolling hills of Eranor. As Agaroth pulled abreast of Siroth, Markus turned and gave him a congratulatory smile. For just a moment, Aram closed his eyes and savored a euphoric feeling he had never experienced before:

Pride.

All his life, he'd considered himself a failure. A weakling. Different. Plagued with odd quirks and bewildered by simple life skills that seemed to come naturally to everyone but him. But he'd been wrong about all that. In the end, many of the things he'd always thought of as weaknesses had ended up being his strengths.

But his moment of validation didn't last long.

Looking ahead, he saw why the prairie behind them had been empty. On the horizon came a scattered glow, the lights of thousands of campfires amassed before the rise of the Hills of Eranor.

The army of Kathrax was not behind them. It was *ahead*.

But hope was not lost, for the allied forces the Dedicants had promised them had arrived in the hills above them and held the higher ground. Though it was hard to determine their numbers from the sky, there seemed to be far fewer campfires in the hills than there were on the plain, which was worrisome.

They flew a wide circle around the enemy army and approached the Hills of Eranor from the north. Around him, wave after wave of dragons descended from the sky, alighting on the ridges of the treeless hills. Agaroth circled, looking for a place to land, and as he did, Aram got a good look at the Wellspring that was called the Heart of the Mother, a lake in the shape of a heart filled with blood-red water. Erupting from the center of the lake was the colossal statue of a woman. Red water wept down the statue's surface in a way that made the woman appear to be bleeding from a thousand cuts. The statue was an Anchor—the Keystone Anchor—and he could feel the tension of the raw power it radiated.

They landed in a cleared area at the forward edge of the camp, where they were met by people who rushed forward to greet them, drawn by the spectacle of the great crimson dragon. To Aram's surprise, the men and women who surrounded them looked to be of various ethnicities and cultures, as though they had come from all parts of the land. They probably had, he realized, thinking of all the Dedicants from the various nations he had met. The sight of so many people was uplifting, and yet he couldn't help but wonder if their numbers would be enough.

Dismounting, he walked with Markus into the crowd. They had to fight their way through the throng as people clamored to get a better view, reaching out their hands toward Aram as he walked by, as though the mere touch of a Champion could bring them luck or fortitude.

It took them several minutes of struggling through the crowd to reach the command pavilions that had been erected on the edge of the hill, surrounded by pickets. The soldiers guarding the enclosure glared at them fiercely, until they recognized their uniforms. Then they stepped aside and went to their knees. Aram just nodded acknowledgement as he passed, for he knew of no appropriate response—or if there even was one.

When they arrived at the entrance to the command pavilion, they were met by a large group of officers gathered from the collected nations. They were joined by Stroud and Lorine, as well as Kedren Devarus, the Wingmaster of the Northern Eyrie.

"Welcome, Ansul," said a woman clad in leathers, coming forward to give Wingmaster Stroud an affectionate hug before turning toward Aram and Markus. "Who do you bring with you?"

"Ladies and Gentlemen," Stroud said, raising his voice to address all the officers gathered in the pavilion. "May I introduce Champion Aramon Raythe and his Warden, Markus Galliar."

Aram bowed to the assembled officers as he had seen Stroud do, Markus following suit. Names and ranks and affiliations were exchanged, though Aram paid them little mind. His attention was commanded by the view visible through the rear opening of the tent, which looked down upon the enemy encampment below on the plain.

A direct line of sight.

Aram felt his mouth go dry, the hairs on the back of his neck standing upright as all of his intuition screamed in alarm.

"We're not safe here," he said.

But nobody heard him, or at least no one listened, for the conversation around him didn't falter.

There was a flash of light from far below.

"Get *out!*" Aram shouted.

He sensed it coming before he saw it: a dazzling wash of light that spread across the fabric of the tent, making the harsh, slanted shadows burn away in a torrent of brilliance. Aram threw his hands up in a desperate attempt to weave a barrier between them and whatever was coming, but something slammed into him, knocking him to the ground. A heavy body landed on top of him, driving the air from his lungs.

WHOOSH!

The world exploded.

The air turned to flame, filling his ears with the roar of fire and screams of agony. Though dazed, Aram got the sense that he was being smothered and then dragged, and no matter how hard he struggled, he couldn't force his chest to move air. But then a weight shifted off him, and he heaved in a great, choking breath.

Shouts and screams came from every direction. Aram heard someone nearby shout, "Get back! Give him room!"

He tried to lift his head to look around, but all he could do was cough. Dark smoke thickened the air, moving over him like a storm cloud. He lay on his side with his knees drawn up to his chest. The screams around him faded, and the smell of cooking meat pervaded his awareness.

"Are you all right?" Markus asked. He was crouched over him, clutching Aram's shoulders.

Aram nodded, drawing in a deep, wheezing breath. Trembling, he pushed himself upright and took in the scene of destruction around him. The command pavilion was gone, reduced to a smoldering pile. Bodies were strewn across the ground around it, most terribly burned. From what he could see, only he and Markus had escaped the interior relatively unscathed.

Spreading his arms, he saw that his dragon scale armor was undamaged—not even singed. "How…?"

"It was pure magic," Markus said. "I Shielded you. But I couldn't Shield anyone else."

Aram's eyes fell on the bodies nearest him, and he realized that one of them was Ansul Stroud. A terrible fear and sadness fell over him, for the eyries had lost yet another great leader. His eyes wandered the surrounding dead, wondering how many others had been slain.

Aram pushed himself to his feet and asked in a flat voice, "Who's next in the chain of command?"

"You are," said a gnarled man clad in flight leathers whom Aram didn't recognize.

He froze as those words sank in. For a moment, all he could do was stare at the billowing smoke. He wasn't a commander. He was young, and all of his training hadn't prepared him for this level of responsibility. He knew how to tie knots and swing a sword, but he knew nothing of the logistics of maintaining an entire encampment or preparing for battle. His throat went dry, and at first, he couldn't find his voice.

"Gather a detail to care for the dead," he said at last, his eyes lingering on the body of Ansul Stroud. "Then find another place for us to meet further back. Out of sight of the plain."

Men moved to carry out his orders. Markus walked with him toward the rim of the hill, drawn toward the sight of the enemy encampment far below. Somewhere down there was the sorcerer who had flung that devastating projectile, and Aram didn't doubt there were others. He scanned the enemy tents for minutes, wondering who and where they were. It could have been Sergan, for all he knew.

The sound of running footsteps made him turn just in time as Calise collided with him, hugging him fiercely. She stepped back just as quickly, looking over every inch of him. Her face was red and glimmering with sweat, her eyes wide and frantic.

"I'm fine," Aram said, trying to reassure her, but for some reason, his words seemed to just make her angry.

"I'll tell you if you're fine," she snapped. Her eyes narrowed, and she peered at him harder. After moments, she finally stepped back and let him go. Turning to Markus, she said, "Thank you for saving him."

Under normal circumstances, Markus would have probably answered her with a joking dig at Aram, but now all he did was shrug wearily, his eyes dim and remote. Aram noticed that Markus's face and armor were coated with soot, so much so that it was hard to see his features. Reaching up, he felt at his own face. If he was as grimy as Markus was, no wonder Calise looked so worried.

Reassured, she left him and ran to where the rest of the healers were caring for the wounded. She knelt first beside a charred form that Aram thought might have been Kedren Devarus, though it was impossible to tell. The man lay in a patch of trampled grass, moaning and twisting in agony. Calise pressed her fingers against his chest, and his thrashing stopped almost immediately.

Aram walked forward, watching in awe as the woman he loved wielded a powerful magic he couldn't begin to understand. Instead of frantically groping at the air, she merely closed her eyes, her features softening, and let her aura flow into the ruined body beneath her hands. Aram moved closer, watching in fascination as the worst of the charring sloughed away from the man, revealing red, raw tissue underneath. The healing continued, the redness fading a bit, until the skin looked more scalded than burnt.

When Calise removed her hands, she was panting, her face bloodless. Aram started toward her, but Markus caught his arm. "She's fine," he said quietly into his ear. "Let her do her job."

Aram forced himself to relax but couldn't help a last glance back as Markus led him away.

A new command pavilion was erected in the center of the camp, well back from the first, out of line of sight of the enemy. As soon as the canvas was stretched over the posts, Aram found himself ensconced within it, surrounded by the leaders of the various nations who had pledged their support to their campaign. Behind the tent rose the glimmering statue of the Anchor, a looming reminder of all they fought for and all they stood to lose.

Aram remained in the tent late into the night, listening to reports and discussing contingencies. He didn't have much to add to the conversation, but found himself listening intently, learning from minds far more experienced than his own. Only when pressed would he offer suggestions that were grounded far more in intuition than knowledge. As the night wore on, Aram found that some of those feelings of intuition were becoming stronger and more urgent, and he wondered if his mind was learning to discriminate between what was just a hunch or an actual interpretation of the strands.

Betharyl, a grizzled woman who led the Ubedian Clan of the Senjian Waste, entered his tent with a contingent of guards and commanded his attention. Ubedid, apparently, was a matriarchy, and most of its leaders were women. Aram couldn't stop staring at Betharyl, who was taller than all of the men gathered in the tent, and just as broad of shoulder. Looking at her, he couldn't help being reminded of Vandra, and the thought made him sad.

"We don't have the numbers, so why are we here?" she demanded.

Remaud, a leathery warrior with long hair and a scarred face, responded, "We're here to fight a war. At least, that's why the Kajidans are here—I don't know about the Ubedians. I say we let the Wings pour dragonfire down upon them," he urged Aram. "We have enough dragons to put them to the rout without having to waste an arrow."

Aram tapped his knuckles against his chin, his gaze lowered in thought. He shook his head. "No. That won't work."

"Why won't it work?" demanded Remaud.

"Because of their sorcerers. I can't fight a battle and maintain light cloaks around all our dragons."

"How many dragons do you think you can protect at once?" asked Markus.

Aram frowned, considering the question, at last offering a shrug. "It depends on how divided my attention is. If I'm sorely pressed, I can't guarantee anything."

The tent broke into a tumult of conversation. It took another hour, but at last they decided on a strategy that Aram thought had the best chance of success, which was to use the advantage of high ground and let the enemy come to them as much as possible. The dragons would be used to provide reconnaissance and harass the flanks of the enemy forces but would not be flown directly over the battlefield.

Eventually, the leaders dispersed to their respective commands. Aram and Markus remained behind, deciding it best to sleep in the command tent, just in case they were needed. One of the officers sent over a supper of roasted venison, which Aram couldn't get down. Nerves made his stomach too tense, and his throat was too constricted to swallow. They sat outside the tent, under the light of the moon, Aram looking on as Markus attacked the meal ravenously.

"You need to relax," Markus advised through a mouthful of venison. "It's not going to do anyone any good if your thinking's addled from hunger."

Aram leaned back against the trunk of a white-barked sycamore. Its leaves carpeted the ground, providing a soft cushion upon which to sit. In his lap, his hands were occupied with a bit of twine, tying little knots over and over into the string, applying all his fierce concentration to it. Tonight, even the twine wasn't helping, not when he knew what dawn would bring. The meeting in the command tent hadn't helped. Too many people had looked to him for direction he wasn't qualified to give. Doubts were beginning to plague him, and he found himself questioning his own judgment, uncertain of his part in any of this. He was terrified that he was going to fail, and that his failure would doom them all. He prayed that feeling was just simple nerves and not his awakening intuition.

The sound of footsteps crunching on leaves made him look up from his knotting to find himself staring into Luvana's face. He was shocked to see her, for no one had told him she was coming. She must have flown dragonback, and he wondered which dragon would have condescended to carry her. Then he thought of Ragath, Vandra's dragon, who would no doubt have wanted to come, seeking salvation or vengeance for his rider. Luvana's expression made him drop the twine and spring to his feet.

"What is it?"

Luvana didn't answer at first. "There's something you need to see."

Markus followed Aram to his feet.

"Come," the Dedicant Mother said, and walked away without answering.

Aram exchanged glances with Markus then hurried to follow Luvana as she walked swiftly back through the dark encampment, winding their way around cook fires and pitched tents toward the charred remains of the first command pavilion. There, a throng of hundreds of people had gathered along the ridge of the hill, all gazing down toward enemy lines. Cold needles of dread pricked Aram's skin as he pushed his way forward through the crowd with a feeling of urgency.

They stopped when they reached the crest of the hill and looked down upon the plain below. The incline was sharp, and it offered a good view of the entire prairie. Below them was a long swath of empty ground between the base of the hill and the perimeter of the enemy encampment, twice the distance of a longbow's reach. Beyond that, the campfires of Kathrax's army danced like a shimmering sea of gemstones.

In the middle of the cleared area, a large pile of wood had been stacked, and within it, tied to a pole, was a restrained prisoner. Aram's body went numb, his breath catching, when he realized he was looking down upon the scene of impending tragedy. All across the crest of the hill, the crowd of onlookers stood silent and still, clenched in the cold grip of dread.

Aram's gaze went to the prisoner tied to the pole. Enemy soldiers were hauling in more wood, stacking it piece by piece around the prisoner's feet as the woman hung limply from the bindings that held her. Wondering if she was already dead, Aram stared at her harder.

He gasped, realizing it was Vandra.

He had only recognized her because of her long raven hair. Blood and bruises covered her face, which was a cruel bastardization of its former beauty. Aram clenched his fists, a terrible, horrified rage hollowing his insides. The crowd around him shifted, and the silence faltered. From somewhere, he heard the sounds of weeping.

"Aram..." Markus whispered.

Below, an armored soldier holding a lit torch approached the woodpile Vandra was staked over.

"You have to do something," Markus gasped.

But Aram was already gathering strands of aether. He started weaving, sending a violent gust of air across the field below, knocking the flame right off the torch. Banners crackled and billowed on their staves for just an instant, but then went still as the gust passed.

There was a long moment of silence.

Then the ranks parted, admitting a man wearing the blue mantle of the Exilari, who carried another crackling torch. He walked forward defiantly, his gaze fixed on Aram as though daring him to act. He drew to a stop before the woodpile and simply waited, torch in hand.

Gritting his teeth, Aram summoned another gust of air. It formed well behind them in the hills before unleashing itself upon the prairie, sweeping over the grass to slam into the encampment of the enemy, staggering soldiers and collapsing tents.

And yet, the Exilar's torch remained undisturbed.

"He's a Shield," Markus whispered in a leaden voice.

Even as he said it, three more men and a woman stepped out from within the ranks of the enemy, positioning themselves between Aram and Vandra. All Shields, Aram knew. He felt the strength and courage drain out of him, for he knew he was defeated. He shook his head, tears of despair collecting in his eyes. Even with all the power the gods had seen fit to give him, there was nothing he could do against that one, tiny flame.

With the slightest motion, the Shield tossed the lit torch into the woodpile.

The flames caught immediately and raced over the fuel, dark smoke pouring upward from the blaze. Vandra threw her head back and howled a hollow and raspy scream that sounded torn from a throat that had already screamed itself hoarse. She continued to scream as her form became one with the flames, just a shimmering distortion within the blaze. Her wails turned to shrieks that clawed piteously at the air.

Until they didn't.

Then another noise rose above the crackle of the fire: the anguished, primal howl of a dragon who had lost its kindred soul. Behind them, Ragath launched himself into the air, spewing a font of white flames like a molten geyser. Enraged beyond sanity, the dragon couldn't hold a course, but careened in a twisting, mindless path toward the enemy. A cloud of arrows rose above the field, arcing toward him, only to become vaporized by the heat spewing from his mouth. White dragonfire, roiling with intensity, slammed into the enemy ranks with the force of a pyroclastic blast, incinerating bodies and melting steel.

The air was filled with the screams of the burning, as though in augmented parody of the grisly execution. Reaching the end of the enemy encampment, the dragon wheeled in the air, spewing fire across the sky, coming back around for another attack.

A strobe of lightning jabbed upward from the ground, spearing Ragath through. Flames gushed from the rent in his chest, and the dragon tumbled from the sky, trailing smoke and fire behind him like the tail of a comet. He crashed at full speed into the center of the encampment, tumbling in a fiery ball that mowed down soldiers and tents, at last coming to a blazing rest.

Both on the hill and on the plain below, a horrified silence fell, and for a long time, the only sound in the night was the crackling of flames. Aram stood gasping, throttled by grief, unable to look away from the blazing mass of the slain dragon. He watched it burn for seconds, transfixed by the spectacle, his vision blurring.

"Aram," Markus said, setting a hand on his shoulder.

Markus's voice finally broke him from his stupor. Wiping his eyes, Aram whirled and trudged away, pushing his way back through the stunned crowd.

A ram slumped down beside the campfire, leaning back against the trunk of an oak tree and staring upward at the black silhouettes of branches above him. He was trembling, aching with a gut-twisting combination of guilt, grief, and horror. Vandra had been his mentor and his friend. She had respected him right from the first and had believed in him even when he didn't believe in himself. She was a formidable warrior and an inspiring friend.

He should have been able to do something. *Anything.*

His eyes burned, and he felt physically ill.

"It's not your fault," Markus said.

Aram's lips compressed, and he stared hard into the fire, letting the world diminish until the flames blotted out all his other senses. "It was just a torch. What good am I, if I can't put out a single torch?"

He could hear the echoes of Vandra's screams in his mind, and the tormented cries of her poor dragon. The image of Ragath plunging from the air kept repeating over and over in his mind. For some reason, the dragon's death bothered him just as much as Vandra's, maybe because of the appalling shock of it.

"You'll make a difference tomorrow." Markus picked up a stone and turned it absently in his hands. "We both will. Tomorrow, we'll pay them back." He, too, was gazing into the flames, but his expression was vengeful. His dark hair hung in his face, plastered there with sweat, even though the evening was cool.

764

Abruptly, Aram rose.

"Where are you going?" Markus asked, twisting around to look at him.

But Aram didn't answer. His throat had tightened to the point that any answer he could have given would have come out a croak. Leaving Markus by the fire, he trudged off into the night, winding his way around tents and campfires. He walked with his head bowed, trying to hide his face so he wouldn't be recognized. The few times people greeted him, his only reply was a nod or a coarse mumble, for he couldn't conjure anything better. He was too tormented by emotions, and there was only one thing in the world strong enough to give him comfort.

He walked as fast as he could toward the outskirts of the encampment, where he knew Agaroth waited. He could feel his dragon's presence in his mind, and he knew that Agaroth was just as troubled as he was. He, too, had been rattled by Vandra's death, though not for the same reason as Aram. He was much more concerned about the number of enemy Shields he had seen, and the threat they posed his rider.

When Aram reached him, he collapsed against his dragon's side, running his hand across Agaroth's red scales and pressing his cheek against him, taking comfort in his presence. He let his dragon's strength seep slowly into him, making up for what he lacked of his own.

"If I fall in battle tomorrow, I don't want you to do what Ragath did," he whispered. "Promise me you'll survive. Promise me you'll find another to share the bond with."

Agaroth growled low in his throat, dismissing the notion contemptuously. He would be powerless to do anything different, and to try to act against instinct would be a shameful attempt to deny nature her wisdom. Their souls were intertwined for a reason, and that reason extended beyond the mere bounds of mortal life.

"But it doesn't have to be that way," Aram argued. "You survived losing Daymar, and you can survive without me too. You're the last of the Great Ones, and this world needs you far more than I do."

He knew the moment the words left his mouth that he had voiced the greatest reason why his dragon would never outlive him. Agaroth was the last of his kind, just as Aram was the last of his, and he could never endure in this world without a soul as great as his to cleave to.

At last understanding, Aram slammed a fist against his thigh, cursing the undeniability of nature. His dragon curled his neck around him, and the warmth of Agaroth's body felt good against his back. But even the dragon's touch could not keep the recurring image of Ragath's fall from haunting his mind.

Eventually, he fell asleep, his dragon curled around him. But it was not a restful slumber, as it was disturbed by frightful dreams. When Aram moaned and thrashed in his sleep, Agaroth drew nearer, resting his head against his chest. Eventually, both dragon and human found some measure of rest, though not peace.

Dawn came.

Only, it was less of a transition from night into day than it was a shift from tension to action. Aram awoke before sunrise and returned to Markus, but the rest of the encampment was already stirring and preparing for the coming battle. Warriors were sharpening their weapons and donning their gear, gathered around campfires eating what may be their last meals.

The sun rose darkly, obscured by thick clouds that threatened rain, a reflection of the grim storm brewing beneath them. Lightning flashed and flickered on the horizon, the sight making Aram shiver. It reminded him of the sorcery that had brought down Ragath, and he knew other dragons would die this day.

Markus looked up from where he sat beside the campfire, acknowledging Aram with a nod. There was no sign of resentment on his face, as Aram had feared, though seeing him there all alone brought him a pang of guilt. Aram sat down at his side. Markus held a wood spit in his hand, roasting strips of meat above the flames.

"I'm sorry," Aram muttered.

"It's all right," said Markus. "Esmir came by and kept me up late into the night. It's probably better you weren't here. At least you got some sleep."

"Esmir's here?" Aram asked. He hadn't seen the old Warden.

Markus tossed a stick into the fire. "He came with Luvana."

Aram shook his head, wondering what Luvana had been thinking, bringing Esmir here, of all people. He reached up and rubbed his eyes. When the meat was done, Markus pulled the spit out of the flames and blew on the meat to cool it down. He tried to pull off a strip but jerked his fingers back.

"Want some?" he asked, shaking his hand.

"No, thank you." Aram didn't understand how Markus could be eating; his own stomach had enough things to handle.

After the meal, they geared up, then Aram waited as Markus kicked dirt over the fire.

Markus drew a deep breath, raising his eyebrows. "Are you ready?"

Aram somehow conjured a weak smile. "Does it matter?"

Markus didn't smile back. "No. I suppose it doesn't." His face grew somber. "Years ago, Master Ebra charged me with protecting you, and I promised him I would. So far, I haven't lived up to that promise very well." Markus's eyes hardened. "Today, I will."

"You've always been there for me," Aram differed. He held out his hand, and when Markus clasped it, Aram drew him into a hug. He was profoundly grateful, for Markus was the best friend any man could ever ask for.

Markus clapped him on the back. "Come on. Better get going before this battle starts without us."

"Oh, it's not starting without us," Aram said bitterly, stooping to pick his sword up off the ground. "I'm not that lucky."

Together, they made their way toward where the front line was forming along the ridge overlooking the plain. There, the soldiers were forming up, archers in the front, arrayed along the swells of the hills. Aram's gaze fell on a woman standing at the end of a row of tents.

Calise.

She stood under the shadow of a maple tree, her arms folded in front of her. Seeing her, Aram felt a rush of joy that bordered on euphoria, and he jogged over to her, taking her in his arms and kissing her softly. When they parted, he stood staring into her face, trying to read the expression in her eyes. It wasn't an emotion he recognized, perhaps a mixture of several.

"Are you upset?" he asked, suddenly wondering if he'd done something wrong.

She nodded, her lips pressed tightly together. "Yes. I'm upset."

He frowned, wondering what he'd done wrong. Then he remembered the story she'd told him about her sister, and he understood. "I won't leave you waiting," he promised, figuring it was a pledge he could keep. "No matter what." Even if he fell in battle, she would know, because Agaroth would die with him.

Calise bit her lip, stepping back and giving the slightest nod. "I want the necklace," she whispered. "The heart knot."

Aram reached up and touched the knotted necklace his father had given his mother before the battle he'd never returned from. He didn't know if Calise knew what it meant, or what it meant to him. He hesitated, almost telling her no, for the last thing he wanted was to leave her the way his da had left his mother, with a twine necklace and nothing more. But he had Markus and Agaroth, and he trusted them.

Aram removed the necklace from his own neck and tied it around hers. Leaning forward, he kissed her one last time, his lips lingering on hers softly. Letting go of the kiss was hard, almost as hard as letting go of her. With one last smile, he turned and jogged back across the clearing toward Agaroth.

Sergan stood behind the front ranks of the Aragharian lines, trying hard not to smell them. The insect-creatures reeked of the void, a sickly-sweet odor that reminded him of carrion. Their limbs clicked when they moved, and their mandibles clattered. He didn't trust them, but then again, he didn't trust anyone, especially not on a battlefield. His gaze wandered to the hills in front of them, to where thousands of barbarians stood in line, waiting to receive them. Behind them stood the looming effigy of the Anchor, a great white statue that wept a crimson fluid down its face.

He rested his hand on the hilt of the Baelsword he wore at his side and felt a stirring deep within, like the cold coils of a serpent constricting around his spine. The sword had a soul of its own, or perhaps what he was feeling was the combined weight of all the souls it had devoured through the years. The Baelsword wasn't his, but he had every intention of using it. He had not come to this godforsaken world to fight for Kathrax. He had come for his own purpose, and he could sense that purpose now, somewhere upon the hill in front of him. Sergan intended to use the Baelsword and Lazair's signet to wring every drop of agony and essence out of Aram, then use the water of the Wellspring to extend his young life. With care and dedication, he could continue extracting essence from him for years to come, a lifetime's supply, even for a glutton like himself.

Sergan could almost taste that sweet vintage on his tongue. He stared down at the vials strapped to the leather baldric that crossed his chest. They were filled with the rank essence of the woman he had burned, and though it tasted foul, it was strong. Between the vials and the Baelsword, he had everything he needed to bring a Champion down. Even better, the Revered Master had sent him reinforcements, and he had four powerful Shields to help his cause.

"I thought your master was going to be here," he said casually to the pale Nimarean man beside him who had once been one of Lazair's henchmen. Sergan wasn't aware of the void-man's true function or purpose, only that he wasn't part of the regular military, and yet people were quick to follow his orders.

"The Divine One will come when he comes," the man said. He reminded Sergan of the zealous maniacs of the Temple of Uthobe in Odessia, who ate the fruit of a sacred tree to induce visions and were known to cut the hearts out of their own chests in sacrifice to their heathen god. This man was nearly as delusional as they were, and Sergan found himself sidling away from him, just as repulsed by him as he was by the insect-creatures.

The sonorous cry of a horn rose from somewhere across the plain, the note rising in crescendo before diminishing again. Hearing that sound, Sergan tightened his grip on the Baelsword's hilt and licked his lips.

Aram saw two men walking quickly toward them, and he halted, turning back. He recognized both of them from the night before. They were commanders, though he had forgotten which nation they belonged to. One of the men was Auld, with long brown hair the same reddish color as Aram's own, his eyes a blazing turquoise. The man with him looked like he could have been Odessian, had he come from the World Above.

"Champion." The Auld man bowed slightly. "Our scouts have reported strange occurrences in the northwest. A gathering of clouds and hailstorms that do not seem natural. Something comes."

Aram frowned, not knowing what to make of the report. It almost sounded like sorcery, though it would have to be incredibly powerful to alter weather patterns. In his core, he felt a coldness stir. He glanced to the north across the troubled plain and saw what the commander was talking about. Dark clouds were visible against the horizon, and he could see that they were moving swiftly. It reminded him of the squalls he'd seen as a boy that used to come in over the ocean, battering boats and chasing the fishing fleet back to the protection of the harbor.

Sometimes a storm was just a storm.

But no, his gut told him. This storm was different.

"For now, have the scouts keep watch and send word if anything changes," he said, pulling his helmet over his head. "That's all we can do."

The men bowed and left, and Aram climbed onto Agaroth's back. He turned to look at Markus, who sat astride Siroth. Markus dipped his head and Aram raised his hand, saluting him back.

"You ready for this?" he asked Agaroth, giving the dragon a scratch.

In reply, Agaroth let out a growl and extended his wings. Backlit by the rising sun, the thin skin that covered the dragon's dark wings was rendered translucent, revealing the intricate patterns of scars and venation within. Agaroth shifted his posture, preparing for flight, the corded muscles of his body rippling beneath his scales. Aram strapped himself into the harness, gripping the dragon's sides with his legs and grasping the black spines that ridged his back.

"Let's go," Aram said, and Agaroth lunged into the air.

His lithe body slithered upward with a sinuous motion, rising and then dipping with every stroke of his wings. Siroth caught up with them quickly and flew at their side, almost wingtip to wingtip. Though not a Great One, Siroth was larger than any other dragon in the Wing and didn't look completely dwarfed by Agaroth's size. Behind them, the other dragons rose from the ground in waves, and Aram twisted in his seat to get a view of them.

Reaching out for the strands of aether that made up the substance of the sky, he started weaving radiant armor to shield them from sorcery. He couldn't cloak them all, only those who would be assaulting the enemy directly. He didn't dare shield too many, for the cost of the weaving would leave him too exhausted for battle.

From somewhere down below, the cry of a horn sounded from the enemy ranks, giving warning that their dragons had been spotted. It was answered by a bellowing war cry that went up from tens of thousands of throats, and the enemy started forward.

Aram glanced at Markus and nodded, then hung on tight as Agaroth swept into a steep, banking dive.

A ram felt his stomach plunge as Agaroth dove from the sky, his hair whipping in the wind caused by the speed of their descent. His body lifted, and the only thing keeping him on the dragon's back were the straps of the harness fastened around him. The ground was rushing up fast, swarming with men and beasts, and just when Aram squeezed his eyes closed in anticipation of impact, Agaroth splayed his wings and leveled off, streaming a gush of brilliant, broiling flames across the battlefield. Aram glanced behind them, awed and dismayed by what he saw. A flaming, blackened swath had been carved out of the center of the enemy army.

Agaroth glided with the speed of the wind above the plain, pouring roiling fire down upon the enemy host. The flames hit like a shockwave, pulverizing bodies and shattering armor. Arrows and spears shot upward from the ground, but none could find purchase in his scales. Reaching the edge of the battlefield, Agaroth leaned into a wide, banking arc, coming back around for another pass.

Behind them, Siroth was just finishing a parallel run, blasting a similar trail of smoke and broiling death through the enemy ranks. Other dragons followed after them, a dozen in all, shimmering with the blazing light of Aram's woven armor.

Agaroth blasted another searing stripe across the battlefield, but as they came back around, Aram saw that the two armies had come together, and the ranks were now too intermixed to rain fire indiscriminately.

Still, the dragons had wreaked real havoc, both in casualties and, certainly, morale.

But now the only way he could be effective was to fight the rest of the battle from the ground.

"Take us down," he ordered Agaroth.

The dragon arrested his flight with a backstroke then remained hovering for a moment in the air, his wings working in complex motions to hold them stationary. Aram gasped as an image slammed into his mind, of he and Markus being overwhelmed in the thick of the fight.

"That's not going to happen," he argued, answering with an image of his own, of Markus and their two dragons fighting at his side.

Agaroth turned his neck and glared back at him with menacing eyes before giving in. He circled the battlefield slowly, searching for a place to land.

"There," Aram said, pointing at a relatively clear area behind the thick of the melee.

Agaroth complied with only the slightest hesitation, spiraling downward to the ground. He landed hard, turning in a circle and gushing flames everywhere, driving the enemy back. Siroth swooped down and landed at Agaroth's side, and Markus slid from his back. He met Aram just as he dismounted, positioning himself in front of him, just as Esmir had taught him.

"What are we doing here?" he yelled, lifting his sword and looking for an enemy to strike.

Aram didn't know. He wasn't sure what he was capable of. But they were here, on a battlefield, and he knew he was about to find out. Already, soldiers were closing in.

Arrows started falling around them.

Aram wove a shield to protect the dragons, thickening the air just as Dedicant Carlova had shown him. He couldn't harden the strands as much as she could, but it was enough to slow any arrows down enough to render them useless. Behind him, the dragons growled and hissed, belching cones of fire toward any soldiers who came too close.

The sounds of screams got his attention, and Aram turned to see that a group of Highlanders behind them had been enveloped by void walkers. It was a situation dragonfire couldn't save them from.

Aram wove braids of aether quickly. Jerking the final knots tight, he dragged all the void walkers backward as one, hauling them across the ground away from their prey. He then cut the strands, shielding his face as every creature exploded all at once. Gore and body parts rained from the air, the sight making him physically ill.

It also enraged the enemy.

Suddenly, soldiers were pouring toward them from every direction, and though the dragons did their best, they had to pick their targets carefully. Aram was hard-pressed to work fast enough, desperately weaving and cutting strands, battering back the soldiers who got through. Soon, the center of the battlefield was awash in dragonfire and searing magic, both combining to form a deadly radius of carnage. Aram walked forward with Markus in front of him, taking more ground, cutting off the enemy rear guard from the melee.

Within minutes, they had secured a wide area of the battlefield, cleared of everything but the dead.

Aram staggered, overcome by a wave of dizziness and exhaustion. Using that much magic was taking too much of a toll on him. He was going to have to back off before he collapsed.

Just then, the air lit up with a shocking flash of light that was gone in an instant, followed by a rolling thunderclap. Aram caught the streak of fire out of the corner of his eye and turned just in time to see a dragon enveloped in flames plunging into the thick of the melee, hitting the ground in a ball of fire.

He closed his eyes, feeling gut-punched.

The dragon had been Wingmaster Lorine's.

Exhaustion was hammering him, and he'd let the dragon's shield slip. Feeling sickened, he tightened the glowing armor around the others. Anger burned deep into his insides. He couldn't keep the dragons shielded forever.

Their sorcerers were the problem. He had to find them and take them out before he collapsed from exhaustion. Aram scanned the field of battle but could see little from their position. Enemy sorcerers could be anywhere spread throughout the plain or even hiding in the rear. Gritting his teeth, Aram suppressed a growl.

They had reached a place where a small, rocky hill protruded above the prairie. Aram decided to climb it, wanting to look down upon the battlefield from higher ground and get a better perspective. He ascended carefully, exhaustion making his legs unstable. Markus helped steady him up the steeper parts, a look of concern on his face.

When they reached the top of the hill, Aram stopped and gazed out over the field. He saw that there was still a lot of the battle left to fight. Most of the fighting was centered below the rise of hills, where a wedge of the enemy was trying to break through the ranks of defenders.

Below, fifty or so men had broken off from the melee and were loping up the base of the hill toward their position. Realizing they had drawn attention to themselves, Aram summoned their dragons but then stopped. Perhaps that kind of attention was exactly what they needed to draw the sorcerers out. He held his ground and waited, letting his opponents ascend.

Markus moved in front of him, raising his sword. "What in the hell are we doing, Aram?"

"Killing sorcerers."

"I don't see any sorcerers!"

"They'll come." Aram felt certain of it.

With that, he started spinning aether, working a quick succession of braids that spiraled out away from them in the air, forming a construction that reminded him of a spider's web, only a thousand times bigger and more complex. Tying it off, he wadded it into a ball and cast it down upon the hillside, aimed at the soldiers advancing toward them.

He was unprepared for the strength of his own creation.

Below them, the side of the hill erupted in a thunderous blast of rocks and hurling debris. Jets of dirt and tumbling boulders shot out from the hillside, arcing upward into the sky to land hundreds of feet away. Aram staggered, almost thrown backward by the force of the blast, and Markus dropped into a fighting stance to keep from falling over. Rocks and scraps of armor shot toward them, and Aram had to harden the air to keep them from being hit. Markus glanced back at him with a look of shock, his face beneath his helmet gray with dust.

Rather than chasing the enemy away, the explosion had the opposite effect—the effect Aram had hoped for. Scores of warriors and insect-like creatures broke off from the main host and scrambled toward their position, drawn like bats to the moonlight. Seeing the threat to his rider, Agaroth spread his wings and roared then sprang into the air and glided to the hilltop. He landed on the peak above them, where he brandished his might and size in a terrifying display. Siroth skimmed to the opposite side of the hill, where he affected a similar posture, glaring down the hillside, ready to ward their other flank.

"They're coming to us, all right," Markus muttered. "Think you can do that again?"

In response, Aram raised his hands, gathering strands of aether and preparing to bind. When the first wave of the enemy broke over the crest of the hill, it was Agaroth who attacked first, lunging forward to blanket the hillside with searing white flames. The insect-creatures nearest were scorched instantly to charcoal. The armor of the men heated red then melted, pooling on the ground in globs of slag. Those further away dropped, enveloped in flames, the insects emitting piercing, whistling noises as they died. When the roar of the fire had ended, the entire hillside was smoldering and blackened.

But there were more coming—far more than Aram had counted on. He knew he had painted a large target on himself, but he'd felt sure they'd send sorcerers to take him down, not throw half their army at him. If this continued, he and Markus would have to abandon the hilltop.

Weary, he tore more tendrils from the air and started to work them. His ability to see in color was nothing short of a godsend, allowing him to handle dozens of complications at once, all flowing together into logical patterns that would have been indiscernible to normal human eyes. These, he flung down the hillside, where they exploded, slicing through men and beasts like scythes reaping grain. Eventually, the waves of warriors stopped coming, instead fleeing the area and in all-out rout.

Seeing that there was no one left to attack, Aram brought his hands up to clutch his throbbing head, feeling dizzy and sick to his stomach. He had never handled so much magic before, had never *imagined* handling so much magic. He couldn't have kept it up much longer. He felt Markus's hand on his arm and turned to look at him

"Are you all right?"

Aram nodded, squeezing his eyes closed until the ground stopped heaving under his feet. "I just need to rest for a moment."

Markus let go and jogged back to where Siroth stood, looming over the blasted hillside like a living gargoyle. Markus grabbed a waterskin that hung from his harness then returned to Aram's side, pressing it into his hands.

"Drink."

Aram tilted his head back and gasped as the sweet taste of Wellspring water touched his lips. He gulped it down, beyond grateful for Markus's foresight.

The water cooled his parched throat and filled him with a comforting sense of relief. It didn't make the ache of exhaustion go away, but it did make it bearable. He had to stop himself from drinking too much, knowing he should save some for later, when he might need it even more. He wiped his mouth and handed the waterskin back.

He crouched down to catch his breath, holding his head in his hands. He stayed there for minutes, until Markus set a hand on his shoulder and pointed toward the scorched plain below.

"What's that?"

Aram stood to look, and just as he did, the entire hill shuddered. A shadow raced over them, and suddenly Agaroth roared and lunged skyward—

—to be slapped back to the earth by a dragon pouncing on top of him. Agaroth roared in anger, twisting his body to right himself as the smaller dragon clamped onto him with its powerful talons and caught hold of his neck with dagger-sharp teeth. Agaroth thrashed his powerful neck in an effort to dislodge his attacker. His tail whipped furiously, beating at the dragon clinging to his back. He succeeded in jarring it loose, but the creature just pounced again, latching onto Agaroth with teeth and talon.

Aram raised his hand and started to bind but dropped the strands when another dragon hurled out of the sky, knocking Siroth off the hillside. Shocked, he scrambled to gather the remnants of his scattered weaving, but before he could pick it up, Markus stepped in front of him, raising his sword.

Five figures were climbing the hill, approaching their position: three men and a woman bearing weapons and shields, as well as another, blue-cloaked figure carrying a sword that glowed with dark strands of power.

Aram had seen that sword before, just as he'd seen the man before. But reconciling the two of them together in one place took him valuable seconds.

The fear that seared Aram's nerves at the sight of Sergan Parsigal was almost crippling. All at once, he was back in the well staring up the shaft at this monster's face. His breath hitched, and he took a jarring step backward.

The sorcerer's eyes fell on him, and a smile bloomed on his lips, the same sardonic grin Aram remembered from all those years before. His gaze went to the sword in Sergan's hand and he felt his courage slip.

Sergan was holding a Baelsword, and the look on his face told Aram that he intended to use it. Aram glanced in Agaroth's direction, but the dragon was still fighting a battle for his life, and another dragon was diving toward him to join the first.

Markus stood ahead of him, turning slowly, first one way then the other, as Sergan's four Shields spread out to approach them from all sides. All four looked strong and proficient with the weapons they held. Any one of them would be capable of threatening Aram, if they could get past Markus. Aram raised his star-steel blade, knowing it would serve him far more than magic, under the circumstances.

"Well, hello again!" Sergan said, taking a step closer.

Two of the male Shields were converging on Markus from different angles while one hung back warding Sergan. The woman skirted the edge of the hilltop in a broad circle, seeking to position herself behind

Aram. Pressured, Markus started backing up, but then thought better of it and held his ground. Aram was having a hard time dividing his attention between Sergan and the black-haired woman with the sword who was inching ever closer.

Behind them, Agaroth let out a snarling roar that broiled the air. Both dragons had wrestled him to the ground, but he wasn't beaten yet.

Sergan said to Markus, "You made a poor choice. I would've made you great. You could have had anything you wanted. Instead, you chose the halfwit." He curled his lip, shaking his head. "What a godsdamned waste."

His Shields had stopped moving and stood their ground, just out of striking distance of Markus's blade. The woman, however, was still edging around the perimeter of the hill, sword raised, her attention riveted on Aram.

"Now you're going to die," Sergan scolded Markus, "and I'm going to spend the rest of my life milking your friend of every drop of essence I can wring out of him." He drew the Baelsword back over his shoulder.

His two Shields struck out at Markus simultaneously, just as the woman swept forward, lunging at Aram.

Aram pivoted toward her, raising his blade to block, but something grabbed his arm, jerking it forcefully back. He lost the split second it took him to recover, and he couldn't avoid the weapon coming at him. The sword grazed his chest, scraping across his dragon scale armor with the sound of a whetstone sliding down the length of a blade.

He wrenched his arm back, bringing with it strands of glittering aether that hung from his hand like a broken spider's web. Sergan had intervened, and Aram was vulnerable without a Shield. In front of him, Markus was hard-pressed to defend against two skilled swordsmen coming at him from both sides, and their dragons were both engaged in battles for their own lives.

Sergan had planned this ambush well.

Aram attacked, weaving a whip of aethereal lashes that struck out at Sergan with scalding tongues of flame. The Shield between them deflected all but one of the lashes, which managed to get past him and score

Sergan on the cheek. The sorcerer cried out and brought a hand up to the cauterized wound that branded his face, cold ire and magic blazing in his eyes.

Aram couldn't weave a second attack because he was too busy blocking the woman's sword, moving through the forms drilled into him in the training yard. But the woman he fought was more skilled, moving with the grace of someone who had practiced with weapons from an early age. She came at him with solid strikes powered by her balance and momentum, which more than compensated for her inferior strength. Her movements were brisk and precise, and she shifted through forms as fluidly as a dancer.

Aram was forced to retreat further from Markus, barely deflecting her lightning-quick cuts. As he backed away, he purposefully kept the woman between Sergan and himself, using her intentionally to Shield anything the sorcerer might hurl his way. But it didn't take Sergan long to realize his strategy. The sorcerer stalked forward, skirting the perimeter of the hill. As he walked, he brought a vial of essence to his lips, drinking it down.

Sergan raised his hand, his eyes glowing with the unholy light of stolen magic. At the same time, the woman came at Aram with a crisp series of attacks.

The wall of solid air Sergan conjured smacked into him with the force of a cyclone, lifting Aram's body and hurling him across the top of the hill. He struck the ground hard, losing his helm in the process. He lay flat on his back, his vision exploding in glittering white sparkles before darkening. He clung to consciousness by his fingernails, but he'd had the wind knocked out of him, and he couldn't move. For seconds, he lay on the ground, stunned and helpless.

They were seconds he didn't have.

The woman fell upon him, driving her knee into his chest. At the same time, the edge of her sword kissed the skin of his neck. Aram gaped at her, his lungs burning for breath. The woman's face was growing dull and dark as his vision faded, and he would've passed out had she not eased her weight somewhat. He drew in a great, choking breath, his sight returning in time to see Sergan coming forward, the Baelsword lowered at him. Aram spun a complex braid, but before he could release it, the woman's sword pressed into his neck.

Suddenly, the woman gasped, her eyes going wide. Her sword retracted from his neck ever so slightly.

Aram stared up at her, confused, until his gaze fell upon the tip of the blade protruding from her chest. She fell on top of him, sliding forward off the end of Markus's sword.

The elation Aram felt was short-lived, for Markus sank to his knees, his gray tabard saturated with blood all down the front of him. His sword spilled from his hand, and he slumped the rest of the way to the ground, his blood-drenched hand groping at his chest.

"No!" Aram gulped.

He heaved himself off the ground and lunged for Markus. But Sergan's boot caught him in the chest, knocking him over. The same boot took him in the jaw, snapping his head back and dropping him to the ground. Dazed, Aram felt something take hold of him, dragging him backward. His arms were pinned by a painful weight, then, the next thing he knew, a cloth was being wound around his face like a bandage, blinding his eyesight so he couldn't bind.

He struggled desperately, but he couldn't shake the weight pressing him against the ground. He had to get to Markus, had to stop the bleeding—every second counted, and each second that passed could be one too many.

A thunderous roar shook the earth, overwhelming Aram's hearing. The weight disappeared from his back, and Aram tore the cloth away from his face just in time to see Agaroth take hold of Sergan and fling him into the air. The sorcerer's body smacked the ground on the edge of the hill, where he lay moaning while the dragon crouched and opened its glowing maw.

WHOOSH!

A torrent of brilliant, roiling flames erupted from Agaroth's mouth, devouring the hilltop. The sound of the inferno was deafening, and even from behind the dragon, Aram could feel the raw heat of the fire scorching his cheeks. He turned his face away, squeezing his eyes closed, as the gushing blast continued for blistering seconds before finally dissipating.

When Aram looked back, all that was left of the hillside was a large area of blackened, smoldering ground with flames still licking along the margins of the destruction. If there were human bones there, he didn't see them. He doubted even bones could have survived that blast.

Mindlessly, he scrambled to Markus and rolled him over onto his back. Markus was unconscious, his blood spreading across his tabard. Aram ripped the material down the front then fumbled with the buckles of Markus's armor, pulling his cuirass off and casting it aside. Beneath it, Markus's arming shirt was saturated with blood like a cloth soaked in wine.

Panicked, Aram drew his knife and used it to saw through the padded shirt, revealing a ghastly wound in Markus's chest. It was a puncture as wide as two of his fingers, and blood bubbled from it at every breath with a horrible wheezing sound. Aram could tell by the pallor of his skin that Markus was already in shock.

Tearing off his mantle, Aram wadded up the fabric and pressed it hard against Markus's chest. Cold panic filled him as he watched the fresh material dampen with bright red blood. He wasn't a healer like Calise, and even if he were, it wouldn't do any good. Markus was Impervious to magic, even the kind that could save his life.

"Hang on!" Aram begged. Everything he remembered about field dressing slipped from his mind, and the only thing he could think of was pressure. He had to maintain pressure.

"Agaroth!" he called. "Siroth!"

Agaroth spun to face him, wings splayed and spines raised. His blazing gold eyes settled on Markus, and he breathed a fiery snort of rage. An image passed through Aram's mind of a black dragon with an injured wing, and he knew at once that Siroth would have a hard enough time flying himself back.

"Help me!" Aram gasped, wrapping his arms around Markus and dragging him toward his dragon. With the help of a large rock and the

judicious use of the leading edge of Agaroth's powerful wing, he managed to get Markus over the dragon's back and climbed up behind him, strapping them both in.

"Fly fast!" he whispered, more of a prayer than a plea. He clutched Markus tight as the two dragons surged into the sky, heading back over the battlefield toward the hills on the far side.

They touched down on the edge of the encampment, where the tents of the healers were located. Seeing them coming, those on the ground scrambled to clear a space wide enough for them to land. People rushed forward to help lift Markus down from Agaroth's back, laying him on the grass, where healers converged on them. Aram crouched at Markus's side, keeping pressure on the wound through blood-soaked bandages. From behind them, he heard the growls of an enraged dragon and realized it must be Siroth, despondent over the condition of his rider.

Calise appeared beside them, gently removing his hands. She lifted the sodden cloth, exposing the still-bleeding puncture. Clamping both her hands over the wound, she closed her eyes and summoned her magic.

She cursed and pulled back.

Aram felt a cold terror grip him in a glacial fist. He grimaced, a sob of helplessness tearing at his throat.

Applying pressure to the bandages, Calise called back over her shoulder, "Someone get me a square of leather and a compress! And Wellspring water!

Markus groaned, but otherwise seemed unconscious. Aram moved back, giving her room to work, and watched from the crowd of onlookers.

Someone came running with the items Calise needed, handing them over. She upended the container of Wellspring water over a square of leather then poured more water into the wound to clean it. Then she bent over Markus, holding the leather square in both hands.

"Breathe out hard," she ordered, and Markus must have heard her, for the wound gurgled and foamed as air gushed through it.

Quickly, Calise pressed the leather over the rent, covering it with absorbent cloth and binding his chest tightly with bandages. They put Markus on a stretcher and were about to carry him to the tents, but Aram stopped them.

"Give me a moment," he said, sinking down at Markus's side. Taking his best friend's blood-wet hand, Aram leaned forward and kissed him on the cheek, for he knew he might never see him again.

"You better fight just as hard now as you did on that battlefield," he rasped, his throat clenched, his eyes burning.

Markus opened his eyes and smiled weakly, squeezing his hand. He stared up at him with a gaze suddenly fierce and determined, conveying a message that Aram had no trouble understanding: that no matter what happened here today, their friendship was the one thing the enemy could never take from them. Aram couldn't hold the tears back as he let go of Markus's hand and stood back, watching the healers carry him away.

He stood and stared after him, then wiped his eyes and started back toward Agaroth. The sounds of battle were growing closer and louder, and he feared their soldiers were losing ground.

"Aram!" Calise cried. "Where are you going?"

He paused, turning back. His gaze ran over her, taking her in, from her blood-slicked arms to her sweat-dampened hair, and he couldn't remember admiring anyone as much as he did Calise at that moment. She walked over to him and reached up to touch his bleeding cheek where Sergan's boot had kicked him in the face.

Aram flinched back. "I've got to get back out there."

Calise shook her head, her eyes widening. "You can't!"

Before Aram could argue, he heard someone behind them exclaim, "By the gods! What is that?"

Glancing toward the sound of the voice, Aram saw that a small crowd had gathered not far away, their attention fixed on something down below. He ran toward them, fighting his way through the crowd to where he had a decent view of the entire plain.

The battlefield spread before him, a large swath of denuded, dark ground. Most of the combatants were collected in about a dozen nodes, where the fighting was most intense. Corpses of men and animals littered the field, and scavenger birds blotted the skies above it, their insistent cries combined into a wall of noise that rivaled the clamor of battle. Smoke rose from all across the plain where fires had been set, and in places where the fighting had been the thickest, the bodies were piled into hummocks. At the base of the hill, a sparse line of defenders were being driven back by a fresh enemy charge.

But that wasn't what had captured the bystanders' attention.

Hovering above the battlefield was a black Greater Dragon even larger in size than Agaroth. Upon its back was a dark figure armored in lacquered plate, holding a shield in one hand and a Baelsword in the other. The dragon descended upon the battlefield, soldiers and therlings scrambling to clear an area for it to land. It touched down upon the plain with a terrifying roar and a frightening display of its massive wings.

Its rider slid heavily from the dragon's back then strode forward into the cleared space and simply stood there, helm tilted, gazing toward them.

Toward *him*, Aram realized with a shiver.

He was too far away to see the dark warrior's eyes, but he could still *feel* them. It was a sensation like worms trying to burrow through his eye sockets, and he had the impulse to claw at them.

"What is it?" someone gasped.

"It's the Archon," Aram answered, for he had seen that terrible figure before during his Trials. "Kathrax."

That thing had killed his father. And now, he felt certain, it had come here for him. Kathrax wanted him, though he didn't know why. He couldn't tell whether the Archon desired merely to slay him, or if Kathrax had some other terrible purpose for him in mind.

A powerful feeling came over Aram, the urge to go down there and confront the Archon face-to-face. No. Not to confront. To *surrender*. It was something he should do, because it was the right thing, the *reasonable* thing. The longer he delayed, the more uncomfortable he became. He shouldn't be here, staring out across the battlefield. He should be down *there*, walking across it toward his master.

"*Gah!*" Aram spat, realizing what was happening.

He shook his head vigorously to rid his mind of the intrusion. People around him glanced at him strangely, their eyes full of worry. Trembling, he turned and strode away, feeling as though his skin were crawling with maggots. He had never felt such an invasion before. The Archon's mental touch had left him feeling filthy and vulnerable.

After cold, solitary seconds, Agaroth's presence returned to dominate his mind, helping Aram shake off the last of the lingering feelings. The dragon was livid, enraged at the enemy's attack on his rider. He reared back and roared, his hot breath searing the air.

Aram paused, glancing back to regard his enemy. He could feel the Archon's strength, and he knew he was no match for it, not alone, not without Markus. He also knew he had no choice but to face it.

Fear is your enemy. Don't surrender to it.

His father's voice echoed in his mind, solidifying his resolve. He gathered his courage, knowing well that without a Warden, he wouldn't have much of a chance against Kathrax. But, like his father before him, he had to stand and face him anyway. Glancing sadly at the line of tents where they'd taken Markus, he set his course for his dragon.

"No, Aram, you can't!" Calise cried, catching his arm. "Not without a Warden!"

Aram didn't know what to do or say. He didn't want to lie to her and tell her he'd be coming back. So he conjured a sad smile and said, "I'm sorry. I am. But I don't have a choice."

"Yes, you do!"

Surprised, Aram saw Esmir hobbling toward them, carrying a longsword in his hands. Aram stared at the old man in confusion, not understanding what Esmir was trying to tell him. He waited precious moments for Esmir to arrive breathless before him, leaning heavily on the blade of his sword.

"You don't have to go alone," Esmir said in a gruff voice, wiping sweat from his brow. "I'll be your Warden."

Aram shook his head slowly, gaping at Esmir in bewilderment. "You can't."

The old man could scarcely walk, much less Shield him against an Archon. The very notion was absurd. He glanced at Calise, seeing his own doubts echoed in her face.

Esmir compressed his lips and raised his chin, looking affronted. "I can't move like I used to, but I can still stand in front of you and block. Who the hell do you think trained you, boy? At the very least, I'm better than nothing."

Aram stared at Esmir before finally nodding. The old Warden wouldn't last a minute, and he was sure Esmir knew it. He was volunteering to sacrifice his life for very little gain. Maybe he felt compelled to, because of Daymar. Regardless, it was a noble gesture, and Aram could not deny him.

"You are much better than nothing," he said, dipping his head. "Forgive me. I'd be honored to fight at your side."

With a grunt, Esmir hobbled past him, approaching the great red dragon who despised him more than any other person in the world. But when he arrived at Agaroth's side, the dragon's golden eyes softened, and he swept his wings back, lowering himself to the ground for Esmir to mount. With Aram's help, the old Warden somehow fought his way onto the dragon's back and strapped himself in, all while managing to maintain a semblance of dignity.

"I've got to go," Aram told Calise, pulling away.

"Not without a helmet," she insisted firmly.

Irritated, Aram turned and scanned the ground. This was a field hospital; surely there must be unused armor lying about. It didn't take him long to spot a helmet tossed aside in a pile of discarded gear. He ran to pick it up, shoving the helmet on his head and cinching the strap. He paused when he reached Agaroth's side, turning back and smiling solemnly at Calise one last time.

Then he followed Esmir up onto Agaroth's back. As soon as he was secure, the dragon flexed his wings and roared a challenge across the battlefield. He leapt into the air, the powerful muscles of his wings pulling them aloft.

From under the shadow of an oilcloth canopy, Markus watched the great red dragon vault into the sky, veering with the grace of a falcon toward the battlefield. In spite of the sharp pain that stabbed his chest with every breath he drew, what hurt worse was the terrible guilt he felt at not being on that dragon's back instead of Esmir. It was a brave act the old man performed, but that was the best that could be said for it. It was *his* duty, not Esmir's. But he had failed Aram just as surely as Esmir had failed Daymar, and this was the result.

Markus's vision blurred as he watched the dragon grow small and distant in the sky. With a sigh, he closed his eyes, thinking back on the strange boy with brown blood and a cave full of knots that he'd rescued from a beating so many years before. As the dragon slipped out of sight behind a long line of hills, Markus sent his thoughts and heart after Aram, the most courageous man he'd ever known.

Calise fingered the twine necklace around her neck as she watched Agaroth descend toward the battlefield. Among the Auld, an eternal heart knot was a sentimental gift from a warrior to his beloved, given on the eve of battle. If the man returned, the necklace was burned as an offering of thanks to the Mother for bringing him home. If the warrior fell in battle, the heart knot would serve as a reminder of his love.

This was not the first time Aram had presented her with this weighty gift. He had entrusted the necklace to her before his Trials, for safekeeping, or so he said. She had accepted the token then, thinking him ignorant of the gesture's true significance. But this time, when he had tied it around her neck, she had seen in his eyes that he knew exactly what it meant.

And he'd given it to her anyway.

Reaching up, she wiped her tears. If Aram came back, then they would burn the necklace together. And if he did not, then it would be hers to cherish and despise for the rest of her life. As her gaze drifted toward the now-empty sky, she clenched the knotted twine in her fingers, holding onto it like a lifeline.

Agaroth's sleek body slipped through the clouds, angling toward the bare patch of ground where their adversaries awaited. The dragon circled once, carefully selecting a place to land, then descended from the air, coming to rest upon a patch of unbroken soil away from the thick of the fighting.

Seeing them, the Archon's dragon dropped into a crouch, raking back its obsidian wings and baring its teeth, raising its hindquarters like a panther readying to spring. Agaroth opened his maw, letting out roiling hot breath, lashing his tail as though trying to goad his nemesis into attacking.

Aram waited until Esmir was down before sliding off the dragon's back. He stood for a moment assessing the situation. The day had darkened considerably; the sun was hidden behind cloud cover. A cold wind breathed a gust of stale air in his face that stank of blood, a rank metallic odor that made his stomach twist.

He stood gazing out over the horrendous landscape, absorbing it in small increments. Everywhere he looked was death and agony, mounds of corpses and moaning wounded. A man to his right was trying to grope his way forward on his belly, calling out for his mother as though searching for her. A woman not far away lay on her back screaming, waving in the air her own severed hand. There was more. Too much more. Clutching his stomach, Aram bent over, trying hard not to vomit. Wiping his mouth, he straightened, a cold hollowness goring out his insides.

That was when he felt the presence enter his mind, like a cold iron spike slipping into him, shoving its way deeper.

Groaning, Aram squeezed his eyes closed as he grappled against that feeling with every fiber of his will, at last succeeding at expelling the assault. Panting from exertion, he opened his eyes and lifted his head, staring straight ahead across the hellish scene into the helmed face of his adversary.

A sudden and all-consuming rage bloomed within him, starting in his stomach and working its way up to his chest, spreading out to all of his extremities. Unbidden, his hand moved for the hilt of his sword, sliding it out of its lacquered scabbard. He held it in front of him as he stalked slowly forward, the star-steel blade shining brightly with the light of the power manifest within him.

Seeing him coming, Kathrax raised his Baelsword, which blazed with dark flames. He reached out toward Aram with his gauntleted hand, palm open, as though trying to grasp him.

He closed his fist.

Before Aram, two demonic creatures materialized in a flash of brilliant light: therlings, conjured from the void. They looked like gross amalgamations of both human and animal parts, as though they were deliberate parodies of all that he fought for. One had goat's horns and a wolf's muzzle, its hands ending in talons, a barbed tail extending from its back. The other looked like a cross between a praying mantis and an elk, with bulbous eyes staring out from an antlered head. The creature's powerful forelimbs ended in claws that clacked like those of a crab, and it pawed at the ground with a cloven hoof, looking ready to gore him.

"This should be my fight," said Esmir soberly.

"It's mine," Aram said, raising his sword in both hands. He didn't wait for the void-creatures to come to him. Instead, he lunged forward, bringing the fight to them.

He struck out with his foot, kicking the goat-thing in the knee, at the same time sweeping out with his sword at the other. The elk parried his strike with its massive rack of antlers. With a jerk of its head, the elk captured his blade and nearly wrenched it from his gasp. Somehow, he managed to maintain his grip on the hilt.

Aram jerked it back and scrambled away, yielding ground but

gaining precious seconds to recover. The goat brayed as it dove at him, a flamberge sword appearing in its hand. Aram blocked the strike it tried to land on him, spinning away fast to avoid being gored by the elk's antlers.

When the goat-thing came at him again, he punched it in the face then brought his sword up, slicing through the thick mane of hair that encircled its neck. Black blood spewed from the wound, and the goat screamed like an agonized child.

Aram sprang back as, enraged, the elk-creature lowered its head and charged at him like a bull. Before he could get his sword up, Agaroth pounced on the elk, closing his talons around its girth and taking it to the ground. While the creature struggled, the dragon started tearing it apart, piece by mismatched piece.

Aram turned to Esmir, flashing the Warden a reassuring smile. But Esmir didn't return the expression, his gaze fixed on something behind Aram.

Turning, Aram saw that a glittering wound had ripped open the air, the threads of the Veil unraveling right in front of him. The earth trembled, almost knocking him off his feet, even as he grappled to close the rupture. But before he could finish tying off the strands, something forced the rift open wider, unravelling the Veil for hundreds of feet to either side.

Esmir cursed loudly, jumping back. Agaroth gave a furious growl, raking back his wings.

Aram started to raise his sword but then froze when he saw what was coming.

In the wide, cleared area around them, a rupture in the Veil had opened, a long wall of brilliant, blinding light that seemed to be sucking the life from the world. Just the sight of it provoked a deep, visceral fear. Unlike the other ruptures Aram had seen, this one did not lead to the World Above. This rupture opened directly into the emptiness of the void between worlds, into the desolation that turned living creatures into hungering wraiths.

Seeing the rupture, Agaroth shrieked and flinched back, a reaction that filled Aram with so much dread that he stood frozen, unable to move. His dragon had been trapped within the void for hundreds of years and knew better than anyone what horrors lay within. As the opening yawned larger, a breeze picked up, air rushing toward the vacuum of the looming maw. The speed of the wind increased as the rupture expanded, until it became a howling gale that whipped Aram's hair against his face and plastered his mantle to his back. Debris carried by the wind rushed past him: leaves and twigs, strips of cloth, clouds of churning dust and tumbling branches.

Out of the gaping rupture emerged four inhuman creatures, stepping out onto the sodden ground of the battlefield. They were not therlings, nor were they void walkers. Aram recognized their kind immediately, and that recognition filled him with fear, chilling his insides.

They were Overseers, or at least of the same mysterious race as the creatures who had supervised his Trials. They stood before him, each twice the height of a man: powerful, otherworldly beings with an arcane and ancient presence, their faces serpentine, their eyes black and vacant. They were clothed in robes that crackled in the wind. The wide rupture closed behind them, sealing itself shut with writhing tendrils of aether.

And yet the Overseers remained, standing in a line before him, cutting Aram off from his adversary.

Aram gripped his star-steel blade firmly in both hands. Esmir walked forward to stand at his side, considering the creatures before them with a mixture of revulsion and disbelief. Raising his sword, the old Warden settled into a fighting stance, ready to step in front of Aram and Shield him with his own body.

Esmir glanced at Aram and met his gaze, and something passed between them, the deep affection shared by a master and his apprentice. The old man nodded, resolve squaring his jaw, his hunched back straightening. A lump formed in Aram's throat, and his chest tightened with heartfelt gratitude. He did not know what he had ever done to deserve such remarkable friends and allies. Vandra and Markus, Calise and Esmir…not so long ago, he had been a boy of twelve who had thought the most he could look forward to was a lifetime spent at sea, surrounded by nets and rigging and solitude. He had thought himself undeserving of friends, and yet, somehow, he'd ended up with the best friends any man could ask for.

As he stood before a line of beings more powerful and sinister than any in the world, he felt comforted to know that he had Esmir at his side. Together, they might be enough, and even if they weren't, he felt certain they would make a good accounting.

A shadow fell over him, and Aram shivered.

It was then that he noticed that the day around them had changed. It was as though the sun had set when he wasn't looking, light draining from the sky. Darkness and shadows had settled in, and the air had taken on a chill. The sky overhead was gray. The sun hung above them in the position of high noon, a black disk outlined by a halo of red, ominous light. He saw that Esmir was staring up at it, too, frowning deeply at the corrupted sun that hung like an ill-portent in the sky. The lines around the old man's eyes deepened, but his shoulders didn't sag, and his grip remained firm on the hilt of his sword.

Aram turned his attention back toward the line of foes, waiting for them to act, uncertain of their intentions.

He didn't wait long.

The creature directly across from him took a step forward, it's inky gaze locking on his.

SURRENDER.

The force of the word trembled the foundations of Aram's mind. He brought a hand up to his temple, clenching his jaw against the pain of it. He could not imagine the strength of the mind that could inject such force into a single word. Every fiber in his body trembled under the weight of it.

"No." He shook his head.

SURRENDER...OR BE BROKEN.

Aram groaned, squeezing his eyes closed as the words raked like claws into his mind. He had experienced these voices within the portal stones, but he didn't remember them being this overwhelming. Or was it the voice of the Archon he was hearing?

Whichever, it didn't matter.

Esmir shot a nervous glance his way. "What's happening?"

"They're going to attack," Aram answered under his breath, his eyes locked on the Overseer's black gaze.

The strange creature inclined its head, as though acknowledging a foe. Then it raised its palm, the other three echoing its gesture.

Sharpened beams of intense blue light shot from their hands, streaking toward Aram. Esmir moved with the alacrity of a twenty-year-old, inserting himself between the assault of magic and the Champion he defended. The spears of light fell upon him and were unmade, disappearing completely. Aram gaped at him in wonder, but only for a second, because the beings were moving quickly, spreading to encircle them. Esmir turned slowly, following the line of creatures as they wrapped around them. Aram put his back against Esmir's, for, Impervious or not, the old Warden couldn't defend him from all sides. When the next series of attacks came at him, Aram met them with his star-steel blade.

Beams of razor-sharp energy reflected off his sword, scattering like sunrays. In the same instant, Aram started weaving, throwing up a web between himself and the Overseers, thick enough that their light couldn't penetrate. A growl of rage trembled his mind, and he could sense their frustration. He could not see them through the shadow-shield, but he could feel them clawing at it, dismembering its fibers.

Aram gathered more strands of aether and wove snarls of knots that he then tore apart, snapping the strands that bound them and releasing all the pent-up energy stored within. One of the reptilian creatures gave a shrill cry as it went down, spewing black blood from a rent in its chest. In retaliation, the others redoubled their efforts, forcing Aram to divert most of his energy and attention into bolstering his shield.

Vaguely, he was aware of the rage of his dragon, and he knew that, behind him, Agaroth was fighting a battle for his life against the obsidian monster. Though he wanted to turn and look, he couldn't, for he was too hard-pressed to defend himself and Esmir.

Focusing all of his concentration, Aram wove an elaborate pattern in the air between himself and the nearest of his enemies. When he finished, he jerked the threads with all his might, snapping every strand all at once and releasing a torrent of power that exploded in the Overseer's face, taking its reptilian head off.

The remaining two Overseers hissed, intensifying their efforts, and powerful ropes of light streamed out of them in blistering rays. But with only two of them remaining, the assault was less than it had been, and Aram felt his confidence surge.

But then another force asserted itself: a darker, more sinister power adding its own menace to the attack. Suddenly, Aram found himself being quickly overpowered by an onslaught of magic unlike anything he had ever imagined. A terrible inferno erupted from the ground beneath them, and suddenly he and Esmir were standing in the funnel of a tornado made of flame.

Aram did his best to draw the heat out of the blaze, but he couldn't stop the flames from reaching them. Behind him, Esmir staggered, knocking into him and throwing him off balance.

"Turn around!" the old man growled over his shoulder. "Hold onto me, boy, and don't let go!"

Aram did as Esmir ordered, wrapping his arm around the old man's chest from behind, hugging him close, so that he could maximize the protection of the Warden's touch.

Seeing their vulnerability, the Overseer in front of them ceased its attack and simply stood for a moment regarding them. Slowly, it raised both hands.

BE BROKEN.

Aram threw himself aside as a slanted beam of light sliced toward him like a guillotine. It hit Esmir in the back and would have sliced any other man clean in half, but not the Warden. It hurt him, nevertheless. Esmir staggered, growling in pain. A line of blood appeared and spread across the cloth that covered his back. He was resistant to magic, but not a True Impervious like Markus. Magic could still harm him, if it was strong enough.

This was.

Emboldened, the Overseers renewed their attack. With the weight of his body, Esmir knocked Aram to the ground and hunkered over him. The old Warden screamed as streams of magic gushed toward him, enveloping him in a molten halo. Somehow, his body repulsed it all, leaving Aram unharmed beneath him.

Growling in pain, Esmir pushed himself to his feet, drawing Aram up after him, blocking the onslaught with his own body. Behind him, Aram wove rapidly, spinning a web of absorbent strands that he threw around them both. But the Overseers' assault was too powerful, and the fibers melted as soon as he wove them. Panicked, he glanced about, searching for Agaroth but not finding him.

Blood coursed from multiple wounds on Esmir's body, and his tunic smoldered from the heat coming off of him. Still, he held his sword in front of him, bearing the brunt of the assault.

But he could not stand forever.

The attack increased in force until it was a blazing blue fire that engulfed them both. Aram did the only thing he could do: he held onto Esmir as tight as he could and did his best to mitigate the damage they were taking. Pressing his face against Esmir's back, he fought to infuse the old Warden with some of his own strength. But it was impossible; Esmir was as resistant to his own magic as he was to the Overseers'.

Esmir held on as long as he could, fighting the onslaught of magic until his body started smoking. Throwing his head back, he howled in pain, the tendons of his neck bulging like overstretched cords. Aram could feel the Warden's skin heat until it was hot to the touch, like the handle of a pot left over an open flame. He hung onto him tighter and wove as fast as he could. But he couldn't weave fast enough.

At last, the old man faltered.

He sank to one knee, dropping his sword. Aram clung on to him, following Esmir to the ground, struggling to hold him upright. With his ear pressed against Esmir's back, he could hear the old man's breath turn to wheezing. He struggled harder to defend him, but there was nothing he could do. Not against that.

"Hang on," he whispered, squeezing his eyes closed as he hugged the dying Warden. "Please hang on."

SURRENDER.

The finality of that word rocked Aram to the core. In his arms, Esmir was dying, and towering above them were two Overseers and whatever presence was bolstering them.

It was finished, Aram realized.

He had failed.

At that moment, the assault ceased.

Aram laid Esmir upon the ground, pressing a kiss against his brow. Then he looked up and stared into the nearest Overseer's hell-dark eyes and climbed defiantly to his feet. His gaze swept past the sinister creatures, coming to rest on the dark form of the Archon, who stood waiting behind them across the field. And then his eyes fell on Agaroth, and he saw that the dragon had lost his own battle. Agaroth lay pinned and bleeding, black chains as thick as Aram's thighs lashing him to the ground. An iron collar was fixed around his neck, and two other bands secured his legs. Over him, the black dragon stood guard, its dark eyes gloating.

The nearest Overseer reached for Aram. He swept out with his sword, but the glowing blade struck the air with a metallic *clang*, the impact jarring the hilt right out of his grip. The Overseer's hand shot out like a snake and caught hold of his neck and, suddenly, the creature was strangling him.

Aram struggled, beating against it with his hands and feet, but nothing he could do remotely affected it. The hand throttling his neck was like a vice, and all his struggles just made it clamp harder. His lungs burned for air, and his vision was going dark quickly. He couldn't see the strands. He could hear himself making pathetic strangling noises, but nothing he could do moved air past that iron grip.

Just when he felt his consciousness give, the steel-cold grip opened and released him. Aram dropped to the ground, where he lay choking and wheezing, his hands clutching his neck. He lay gasping for seconds, until he finally gained enough presence of mind to wonder why the creature had released him.

Raising his head, he looked behind him and was startled to find both creatures dead. Something had cut them down, sliced them clean in half. They lay in murky pools of dark blood, their monstrous eyes frozen like obsidian glass.

Aram scrambled to his hands and knees, looking to see what could have felled such monsters. He started to struggle to his feet, but as he did, something slammed into him from behind, knocking him back to the ground. He fell next to his sword and reached for it. But as soon as his hand closed around the hilt, the ground disappeared beneath him, and suddenly he was somewhere else.

Dazed, Aram looked up to find himself lying on the ground at the Archon's feet, staring up into the slanting eye slits of a great helm adorned with long, spiraling horns, the head fixed to a black-armored body much larger than a mortal human's. The shadows beneath the helm regarded him with cold consideration, and that gaze filled him with a terrible feeling of failure. Slow degrees of desperation crept over him, as he became aware of just how thoroughly he'd been beaten. He had faced this enemy before, and he knew what it was and what it could do to him. This was the Archon who had killed his father and imprisoned his soul.

Kathrax fixed him with a shadowy stare, but Aram refused to surrender to it. Summoning every last scrap of courage that he had, he pushed himself to his feet.

The Archon made no move. He stood with his Baelsword planted in the ground, his gauntleted hands resting upon its two-handed hilt. The sword itself was as tall as Aram. It blazed with shadowy flames that coruscated over the steel in a way that was hauntingly beautiful. Aram stared at those dark flames, mesmerized, for he knew now what they were. Kathrax's sword drank the spirits of those it brought down, and the torment of those spirits was the source of its dark power. His own father's soul was in there somewhere, fueling those black flames.

SURRENDER.

It was that same tremendous voice, shuddering through his head like a thousand thunderclaps.

"No," Aram said, drawing his sword back over his shoulder and winding his arms.

The Archon didn't move, despite the fact that Aram stood within striking distance. Just as when he'd faced this enemy within the Shadow Realm, Aram had the impression that Kathrax judged him too insignificant to be regarded as a threat.

Aram's gaze fell upon the Baelsword, and his heart sank.

It wasn't the Archon's intent to take his life. Kathrax wasn't interested in another corpse.

He wanted Aram's soul.

Feeling suddenly sickened, Aram at last understood. With Sergan dead, Kathrax had only one way to defeat the wards of the Anchor, and that was with the pure essence of a Champion. With that, he could deliver a mortal blow to the Heart of the Mother and strike down the Veil that cleaved the earth. But it was more than that.

Luvana had told him the Archons had been feeding for centuries on the souls of the Gifted to ignite within them the spark of divinity. And

Kathrax was so close to accomplishing that goal...Aram could physically feel the Archon's thirst for him, for the potent soul of a Champion would all but assure his ascendance.

With that knowledge, Aram felt the rest of his strength leave him all at once. He had played right into the Archon's hand, delivering to him exactly what Kathrax needed. Now, there was only one last choice to make, and that was whether to surrender or go down fighting. He had no chance against such a monster, not without a Warden. No matter what he chose, he would lose either way. And with the Anchor destroyed, the Auld would become the hunted, and the Exilari would fill their cellars with them.

A vision filled his mind, the kind Agaroth would send him. Only, his dragon would never afflict him with images so unbearable. In his mind, he looked out across the wasteland that had once been the Hills of Eranor. He saw his friends and allies being herded into lines and driven toward ruptures in the air. It took him a moment to understand what was happening to them, and when he did, it was all he could do to keep from vomiting.

They were being driven into the void. All of them.

"No..." Tears filled his eyes, and he shook his head. "Oh, gods, no..."

Through clouded eyes, he regarded the monster before him. He couldn't let that fate come to pass. He had a decision to make. It was an easy decision. Easy, but hard, nevertheless.

He drew his dagger and angled it at his own throat.

"Aram! No!"

He froze, the familiar voice cutting his motion short.

A gust of wind buffeted him as a black dragon dropped out of the sky, landing right behind him. Markus slid from Siroth's back and stood feebly, his left hand clutching his sword, his right arm bound in a sling. He was pale and weak and frail, but he was *there,* limping toward him. Aram gaped at him in shock, almost too stunned to react.

He resolved not to waste that split-second Markus had given him. Dropping the dagger, he lifted his sword and reached out with his mind, gathering every fiber within reach. Using the star-steel blade as a focus, he conjured a blazing ball of energy that he hurled at Kathrax. It impacted like a meteor, clinging to the Archon's body like naptha, burning with savage, searing flames.

Kathrax raised his hands, and the flames extinguished. Immediately.

Before Aram could react, the Archon produced a fiery sphere of his own, flinging it toward him. It would have killed him, had Markus not intervened. He staggered into the path of the flames, letting the blaze envelop him. And as it did, it hissed and steamed and died as surely as if someone had drowned it.

The Archon howled in fury.

Emboldened, Aram conjured a lance of solid air and cast it as hard as he could, not at the Archon, but at his dragon. The beast roared in pain and shock as the lance of magic buried itself in its massive chest, piercing its heart. Its eyes blazed for an instant with a brilliant golden light as the shadows left them, but then that light faded forever. The dragon's serpentine body went limp, the life gone from it.

Howling, Agaroth surged against the bonds that held him, straining against them with every muscle. Aram ran to him and, raising his starsteel blade, brought it down with all his strength on the band anchoring his dragon's neck to the ground.

The massive band snapped. With a roar of fury, Agaroth shook off his bonds and vaulted into the sky, spewing roiling flames, then turned and descended upon Kathrax.

The Archon swept his hand around as if flinging something at the dragon, but before he could finish the gesture, Agaroth landed on him, toppling him backward and gushing broiling fire into his face.

Kathrax threw the dragon off him, and Agaroth tumbled through the air as though hurled by a giant. His enormous body slapped hard against the earth, sending up a wave of dust and showering debris. Before the dragon could rise, an invisible rope latched onto Aram and jerked him forward. The next thing he knew, his body was pressed against the Archon's chest, being used as a shield against his own dragon. Ready to spring, Agaroth backed down, looking suddenly uncertain.

Kathrax's hand snaked up, grasping Aram's face and wrenching his head around until he was forced to stare into the shadows of the dark helm. Aram squeezed his eyes closed in panic. Markus stood only paces away from him, somehow still on his feet, yet neither his Warden nor his dragon could come to his aid. Reaching out with his mind, he tried desperately to weave a binding, but Kathrax simply unraveled it. Desperate, Aram tried again, with similar results.

He sagged helplessly, stung by the realization that Kathrax could dismantle any binding he wove.

Unless...

Unless he didn't weave.

What if he *un*-wove?

Looking up at the Archon, Aram could see the strands of aether that anchored Kathrax in a complex pattern to the warp and weft of the world. Reaching out with his mind, he started plucking at those strands, picking them out of the tapestry of the world one thread at a time.

Realizing what he was about, the Archon howled, shoving him away. Aram landed on the ground and rolled, lurching to his feet. He stalked forward, his mind working furiously to sever the strands of the world faster than Kathrax could bind them back together again. He found himself locked in a contest of skill, and very quickly, it became clear that Aram could rip the strands that wove him far faster than Kathrax could repair the damage.

But Kathrax must have realized that also.

So he retaliated by doing the same to Aram.

Aram cried out in pain as his own tethers to the world were severed, but he couldn't stop working. Instead, he plucked more furiously at the Archon's tangled soul, unraveling Kathrax with the speed of a master butcher. The Archon shivered, becoming insubstantial. A few more tears and Kathrax fell to the ground with a mental howl of pain that shook both earth and heavens.

Kathrax was coming undone. Just as his spirit was unraveling, so was his body, his armor becoming worn and tattered, aging centuries in seconds, his motions faltering.

Thread by thread, Aram picked Kathrax out of the pattern of existence, until he reached a point where the rest of what was left started unravelling all on its own. The Archon's mental thundering lessoned, until it was reduced to audible groans that faded as Kathrax himself faded from the world, leaving behind only a scorched hole in the fabric of the pattern.

As he watched his enemy perish, Aram felt his own soul unraveling. The last of the strength left him, and his body spilled to the dirt, where he lay twitching, his muscles and reflexes gone beyond his control.

But then a heavy weight fell atop him, crushing his belly against the earth, and he felt Markus's strong arms encircling him, hugging him close.

"I won't let you go, I won't let you go…" Markus repeated over and over in ragged breaths wracked by sobs.

Markus's voice faded, even as his Shielding presence tethered Aram's spirit to the earth. Aram let exhaustion claim him. His eyes slid closed, and he collapsed into the fierce embrace of his friend. His Warden.

His champion.

A ram opened his eyes to the muted light of an oil lamp. Gradually, he became aware of the sounds of people moving around him, of hushed voices speaking in quiet conversations. The strong odor of blood mixed with herbs told him that he was in one of the hospital tents. His body hurt all over, especially his right side. He tried moving his arm but winced from the pain. It was like a thousand tiny claws digging into his skin all at once.

"Welcome back," said a soft voice.

Aram turned to see Calise smiling down at him, her face the most beautiful sight he had ever beheld. She was sitting in a chair beside his bed, clutching his hand. Her soft fingers stroked his, and he squeezed them back.

"Hey." He smiled up at her, the sight of her freckled face making him feel dizzy with relief, for it meant that he was still alive. He thought he remembered dying, but that couldn't be right, for Calise was with him, holding his hand. Then he remembered Markus falling upon him, Shielding him from death, and an intense fear lanced through him, making him gasp.

"Markus—"

He tried to sit up, but Calise's hands on him kept him down.

"Lay back. Markus is fine. He's resting."

Aram closed his eyes, euphoric with relief, his pulse hammering in his head. He didn't understand how Markus could have survived all that. He had more grit and nerve than anyone else Aram had ever met.

"What about Esmir?" he whispered, though he dreaded to hear the answer.

"He's going to be all right," Calise smiled fondly. "It would seem you have two very tough Wardens."

Aram could hardly believe it. The fact that any of them were still alive was nothing short of miraculous, far more than he dared hope for.

"I do," he whispered, his voice thick with emotion. Without Esmir and Markus, he wouldn't be alive. Both Wardens had kept him standing long after he should have fallen.

"What about the battle?" he asked.

"We won." Calise ran her hand soothingly through his hair, smiling proudly. "We lost a lot of people, and we lost a lot of dragons, but nowhere near as many as we would have lost without you and Markus and Esmir."

At the mention of dragons, Aram was reminded of the other companion who had fought at his side. He knew that Agaroth still lived, for he wouldn't have survived had his dragon fallen. Aram could sense him in the back of his mind, the same way he was aware of his own body parts. Just like him, Agaroth was in pain from many wounds, but also like him, he would heal in time.

"I want to see my dragon," he said.

But Calise set a hand on his shoulder and wouldn't let him up.

"Agaroth is fine. He got a little chewed up, but he'll make a full recovery. I think he's more worried about you than anything."

"I'm fine," Aram muttered absently.

"Really? Then why am I running out of burn salve?"

Burn salve? Startled, he glanced down at himself, for he didn't remember getting burned in the fight. He wasn't wearing a shirt, and his body was covered only by a light wool blanket. Tugging it down, he saw that the skin on the right side of his chest was covered in lacerations. The damage extended to his shoulder and down the length of his arm. Staring at the wounds, he couldn't imagine what had caused them. The last thing he remembered was his spirit coming undone as Kathrax attempted to unravel him from the world. Perhaps this was the physical result of such a confrontation. The harder he stared at the small slices in his skin, the more they looked like fine brands seared into his flesh rather than cuts.

"It's healing, but you'll have scars," Calise informed him.

Aram didn't doubt it. "Scars are fine. They're better than the alternative."

Looking back at her, he noticed Calise was still wearing the twine necklace he had tied around her neck. Reaching up, he lifted it out of her collar and ran his thumb over the heart knot. The twine was dark and discolored from years of being worn, first by his mother and then himself...and now by the woman he loved.

"You're still wearing it."

"Of course I am." She smiled affectionately. "You haven't taken it off me yet."

"Is that what I'm supposed to do?"

When she nodded, he reached up with both hands and reverently untied the small knot he had used to secure the necklace. He didn't know why he'd chosen the sheet bend knot at the time, out of all the other knots he could have picked. Most people probably would have tied a square knot. But Aram wasn't most people, and he knew that the square knot was the ficklest knot of all, and he would have never trusted Calise's heart with one. The more he thought about it, the more the sheet bend did seem like the most appropriate knot he could have tied. After all, he had grown up in a fishing village, where the sheet bend had a special significance. It was the primary knot used in the making of fishing nets, and he had spent a good portion of his childhood working them.

Drawing the twine necklace from Calise's neck, Aram whispered, "Thank you for wearing this."

"It was my honor." She straightened, tucking her hair back. "Now, do you know what we're supposed to do with it?"

Aram nodded, looking down at the twine in his hand instead of at her, contemplating the necklace sadly. "Aren't we supposed to burn it?"

"So, you *do* know what that necklace means." Calise's eyes narrowed.

"I do. My father made that necklace. He gave it to my ma before he died."

She frowned at him hard, scrunching her brow. "Then do you really want to burn it?"

No. He really didn't want to. The necklace was the only thing he had left of his parents. It was his most treasured possession, and the most sentimental. He sighed and shook his head.

She stroked her hand through his hair, smiling sadly. "That's all right. We don't have to." She bent forward and kissed his brow. "I'm going to go check on my other patients. I'll come back. In the meantime, I want you to get some sleep."

Clutching the necklace tight, Aram did as his healer ordered, smiling as he closed his eyes.

The next time he awoke, it wasn't Calise at his bedside.

It was Esmir.

Aram couldn't believe it. The old Warden looked hale and more energetic than Aram could remember ever seeing him. There was a life in his eyes that hadn't been there before, and Aram couldn't imagine what had put it there. He looked like a man who'd been resurrected from some dark fate.

"Esmir!" Aram cried, his joy coloring his voice. He tried to sit up, but pain made him think better of it.

"It's good to see you alive," Esmir said with a warm smile.

"It's good to *be* alive," Aram assured him. "And I wouldn't be, without you. What you did…" He shook his head in amazement. He still didn't understand how the crippled old Warden had stood at his side against an Archon. It was almost as though Esmir's body had forgotten that it was old, returning to a time when he'd been the Warden who fought at Daymar Torian's side. And for those few minutes, Aram thought, Esmir had been that man again.

"What I did is nothing compared to what *you* did." Esmir fixed him with a proud smile. "Other than Erok, you are the only person in all of history to have ever brought down an Archon."

"Yes, but you—"

Esmir patted his hand. "Don't. Don't try to belittle your accomplishment. You do that far too often."

Aram went silent, for Vandra had said something of the like to him once. It wasn't that he meant to belittle what he did, or be falsely humble, it's just that he didn't know how to talk about an accomplishment without seeming to brag. There is a fine line between acknowledging a victory and being boastful about it, and he had no idea where that line was.

"I wish Vandra could be here," Aram said dismally, struggling to picture her face in his mind, the way she had looked the last time he'd seen her. He knew that's the way she would want to be remembered, though he was sure her execution would haunt his memories for many years.

"She *is* here," Esmir said. "Listen."

Aram didn't know what he was talking about, but he did as the man asked and closed his eyes and listened. For a long time, all he could hear was the sound of people moving about the hospital tent. Somewhere, a person was moaning softly. Another was coughing. Someone else was sleeping, the sound of their breathing loud and even. Outside, the wind was blowing. A gust came up, shuddering the fabric of the tent and crackling a flap that hadn't been tied down.

"I don't hear anything except the wind," Aram said, opening his eyes.

Esmir smiled. "The Auld believe that when a person dies, their soul becomes the wind."

"The wind?" Aram scrunched his brow. "Really?"

"Really. Think about it. Think about all that the wind is and all that it does. Where it goes. Where it comes from. The wind knows everything, for it travels everywhere, and it's with us always. It endures. It feels. It speaks. Sometimes it whispers. Sometimes it rages. Give it a listen sometime. See what it tells you. You know what the best thing is about the wind?"

"No. What?"

Esmir smiled a confident smile, opening his palm. "More than anything else in this world, the wind is truly free."

Aram found himself nodding slowly, for it was a comforting belief. He hoped that Vandra was truly free like the wind. Her and Master Ebra, and all the other people who had gone ahead of him, even his da.

But then a heavy sadness clamped down on his heart. "My father's soul didn't become the wind," he said softly. "It's trapped forever in Kathrax's Baelsword."

A long silence followed his words as Esmir's face grew stony and silent, his gaze averting. He stared hard at the side of the tent for a long time, suddenly looking his age. At last, he heaved a long sigh.

Patting Aram's arm, he said, "It doesn't have to be forever. I'll send some people out to look for it."

"To do what with it?" asked Aram.

Esmir didn't answer, but left without another word, leaving Aram feeling alone and sad. He closed his eyes but didn't fall back to sleep. Instead, his mind sought Agaroth for the comfort of his dragon's presence.

He lay in bed for the rest of the day as Calise came and went from his bedside. He listened to the sound of the wind outside and the noises of the encampment being broken down. The battle was over and so was the war. There was no sense for them to remain here any longer. The armies of the other nations would want to return to their homelands, and the dragons would be anxious to get back to their eyries. As for himself, Aram couldn't wait to get back to Skyhome. He wanted nothing more than to be back in his eyrie with Markus and their dragons, swapping stories over drinks.

He slept through another night and most of the next morning. By dawn, he was feeling much better and was able to sit on his own for short periods of time. His friends came to see him, encircling his bed with euphoric smiles and battering him with questions until Calise finally drove them out. Iver lingered behind after the others left, sinking down at Aram's bedside and taking his hand.

"Thank you," he said, bowing his head gravely. "I'm so sorry for not believing in you."

"It's all right." Aram smiled weakly. "I didn't really believe in myself."

Iver raised his head and caught his eyes firmly. "I'll never doubt you again. Never. Anything you need...I'll always be there." With that, he rose with a muttered word of gratitude for Calise.

Aram sank back in his bed and closed his eyes, glad for the visit by his friends, for they had lifted his spirits somewhat, though not as much as they should have. He was growing worried because Markus still hadn't awakened. Calise had tried to assure him that was normal for someone as injured as Markus was. She said he was improving by the hour, and that his wound was not festering.

When he was feeling up to it, Aram had Calise help him over to Markus's bedside. He sat in a chair beside his sleeping friend for the rest of the day. With nothing better to do, he recounted stories of their years together, stories that he thought Markus would find funny if indeed he could hear them. Some of the stories he told made him laugh, while others brought tears to his eyes. Markus just slept the whole while, his face peaceful, his breathing deep and regular.

"It's good to see you out of bed."

Aram turned and was shocked to find himself looking at Luvana. He almost didn't recognize her, for she seemed so thoroughly out of place in a hospital tent. She was wearing her blue headscarf, her gray hair neatly braided. He couldn't imagine what she was doing here. She slid into the chair opposite him and, looking at Markus, addressed Aram softly:

"I came to thank you. And to apologize."

Aram frowned. "Apologize for what?"

"For your father. And for keeping the knowledge of him from you."

Aram averted his eyes, for he knew this was not the time for anger. He swallowed heavily, though it was a heavy knot to get down.

"I forgive you," he said at last, and tried to mean it, even though he knew it would still be some time before the last vestiges of his resentment faded.

"Thank you. And thank you, too, for all that you've done. You do indeed have the heart of a Champion."

Aram nodded, unable to look at her, for her words moved him more than he wanted her to know. Unlike Vandra, Luvana had never respected him. But, somehow, that made the respect she paid him now even more meaningful.

She stood and left. As she was headed out the opening of the tent, Esmir came in and, to Aram's astonishment, the two paused and traded pleasantries. Aram squinted at the old Warden as he crossed the tent and lowered himself into the chair the Dedicant Mother had just abandoned.

"So, you and Luvana are on speaking terms now?" Aram raised an eyebrow.

"It seems I've redeemed myself in the eyes of the Council." Esmir chuckled. The youthful glint was back in his eyes, and now Aram understood the source of it.

"Remind me to never fall out of the Council's good graces, if this is what it takes to be redeemed," Aram said.

"Would you guys stop talking so loud?"

The sound of Markus's voice made Aram break out in a smile of joy. "Hey! You're awake!"

"I'm not sure if that's what you call it," Markus muttered, cracking open an eyelid and giving Aram a weak grin.

Aram would have hugged him, if he could be certain it wouldn't hurt his friend more.

"I can't believe what you did!" Aram exclaimed. "I don't even know how the hell you *did* it!"

"We'll just say that it was against his healer's advice," said Calise, coming up behind them. "I just about tied him down. But he had a sword, and I didn't."

Markus shrugged. "Maybe it was stupid. But I did save your life."

"You did," Aram agreed. "And I'll never stop being grateful."

At that, Markus started coughing, which Aram thought must be horrifically painful.

Calise pointed across the tent. "All right, time for you to get back to bed! If Markus bursts his stitches, I'm not sewing him back up again!"

Aram frowned at her. "Why not?"

Esmir and Calise exchanged glances, and suddenly Markus's coughing seemed more like laughter.

Calise grinned. "It was a joke."

Instantly embarrassed, Aram offered an apologetic smile. "Sorry."

Bending, she gave him an affectionate hug. "It's all right. It's one of the things that makes you *you*. And I wouldn't have you any other way."

EPILOGUE

Aram shivered as he walked down the dark, pre-dawn streets of Hearth Home with Calise and Markus at his side. The air was cool and crisp, and, to him, it seemed that their footsteps echoed more hollowly than they should. The sounds reverberated off the surrounding walls, amplified by the quiet and the stillness of the empty streets. Even the roosters hadn't awakened yet, and this early in the morning, not even the bakers were about. It had been a while since he'd strolled Hearth Home's empty streets this early in the morning—not since the last time he'd visited the Brausas' workshop, when he'd helped Onsel Brausa finish forging his star-steel blade.

By the time they arrived at the door of the smithy, the horizon in the east was just beginning to warm, though stars still dominated the rest of the sky. Aram paused on the door's threshold before knocking, taking a few moments to gather his feelings. In his hands, he carried a long parcel shrouded in dark cloth, and it bore down on him with a soul-crushing weight.

"You can do this," said Markus, patting his back.

Aram knew he could. It was just far more difficult than he'd thought it would be. Squaring his shoulders, he raised his fist and rapped twice upon the oaken door. It seemed forever before he heard the sound of footsteps on the other side. But at last, the door opened, and Onsel Brausa stepped aside to let them pass.

"Is that it?" the swordsmith asked in a lowered voice as his gaze took

814

in the darkly wrapped bundle in Aram's arms.

Aram nodded, unable to trust his voice. Calise gave his shoulder a reassuring squeeze. He smiled at her in thanks, for he didn't think he could do this without them.

"Let's head on back," Onsel said, his voice full of trepidation.

They followed the swordsmith into the back of the building. It was too early in the morning for any of the apprentices to be in yet, so the workshop stood empty, its forges cold. The room was suffused with a strong odor that Aram found comfortingly nostalgic, for he had learned to associate it with the excitement he had felt when working on his blade. It was a pleasant mixture of coal, steel, pitch, and sweat, and for some reason, it put a metallic taste in his mouth that would stick there for hours long after he left, reminding him of the feel of the forge.

He followed Onsel to the back of the smithy, where the star-steel forge sat in the corner. It was the hottest forge in the Brausas' work-shop—maybe in the whole world. Aram just hoped it would be enough.

"Set it here," Onsel said, indicating a large anvil that was fixed to the floor. His face was already glistening with sweat, and the forge hadn't even been heated yet.

Aram did as he bid, setting the parcel down across the anvil then stepping back, glad to have it out of his hands. He glanced at the sword-smith, feeling suddenly uncertain.

"What now?" he asked.

Onsel Brausa's eyes were fixed on the dark drape of cloth, his face paler than Aram ever remembered it being. "Now we light the forge. Do you remember how?"

He did. Aram moved immediately to a stack of thin metal rods and selected one, then took one of the small hammers that were hanging by pegs from the wall. He glanced at Markus for reassurance, for there was a heaviness on his chest that pressed down so hard it made it almost difficult to breathe.

Markus nodded at him. "Go ahead. You've got this."

Aram moved to the smaller anvil next to the star-steel forge and held the rod against it at an angle. Then, raising the hammer, he began striking

the rod soundly. The bright sounds of the small hammer rang metallically off the walls. As he struck the end of the rod, it gradually lengthened
and sharpened to a point, and Aram could feel the heat coming off of it.

"Here!" Onsel said, handing him a strip of parchment.

Aram set the hammer down and held the parchment against the heated end. The strip ignited almost immediately, a strong flame rushing
over the parchment. Quickly, Aram dropped it onto a small stack of kindling, bringing the star-steel forge to life.

The flames raced over the coals with a hissing crackle. At a nod from
Onsel, Aram moved to the piston and started working the bellows,
pumping air into the forge until the fire lapped hungrily at the air above
it.

"What kind of coal's in there?" Markus asked.

"Crushed dragon bone," Onsel answered. "The hottest-burning fuel
in the world."

Satisfied, Aram fed the forge slowly with air, watching the flames
evolve through a wide range of colors, starting with red then progressing to cherry, deepening to a dark orange then yellowing before flaring
brilliant white.

"There," Onsel said at last, and Aram let go of the piston.

Moving away from the bellows, Aram asked, "What now? Do I just
put it in?"

The old swordsmith produced a rag and mopped his brow, his face
set in grim lines. He nodded at the forge. "Go ahead."

Aram hesitated, powerful emotions filling his core with a terrible
ache. For a moment, he couldn't move, but stood collecting himself.
Eventually, he found his resolve. He went to the long bundle he had laid
across the anvil and drew the dark fabric back with a trembling hand.

As soon as the Baelsword was exposed to the air, dark flames erupted
all along the length of the blade, fed by the torment of the souls locked
within the steel's crystals. It was a terrible feeling, staring down at the
darkness that radiated from that blade, the sight carving a hole out of
him right through his heart. Aram felt Markus's hand on his back, lending him the strength he needed.

Gripping the Baelsword's hilt in both hands, Aram walked with it to the forge and thrust it into the glowing coals.

Immediately, the forge erupted with an explosion of flames that took Aram completely off guard. The forge blazed violently with every color of the spectrum, reminding Aram of the terrible colors of Sergan Parsigal's tainted aura. It seemed as though a battle were being waged within the forge between the sword's dark flames and the dazzling colors of the fire fed by the dragon-bone coals. Gradually, the dark power of the sword was overcome, devoured by the beautiful many-colored flames of the forge.

The Baelsword's hilt was consumed first, catching fire and charring to black before turning gray and crumbling to ash. For a long while, the steel of the blade itself didn't change color, and Aram was beginning to fear that it wasn't going to heat. He pumped the bellows, feeding the flames until, at last, the Baelsword's steel finally began to warm, turning a deep shade of brownish-red. As Aram watched the sword heat in the coals, he was filled with a complex mixture of emotions.

Onsel moved forward and took over the bellows, adding air to the forge. The steel glowed brighter, gradually progressing through slow degrees of red into orange and then finally arriving at yellow, when it abruptly caught fire with an eruption of crackling sparks.

Slowly at first, the blade began deforming. The glowing edges lost their shape, dripping bright golden drops of liquid steel into the forge. Fire gushed as the melting blade released its tattered collection of souls, which escaped the forge in a hot wind that gusted past them. Aram threw his head back and gasped as the wind swept over him, for he could feel those souls moving through him, pressing upon his heart a strong sense of gratitude.

As he watched the Baelsword succumb to the flames, his eyes filled with tears of sadness and relief, for he knew that his father's spirit was finally free.

"Goodbye, papa," he whispered.

Swallowing a heavy lump in his throat, he reached up and untied the twine necklace around his neck. When Calise saw what he meant to do, she looked at him in concern. But Aram gave her a reassuring smile, so she leaned into him, taking his hand. With Markus looking on, together they raised the eternal heart knot necklace over the forge and surrendered it to the flames, a symbol of love, hope, and thankfulness.

When they left the forge in the light of morning, the streets of Hearth Home were filled with people waking with a newfound sense of security that hadn't been known in hundreds of years. For all of them knew that, for the first time in centuries, their world was finally at peace. Above them, a beacon fire blazed in the Heights, signaling to all the world that a Great One and his Champion watched over them.

THE END

SPECIAL THANKS TO:

The Ladies of NOFFA, my beautiful and inspirational Turtles

The Terrible Ten, although there are more than ten of you

Phil Tucker, for hours and hours of discussion on story structure

Matt Presley, for Zoom calls and advice on world building

Sarah Chorn, my glorious editor I'll be eternally grateful to

Dave Langlinais, for his blacksmithing knowledge and advice

Alec Hutson, for super-sleuth typo hunting

Clifford W. Ashley, author of *The Ashley Book of Knots*, my knotting inspiration

FURTHER THANKS TO MY BETA READERS:

Mary Elizabeth Koch • Jouko-Tapani Torkkeli • Sue Brouillette
Andrew McVittie • Lana Turner • Dave Jenkins • Kevin Rowe

Made in United States
North Haven, CT
01 March 2022